Bertie:

The Complete

Prince of Wales

Mysteries

Books by Peter Lovesey

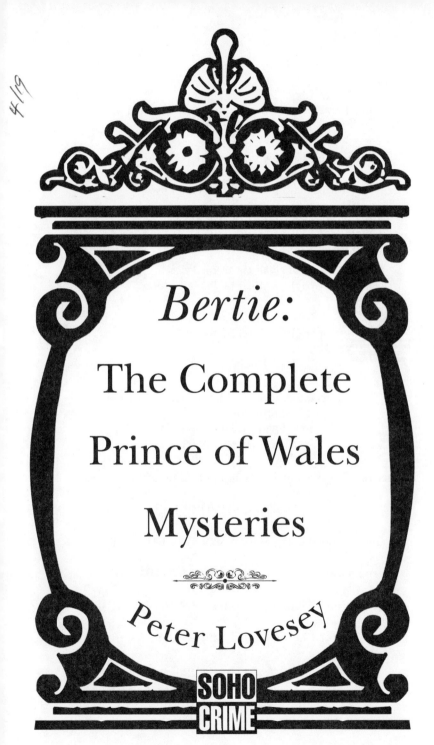

Bertie:

The Complete

Prince of Wales

Mysteries

Peter Lovesey

SOHO CRIME

Bertie: The Complete Prince of Wales Mysteries

Introduction © 2019 by Peter Lovesey

Bertie and the Tin Man
Copyright © 1987 by Peter Lovesey

Bertie and the Seven Bodies
Copyright © 1990 by Peter Lovesey

Bertie and the Crime of Passion
Copyright © 1993 by Peter Lovesey

This collected edition first published in 2019 by
Soho Press, Inc.
853 Broadway
New York, NY 10003

Library of Congress Cataloging-in-Publication Data is available.

ISBN 978-1-64129-049-4

Bertie and the Tin Man: eISBN 978-1-64129-050-0

Bertie and the Seven Bodies: eISBN 978-1-64129-051-7

Bertie and the Crime of Passion: eISBN: 978-1-64129-052-4

Printed in the United States of America

10 9 8 7 6 5 4 3 2 1

Contents

Bertie:

The Complete

Prince of Wales

Mysteries

Becoming Bertie

AN INTRODUCTION BY PETER LOVESEY

The detective memoirs of Bertie, the Prince of Wales, appear here as a single volume for the first time and I was asked to explain how this self-appointed sleuth arrived in my writing life and took over.

My career as a crime writer began with eight novels featuring Sergeant Cribb, a Victorian policeman who, unlike Bertie, was pretty good at the job. Each story unfolded against a background of some Victorian sport or pastime and I immersed myself in accounts of go-as-you-please races, bareknuckle boxing, the music halls, séances, river trips, the seaside and waxworks. A TV series was made and my wife, Jax, and I wrote a further six plays featuring such events as a wedding, a school reunion, Christmas carol–singing and the London Zoo. TV was a wonderful boost, but it quickly used up my stock of ideas for future books. Worse, I found that the characters I had in my imagination had been dulled by the power of the TV images and the brilliance of the acting. I wrote no more Sergeant Cribb novels.

Nine years later, I came across a book about Fred Archer, the foremost jockey of the nineteenth century, the rider of more than 2,700 winners. At the high point of his career, aged 29, he spoke his last words—"Are they coming?"—put a gun to his head and killed himself. Any crime writer would find such a scenario irresistible. Why did poor Fred do it and who were the mysterious "they"? Horse racing was a sport I hadn't considered as a setting when I was writing the Cribb series. How about writing a Victorian version of a Dick Francis thriller? But I couldn't see Sergeant Cribb as the protagonist. I needed a new detective.

The largest wreath on Archer's coffin when it was driven through Newmarket to the grave had been from his royal patron, the Prince of Wales. In one of those lightbulb moments I pictured Bertie as my sleuth. There were clear advantages to having the future king on the case. Obviously, he must have taken an interest in the mystery. He could call on Scotland Yard for help if needed. Equally he had the power to send them packing. He knew about racing and he had limitless time to devote to an investigation. But would he be any good?

Probably not.

At this stage of his life, in 1886, he was 45, more renowned for indulgence than intelligence. He had a sense of his own destiny and a liking for ceremonial affairs, but his mother, the queen, denied him the opportunity of reading state papers and he frittered much of his life away in gambling, shooting game and being unfaithful to his long-suffering wife, Princess Alexandra. I couldn't imagine him as a serious investigator, but he would relish the chance of playing private detective.

Bertie as an inept sleuth intrigued and inspired me. This would be his case and his book and his voice would tell the tale. Up to then I hadn't written a book in the first person. Already Bertie was taking over.

I promised myself I would portray him as truthfully as I could, allowing that there was no evidence he had ever investigated a crime. The scandals, the mistresses and the gambling, were well-known. But the qualities that eventually made him a successful king were evident as well. He was confident, good-humored, a fine organizer and far more forward-thinking than his mother.

I still have a thick file of all the notes I made on Fred Archer. I travelled to Newmarket and saw the section devoted to Archer at the National Horse Racing Museum and photographed the silver revolver that fired the fatal shot. I visited Falmouth House, where the suicide took place, and I walked the funeral route and found the impressive headstone. The events of 1886 became more immediate to me. I wanted as far as possible to do justice to the memory of the tragic jockey. I would devise a fictional plot that worked within the constraints of the real events of a century ago.

There were enough strong individuals around Bertie and Archer in real life to allow me to involve them in the plot rather than creating imaginary characters. And I would set the story in real places. If the events came to life for me, I reckoned my readers were more likely to believe in them.

My working title was *Are They Coming?* But by the time I had written the book I wanted something closer to the jovial heart of the story. Fred Archer had been known to the racing public as the Tin Man because he was said to have been careful with his money. I opted for *Bertie and the Tin Man.*

The book was enthusiastically received. The quote that pleased me most was from Peter Grosvenor in the *Daily Express*: "It's Dick Francis by gaslight."

I hadn't thought about writing a sequel until a review came in from Marilyn Stasio in *The Philadelphia Inquirer*: "One doesn't wish to put that nice Sergeant Cribb out of a job; but we can't wait to go out on another case with dear Bertie."

Nothing as ready-made as the Fred Archer tragedy suggested itself, and I wrote another book set in 1946 and called *On the Edge* before returning to Bertie. The inspiration this time was the Queen of Crime. I knew the centenary of Agatha Christie's birth would be celebrated in 1990. Like most other crime writers, I admired the audacity and ingenuity of her plotting. A whole group of her books featured lines or themes from nursery rhymes: *Three Blind Mice*; *Hickory Dickory Dock*; *One, Two, Buckle My Shoe*; *Five Little Pigs*; *A Pocket Full of Rye*; *Ten Little Indians* and *Crooked House*. In tribute perhaps I could devise a Bertie story using a well-known rhyme.

I was lucky to find one that the prolific Agatha hadn't used. It was the rhyme beginning *Monday's child is fair of face.* Suppose I substituted the word "corpse" for "child" so that the next line would be *Tuesday's corpse is full of grace.* And so on, through the days of the week. The next step would be to plot seven murders that fitted the predictive words of the verses. The setting was ready-made: a stately home; and the occasion a house party of the kind Bertie regularly dignified with his presence. Happily for my plan, Agatha Christie was renowned for her country house murder mysteries.

I planned the book carefully. Early on, it became obvious to me

that the characters—seven of whom would be murdered—couldn't
be based on real people. But I would make sure that the setting
(I'd better not say which house and estate I portrayed) was accurate and the social conventions of a shooting party were followed.
Well, I finished in good time for the centenary. I was
vice-chairman of the Crime Writers' Association that year and
we held our annual conference at the Grand Hotel, Torquay,
and visited Greenway House where the great writer had lived.
A huge banquet and fireworks display was hosted by Agatha
Christie Limited at the Riviera Centre and among the guests
were the actors Joan Hickson (Miss Marple) and David Suchet
(Poirot). *Bertie and the Tin Man* was published to quite a fanfare
from the press.

And—would you believe it?—not a single reviewer picked up
on the fact that *Bertie and the Seven Bodies* was intended as a nod
to Agatha Christie. I felt much the same as Bertie when his best
intentions had misfired.

Three years went by. I busied myself with a new character, a
modern policeman called Peter Diamond, the head of CID in
the city of Bath. This was a departure. Up to then, all my crime
writing had been set in the past and I wasn't entirely confident I
knew enough about police procedures to embark on a contem-
porary series. Diamond resigned at the end of *The Last Detective*
and became a freelance sleuth on a mission to Japan in *Diamond
Solitaire*. Both books were popular and the first won the Anthony
Award, yet I couldn't see a way forward. Diamond was no amateur.
He had hit the buffers.

I heard the call of Bertie again. He was an amateur, of course,
but on his own terms.

Pumped up, I wrote the third book of the series, *Bertie and
the Crime of Passion,* set in Paris in 1891. The Prince had a great
partiality for France and visited there as often as possible. As early
as 1881, he had paved the way for the *Entente Cordiale* by meeting
the French statesman Léon Gambetta at the Château de Breteuil
and discussing an alliance between the two countries to oppose
Germany's imperialism. Twenty-three years later, as King Edward
VII, he insisted against the advice of the British cabinet on making a state visit to Paris that boosted Anglo-French relations and
undoubtedly helped the politicians on both sides of the Channel

to sign their famous declaration of 1904. In the years between, he achieved some *ententes* in private with the famous actress Sarah Bernhardt. Bertie's love of Paris and the ladies of France was the inspiration for the new novel.

This one wasn't to be a story of serial murder. Most of the characters were survivors, so Bertie was able to interact with some of the people who really did frequent the Moulin Rouge: Louise Weber, known as La Goulue, and her partner, Jacques Renaudin, known as Valentin le Désossé, and the artist Toulouse-Lautrec. He would also lock horns with the celebrated detective Marie-François Goron, *chef de la Sûreté*. If I say more this will turn into a spoiler instead of an introduction.

That's enough of me. Bring on Bertie, the sleuth who outwits Scotland Yard and the Sûreté and is at least the equal of Hercule Poirot—if he is to be believed.

Bertie and the Tin Man

CHAPTER 1

The Tin Man asked, "Are they coming?" and reached for his revolver.

His sister Emily made no response. She stood at a bedroom window of Falmouth House, near Newmarket, staring down at the curve of the gravel drive between the lawns. It was Monday afternoon, 8 November, 1886, about twenty past two. She made no response because she didn't understand the question.

She was bone weary, but profoundly relieved that her brother had rallied after a frightening weekend. On Thursday evening he had come back from the races at Lewes complaining of a feverish chill. Next day his temperature had soared dangerously. Two doctors had seen him, and a nurse from Cambridge had been engaged. Not until Sunday evening had his temperature started to drop. Last night, thank heaven, he had slept. This morning he had sat up in bed when his regular doctor called. His temperature was right down. Some of his friends had called to see him and he had chatted happily. A few minutes ago he had told Emily to send the nurse for lunch.

"Are they coming?" What did he mean by that?

Emily heard a sound behind her. She turned.

The Tin Man was out of bed and striding toward the open door in his nightshirt. He had the gun in his left hand.

Emily's throat contracted. She put her hand to her neck and cried out, "What are you doing?" She darted across the room toward him.

He backed against the door and it slammed shut.

She froze.

He had lifted the gun and pointed it toward his own face.

Until such a crisis occurs, nobody can know how they will react. Emily fought her paralyzing fear, flung out her arm and tried to stop him. She succeeded in pushing the gun aside. He grabbed her with his right arm, gripped her around the neck and thrust her against the door. They wrestled for what seemed like a minute.

She shrieked repeatedly for help.

He tightened the grip. Emily's arms flailed uselessly. Considering how ill her brother had been, his strength was extraordinary, superhuman. He held her on his right side while he turned his face to the left and moved the muzzle to his mouth.

She was powerless to stop him. She could only scream.

He spoke no other words. He pulled the trigger and the shot hurled him backward. He hit the floor.

Sobbing hysterically, Emily staggered across the room and tugged at the bell rope.

Were they coming? It no longer mattered to the Tin Man.

CHAPTER 2

Sandringham
31 DECEMBER, 1886

I must say, it's a queer thing to be sitting in my study on the last day of 1886, addressing someone not yet born, but that is what I take you to be. That is what you had *better* be. As for me, I am a dead man, or will be when you read this. And grossly libeled in the history books, I shouldn't wonder.

Not to prolong the mystification, my name is Albert Edward, and among other things notable and notorious, I am the Prince of Wales, the eldest son of Her Gracious Majesty Queen Victoria. To please Mother and Country, I wear a straitjacket. This uncongenial garment is known as protocol. It obliges me to consign this intimate account of certain adventures of mine to a secure metal box in the Public Record Office for a hundred years. So I can confidently inform you that I am dead. As are all the other poor, benighted spirits I shall presently raise.

Good day to you, then. Not a bad day to commence putting pen to paper. Christmas festivities over; too much fog about for shooting; flat racing finished for the year; and a certain lady who has been known to make agreeable incursions upon my time and energy is occupied for a season on the New York stage.

In case it surprises you that the Heir Apparent's waking hours are not filled with official engagements, allow me to state that I do my share of laying foundation stones, inspecting lines of guardsmen and handing prizes to clever dicks in universities. I do my share and the Queen's as well, for it's no secret that the Empress of India practices her own variety of *purdah*. The year of 1887 will be the fiftieth of her reign, her Golden Jubilee, and who do you think is acting as host? The royal families of four continents will be in attendance, and my most daunting task is to persuade the principal subject of all the rejoicing to emerge from her drawing room at Windsor for an afternoon.

What a job! Like putting up a tiger without elephants or beaters. Steady, Bertie. This is a memoir, not a letter of complaint.

It was seven weeks ago that I was given the shocking news that prompted me to turn detective. Yes, *detective*. Does that surprise you? It surprised me. I wouldn't have dreamed of such an eventuality until it grabbed me by the beard and fairly hauled me out of my armchair. Yet now that I reflect upon it, I see that my unique position fitted me admirably for the challenge.

On the afternoon of 8 November, 1886, the first report reached London by wire from Newmarket that Fred Archer had killed himself. You cannot imagine the sensation this caused. Archer, the greatest jockey ever to grace the Turf—and I am confident that you, a century on, will know his name, even though you have never seen his like—had blown his brains out with a revolver bullet. He was twenty-nine years old. This year he had won his fifth Derby, his twenty-first Classic.

How shall I convey the shock that devastated the nation?

Archer was a legend. Crowds gathered to catch a glimpse of him wherever he appeared. Women he had never met pressed passionate letters into his hand. Every owner in the kingdom wanted to retain him. He rubbed shoulders with the highest in the land. Well, the second highest, at any rate—Mama not being a frequenter of racecourses. Here, I must own to a personal interest. In April, 1886, Archer rode a doughty little filly by the name of Counterpane to victory in a Maiden Plate at Sandown Park: my first-ever winner on the flat. We were given a rousing ovation from the public. Sadly, two weeks later, Counterpane broke a blood vessel and dropped dead. I bore it with philosophy, yet looking back, I wonder if my filly's untimely fate presaged the tragedy that befell her rider.

I am told that when the dreadful news of Archer reached London, Fleet Street was impassable for the crowds massed outside the principal newspaper offices. Special editions of the evening papers carrying the bare statement that the great jockey was dead sold out in minutes. Extra-special editions were printed and the sheets were snatched unfolded from the bundles faster than the boys could hand them out.

It chanced that the day following, 9 November, was the forty-fifth anniversary of my birth. As usual, flags were hoisted across the land, gun salutes were fired and church bells rang out peals at intervals from an early hour, but the gun crews and the bell ringers might as well have stayed in bed for all the attention my birthday received. One topic, and one alone, engrossed the nation. In the city, members of the Stock Exchange fought with umbrellas for the first edition of *The Times*.

Those who obtained a copy read in the leading article, "A great soldier, a great statesman, a great poet, even a Royal Prince, might die suddenly without giving half so general a shock as has been given by the news of the tragical death of Fred Archer, the jockey."

How true! I was as shaken as any man, although I cannot forbear from pointing out that the remark about a Royal Prince was in deplorable taste, particularly on my birthday. One never knows what unpleasant shocks lurk unsuspected in the newspapers. I still bristle at the memory of learning in 1876 from *The Times of India* of the proposal to confer the title of Empress on my mother. Neither she nor Disraeli (who accepted his own earldom the same year) had thought fit to tell me about the Royal Titles Act, and I protested vigorously to both, I promise you. In no other country in the world would the next heir to the throne have been treated with such disregard.

Notwithstanding my misgivings about the press, I wanted to know about Archer. I turned out before breakfast and pedaled my tricycle furiously up the drive at Sandringham to meet the delivery boy. Gave him a shock, I fancy. I didn't read the remarks in *The Times* at that juncture. It was all graphically reported in that more congenial organ, *The Sporting Life*.

"Many happy returns of the day, Bertie, my dear," piped my first lady as I repaired to the breakfast room. Dear Alix had made an exceptional effort to be on parade. I can reveal to posterity that the Princess of Wales is not noted for punctuality.

The table was heaped with presents in brightly colored boxes tied with ribbon. A jug of Duminy, *extra sec*, was by my place and a servant hovered for my order. Alix was cooing like a basket of pigeons.

"My birthday is blighted," I informed her.

I must explain that Alix was not aware at this juncture of the tragic tidings from Newmarket. The previous evening, she had retired early. I was entertaining certain of my birthday guests until late. I heard the news of Archer from Knollys, my secretary, about 1:30 A.M.

Alix turned pale. She is inclined to anemia, anyway, and now she was more starched than the tablecloth. "Not another scandal, Bertie?"

"Absolutely not. The very notion," I protested in an outraged tone.

"Then what can have happened?" She put her hand to her collar as another thought occurred. "It isn't—tell me it isn't—bad news from Windsor." Inopportunely, a hint of color returned to her cheeks.

"So far as I'm aware, Mama is in the pink of health," I answered coolly, and then repeated, "The pink of health." (Alix is rather deaf.) "'Long to reign over us,' as the Anthem perpetually reminds one."

She sighed slightly and leaned back. "What, then?"

I tossed her *The Sporting Life.*

"Took his own life?" she read aloud in that Danish chant of hers that makes everything she says sound like Little Jack Horner. "What an unexpected thing to do."

"Due to an aberration of the brain, if the report is to be believed," I explained. "The poor fellow was apparently suffering the effects of typhoid."

"*Apparently.* You sound skeptical."

"I am," I admitted, adding in a measured voice, "I am not unacquainted with the symptoms."

"Of course, my dearest," Alix affirmed with eyes lowered, doubtless recalling how my father, Prince Albert, rest his soul, died of the dread disease and I myself had practically succumbed to it when I was thirty.

I made a rapid summation that saved her the trouble of reading further. "It seems that yesterday morning Archer was pronounced better and was speaking normally to his friends and family. Sometime early in the afternoon, at Archer's own suggestion, the nurse left the room to get some lunch. Mrs. Coleman, his sister, remained in the bedroom. She crossed the room to look out of the window, and Archer got up from the bed with a revolver in his hand. She ran to him and struggled with him, but he put it to his mouth and shot himself."

"Dreadful," said Alix.

"*Rum* is the description I would use," said I. "I shall cogitate on this."

I sent word to the chef to prepare a full breakfast, as for a day's shooting. That is to say, bacon and eggs, and plenty of them, followed by Finnan haddock, followed by chicken, followed by toast and butter, helped down with plenty of coffee. With me, breakfast has to be like the evil thereof in the Bible: sufficient unto the day. I had a strong premonition that this day would make heavy demands on my constitution.

Breakfast was not long in coming, or going. I eat swiftly, and with relish.

To please Alix, I unwrapped a box of Corona y Coronas and a pair of carpet slippers that she unsportingly informed me were exclusively for use in my bedroom at Sandringham, and then I was left to ponder further the strange suicide of Frederick James Archer.

Typhoid?

I can vouch for its dramatic effect upon body and brain. When it poleaxed me, toward the end of 1871, I was delirious for days. I am told that I shouted at my attendants, hurled pillows across the room and broke into songs of the sort that you won't find in the English hymnal. Poor Alix had to be restrained from staying in the room with me on account of certain names I uttered in my ravings. Once she tried to enter secretly on hands and knees, and I felled her with a pillow. I was quite oblivious of my conduct, you understand. Even my devoted Mama the Queen was obliged to shelter behind a screen. I hovered between life and death for weeks on end. As the poet dramatically expressed it:

Across the wires, the electric message came:
"He is no better; he is much the same."

WHEN I *DID* RECOVER, THE whole Empire breathed a sigh of relief. There was a service of public thanksgiving in St. Paul's.

In Archer's case, if the account were true, there were no symptoms of delirium on the day of the tragedy. He so impressed his friends that they left him in the charge of the nurse and Mrs. Coleman. He calmly dispatched the nurse to lunch and then dispatched himself with a bullet. A queer case of typhoid, if you want my opinion.

I summoned Sir Francis Knollys. Where would I be without Knollys? A more loyal secretary never picked up a pen. A bit of a stuffed shirt now that he's past fifty, but a regular pal in a scrape, and we've weathered a few in our time. I could a tale unfold of Francis and his collection of garters, but he's saved me from a few warm moments, so no matter.

"I propose to attend the inquest," I informed him.

"The inquest?" he repeated obtusely.

"Into Archer's death. There will have to be one. Kindly make the arrangement, Francis."

"Of course, sir." He hesitated. "I presume you would wish your attendance to be unofficial?"

"If you mean a seat at the back, see that it's well padded."

I opened another present while he went to make inquiries. Mama had sent me the usual cuff links and a copy of *The Golden Treasury*, with the marker pointedly inserted against a poem entitled "A Renunciation." Hope springs eternal in my mother's breast.

Knollys was back before I had time to open another wrapping.

"It's today, sir. The inquest is this afternoon."

"That's uncommonly quick. I wonder what the hurry is."

"Unfortunately, you have a full day of engagements."

"When haven't I?"

"The Mayor of Cambridge is coming this morning to discuss the Imperial Institute Fund."

"Put him off, Francis. I'd much rather attend the inquest."

"The laborers on the Royal Estate are due to assemble in the mews for the customary dinner in honor of your birthday."

"The laborers? For God's sake, they don't require me in attendance to give them an appetite."

"Then there are your birthday guests: Lord and Lady Randolph Churchill, the Comte and Comtesse de Paris, Prince and Princess Christian—"

"Where precisely is this inquest taking place?"

Knollys made no attempt to muffle the sigh he gave. "New-market, sir. At Archer's private residence."

"At what time?"

"Two o'clock."

"Then I can be back by six at the latest. The Princess will entertain my guests, and I'll see them at my dinner party. Order the carriage."

Although I could think of jollier reasons for visiting Newmarket, I wasn't going to miss this morbid matinee for anything. Fred Archer had been in a few fast finishes in his time, but an inquest within twenty-four hours of his death was remarkable going, even by his standards.

As for my birthday visitors, I reflected as my carriage bowled along the road to Newmarket, I had no conscience about abandoning them for the afternoon. Randolph was fortunate to be received at all (and knew it) after his contemptible behavior in years past over some innocent letters I once penned to Lady Aylesford. (While I was abroad, in India, he came to my wife Alix with threats that he would publish them unless I brought my influence to bear on a divorce case in which his brother was the guilty party. I was so incensed that I challenged him to a duel, which of course he was not man enough to accept. For eight years after, I refused to dine at any house where he was invited.) Of my other guests, the Comte de Paris had come only to shoot pheasant. And the appalling, one-eyed Christian came on sufferance, because he was married to my sister Lenchen (Helena). Setting aside our family difference over Schleswig-Holstein, the man was bereft of the most basic tenets of social behavior. His favorite party piece was to produce his several spare glass eyes at dinner and range them on the table. If that didn't sufficiently disgust the company, he would pass around the bloodshot one he wore when he was suffering from a cold.

The Archer residence, Falmouth House, turned out to be an impressive mansion for a jockey, a multi-gabled redbrick structure in its own grounds on the Bury Road. He had built it three years before when he married the daughter of the trainer, John Dawson. But it proved to be an ill-fated home for the couple. Their infant son died there a few hours after birth in January, 1884, and the following November, his wife also died after giving birth to a second child. And now Falmouth House had seen a third fatality within three years of being built.

My carriage was met by a fellow in a Norfolk jacket whom I took to be one of Archer's family until he announced himself as Captain Buckfast.

Buckfast. Mark his name. I knew it from the racing calendar. He owned and raced horses, and was a close friend of Archer's. I assumed he was sent by the family to meet the royal visitor on account of his army rank. That's the usual form: find an ex-officer and push him forward. Buckfast was adequate to the task, if somewhat diffident. I would have said he was past forty, but my estimates of age have given me several unwelcome surprises of late. I find that I'm classing men of my own age as some years senior to me. I shall have to revise my estimation of what forty-five actually means in terms of thinning hair and thickening elsewhere. If you want to picture Captain Buckfast, he was possessed of a military man's mustache with waxed ends, behind which lurked a less dramatic countenance, brown eyes set widely apart and pale lips that didn't propose to smile without excessive encouragement. His most interesting feature was a crippled left arm that I learned later had been practically hacked off with a spear in the Zulu War.

Not wishing to advertise my presence, I sent the carriage away and asked Buckfast about the arrangements. Once I had established the plan of the house, I had him show me to the bathroom. I'm pretty adept at hide-and-seek in country houses. After a quiet cigar, while the coroner went through the preliminaries downstairs, I planned to make my way to the dining room adjacent to the drawing room. From there, I could follow the proceedings through an open door without being observed by the press.

It didn't go quite as planned.

The cacophony of voices downstairs increased as more people arrived. Apart from the coroner and his officials, there were witnesses, the family, the jury and the press. When I judged from a sudden abatement of the noise that the inquest had begun, I leaned over the landing rail and heard the jury sworn in. The words weren't audible, but I could tell the different tones of voices. I soon picked up the measured accents of the coroner.

I decided to make my move down the stairs. Unfortunately, I

had only reached the third or fourth when I heard the scraping of chairs.

I stopped as if petrified.

A door opened, and people came out into the hall below. They started up the stairs.

Mercifully, I was obscured from their view by the bend in the stairway. I turned and reclimbed those four stairs and pushed open the nearest door.

I was in a bedroom, which didn't surprise me. The room was occupied, which did. The occupant was lying in an open coffin. I was alone with the mortal remains of Fred Archer.

But not for long. The jury was coming upstairs to view the body.

CHAPTER 3

My first instinct was to look for cover. I had the choice of a large mahogany wardrobe or the space under the bed. Neither struck me as suitable. If a lady's honor were in jeopardy, I wouldn't think twice about climbing into a wardrobe or taking my chance beside a chamber pot, but this wasn't that sort of emergency.

I glanced toward the curtains and dismissed that possibility as well. I wasn't a performer in a French farce. My status in the nation obliged me to conduct myself in as dignified a fashion as circumstances permitted. There was nothing I could do except abandon all ideas of remaining anonymous.

I took up a regal stance (left thumb tucked behind overcoat lapel, right hand holding stick, hat and gloves at waist level) beside the coffin as the coroner led the jury into the room. He was giving them encouragement in a well-practiced manner. ". . . a dismal, but necessary, formality. However, gentlemen, the appearance of the deceased is not so disturbing as you might anticipate, the bullet having passed through the mouth and exited at the back of the head. So, if you please . . ."

They lined up on either side. To my astonishment, no one looked twice at me. They simply joined me beside the coffin. I could only assume that their melancholy duty had blinded them to everything else, even an encounter with the Heir Apparent.

The coroner made a small lifting gesture with his fingers that

I supposed for a moment had some ritualistic significance. Then he repeated, "If you please . . ." and it dawned on me that he was gesturing to me.

Here I must intrude a sartorial note. In keeping with the somber occasion, I had dressed in a dark overcoat with black velvet revers and black necktie, and I was carrying a silk hat and black kid gloves. Either the coroner had taken me for an undertaker, or he was giving me the opportunity to pass myself off as such.

I didn't need any more bidding. Obligingly, I bent forward and lifted the piece of linen that covered poor Fred's face.

He was a pitiful sight. The last time I had seen him was a fortnight before, directly after he had lost the Cambridgeshire in a desperate finish, and he had looked extremely dejected then, far too troubled for a man who had won the Derby earlier in the year. It sounds trite to say that he looked decidedly worse now, and I had better explain myself better. It was unmistakably the Archer profile: the broad forehead, well-shaped nose, prominent cheekbones and neat, determined jaw. Still, essentially, a young man's face. I daresay rigor mortis produces strange effects, and no doubt what I noticed was nothing remarkable, but I swear that there was an expression on the features. An expression of terror.

"The jury may wish to examine the back of the head," the coroner said to me, jolting me out of my thoughts. There was no doubt of it; he took me for an undertaker.

I was starting to wonder if I was equal to the job when one of the jurymen, bless him, spoke up. "I suggest we defer to the medical evidence on this. None of us are used to looking at bullet wounds."

There were general murmurs of support.

"Very well," said the coroner. He turned to me. "In that case, that will be sufficient."

I replaced the sheet immediately, and took a step back.

"While we are here," the coroner told the jury, "kindly observe the window where one of the witnesses, Mrs. Coleman, will tell you she was standing before the fatality occurred. Also the night commode beside the bed where the revolver was apparently kept. And the hearth rug upon which the deceased fell. And now, with your cooperation, I propose to resume the inquest downstairs."

They shuffled out without another word between them, leaving me with the corpse. I must confess to feeling slightly piqued that they hadn't recognized me, but on balance it had turned out well. And the story of Bertie the undertaker would go down famously at my birthday party.

Looking back on my career as an amateur detective, I see that it really began when I was left alone in Archer's bedroom. Purely by accident, I'd been afforded a splendid opportunity of searching for clues to the mystery of his sudden death. I'm not given to rummaging through other people's possessions, you understand, but as the man in question was in no mind to object, I made an exception here. So before following the others downstairs, I opened the wardrobe.

The late Mr. Archer had a fine collection of suits, which I methodically searched. Unhappily for me, he also had an efficient valet who had emptied the pockets. I didn't find so much as a spare button. I turned to the tallboy beside the washstand. Nothing of interest to an investigator had been left there. I searched the small chest of drawers and the night commode without result. There wasn't a letter or a visiting card to be found. Not even a betting slip. I couldn't believe that any man led such a colorless life, least of all the most famous jockey in history. Someone had diligently removed every personal item, even photographs. Every bedroom I've ever slept in—and I speak from not inconsiderable experience—has had its display of family photographs on the tallboy: Mama and Grandmama and the Great Aunts and Our Wedding (which I generally turn to the wall). In this room of death there wasn't a picture of the late Mrs. Archer, or even the child so tragically orphaned. I left without a clue, but with my curiosity vastly increased.

Captain Buckfast was giving evidence as I descended the stairs. I moved unobtrusively across the hall and into the empty dining room, where a chair had been thoughtfully provided close to the open door. I was afforded a view of the coroner and the witness without exposing myself to the eyes of the press.

"About four years," Buckfast was saying.

"You were very intimate with him?"

"Yes, sir."

"You visited him frequently?"

"Yes."

"And accompanied him to America on a visit?"

"That is so."

"That was toward the end of 1884, after his wife died?"

"Yes."

"And you have formally identified the body upstairs as that of Frederick James Archer?"

"Yes."

"Now, would you tell us when you last saw him alive, and how he appeared?"

The invitation to provide some information of his own appeared to throw the worthy captain slightly off-balance. He was happier with one-word responses. "I was with him until about noon yesterday. He appeared to be much improved, so I went out. When I returned shortly after two, I heard that he had shot himself."

"Did you ever hear him speak of suicide?"

"Never."

"Did you think he was a man likely to do such an act?"

"No, sir."

"You had conversation with him in the morning?"

"Yes."

"Did he say anything that might have indicated such an intention?"

"No, sir."

The coroner paused. Buckfast stood rigidly waiting for the next question. If someone had shouted, "About face," I am sure he would have obeyed.

"You noticed nothing unusual in his conversation?"

"Only the wandering."

The coroner leaned forward to catch the word. "The what?"

"The wandering. He would converse to a certain extent and then seemed to wander."

"I see. How would you describe his state of mind when you left him at noon?"

"Happy and contented."

"Really?" The coroner picked up a pen from the silver inkstand in front of him, dipped it in the ink and made a note. He resumed, "The deceased had recently been depriving himself of food. Is that correct?"

"Yes, sir."

"Why, exactly?"

"He was wasting for the Cambridgeshire. He rode St. Mirin at eight stone, seven pound."

"This was an exceptionally low weight for the deceased to achieve?"

"Yes."

"He was a tall man for a jockey?"

"Five feet, eight inches."

"By 'wasting,' you mean shedding weight by starving himself?"

"And other methods," volunteered the captain.

"Could you be more specific?"

"He used Turkish baths. And his mixture."

"His mixture?"

"A potion he took."

"Of what, precisely, did this potion consist?"

"I couldn't say. He was very secretive about it."

"It was purgative in effect?"

"I think you'd find it so."

The coroner gave a thin smile. "I am most unlikely to try. Thank you, Captain. I have no more questions for you, unless the jury wishes to ask you anything."

A chair was found for the next witness, Mrs. Emily Coleman, the jockey's sister. She was deeply affected by the tragedy, and even the simple formality of identifying herself caused her difficulty. In appearance and manner she reminded me slightly of my youngest sister Beatrice, with her forlorn, yet winsome, look.

After an interval while we all shifted uneasily in our chairs, Mrs. Coleman found her voice, and then it was difficult to stop her.

"I live here, in my brother's house, and I was with him when he died. I have been with him constantly since he was brought home from Lewes races on Thursday."

"That would have been the fourth of November," the coroner put in to assist his clerk, but the lady hadn't paused.

"I didn't think he was very ill that evening, and he went to bed about half past eleven. The next day, he was unable to get up, so I sent for Dr. Wright, and he took his temperature and it was so high, he said he wanted a second opinion, but Fred refused. Dr. Wright spoke to me and insisted that Dr. Latham was sent for from Cambridge on the Saturday—"

"Sixth of November," interposed the coroner.

". . . and by this time poor Fred was wandering in his mind. He seemed to forget things he had said a few minutes previous. He wouldn't take his medicine. He just kept asking for his mixture. The doctors said he was suffering from a severe chill. They arranged for two nurses to come and help me. The funny thing was that by Monday he appeared to be much better. I had several long conversations with him."

At the rate she was pouring out words, I could well believe it. How much the patient had been allowed to contribute was another question.

"Although he was better, he still wandered in his mind at times, and he was very anxious whether he was going to get over it. Then about two o'clock he said he wanted to speak to me alone. He told me to send the nurse away, which I did."

"So we are coming to the fatal incident," said the coroner in a fortissimo observation that finally induced Mrs. Coleman to pause in her narrative. He was enabled to add, with less bellows, "Tell me, did you notice anything peculiar in his manner?"

"No, he was quite normal. It was nothing unusual for him to ask me to send one of the nurses away, and I thought nothing of it. After she'd gone, I walked toward the window and looked out. Fred suddenly said, 'Are they coming?' Then I heard a noise, and when I turned, he was out of bed and walking across the room, near the door. To my horror, I saw that he had a gun in his hand. I ran toward him and tried to push the gun to one side. He put one arm around my neck and thrust me against the door. I don't know where he got the strength from. He had the revolver in his left hand. Then he put it to his mouth and . . ." Mrs. Coleman bowed her head and sobbed.

At a nod from the coroner, another woman stepped forward to comfort the witness. I think we all felt profoundly sympathetic. No one who had heard the account could have failed to picture the horror of what Mrs. Coleman had endured. I could imagine what the more lurid newspapers would make of it.

When the lady had recovered sufficiently, the coroner said, "There are just a few more details the court requires from you. During this scene that you have just described, did the deceased utter any other words?"

"I've told you the only words he spoke."

"'*Are they coming?*'"

"Yes, sir."

"Did you speak to him?"

"I had no chance. I was screaming for help. Nobody heard me, because the door had closed in the struggle. I got help eventually by ringing the bell."

"How long did the whole transaction take, would you estimate?"

"Not above two minutes, sir."

"And how would you account for it?"

"He seemed to be seized with a sudden impulse. I can't put it better than that."

That concluded Mrs. Coleman's evidence. She was helped away from the chair.

What would you, dear reader, have been thinking at this stage? From the evidence given by Captain Buckfast and Mrs. Coleman, did Archer's behavior sound like a fit of delirium or an aberration of the brain, as the press had suggested?

The crime of suicide presents us with a dilemma. On the one hand, it is an abominable act, punishable by law if the miscreant is unsuccessful in his attempt. On the other, we feel the profoundest sympathy for the close relatives of an individual who has taken his life. This lures us into hypocrisy. If a man is stopped before he pulls the trigger, we send him to prison. If we are too late, we look for signs that he was temporarily insane. From the evidence thus far, it appeared likely that Archer knew what he was doing. I looked forward with interest to the medical witnesses.

First, however, we had Archer's valet, Harry Sarjent. It was he who had first answered the bell and come to the aid of Mrs. Coleman. He explained how he had seen his master lying on the hearth rug, and how he had picked up the revolver that had fallen from Archer's hand. His evidence was all about the gun. About a month previously, Archer had become nervous about a recent burglary in Newmarket and sent his revolver for repair. It had been given to him as a present by a grateful owner. He had loaded it himself and given the valet instructions to put it in the night commode beside his bed when he was at home. At other times, the valet was directed to sleep in the house, with the gun beside him. When Archer had returned from Brighton on the Thursday, the valet, in accordance with instructions, had deposited the revolver in the drawer of the commode.

The nurse, Charlotte Hornidge, came next, and she couldn't have been above nineteen, with a high color to her cheek and black curls thrusting from her cap, far too pretty a creature to empty a bedpan, in my estimation.

The coroner agreed with me, from the way he took off his glasses and cleaned them two or three times.

"I was sent to dinner at seventeen minutes past two," stated Nurse Hornidge, which impressed us all. Here, we thought, is a meticulous witness, as well as a decorative one. "Mr. Archer suggested it to Mrs. Coleman."

Perhaps poor Fred was out of his mind, after all, I thought. Any sane man would have sent his sister to dinner and asked the nurse to remain.

"I had hardly been downstairs one minute when the bell rang violently," she continued confidently. "I also heard cries of help, and a sound as if a pistol had gone off. I dashed upstairs and saw the patient lying on the hearth rug, quite dead. Mrs. Coleman was screaming. The valet was also present. He was just ahead of me."

"You say that your patient was dead, my dear. Did you examine him?"

"I saw that he was bleeding in his mouth. I looked in his eyes and felt his pulse, but I didn't examine him further. I waited for the doctor."

"Eminently sensible," commented the coroner with an ingratiating smile. "Now perhaps you would say something about his state of mind, as you perceived it that morning. Was he rational, so far as you could tell?"

"Oh, yes. When I spoke, he always answered rationally, but he was very low-spirited when I was nursing him. I remember a conversation when he told me he thought he was going to die. I told him to cheer up, because there was no reason to think he would die. He replied, 'I wish I was of your way of thinking.'"

"But you still found him rational? He didn't appear to you to wander in his mind?"

"No, sir."

"Not in any way at all?"

"Not in the least."

"You're quite certain?"

"Utterly."

I may be mistaken, but I thought the coroner sounded slightly less enchanted by Nurse Hornidge when he thanked her for her testimony and told her to return to her seat.

The final witness stepped forward. Dr. J. R. Wright of Newmarket was a silver-haired, crisply spoken man, who must have appeared many times before the coroner. His manner of giving evidence carried authority.

"I was Mr. Archer's medical man for fourteen years. He had pretty good health. I have never attended him for a serious illness until this case of typhoid. I was called to see him last Friday morning, the fifth of November, and I found him in a high state of fever, extremely restless. I prescribed for him and saw him again at two. By then the fever symptoms had increased. Indeed, his temperature was so very high that I suggested having a second opinion. The patient declined, but I took it on myself to send for Dr. Latham from Cambridge."

"He is an authority on fevers?" inquired the coroner.

"He is a colleague whose opinion I value," stated the doctor in a tone that made the question seem superfluous.

"Kindly proceed."

"Dr. Latham sent his carriage for me the next morning at seven-thirty. We examined the patient together. He was no better. His temperature was the same, and he was not prepared to be cooperative."

"In what way, Doctor?"

"He told us he didn't require another medicine. He wanted his wasting mixture."

"Why was that?"

"He had a delusion that a dinner he'd eaten three days ago was still in his stomach."

"Ah," said the coroner, removing his glasses and placing them on the table. "His mind was wandering."

"It is not unusual in cases of fever."

"I'm sure. Pray go on, Doctor."

"Dr. Latham attended again in the afternoon and told the patient he had typhoid fever, and he then became more quiet."

"You agreed on the diagnosis?"

Dr. Wright answered, "There is no question of it. Admittedly, the patient appeared to rally during the course of the weekend and his temperature fell on Sunday afternoon, but this is not uncommon. In fact, on Monday morning, he was better."

"When you say 'better,' do you mean that his temperature was normal on the morning he died?"

"Fluctuations in temperature are to be expected," answered Dr. Wright.

"I must have a more precise answer to my question, Doctor."

"The patient's temperature was normal yesterday morning."

"How was his behavior?"

"He was very low-spirited. He told me continually that he would die. I had a reassuring talk with him and left about nine-thirty. I was called back in the afternoon, about two-thirty. When I saw the deceased, he was on his back on the floor, covered with a sheet, quite dead. There was a wound at the back of his mouth. On examining the back of his head, I found an opening between the two upper cervical vertebrae. I was shown the revolver, and I have seen the bullet found on the dressing table, and I have no doubt that it was the bullet that passed through the spinal column, causing death."

"I am sure the jury has been greatly assisted by your evidence, Doctor. I have just one or two questions more concerning the state of mind of the deceased."

The doctor didn't need to have them. He knew what was wanted. "I would say that he was not delirious in his fever, so much as disconnected in his thoughts. It seemed from the commencement of the illness to take the form of depression. One must also take account of the weakened state he was in from reducing his weight by unnatural amounts. This, followed by the fever, so disordered his brain that he was not accountable for his actions. In other words, he was temporarily insane when he committed the act."

Approving murmurs were heard. It was as if the doctor had spoken for the whole of Newmarket, and there was no question what the jury's verdict would be.

Fred Archer was found to have committed suicide while in a state of temporary insanity induced by typhoid fever.

CHAPTER 4

Hold on to your hat and keep your wits about you, for we're about to make a backward leap. After that depressing inquest, I propose to treat you to a breath of fresh air and some sport. Of the four-legged variety, naturally. We'll project ourselves back a fortnight, and bring poor Archer briefly back to life, put him on St. Mirin and look at his last ride of consequence, the 1886 Cambridgeshire. My weakness for the Turf is well known, so in case this smacks of self-indulgence, let me assure you that the race is fundamental to the crime I shall unfold.

To Headquarters, then, on Tuesday, 26 October (Headquarters being the name by which Newmarket is affectionately known to all patrons of the Turf). A day for topcoats and mufflers: chill, slate gray and with a stiff breeze blowing off the fens. Not that October weather would deter the race-going public. They came in their thousands, trainloads from Liverpool Street and St. Pancras, the Midlands and the North. Personally, I avoid traveling on the day of a big race if I can possibly help it. I arrive on the first or second day of the meeting and stay overnight in my rooms in the Jockey Club. If affairs of state compel me to travel on race day, I make an outrageously early start. It's either that, or trail the last five miles in slow procession between the four-in-hand full of jovial "men" from Cambridge, and a trap containing a farmer and his giggling daughters. No thank you.

I wouldn't mention this to the good people who live there, but between ourselves, the town of Newmarket is a fearful disappointment when you first see it. It's little more than a stretch of the London to Norwich Road lined with dull buildings, most of them modern. The only edifice of interest is the Jockey Club, and that chooses to sit with its back to the High Street.

Mercifully, there's more to Newmarket than its buildings. From first light onward, the High Street echoes to the clatter of hooves as the trainers lead their strings to the gallops. See the breath on the morning air and the shimmer of well-groomed flanks and you'll know what animates this place. It has been linked with the horse ever since Queen Boadicea in her chariot led the Iceni against the Romans, but the credit for making it the headquarters of racing should be awarded to the Stuarts. That shameless old reprobate, King James I, built a palace and royal stables here and was rebuked for spending too much time at the races, as were his son and grandson, Charles I and II. They have my sympathy. Do you know, my mama the Queen has never patronized a Newmarket meeting? Before I was old enough to declare an interest, she had the old palace of Newmarket auctioned. It was demolished by the purchaser, and now a Congregational chapel stands on the site.

On this Cambridgeshire day, the High Street was practically impassable by noon. There is always a throng outside the Subscription Rooms, where the principal bets are laid. I had made sure of getting reasonable odds the previous night, so for the purposes of this narrative we can proceed at once to the Heath.

The Cambridgeshire is the last great race of the season, with a character all its own. It gives the final chance for a horse to impress before it goes to winter quarters, an uphill one-mile, two hundred and forty yards for three-year-olds and over, where sprinters and stayers can try conclusions. Fortunes are staked on the outcome. For a betting man, the good old Cambridgeshire has more to commend it than the classics. Form and the handicapper aren't infallible, thank the Lord, and there's a rich history of sensations. Catch 'em Alive was the winner in 1863, but in the weighing room afterward, calamity! His jockey couldn't draw the weight. They were about to disqualify him and award the stakes to the second, when someone thought of examining the scales. Would you believe it, some blackguard had tampered with them by fastening sheet lead to the bottom of the weight-scale. Another drama that outraged

many was Isonomy's two-length win at 40-1 in 1878, after that foxy
old trainer John Porter kept his form from the touts for a twelve-
month. Fred Gretton, the owner, is said to have netted £40,000.
Is it any wonder that I sent my horses to Porter? And I'll give you
one more Cambridgeshire controversy: Bendigo's win by a head
in 1883, believed by no one except his backers, and precious few
of them, if truth be told.

Back to 1886. The day couldn't have started in finer style. My filly,
Lady Peggy, easily carried home my colors at 10—1 in the Maiden
Plate for two-year-olds, putting the crowd in bonny humor and one
hundred guineas in my pocket. Amid a chorus of loyal acclaim, I
took myself and several of my party down to the unsaddling.

Archer was the jockey. For me, nothing can equal the pleasure
of leading one of my own into the winner's enclosure, and I don't
mind admitting that my heart swelled when the champion jockey
dismounted and stood beside me and my steaming filly. As I write
these words, I have a tinted photograph on my desk that brings it
vividly to mind, Archer in my colors, the purple with gold braid
and scarlet sleeves, and the gold-fringed black velvet cap.

I'm racking my memory to see if I can possibly recall any sign
that he was under strain. It's difficult. The pinched look is common
to all jockeys except boys, and Archer, as you know, had wasted
more than usual to make the weight for his Cambridgeshire ride.
He was an inch and a half taller than I and weighed all of six
stones less (though I've never aspired to be a jockey).

The only sign of anything untoward was that he was talkative.
I must tell you that the greatest jockey in history wasn't noted for
his conversation. He generally saved his breath to cool his porridge, as the saying goes. Yet here in the unsaddling enclosure,
surrounded by the usual gogglers and fawners, I was treated to a
regular torrent of words.

"She's a plucky one, your Royal Highness," says he. "I wouldn't
call her a classic prospect, but she'll earn some tin if you pick her
races carefully. Tidy work over the last furlong, wasn't it? When I
started to ride her with my hands, she half stopped and pricked
up her ears as if she wondered what it meant. Then she did all I
asked. Wasn't it a tonic to watch?"

"Emphatically," I answered. "But let's give the jockey some
credit as well."

"Thank you, sir."

"You must be feeling confident," I commented, fishing for information.

"Cock-a-hoop, sir."

"So should I chance a tenner on St. Mirin?"

"Every tenner you can spare, sir. I haven't won a Cambridge-shire yet, but I've never had a prospect like today."

Lord Edward Somerset, the owner of the favorite, Carlton, happened to be one of my party, and close enough to hear this. "Get away, Fred!" says he. "You won't beat my colt and you know it. Yours hasn't learned how to gallop. Alec Taylor tried them together and Carlton took it by a street."

"I heard, my Lord," commented Fred impassively, as he loosened Lady Peggy's girth, "but did you take the riders into account? The lad on St. Mirin was a novice."

"Where did you discover that?" asked Somerset, flushing to the tips of his ears.

"From the horse's mouth," responded Fred in all seriousness. He paused before he added, "The poor beast was never off the bit." With that, he lifted off the saddle, touched his cap and left me laughing, and Edward Somerset purple faced.

"Pig obstinate," Edward commented when the jockey was out of earshot. "He was offered the ride on Carlton and he refused."

"Do I detect a dwindling of confidence?" I asked.

"Not on your life."

Nonetheless, I dispatched one of my party to Tattersall's ring to put fifty on St. Mirin at 10-1. In the Subscription Rooms the previous evening, I'd already backed an elderly outsider, The Sailor Prince, at 25-1 for sentimental reasons (he was the son of a horse called Albert Victor, and *my* A. V. went through Dartmouth, and my other boy George is in the Navy still).

Edward Somerset's story of the trial between Carlton and St. Mirin was true, and pretty common knowledge. Both colts were trained at Manton by Alec Taylor and regarded as useful three-year-olds. One morning on the Marlborough Downs, observed by touts from all the sporting press, he raced them over a measured mile, and Carlton came out an easy victor.

Why, then, was Archer so confident of St. Mirin taking the Cambridgeshire? And why so talkative? Uniquely in his career, he had made sure every newspaper blazoned his confidence: "The crack jockey fancies his mount immensely."

Certainly St. Mirin was well sired, by that plucky Derby winner, Hermit, out of Lady Paramount. It had promised well, but hadn't won anything as a two-year-old. If I'm any judge of horseflesh, it was too light about the loin and flank to possess much stamina. I like an animal with something behind besides ribs.

My thoughts returned to St. Mirin's hindquarters when the Cambridgeshire entrants were paraded in the saddling enclosure known to all Turfites as the Birdcage. Prominent there was the animal's owner, the Dowager Duchess of Montrose, as formidable a female as ever graced the Turf. She is known unkindly, but not inaptly, as Six-Mile Bottom, and if St. Mirin had been half so generously endowed as she in that portion of the anatomy, the race would have been as good as over.

Did that strike you as an ungallant observation? The fact is that Carrie Montrose had long since put herself beyond the pale. Before I was born, she scandalized society by insulting my mother the Queen. This was over the so-called Bedchamber Plot in 1839, when Mama, encouraged by Lord Melbourne, stoutly refused to dismiss certain of her Whig ladies-in-waiting, and so frustrated Peel in his attempt to form a Tory administration. Mama doted on Lord Melbourne, you know, and thanks to her firmness, he was returned as Prime Minister. At the Ascot races she invited Melbourne to sit beside her in her carriage for the drive up the racecourse. This was all too much for the young Duchess of Montrose and another Tory woman. They stepped brazenly forward and hissed the Queen. Mama was incensed. She said such creatures deserved to be horsewhipped. If you ask me, there was intemperance on both sides. Mama wouldn't like it said, but she and Carrie Montrose have much in common. The difference is that Carrie's tantrums take place in public.

On this Cambridgeshire afternoon, the Duchess had wrapped herself in a sable coat that must have decimated the wildlife of Canada. She was haranguing Archer as he waited to mount St. Mirin, and half the racecourse could hear it: "I want no sleeping in the saddle, Fred. He's a horse in a million and I adore him, but don't spare the whip if he slackens."

Stony faced, the greatest jockey of the age kept his eyes on the horse in a million. No one knew exactly how much the Duchess had paid him as a retainer, but it was close to five figures for a claim of any sort, so he was well compensated for any embarrassment.

On the far side of the Birdcage, Edward Somerset issued final instructions to the elder of the Woodburn brothers, who was riding Carlton, with only six stone, thirteen pounds, compared with St. Mirin's eight stone seven. In Tattersall's ring, Carlton remained the clear favorite, although his price had lengthened slightly. St. Mirin, for all the confidence bestowed in him by Archer and his owner, was some way down the betting. Melton, the 1885 Derby and St. Leger winner, was being heavily backed at 100-6, in spite of his in-and-out form and the nine stone, seven he was handicapped. Tyrone, of whom I knew little, had come in at 8-1. St. Mirin's on-course price had lengthened to 100-8.

The signal was given to mount, and we patrons of the Turf made the best speed we could to our points of vantage. I called for my hack and cantered up the hill to the finishing post. The Cambridgeshire, I must explain, takes a different course from the rest of the day's program. It starts near the new stand at the Rowley Mile and proceeds up a stiff rise, "on the collar" all the way, to the part of the Heath known as the top of the town. A forty-minute interval is given after the finish of the previous race to allow the public to foot it up the hill, but few who make the effort are likely to be satisfied with what they see. A really good view of the Cambridgeshire is difficult to come by. You need to be on the roof of a brougham at the very least to look down the steep gradient to the start. The carriages reach all the way past the rails. I'm afraid the groundlings catch only a glimpse of the jockeys' jackets, unless they miss the finish altogether and station themselves opposite the Red Post, about two furlongs from home.

My carriage was by the winning post. Good-humored shouts and applause hailed me as I clambered up to the box seat and focused my race glasses on the advance flag at the start. The starter's assistants were still trying to get some semblance of order into the field, so I put down my glasses and took a warming sip of brandy. I defy anyone not to feel dry-mouthed with anticipation at the sight of that emerald band of freshly mown turf stretching away across the Heath.

Carlton or St. Mirin?

Lord Edward Somerset or the Duchess of Montrose?

Sixteen had cantered to the start, one of the smallest fields in memory. I mounted the roof of my carriage and got another cheer. I secured my top hat more firmly, for there was the devil of a wind blowing up the course, likely to trouble all but the strongest. Several others of my party who had joined me on the roof did likewise.

I held my glasses steady and picked out the start again.

They were moving toward the tapes. There was some hesitation as one reared up and tried to turn. The jockey was quick to assert his control.

The flag fell. The familiar, irresistible shout went up.

I trained my glasses on the multicolored line as it stirred and rippled like the tail of a kite. Without a doubt they were charging up the course, yet they scarcely appeared to progress at all. For an agonizing interval it was impossible to tell who had taken up the running, then the name Carlton was on everyone's lips. I shifted my glasses to the left. The colors of Mr. Somers, as Edward is known—blue, with white diamonds—definitely showed in front on the lower ground. It was already obvious that Carlton was setting a scorching pace. They had all settled down to their work, and I couldn't make out who was second for a long time.

Then I glimpsed St. Mirin, tucked in usefully behind the leader; you'll understand that I have a sharp eye for a scarlet sleeve, and the Montrose colors are all of that hue. Tom Cannon, on Melton, was close up. The three favored horses had chosen to make their running together on the lower ground, pursued by several others, while another group, including Tyrone and The Sailor Prince, had elected to strike out on the right.

As they approached the Red House, the favorite still led, and those wily horsemen, Archer and Cannon, were preparing to challenge. I gripped my glasses and shouted with the crowd. I could see young Woodburn desperately trying to liven Carlton with some rib roasters, but Somerset's colt appeared to be straining to master the hill.

The three fixed in my focus were raising a veritable cloud of steam. The wind and the gradient were taking a toll of them all, and there were still two furlongs to run. Carlton's stride was visibly shortening. Was St. Mirin's? I feared so.

To another roar from the crowd, Melton moved out to challenge the leader. Cannon's *eau-de-Nil* jacket appeared to show in front. He was sitting well. Melton had a glorious action and Tom didn't need to be told he was on a good thing.

Then, by Jupiter, the scarlet of St. Mirin showed! He drew level with Carlton. He challenged Melton. He dashed into the lead. Too soon? I wondered. Better than being boxed up, I tried to tell myself. I ground my teeth in apprehension at Archer's temerity. I'm a dreadful faint heart when watching something my money is on.

Tom Cannon is no slouch. He has collected every classic in his time. In 1882, he took the 2000 Guineas, the Derby and the Oaks, and he's been runner-up to Archer as champion jockey more times than I cared to remember at this stage of the race. He was making a fight of it now.

The whips were out. They were so close that I could hear the drumming of hooves and see the mud kicked up. Carlton appeared to have shot his bolt, which subdued some of the crowd, yet there was still a tremendous din around me.

I suffered agonies as Melton edged closer to St. Mirin. Cannon has a reputation for gentle handling, yet I tell you, in that final furlong he flogged his mount as soundly as ever Archer punished a horse. Nor, it goes without saying, was St. Mirin spared the whip. Whatever the result, Carrie Montrose would have no cause to complain, for Archer obeyed her instructions impeccably.

And I should have trusted him to find enough. Who else but Archer would one depend upon to get up in a neck-and-neck finish? He was the master. When the horse was off the bit and dashing full pelt for the post, Fred knew precisely when to use the whip and how to stand on the stirrups and get so far forward that it was practically his cap that first crossed the line.

Fifty yards from home, Melton faltered. In his Derby year, he might have held on, but as a four-year-old carrying top weight he couldn't sustain the effort. He threw up his head, and I knew he was beaten.

What a fright he had given me!

I lowered my glasses and cheered St. Mirin and his rider.

How often has it been borne home to me that nothing in this sport is certain? From nowhere, it seemed, a blur of black and Indian red appeared on the far side. Something was challenging St. Mirin on the top ground. It had come out of the ruck and was finishing faster than Carlton and Melton. Damn my eyes, it was faster than St. Mirin!

Archer must have seen the danger at the edge of his vision. His head didn't turn, but he used the whip again. St. Mirin and its challenger passed the post together. I was opposite the line and I couldn't separate them.

"What was it?" I demanded of one of my party.

"The Sailor Prince, sir."

The Sailor Prince! My outsider at 25-1!

Do you see what I meant about the Cambridgeshire? This animal's form was laughable. It was the oldest horse in the field, a six-year-old that had run the race twice before and never finished better than ninth!

The crowd had lapsed into the buzz of anguish and frustration that follows an unexpected result. Few had backed either St. Mirin or The Sailor Prince, but I was doubly satisfied. Whatever the outcome, I'd picked the winner. Now, which would it be?

These things always take longer than you expect, and I hate suspense, so I got down from my carriage to seek an opinion from the jockeys.

By the time I arrived in the weighing room, Archer was stepping off the scales, pale, flecked with mud, eyes downcast.

"Well, Fred, what's your opinion?" I asked straight out. "Come on, man, don't play the oyster."

Hearing my voice, he looked across, twitched his features into something that was intended for a smile, and said without much exultation, "I believe I held him off, sir."

I noticed Tiny White, the lad who had ridden The Sailor Prince, give a slight shake of the head, but nothing else was said until we all stood outside waiting for the numbers to be hoisted in the frame. Then Sir George Chetwynd came up to Archer and asked his opinion, and the champion contradicted his earlier verdict and said, "I was beaten. I allowed Tom Cannon to kid me."

He was right. A moment later The Sailor Prince was declared the winner by a head. It was the oldest horse ever to win a Cambridgeshire.

I told Archer to have no regrets on my account, as I'd backed the winner, and then I asked him the meaning of his remark about Cannon.

"I shouldn't have taken him on so early," said he. "Mine had nothing more to give when the outsider made its run."

"You didn't disgrace yourself, Fred," I tried to assure him.

He gave me a bleak look and spoke the last words I ever heard him utter: "I wish I agreed with you, sir."

I took it as a typical Archer remark after losing a race he believed he should have won. Poor beggar, I thought, you've got another rough ride in prospect when Carrie Montrose catches up with you. I wouldn't care to receive one of her tongue-lashings. Almost as daunting as a summons to Windsor after a night out with the Marlborough House set.

I don't know what Carrie had to say to Archer, but that same evening she sold St. Mirin, the colt she "adored," to the Duke of Westminster for 4,500 guineas.

And the real story of the race had yet to come out.

CHAPTER 5

After the inquest, I remained for some time in the dining room of Falmouth House, not wishing to reveal myself to the gentlemen of the press. Looking at my surroundings, it seemed eminently reasonable that Archer should have decided to equip himself with a revolver, for the sideboard practically groaned with silver trophies and the walls were crowded with paintings. Four of his Derby winners were represented there in oils, with the prime position over the mantelpiece awarded to Arnull's portrait of Bend Or, and no wonder, considering the phenomenal manner in which the big chestnut colt overcame Robert the Devil in 1880. Did you ever hear the story of what happened to Archer before that celebrated race? If you're a serious reader (i.e. without a sense of humor), you have my permission to skip the next paragraph or two, because it has no bearing on the mystery, but if, like me, you are partial to a spot of amusing gossip, read on.

To some, Fred Archer was a paragon among jockeys, but the plain truth is that he was uncommonly hard on his mounts. He didn't hesitate to use whip and spurs to vitalize a horse unwilling in its work, and one, aptly named Muley Idris, took its revenge one morning after a training gallop. It seized his right arm in its jaws, swung him off his feet and would have trampled him if someone hadn't come to his rescue. The limb was a fearful mess and the Derby was only three weeks off. Archer's doctor referred him to Harley Street, and the specialist he saw happened to be

Sir James Paget, a man so ignorant of sport that if you mentioned Epsom, he thought of a laxative remedy. Sir James dressed the wound and put the arm in a splint and told Archer it should be better in three weeks.

"But shall I be right for the Derby?" Fred inquired.

"I think you can go."

"Yes, but can I ride?"

"Better drive, my boy, better drive."

With admirable self-control, Fred said, "I fear, sir, you have not realized who I am."

Sir James peered at his pad and said, "I see I have the honor of receiving a Mr. Archer . . ."

"Yes, Sir James," said Fred, "and I think I should tell you that what you are in your profession, I am in mine. If I ride Bend Or, I could earn in the region of two thousand pounds."

"Two thousand?" said the consultant, after a thoughtful pause. "And you say we are coequals. I've never charged that for a horse bite, but for you, Mr. Archer, I'm willing to make an exception."

To complete the story, Archer started that Derby with a near useless right arm supported by an iron splint. Around Tattenham Corner, he was in fifth place, six lengths adrift of Robert the Devil. In the last furlong, he reached for his whip, but the pain in his arm obliged him to drop it at once. Miraculously, by dint of voice power and extraordinary horsemanship, he persuaded Bend Or to shorten the advantage yard by yard and finally get its nose in front. He remarked to me later, "Bend Or wasn't the best I ever rode, sir, but he was the gamest. We pulled that one out of the fire."

Dedicated detective story readers, resume here. Quite properly, the room also contained a bronze statuette, on a table against the window, of that beautiful animal, St. Simon, which missed its chance to run the Derby, but retired unbeaten and never seriously challenged. The sculptor, I noticed, was Boehm, of whom more anon. I was still facing the window when I said aloud, "Rather a pantomime, wasn't it?"

Captain Buckfast (I'd spotted his reflection as he entered) answered, "I beg your pardon, sir."

"The inquest," I enlightened him. "A performance of make-believe—with the ending everyone wanted." Since he didn't respond to this neat analogy, I turned and said, "You don't really believe the verdict, do you?"

I was being unfair, I admit—his future monarch inviting him to question a British jury's decision. The poor fellow was struck dumb. His mouth gaped, and his brown eyes registered something between mystification and panic. To restore confidence, I issued an order (which never fails with the military): "Show me over the house, Captain, and I'll explain. Has everyone departed except family and servants?"

They had, and I started my tour of inspection in the cellars. My respect for the late owner increased even more when I saw his champagne—I would estimate over two hundred dozen of vintage stock, tidily racked. "He took it in moderation," Buckfast assured me in the reverential voice one uses of the recently departed.

"At what hour of the day?"

"Lunch, sir."

"And of what did his lunch consist?"

"A glass of this and one sardine."

"One sardine?"

"Yes, sir."

"And after that? A dose of castor oil?" I quipped.

"No, sir. That was for breakfast."

He was completely serious. I decided not to pursue the intimate workings of Archer's digestion. "If I recollect, you said in your evidence that you have known him four years."

"Yes, sir."

"As a friend?"

"I like to think so."

"A friend in whom he confided?"

"On occasions."

I was doing no better than the coroner at drawing him out. I must have pulled a face, because he added defensively, "I'm known for my discretion, sir."

"Of that I have no doubt. Would you go so far as to say that, since the death of his wife last year, you were closer to Archer than anyone else?"

"I would, sir."

I waited.

Eventually he cleared his throat and volunteered, "I looked after his business affairs, his racing engagements and so forth."

My silence was more productive than my questions.

He added, "When I say 'looked after,' I must make it clear, sir, that Fred made his own decisions. He simply left the paperwork to me."

"So he wasn't much of a hand with pen and ink?"

"He was illiterate. He could barely scratch his own signature."

We moved upstairs to the drawing room where the inquest had taken place. This, too, was hung with oils and engravings, including portraits of two of Archer's patrons, Lord Falmouth and the Duke of Westminster. Then my attention was diverted by a familiar item on a card table, a silver cigarette case mounted on a crude chunk of metal that an inscription informed us was a portion of a shell that had burst on the deck of the gunboat *Condor* when my old pal Charlie B. (Lord Charles Beresford) found fame at the bombardment of Alexandria. I have an identical one. Lord knows how many Charlie distributed.

I made some witty remark about it to Captain Buckfast and he began to relax a little. He escorted me around the room, pointing out the Classic winners, and we exchanged memories of some of Archer's notable triumphs. Buckfast took a rather touching pride in each success. His reserve, I decided, wasn't born of stubbornness, so much as loyalty to a great man of the Turf who happened to have been his friend, and I liked him better for it.

"Fred's record will take some beating," I remarked, fresh from reading the obituary columns. "Thirteen years in succession as Champion Jockey and over 2,700 winners."

"Twenty-one of them Classics," Buckfast chipped in.

"Pity about the suicide," I added casually. "I can understand the decision to arrange the inquest so soon—or I think I can. Was that your doing, Captain?"

"The family's," said he. "Mr. Archer, Sr., and Fred's brother, Charles. Once this appalling thing occurred, they wanted to, em—"

"Bury him as soon as possible?"

Buckfast cleared his throat and murmured confidentially, "He was used to the intrusions of the press, but the family are not."

"Quite. They don't want the newshounds in full cry."

"Exactly, sir."

I nodded and remarked, "I think everyone cooperated admirably."

He either missed my irony or decided to let it pass. He smiled a little awkwardly and said, "Would you care to see the Turkish bath, sir?"

The Turkish bath, where by all accounts poor Archer spent the greatest part of his time at home, was an outhouse beyond the kitchen containing two tiled rooms. We presently stood in the hot-air chamber among the plumbing and wooden slats, and in that more secluded place talked of the real significance of the inquest.

"I should like to expand upon my earlier remarks," I offered. "I've no reason to believe that anyone at the inquest was dishonest. I merely observe that some of the evidence was inconsistent. Let's take the nature of the illness that had afflicted poor Archer."

"Typhoid fever."

I arched an eyebrow. "So the doctor conveniently informed us. Conveniently, because it is well known that typhoid induces hallucinations of the brain. I suffered it myself."

"The whole nation suffered with you, sir."

"How kind of you to mention it."

After a suitable interval, Buckfast asked, "Are you skeptical of the diagnosis, sir?"

"Perhaps you recall the doctor saying in evidence that he and his colleague diagnosed typhoid on the Saturday afternoon."

"Yes, indeed."

"How strange, then, that Mrs. Coleman wasn't informed. She believed her brother was suffering from a severe chill. Isn't that what she said?"

"There seems a discrepancy, certainly . . ."

"When were *you* informed that he was suffering from typhoid?"

"Yesterday, sir."

"After he shot himself?"

"Well, yes."

"Not on Saturday, when the doctor claimed the diagnosis was made?"

"No, sir."

"Doesn't that strike you as queer?"

Buckfast hesitated. "I'm in no doubt that he was very ill at the week's end, sir. Feverish. A very high temperature."

"Undoubtedly," I concurred, "for a couple of days. He was poorly on Saturday and Sunday, but yesterday he was sitting up having conversations."

Buckfast nodded. "Perfectly true, sir."

I said in a reasonable tone, "It sounds most unlike the typhoid I experienced. I was at death's door for three weeks. A severe chill I can believe, but typhoid . . ."

Buckfast stood erectly, saying nothing.

"Of course," I went on, rather enjoying this (you can see me blossoming as a detective, can't you?), "if one were to stand logic on its head and reverse cause and effect, a possible expla-nation emerges. Suicide equals brain fever equals typhoid. A well-intentioned family doctor may see it as his duty to confirm such a diagnosis."

Buckfast thought it proper to defend the medical profession. "There was the matter of the wandering."

"Ah, the wandering," said I. "Everyone was at pains to mention the wandering. It is, after all, a well-known symptom of typhoid. Everyone, that is to say, except the nurse."

"I thought she spoke of it," said Buckfast with a frown.

"The coroner did, when the nurse was giving evidence. He particularly asked her whether the patient wandered in his mind. She denied it. She said she was utterly certain that he didn't."

"Perhaps she was absent from the room when it occurred," the Captain responded.

"Possibly," said I, and then suggested, not without irony, "Shall we move on? The ventilation in this place leaves something to be desired."

We removed ourselves to the conservatory, passing Mrs. Cole-man on the way. I don't think she could have overheard us in the Turkish bath. She effected a passable curtsy, and I returned a nod, as one couldn't smile in the circumstances. In feature and build she was very like her brother had been, though better nourished. She was still red-eyed from weeping, reminding me that the family wouldn't be overly pleased at having the inquest verdict questioned. However, if Archer, as I suspected, had been terrorized into taking his own life, someone was responsible and should be made to answer for it.

Among the ferns and palms I rapidly located the only bentwood chair furnished with cushions, and dispatched Buckfast for a bottle of Archer's vintage bubbly. As I reasonably pointed out, the owner had no more use for it. Knowing Archer's reputation for tightness—not for nothing was he known as the Tin Man—I privately doubt whether he would have offered us so much as a glass of beer while he was alive, but I don't believe in speaking ill of the dead, so I gave him the benefit of the doubt and uncorked his champagne when it was brought. I also offered Buckfast a cigar. Not often do I hand out my specials to virtual strangers. However, a notion was forming in my brain that the Captain could be of service to me. When he had poured me a glass, I invited him to take the stool opposite. Without fuss he wedged a matchbox between his knees and struck a light with his good hand and offered it to me. The hand shook a little as it approached my cigar, but whose wouldn't? All in all, he exemplified what is best in the British army officer: resource, good manners and loyalty to the Crown.

"Tell me about yourself," I invited him warmly. "Are you a family man like me?" (That *like me* is my way of putting a man at his ease.)

"No, sir." (It doesn't always succeed.)

"What is your status, then?"

"I'm a bachelor with rooms in London. Jermyn Street."

"A good address," I told him. "Not far from mine. I have a place in Pall Mall."

"I know, sir."

"And you had some time in the army? The Guards?"

"Cavalry, sir. The 17th Lancers. I was wounded in the Zulu War, at Kambula."

"Rotten luck."

"I got in the way of an assagai."

I shook my head in sympathy. "A savage beast."

"It was a spear, sir."

"I was referring to the native who threw it, Captain. So you returned to England—on a generous pension, I hope?"

"It suffices, sir. I have a modest private income."

"And you know enough about racing to earn a penny or two?"

He gave the suspicion of a smile. "One never knows enough, unfortunately."

"How true!"

He added, "I owned a colt that won the Guineas and came second in the Derby."

"Oh? Which was that?"

"Paradox."

I was more than a little impressed. He was speaking of one of the outstanding thoroughbreds of recent years. "You owned Paradox? I thought Brodrick-Cloete owned Paradox."

"I sold it as a two-year-old."

"Pity. What did you get for it?"

"Six thousand. I bought it as a yearling for seven hundred."

"Not bad! I can see why Archer cultivated you. Let's drink to Paradox." We touched glasses and I looked searchingly into his eyes. "I want to confide in you, Captain," I informed him without ceremony. "From all I heard this afternoon, I don't believe Archer was deranged by typhoid. I think he shot himself deliberately. Does that shock you?"

He was silent for a moment. "Why should he do such a thing, sir?"

I lowered my glass and leaned forward. "That's the crux of it, Buckfast, that's the crux of it. I'm hoping you can enlighten me. We heard he was low-spirited. Is that true? When you left him at midday yesterday, he was happy and contented. Weren't those your very words?"

"Well, yes. That was my clear impression, sir."

"Yet the doctor and the nurse reported that he was low in spirits. He told them he was going to die."

Buckfast lowered his eyes for a moment and rested his chin on his fist in an attitude of thought. "They must have been speaking of much earlier. The doctor left by half past nine. By noon, when I went out, Fred was much improved. You could ask Mrs. Coleman."

"I don't think we should trouble her now."

"I wouldn't have dreamed of going out if I'd thought he was depressed, sir. I cared about Fred. I've seen him through some dreadful times—slanderous attacks by people who should have known better, the deaths of his first child and his wife. I took him to America to recover from the grief. When you've seen a man in the depth of despair, you know the signs. He was at peace when I last saw him. I swear it."

From a normally reticent man, this was a singularly moving

speech. Buckfast had gone quite pink as he uttered it. He took out a handkerchief and wiped the corner of his eye.

I refilled his glass. "Now that he's gone, what do you propose to do?"

"I've hardly had time to consider, sir. I've been showing the coroner over the house and preparing for the funeral. After that, no doubt I'll be asked to assist the executors in going through his papers."

"After these duties have been dispensed, would you consider rendering a service to me?"

He didn't move a muscle, but his eyes shone like the Koh-i-Noor. I believe he thought I was about to offer him a position as my racing manger. "Whatever you deem that I'm capable of performing, sir."

I said, "I, too, had a strong regard for Archer, and I'm not satisfied that what we heard today was the whole truth. I shall be making some inquiries of my own—in the strictest confidence—and you are best placed to assist me in this enterprise."

He looked a shade crestfallen, I thought, but to his credit he said at once, "It will be my honor and my pleasure, sir."

"Not much pleasure, I suspect," said I.

"What can I do to help?"

I put aside my glass and sat forward. "Of all the words that were spoken at the inquest, three intrigue me mightily. Why? Because they were the last that Archer ever spoke."

"'Are they coming?'"

I nodded. "A simple question, but what a dread significance it has in the circumstances. 'Are they coming?' What could he have meant by it? The coroner seems to have missed the point completely. Presumably he dismisses the words as the rambling of a demented man. Demented? Or tormented? That is what we have to discover, Captain."

His eyes had widened. "So you believe he was expecting someone to come to the house, sir? Someone real?"

I answered, "I doubt if he was referring to the Four Horsemen of the Apocalypse. Mrs. Coleman was at the window looking out, and Archer thought she'd seen some visitors who so alarmed him that he reached for the gun. Captain, have you any notion who they might have been?"

He shook his head. "Every jockey is vulnerable to criminal elements, sir. There are plenty of low types on the fringe of racing."

I nodded. We both knew the temptations open to jockeys, and Archer had more than once been asked to explain a curious result, but he had satisfied the Turf authorities each time. In sixteen years of racing he had only once been suspended, and that was when he was a lad of fourteen.

I asked, "Did he have any enemies among the jockeys?"

"Not that I ever heard. Rivals, yes. Fordham, Cannon, Wood. He gave no quarter on the racecourse, and they knew it. But they respected him."

I took out my watch. I'd already lingered longer than I intended. My birthday guests would assemble in the anteroom at Sandringham in under three hours. "Very well. We obviously have some serious detective work ahead of us. Are you game? You're at liberty to say no if you wish."

"I'll do anything I can to be of assistance, sir."

"Good. What's your Christian name?"

The question discomposed him a trifle. "Charles, sir."

"Is that what your friends call you?"

"They call me Charlie, sir."

"That's good enough for me. Well, Charlie, I'm Albert Edward. Bertie to my intimates, but you'd better continue to call me sir."

"As you wish, sir."

"These are your instructions. Search your memory minutely for any incident concerning Archer that might suggest he was under threat. You say his executors will want your help in sorting through his papers in the next few days. Study those papers before you hand them over, even if it means staying up all night. Look for anything of possible significance in the accounts, the correspondence, his betting book. I shall want a report when I see you next, and, I hope, some promising avenues of inquiry."

"Will that be at the funeral, sir?"

"I think not, Charlie. I'll be sending an equerry."

"Then how shall I report to you? By letter?"

"Lord, no. We'll meet privately. This is a highly secret investigation." I got up and reached for my hat. "What was the name of that valet—the fellow who placed the revolver in the night commode?"

"Sarjent, sir."

"I'd like to see him if he's still about. And would you have my carriage called? It's waiting in the lane beyond the church."

I have a reputation for being fastidious in regard to dress, and I suppose it's justified. I don't have a large wardrobe by the standards of European royalty, but what I have is the best, and I make a point of keeping it so. When Sarjent arrived, I said, "Do you know who I am?"

I needn't have asked. He was out in goose pimples at the sight of me, a tall, willowy young man of about twenty-five. "I believe so, your Royal—"

"How long did you work for Mr. Archer?"

"Four years, sir, first as a groom."

"He must have thought well of you. It was your job to guard the house when he was away?"

"Yes, sir."

"Did you ever notice anything suspicious? Intruders, that sort of thing?"

"Never, sir."

"What exactly did Mr. Archer say when he asked you to guard the house?"

"He said he didn't want it burgled while he was away, sir."

"A reasonable sentiment. And are you as good a valet as you are a guard?"

"Yes, sir."

"Then take this hat and coat and brush them soundly. I want them back in ten minutes, in the front hall."

He was back in less, which was unfortunate, as I was just emerging from the cloakroom to a fanfare of rushing water. When he had helped me into the coat, he dropped the florin I tipped him with and retired blushing.

My co-investigator, Charlie Buckfast, made a more timely entrance.

To round off our business, I told him in confidence, "I'll arrange to see you in London in a week or so. Occasionally I have engagements in the metropolis, of a private nature."

He said impassively, "My rooms in Jermyn Street are at your disposal anytime you wish, sir."

I winked and said, "I have hopes of you, Charlie."

CHAPTER 6

A nd now we shall trip the light fantastic together. Consider yourself invited to the County Ball at Sandringham on Friday 12 November, 1886. Let's rattle the chandeliers with my favorite dance, the Triumph. It's meant to be danced with vigor, you know, and Signore Curti and his instrumentalists will give no mercy until I signal them to stop. In case you were thinking of sitting out, I must warn you that I'm a tyrant in my own ballroom. No one is permitted to shirk.

I take Lady Randolph Churchill's hand and lead her on to the floor. If I'm any judge, Jennie's spirits need a lift. She's been unusually subdued since she arrived, and the whisper is that she and Randolph were barely speaking before they got here. The age-old problem. I wouldn't be Randolph for all the tea in China when she shames him with those exquisite violet-tinted eyes. But through the white lace gloves, Jennie's hand is warm to my touch, and I feel not the slightest tensing of the fingers when Randolph turns to Lady de Grey and invites her to make up a set. Cunning old Randolph, a politician in all things. Gladys de Grey is a black-haired beauty straight off a Goya canvas, all passion and fire, but she was married for the second time last year, and is so besotted with her noble earl that she's the safest woman in the room for Randolph to be seen with.

Before Curti raises his baton, I spot a few malingerers behind the columns where they're apt to take cover when the Triumph is announced. "The footmen have instructions to take the names of all deserters!" I shout, and repeat the phrase in French for the benefit of the Duc de la Trémouille. It terrifies him into snatching the plump forearm of the wife of the Lord-Lieutenant and hauling her into a set led by my dear wife Alix and the Comte de Paris.

I smile at Jennie. "Ready, my dear?"

"Whenever you say, sir."

Is that meant to be suggestive? I can't be certain, but I give her the look that never fails to redden a pretty cheek. Then I nod to Curti, and the opening chord is sounded. Every gentleman bows, every lady curtsies, and that is the first and last stately movement in the dance. We hurtle into the briskest gallop you can imagine, skirts and coattails flying. Jennie and I lead the set, down the middle and up again, past a blur of red and black jackets and taffeta gowns of every color. She is obliged to cling to me in order to stay upright, and I won't deny that this is one of the attractions of the dance. In this account of my adventures I mean to be frank about liaisons, and I shall be, so you must take my word for it that I've never bedded Jennie—our intimacies are exclusively platonic. That is, up to the time of writing.

We stand back to watch the less boisterous dancing of the next pair, the Comte and Comtesse de Paris, who are my principal guests. Poor dears, they have been living at Sheen House since their expulsion from France. Who would be a pretender to the French throne? Mind, even a staunch anti-Republican must have reservations about the Comtesse, who smokes a pipe (not during the dance) and helps herself to my cigars on every imaginable pretext.

My sympathies toward the royalists from across the Channel are well known, and in certain circles notorious. When I offered Chiswick House to the Empress Eugenie after the fall of the Second Empire, I was called to Windsor to explain myself. I was informed that my action was diplomatically inept, which gave me an opportunity to respond that as I was never taken into the confidence of the diplomats, I could scarcely be blamed for upsetting them.

As we progress, I glance at Jennie, but her eyes are on Randolph or the lady he is dancing with, so I turn my gaze toward the far end of the ballroom, where I meet a penetrating look from a face ravaged by sixteen years of heroic service to me: Sir Francis Knollys. Who would believe that Knollys was capable of diverting me from the fascinating Lady Churchill? This, you see, was the day of Fred Archer's funeral at Newmarket. Impossible for me to attend, so I sent a gigantic wreath and Knollys. And now I'm extremely impatient for his report.

I decide to exercise the prerogative of mercy and limit the reprises of the dance to two, and my guests limp to the nearest chairs. Unfortunately, supper is not due for twenty minutes. When I have returned Jennie to her spouse, I tell Signore Curti to give us a slow quadrille, which at least will supply an opportunity of communication. Then I beckon to Knollys.

We make up a square consisting of myself and Alix, Prince Christian and my sister Lenchen, the Comte and Comtesse de Paris, and their young daughter Hélène, the Princesse d'Orléans, partnered by Knollys. The tempo is undemanding, so each time I step sufficiently close to Knollys I can discreetly slip him a question.

"A fitting send-off for the Tin Man?"

"Indeed, sir. Upward of thirty carriages."

"Plenty of wreaths, I daresay?"

"More than I could count. They blocked the hall and stairway of the house."

At this, Knollys steps aside and I find my uncouth brother-in-law fixing me with his one good eye. Christian has aspirations to be a Turfite, and he must have overheard, because he says in a voice audible to the entire set (save possibly Alix), "You must be speaking of the dead jockey. Where was the poor fellow buried?"

Lenchen flaps her hand at her clodhopping husband and says, "This is hardly a topic for the ballroom, my dear."

Knollys, embarrassed, mumbles something about the local cemetery, and young Hélène says brightly, "Cemetery? *Que veut dire ceci?*"

Alix, who picks up the child's piercing remark, and is always grateful of an opportunity to join in the pleasantries, provides our French guests with a definition of the word, and then supplements their vocabulary with some others, such as *mausoleum, sepulcher* and *crypt.* Meanwhile, I'm close enough to Knollys to ask, "Did you make a list of the wreaths?"

"So far as possible, sir."

"Apart from mine . . . ?"

"Lord Falmouth, his first patron."

"Naturally, and . . . ?"

"The Duke of Westminster."

"Oh, where?" says Alix, looking around the room. "I haven't seen him."

"The Marchioness of Ormonde," continues Knollys, who is as accustomed as I to Alix going off on tangents. "Count Kinsky."

"So 'andsome!" murmurs the Comtesse, equally at sea.

"Sir George Chetwynd."

It amounts to a catalog of the racing aristocracy. After I've heard it out, I say with confidence, "My wreath was the largest, I presume?"

The sequence of the dance constrains me to wait for an answer, and when it comes, it's Knollys at his most diplomatic: "Yours had pride of place, sir."

I blink in surprise. "Not the largest?"

He shakes his head.

I say in his ear as we pass, "Tell me, who so far forgot himself as to send a wreath larger than mine?"

"The Dowager Duchess of Montrose."

"Carrie Montrose!" I say in outrage.

"Who is this Montrose?" asks the Comtesse.

"Mes sentiments, exactement," I tell her.

Supper is taken in the dining room. The band of the Norfolk Regiment play Bizet, while I play host to my French guests—not to mention the three hundred others who swoop on the *Mousse de Saumon aux Concombres* and the *Ortolans à L'Aspic* as if they haven't seen food in a fortnight. I suppose the dancing gives them an appetite. The Duc de la Trémouille attacks the *Noisette d'Agneau à l'Anglaise* as if he were taking revenge for Waterloo.

After the strawberries, the plates are cleared, coffee and cigars are handed around and I become an object of surpassing interest, for no one may rise to respond to a call of nature until I get up from my chair.

I stand and make an expansive gesture that signals relief for all who need it. This is also the cue for frisky debutantes to slip away from their chaperons and make assignations in the corridors.

I cross to the table where Francis Knollys is seated with some kindred spirits, among them Christopher Sykes and Lord Arthur

Somerset, who is known to us all in the Marlborough House set as Podge.

Before the dancing resumes, I mean to obtain a more coherent account of the funeral. The cortege, Knollys informs us, consisted of six funeral carriages of family mourners, the hearse itself, a large brake loaded with wreaths and floral tributes and up to twenty private carriages. Although the principal racehorse owners had not considered it appropriate to attend, the Turf was honorably represented by Mr. Tattersall, of the famous firm; John Porter and Tom Jennings, two of the most distinguished trainers of recent years; Tom Cannon, Fred's old rival in the saddle; and my co-investigator, Charlie Buckfast. Wholly unfit to be included in such company (I'm compelled to mention the monster because he will figure in our story) was Abington Baird, the notorious amateur rider known as the Squire.

The cortege left Falmouth House at 2 P.M. and drove the mile or so into town along the road beside the Heath, past a continuous line of stable lads, who showed touching respect for the great Fred by posting themselves like guards of honor at a state funeral. In the long main street of Newmarket, where every shop was closed, with blinds drawn at all the windows, the townsfolk stood three and four deep, oblivious of the rain. The tide of people at the cemetery gates delayed the cortege for some minutes, for the police had stopped the public from entering. Only the immediate family entered the small chapel for the funeral service. Then Archer was laid to rest in a plot lined with laurel leaves and white chrysanthemums, beside the graves of his wife and infant son. I heard that his father was too distressed to attend.

"Was anything said about the suicide?" I ask Knollys.

"By the vicar, sir?"

"By anyone at all."

"It was generally spoken of as a dreadful tragedy."

"Not as a mystery?"

"Not that I heard, sir."

"Podge" Somerset has been listening keenly, yet draws back now and takes an unwarranted interest in his cigar, as if it just flew into his hand. I'm not standing for that kind of evasion.

"What do you know about it?" I ask.

"Nothing worth saying at all," he hedges.

"Out with it, Podge. You may be well padded, but you're very transparent."

He flushes scarlet. "I would only care to comment, sir, that I'm not surprised Archer shot himself. He was in very bad odor after the Cambridgeshire."

"Oh? Who with?"

"My brother Edward for one."

"What does Edward have to complain about? His horse was well beaten."

"It was stopped."

I stare at him in amazement. He's telling me that Carlton, the 4-1 favorite, was not allowed to win. You often hear ill-founded accusations after a favorite fails to please, but this comes from the owner. If true, it warrants a Jockey Club inquiry, at the least.

I'm trying to follow the logic of what he's just suggested, but he's lost me. Even if Carlton *were* stopped, why should Archer be blamed? Woodburn was the rider, not Archer.

He explains, "Woodburn was bribed by Archer to throw the race."

I'm speechless.

He adds, "Since his wife died, Archer had nothing to live for except his racing. Winning the Cambridgeshire became his obsession. He would use any means. He decided Carlton was the main threat, so he paid Woodburn to lose, but he reckoned without the outsider. He was devastated. That's why he killed himself, Bertie."

After a moment to contain myself, I say, "Podge, do you know what you're suggesting—that the greatest jockey in the kingdom was corrupt?"

"I say it, sir."

Christopher Sykes, that beanpole of a fellow with sad eyes and the longest face you ever saw, who was manifestly sent into the world to be a victim of practical jokes, and unendingly tries to convince me otherwise, asks Podge, "Have you spoken to Woodburn? Have you accused him to his face of taking a bribe?"

"My brother has."

"And . . . ?"

"The man denies it. Naturally he would. His livelihood is at stake."

"Then you have some other proof?"

Podge begins to flounder. "Not exactly proof, but I'm darned sure we could obtain it if we tried. Now that Archer's dead, it seems churlish to pursue it."

At this, I see red. "That's decent of you, I must say! You and your brother slander a man who is scarcely in his grave and then admit you haven't a shred of proof to support you. But you're such fair-minded fellows that you're not even proposing to supply the proof. Fair-minded, my arse! You're a muckraker of the worst sort, Somerset, and I've heard as much as I can stand."

With that, I march back to the ballroom, and as I go, I'm sorry to say, I strike panic into numbers of my guests, who step backward and press themselves against the wall—always a sign that I'm glaring at people. You may think I was unduly harsh on Podge considering that I'd practically commanded him to expound his theory. Perhaps I was. I had a strong respect for Archer. In my opinion he was neither bad, nor mad, and I shall prove it.

While the first waltz after supper is in progress, I compose myself by sitting with the Earl and Lady de Grey, or Fred and Gladys as I know them. Fred is the best shot in England, and that's saying a lot, but it *is* the lot, so far as anyone is aware, except possibly Gladys. She dotes on him, so perhaps there's more to the little man than we give him credit for, though between ourselves, he caught her on the rebound, lucky fellow. She was married first to the fourth Earl of Lonsdale, who treated her disgracefully. His sudden death was a blessed release for Gladys. She's still only twenty-seven, and, I don't mind repeating, a fascinating creature. I ask her to dance.

I'm still brooding over Podge's monstrous allegation. Even supposing the unthinkable were true, and Archer actually did pay a bribe to another jockey, the thwarting of his plan was hardly grounds for suicide. All right, the Cambridgeshire was about the only race of note that he never won, and the wasting he was willing to endure to make good the omission was extraordinary, even obsessive, to use Podge's phrase. Yet at twenty-nine he could have looked forward to other Cambridgeshires. Plenty of jockeys go past forty. Why stake his reputation, indeed his life, on the outcome of this one race?

Gladys de Grey interrupts my brown study by remarking, "Perhaps in this case feminine intuition may be of assistance."

I frown. "What makes you say that?"

She smiles. She looks bewitching in a diamond tiara, with a rope of antique pearls wound in triple around her neck and suspended in a long loop from her bare shoulders across her bosom to the level of her waist. She tells me, "Like every other woman in the room, I've been watching you, sir. It's evident that you have something on your mind. Would I be right in divining that it is not unconnected with a sad event at Newmarket?"

"Good Lord, Gladys, how the deuce . . . ?"

"I have my sources."

I affect a stern look. "Don't be evasive with me, young lady, or . . ."

Another smile dawns. "Or what, Your Royal Highness? How do you deal with evasive females—shut them up in the Tower, or is that a thing of the past?"

The dance is coming to an end. I signal to Signore Curti to prolong it, and I confide to Gladys, "The punishment I propose for you is far more severe than a spell in the Tower. I shall force you to dance with me until you promise to cooperate."

She says solemnly, "How could I *not* cooperate with a man who dances as divinely as this? I am utterly at your mercy, sir. I shall tell all. I saw you in earnest conversation with a certain gentleman who arrived late for the ball, so I asked Charlotte Knollys where her brother had been today."

"Ah."

She sighs. "Now you're no longer impressed."

"Untrue. Let's put this intuition of yours to the test. Where would *you* look for an explanation of Fred Archer's suicide?"

She raises her eyebrows as if the answer is obvious. "*Cherchez la femme*, I should think."

I stop dancing and cause a shunt down the length of the ballroom. "A *woman*. Archer had no time for women."

"He married one," says Gladys flatly.

"Yes, but she died."

". . . leaving him alone in the world with a beautiful house and oodles of money. Of course there was a woman ready to fill the gap."

"Name her, then."

Gladys smiles wickedly and recites a verse that was current a year or two ago:

"Isn't Craw a lucky boy
With Carrie Red and Corrie Roy?
Corrie Roy and Carrie Red—
One for the stable and one for the bed."

I'd better translate. "Craw" was the late Stirling Crawfurd, a distinguished figure of the Turf, and Corrie Roy won the Cesarewitch for him. "Carrie Red" was his buxom and energetic wife.

I say with a gasp of disbelief, "Carrie Montrose?"

Gladys nods.

I've given up any pretension of dancing. I lead her to the side of the ballroom. "Gladys, that's grotesque! Carrie Montrose must be almost seventy!"

"Sixty-eight. Why is it grotesque if an old woman desires a young man, when the reverse is so acceptable?"

I sidestep that one. "Are you serious—about Carrie Montrose?"

Her brown eyes lock with mine, and she almost dares me to challenge her. "Believe me, she was actively pursuing him. She offered to marry him."

"How can you know this?"

"I listen, Bertie. What else is there for a respectable married lady to do but take an interest in what the not-so-respectable ones are doing?"

She follows that with a penetrating look. The fact has not escaped me that she has addressed me for the first time as Bertie. I escort her back to the best shot in England, thinking, after all, that they are well matched.

CHAPTER 7

The ball ended officially at 2 A.M. on Saturday morning. After the last carriages had left, my houseguests amused themselves for a while with my barrel organ, until, toward 3 A.M., I bade good night to the ladies and led the gentlemen to the smoking room. I have noticed many times that there's nothing like a smoking-room party in the small hours to bring out the true character of one's associates. Randolph got up a noisy game with the French in the bowling alley next door; Christian sank into my favorite armchair and snored; Knollys went straight to the brandy; Podge Somerset, wishing he were a million miles away after his dressing-down, wandered about the walls studying my Leech pictures as if he had never set eyes on them in his life; and the Great Xtopher (Sykes) tried to prove himself indispensable by poking the fire.

Sykes it was who brought up the subject of Archer again. I suppose he was interceding on Somerset's behalf, trying to suggest that there might after all be something in the story of bribery, although you can never be certain with Christopher. He's learned to distract me when the brandy is being served. One evening after dinner at the Marlborough Club, when tedium was setting in, I acted on a whim and tipped my glass of brandy over his head. Nothing remarkable in that, except that the fellow bore it like a philosopher, letting the liquid trickle down the length of his face and beard onto his dress shirt and dinner jacket, before turning a damp face to me and saying in his solemn voice, "As your Royal

Highness pleases," and causing every one of us to howl with laughter. I'm still helpless if I picture it. Naturally, it became a party turn. Now no evening is complete until Sykes has been dowsed with brandy, a full decanter if possible, or had my cigar stubbed out on the back of his hand. His response is always that impeccably obliging, "As your Royal Highness pleases," and hilarious to hear.

Before a glass was put in my hand, he said, "There was something I meant to mention earlier, sir, about the Cambridgeshire, but the opportunity passed."

I eyed him without much show of interest.

He moved as close as he dared. "Touching on the possibility—the remote possibility—that the race was not to the fastest, so to speak, I heard from a certain source that a personage not unknown in Turf circles made a tidy sum by backing the outsider that won."

"So what?" I commented. "I backed it myself at 25-1."

"Sir, this individual netted fifty thousand on the race."

"Fifty thou?"

"He spread his investment over several bookmakers. He dined at Romano's the same evening and was boasting to all and sundry about his coup."

"Well, don't be so blessed mysterious, Christopher. Who was this lucky blighter?"

"Baird, sir."

After a moment's hesitation I said warily, "Do you mean Abington Baird? The Squire?"

Sykes gave a nod and followed it with a grave stare—and no one in my circle can stare more gravely than he.

I'm not sure how I received this information. I may have whistled, or vibrated my lips like a horse, or uttered a profanity. At any rate, I took the point about Baird. If that monster of iniquity had backed the winner, questions indubitably had to be asked.

It won't have escaped you, I'm certain, that Baird's name has already been raised. He was mentioned to me by Knollys as one of the mourners at Archer's funeral. And now, in case you suspect me of prejudice, I shall enlighten you about Mr. Baird's reputation.

He is a young man still in his twenties, of immense wealth, some three million pounds, which he inherited on his twenty-first birthday. His father and uncles, the seven sons of an impoverished Scottish farmer, built their fortunes out of coal, iron and the railways. The family firm of William Baird & Company now owns and mines vast areas of Western Scotland, and those brothers who founded it represent all that is estimable in the Scots character: energy, enterprise and foresight, governed by thrift and piety.

Unhappily, none of this except the money was passed on to the next generation—by which I mean George Alexander Baird, known in racing circles as Mr. Abington or the Squire. He was sent to Eton and Cambridge to be educated as a gentleman and drove his tutors to the point of despair. If rumor is true, he didn't attend a single lecture while up at Magdalen. He went elsewhere for his schooling, to gambling dens and low public houses and penny gaffs. He consorted with women of doubtful repute. He surrounded himself with an odious gang of roughs and pugilists and took a fiendish delight in giving offense to decent people. One of his favorite tricks upon entering a restaurant or public house was to knock off a stranger's hat or snatch his cigar. Were the victim so rash as to protest, he was liable to have his nose bloodied by one of the Squire's pugilistic following. The latter, I may say, included Mitchell and Smith, champions of England.

It occurs to me on reading over the previous paragraph that certain newspapers obsessed by stories of indiscretions in high places might be tempted to make invidious comparisons. They had better be advised that there is an absolute distinction between private high spirits and public rowdyism.

One would not claim to be a saint, of course, any more than asserting that Baird has utterly gone to the devil. The Squire's saving grace is that he is a capital horseman, probably the finest gentleman rider (I use the word *gentleman* only to distinguish him from professional jockeys) in the kingdom. While at Cambridge, he maintained a string of hunters, took part in the University Drag, and inevitably rubbed shoulders with Newmarket trainers. The Turf excited him as nothing else. His chief ambition was to emulate Fred Archer. To this end, he first became an owner and spent vast funds on acquiring good horses to ride. He followed Archer from meeting to meeting, studying his style and tactics. Ultimately, he persuaded the champion to tutor him, blithely paying, it is said, the most extravagant fees ever asked for riding lessons, for the Tin Man was never cheaply bought. The Squire got good value, however; he learned how to steal that precious yard in a close finish, and equally how to catch the judge's eye by getting up on the horse's neck. Last year, he rode almost thirty winners. Yet the outlay on his racing must vastly exceed the returns. He keeps horses all over the country—many registered under other names—on the principle that when there is a meeting in the vicinity, he will always have a ride available. He has not the foggiest idea how many he owns. Each time a selling race takes place at a meeting he attends, he buys the winner. When Lord Falmouth's horses were put up for sale a couple of years ago, the Squire went through the catalog with Archer and outraged the Turf aristocracy by buying the pick of the collection. So it was fitting, if not in character, that the Squire should have attended Archer's funeral.

There is no question that he admired Archer—reason enough, one would think, to pay final respects, even if he wasn't well-known for respecting anyone. Yet this story of a thumping win on the Cambridgeshire, coming after Podge's bizarre accusation, troubled me deeply. Was it possible that Archer had known something and tipped The Sailor Prince? The Squire must have felt confident, to go to the trouble of spreading his bet over several bookies. A win of fifty thousand was fairly small beer to a millionaire, but it impressed the world at large. His main reward was the prestige of picking the outsider, and he'd made sure it was public knowledge. The Squire craved esteem as a Turfite, so no wonder he had broadcast his success in Romano's. The question was whether he regretted making it public now, in the light of Archer's violent death. Had his boasting in some way precipitated what happened? Was it out of guilt that the Squire had made his appearance at the funeral?

I inquired of Sykes, "How did you hear about this?"

He nervously fingered his beard and glanced about the room. "From my sister-in-law Jessica, sir. She got it from one of her acquaintances."

I chuckled. "That can't be right."

"Why not, sir?"

"Jessica doesn't have *acquaintances*, does she?"

Christopher reddened. His elder brother, Sir Tatton Sykes, had married the lively Jessica Cavendish-Bentinck when she was eighteen, he forty-eight. Ten years on, Tatton was mentally in his dotage. He subsisted on milk puddings and early nights. Jessica, still in her prime and believing there must be more to life than a bowl of tapioca and sweet dreams, leased a large house in Grosvenor Street and gives some of the gayest dinner parties in London. To the gossip-mongers, Lady Tatton Sykes is known as Lady Satin Tights, and I don't think she minds a bit.

Poor Christopher! It all but choked him to mention his scarlet sister-in-law. He said, "Her informant was a, em, gentleman friend who happened to be in Romano's the evening Baird was there."

"Am I not to be told his name?"

"In all humility, sir, it might be more profitable to know the name of the young lady who was at Baird's table."

"Conceivably. Who was that?"

"She calls herself Miss Bliss, I believe. They appeared to be on intimate terms."

"Miss Bliss? Sounds ominously like one of the sisterhood."

"I understand she has not descended to that, sir. She is a music hall artiste."

I was so grateful for this information that I refrained that evening from pouring brandy over Sykes. If inquiries had to be made, Miss Bliss, the music hall artiste, sounded a more approachable subject than the Squire. My heart had sunk at the mention of that reprobate's name. Can you imagine my situation trying to conduct a discreet conversation with such a loudmouthed barbarian?

In bed that night I decided on my course of action. I was due to visit London the following weekend. On the pretext that Satan finds some mischief still for idle hands to do, my dear mama and her advisers are indefatigable in devising ever more obscure ways of occupying my hours. The latest is the Wellington Statue Committee. I ask you! Some years ago Wyatt's hideous equestrian statue of the old Duke was removed from the arch at Hyde Park Corner and carted off to Aldershot, and ever since there has been a debate as to what should be put in its place. The committee was formed to devise a competition to find a less objectionable replacement, and I was considered the ideal chairman. If I learned anything from this experience, it was that sculptors and soldiers should be kept apart.

Did you detect a note of bitterness there? This has been a momentous year in the destiny of the nation, with two changes of government and the great debate over Gladstone's Home Rule Bill. As the future King, I wish earnestly to keep abreast of the affairs of state, yet I am compelled to wheedle tidbits of information from ministers like Lord Rosebery and Sir Henry James, who happen also to be my friends. They and I are obliged to be so damnably furtive about the business as to feel a sense of guilt.

Anyway, the great decision over the Wellington Statue took me to the Smoke. On these occasions, I stay at Marlborough House, where congenial companions are always within call and the servants are handpicked for their loyalty. This time, I sent word to Captain Charlie Buckfast that I would call privately at his rooms in Jermyn Street on Friday night.

Then I made preparations. I surprised one of my gardeners by asking to borrow a set of his oldest clothes. Having kitted myself in boots, kersey trousers, doeskin waistcoat, serge jacket, great-coat, muffler and billycock hat, I left Marlborough House on Friday evening by the tradesmen's entrance and walked to Jermyn Street. It is a little-known fact that I am not unused to walking the streets of London in the clothes of a workingman. A year or two ago, in my capacity as member of the Royal Commission on the Housing of the Working Classes (another of HM's ideas for filling my time), I ventured incognito into some of the worst slums of St. Pancras. I can tell you I felt safer on that occasion than I did this evening walking through St. James's. I got some decidedly antagonistic looks.

Captain Buckfast lived above Boyd's, the fruiterers. I was obliged to step over two boxes of oranges to reach his door—a change from a red carpet. I was starting to congratulate myself on the success of my disguise when the door was opened by a butler who promptly bowed so low as to show me his back collar stud. I muttered, "Not here, you buffoon," and it so shocked him that he broke wind. This is one of the hazards of bowing, as anyone who has attended an investiture will know.

When I got upstairs, Buckfast at least had the grace to look bewildered at my appearance. The first thing I asked was whether this was his regular butler, and he admitted that he'd hired him for the occasion. I was highly displeased, and I let him see it.

I tersely instructed him to give the man his marching orders, not for what had occurred downstairs, which can happen to the best of us, but because, damn it, I had specified a private visit. While he dealt with that, I took stock of the place: very much the ex-soldier's, neatly arranged, with colored engravings of cavalry officers at symmetrical intervals around the walls; zebra hides on either side of the fireplace; some native spears, a Zulu drum; and, reflecting his Turf connection, a painting of Paradox, with Archer up. I picked a spill from a Chinese vase on the mantelpiece, lighted it and started a cigar.

"Can I rely on you at all?" I asked when Buckfast returned, full of apologies. "Did you find out anything at the funeral?"

"I have to admit I didn't, sir. The weather was most inclement."

How that had obstructed him, I didn't ask. "Have you sorted through Archer's papers, as I asked?"

"Yes, sir."

"And . . . ?"

"I found nothing irregular."

"But you can tell me how much he was worth?"

"Somewhere near sixty thousand pounds, I would estimate."

"Are you sure? I read a couple of years ago that he had a quarter of a million."

Buckfast shook his head. "An exaggeration, I'm certain, sir. He was never worth as much as that. Of course, he sank enormous amounts into building Falmouth House."

I waited to see if anything else was forthcoming, but it wasn't. If you got three sentences together out of Charlie Buckfast, you were doing well. I admonished him gently. "Charlie, you disappoint me. How are we going to form an investigating team if all the discoveries are down to me?" Not without relish, I told him first about the Somerset family's suspicions over the Cambridgeshire result, then the Squire's boastings in Romano's. "Do you know the Squire, Charlie?"

"He's no friend of mine, sir."

"I'm glad to hear it. But he was a friend of Archer's, so you surely met him on occasions?"

Buckfast shook his head. "I'm not sure that Fred ever thought of Baird as a friend. Most times, he was an infernal nuisance. Never missed a chance to claim acquaintance."

"What about this story, then? Is it possible that Archer told him to back The Sailor Prince?"

He put his face through a series of pained expressions as he tried to come to terms with this odious suggestion. "I suppose it's not impossible."

I had the advantage of him. I'd already thought the unthinkable. "The opportunity was there at the Newmarket meeting. They were both on the racecourse all the week."

Charlie Buckfast's blood pressure was rising visibly. He blurted out, "I can't believe that Fred stopped his horse, sir. I simply can't believe it. His whole career would be at risk. He'd rather be dead than . . ." He let the words trail away as he realized what he'd said.

I told him, "I think a visit to the music hall is indicated."

CHAPTER 8

Let's give Buckfast his due: his mustache twitched at the prospect of the Heir Apparent visiting a common music hall, but otherwise he took it as an ex-officer should. "I presume, sir, that this must be in the course of duty."

"You have it, Charlie."

I told him about the connection (if that doesn't sound indelicate) between the Squire and Miss Bliss. He confessed he had never heard of Miss Bliss.

"Nor I."

"How shall we find her, then?"

I smiled in a cryptic fashion. "Last Sunday morning, Charlie, I attended Divine Service at Sandringham in the company of Lord Randolph Churchill, Prince Christian and a handful of red-eyed survivors of the County Ball. The Sub-Dean of the Chapel Royal was sent from Windsor to give the sermon. For a text, he used the parable of the ten virgins—not the most fitting choice. I could have taken it irreverently, Charlie, but I did not. I listened to the word of the Lord, and in future I shall apply it in my daily life."

"To be a wise virgin?" said Buckfast.

I gave him a sharp look. "To be prepared."

"Ah."

"A sound principle for detective work, wouldn't you agree?"

"Absolutely, sir."

"So today I have come prepared. I sent for a copy of that useful periodical, the *Era*. I studied the music hall notices, and I find that a Miss Myrtle Bliss is appearing twice nightly at Mr. George Belmont's hall, the Sebright, in Hackney Road."

"Hackney Road?" Buckfast mouthed the words in a whisper, as if they ought not to be spoken aloud. He was so dismayed that he quite omitted to compliment me. For the benefit of my readers in the provinces, the road in question runs from Shoreditch out to Cambridge Heath, not the worst of East London, by any means, but still a locality where people of Buckfast's class—not to mention mine—venture at their peril.

The reason for my workingman's attire was now apparent, and we presently attended to his. We opened a trunk and found a Chesterfield overcoat that he hadn't worn since the seventies and a pair of army boots that we dipped in water to remove the shine. The hat was more of a challenge. We were obliged to use the only black bowler he possessed. After crushing it out of shape and liberally applying goose fat and ash, we finally had a titfer sufficiently shabby.

I looked at his cavalry mustache and said, "That's got to come off."

He was aghast. "It took years to cultivate, sir."

He was so reluctant to submit to the scissors that I was persuaded to see what difference it would make to dismantle the spiked ends. We softened the wax over a bowl of steaming water and I prised the hairs apart with a silver toothpick. He bore it with fortitude. I assured him when it was done that the bedraggled effect was pure working-class.

We left Jermyn Street about eight o'clock. I first proposed that we take a cab to Shoreditch High Street and hoof it from there but quite failed to realize that no cabman would stop for the likes of us in clubland, so we were compelled to walk to Oxford Circus to look for a bus. All this was novel to me, and I enjoyed it immensely.

"This strikes me as more dangerous than Hackney Road," I remarked as we strode up Regent Street in our hobnailed boots, getting distinctly unfriendly looks from the well-heeled West Enders.

"It might be safer if you stepped aside and gave them precedence, sir," Buckfast suggested.

He was right, of course. The habit of a lifetime is hard to break.

While we waited in Oxford Street for the Clapton bus, I admitted, "This may be a wild-goose chase, Charlie."

He responded with impeccable good manners. "Speaking for myself, sir, it's a privilege, whatever the outcome."

The fat woman in front turned and took a hard look at both of us. I fear we were not wholly convincing as members of the great unwashed. I won't go into the embarrassment created on the bus when I proffered a sovereign for our two threepenny fares. Thank heavens Buckfast had a spare shilling.

As it was not a particularly cold evening, we sat on the upper deck, where we could talk more freely. And talk more freely Buckfast did, after I offered him a cigarette, quite abandoning his usual reticence. He was interesting on the subject of Fred Archer's relations with the fair sex. He told me that eager females went to extraordinary lengths to contrive meetings with Archer up to the time of his marriage and beyond. I don't know what it is about the ladies who patronize racing, but many a jockey had been offered an extra ride after the last race, if you'll pardon a smoking-room expression. Fred, of course, was better looking than most with his dark hair, glittering brown eyes and superior height. According to Buckfast, he often had invitations of the most brazen character pushed under his door. As a matter of routine when booking into hotels, he would ask the staff not to reveal his room number to inquirers of either sex. Even so, he was often obliged to change hotels to avoid his fair pursuers.

"Charlie, my dear fellow, you make these women sound like the hounds in full cry," I commented.

"Sometimes they were."

I pondered a moment. "Now there's a thought."

"What's that, sir?"

"'Are they coming?'"

I meant the remark in jest, but I didn't see Buckfast smile under his drooping mustache. I suppose as a military man, he lacked imagination. Personally, I was highly amused by the vision of a pack of lustful ladies advancing on Archer's house.

I asked, "Did he never allow himself to be caught?"

"Setting aside his marriage?"

"Naturally."

"No, sir. To my knowledge, he resisted them all. He was unfailingly charming, but implacable."

"I wonder why."

"There were more important things, sir."

"Winning races, you mean?"

"And holding on to his money. Women don't come cheaply."

The bus took us along Holborn and through the city, past Liverpool St. Station and out to Shoreditch. As it started along Hackney Road, we looked out for the lighted front of the music hall. Progress was slow along the narrow thoroughfare, for most of Shoreditch seemed to have left its shopping until late, crowding the barrows at the curbside and crossing the road without the least regard to traffic. Tantalizing aromas of hot soup, pies and roast chestnuts wafted up to our level, and I was so distracted (not having taken Buckfast up on his offer of a meal) that I missed the Sebright when it finally came in view. My hawk-eyed companion pointed it out, a narrow entrance framed by crowds of plaster cherubs festooned with colored lights.

We left the bus and were immediately accosted by two painted females reeking of cheap scent, one of whom linked her arm in mine and said, "Gerna tike me in, Tubby? Yer won't be sorry, m'darling."

I said firmly, "That's open to question, madam, and I don't propose to risk it."

To which she retorted, "Listen to 'im. *'Don't propose to risk it.'* Oojer think y'are, then? Lord Muck?"

I didn't enlighten her. We shouldered a passage through the throng of orange sellers, piemen and whores, paid our shilling for a seat in the front and passed inside.

I'm glad to report that the Sebright is a music hall in the old style, with tables for the patrons, where you sip a pot of beer and sup on pease pudding or pigs' trotters if you wish, while the performers entertain from the platform. I say "the old style" to distinguish it from such aberrations as the revamped London Pavilion, which are increasingly appearing in the West End. What a confounded liberty to masquerade as music halls when they force you into a row of tip-up seats with just a ledge to hold your beer glass and, as likely as not, with your view obstructed by the hat in front of you. It appears to me that the managers are interested only in cramming as many people as possible into their dreary "palaces of variety." From which you'll have gathered that I'm a stout supporter of the traditional halls. Years ago, I made a private visit to Evans's in Covent Garden and watched the show from a screened box, and I was ravished by the experience. I've been many times since, to all the more accessible halls. And I regularly invite my favorite artistes to perform at Sandringham and Marlborough House, though I'm bound to say that private entertainments lack something in atmosphere. One's dinner guests can be so infernally stuffy.

Buckfast and I found a convenient table out of the glare of the lights, yet not too close to the promenade. This, I may say, was my first experience of music hall as an anonymous member of the public, and I relished every moment. We took a chance on sausages, fried onions and mash, and helped ourselves to mustard from an enormous, gruesomely encrusted jar. What a toothsome treat it made! And what a splendid novelty to eat a meal with one's hat on!

No one in a regular music hall pays undue attention to what is happening on the stage until the top billings appear. There's a steady din of conversation punctuated by laughter; the waiters and potboys move among the tables; and the patrons are at liberty to get up from their seats and promenade. In fact, Belmont, the proprietor, was touring the auditorium during the acts, cigar in hand, saying to the patrons, "What do you think of that for thirty bob a week? Not bad, eh?"

I was mainly occupied in clearing my plate and ordering a second helping, but of course I kept an ear open for the chairman's announcements. He was on a raised chair at a table just in front of the orchestra, at the foot of the stage. Thus far, he'd introduced Sam Redman, a comic with blackened face who spoke on a monotone and hardly paused for breath; Marie Lloyd, the singer of "The Boy in the Gallery," said to be no older than sixteen; and a pair of lady gyrists or "voltas," who swung from ropes suspended over our heads and did nothing remarkable except show their legs in pink tights. Most of the turns, it has to be said, would have been hooted off the stage in a better class of hall. But then music hall isn't only what happens up there on the stage; everyone is noisily involved, from the chairman in his white tie to the brawny stevedore out for the evening with his doxy.

I won't tax your patience by taking you right through the bill. Sometime toward ten o'clock came the rap of the hammer followed by, "And now, ladies and gentlemen, beauty and obedience—the adorable Miss Myrtle Bliss and Cocky."

"And Cocky?" I piped in surprise. I hadn't expected a double act. I spoke more audibly than I intended.

"And Cocky, old cock," retorted the chairman, to hoots of amusement from the audience.

I was about to shout something back when Buckfast silenced me by pushing a cigarette between my lips. He was right, of course. I'm occupationally accustomed to being the center of attention. It was no way for a plainclothes detective to behave, and once I was over the affront, I appreciated what he'd done. Charlie Buckfast was going to be a valuable companion, for all his want of humor.

As he struck a match for me, I said for his ears only, "I was expecting her to be a singer."

"And I, sir," he agreed.

How mistaken we were! Miss Bliss was a bird trainer, would you believe, and Cocky was a white cockatoo that performed like a human with bits of apparatus, including a miniature tricycle and a tiny drum. To be truthful, it wasn't a very arresting turn until, through no fault of mine, I became part of the performance.

This was how it happened. The spotlight unexpectedly shifted from the stage to the audience, dancing about our heads, and then, for some reason unfathomable to me at the time, settled on our table. Thereupon Cocky gave a piercing screech and flew straight toward me, nipped the cigarette from out of my mouth, soared into the gods and presented it to someone in the gallery. That got the biggest cheer of the evening. Apparently it was one of his regular tricks.

I must have made quite a spectacle of myself, for it's no joke to find yourself with the limelight shining down on you and a large cockatoo flying toward your face.

Miss Bliss made a show of scolding the bird and told it to say sorry to the gentleman, but I flapped my hand to show I wanted nothing more to do with Cocky. The evil creature turned its back and said something I didn't catch that got belly laughs all round.

I haven't told you yet that Miss Bliss was an uncommonly pretty black-haired creature in a fetching lemon-colored gown with a silver girdle. She had white, elbow-length gloves and a large white hat with a pale yellow ostrich feather. When the act finished, she gave me a most disarming smile.

I called a waiter and asked him for pencil and paper. At the feel of a florin pressed into his palm, he was eager to oblige.

"My dear Miss Bliss," I wrote, "I write as one who was not only captivated by your charming performance this evening, but was privileged to take a small part. I was the smoker of the cigarette that your parrot cleverly snatched away. I consider myself honored to have contributed in a small way to your success tonight. And I would be doubly honored if you would agree to join me and my companion for supper."

I folded it and handed it to the waiter.

"Who is it for, mate?" he asked.

I was about to tell him curtly that he was no mate of mine, when Buckfast chipped in with, "Miss Bliss, the young lady who just performed."

"Myrtle? You're too late." He grinned and added, "The bird has flown—and Myrtle with it."

"What?"

"She must have left the building by now. She appears at the Royal Eagle in half an hour."

"Damnation!" I *knew* that music hall performers appeared on several bills the same night. If I'd studied the *Era* systematically, instead of chucking it aside the moment I found her name on the bill for the Sebright, I'd have known she was likely to be rushing off to another hall. So much for my resolve to be a wise virgin.

"Where the devil is the Royal Eagle?" I demanded.

"City Road—as if you didn't know."

Buckfast said sharply, "If we knew, there would be no point in asking."

"Strike a light, mate—don't you know the song? 'Up and down the City Road, in and out the Eagle; that's the way the money goes—'"

I said, "Is it far?"

"No. Hoxton. You can walk it in twenty minutes, easy."

Easy was not the word I would have used as we shouldered our way through the crowds along Hackney Road, stepping over drunks and beggars and being importuned repeatedly by pimps and opium dealers. Stopping to ask for directions was positively dangerous in such a neighborhood, and thank heavens we were fortunate in the persons we consulted. Resolutely, we persevered as far as Old Street and so through to City Road, which was no more salubrious, I may tell you.

The Royal Eagle was another honey pot for streetwalkers and hawkers of every description. Before we went inside, I glanced at the bill and saw that Myrtle Bliss was indeed performing, with "feathered friends." Her name was at the bottom of the bill here, which meant second billing. Top, I noted wryly, was "Marvelous Disappearance of a Lady."

We moved around the side of the building to the pass door. It cost me a sovereign to gain admission that way, and even then the harridan on guard tested the coin with her teeth before she would let us through. Miss Bliss, we were advised, had her own dressing room at the top of the stairs. Luxury, indeed! The reason was shortly explained.

When I knocked, there was a screech from Cocky, or so I assumed, but it was followed by a pandemonium of squawks and shrieks. I opened the door and stepped into a veritable parrot house. It was a riot of color and earsplitting noise. There must have been six large parrots the size of Cocky; and uncountable smaller ones perched on every conceivable place where claws would grip. They screamed and swayed and flapped their wings. One of them called out, "Shut the door!" and I obeyed.

Miss Bliss spoke from behind a Japanese screen. She had to shout to get any hearing at all, and it was apparent that she mistook us for some other person. "Didn't I tell you not to come in sudden like that? You know it starts them off. Oh, stow it, Binky. You'll give me another headache." And when Binky persisted, "All right, you noisy perisher, I'm going to strangle you now!"

Suddenly she was no longer a disembodied voice. In fact, there was rather more body than either Buckfast or I were prepared for, because she was wearing only a bodice, drawers and stays when she darted out in pursuit of the noisiest parrot, an evil-looking red-and-yellow macaw perched on a chair back. She threw a towel over it and thrust it into a cage, where it abruptly stopped its hullabaloo. That bird was no less startled, I can assure you, than Captain Buckfast and I.

The shock was not unwelcome. Myrtle Bliss, in stays, was by far the prettiest sight we'd had all evening. Her figure revised the laws of science as I understood them. It was buoyancy without immersion, mass that defied gravity. And to run your eyes along the length of her legs was to understand infinity.

Unabashed, she glared at Buckfast and me and said, "Who the blazes are you?"

I said, "The Prince of Wales." I hadn't intended to give myself away, but I'm a creature of impulse. I adore surprising pretty young women, and at that moment I wanted nothing else but to make Myrtle Bliss shriek like her birds and take cover behind the screen.

It didn't happen. She said, "And I'm Florence Nightingale. Who's this—the Archbishop of Canterbury?"

Buckfast said, "Madam, take care how you speak to His Royal Highness."

She hesitated, and then said, "You're a couple of loonies. Stay where you are. These birds have got sharp beaks, you know."

I said, "I know from experience, my dear. One of them had my cigarette in the Sebright."

She clapped her hands and said with manifest relief, "*That's* who you are, you artful beggar! I thought I'd seen your face before. For a moment I thought you *was* the Prince of Wales."

I gave Buckfast a restraining look. Now that it was established that we weren't lunatics, but artful beggars, Miss Bliss seemed ready to be friends, and I had no objection. I could understand why the Squire had treated her to supper in Romano's. She was about twenty-four, I would guess, with glittering brown eyes, black hair in ringlets and a most engaging smile. I said, "We'd like to take you out to supper."

She giggled, fingered her drawer strings and said, "Dressed like this?"

To show decorum, I said, "Good Lord, no. We'll wait downstairs."

Buckfast, still thinking along more practical lines than I, asked her, "What will you do with your parrots?"

She said, "I'll put them to bed first."

Cautiously, I asked, "Where precisely?"

"Here. They sleep here while I'm engaged. All except Cocky. He comes home with me." She gave me a saucy look. "He's very privileged."

Buckfast said in a shocked voice. "Do you propose to bring the cockatoo to supper?"

She said, "We'll go to Mr. Hollis up the road. He's used to Cocky."

So it was settled, and I was thankful; none of the places I knew for supper would have welcomed us dressed as we were, with or without the bird. In Hollis's oyster house in the City Road, Cocky perched on a coatrack and observed a discreet silence.

Myrtle (we were soon on familiar terms) had put on a large black plush hat with a dash of crimson in the trimming, a black dress cut distractingly low at the front, and ruby-colored beads and earrings. She was liberally scented with frangipani. She sat facing Buckfast and me at a table screened on three sides by dark-stained wooden boards.

We ordered, talked for ten minutes about Cocky, who it emerged was a greater sulfur-crested cockatoo, and then I brought the conversation around to animals in general and racehorses in particular. Myrtle admitted to liking a "flutter on the gee-gees" when she could afford it. So I told the story of my old friend Sir Ernest Cassel, when he started as an owner and asked Lord Marcus Beresford's advice as to what should be inscribed on the side of his horse boxes. Ernest is justly proud of his knighthood and wanted to know whether it would be appropriate to add the letters K.C.M.G. after his name. "Oh, it's quite clear," said Marcus. "You put K.C.M. on the outside, and the gee goes in the box."

Myrtle gave a screech of laughter that startled even Cocky, and I followed up my story by asking whether she'd won anything on the horses lately.

"As a matter of fact, I have," she told us. "I backed the winner of the Cambridgeshire."

"The Sailor Prince?" said I, trying to sound surprised. "How very clever!"

"Bertie, I knew it couldn't lose," she admitted. "A gent of my acquaintance told me to put on every penny I had. I didn't do that, but I stumped up a week's wages and got a very good price."

"This gentleman—was he by any chance Mr. Baird, the Squire?"

She was saucer-eyed. "How did you know?"

"Oh, it's common knowledge that he fleeced the bookies, and good luck to him." I winked across the table. "Do you happen to know his secret, Myrtle?"

"What?"

"I mean, where he got his information."

She said with awe in her voice, "For God's sake, keep your voice down, Bertie. He'd kill us both for gabbing about it in a place like this."

I said, "Later, perhaps—in another place?"

She said flatly, "You're an optimist, and no mistake."

She refused to be pumped any more on the subject of Baird, so we did full credit to Hollis's oysters, and very scrumptious they were, fresh from Colchester that morning. Without thinking anything of it, I ordered champagne. What else can one drink with oysters? Hollis first offered us quinine water, which I informed him wasn't fit for the parrot to drink. I insisted on champagne and suggested he send out for it. He wanted some assurance that we could pay for it, so I took out a handful of sovereigns and gave him one.

This transaction was productive in more ways than one, because I happened to notice Myrtle's eyes on the money, and her pupils had dilated like a hunting cat's. So, I thought I understand what excites you, young lady, and what drew you to the Squire.

Hollis was gone for a long time and finally returned with a bottle of non-vintage with a very inferior label that cost me five shillings. Once or twice in the next hour, as Myrtle and I conversed merrily about the music hall and our favorite comic turns, with Buckfast out of his depth, I felt the touch of Myrtle's shoe against mine, and believe me, it wasn't accidental. When the time came for us to leave, and Buckfast obligingly went to collect our coats, Myrtle leaned toward me and said, "Can't you get rid of that old poopstick?"

I murmured, "With the greatest of ease."

While Myrtle was retrieving Cocky, I told Buckfast in the kindest terms that his duties were over for the night, and I would pursue the inquiry independently.

"Is that altogether wise, sir?" he asked.

"Charlie," I responded, "this is an avenue that only one of us is at liberty to venture along."

So we parted outside, Buckfast to try his luck at the cab stand and I to try mine with Myrtle. She had lodgings in Mile End Road, not the best of addresses, but convenient for her music hall engagements, and, she volunteered with a playful pull at my beard, blessed with a very understanding landlady.

Myrtle made no bones about inviting me in. We groped our way up a creaking staircase to the top floor, and she asked me to hold Cocky while she found her latchkey.

She let us in and reached for matches and a lamp, which presently showed me an attic room of modest proportions containing a bed, wardrobe, table, washstand and T-shaped perch, where I thankfully transferred Cocky. In the absence of any chair, I stood awkwardly holding my hat while Myrtle found some seeds for the bird.

That done, she turned to me and said, "Well, Bertie, it's too perishing cold to stand about. I'm getting straight into bed." She then started unbuttoning her dress.

You may think that good taste demands I should end my chapter here, but there is more of significance to tell, even at the cost of some embarrassment to myself. As you peruse these lines, kindly remember, as I endeavored to, my serious purpose in being there.

I decided that now might be the last opportunity for questions, so as Myrtle continued to disrobe, I said, "You hinted in the oyster house that you knew why The Sailor Prince was a certainty for the Cambridgeshire."

She lifted her skirts over her head and said, "Lord bless you, Bertie, you're not going to talk about horses now!"

I said, "I understood that *you* were going to."

She was down to her stays again. She draped the dress over the bed rail and said, "You'll have to ask the Squire."

I said, "That's no answer, Myrtle."

She came over to me and casually started unbuttoning my coat and jacket. "You're used to wearing better togs than these."

"Don't be evasive, miss."

She said with gentle mockery, "Masterful!" and started on the waistcoat. "Bertie, all I know is that it was a very close secret. The Sailor Prince was a much better horse than the bookies knew. The Squire spread his bets so as not to spoil the odds." My overcoat, jacket and waistcoat joined her garments on the bed rail.

"Was it a fixed race?"

"Would you loosen my stays?"

I obliged, manfully endeavoring to keep the investigation foremost in my thoughts.

As Myrtle eased the corset over her hips and stepped out of it, she offered, "I could try and find out, if you want."

"When will you see the Squire again?"

"Tomorrow."

At this juncture in the proceedings, my concentration wavered. It's no secret that I've battled gamely all my life with mixed success against my amorous nature. The sight of Myrtle in chemise and drawers would have made a saint think twice about paradise, but I had more to endure than the visual provocation, for she had hitched her thumbs under my braces and slipped them off my shoulders. The borrowed trousers dropped like a flag at sunset.

She commented, "Nice underwear. Why don't you take it off?"

"I don't trust your cockatoo."

She shook with laughter. "Oh, Bertie, he only takes cigarettes!" She wrenched off her remaining clothes and stood gloriously, glowingly naked. "Come to bed as you are, then."

Such cheek. Such cheeks.

The cultured element among my readers will be relieved to learn that I didn't do quite as the lady suggested. I first removed my boots.

How long it was before we were interrupted, I cannot say, except that it was not long enough, either for Myrtle or for me. There had been steps on the stairs several times already, so we paid no attention to a particularly heavy-footed approach until the door was thrust open without even the courtesy of a knock and someone staggered in, collided with Cocky's perch and knocked it over and crashed on me like the Tay Bridge.

Myrtle, heaven knows how, managed to squirm from under me and ignite the lamp. The cockatoo, quite berserk, was on the pillow pecking tufts of my beard. The intruder was lying across my back in a posture I shall not attempt to describe.

When the light came on and Myrtle bravely removed the bird, I managed to extricate myself. Our uninvited guest was fortunately not a heavy man.

In fact, he was a famous gentleman rider. We both knew him.

"The Squire!" whispered Myrtle.

He opened his eyes and said, "Where am I, Marlborough bloody House?"

Then he shut them again. He was as drunk as the moon in a puddle.

CHAPTER 9

Considering my situation at the end of the last chapter, it may surprise you to learn that I duly attended the Wellington Statue Committee meeting on Saturday morning. I have always been punctilious in attendance to my duties. *Ich Dien,* as you probably know, is the motto of the Prince of Wales. I serve, no matter what has occurred the night before, never ceasing to amaze my intimates when I rise early after a demanding night. But there's nothing remarkable in it. With me, it comes down to priorities—generally, pressure on the bladder.

This was the committee's first opportunity to examine the plaster models submitted by the sculptors. After a couple of hours, dusty debate over whether the likeness to Wellington mattered more than the anatomy of the horse, we chose Mr. Boehm's design and adjourned to brush the plaster off our suits. The momentous decision as to which direction the statue should face was postponed until the following Saturday, when we agreed to reconvene at Hyde Park Corner. Such are the great affairs of state which occupy me. Prime Ministers of each persuasion, Disraeli and Gladstone, have repeatedly urged the Queen to initiate me into the responsibilities to which I am heir. I am still not permitted to see the contents of a Foreign Office dispatch box. Every impediment possible is put in the way of my travels. "Any encouragement of his constant love of running about," Mama wrote to Disraeli, "and not keeping at home, or near the Queen, is earnestly and seriously to be deprecated." Yet what incentive am I given to keep at home?

When the meeting was over, I told my coachman that I had some shopping to do in Jermyn Street, and after he had conveyed me there I would not require him to wait. He's a trusted servant, totally discreet. How one relies upon such people! Many's the time he's driven me to addresses I wouldn't care to see printed in the Court Circular.

Charlie Buckfast opened his own front door this time, and I don't mind admitting that I chuckled at the sight of him, for I'd caught him repairing his mustache. One side was waxed, and the other hung limp.

I said, "Is it as late as that?"

He didn't understand.

I said, "Your face is at half past three."

Once inside, I settled into one of his leather armchairs and allowed him to continue with the repairs while I gave an account of the night's adventure. In all important respects, it was a truthful account. If you notice any small discrepancies in what follows, it is because I have always believed that good taste ought to govern one's conversation.

"Once I had escorted Miss Bliss back to her lodgings," I explained, "I commenced to examine her—in the legal sense of the word, you understand. That, after all, was my reason for being there."

Buckfast stood in front of his sideboard mirror combing the unkempt half of his mustache. "That goes without saying, sir."

"Naturally, Charlie."

His eyes met mine through the mirror. "And was she . . . forthcoming, sir?"

"My word, yes—it was give-and-take for the best part of an hour, Charlie."

"Did something emerge?"

I gave a sniff. "I rather think that your wax is becoming overheated."

He snatched up the fireplace tongs and rescued the tin from the edge of the grate.

I told him as he teased out the whiskers again and twisted them, "Myrtle and I were rudely interrupted in the middle of our exchange. Someone burst through the door, staggered across the room and fell onto the bed."

"Good Lord! That must have been uncomfortable, sir."

I said with emphasis, "I got up from the chair where I was seated and went to the bed to protest. The man was obviously drunk, as one would expect. But I did not expect to recognize him, Charlie. It was Abington Baird, the Squire."

Buckfast turned from the mirror, and the mustache sagged again. "But how on earth . . . ?"

"He'd made an arrangement to meet Myrtle on Saturday, and she assumed he meant Saturday night, after she finished her music hall engagements. She wasn't prepared for the small hours of Saturday *morning*, and nor was I. I mean, one simply doesn't blunder into a lady's room like that in the middle of the night. It's not as if it were a house party."

"Outrageous," Buckfast agreed. "Did he recognize you?"

"Oh, yes. He wasn't *that* inebriated."

"What did you do, sir?"

"What did I do? My first instinct was to leave at once. Heaven only knows what a scoundrel like Baird would make of one's predicament, however innocent the explanation. Then I had a second thought. Up to this moment, I'd been extremely reluctant to confront the fellow, whatever his involvement in the Archer mystery. Now, I had the advantage of him. For once, he was away from his gang of roughs and pugilists. Like most bullies, he's a different man deprived of his support. I told Myrtle to bring me the jug of water on the washstand. She was splendid. She knew what to do."

"Tipped it over the Squire?"

"The lot. Sobered him up in seconds."

"Stout work! Was he willing to answer questions?"

"*Willing* is not the word I would use. He was persuaded."

Buckfast gave one of his rare smiles. "A little arm-twisting, sir?"

"No, no. I abhor violence. I gave him a cigarette and stepped back like a bombardier." I grinned, but Buckfast was slow to comprehend, so I explained, "Cocky the cockatoo performed his music hall turn."

"Ah."

"The Squire cooperated splendidly after that."

"So you were enabled to question him about the Cambridge-shire?"

"I was. First, I confirmed that it was true that he won all that money on The Sailor Prince."

Buckfast remarked without much tact, "I thought everyone in London knew about that."

"Captain, any detective worth his salt checks everything at the source."

He colored perceptibly.

"I proceeded to ask what caused him to repose such confidence in a horse at 25-1. He gave an offensive laugh. I've never been so close to the man before. He has a profoundly disagreeable coun-tenance, Charlie. Those thick lips like saveloys under that snub nose. Quite revolting."

"What was his answer, sir?"

"He said he'd heard that I backed The Sailor Prince myself. I told him *my* reasons were entirely sentimental, making clear by implication that his were not."

"How did he respond to that?"

"With an enormous belch."

"How disgusting!"

"Quite."

"Did you persist, sir?"

"Of course, Charlie. I'm a serious investigator. I asked Myrtle to bring Cocky's perch a little closer to the bed, and that worked wonders. The Squire told me that The Sailor Prince had been showing better staying power in training this season than it had ever possessed before. It was a revelation. William Stevens, the Compton trainer, couldn't explain it, but he had the sense to keep its form from the touts."

"Stevens? I can believe it," said Buckfast. "The Stevens brothers are up to every kind of trick."

"They entered it for the Liverpool Summer Cup and told the jockey to drop in on the rails behind the leader and not try anything spectacular. The Sailor Prince finished well up in third, behind the two dead heaters, but it could have won at a canter, given its head."

"So it didn't attract much attention."

"Exactly, Charlie. They didn't race it again before the Cam-bridgeshire."

There was a pause while Buckfast once more performed the twisting operation. He faced me, fingers pinching the spike into shape. "Is that approximately even, sir?"

I nodded, and he applied the wax.

Finally he turned from the mirror fully restored and remarked, "When you said 'they' didn't race the horse again before the Cambridgeshire, who exactly did you mean, sir?"

Charlie Buckfast was nobody's fool.

I told him, "That's the crux of it. When the Squire was speaking about the way the horse was prepared for the race, he didn't use *they*, he used *we*. The first time I remarked on this, he told me he kept some horses of his own with Stevens, and he regarded the Yews at Compton as a home away from home. He said he'd often watched The Sailor Prince at work."

"Who is the registered owner, sir?"

"William Gilbert, of Ilsley."

"Ah."

"Do you know him?"

"I know that he's a neighbor of the Stevens brothers."

"Well, you've obviously worked it out," I said. "The real owner of The Sailor Prince is the Squire, and it's registered in Gilbert's name."

Buckfast was impressed. "Did you get him to admit as much, sir?"

"With a little help from Cocky. He has scores of horses registered in other people's names, and pays handsomely for the privilege."

"That's a tremendous risk, isn't it? He could be disbarred from racing if the stewards got to hear of it."

"Yes, but remember what happened the last time he was warned off."

(Here, I'd better supply the story, for although it's well known in Turf circles, I doubt if it will pass down into history. The Squire, like his idol, Archer, is an aggressive, not to say ruthless, rider. His behavior on and off the racecourse has made him countless enemies among the racing fraternity, and no wonder, for when he isn't showing the way home to their horses, he's gallivanting with their wives, most of whom go quite giddy over him—or, more likely, his millions. Matters came to a head in a Hunters' Selling Flat Race at Birmingham in 1882, when the Squire won at a canter and was accused of foul riding by the rider who had finished last, and happened to be Lord Harrington. The Squire had apparently made abusive remarks about Harrington's riding and threatened to put him over the rails. When it was over and Harrington protested, the Squire said, "I thought you were a bloody farmer." As a consequence, he was reported to the Jockey Club and we decided to teach the blighter a lesson. We warned him off every course in the country for two years. How do you think he responded? He had the infernal cheek to let it be known that he proposed to buy the Limekilns—the gallops at Newmarket that are the finest anywhere, and practically hallowed ground. We in the Jockey Club were horrified at the prospect. Imagine this outlaw in a position to dictate which trainers used the gallops. He might have fenced the Limekilns off, or even plowed them up! We were compelled to enter clandestine negotiations with the Squire to secure the lease on terms that wouldn't beggar the club, and of course, he was reinstated before his ban was up.)

Buckfast said, "I daresay he secretly bought The Sailor Prince during the time he was warned off. It repaid him handsomely."

He poured me a glass of dry sherry and asked what else I'd learned from the Squire.

I responded judiciously, picking my way with care. I had a job for Buckfast that he might not welcome. I'm not renowned for my tact, but I felt some subtlety was wanted here. "He spoke up for Archer, wouldn't hear a blessed word against him. He said Fred had nothing to be ashamed of over the running of the Cambridgeshire. That rumor Lord Edward Somerset is putting about, to the effect that Fred paid a bribe to stop the favorite, Carlton, is a diabolical slander, in the Squire's opinion. Fred was offered the ride on Carlton, and he turned it down because he was convinced St. Mirin was the better horse."

"He's right about that," Buckfast conceded. "Fred thought he was on a certainty."

I continued in the same vein, "The Squire said he had a friendly exchange with Archer on the day of the race. Archer advised him strongly to back St. Mirin."

Buckfast put aside his sherry as if it were poisoned.

"Charlie, you look skeptical," I said. "As a matter of fact, Fred gave me the same tip."

He cleared his throat in a way that signaled disagreement.

"Out with it, man," I said.

"Well, sir, I have no doubt that Fred gave you a tip, but I question whether he was so generous to the Squire. They were not the bosom friends that the Squire would have you believe."

"The Squire was Fred's protégé," I pointed out. "Have you forgotten the riding lessons?"

"The most expensive riding lessons I ever heard of. Purely a business arrangement," said Buckfast dismissively. "The Squire paid well, and Fred was never averse to earning some extra."

"Fred in his capacity as the Tin Man," said I.

"Exactly."

I remarked as if the thought had just occurred to me, "Wasn't there talk a year or two ago of Archer and the Squire going into partnership in Newmarket? A joint racing establishment?"

Buckfast winced as if I'd struck him. "The talk was all on one side, sir. Fred would never have sullied his reputation in such an ill-starred venture. He was furious with the Squire for putting the story about. People believed it, unfortunately. The Duke of Portland was one."

"Silly arse," I said. (Arthur Portland had acted prematurely when he heard the gossip and ordered Archer to send back his cap and jacket. Fred never rode in the Portland colors again.) "What you're saying is that the Squire was an embarrassment to Fred. Last night, he was claiming to be his one true friend."

"That's utter bilge—begging your pardon, sir."

I said teasingly, "Do I detect some personal animus here, Charlie?"

He answered, "I have never met the Squire, sir. I have always contrived to keep out of his way. I doubt if he's aware of my existence."

"Perfect," I said, and never meant it more sincerely, "because I want you to follow him."

His face was a study. I could have thrown a penny into his mouth. "Follow him?"

"Go to the places he frequents. They shouldn't be difficult to locate. The Greyhound at Newmarket is one. Romano's in the Strand is another. Where there's a barney going on, it's ten to one you'll find the Squire and his crew. Have another glass of sherry, Charlie. You look as if you need it."

He said, grappling with the unthinkable, "What would be my purpose in being there?"

"It stands out, doesn't it, Charlie? The Squire isn't being honest with us. You just told me he was talking utter bilge. We can't let him get away with it, can we?"

Buckfast rubbed the side of his chin and wetted his lips. "I suppose if you think he had some influence on Fred's suicide, sir . . ."

I said, "Never mind what I think. What do you think?"

After a moment's consideration, he answered, "He's a dangerous man."

"Undeniably."

"And it isn't just the Squire. There are all those others—Charlie Mitchell, Jem Smith—men whose profession is physical violence. They follow him everywhere. You must have seen them on the racecourse, sir."

"I saw them in the City Road last night," I told him.

"They were there?"

"Waiting under a lamppost for the Squire to complete his assignation with Myrtle. She spotted them from the window, at least a dozen of the ugliest specimens of humanity I have ever seen. It was quite impossible for me to return to Marlborough House, as I intended."

"What did you do?"

"I remained there all night."

"With Myrtle and the Squire?"

"Not with the Squire. After an hour, we encouraged him to leave. I helped him downstairs and bolted the door after him. It was the only possible course of action. His mob cheered him raucously when he appeared, and presently moved off, thank heavens."

"But you remained?"

"Solely to protect a lady at risk, Charlie. I don't underestimate these ruffians, and neither must you."

"No, sir."

"You're there to observe, not to provoke any unpleasantness. Be inconspicuous."

His hand went protectively to his mustache.

I said in a mild, reasonable voice, "It's got to come off, hasn't it, Charlie?"

"Off, sir?"

I nodded.

He was aghast. "Completely?"

"Every whisker."

He turned back to the mirror and regarded himself. "I suppose it is a prominent feature."

I said, "At two hundred yards or less. Heaven knows what the Squire and his gang would do with it if they suspected you of eavesdropping."

There was a moment's horrified silence.

I added, "Myrtle offered me her services as a spy, but I'd much rather rely on you, Charlie."

He went to a drawer and took out a pair of scissors. Such is the devotion to duty of the British cavalry officer.

As he snipped, I said, "I wouldn't want you to think that I shall be out of the front line, Charlie. I intend to mount an assault on a different flank. I shall arrange to visit the Dowager Duchess of Montrose."

He cut off a huge handful of whiskers and said, "The Duchess? Whatever for?"

Echoing Gladys de Grey's remark, I said, *"Cherchez la femme,* Charlie."

CHAPTER 10

Each Sunday afternoon, the affairs of State permitting, I make it my custom to tour the Sandringham estate. My weekend guests—there are always guests—are at liberty to join me if they wish, but old friends (the Earl of Carnarvon, Lord Herschel and Sir Henry James on the occasion of which I speak) generally feel at liberty to leave me to it. Upon a bleak November day, the twenty-first, I muffled myself like a cabman, for a brute of a wind was blowing off the Wash. In such conditions I generally head for the greenhouses, only there isn't so much as a rotten tomato to see at this end of the year. So we resorted to the sawyer's yard, where there is always a fire burning, and it was there that I discovered a lad scarcely above twelve years of age reading a copy of *Reynolds's Newspaper*.

I don't know if you will have heard of *Reynolds's*. I hope to heaven it will be defunct and forgotten by the time these lines are read, for it is a vile publication, a rag that promulgates wicked libel and defamation week by week in the name of socialism. Lest you think I exaggerate, let me quote from an article of last May referring to my son Eddy, destined one day to be King:

> . . . *A duller, a stupider lad never existed. He cannot even read with any degree of grace or dignity the written speech which is put into his hand and which is reported next day in the newspapers as his own.*

Now, while I am the first to admit that Eddy's powers of concentration leave something to be desired, it is a matter of record
that after his naval training the boy was admitted to Trinity Col-
lege, Cambridge, and is soon to be offered a commission in the
Tenth Hussars. How can any responsible journalist pen such
vitriolic stuff when we, Eddy's devoted parents, are doing all
in our power to prepare him for the responsibilities of State? I
can tell you, poor Alix would be inconsolable if she knew the
scurrilous abuse that is read each Sabbath in millions of homes
up and down the country.

That was not all. Judge for yourself the quality of the journalism
as I quote the remainder of the same article:

> *The Prince of Wales and other "members of the royal family" who*
> *venture to favor the public with their views upon current topics*
> *have also their speeches prepared for them by the official speech*
> *writer. You have only to dress up a donkey or an ape, and call*
> *it "king" or "royal," and half the females in the land will start*
> *into a paroxysm of admiration, praising the lovely ears, and the*
> *finely molded hoofs and the delicate skin, and the refined ways,*
> *just the same as if it were the most Godlike of created beings.*
> *Many of these poor people are ready for a lunatic asylum; but*
> *of course, so long as they are merely in the stage of idiocy, and*
> *their friends consent to support them at home, the State need not*
> *burden itself with the charge.*

So you can understand my reaction when I chanced upon the
young sawman reading *Reynolds's Newspaper*. I snatched it from his
grimy hands and soundly boxed his ears with it. Then I warned
him that he could seek employment elsewhere if he was ever
again found with it in his possession on my estate. He was quick
to understand. He assured me that he only read it for the racing
results. How I wish my Eddy were so quick-witted.

The head sawman, who is not slow, either, took the opportunity
to divert any blame coming his way by offering to beat the boy
and burn the offensive paper. I didn't allow it. As I explained,
I had already administered a summary chastisement. As for the
newspaper, it was the lad's property, albeit at a cost of one penny,
and I proposed to teach our young socialist a lesson in practical

politics. I respected property, so it was against my principles to permit his newspaper to be destroyed. I would confiscate it instead. I handed it to Jarvis, my estate manager, promising the boy that when he left my employ, which need not be for many years if he improved his ways, he could ask for his paper to be returned, and it would be handed to him.

At the end of the afternoon, Jarvis asked what he should do with the wretched newspaper, and I was somewhat at a loss until I thought of Knollys. "Hand it to Sir Francis," I said. "He will commit it to some place of safekeeping."

Next morning, after my guests had made their farewells and been conveyed to the station, Knollys buttonholed me in the front drive.

"That, em, copy of *Reynolds's Newspaper*, sir."

"Of what?" I said, hazily recalling the incident. The previous night, I had yarned with my guests in the smoking room until the fire turned to ash. "Ah, yes. You put it somewhere safe?"

Now it was Knollys who became vague. "The newspaper, sir?"

"What else? We're not talking about pink elephants, Francis."

There was an uncomfortable pause, then Knollys responded, "The newspaper in question was handed to me, sir. I was given to understand that you had suggested I took charge of it."

"So I did."

He said in that disapproving tone that bears an uncanny resemblance to my mother's, "It is not a pleasant organ—not the organ one would desire to see at Sandringham, sir."

"Emphatically not," I agreed.

"One would not wish Her Royal Highness or the young princesses to discover it by some mischance."

I didn't like the drift of this. I gave a grudging nod.

He continued, "After it was given to me, I examined it page by page. Some of it was extremely offensive. The remarks about Your Royal Highness—utterly uncalled-for."

I said, "I haven't seen them."

Knollys declared forcefully, "Nor will you, sir. I took the liberty of destroying them."

"You *what*?"

"I cut out the only possible item for your scrapbook—and burned the rest."

I was outraged. I shouted, "Damn you, Francis! You had no right. You're worse than incompetent. You're a destroyer, an anarchist," but really I blamed myself. After my homily in the saw yard on the sanctity of property, I should have made sure that the confounded newspaper was put away safely. If the boy grew up to start the revolution, mine would be the responsibility.

Knollys was white at the gills. I suppose I had been too heavy-handed. To soften the rebuke, I said, "You might as well show me the piece you decided to keep. Is it amusing?"

He said, "I wouldn't describe it as such. It is one of the leading articles."

"The subject?"

"The late Mr. Archer and his will."

I pricked up. "Then I should like to see it at once."

He fetched the scrapbook from his desk. The cutting was already pasted in. Under the title "A Jockey's Fortune," it announced that on reliable authority Fred Archer was stated to have left a fortune of over a hundred thousand pounds. Most of what followed was tedious and predictable socialist claptrap about the racing fraternity making piles of gold while the laboring classes starved, without a word about the thousands who are afforded employment by the sport. Archer, it suggested, was a poor stable boy who should have remained poor. He had betrayed his class by hobnobbing with "lords, dukes and even princes, while by certain of his countrymen he had for years been worshiped as a sort of demigod."

I looked up and remarked to Knollys, "The usual joyless propaganda."

He said, "If you read on, sir, I think you may find something to interest you."

I did. It was the very next sentence: "A certain frowsy old dowager duchess of sporting proclivities is said to have been nearly marrying him."

Carrie Montrose.

"My word," I said, spluttering with laughter, "I wonder if she's seen this."

Knollys commented dryly, "I wouldn't care to be the one who drew it to her attention, sir."

I was chuckling over Carrie's sporting proclivities for the rest of the morning, and it was quite some time before I began to grasp the importance of the statement. Lady de Grey had told me that Carrie Montrose, at the advanced age of sixty-eight, had been pursuing Archer with a view to matrimony and I had scarcely believed it, yet here it was in a newspaper read by millions. Strange things happen, but I doubted whether *Reynolds's Newspaper* employed Gladys de Grey to write its editorials.

In point of fact, *Reynolds's* went much further than Gladys had suggested. The Duchess was "said to have been nearly marrying" Archer. Amazing, if true. I should say amazing if Archer had seriously entertained the match. Granted, Carrie was extremely rich and had inherited from her second husband possibly the finest racing stable and breeding stud in the country. Granted, Archer had an eye to making money. Moreover, he was a lonely man since the death of his wife. And Carrie had flattered him by stumping up an enormous retainer for years. Granted, all that. I still couldn't picture them as bride and groom, sixty-eight married to twenty-nine. Six-Mile Bottom carried over the threshold by the Tin Man.

However, I was glad to have the information, for whatever it was worth. It gave my forthcoming meeting with Carrie an extra piquancy. She didn't know it yet, but she would be entertaining me and Charlie Buckfast to dinner at her town house in Cheyne Walk the following Saturday. The arrangements had to be discreetly handled, so it was all being done through Sykes's sister-in-law, Jessica, who was known to Carrie. I hadn't mentioned it to Knollys. Fortunately, he still has sense enough not to interfere in my private dining engagements.

Nor does he open my letters. I mention this because on Tuesday when the post was brought to me, there was a pungent aroma of lavender emanating from the stack. Intrigued, I picked out the source, a scented envelope of a most vulgar shade of blue, with a London East postmark and the word *Pursonall* doubly underlined above a curiously misspelled attempt at my name and address. I was not long in deducing that it came from Myrtle Bliss.

She had first written *Your Royl,* then scored it through and substituted *Dear Burte.*

Wot a jolly time we had Fridy nite! Arnt you a sorsy begger and no mestake! Wooden it be a lark to meet agen? I bin invited to

Noomarkit Sundy with the Sqyre so if you want to here all about
it, be shore to cum and look me up next week-Chewsdy about 11.
Cocky sez bring yore smokes. Hes got a new trick to shew you.

Love,

M

Much as I appreciated the sentiments in general, the style and
orthography shocked me—in fact, caused me to ask myself how I
could have been so impetuous as to encourage such an attachment.
At the risk of appearing snobbish, I must say that on paper the
lady lost most of her charm. All things considered, I preferred to
rely on Charlie Buckfast for news of the Squire. I didn't respond.
If I have learned one lesson in life, it is that letter writing to the
fair sex, whether they are literate or not, is fraught with snares.

That apart, the main excitement of the week was the safe delivery
on Monday, 23 November, of a son to my youngest sister Beatrice.
I visited her at Windsor on Wednesday (not to mention Mama,
and I prefer not to, for it was the usual sermon on self-restraint).
I traveled back to Sandringham for my youngest daughter Maud's
seventeenth birthday party on Friday. Birthdays are joyous occasions, and I would be the last to complain, except that with seven
in our family and over thirty nephews and nieces we do little else
but send cards and eat cake. I left for London late that night for
the inevitable meeting on Saturday morning of the Wellington
Statue Committee.

I was eager to hear from Buckfast after his week as a shadow
to the Squire, and I'd arranged to call at his rooms in Jermyn
Street at six o'clock on Saturday evening, in good time to have his
report before we left for our dinner engagement with the Duchess.
Inconveniently, he was not at his address when I arrived, and I
was obliged to stand for twenty minutes exchanging pleasantries
with the greengrocer about the nourishment in potatoes. I'm a
great advocate of the humble potato.

When a four-wheeler eventually pulled up and a fellow
stepped out, I had difficulty at first in recognizing Charlie
Buckfast. Without the mustache, and in an ill-fitting Norfolk
jacket and cap, he could have passed for a loader at one of my
Sandringham shoots, except that he ignored me totally and
stared up and down the street before he put the key in the

door. He didn't even have the elementary good manners to step back and let me enter first. He fairly bolted inside and left me to make my own way in and close the door after us.

I would certainly have taken objection if I hadn't seen his expression. I'm well used to looking at nervous faces. I come across them all the time, like red carpets and the smell of fresh paint. Charlie's wasn't merely nervous; it was *hunted*. And the first words he spoke when we got upstairs had a horrid familiarity.

"Are they coming?"

I was standing by the window. I stared at him for a moment. Then I turned and looked out.

He said, "Don't move the curtain, for God's sake!"

Below, in Jermyn Street, the growler had moved off. Someone in a dark green ulster and billycock was coming out of the tobacconist's opposite. A couple in evening capes were crossing the road. I could see nothing to provoke such alarm in my co-investigator, and I told him so.

He said, "They followed me up from Newmarket. They looked right into the compartment before the train left, and I saw them get on as it was pulling out. At Liverpool Street, I jumped off the train before it came to a halt and fairly sprinted to the barrier, with them in open pursuit."

"Good Lord! Who were they?"

"Two of the Squire's henchmen, his minders, as he calls them. One is a prizefighter, built like an ox. He's fond of displaying his scars, and the scars are confined to his fists, from battering his knuckles against other men's skulls. The other is taller and younger, with the coldest gray eyes you ever saw. Can you see them yet, sir?"

I glanced down at the street again. "Hide nor hair, Charlie."

He waited, expecting any second to hear me say otherwise. "Please God, I gave them the slip. I changed cabs near St. Paul's."

"Do they have any idea who you are?"

"I think not. But I'm a marked man. Last night, there was dogfighting in the back room of the Greyhound. He has this murderous Staffordshire bull terrier called Donald, which he unleashes on any of the local strays his men can round up. I wouldn't call it fighting—more like ratting. There's betting on how long they last."

"And you were there to see it?"

"No, sir. I took the opportunity to break into Bedford Lodge, the Squire's headquarters."

"You broke into the Lodge! By jove, Charlie, I salute you. Are we on to something?"

Buckfast had poured two whopping brandies. He handed me one, stealing a glance out of the window at the same time. "I'd stake my life on it, sir. I've been listening all week to the Squire's bragging. If half of it is true, Fred Archer must be stoking the fires of hell. The Squire says there isn't a jockey in England who can't be squared. He says Archer and Charlie Wood were in his pocket and now he wants Cannon."

This was devastating. I said in a voice thick with shock, "Archer accepted bribes from the Squire? Is that what you're telling me, Charlie?"

"That's what I heard more than once, sir. He and Wood were regularly pulling races, and the Squire was putting up the money."

I felt a wave of nausea at the very idea. Rumors of a conspiracy, a "jockeys' ring" involving Archer and Wood and certain "professional backers," had surfaced two years ago but were disbelieved by all except that vengeful old Turfite, Sir George Chetwynd, whose own runners had been afflicted that season with in-and-out form. Chetwynd had gone so far as to interrogate the two jockeys (they denied the charge) and publish a notice in the sheet calendar of the Jockey Club asking the stewards how they proposed to deal with the allegations. The stewards responded that they required clearer evidence of malpractice, and for a time Chetwynd was in uncommonly bad odor over the business. Now, apparently, his complaint was vindicated.

The last thing I wanted was to drag Archer's name through the mud.

And there was worse to come from Buckfast: "The Squire claims that he didn't need to put up large bribes once the jockeys had taken the first payment, because they were terrified of a Jockey Club inquiry. Their livelihoods were at risk. They had so much to lose."

"Unlike the Squire, whose reputation reeks to high heaven," I commented acidly.

"He bought his way out of suspension once. He could do it again," said Charlie.

"No doubt of that. With his millions, he has the Jockey Club by its ears. What I don't understand is why he bothers to cheat. What's in it for him?"

"The same thing puzzled me, sir," Charlie admitted. "My first thought was that he took a malicious delight in fleecing the book-makers. Then I heard him say something else, a remark that made me see the logic in what he was doing. He said Fred was an idiot to blow his brains out just when he was offered the finest opportunity of his life."

"Opportunity? What kind of opportunity?"

"A partnership with the Squire."

I closed my eyes and said something sacrilegious.

Charlie gave a shrug. We both remembered the talk of a joint racing establishment. And you, my reader, ought to remember it, too, if you're paying attention, because I mentioned it in the last chapter.

Charlie said, "The bribes were just the bait. The Squire was planning from the start to trap Fred into signing an agreement. He idolized Fred. To be a partner with him was recognition, the supreme accolade. A contract was drawn up and Fred was being blackmailed into signing it. The Squire kept saying that he still had the document and he couldn't bring himself to destroy it. That's why I broke into Bedford Lodge."

"To steal it?"

Charlie looked slightly pained. "To annex it, sir. I managed to force a window in the boxing saloon and gain access to the main part of the house. The lights were burning in every room, but no one appeared to be about. I was looking for a study, or at least some room where a writing desk was situated. The entire house is in a disgusting state, with empty bottles and glasses and cigar butts and half-chewed bones strewn about, and the fireplaces heaped with ash and cinders."

"Didn't you find anything?"

"I gave up looking downstairs, sir."

"You tried the bedrooms?"

Charlie nodded. "I thought possibly the Squire would keep any-thing of value beside his bed. I located his room without difficulty. Unfortunately, it was occupied at the time."

"He was at home in bed?"

"Not the Squire, sir. Two of his men, naked as cuckoos."

"Fellows?" I pictured the scene all too shockingly. "Whatever next?"

"They were a pair of his pugilistic friends, believe it or not, sir—the two who are currently pursuing me."

"Charlie," I said sympathetically, "I understand everything now."

And everything, to put it at its most tame, was unsatisfactory. In spite of our strenuous efforts on Archer's behalf, his reputation looked blacker than when we had started. We still had nothing of substance to assist us, and Charlie Buckfast couldn't any longer be used to keep tabs on the Squire.

He asked me what I proposed to do, and after a moment's reflection, I fished the scented letter from my pocket and allowed him to read it. "I want this thing settled," I said. "If there *is* a document proving that the Squire was pressing Archer into a partnership—and poor Fred shot himself rather than sign—I shan't rest until I've seen it. I think we shall have to resort to Myrtle Bliss."

Charlie looked exceedingly dubious. "She's just a music hall performer, sir. She doesn't have my background or military training."

"She has one incalculable advantage over you, Charlie—the entrée to the Squire's bedroom."

He couldn't argue with that. I suggested it was time he dressed for dinner with the Duchess. At the prospect of venturing out again, he made a few demurring noises, but I was swift to remind him of his obligations as a gentleman, not to say an ex-officer. He withdrew to his bedroom.

It was toward half past seven when we left. I manfully offered to step into the street first, and when I'd made sure there was no one suspicious lurking, I hailed the first hansom that came along and negotiated a fare. Charlie crossed the pavement at speed and climbed in, and we set off at a canter in the direction of Chelsea.

Never having visited Carrie Montrose before, I was unable to give the cabman precise instructions as to the location of the house. The street is numbered, but who wants to own a house that is known by a mere number? The Duchess's is named Sefton House, after her late husband's Derby winner. We had some difficulty in locating it, a common enough experience in a public carriage, when the wily cabdriver takes every advantage to relieve you of more than the fare you agreed. We were driven the length of the Walk—quite half a mile along the Thames embankment (for the houses overlook the river)—and most of the way back before he stopped the horse outside the Duchess's gate. I handed him the one and six we had agreed, and a threepenny tip, and he had the cheek to demand sixpence more for the extra distance. Buckfast and I had already got out, and I was damned if I would be tricked into paying any more. The driver's revolting language disgusted me, and I asked him for his number, which I was unable to see in the darkness. It was a disagreeable, but not uncommon, scene. Buckfast, evidently embarrassed by the business, opened the wrought-iron gate of Sefton House and went through.

Next, I was conscious of a strangled shout that I swear uncurled the hair on the back of my neck. The voice was Charlie Buckfast's, manifestly in trouble, and it came from inside the garden of Sefton House. I guessed at once what was happening, for I called upon the cabdriver to render assistance, whereupon the cowardly fellow whipped up his horse and deserted me. The sounds of heavy blows came from the other side of the high brick wall. I looked up and down the Embankment, but no help was within call. A groan of unspeakable character was conveyed to me as I considered how to act.

I flattened myself to the outside of the wall. Criticize me if you wish, but isn't it beyond dispute that most heroes are people with no imagination? As a sensitive man, I was graphically, painfully aware of what was happening to my unfortunate associate, and it was presently confirmed when two roughs came through the gate dragging the dead weight of poor Charlie, his heels scraping the ground. Both were muffled to the ears and wore long coats and billycock hats. One had the build of a prizefighter, with a back like a leather armchair. The other was taller, better proportioned. I can't be more precise. That stretch of Cheyne Walk is almost unlit.

In fact, I entertained a slight hope that the lighting was so poor that I wouldn't be spotted, but it was not to be. The squat man looked my way and shouted, "Get him!"

Thinking back, my best chance was probably to have dashed through the gate and up the path to the front door of Sefton House. The Duchess or one of her staff might well have heard the commotion and opened the door in readiness. Instead, I rashly started along the Embankment toward the Albert Bridge. Running is not a pastime at which I excel. In the first two strides I lost my hat. I lost my breath in the next and was collared from behind by my pursuer. When I say "collared," I mean it literally. I was grabbed by the collar and practically garotted into the bargain as an arm like a rifle butt clamped against my throat.

The brute hauled me back toward his confederate, who, to my horror, was in the act of pushing Charlie Buckfast over the Embankment wall into the Thames.

I shouted. "You'll kill him!"

The only response was the tightening of the clamp on my throat.

I saw Charlie tipped over the wall. I heard the splash as his body struck the water. There was no cry. Whether he was conscious, I cannot say. He put up no fight, and that's not the way a cavalry officer would want to go.

It was two against one now.

The shape of the figure by the wall was outlined for a moment against the moonlight reflected along Battersea Reach. It was positively simian in aspect.

I tried to speak, but my vocal cords were unable to function under the pressure.

The ape shuffled toward me and grabbed one of my arms. I was propelled toward the Embankment wall and thrust over it, head down, ten feet above the jet-black, glistening water. For a second or so, my legs were held, and I prayed that my attackers would show mercy and drag me back to safety, for I'm not a strong swimmer.

Managing at last to find my voice. I gasped, "I am the Prince of Wales."

They dropped me into the Thames.

CHAPTER 11

Whoever wrote that line "Sweet Thames, run softly, till I end my Song," should have been dropped headfirst into the evil river. His song would have ended there and then.

I can tell you from personal experience that *sweet* is not an accurate description of the Thames. I would allow brackish, foul and emetic, but not sweet. We are told that Mr. Bazalgette's marvelous system of drainage has transformed the river from an open sewer to a natural waterway, and all of London is grateful to him for that, so I shall put the blame on Nature for the unendurable taste of the pints of noxious fluid I swallowed that November night.

I spluttered and floundered. My clothes and shoes weighted me, and I was in the gravest danger of drowning. I have absolved Mr. Bazalgette of responsibility for the state of the water, but the same gentleman is guilty of another charge, for he designed the Embankment, and there isn't a decent handhold for a drowning man to grasp along its entire length. I can remember when it was a wharf equipped with iron hooks and rings and even lengths of rope dangling helpfully. Since Bazalgette's improvements, the hapless struggler in the water is confronted with massive granite blocks forming a rampart, an unscalable wall where his hands claw unavailingly at weed and slime.

If you ask what kept me afloat, I am convinced it was willpower. I was damned if I would allow myself to perish in such squalid circumstances. I'm told that a drowning man sees his whole life pass across his brain like a magic lantern show. I can only speak for myself and tell you that I had a vision of the editor of *Reynolds's Newspaper* at work on a gloating obituary on the moral of my sinking into the sludge. That vision saved me. I struck out like Captain Webb, the channel swimmer, in sight of Calais.

For perhaps fifty yards, I kept up a resolute breaststroke, until, praise be, my hand came in contact with a solid obstruction, a wooden structure, a floating jetty used by the penny steamers. I grasped the post on the nearest corner. It was as sweet an embrace as any in my experience.

I succeeded in dragging myself out at the second attempt and lay blowing like a grampus for an interval of uncertain duration, utterly spent, nauseated from the intake of water. At length, I propped myself into a sitting position and listened for voices above. If my attackers were waiting up there and found me alive, they wouldn't hesitate to throw me back. Hearing nothing for some while, I crawled across the jetty and located the steps leading up to the Embankment wall. Water streamed from my clothes as I ascended. Near the top, I paused and listened.

Not a sound.

I raised my head to the level of the wall. There wasn't a living soul in sight. I clambered over and staggered across the road toward the houses of Cheyne Walk. At the gate of Sefton House, I listened again before entering. All was silent. I tottered up the path and rang the Duchess's door bell.

It was answered by a maid in uniform. She took one look at me in the porch light, said, "Jerusalem!" and slammed the door in my face.

Admittedly, I was an unprepossessing spectacle. My head and evening jacket were coated in mud, slime and waterweed. One sleeve had torn at the seam as I'd pulled myself onto the jetty. I had lost my bow tie, hat, both shoes and one of my gloves. A pool of water was forming at my feet.

I pressed the bell a second time. When there was no answer, I crouched and shouted through the letter slot, "This is the Prince of Wales. Let me in at once!"

I watched and listened for the response, and my announcement certainly elicited some excitement in the house. Presently the light in the hall grew dimmer as a bulky form stepped toward the door.

A pair of eyes met mine on the other side of the opening, and the voice of the Dowager Duchess of Montrose said, "If you don't get off my doorstep this minute, I'll call the police to you!"

This had descended to farce.

As if I had not heard, I inquired, "Did you, or did you not, invite me to dinner?"

There was a pause.

The door eased open a mere two inches. Her face glared through the gap. She flung the door wide open and said, "You're a caution, Your Royal Highness! You and your practical jokes."

I lurched across the threshold, far too weak to argue.

She curtsied, caught a whiff of the river, and abandoned decorum. "God help us, the smell of him! Stay where you are, Your Highness. Don't move a step in those filthy clothes, and keep away from the wallpaper." She sent the maid for newspapers and a bath.

You won't wish to be put to the blush by a copious description of the next few minutes any more than I will. Suffice to say that such is the force of the Duchess's personality that I was persuaded to stand on a copy of the *Morning Post* and strip to my sodden undergarments. She contrived in the cause of decency to place her ample form between me and the team of domestics who carried a hip bath into the hall and filled it with jugs of steaming water from the kitchen, whereupon they all retired, leaving me to complete my undressing in privacy and step into the water. Despite the novel surroundings, never was a bath more welcome.

While soaping my hair, I had a most disquieting thought.

Charlie Buckfast.

Suppose he had not drowned and was afloat in the Thames, expecting to be rescued! It seemed unlikely, for I'd heard no sound when I was in the river, but I couldn't in all conscience abandon the poor fellow if he had the slightest chance of survival. I sat forward in the bath and shouted for the Duchess.

It occurs to me that you may feel I was tardy in bringing my thoughts to bear on Charlie Buckfast. If so, I beg to remind you of what had just occurred. Not merely had I made a miraculous escape from the Grim Reaper. Down there in the Thames, the destiny of the nation had been in jeopardy. By triumphing over death, I had preserved the line of succession and ensured, God willing, that I will be spared to undertake the great responsibility for which I have been preparing all my life. I won't say I was fully conscious of these matters at the time, but afterward they tended to crowd out other thoughts.

Let's give credit to Carrie Montrose, for when I called her name, she appeared very rapidly from behind one of the half-opened doors leading off the hall. Unfortunately, she was not so rapid in apprehending what I was saying. My concern about Buckfast made no appreciable impression. She was not interested in Buckfast. Incredibly, she still appeared to believe that the episode was one of the practical jokes for which I am well known. Worse, silly woman, she had somehow convinced herself that I had devised it with the wicked intention of revealing myself to her in a state of nature. She was pink with excitement.

I told her, "Captain Buckfast may be drowning at this minute!"

She said with a most inappropriate outburst of laughter, "You should be on the stage. You're better than Henry Irving." She wagged a finger at me. "Let's stop pretending, shall we, Your Royal Highness—or may I call you Bertie? You came alone."

In desperation, I howled, "Duchess, will you kindly order your servants immediately to conduct a search along the riverbank?"

She hesitated, frowning, and I entertained a fleeting hope that she understood. Then she said, "Do you really want me to get rid of the servants, Bertie? So early in the evening?"

As I've mentioned more than once, Carrie Montrose is a lady of mature years. Moreover, she is built like a barge horse and colors her hair a revolting shade of orange. She wears it high, in tight curls bunched over her brow, topped, for this occasion, by a cluster of pink and green ostrich feather tips. Her dinner gown was of tomato-red velvet with lace epaulets and a profusion of roses, butterfly bows and gathered frills extending over what one prefers to assume was a bustle, to end in a long train. She wore white gloves and carried a Japanese fan. The effect was as bizarre as our conversation.

I said, "A man may be drowning out there. Hand me a towel, for pity's sake, and I'll give the order myself."

Still refusing to believe me, she said, "Don't you care about dinner? It will be ruined."

I'm afraid I said something unparliamentary about the dinner. But this was an emergency that demanded more than mere words. Since no towel was forthcoming—and to make clear how serious I was—I stood up in the bath. I've never been coy about my body. I've nothing to be ashamed of (quite the contrary) and I made no attempt to cover up. I folded my arms across my chest and faced her.

For once in her life, the redoubtable Duchess of Montrose was bereft of speech. She opened her fan and covered the lower part of her face in awe. I took it to be awe, anyway.

I said, "Will you speak to the servants, or shall I?"

She shot out of the hall and gave the orders. I lowered myself thankfully below the water again, for it was drafty.

When my hostess returned, she was holding a bath towel which she told me had been warmed. She also provided me with bottle-green silk pajamas, a woolen dressing gown in a Tartan design, and slippers. I assured her that I was in a fit state to use the towel without assistance, and she withdrew to the sitting room, leaving me to ponder how it was that an elderly widowed lady living alone could produce a completely new set of gentlemen's night clothes, in my size and precisely the materials and colors I most favored.

But to more serious matters. Dreadful to relate, when the servants returned, they had no news of Charlie Buckfast. Five of them had searched with lanterns for upward of an hour. They said a strong tide was running now and it was likely that he had been carried far upstream. Recalling how I had insisted on his accompanying me, in spite of his apprehensions, I felt conscience stricken. I retained a slender hope that by some miracle the shock of immersion had brought him around, and like me, he had managed to swim to the landing. Optimism leads one at times to make the most improbable assumptions, for I had conveniently overlooked poor Charlie's crippled left arm.

The Duchess, cognizant at last of what had happened, said, "Shouldn't we send for the police?"

This wasn't a suggestion I welcomed. I am the first to applaud the work of the men in blue, but I expect them to perform it without reference to me, except over matters of ceremony. It would be unthinkable for the Heir Apparent to become involved in a police investigation. I was once called as a witness in a case of divorce, and although my part in the sad affair was entirely innocent and trivial, I can't begin to tell you the rumpus my appearance caused—and that was in the civil courts. Imagine the field day the press would have reporting that the Prince of Wales had been involved in a brawl on the Thames embankment. And—perhaps even more shocking—that he had been on a private visit to the Duchess of Montrose.

In hot water such as this I mix my metaphor and grasp at any straw. I deflected the Duchess by asking for a servant to be sent to Jermyn Street to see if by some miracle Captain Buckfast had escaped with his life and returned home. This was arranged. The same man was instructed to call at Marlborough House to collect a change of clothes for me.

Without much concern for the delicacy of my position, Carrie Montrose persisted. She pointed out that what I had witnessed was murder, or attempted murder at the least, and it would be next to impossible, not to say an offense, to keep it secret. The attackers ought to be apprehended as soon as possible. Captain Buckfast was a fine gentleman, a Turfite, and she had the highest regard for him. And as a loyal subject of the Crown, she could not allow the Prince of Wales to be thrown into the Thames outside her own doorstep. She had another suggestion. By a happy chance, one of her neighbors was the Metropolitan Police Commissioner, Sir Charles Warren, "a most approachable gentleman, and totally discreet." Wouldn't it be sensible to speak informally to Sir Charles about the attack? He, of all people, was capable of handling the matter in the strictest confidence.

When the servant returned with news that Captain Buckfast's apartment was in darkness, and there was no answer to the door bell, I consented to send for Warren.

This left me a desperately short time in which to change my clothes and decide how much I would tell. Should I reveal, for example, that Buckfast had spent the past week shadowing the Squire, and that our two assailants were almost certainly the men who had pursued him from Newmarket? It was bad enough having my name linked with Carrie's, but the Squire's as well? I shuddered.

In that divorce case I just mentioned, counsel advised me to answer the questions truthfully and volunteer nothing that was not asked. It is a sound principle.

Sir Charles Warren arrived dressed unnecessarily in full uniform, from cocked hat to high boots, and with all his decorations displayed, which at half an hour's notice was an impressive tribute to his military training. I'd met him thus arrayed on a couple of occasions, but you don't get much chance to assess a man when he bows and you wish him good day and move on to the next to be presented. He is a soldier, a Royal Engineer, who rose to the rank of general, and his appointment to the police was quite recent. He was brought in as Commissioner to deal more effectively with public demonstrations after his predecessor allowed the unemployed to run riot through Oxford Street, breaking windows and looting shops. Sir Charles had useful experience in Bechuanaland, dealing with unruly Boers. He is not a man to tolerate bad behavior.

We went into the dining room to eat. Sir Charles's appearance is intimidating, but so, I am told, is mine. He has a massive mustache in the Prussian style, curling below the edges of his mouth, a truly exceptional silver-brown growth that is distractingly different in color from the hair on his head, which is jet-black and pomaded into a severe, straight line across the forehead. As if that were not sufficiently arresting, he sports a monocle that causes him to frown. However, I am perfectly capable of frowning too.

I sometimes find it expedient in dealing with generals to gain a moral victory at the outset, so I advised him that the K.C.M.G. that he correctly wore suspended from his neck was partially obscured behind his sash, which was at least half an inch broader than necessary. Surprising how often my knowledge of decorations and ceremonial comes to my aid. It quite discomposed him.

While the meal was being served, I took the opportunity to point out that Warren was fortunate to be dining with us. If our worst expectations were confirmed, he was about to eat a dead man's dinner.

He was in the act of swallowing a piece of bread. He had to take water to help it down.

At his request, after the servants had left us, I related my story, describing the two attackers as well as I was able, but venturing no opinion as to their possible identity or purpose. I said that poor Buckfast had taken the worst of the assault and in my estimation was unconscious when he was dropped into the river. I told Warren that I was communicating this intelligence to him out of a sense of duty, and I trusted that he had due authority to start immediate inquiries—but in the strictest confidence. I said if it became public knowledge that I had been attacked and almost murdered, I wouldn't answer for my mother the Queen's health. Such news had been known to induce heart attacks in elderly parents.

He was on pins and needles at this. "Are you inviting me to investigate this dreadful assault myself, Your Royal Highness?"

"Who else should I ask?"

"But I am a soldier by vocation. An engineer. A surveyor. I'm not trained as a detective, sir."

I said, "Come now, you're the most senior policeman in the land."

He had the effrontery to tell me, "The principal reason for my appointment, as I was informed, sir, is to marshal the police to subdue the unruly elements in society."

Seeing red, I told him forcefully, "And I am marshalling you, sir, to find the unruly elements who viciously attacked a member of the Royal Family, and possibly killed his companion. Is that clear?"

He went so rigid that his monocle sprang out of his eye. "Crystal clear, sir."

The Duchess said, "You don't appear to have eaten much, Sir Charles. Would you care for some horseradish sauce on that?"

He said, "No thank you. It would not restore my appetite."

He left soon after.

I thought it judicious at this stage of the evening to announce that I could not remain much longer. Carrie took it in good part and escorted me to her smoking room for a final cigar. She enjoys a smoke as much as I. It was a large room, wainscoted halfway in dark oak and hung with all manner of racing paraphernalia, jockey's silks in the all scarlet, whips, stirrups, framed race cards and portraits of her notable winners—though she has yet to win a classic, the famous Sefton having belonged to her late husband.

As she poured me a cognac, she remarked, "I made an ass of myself earlier—a regular moke."

I said graciously, "I shall remember only how kind you were."

She sighed heavily and said, "I've buried two good husbands and I ought to be satisfied."

I felt unable to comment on that.

She added, "I'm impossibly high-spirited."

I said, "Not at all."

We were silent for a while. Then she said, "Tell me, Bertie, what *was* your purpose in coming here?"

My purpose in coming here? It seemed remote now, and no longer of any importance. "I wanted to talk to you about Archer."

"Poor Fred?" She took out a handkerchief and dabbed her eye. "I don't know if I can bear to talk about Fred."

I said, "In that case, please don't."

She pressed the handkerchief to her nose and blew into it. "We had an understanding, Fred and I. We each had great losses to bear."

I said insensitively, "He was a heavy gambler." You see, my mind was elsewhere, following Sir Charles Warren on the trail of two assassins.

She said, "I meant bereavements."

"Oh."

She went on, volunteering information that I would earlier have been overjoyed to elicit. "We could have been a great comfort to each other, Fred and I."

"Really?"

"I decided to marry him. Then he shot himself."

I stared down into my cognac, telling myself how appalling it would be even to begin to smile. I managed to say, "Why?"

She frowned. "Why marry him?"

"No. Why did he shoot himself?"

She answered, "Everyone knows. It was the typhoid. It turned his brain." Her eyes widened. "Didn't it?"

I said, "Archer rode your horse, St. Mirin, in the Cambridgeshire."

She asked, "What does that have to do with it?"

I said, "There are stories that he staked his entire career on that race."

"I haven't heard them."

"He is said to have bribed Woodburn to stop the favorite."

She shook her head in disbelief. "Who told you this?"

"Arthur Somerset, the owner's brother."

"The Somersets ought to be brought to court for putting such lies about. Their horse shot its bolt. Why can't they admit it? We were all beaten by a good old stayer with a bit in hand at the finish, Bertie, and I say good luck to the owner."

After this generous tribute, I couldn't resist saying, "Do you know who the owner is?"

"Of The Sailor Prince? Willie Gilbert."

"He's the *registered* owner."

She tensed like a predator picking up a scent. "Are you implying that someone else was behind that damned outsider?"

"Abington Baird—the Squire."

"What?" She dashed her brandy into the fire and hurled the glass across the room. "If that monster fixed the race, I'll kill him. So help me God, I'll throttle him with my bare hands!"

She looked capable of it too.

CHAPTER 12

Carrie Montrose had kindly instructed one of her servants to hail a cab, and a four-wheeler was waiting by the gate when I took leave of her. The cabdriver's bored "Where to, guv?" told me at once that he hadn't been advised of his passenger's identity, which fitted my plan.

"Hoxton, if you please. The Royal Eagle Music Hall."

"Be almost over, time we get there."

"That's of no consequence," I told him forthrightly.

"All right. Keep your 'air on."

He flicked the whip and we trundled off. I didn't mind missing the whole of the bill, so long as I was in time to catch Myrtle Bliss before she left. I had not forgotten, you see, that the Squire had invited Myrtle to Bedford Lodge on the morrow, Sunday, and she had offered, in her quaint, lavender-scented note, to tell me what happened. I'd been inclined to spurn the offer until this evening, when Charlie had returned from Newmarket with the Squire's men in hot pursuit. After that, Myrtle's help became essential to my purpose. Not only would I agree to her proposal; I would persuade her to be more than a mere observer—to act, in effect, as my spy. I meant to have the names of the murderous pair at all costs, and with due respect to Sir Charles Warren and the Metropolitan Police, Myrtle provided my best chance.

Rest assured that I had not underestimated the risk she would be taking. I intended to warn her personally how dangerous were the Squire and his "minders."

The crone on guard at the stage door remembered me—or the sov she'd taken off me on the last occasion—and went so far as to beckon me over as I stepped down. It emerged that one of the performers had asked her to find a cab, a four-wheeler at that. I informed her that mine was not for hire. I'd already instructed the driver to wait for me.

She wasn't pleased. She reviled me with an unrepeatable obscenity, thus ensuring that she got no gratuity this time. I thrust myself past the door and inside. As luck would have it, I met Myrtle on the stairs, burdened with several cages containing her feathered troupe. Spotting me, she put them down, the better to curtsy as I thought, and instead leaned forward, kissed me lightly on the tip of my nose and said, "Lord bless you, Bertie. Just when I needed an extra pair of hands."

I've cut people dead for less, but I was so relieved to see her that I merely observed, "I thought the birds remained here."

"No, love. I finished tonight. Got to move out. Would you be a darling?"

I capitulated. I replied benignly that I was famous for being a darling. My four-wheeler was at her disposal. I carried the cages out to the street and stacked them inside.

Myrtle squeezed my arm and said, "You *are* a darling. There's six more upstairs. And three perches and a trunk."

Oh, yes, I was a darling, and no mistake, but those parrots upstairs hadn't been told. They screeched and fluffed up their feathers and thrust their vicious beaks through the bars when my hand reached for the ring on top of the cage. Only by removing my overcoat and throwing it over each cage before I lifted it did I succeed in getting any cooperation. Then, when the birds were docile and downstairs, the cabbie started complaining. He objected to having his vehicle filled with bird cages. He wanted the parrots to travel outside, on the roof, but Myrtle was reluctant to expose them to the chill night air, a message she articulated in a few choice words that flattened the cabbie like a mangled shirt.

The trunk and perches traveled on top, and the rest of us inside, in earsplitting proximity: six large parrots or cockatoos; sundry parakeets, lovebirds and lories; and two people, one in voluminous skirts and camel's-hump bustle. My face was within inches of a large red-and-green macaw, "a proper old softy" according to his owner, a description I ventured to think didn't apply to his beak as he tried repeatedly to bite me through the bars. He had an obscene black tongue like a spike, and his eye was positively evil. Bertie, I thought, how do you do it? How do you keep copping it like this, when you try so hard to stay out of trouble? We were conveyed to Mile End Road and deposited with our aviary and baggage on the pavement outside the house where Myrtle lodged. I settled with the cabman. After he'd pocketed his tip, he rudely commented, "Far cry from Cheyne Walk, ain't it?"

I sniffed and looked away.

It was close to midnight, yet the street teemed with life—predominantly life of the lowest order. I was presently hemmed in by ragged children and thin-faced women of doubtful occupation curious to look at the parrots, to know if they talked and if I would bring one out and put it on a perch. Myrtle, I should explain, had already gone inside with Cocky. My task was to guard the other birds, who in my opinion were well capable of defending themselves.

Someone remarked that I looked like the Prince of Wales, and I retorted genially that everyone said that. Another woman, over rouged and stinking of patchouli, said if I was the Prince of Wales, she was Mrs. L. (a lady of my acquaintance I prefer not to name), and wriggled her body in a most vulgar, suggestive fashion, going so far as to attempt to embrace me. Fortunately at this juncture Myrtle scythed her way through the crowd and grabbed the woman's hair, shouting to me, "She's got your bleedin' watch and chain," and sure enough, the thieving hussy had, though it would not have been of any use to her as a timepiece, for it was full of Thames water. I grabbed her wrist and recovered it, and she ran off, leaving Myrtle with a handful of black hair.

I took over the portering and by stages removed everything upstairs. By this time, I was becoming increasingly conscious of the river water I had swallowed. I asked for the bathroom and was handed a chamber pot. With a silent prayer that it would be equal to the demand, I put it to use, while Myrtle busied herself with her hat. Once I was comfortable and she presentable, we left the birds in noisy occupation and went out, pausing only to empty the pot at the communal privy in the yard—not a place to linger in.

In the quiet of a private room in a city restaurant where I occasionally treat a companion to supper, I took Myrtle completely into my confidence. Her large brown eyes regarded me steadily as I related my efforts to learn the truth about Archer's strange death, and how I had deputed Charlie Buckfast to keep watch on the Squire. I told her quite candidly how Charlie had broken into Bedford Lodge in search of evidence and surprised two of the Squire's men in bed together. She giggled for some time at this, until I shocked her with news of the ferocious attack in Cheyne Walk.

"He's dead?" she said in disbelief. "Your mate Charlie Buckfast has snuffed it?"

"I'm afraid so. I saw him thrown into the river. He was in no condition to save himself."

"Cripes."

Myrtle didn't indulge in false sentiment. After all, she had last described Charlie to me as an old poopstick. She had integrity, for all her rough edges.

She asked, "What did they look like, these two?"

"My dear, it wasn't easy to see, but they fitted Charlie's description of the men who followed him from Newmarket. A broad fellow, built like a gorilla, and a taller one, something over six foot, I'd say. They were muffled and wearing long coats."

After a moment's thought, she said, "So what's it all about, Bertie? Two Mary Anns caught in bed? Is that what Charlie was killed for?"

I shook my head. "It doesn't seem likely. I can understand them taking offense. They might have given chase. Even attacked him. But murder—that would be excessive."

"Are you sure it was murder?"

I nodded gravely. "They knew Charlie was out to the world when they pushed him over the Embankment."

She was thinking again, resting her pretty chin on a small, clenched fist. "But they didn't do *you* in. Why didn't they treat you the same as Charlie?"

"I nearly drowned," I pointed out.

She said, "They could have made sure."

"What charitable things you say!"

She laughed and put her hand over mine. "Bertie, you know

what I mean. They was after Charlie. They had no quarrel with you. You just got in the way, so they chucked you in and all."

She was a sharp thinker, and probably right. I sighed resignedly. As the second highest in the land, it's somewhat demeaning to admit that you got in the way, so you were chucked in and all, but that, express it how you will, was the likeliest explanation.

The champagne buoyed me up, a good Veuve Clicquot, infinitely kinder to the throat than the poison we'd imbibed on our previous supper engagement. It went down famously with pigeon pie. I was glad of a bite. I hadn't acquitted myself too well at Carrie Montrose's table, after swallowing half the Thames.

Myrtle, too, had a decent appetite, and we called for second helpings. We were seated side by side on a double-ended sofa of the sort thoughtfully provided in private rooms, and the waiter was clearly intrigued that my guest hadn't yet removed her hat, but there was more on our minds than spooning.

In privacy again, I said, broaching the subject with extreme tact, for I know the feminine mind, "There may be another interpretation of these events. It's possible, is it not, that the two men were sent to kill Charlie Buckfast?"

She frowned.

I said, "They could have been acting on instructions."

"Whose instructions?"

"The Squire's." I planted a firm, restraining hand on her arm. "Before you raise the roof, my dear, will you hear what I say? If the Squire got to learn that a man had kept him under observation for a week and actually broken into his house, wouldn't he ask himself what that man was looking for? And mightn't he suspect it was something incriminating? And if so, mightn't he want that man silenced for good?"

Myrtle had turned as white as my shirt. I might have just walked over her grave. She shook her head. "He's a rogue, I grant you, but he's never a murderer. Never."

I said, "He's a blackmailer. And what's more, he thrives on blood and violence. What else is fistfighting?"

"It ain't killing, Bertie."

"Dogfighting is. And cockfighting."

Myrtle gave me a withering look and said, "How many grouse do you shoot in a day?"

I capped that with, "Have another slice of pigeon pie," and she gave a reluctant smile. "To return to the Squire," I said, "if he *did* give orders to two of his roughs to dispose of Charlie Buckfast, and they discovered they had me—a second man—to reckon with as well, isn't it logical that they behaved as they did? They made sure of killing Charlie and left me to take my chance in the water. They hadn't been told to commit a double murder."

She was still unwilling to cast her friend the Squire as a murderer. "Why would he want Charlie killed?"

"I told you. Charlie found out about the blackmail."

"Bertie, the Squire's been called all kinds of things—a bully and a cheat and a public nuisance. What's blackmail? One more thing on his list."

"No."

She was surprised to be challenged. She glared at me defiantly.

I said, "This wasn't one more thing on the list. The Squire may seem like a fellow who respects nothing and nobody, but don't be deceived. There was one man he idolized."

She knew at once. "That jockey—Fred Archer."

"Yes. He took riding lessons from Archer. He adopted his style and learned how to get the best from a horse and how to 'kid' the other jockeys. As a result, he's the best gentleman rider in the country. But it wasn't enough for the Squire. He wanted to be Archer's equal. He wanted a partnership. His dream was to own a racing stable with Archer, but Fred wouldn't hear of it. So what did the Squire do? He devised a plot to entrap Archer. He got him implicated with others in a jockeys' ring, a conspiracy. And the sole purpose of this was to make Fred vulnerable to blackmail."

Myrtle took in a short, audible breath and a tear slid down her cheek. All her defiance had evaporated in the face of my ruthless exposure of the Squire's duplicity.

I said, "Charlie Buckfast overheard talk of a document, a contract: the proof that only Fred's signature was wanted to seal a partnership."

She understood. "That was what Charlie went into Bedford Lodge to find?"

I gave a nod. "Can you imagine how the Squire must have received the news that Charlie had broken in? He'd hate the world to find out that he hounded his hero to death. That's why Charlie had to be silenced."

Myrtle bit her lip. She had gone so rigid that her stays creaked. I topped up her glass, understanding her distress.

At length, she said bleakly, "What do you want me to do, Bertie?"

Her forlorn expression moved me profoundly. How would I ask her to betray the man who, for all his wicked ways, had plainly claimed a place in her affection? How could I conceivably expose this trusting young woman to such danger?

Only with profound misgivings and the assistance of Veuve Clicquot '78.

You see, as I explained to Myrtle, nothing would have prevented me from undertaking this perilous mission myself, except that I am so damnably well known. It's next to impossible for me to creep along corridors in strange houses without being recognized.

When she had agreed to make a search of the Squire's bedroom and obtain the contract, she said, "It's a queer thing, Bertie. You say the Squire idolized Fred Archer."

"Emphatically."

"And Charlie Buckfast was devoted to him."

"Yes, he did everything for Fred except ride the horses."

"And you're just the same. You can't forget him. You've got this bee in your bonnet about his suicide."

"If you wish to put it that way."

"Then tell me this: What is it about Fred Archer? What made him so special?"

It was a profound question, worthy of a thoughtful answer. I daresay to the more discriminating among my readers that the same question may have crossed your mind as you read these pages. After reflection, I told Myrtle, "It's not easy to explain. In some respects, he was obnoxious. A tyrant on the racecourse, particularly with boy jockeys and less experienced riders. He insisted on weighing out first, to get the prime position at the start. His language in a race would make your hair curl. And he gave his horses no mercy. He frequently drew blood with the whip and the spurs.

"He was a mean beggar too. They called him the Tin Man. He'd take the pennies off a dead man's eyes. Yet his gambling was out of control at times. He was proud, unsociable, lacking in humor, and generally unprepossessing. He was a bag of bones, of course.

He neglected his health in the cause of racing. He'd neglect anything in the cause of racing, as I'm sure his wife and infant daughter discovered. But in spite of all that, he was a man in a hundred million. The finest jockey who ever lived. Uneducated and illiterate, but a genius. Intelligent, yes. Highly intelligent. After a race he would tell me not only how his own mount fared, but how everyone else performed. And no braver man ever lived—which is why I still can't understand him killing himself."

"It takes a brave man to do that," Myrtle remarked.

"But a braver man would face up to his problems—wouldn't he?"

She didn't reply. She said, "I never met him. Tell me about his eyes."

"His eyes? Yes, they *were* remarkable. They were deep set and heavy lidded and appeared to be looking inward, except when something caught his interest. Then the light leapt from them. They were very expressive then. I won't forget them."

She said, "You can tell a lot from the eyes."

To which I replied, "And I can tell from yours that you're ready for bed."

Whereupon I saw something else in them: a gleam that didn't amount to panic, but wasn't far short of it.

I knew what had crossed her mind. As it happened, I was in no condition myself for fleshly pleasures after my strenuous evening. So I said, "To be more accurate, I suspect that you're ready for sleep, and who am I to deny it when I've set you such a daunting task tomorrow?"

I escorted her back to her lodging and was in my own bed in Marlborough House by 2:30 A.M.

CHAPTER 13

Yes, thirteen—the unlucky number. When I arrive at a dinner party, I always count the places at the table. If they number thirteen, I call for my coat. In practice this hardly ever happens, because Francis Knollys advises my hostess in advance that thirteen will not be tolerated any more than crossed knives or spilled salt. I won't have my mattress turned on a Friday, either.

These superstitions of mine may sound ludicrous to some, yet there's no denying that Chapter Thirteen contains an unpleasant shock. I mention this for the benefit of readers of a delicate disposition.

But I must not anticipate . . .

I left London for Sandringham on Sunday, 28 November, and put myself in a thunderous mood by purchasing a copy of *Reynolds's News* (why do I punish myself?) to read on the train. You wouldn't think the birth of an innocent child (my dear sister's) a subject for political comment, but then you underestimate the socialist propagandists. "The Queen has now thirty-one grandchildren," observed the writer, "and the people are of the opinion that this is more than a sufficient number of paupers of the royal and expensive sort. A much more joyful thing to the people than the birth of this boy would have been to hear that his father had fallen into some sort of useful occupation and was in a position to provide for the progeny he sends into the world." What vindictive drivel! Who are they to voice the opinions of the people any more than

I? I screwed up the disgusting rag and tossed it out of the window and picked up the *British Medical Journal* instead.

Lest anyone suspect that I have morbid interests, let me hasten to declare that I am not a regular reader of the medical press. I happened to have a copy with me that was more than a week old. Francis Knollys had slipped it into my attaché case with the suggestion that I would find something of interest inside, and I had not troubled with it until then. It turned out to be a comment on Fred Archer's suicide. Speaking of the alleged typhoid that afflicted the jockey, it read, "This disease is so associated in the minds not only of the public, but the medical profession, with prostration and low, muttering delirium that the fact that acute delirium with delusions, usually of a suicidal character, sometimes comes on during the early stage, will be new to many." I trust that the irony of this piece is not lost on my readers; more support, if any were needed, that the tragedy was not medical in origin.

At Sandringham on Monday morning, I commended Knollys on finding the piece. The trouble he'd taken to bring it to my attention was, I had decided, an indication on his part that he now accepted my involvement in the matter, even if he could not wholeheartedly support it. I asked him what engagements I had this week. Before he answered, I added, mindful of Myrtle, ". . . because I propose to spend Tuesday and Wednesday in London."

There was a pause of the sort that novel writers describe as pregnant.

He said, "Might I be so bold as to inquire, sir, if that is an engagement of a private nature?"

"It is, Francis. And it can't be ducked."

"I see." He gave me that look.

"Well, man," I said, "what's the difficulty?"

"Wednesday, sir, is December the first."

"Good thing too. November has been a brute."

He coughed into his hand. "I took the liberty of ordering the usual red roses, sir."

Oh, my hat! I thought. *Alix's birthday.*

I said, with an effort to keep my dignity, "This year I have decided to take Her Royal Highness to London for her birthday."

"But she always likes to spend it here, sir."

"I shall persuade her otherwise."

"As you wish, sir."

"As *she* will wish—when I have explained what I propose."

"Undoubtedly, sir."

I marched to the window and stared out at the frost. "I must admit to some difficulty in choosing a suitable present. Can't just give her the damned roses."

"A choker, sir?"

"You have it, Francis! The good old dog collar." I should explain that Alix has a small blemish on her neck, of which she is inordinately self-conscious, so she contrives to keep it covered. Fashion being so imitative, every well-dressed woman in the land now sports a high collar or choker, and all in consequence of one small brown mark on Alix's neck.

After a short interval while I wrestled with my memory, I said, "Didn't I give her a choker last year?"

"Yes, sir, but you could choose different stones."

I told him to arrange it with Garrard's, our usual jeweler, after consulting his sister Charlotte, who is Woman-of-the-Bedchamber.

At luncheon, I announced to Alix that I proposed taking her to London on her birthday.

She twisted her pearls around her finger, always an ominous indication. "Aren't I going to have my usual party at Sandringham?"

"Not this year. I'm taking you to the theater."

Her lower lip quivered, and I knew that tears would follow, but I'm glad to report that they were tears of joy. "Bertie, what a dear husband you are, full of surprises! What are we going to see?"

Fortunately, I'd taken the precaution of studying the newspaper. "A new comic opera called *La Béarnaise,* with Miss Florence St. John and Miss Marie Tempest. It's said to be the equal of anything by Offenbach."

"A comic opera. What fun!"

"You're pleased?"

"Indescribably." She hesitated. "Bertie, do you know what would make the evening complete for me?"

"Supper at Romano's?"

"What I should really like would be to take our turtledoves with us." (This affectionate term is one we use for our daughters, the Princesses Louise, Victoria and Maud.)

"Why, yes," I said as enthusiastically as I was able while thinking how to escape to Mile End Road on Tuesday evening. "It will do them good." (They are shrinking violets, all three, and I can't fathom why, with a papa like me. I'm told they are unkindly known in society gossip as their Royal Shynesses.)

Alix further complicated matters by suggesting we travel to London on Wednesday, but I scotched that with a white lie that solved my difficulty. I said I'd been invited to attend a meeting on Tuesday evening of the Queen's Jubilee Committee for the East End. It would probably drag on until late, but I felt bound to give it my support.

So the five of us, and my little dog Peter, and Knollys and his sister, took the train from Sandringham on Tuesday morning.

In the entrance of Marlborough House stands a stuffed baboon holding a tray on which the letters are left. This morning the poor thing was laden to its snout with birthday cards. Alix wanted to open them at once, but I insisted that she wait until Wednesday. Nor would I allow her to unwrap any of the parcels heaped against the wall. She's like a child at these times and begged me to allow her to read the addresses and see if she could guess who had sent them. In a moment, she announced, "It isn't fair. The biggest one is for you, Bertie!"

"Are you sure?"

She was holding a cardboard box large enough to contain a framed painting. I frequently receive unsolicited daubs from artists seeking royal patronage. However, from the way Alix was handling this, it didn't weigh as heavily as a picture. I said, "I expect it's for you, really. Someone's made a mistake."

"It says 'personal' on the label."

"Let's unravel the mystery, then." I cut the string and took off the lid.

"Tissue paper," said Alix. "Something special, obviously. Perhaps it *is* for me."

I drew back the wrappings and discovered my evening shirt, freshly laundered. And the suit I had worn when I fell in the Thames, now cleaned, with the torn sleeve invisibly mended.

I muttered, "My laundry."

Alix said in a puzzled voice, "But you don't send your clothes to the laundry." She delved into the wrappings and took out my socks and suspenders. Then my merino wool vest and nether garment.

And a solitary glove. All beautifully cleaned. On this evidence, one could recommend Carrie Montrose's laundry to anyone, but at that minute I wished they had lost the lot.

I said, "It must be a practical joke," and my daughters supported me by giggling behind their hands. Alix likes a joke, too, but on this occasion she declined to join in.

I blustered on, "I'd like to know who did this. Charlie Beresford, I shouldn't be surprised."

Alix said in disbelief, "Your clothes, Bertie? Your intimate garments. How could Charlie possibly have acquired them?"

"From Knollys!" I declared in desperation. "Francis! Explain yourself."

But he had vanished. There are no flies on Francis.

I said, "Infernal liberty! I'll take it up with him later. Clever jape, though. Charlie B had better watch out. I'll settle the score when I can think of something fiendish enough." I stuffed everything back and replaced the lid, saying to Alix, "I think it would do no harm to open your presents, dearest. You're bound to get many more tomorrow." As she reached for a parcel, I made as dignified an exit as I could, with the box under my arm.

Of course I said nothing to Francis when I caught up with him, except to make quite sure that a glittering choker was on order.

The day did not improve for me. It emerged that Sir Charles Warren was waiting in an anteroom in his cocked hat. He had "an urgent and confidential matter" to communicate. I asked Francis to step outside and send Warren in.

The commissioner preferred to remain standing. His eyes gleamed as brightly as his medals. "Yesterday evening, Your Royal Highness, we recovered something from the river."

He punctuated his statement with a dramatic pause. I waited for it to end.

He resumed, "When I say 'we,' I mean Thames Division. We found the body of a man answering Captain Buckfast's description."

I'd feared this, of course, but I still felt my skin prickle. I suppose I had hoped for a miracle. I asked, "Truly? Where was the poor fellow found?"

"In Battersea Reach, sir. It was a stroke of luck."

"Luck? That's a rum word to use in the circumstances, Commissioner."

He didn't flicker an eyelid. "I mean, it was lucky that we recovered him, sir. In this cold weather a body tends to sink and stay on the riverbed for weeks before it rises. A bargeman happened to notice the heel of a boot projecting above the water level. Boots don't usually float, so he took out a boat hook and made contact with something larger. He informed Thames Division, and they advised me." Warren added on a note of self-congratulation, "I had already asked to be notified of every corpse recovered from the river."

"Are there so many?"

"Twenty and upward, week in, week out, sir. Most of them are suicides or accidents. The watermen bring them in usually. We pay them a shilling for their trouble."

I said, "Are you certain that this is Captain Buckfast?" Then I added hastily but emphatically, "It would not be appropriate for *me* to identify the body. There might be a constitutional difficulty about my attending a coroner's inquest."

Warren said reassuringly, "That has already been done, sir. I sent for two witnesses, people who knew Buckfast well: a Mr. Harry Sarjent of Newmarket, who was the late Fred Archer's groom and valet, and John Parker, his gardener."

"Sarjent is a capable fellow and a good witness," I said, recalling how he had performed at Archer's inquest and afterward brushed my hat and coat.

"You know him?" said Warren in some surprise.

Resourcefully, I answered, "I read his evidence in *The Times*."

"Ah."

"So there can be no doubt that this was Captain Buckfast?"

"Regrettably, none, sir. They identified the clothing first. Then they were asked to examine the personal effects. His pocketbook containing several of his visiting cards was still in the jacket, and a badge of the Seventeenth Lancers was attached to his watch chain. Finally, they viewed the body. They both remarked on a strange fact."

"What was that?"

"The man pulled from the Thames was clean-shaven. My information is that Captain Buckfast possessed a particularly fine mustache."

"That is correct."

I believe I mentioned the whiskery exuberance of Sir Charles Warren's own upper lip. In speaking of Buckfast's loss, his hand crept protectively toward it.

I explained, "He recently shaved it off. I should have mentioned it."

"The identifying witnesses were both certain that the dead man was Captain Buckfast, sir, with or without the mustache. And there was clear evidence of the attack that you described. Bruising about the head and shoulders." Sir Charles took a deep, significant breath. "There can be no doubt, sir, that I am dealing with a case of murder."

"No doubt whatsoever, Commissioner."

Warren cleared his throat. "Then with your permission, sir—"

I raised my hand to interrupt. "Before we go any further, Commissioner, I would like to make something very clear to you. You have my permission to pursue this in whatever way you choose, so long as you keep me out of it."

There was an uncomfortable silence.

Warren ended it by saying stiffly, "I was charged with certain responsibilities when I became Commissioner, sir, and the first of these was to prosecute crime. Murder is the worst of all crimes."

I remarked, "I believe you also swore an oath of loyalty."

"To the Sovereign, sir, if you'll forgive me."

I said, "*I* might forgive you, but will the Sovereign, if you provoke a royal scandal? With due respect, Sir Charles, I know that gracious lady rather better than you, and in her view there is one crime even more iniquitous than murder, and that is indiscretion—indiscretion by responsible individuals whose loyalty ought to be unswerving. Do I make my meaning clear?"

There had been a stirring of defiance, but I'd scotched it. One is obliged to, in such situations. Sir Charles Warren was new in the job, and no match for me. That speech is always a winner, whether you're dealing with a protesting husband or a bumptious policeman.

After Warren had marched out, I spent some quiet minutes thinking about poor Charles Buckfast. I doubted whether his death would touch many people, and he was unlikely to receive an obituary notice from *The Times*. On the other hand, he was a Turfite who had never brought disrepute to the sport, and by all accounts he had been a loyal friend to Archer. He had served me loyally too. He wasn't much of a conversationalist, and I wouldn't rate him as the wittiest companion I've known, but he was brave and dependable, qualities not to be underrated in detective work. Notwithstanding the tragedy, you see, I was still thinking as an investigator, implacable in my resolve. This brutal murder wasn't going to stop me; rather, it spurred me on. I owed it to Charlie to bring the case to a successful conclusion.

What next, then?

First, I required another assistant. After all, there are certain investigative duties it would be unthinkable for me to undertake alone. I needed someone of unquestioned loyalty, a good observer, brave and capable of outwitting the Squire and his murderous gang.

Why not a woman? Why not Myrtle Bliss?

In relation to the Squire, Myrtle had certain physical advantages over Buckfast that I've hinted at before. True, she was not much of a hand with a pen, but I didn't require her to write out reports or take evidence. She was very responsive to me, which is a mark of intelligence.

In a sense, she was already on probation for the job. This evening, I would hear what she'd gleaned from her assignation with the Squire on Sunday. If it was of any use, I'd take her on as Buckfast's replacement. I didn't mind paying her the wage she'd get from the music halls.

I took an early dinner and left Alix to an evening of whist with our turtledoves. She urged me not to return too late from my Jubilee Committee meeting. As we sleep in separate rooms (and have for the past fifteen years), I was most unlikely to disturb her, but I assured her that I would escape at the first opportunity because I wanted to be at my brightest on her birthday.

I crossed the street to my club, the Marlborough, and consulted the *Era*, to see where "Miss Bliss and her Feathered Friends" were performing this week. I had a notion that I might visit Myrtle's dressing room, but when I saw where she was engaged, I changed my mind. The Bell Music Hall is situated along St. George's Street, in the dockland area of the East End, a street so notorious as the old Ratcliff Highway that its name was altered in an attempt to whitewash its reputation. A more notorious and dangerous locality could not be imagined.

So I remained in my club for a couple of hours and inevitably got caught in conversation and stayed longer than I intended. When I finally escaped, it was after ten. I hurried down to the rank in Piccadilly and asked the first hansom driver if he could get me to Mile End Road by eleven.

He trotted out that favorite saying of his trade: "That's all right, sir—Archer's up!"

I smiled grimly and said I hoped he was.

I don't mind confessing that for some unfathomed reason that November night in the cab, I felt uneasy. "Archer's up!" must have been said a million times and more to impart confidence. It troubled me. There's something about the arrangement of a hansom, with the driver aloft and out of sight behind you and only the apron over your knees and the horse's rump in front, that can give you a feeling of isolation. With a fog thickening every minute, blotting out the lamplight, your imagination doesn't need much to take a macabre turn.

Progress was slow through the city. It was well after eleven when we got to Mile End Road. I instructed the cabbie to wait while I went upstairs. My knock on Myrtle's door elicited no response. She was not back from the Bell.

I won't prolong the description of what, for me, was a tedious wait for more than forty minutes. I went down to the street and talked to my complaining driver. He told me he went off duty at midnight, so I gave him a half-crown and promised a sovereign at the end of the hire. I was as cold and depressed as he was.

Having come this far, I was in no mood to give up. "Chewsdy about 11" was what Myrtle had written, and dammit, I'd rearranged Alix's birthday to make the appointment.

When I heard the chimes of midnight, I told the cabbie to take me directly to the Bell.

This is the hour when the lodging houses have taken their quota, and unfortunates and ne'er-do-wells by the thousands wander the streets of the East End looking for staircases and doorways where they can huddle down for the night. Foreign seamen stagger out of the dancing rooms and public houses. It is the worst time for a young woman to be walking home, yet I doubted whether Myrtle could find—or afford—a cab.

To search for her in the fog was out of the question, so we

made haste through Whitechapel, turned south across Commercial Road and Cable Street (all sinks of iniquity), and into St. George's Street, where my heart sank. The Bell was already in darkness when we halted outside. I climbed out and crossed the pavement to the front. The doors were bolted, and several ragged families, cadaverous men and women with babies in arms, had already taken up residence against them. A creature of hideous description attempted to importune me.

I looked for the stage door, in hope that some of the artistes might still be leaving by that means. The door was closed, and the entrance filled by a huge man—probably a stevedore—who told me forcibly to be off, because that was his "doss."

I returned to my cab and discovered the driver in animated conversation with a youth of markedly better appearance than the other denizens of this locality. It appeared that this uppish young fellow proposed to hire my vehicle. I stepped forward to disabuse him of the intention and discovered that he was the assistant manager (probably the barman, in reality) of the Bell and had just locked up for the night.

I asked when Miss Bliss had left, and he ventured the opinion that she must have departed at least an hour ago. No one was still inside.

I asked if he had actually seen her leave, and he had not. I said she had not come home, which led him to assume I was her father, which I found rather tiresome.

Quite off the cuff, I concocted a most ingenious story. I said I was a veterinary doctor and I'd been treating one of Myrtle's parrots. This evening it had died, and I feared that the cause was psittacosis, which can affect humans, sometimes with fatal results (this useful information I had learned from my dear mama, who keeps an aviary at Windsor and won't go near the parrots). It was a matter of the utmost urgency that I should examine the other birds.

Really, of course, I wanted to gain admittance to Myrtle's dressing room to see whether she had left me another of her lavender-scented notes. She couldn't possibly have forgotten our arrangement.

Upon receiving an assurance that he could share my hansom if he let me in, the young man took out his keys and made a determined move toward the family encamped at the front doors. They let us through. He said he would show me Myrtle's dressing room, which he didn't propose to enter himself, in view of the risk to his health. He found a couple lanterns and led me through the auditorium to a door at the side of the stage. The dressing rooms were to our right. Mrytle's, I was informed, was the last one, and would I kindly make my own way back to the front of the building when I had finished?

I stepped to the door, opened it and shone my lantern inside. Two or three of the birds were picked out, sleepy, silent on their perches. Cocky rocked from one claw to the other and stared at the light, flexing his yellow crest.

I moved the lantern lower and had a momentary shock as the beam flashed back at me from the mirror over the dressing table.

This all happened within a few seconds, yet I recall it vividly as a series of impressions that might have taken minutes.

I thought dully, Cocky shouldn't be here. She always takes him home.

Then I saw Myrtle's corpse on the rug in front of me. There was blood. There was a hole in the side of her head.

I thought, I've got to get out. I can't be found here. Whatever this means, it's no place for me.

If that demonstrates a want of compassion, so be it. The compassion came later. In the shock of discovery, you think only of practicalities.

I backed out, and as the lantern beam flickered across the room, a voice said, "Hello, Bertie."

There was no one there.

Cocky repeated, "Hello, Bertie. God bless the Prince of Wales."

Myrtle's letter: "Hes got a new trick to shew you."

A new trick be damned. He'd give my name to the police.

I would have to take Cocky with me.

CHAPTER 14

Having persisted with me to this point, you know that I don't shirk the facts of life when they are necessary to my narrative, and now you know that I treat the fact of death with the same candor.

I thought of issuing an instruction to the printer to mark the previous chapter with a black edge as a token of respect, and also as a warning to the unwary. After much heart searching I abandoned the idea. I have the greatest difficulty in bringing myself to read anything surrounded with a black edge, so how could I ask my readers to face what I could not?

Forgive me. After a death has occurred, one's instinct is to talk about anything but the dreadful fact itself. I'm coming to it now.

I am at a loss to find words adequate to the horror of that grim November night. Don't imagine that my life of privilege has spared me from bereavement. I am not unaccustomed to the death of close friends and members of my family. I know the process: the sense of shock, overtaken by numbness, turning to grief as the mind begins to accept what has happened. After that, despair may set in, or even loss of faith.

Myrtle's violent death affected me in other ways. I was gripped by horrid sensations. I was appalled, afraid, and worse, I was convinced that I was responsible.

Responsible? you ask.

Allow me to explain. The killing of Charlie Buckfast had taught me how dangerous it was to tangle with the Squire and his gang. I was shocked beyond words at the viciousness of that attack. I was deeply distressed about Charlie, and I regretted sending him to Bedford Lodge. I'd miscalculated badly. On the other hand, I didn't feel directly responsible for his death. No one could have foreseen that we were dealing with murderers.

Myrtle's death was squarely on my conscience. True, I'd alerted her to the dangers. I'd told her that Charlie had been killed. But I'd still recruited her as my spy, knowing she was willing to take the risk. She had been blessed, or fated, with the confidence of the young. She had been generous hearted and unafraid, and I'd taken advantage of her cheerful acquiescence with this dreadful consequence.

Let us return to that room of death. As I related, immediately after the discovery, my reaction was to flee from the scene.

Cocky said for the sixth or seventh time, "Hello, Bertie," and I knew I must attend to him first. I put down the lantern and transferred him to a cage. When I grasped him, he gave a screech, assuming, I suppose, that my purpose was strangulation. He submitted quite readily to being pushed through the wire door and was silent thereafter.

It was out of the question to escape by the way I had entered. The cabman and the assistant manager would be waiting at the front of the building. As yet, they had no suspicion of my identity. To the cabbie, I was just a "fare" he had picked up in Piccadilly; to the young fellow, an animal doctor. After what I'd just seen, it was vitally important that they remained in ignorance. However, I was in no state to keep up the pretense, and I was damned sure Cocky would give me away if they heard him.

I climbed out of a window in the property room by means of a conjurer's card table. My feet located a convenient cask in the yard outside and I remembered to reach for the parrot cage before descending to *terra firma*.

My ulster was heavily stained with some sort of grease from the window frame, and I ripped the bottom of one trouser leg, which was all to the good when I got out among the ragtag and bobtail of St. George's Street. Do you know, I believe I have Cocky to thank for saving me from being attacked and robbed? With the parrot cage and my beard, you see, I passed for a seaman.

I received numerous invitations from tarts who called me sailor, but the thieves and garotters let me pass on the assumption that a seafaring man is likely to put up a fight.

Without much idea of direction, I stepped briskly ahead, alert for the sudden attack from behind. Groups of roughs were standing at many of the corners. Without being too obvious about it, I quickened my step and crossed to the other side whenever I saw such a gathering, and, I'm ashamed to say, I did the same when I spotted a constable's helmet. However, the thought did not escape me that we owe a great debt to our gallant police, nightly patrolling these festering thoroughfares.

The scene stretched ahead, it seemed unendingly, tenements looming on either side, passageways cluttered with what might have been rubbish heaps until one heard a baby cry or a man mouth an obscenity. Doors were thrust open without warning, and bodies would stagger across my path in a shaft of light. Still the street women pestered me with offers that turned to taunts and curses as I stepped aside and hurried past.

My entire future was reduced to reaching the next lamppost in safety.

I marched on as rapidly as my steps would take me and at last discerned a slight improvement in the dress and behavior of people I passed. The street widened. Then, praise be, I recognized Tower Hill—not usually an auspicious locality for one of the blood royal—but a haven to me that night, for there, to my profound relief, I succeeded in stopping a cab. He wanted extra, of course. Had he known, I felt ready to offer him half the kingdom. He put me down in the Mall, and I returned to Marlborough House about one 1:45 A.M.

Knollys must have heard me, for he came down in dressing gown and carpet slippers as I was calming my nerves with a dram prior to retiring. Without asking, he poured one for himself.

He said, "This is bloody early for you." We don't mince words in the small hours, Francis and I.

I nodded.

He said, "Your trousers are torn. How did you do that—climbing out of a window?"

"It's really no concern of yours."

That should have been enough. However, when Francis is

inquisitive, he finds it hard to stop. "The husband came home unexpectedly, then?" He takes it as read that I devote my nights to adulterous adventures.

I ignored the question.

He persisted, "It's before two."

I said, "So far as you're concerned, Francis, this is before midnight."

He finally felt the frost in the air, for he paused before informing me on an appeasing note, "Her Royal Highness retired at eleven."

"In that case, I was back by a quarter past."

There was another interval while he took stock.

He resumed, with due formality, "The choker is wrapped and on your desk, sir. There is a card. It wants only your inscription."

Alix's birthday. After this evening's excursion into hell, how could I bring myself to think about a birthday?

I undertook to write something in the morning.

Knollys asked me what was under my coat (which I had taken off and draped over the parrot cage).

There was no possibility of denial, so I answered casually, "A talking cockatoo."

He commented, "What a splendid idea, if I may say so."

"Really?" I said, bemused.

"As a birthday present."

He was right. It was a capital idea, and I was pleased to take credit for it in the morning. Have I told you that Alix adores animals and birds to a quite ridiculous degree? One afternoon on our voyage up the Nile some years ago, she was reclining on a chair in a shaded area of the deck when she felt something cold up her skirt, nuzzling her knee. It was the nose of a black ram, which had slipped its tether in the kitchen quarters and wandered out of bounds. Instead of taking fright, Alix was enchanted. She offered the beast a sugar lump and sent for more. When she learned that she'd made a pet of tomorrow's dinner, she was horrified. That sheep traveled all the way back to Sandringham with us and lived for some years after.

So you can understand why Cocky was such a success as a birthday present. She took him out and allowed him to perch on her arm. When he said, "God bless the Prince of Wales," Alix whooped with delight. She convinced herself that I'd bought the bird weeks ago and had been giving him secret elocution lessons.

She took this as evidence of my devotion and went quite watery eyed as she told me so. I decided not to enlighten her that Cocky could also ride a tricycle, walk a tightrope and snatch cigarettes from the mouths of theatergoers.

As for the jeweled choker, she didn't give it a second look.

During the morning, there were several callers, much to my agitation, for I fully expected the cocked hat and monocle to appear around the door at any second. I'd convinced myself that my cabman or the young fellow from the Bell had recognized me and named me as the likely murderer. As the last person to visit the scene of the crime before the body was discovered, I would have plenty of explaining to do. However, the visitors without exception had come to greet Alix, and when Oliver Montagu arrived for lunch, I knew I would have some precious time to myself. (Oliver is hopelessly in love with Alix, and has been for about twenty years. The affection is mutual, and I allow it, knowing well that Alix has never conceded the ultimate favor and never will. I think she's forgotten how.)

In the quiet of my study, I agonized over my predicament. By now, someone, some cleaner or janitor, must surely have looked into that room of death and called the police. A description would presently be issued of the bearded, well-spoken and handsome gentleman with an intriguing trace of Germany in his accent who had fabricated a story to gain admission to the room. Theories would abound: that he had arranged a secret rendezvous with his victim; or that he had killed her earlier in the evening and was returning to the scene of his crime, as all murderers are said to do, if only to cover their tracks.

You may think that as a potential suspect, I would have an advantage over a commoner. The contrary is true. If the Prince of Wales shaved off his beard to avoid detection, every newspaper in the land would make a sensation of it. I would find it impossible to disappear into a crowd, or secretly take a passage to France. I was a sitting duck.

Knollys came in toward noon. His worried countenance was no comfort at all.

"What is it?" I asked.

"A difficulty, sir . . ."

My heart raced.

". . . and I am most reluctant to mention it on this happy day."

I said, "Don't stand on ceremony with me, Francis. Is someone outside?"

"Well, yes."

"Is it Sir Charles Warren?"

He frowned. "No, sir. It is Sir Frederic Leighton."

"Fred Leighton?" I couldn't begin to think what would bring the president of the Royal Academy to see me without making an appointment. He was a dinner-party acquaintance who had more than once turned his talent to supervising the decorations for a fancy dress ball we gave: a useful fellow to know but without much sense of fun—hardly one of the Marlborough House set. "What does he want?"

"It appears that criticisms have been voiced in certain quarters of the Academy sir, and he wishes to bring them to your attention before they become public."

"Criticisms of what, precisely?"

Knollys coughed.

I glared at him. "Of me?"

He swayed back and lowered his eyes.

"Of what am I accused?" I asked.

"Of favoritism, I gather, sir."

"*Favoritism?* In what connection, for God's sake?"

"The Wellington statue."

Imagine! I was in imminent danger of being hauled off to Scotland Yard to answer questions about a murder, and Fred Leighton wanted to talk to me about the Wellington statue. As if I hadn't sacrificed enough of my time already on that tedious committee.

"Begging your pardon, sir, Sir Frederick insists he has a duty to impart this information to you." Knollys was so patiently unhappy that I began to feel sorry for him.

"To keep me in the picture, in other words," I quipped, and felt a shade more affable. "Very well. Tell him he can make a lightning sketch, Francis."

As I expected, the whole thing was the silliest nonsense. Artists are supposed to have a sense of proportion, which of course they completely lack. It emerged that certain dissidents in the R.A. were complaining because the Wellington statue competition had been awarded to Edgar Boehm. They said his plaster model was inferior to several others submitted, and it had come to their ears that I, as chairman, had championed Boehm and influenced the decision.

Holding myself in check, I asked Leighton why a chairman should not state his views, and he said there was a suspicion (which he did not share, of course) that my support of Boehm was more a matter of pro-German bias than artistic judgment.

I rocked with laughter at this, and it quite took the wind out of Leighton's sails. I told him truthfully that Boehm's nationality hadn't influenced me in the slightest. As a matter of fact, he wasn't a German at all. He was a Viennese who had become a naturalized Englishman over twenty years ago. I suggested that Leighton impart this information to his petty-minded members. As he was going through the door, I gave him a Hanoverian boot up the backside by telling him that paint and politics don't mix.

I felt better for that encounter. It helped me through lunch. I ribbed Oliver Montagu once or twice, and I was kindness itself to Alix, even managing to feign surprise when she told me how Cocky had stolen Oliver's cigarette.

Some fitful rays of sunshine broke through in the afternoon, encouraging me to take my dog Peter for a walk in the grounds while Alix drank tea with her swain. As the hours went by, and Sir Charles Warren failed to appear, I began seriously to entertain the hope that I'd not been reported to Scotland Yard. Instead, my thoughts took a more constructive turn. I considered what was to be done about Mr. Abington Baird, the Squire.

The thought of him caused me to clench my teeth and give a jerk to Peter's lead, so that the innocent animal reared up unexpectedly on its hind legs. The Squire was a killer by association, if not with his own hands. For reasons that are too obvious to repeat, I couldn't tell everything to the police, which left me with a heavy responsibility.

Do you appreciate my difficulty?

I asked myself whether, unaided, I was capable of taking on the Squire and his murderous gang.

Of course not.

If I enlisted help, who could I trust?

The Marlborough House set? Emphatically not.

The Freemasons? I am, of course, the Most Worshipful Grand Master of England, and my fellow Masons are pledged to support

me. The brotherhood would be more discreet than the likes of
Charlie Beresford and Podge Somerset. Unfortunately, the second
most eminent Mason in London happens to be Sir Charles Warren.

Not the Freemasons.

I was compelled to act alone. But how? And what was to be done?
There was nothing else for it: I must see the Squire in person.
I required something more than circumstantial evidence that
he had hounded poor Archer to death and ordered the killing
of Charlie and Myrtle. He was an incurable braggart, so I was
damned sure I'd have no difficulty persuading him to talk. My
object would be to obtain a confession, a signed statement of
his guilt, together with the names of his accomplices. I'd send
it to Warren, and the case would be concluded without any
reference to me.

Was this a pipe dream, or was I capable of making it happen?

That evening, we went to the theater as arranged, and I believe
Alix and our daughters enjoyed the operetta. I remember little of
it, for I was plotting and scheming more inventively than anything
that happened on the stage.

My reasoning went like this: I was determined to extract a
full confession from the Squire for the deaths of Archer, Charlie
Buckfast and Myrtle. Clearly, it would be folly for me to go to
Bedford Lodge. It would be folly of another sort to summon him
to Marlborough House or Sandringham. So the confrontation
had to be on neutral ground. And he had to be persuaded or
induced to come there without his henchmen. First, I thought of
the Jockey Club, but there are too many sharp ears there. The
meeting place had to be private.

Neutral ground, where he'd feel secure.

Before the National Anthem was played for the second time,
I'd chosen it.

With that off my mind, I gave the rest of the night to Alix. As
soon as we were home, we challenged Knollys and his sister to skittles and trounced them three times over. Then it was blindman's
buff with the Princesses, followed by General Post, followed by a
riotous game of hide-and-seek all over the house. For a woman
of forty-two, my dear wife has exceptional energy. She prefers
rough games, when everyone shouts at the tops of their voices,
to playing cards, when she can't hear the calls. I'm sure she went

to bed exhausted and happy, and that pleased me, for I'm very attached to her.

The following morning, I set my plan in motion. When Knollys came in with my list of engagements, I told him I had another to fit in.

"What is that, sir?"

"I want to see the Great Christopher."

"Mr. Sykes, sir? That might be difficult. I've had to make some adjustments already, to free you this afternoon."

I said, "I'm not concerned about this afternoon, Francis. I want him here as soon as possible."

"Yes, sir."

I took my time trimming a cigar. "What's the difficulty, then? What's upsetting my afternoon?"

He shuffled his papers. "Her Majesty the Queen, sir. Sir Frederick Ponsonby called on the telephone from Windsor. Her Majesty wishes to see you privately at three."

A butterfly fluttered in my stomach—the species known as the monarch. "It's an urgent matter, then?"

"So it would seem, sir."

CHAPTER 15

Two items on different pages of *The Times* caught my attention that same morning. Among the announcements of recent deaths I found the name Buckfast, "Captain Charles of Jermyn Street, formerly of the Seventeenth Lancers." No information was revealed about the circumstances of Charlie's passing. It was simply worded ". . . suddenly, in London, on 27th November." *Suddenly* was no exaggeration, poor fellow. The funeral was to take place privately at Highgate on Friday morning. I jotted a memorandum to Knollys to be sure to order a wreath.

The second item was a report tucked away at the end of the column of police intelligence:

MYSTERIOUS DEATH OF A MUSIC HALL ARTISTE

The body of a young woman well known as a music hall performer was discovered in a dressing room of the Bell, St. George's Street, East London, yesterday morning. She had been shot in the head. She was identified as Miss Myrtle Bliss, aged twenty-three, a bird trainer. The Whitechapel Police have announced that they wish to interview a man who gained admission to the hall after it closed on Monday evening. He is described as aged about fifty, of foreign extraction, short and portly in appearance, bearded, and wearing a brown ulster and Homburg hat.

My first reaction was to snort at the description. Then, having seen in cold print that I was in effect a wanted man, I took a different view. The gross distortions could work to my advantage. They were certain to confuse the public, which I was confident didn't think of its future King as foreign in extraction, or fifty, or the other libelous things. The only accurate information was the hat. Even my ulster is more gray than brown. Pity the Whitechapel police, and pity all fat foreigners over fifty!

Actually, there was something that troubled me more than the police, and that was the summons from Windsor. If my mother the Queen had heard of my adventures in Chelsea and the East End, I'd be better off behind bars with a ball and chain attached to my leg.

For distraction, I started some paperwork. The field for the Prince of Wales Steeplechase at Sandown Park wanted my undivided study. An animal called Hornpipe took my fancy. On the memo to Knollys I added, "£25—Hornpipe, 1:30, Sandown." A distracting thought came to me: What if Knollys took this as the message to be attached to Charlie Buckfast's wreath? I daresay as a racing man, Charlie might have appreciated the sentiment.

Christopher Sykes was announced before I'd made my choice for the two o'clock. Let's give credit to the Great Xtopher: he answered the summons and was over from Hill Street inside the hour, dipping his vast head toward me like a buffalo at the water hole.

"Splendid!" I greeted him. "I was hoping you'd be in London. Do sit down and stop staring at your shoes, Christopher. There's nothing offensive on them, is there?"

Perching himself on the extreme edge of an upright chair, he said, "Your Royal Highness—"

"Before you go any further," I interposed, "we've known each other long enough to dispense with that. I'm looking for some help."

"Whatever you require, sir."

"You'd better hear about it first. I'd like you to throw another of your house parties at Brantingham Thorpe."

Brantingham is Sykes's pile in Yorkshire, a Jacobean manor house near Beverley, the town he represents in Parliament. It's convenient for Doncaster racecourse, so we always get up a party in September.

He winced with the honor of it. "Another house party, sir. What a capital thought! Do you have the New Year in mind?"

"The weekend after this."

He swallowed and tried to stay calm. "So soon?"

"Unavoidably," I said. "People will be delighted to come, I'm sure."

"Yes, indeed." He had twisted his long legs into an extraordinary shape that reminded me of barley sugar. "Then I had better attend to the invitations at once. Do you have any particular guests in mind, sir?"

"Your sister-in-law Jessica, for one."

"Jessica?" The legs tried for another twist and failed. "I expect she would come . . . if invited." Now he was sucking his cheeks like a saint undergoing martyrdom. "You know her reputation, sir. She's considered fast."

"Yes," I said tolerantly. "She has some fast friends as well. Have a discreet word with her, Christopher. Ask her to recommend half a dozen of the giddiest girls in London."

He dropped his hat.

As he bent to retrieve it, I explained, "I want this house party to be a romp, a veritable romp. Oceans of fizz, of course. Log fires in all the rooms. Colored lights. A German band. A performing bear."

He straightened and blinked. "A bear at Brantingham, sir?"

I made an expansive gesture. "Well, an Irish fiddler, if you like. Or a sword swallower. Anything to jolly up the ladies."

Sykes looked ready to ask for the last rites.

I said, "Have you got a bellyache?"

He shook his head.

"Chilblains, sciatica or piles?"

"No, sir."

"Well, then, what's the trouble?"

He gulped and said, "All these active young women, and just you and me?"

He's extremely obtuse on occasion. I said, "Most of Jessica's friends are married, aren't they? Let them bring their husbands. That won't cramp their style if they're the sporting girls I take them for. Besides, there are one or two others I want you to invite."

"Personal guests, sir?"

I smiled. "Depends how personal you want to make it, Christopher. There's a charming little creature by the name of Lady Florence Dixie I'd like you to meet. Over rouged by some standards, but full of dash. She has a pet jaguar which she takes for walks in Kensington Gardens."

He had the grace to say feebly, "How exotic."

"Invite her, then."

"Oh, I didn't mean—"

"And there's one more guest I must have on the list."

"Mrs. Langtry?" ventured Sykes.

I gave him a glare. "Heavens, no. She's in America. Besides, I wouldn't let Lillie anywhere near a house party like this. I'm referring to a gentleman—Mr. Abington Baird, the Squire."

Sykes stiffened like a rabbit at the sound of gunfire.

I said, "I understand your apprehension, Christopher. He's an odious fellow."

"Infamous," whispered Sykes.

"Christopher, I'll put my cards on the table. I need to have a meeting with the Squire, man-to-man. A meeting of the utmost importance. I don't exaggerate when I say that it's a matter of life and death. Brantingham Thorpe is to be the setting for that meeting."

"But the other guests? All those excitable ladies?"

"The bait, so to speak."

"Bait?" repeated Sykes, as if he didn't understand the word.

"The Squire is an absolute Lothario."

"Oh."

"When you issue the invitations, don't mention that I'm coming. Don't breathe a word to anyone. Tell the Squire that some of the most adventurous ladies in London are desirous of meeting him, and make it clear that the invitation is for him alone. We don't want his pugilistic friends aiming punches at your Ming vases."

By this time, Sykes was too far gone to worry about his vases. I dismissed him gently, and he glided out like a sleepwalker.

Reader, you may sympathize with Sykes. I do, myself, when he is absent. I have the greatest difficulty in explaining why the sight of the fellow turns me into such an ogre. It's utterly against my nature, as you must have divined by now. Anyway, you might think there was some sort of justice at work later that day when I traveled to Windsor for my audience with the Queen. I was in a state of trepidation close to panic. The boot was on the other foot—and my dear mama has a kick like a mule.

A carriage was waiting in the yard at Windsor station. During the drive I rehearsed my speech for the defense. Give nothing away, I had decided. Don't get boxed in by detail. Steer the discussion toward the general issue of one's role as the Heir Apparent.

It was a closed carriage, so I spoke aloud, addressing the empty seat opposite, reminding it that the best years of my life would be wasted if I continued to be excluded from affairs of state. Ten years ago, my brother Leopold, rest his soul, was handed the Queen's Cabinet key. At the age of twenty-two he was permitted to open the secret dispatch boxes. Here was I, at forty-six, the future King, still denied that privilege. Was I so irresponsible, so neglectful of my duties? Had I mismanaged any of the twopenny-halfpenny committees I had been deemed worthy of chairing?

On second thought, this sounded too much like a complaint. One needed to make it more assertive. I am in the prime of my life, Mama. I am capable, healthy and energetic. I shall not be wanting when I am called upon to begin the great task ahead. Of course I wouldn't wish it to be one day sooner than the Almighty in His wisdom decrees, but you will not need reminding that you are now in the fiftieth year of your reign. Is it not time that I shouldered some of the burdens of State that you have borne so ably all these years?

That was better.

I must have been venting hot air, for the carriage window had steamed over. I cleared a peephole and saw trees. Too many trees. This wasn't the drive to Windsor Castle.

I was being brought to Frogmore, to the Mausoleum.

Bertie, I thought, this does not augur well.

It was twenty-five years since the death of my father, Prince Albert. Twenty-five years to the month. In the family, we speak of December 14 as "Mausoleum Day," when we congregate annually to pay our respects, but Mama is to be found at the "dear resting place" as often as you or I take the dog for a walk. On any occasion or anniversary of the slightest significance, she will find time to visit there. On the day before our wedding, Alix and I were taken into the shrine for Mama to link our hands and tell us that Papa gave us his blessing. I mistakenly took this as a sign that I was forgiven for past misdemeanors. I'm afraid she will always blame me for Papa's last illness, even though Dr. Jenner blamed the drains at Windsor. (Without wishing to belabor a story familiar to many, I should explain that my father felt obliged when feeling greatly out of sorts to visit me at Cambridge to admonish me for bringing disgrace on the family with an actress who was introduced to my bed in the Curragh Camp as a jest by brother officers of the Grenadier Guards; this at a time when my parents were pressing me to become betrothed to Alix. Papa's cold developed into typhoid, and Mama, in her distressed state, refused to send for me, so I was only enabled to come to my father's deathbed when my sister Alice sent a telegram without Mama's knowledge.)

My maternal grandmother, the late Duchess of Kent, has her own mausoleum at Frogmore. She had died earlier the same year, which undoubtedly compounded my mother's grief. There had been a rift between them for years, which I need not go into here, but Mama felt the bereavement keenly. She refused to leave Frogmore and the room where her mother died. She accused me of being heartless and selfish for writing to her on mourning notepaper with insufficiently wide black edging. When I tried to comfort her in person, she said I showed insufficient grief. She said I lacked the brains to feel emotion. All in all, you will understand why Frogmore is not my first choice for a tête-à-tête with Mama.

We drew up at the Mausoleum, which is about as cheerful in conception as taste will allow, for my mother wanted a living memorial rather than a *Sterbezimmer,* a death chamber. The stonework is light in color and the interior is ornately decorated, with profuse gilding that catches the light from many arched windows, though in December the main source of illumination is the gas.

Inside, the chill gripped me and I remembered all those December vigils beside the tomb, looking at my brothers and sisters in prayer, wondering which of us would go down with pneumonia first.

Just inside the entrance, an Indian servant gave me a shock when he moved out of the shadows, bowing and making a gesture toward the inner chamber. I stepped forward, my shoes making such a fearful clatter on the marble floor that I didn't hear my mother the Queen greet me. However, I saw her in the gaslight, a small veiled figure beside one of the four sculptured angels who guard Papa's tomb.

I just said, "Mama, dear." It didn't seem fitting to add, as I generally do, ". . . what a pleasure!"

She regarded me for a moment through her veil and sighed heavily. Her mood evidently matched her widow's weeds.

I remembered to say, "Dear Alix sends her love."

Mama is fond of Alix. She asked, "Did she have her birthday?"

I don't know what answer this was meant to evince. If it was negative, poor Alix would be dead. I said as heartily as circumstances allowed, "Never a better one."

"I expect she received the small present I sent."

"My word, yes!" I had no idea what it had been. "So very acceptable! She uses it constantly."

"Bertie, you are being deceitful again. Let us pray."

So we got on our knees and Mama led us in prayer. We prayed for Papa and all departed souls. We prayed for the Church and Parliament and the armed forces, the farmers and the fishermen, my brothers and sisters and all the family. We prayed for our servants and our pets. Then we prayed for truth to enter our hearts.

"Amen," said Mama at last; then, in the same breath, turning to face me, "She uses it constantly! I sent her a dog basket for the Pekingese. Now, Bertie, I want to speak frankly to you."

I asked, "May we get up first? My knees have gone numb."

So we promenaded around the tomb. She said, "It is necessary for me to speak to you about a person."

I should explain that in Mama's vocabulary, a person is not a person at all as you or I would understand it, but an undesirable, a reprobate, a monster of iniquity. I rapidly reviewed the persons I had encountered in the last week or so: Myrtle, the Squire, Carrie Montrose. Any of these would qualify for Mama's censure.

I asked as casually as I was able, "Do you mean somebody of my acquaintance?"

"Certainly."

"A lady?" An unproductive question, I realized as soon as I asked it, for a person might be female, but she could never be a lady.

"Certainly not."

There was an interval while we walked and said nothing. Oddly,

Mama appeared reluctant to pursue the subject, now that she had started it.

"A titled person?" I inquired.

She made a sound in her throat, a stifled laugh that carried no joy and humor. Irony, perhaps. She said bitterly, "It wouldn't surprise me if that's next."

Now I was all at sea. I said, "I'm afraid I don't know who you mean."

"Mr. Boehm."

"Boehm the sculptor? Edgar Boehm?"

"Who else?"

The relief! I almost did a dance of triumph around my father's tomb. I said, "Does this have something to do with the Wellington Statue Committee?"

"Isn't that evident?"

"And our choice of Edgar as the winning sculptor? Is there a difficulty?"

She cried out with such force that the black ostrich feathers quivered on her hat. "You call him by his Christian name, as if he's an intimate! I can scarcely bring myself to speak of this person at all."

I was baffled. Edgar Boehm was an old friend of the family. Papa, himself, had sat for him and approved the bronze busts he had made. His sculptures of several of us had appeared in the Royal Academy Exhibition. I so liked the 1872 equestrian statue of me as Colonel of the Tenth Hussars that I invited him to make a bust of the Princess Maud, which he charmingly entitled "Little Harry," our family name for her. In 1878, he created a figure of me on horseback described in the catalog as colossal. I presented it to the City of Bombay in celebration of my visit to India. He'd even sculptured my mother the Queen in marble.

I said, "Forgive me. I had no idea he had given offense to you."

She said, "Not only to me. To his fellow artists. I am informed that an approach was made to you yesterday morning."

The Queen is possessed of sensitive antennae. She might appear to be shut away from the world, but she has her ways of gathering information. As a detective, I was a mere beginner beside her.

I admitted, "Sir Frederic Leighton came to see me on the matter, yes. There is apparently some feeling in the Academy that I influenced the committee unduly."

"Did he ask you to alter the decision?"

"He didn't put it so plainly as that."

"Did you make any promises?"

"Not exactly promises," I prevaricated. "However, in view of your feelings on the matter, I shall reconvene the committee as soon as possible. It's not too late for second thoughts. We rejected some very acceptable designs."

To my dismay, she stopped, shook her fist and said, "Imbecile!"

Telling myself to stay calm, I said, "Mama, I've just explained. I can get the decision rescinded."

She said, "I *don't want* it rescinded! Leighton is a mischief maker who ought to be stripped of his title. The decision must stand. Boehm is the winning sculptor. Is that understood?"

It was noted, but by no means understood.

We made another circuit of the tomb before she would say any more. Then she sighed again and added, "I can understand your silence. The fact of the matter is that something occurred in the past, something that now enables Mr. Boehm to insist that we favor him."

"Ah."

"Your committee made the correct decision. We cannot allow that nincompoop Leighton to question it."

I dug deep into my memory, to Balmoral in the summer of 1870. A family crisis. I had been summoned to talk some sense into my sister Louise, who had fallen in love with a commoner: a personable thirty-five-year-old sculptor by the name of Erasmus Boehm. He changed it later to Edgar, which had a more English ring to it. Louise was twenty-two at the time, a talented artist and very suggestible. The romance had started innocently enough. The Queen had invited Boehm to Balmoral to make a sculpture of John Brown, the gillie to whom she was foolishly attached. Boehm had moved in with his mallet and chisel for three months. He was attracted to Louise and was soon giving her lessons in clay modeling and, I gather, much else besides. One morning Mama decided to see what progress had been made on the statue of Brown. She found Louise alone in the studio with Boehm.

In the pandemonium that followed, Louise declared her undying love for the sculptor. The Queen for once was speechless, so I was called in to read the riot act while Mama diverted her fury into finding a suitable husband for this wayward daughter. Boehm couldn't possibly marry into the family; he was a Royal Academician, and that was the only thing royal about him. I'll say this for him: considering his situation, he conducted himself with dignity and charm, or I'd never have continued to commission his works.

Louise was married to the Marquess of Lome the following March. I'm afraid it's an unhappy match. They are childless and lead virtually separate lives. Under Boehm's unflagging tuition, Louise has become a very proficient sculptor.

I presumed that the entire episode must have been forgotten and forgiven by Mama, for she certainly sat for Boehm two or three years after. Personally, I find a lot to admire in the fellow. Whether he actually rogers my sister I can't tell you, but at least he has the manners to keep it to himself.

Or—a disquieting thought came to me—had he used it to gain advancement?

I asked my mother directly, "Does this have to do with that episode at Balmoral, the year Boehm made the statue of Brown?"

She said bitterly, "Do you need to ask?"

I said, "So is he willing to threaten a lady's reputation to gain advancement? That's deplorable!"

"Detestable!" muttered my mother.

I said, "But I had the impression that he was quite devoted to Louise."

She lifted the veil and stared at me with her pale blue eyes. "It has nothing to do with Louise. Absolutely nothing." She jerked down the veil and walked on, out of the room containing my father's tomb.

I followed, mystified.

Outside in the anteroom, she paused briefly beside the plaque she had insisted be installed there to the memory of John Brown, the insinuating, coarse-mannered Highlander I've already mentioned.

Nothing was said, and the Queen walked out of the Mausoleum, but I was no longer mystified. It wasn't my sister's reputation that was under threat as a result of Boehm's sojourn at Balmoral in 1870, but my mother's.

CHAPTER 16

In a private room at the Marlborough Club on Friday evening, 3 December, I spent several hours with Christopher Sykes planning the house party at Brantingham Thorpe. I learned that the invitations had already gone out; a small orchestra had been engaged; and the domestic staff at Brantingham was preparing the rooms and the menus. As ever, the great Christopher had spared no effort, for all his misgivings.

What, then, was left to occupy us for so long in the Marlborough Club? It was, of course, the *raison d'être* of the party: the ensnaring of the Squire. If Sykes is unequaled as an organizer of parties, I may modestly claim a fair reputation as a hunter. One day in Nepal I shot six tigers, two of them man-eaters. I have bagged the fastest land animal in the world, the cheetah; and the largest, the elephant. In Bavaria, I was once in a party of ten guns that beat all records by shooting over twenty thousand partridges in ten days. I am the first to admit, however, that when the hunter pulls his trigger, it is only the final act in a process involving a small army of gamekeepers, beaters and loaders: hence the absolute necessity of planning. And hence our deliberations in the Marlborough Club.

So I approached the task as a hunter, taking account of the feral instincts of my quarry. The Squire was more dangerous than the tiger, more stealthy than the leopard. I suppose if one took into account the nature of the killings, he was akin to the vulture, relying on others to make the attack, but it would be foolhardy to fit him into any category. He was certainly capable of killing me if I gave him the opportunity.

I remained in London until Tuesday the seventh, diligently attending to my official duties while preparing for the dangerous encounter to come. A pleasing ceremony was enacted at Marlborough House that morning when Prince Komatsu of Japan, representing the Emperor, conferred on me the Insignia of the Imperial Japanese Order of the Chrysanthemum. Alix, who is as ignorant about Japan as she is about ceremony, couldn't understand why they hadn't chosen some more suitable flower, like the daffodil (for Wales, you see?). I told her they picked the chrysanthemum for me because it was large, round and shaggy, which shows that my humor hadn't deserted me under the strain.

Late in the afternoon, we left the metropolis to be the guests of the Danish minister and his wife, Madame de Falbe, at their splendid seat at Luton Hoo. I looked forward to some good shooting and Alix to jabbering in Danish to her heart's content. I'd already arranged to absent myself from the party on Saturday. Affairs of state, I'd told my host. Alix was sure to have something sarcastic to say in Danish about my affairs of state, but this time she would be mistaken.

And now, by the power of the pen, I'm going to transport us to Brantingham Thorpe on the evening of 11 December. Take it from me, the railway journey from Luton to York on a Saturday afternoon doesn't bear description.

My arrival was enshrouded in secrecy. Fortunately, I'm quite an old hand at entering houses by way of the mews or the servants' door. Muffled to the eyebrows, I stepped from the station fly straight through the woodyard into the kitchen, where a trusted butler with a candlestick showed me up the back stairs, through a baize curtain to the wing where Sykes accommodated his guests.

We had arranged that I should occupy the Beverley Room, an oak-paneled bedroom of modest proportions with, I was satisfied to discover, a blazing log fire and, even more welcoming, a table set for supper: toast and anchovies, oysters with brown bread and butter, chicken breasts and baked ham, quails' eggs, frog's thighs in jelly, a variety of cheeses and a large bowl of gooseberry fool. After the butler had poured me some Chablis I dismissed him and set to, for I was famished.

Some appreciable time passed before I was conscious of anything but the needs of the inner man. When I was round to the port and cigars, my ears picked up the strains of the orchestra from downstairs. An eightsome reel. By this time the house party was going full bat, and the most sociable fellow in the house was closeted upstairs! It was enough to make a parson swear.

I knew precisely what was happening. The guests, including our quarry, the Squire, had arrived much earlier than I. An afternoon around the piano had given the ladies, in their tea gowns, an opportunity to parade their talents, and the gentlemen to assess them. The flirtations and light behavior had begun in earnest over dinner, when Lady Jessica and her winsome friends had appeared in alluring décolletage. After five or six courses and wines, the ladies had retired to refresh their scent and prepare themselves for the excitements in prospect, while the gentlemen plotted their conquests over brandies and large cigars.

Reader, as I was chiefly responsible for establishing the weekend house party as a vogue in society, I had better explain the rules of conduct. You must understand that the main object is fun and games of an adult (not to say adulterous) character, so infinite care is taken over the invitations. The discerning host makes sure that his guests are sportively inclined, attractive and amusing, and upon this the success of the weekend depends. No less in importance is the allocation of bedrooms. Husbands and wives are not expected to sleep together. Everyone is allotted a single room. Spouses are then enabled to follow their fancies independently, provided of course that the wife has previously satisfied convention by bearing her husband a male child. Wives without sons are off-limits to gentlemen of honor, as are unmarried girls. If a liaison is well known, the fortunate couple may be provided with rooms in reasonable proximity. Otherwise, as in this case, it is a fair field and no favor.

As for me, this night had something less delectable in prospect. I would remain in the Beverley Room awaiting the moment when the Squire would spring the trap.

Downstairs, I heard Sykes shout, "If you please, ladies and gentlemen, if you please!" As master of ceremonies, he was endeavoring to intersperse the program of dancing with after dinner games. The high-spirited crowd we'd invited would not be much subdued by its po-faced host. Charades and Dumb Crambo would rapidly give way to games like Sardines, involving hiding, romps and forfeits. Forfeits galore! There's something in the English character that relishes embarrassment, either to oneself or others. That's why the majority of parlor games are designed for the express purpose of extracting forfeits.

As always, the climax of the evening would be "crying the forfeits." Everyone compelled to pay a forfeit hands to the host some personal article, such as an item of jewelry, a key or a watch. Some who have collected several forfeits are obliged to deposit more than one item. These possessions are redeemed when the forfeits are completed to everyone's satisfaction.

The forfeits are cried by two of the guests. One, known as the forfeit master, is seated, with the articles in his lap. The other (generally a lady) is blindfolded and must kneel before the first, who picks an object and holds it aloft, crying, "Here is a thing, and a very pretty thing. What shall be done by the owner of this very pretty thing?" The blindfolded lady asks, "Is it a lady's or a gentleman's?" She then names an appropriate forfeit, and the hapless owner performs the undignified task. A boisterous party can result in singular frolics.

I've gone to some trouble to explain how it works because I proposed to use the crying of the forfeits to implement my plan. I was relying on Sykes to set the whole thing in motion. During the evening he would closely observe the Squire to see which lady aroused his passions most. When he was certain, he would slip out of the room and take out a silver chain and locket provided by me. Inside the locket would be a slip of paper inscribed with these words: "The Beverley Room tonight, handsome Squire. I will be waiting impatiently." Sykes would append a forged signature—that of the lady admired by the Squire.

Do you see the trap? The Squire is called upon by Sykes to be the forfeit master. The trinkets, including the locket containing the note, are heaped in his lap. Naturally, when he holds up the locket, nobody will claim it. Intrigued, the Squire will open it and read the message.

So I had to be patient. If patience is said to be the beggar's virtue, is it so remarkable that a prince should be without it? I hate inactivity, and I didn't expect my visitor for at least a couple of hours. Sykes had providently arranged for a stack of magazines and newspapers to be left out, and I settled down to pass the time with these, closing my ears to the sounds of high jinks downstairs.

I picked up *The Sporting Life*, grateful that someone understood my taste in reading. I studied the results from Sandown Park. No winners from yesterday—not even a place. Steeplechasing doesn't have the same appeal as the flat for me. There are enough imponderables in a flat handicap, without putting in jumps as well.

An item about Archer's will caught my eye. A rather surprising item. His estate amounted to £60,000—a sizable fortune by most standards, but distinctly less than anyone had predicted, except Charlie Buckfast. The smallest estimate that I'd seen in the press was the figure of £100,000 in *Reynolds's Newspaper* and some had put it as high as half a million. The principal beneficiary was Archer's infant daughter, Nellie Rose, who was now in the care of her grandparents. Eight other relatives and friends received legacies.

Unable to concentrate any longer on the papers, I smoked two or three cigars, musing on Archer and the tragedies that had beset him. Even after his passing, death had claimed more victims, as if still exacting payment for his genius. Who was to say that the price had yet been paid?

I shivered, and it wasn't because I felt a draft.

My morbid thoughts were banished by a shriek from downstairs, followed by wicked laughter. In the intervals between dances, Sykes was still manfully attempting to direct the parlor games. Judging by the hysterical response of certain of the ladies, he was either having a brilliant success or a ludicrous failure. How tempted I was to surprise them all! Frankly, Lady Florence Dixie was wasted on Sykes. She's a bubbly, mischievous minx, and I've never found an opportunity to plumb the depths of her mischief. Once she formed a quadrille at Blenheim with Bay Middleton and another pair who included Gladys de Grey (then Lady Lonsdale). She took one look at the elegant Gladys and piped, "Why can't I be as tall as you?" and sprang high in the air like an acrobat.

Sometime after midnight, the music stopped. For me, the evening was about to begin. I tossed my cigar butt into the fire and got up from the armchair, listening keenly. I took a few deep breaths, bracing myself for a set-to with the Squire. My skin prickled and my hands shook a little when I clenched them. One doesn't get much hand-to-hand combat in Court circles. At least, I thought, I'll have surprise on my side.

Presently I heard a sound below my window. I drew back the curtain a fraction and saw the band loading their instruments into a van. The task took about ten minutes. They whipped up the horse and left.

Next, much giggling on the stairs and the swish of skirts as the ladies came to bed. I crept across the room to listen. When their voices grew more distinct, I heard one say plaintively, "He's divine. But he'll never know where I am."

A reassuring voice told her, "Daisy, darling, he's only got to find his way along here. It's really quite light in the moonlight."

"And so is Daisy!" remarked another, to screams of laughter.

A relative silence ensued for up to an hour before the party in the smoking room broke up and heavier steps trod the stairs. The stronger sex are tight-lipped at such times. I heard a few murmurs of, "Good night, old boy." Doors were closed and that was all.

Good taste decreed a further interval of at least half an hour before the first noctambulation. Like everyone else, I daresay, I opened my door a fraction and waited for the creak of a board. I turned down the light to the merest blue flicker.

I had taken up a position to the left of the door, with the intention of grabbing the Squire the moment he entered. I'm not very adept at wrestling, but I was confident of handling a fellow who tips the scales at under ten stone. Besides, the indispensable Sykes was located just across the corridor, ready to come to my assistance as soon as I gave the shout.

I exercised commendable patience in the next twenty minutes or so. Eventually I was conscious of a movement somewhere nearby.

I strained to listen.

The first tiptoed steps came along the corridor, rapidly, supremely confident where they were going. I pressed myself to the wall. The steps came level with the Beverley Room—and failed even to pause. I heard a soft click as a door opened and closed, followed by a muffled greeting, then silence again.

After a tense hiatus, someone else made a move, padding determinedly in my direction.

I held my breath.

He actually stopped outside my door. He was so close that I could hear his breathing. I heard him sniff. He was taking an unconscionable time to come in. I could barely restrain myself from flinging open the door and snatching him inside.

Then—would you believe?—he crept away!

It's true—the footsteps retreated along the corridor.

For all the tea in China—why?

The door of the Beverley Room was labeled plainly enough, and he'd had no trouble seeing it, because, as the ladies had remarked, the corridor was aglow with moonlight. A shaft extended through the gap in the door and across the carpet. My eye followed it back to the door, and that was what caused me to notice something on the floorboards. First I thought it was some creeping thing, but common sense told me that the Brantingham Thorpe cockroaches couldn't be quite so large.

I stooped and picked it up.

My locket and chain. He'd chucked it down in the doorway. I felt like a woman spurned.

What the devil had gone wrong? This was utterly, maddeningly out of character. The Squire had no business behaving like this. He was about as coy as Casanova.

An ugly suspicion uncoiled itself: Had Christopher Sykes botched the plan in some way?

I unfastened the locket and took out the slip of paper and read the message. It was certainly the invitation I had written. And, just as I'd directed, a signature had been added: "Jessica."

I couldn't fault Sykes. He'd done precisely as I'd ordered, even though it had meant admitting that his own sister-in-law was the Squire's choice for a bedmate.

So I had nobody to blame. The plan had failed, and I couldn't fathom why.

Then I turned over the piece of paper and saw a message written on the reverse: "You should give up cigars—they don't become a lady."

The Squire had smelled the fumes.

All these elaborate preparations, all the thought I'd put into this weekend, and my plan had foundered because I can't resist a smoke.

I called softly for Sykes, and he rushed in, armed with a poker.

I told him it wasn't required and explained why. I am bound to say that he appeared more relieved than angered.

"Better sleep on it, sir," he suggested. "We'll think of something else in the morning."

I said, "Stop talking like my old nanny, Sykes. I mean to settle this tonight."

"Tonight?" He looked even more troubled than usual.

"At once."

"But what can you do, sir? He'll be on the alert now."

I said grimly, "He'll be on the first train back to Newmarket if we don't detain him."

I asked Sykes for the name of the Squire's bedroom. Then I sent him to station himself with his poker at the foot of the stairs in case there was a chase. I proposed to step into the lion's den.

The room was called York, and it was situated on the same floor as mine, around two turns of the corridor. You'll have to take my word for it that an Indian scout could not have crept through the house more stealthily than I did. I might have been walking on eggs. Yet I'd defy anyone to master the loose boards in Brantingham Thorpe. When I felt the ominous movement under my shoe, it made more of a rasp than a creak. I tensed.

An enticing murmur of feminine origin responded from a door left ajar. I refused to be distracted.

I hesitated at the first turn, and it was a good thing I did, because a figure in a dressing gown was moving quite rapidly toward me. He had too much girth to be the Squire. He was making such a beeline that I guessed the bathroom at the end of the corridor was his destination. Haven't we all been so afflicted soon after going to bed?

I stepped back fast, through that open door from which the murmur had emanated, pulling it almost shut.

The lady's voice asked at once, "Is that you?"

I answered, "No."

She said generously, "I don't mind."

The loose board outside gave a startling screech, and to my consternation, the door opened. The fellow in the dressing gown walked straight past me toward the bed.

The lady in the bed asked in an interested voice, "Are there two of you?"

I said, "Yes, and this one is leaving." Which I did.

My second noctambulation was conducted with more purpose. I abandoned all stealth, stepped out boldly and located the York Room. The door was closed, so after putting my ear against it and hearing nothing, I tried the handle. It turned readily enough, but the door wouldn't yield. I was locked out—or the Squire was locked in. I rapped and got no response.

What wretched luck!

I knocked more firmly, knowing in my sinking heart that the Squire wouldn't respond, whatever I tried. I didn't want the whole of the house turning out to complain at the disturbance, so I reluctantly returned to the Beverley Room.

I let myself in and was reaching for the port when my collar was gripped from behind and jerked upward, practically choking me.

I must have made quite a racket, because my assailant said in a voice I didn't recognize, the coarse, throaty growl of an uneducated man, "Stow it, Teddy, or I'll shove your face through the wall."

Being a prudent man, I stowed it, and for my cooperation I was flung onto the bed. I cracked my head against the wooden headboard and saw a fireworks display worthy of the Crystal Palace.

CHAPTER 17

Through the pain, I said, "Do you know who I am?"

My assailant put a face of unexampled brutality within a couple of inches of mine and said, "Yes, Your Worship. You're the Prince of Wales. And I'm Charlie Mitchell, the Champion of England. You got a title and so have I. The difference is, I had to fight for mine."

This is impossible, my beleaguered brain told me. The Squire was told to come alone.

Mitchell, you'll recall, was the Squire's chief henchman, the most famous prizefighter in England. This notorious pugilist had been smuggled into Brantingham Thorpe to deal with me. He had been to America in 1883 to try conclusions with John L. Sullivan, the world champion. Swarthy in appearance and clean-shaven, without a glimmer of intelligence to animate his menacing features, he reminded me strongly of my odious brother-in-law, the Marquess of Lome.

Bertie, I said to myself, unless you're nimble witted you're about to go the way of Buckfast and Myrtle.

I asked him good-naturedly, "Do you want money?"

Mitchell replied with a sneer, "You can make me a Knight of the Garter if you want." With that he forced what I prefer to believe was an unused handkerchief into my mouth to serve as a gag and grabbed my own silk scarf from the coat hook on the door and pressed it across my face, tugging my head upward to tie a knot behind. His hands felt like well-scuffed shoes. He pushed me onto my front and bound my wrists. Then he warned me super-fluously, "Don't give no bother, right? We're going downstairs."

He's planning to murder me in the grounds, I decided. It's less likely to disturb the people in the house and he can make his escape more easily.

He gripped my left arm by the biceps and swung me off the bed and toward the door. His strength was terrible to contemplate.

There was one chance of salvation, and I dared not put much hope on it. Christopher Sykes was waiting at the foot of the stairs with a foot-long poker. Even from his vast height, Sykes would need to wield the poker with prodigious strength and speed to fell Charlie Mitchell with one blow. As sure as the Creed, he wouldn't get a second try. But if I were alert and agile, it might enable me to escape.

Unfortunately, it did not, for instead of turning toward the main stairs, Mitchell steered me to the left, and by now every bedroom door was closed. We passed the Squire's without pausing, turned right, through the baize door and down the servants' stairs to the kitchen, which was deserted except for a couple of cats.

Mitchell unbolted the door and marched me across a cobbled yard, past the stables. A clear sky gave us strong moonlight and penetrating cold. Bareheaded and without so much as an overcoat, I was horribly reminded that royal executions always seemed to happen during the most inclement time of the year.

Across the yard was a high, gray building with a tiled roof already glittering with frost. The coach house, I decided, and this was confirmed when Mitchel kicked open a door and pushed me inside. Coach house or slaughter house?

There were four or five vehicles in front of me, and beyond them one with its lamps lighted. I didn't have much time to study my surroundings because a figure in a topper and greatcoat stepped out of the radiance and swaggered toward us. The insolent grin framed by sandy-colored muttonchops was really no comfort, although I hadn't expected the Squire to be in at the death.

He whisked off the hat and swung it in front of him in an insolent, exaggerated bow. Addressing Mitchell, he said, "Charles, my dear fellow, there's no need to hold on to the Prince like a punt pole. We're not likely to lose him now. And take that scarf off his face. He looks like a bank robber. It's enough to get us all into trouble."

Mitchell untied me and removed the gag. I spluttered as the air entered my throat again.

"God save us, Your Royal Highness, I don't like the sound of that," commented the Squire. "You'll be catching your death if we don't look after you. Why don't you step into my private brougham? There's a blanket inside that you can put around your shoulders."

I wasn't fooled by his show of concern, but I was so relieved to be offered anything less than a bullet through the head that I didn't think twice about acting on the suggestion. I climbed into the coach (you're right, it was the one with lighted lamps, but that didn't seem significant at the time), grabbed the blanket and wrapped myself in it.

The Squire came in after me, took the seat opposite and shut the door. The light entering the window picked out the dissipation in his face, though I knew him to be barely twenty-five. His rubbery lips were held in a permanent sneer and his eyes were so pouchy that he might have been sparring with Mitchell.

"Now we're alone, Your Royal Highness," he said, "I'll speak out. I'm bloody insulted."

It was some comfort that he proposed to speak at all. My best chance of a reprieve was to keep reminding him who I was, so I said, "I'll thank you to show some respect."

"A fat lot of respect you showed me," he returned, "trying to pull a threepenny-novel trick like the message in the locket."

I looked away. I wasn't obliged to listen to his ranting.

But out of curiosity I did. He continued, "Your toadying friend Sykes obviously didn't throw the house party for his own amusement. I knew you'd be here, and I knew why. It's about Myrtle, isn't it?"

Astonished that he had the gall to raise the subject, I said, "Yes. Since we're speaking out, Mr. Baird, I want to know why you killed her."

He gave me a stare I can only describe as maniacal. "I killed her? You're accusing *me* of killing Myrtle?"

"You or your pack of jackals."

He protested in a rush of words that didn't impress me at all, "No one talks to me like that. No one. She was my girl, my guest at Bedford Lodge. A peach of a girl. I wouldn't hurt a hair on her head."

"Your henchmen did."

"That's a vile suggestion!"

"It was a vile crime," said I. "They also attacked and killed Captain Buckfast. Before you deny it, I was there. They threw me in the Thames—me, the Heir Apparent—and I might very well have drowned with him."

With about as much concern as a fishmonger feels for a lobster, he said, "Are you telling me that you were there when Buckfast was killed?"

"Can I put it more plainly?" He still appeared to doubt me, so I added, "Didn't your two thugs tell you?"

He was silent for some seconds. I wouldn't go so far as to say I'd delivered a knockout punch, but I might have winded him.

Outside, Mitchell had unbolted the large doors at the end of the building, and someone else led in a pair of grays.

The Squire began again on a more conciliatory note, "I'm trying to make sense of this. What reason would I or my friends have for killing Buckfast and attacking you?"

Some bluff on his part was to be expected, and I didn't have much patience with it. I said, "This show of innocence doesn't impress me much, Baird."

"You see?" he said. "You accuse me, and you can't explain why."

"Of course I can explain why!" I told him angrily. "We were too close to the truth about your dealings with Fred Archer."

"Dealings? What dealings?"

By now, the force of the argument had taken hold of me, "Buckfast spent a week in Newmarket collecting evidence. He broke into Bedford Lodge—"

He repeated rudely, "What dealings?"

I glared and said, "The blackmail that drove him to shoot himself."

"Blackmail!" he said, doing his best to sound outraged.

"You corrupted Archer with bribes, and then threatened him with exposure."

"I did not. Fred never took a bribe in his life."

How ironic that I, who had started out believing Archer was incorruptible, should find myself recounting his sins to this loathsome humbug. I said, "He was regularly pulling races and you paid him to do it. He was in your pocket, to quote your own words."

"Who told you I used those words?"

"Buckfast. He heard you bragging all over Newmarket."

"Then he lied."

"Why should Buckfast lie to me? As a matter of fact," I added, voicing a suspicion I'd been saving for this encounter, "I now understand why the running of the Cambridgeshire was so peculiar. You and Archer rooked everyone."

"There was nothing fishy about the Cambridgeshire," he insisted. "I kept my horse's form from the bookies, that's all."

"Really? How many jockeys are capable of beating Archer in a close finish? Two or three at their best? Cannon, perhaps, and Wood. Who was on your animal—Albert White? Come now. *Albert White!* He wouldn't live with Archer in a fair-run finish. Fred obviously let him get up. And what happened to Carlton, the favorite? It finished nowhere. Why? Because you bribed its jockey, Woodburn."

He said defiantly, "I paid Woodburn nothing."

"If it wasn't you, it was Archer who handed over the money. You had Archer on a string. You were all ready to take him on as a partner and bleed his reputation white."

He said, "There's no evidence for any of this."

I said, "But there is. That's why Buckfast broke into Bedford Lodge."

"When was this?"

"Two weeks ago last night. The night you went to the dogfight at the Greyhound."

My grasp of the facts was manifestly beginning to trouble him. He said tamely, "We're often at the Greyhound."

I said, "He got into your room and surprised two of your men . . ."

"In my bedroom?"

". . . in a state of nature and in a proximity that was anything but natural."

He snorted his disbelief.

I said, "The same men followed Buckfast to London on Saturday and made that murderous attack."

He asked me to describe them, which was a change from all the denials, and some indication that I'd impressed him. When

I'd given as good a description as I was able, he said in a more subdued manner, "If there's a grain of truth in this, I'll see those men hanged. I don't know who you mean, but I'll question every one of my associates."

"Don't shift the blame, Mr. Baird," I told him sternly. "I still hold you accountable for three deaths."

"Three?"

"Archer, Buckfast and Miss Bliss."

"You're talking rubbish," he rasped. "By Jesus, you're wrong from beginning to end and I'll prove it." He thrust open the carriage door and called, "Get those bloody horses between the shafts and drive away."

CHAPTER 18

That ride through the night in the Squire's brougham was an experience I wouldn't care to repeat. We careered up the drive of Brantingham Thorpe as if pursued by wolves. I fully expected us to throw a wheel at any minute. No such premonitions afflicted Charlie Mitchell, on the box beside the coachman shouting to him repeatedly to whip up the horses.

Inside, so buffeted that only with difficulty could I remain on the seat, I inquired where we were going so late and at such speed. The Squire refused to tell me. He had retreated into a churlish silence, which angered me greatly. If anyone had cause to feel aggrieved, it was myself.

We veered left at the main road with a tremendous grating of iron on grit, and an alarming possibility presented itself. I knew of nothing in this direction except the north bank of the River Humber. My fortunate escape from drowning in the Thames was all too vivid in my recollection. On that occasion, I'd saved myself with a few rapid strokes of the dog paddle, but the Humber is up to two miles across in places. If they proposed to make a better job of annihilating me this time, the vast, deserted reach to the south of Brantingham Thorpe would be ideal for their purpose. My body might never be found.

How I regretted speaking out so forthrightly about the Squire's guilt! I've never been noted for guarding my tongue. Time and again it has got me into hot water. Hot or cold, I can't abide the stuff.

Bertie, I thought, this cannot be tolerated. If ever the silver-tongued charm of the Saxe-Coburgs had a challenge, this is it. So I suppressed my jitters and summoned up a fraternal smile. "Mr. Baird," I said civilly, "whatever our differences, we both respected Fred Archer as the greatest jockey who ever lived."

He ignored me.

Doggedly I continued, "That is why I chose to interest myself in the mystery of his suicide."

He stared through me.

I added in the same conciliatory vein, "However, I am coming around to the view that it might be sensible to dismiss the whole unfortunate matter from my mind."

Do you know what this more than generous offer elicited from the Squire? Nothing, not so much as a raised eyebrow. The man was impervious to charm or compromise, and I refused to grovel until it was absolutely necessary.

I lapsed into silence again and endeavored to control my anger by applying my mind to other things. What would an experienced detective be doing now? Studying the scene from the window to learn where he was being taken.

I peered out. My view gave me precious little information. I could see no water yet, and I reckoned at the furious rate we were traveling that we ought to have reached the Humber by this time. Presently a sharp turn to the left gave me a slight pretext for optimism. The steadier rumble of the wheels suggested we were on a trunk road. We might, after all, be traveling east, toward the town of Hull.

It transpired that we were not. My sense of direction had failed me utterly, for we were approaching Beverley. I knew it was Beverley, because in the moonlight I saw the familiar outline of the twin towers at the west front of the Minster. When I say "familiar," I should own that I've never worshiped in the Minster; I usually pass it on my way to the racecourse. It is on open ground to the south of the town.

We drove farther in and stopped by the market cross, where-upon Mitchell got down for a consultation. He asked which street we wanted, and I leaned forward to listen. I heard nothing of value because the Squire simply swore at him and ordered him to change places. Mitchell needed no second bidding. When he climbed in, I saw that the front of his overcoat had acquired a thick covering of frost.

Our destination proved to be a terraced house in a narrow street off the marketplace. Automatically, I made ready to get out as the carriage stopped. Mitchell growled and wagged his finger at me, and I subsided again. The Squire marched over to the door of the house and knocked. I wondered what reception he'd get at this hour, for I'd heard a clock striking three as we came through the town.

Almost at once, a window opened upstairs. Inconveniently, I couldn't hear what was said. After a brief exchange, the Squire came over to the brougham, opened the door and ordered me out.

The purpose of all this exercised me greatly, and my brain grappled with some horrid possibilities. If I wasn't to be drowned this time, perhaps my fate was to be struck on the head and buried in the backyard. Or did they intend to stuff me into a tin trunk and bury me at sea?

As I crossed the cobbles with the Squire, he said, "I haven't told him who you are."

"The ignorance is mutual," I answered.

But I *did* recognize the face when the door was opened by a diminutive, rat-faced young fellow in a nightshirt. He was probably under twenty years old. His features were pinched by sleep and I couldn't see much of his eyes, but I knew him. I'd seen him often. The deuce of it was that I couldn't think where, or who he was.

The Squire told him brusquely, "This won't take long. Where can we talk?"

"In the back room, Mr. Baird, so long as you keep your voices down."

I was still unable to place him. The voice came in a throaty rasp that wasn't familiar. I have no ear at all for accents.

He led us—that is to say, myself, the Squire and Mitchell—through a damp-smelling passage to a small room where the embers of a fire glowed faintly. A linnet in a cage twittered at our host when he lighted an oil lamp. The flame showed us a few sparse furnishings. I claimed a wooden armchair nearest the dying fire, and the others found stools on either side of a small, square table covered with oilcloth.

In the better light, I stared at the youth I have called our host, searching for the clue that would tell me where I'd seen him. My first impression of him as "rat-faced" was, perhaps, uncharitable, but if you had seen his beady eyes, sharp nose and protruding teeth, you would undoubtedly have reached a conclusion not very different from mine. Curiously, for all his lack of stature, I had an idea that I was accustomed to looking up at him.

This I found puzzling, for people are meant to look up at *me*. I'm invariably elevated above the public on some form of dais or rostrum. Even at the races, I stand on a carriage for a better view.

The races.

"Got it!" I blurted out. "You're a jockey!"

He raised his hands in alarm and said huskily, "Stash it, mate. My landlady's asleep upstairs."

The Squire nodded to me and said, "It's Woodburn."

"Woodburn—of course!"

The scene at Newmarket surfaced in my memory. I saw the field charging up the hill again, sharpening into focus in my glasses. Woodburn was the rider in blue, with white diamonds, on Carlton, the favorite, and he was leading the gallop, with Melton and St. Mirin tucked in behind. He had nothing to give when they challenged. He was a terrible disappointment to the crowd.

There was the sound of someone—presumably Woodburn's landlady—shifting in bed upstairs. The jockey put a finger to his lips and pointed at the ceiling.

The Squire ignored him. He had decided at last to explain the purpose of this bizarre meeting. "Woodburn does winter work up here with Tom Green, the Beverley trainer who looks after some of my horses. I'm giving you the opportunity to question him, Your Royal Highness."

I was so overwhelmed that this was indeed Woodburn the jockey, and not (so far as I was aware) an assassin or a disposer of corpses, that for a moment I couldn't think what I wanted to ask him about.

The Squire prompted me. "About Fred Archer," he added.

"Archer, yes." I nodded vigorously. What I needed now was a strong drink to marshal my thoughts. Unthinkingly, I turned to young Woodburn and asked, "Would you have such a thing as a cognac?"

Woodburn screwed up his face and demanded of the Squire,

"Is this one of your famous practical jokes, Mr. Baird? I mean, am I really supposed to take this old geezer for the Prince of Wales?"

The Squire answered tersely, "It's no joke."

"You can't deny that there's a likeness," Woodburn blundered on inanely, although I suppose he couldn't be blamed for persisting in his error. A few minutes ago he'd been soundly asleep. I think if my mother the Queen had been there beside me in her coronation robes he still wouldn't have believed it.

To me, the Squire said irritably, "Get on with it, blast you."

No doubt, sensitive reader, you are appalled that anyone could address me so. You may imagine my feelings. For the present, I contained them, for I had collected my wits. I realized I had been handed a perfect opportunity to test the truth of the Squire's claim that neither he, nor Archer, had paid a bribe to Woodburn. I was confident that he would get his comeuppance very shortly.

Addressing Woodburn, I said, "I want some honest answers from you, my lad. I want to get to the bottom of the Cambridgeshire result."

Woodburn looked extremely alarmed, as I had expected. He said, "The Cambridgeshire?" Turning to the Squire, he asked, "What is this, Mr. Baird—a stewards' inquiry?"

I answered grimly, "It's a great deal more than that. You rode Carlton, the favorite, and it ran like a selling-plater. I want to know why."

He squirmed on his stool. "Even a good colt has a bad run sometimes."

Ignoring that evasion, I plunged in and asked, "Is it true that you took a bribe from this gentleman?"

Woodburn blinked and looked at the Squire and then at me as if I'd impugned the Archbishop of Canterbury. "From Mr. Baird? Never."

At this, the Squire thrust out his fat lower lip in triumph, and I reflected how futile an exercise this was. Of course, Woodburn would stand by the Squire if they were both in league.

"From Archer, then?" I suggested.

"Fred Archer?"

"Don't try me, Woodburn."

He said, "Fred was offered the ride on Carlton, and he turned it down."

"You haven't answered my question."

The Squire sprang to his defense. "But he has. If Fred turned down the ride, he must have known St. Mirin was a better colt."

"Not necessarily," I said. "There was a trial before the Cambridgeshire, and Carlton beat St. Mirin easily. What do you say to that, Woodburn?"

The jockey nervously wetted his lips. "Fred wanted the ride on Carlton, but he was under an obligation, sir."

I noted the *sir*. I was making an impression. "An obligation. To whom?"

"St. Mirin's owner, the Duchess of Montrose. She's a very forceful lady."

"I'm aware of that."

"I was over in Ireland with Fred for the Curragh October Meeting, and I was there when he opened a telegram. It said: 'My horse runs in the Cambridgeshire. I count on you to ride it. Montrose.' For Fred it meant getting his weight down to eight stone six. That's terrible wasting for a man of his size."

I said, "You're still avoiding my question. Did you or did you not take a bribe from Archer?"

A look appeared in Woodburn's eyes that I find difficult to describe. There was embarrassment there, which I expected, and defiance. And there was something I didn't expect: fear, amounting almost to panic.

The Squire must have noted it, too, for he took this as the cue to indulge in some blatant leading of the witness. "For God's sake! Fred was straight as a die. Answer the bloody question, man!"

"I can't," said Woodburn. "I dare not."

"Why?"

To everyone's amazement and confusion, Woodburn said, "He could be listening."

After a breathless interval I inquired, "Who exactly do you mean?"

"Fred."

There was another stunned pause.

Trying to sound reasonable, Woodburn explained, "I'm not really a believer in such things, but when people I know—honest, reliable people—tell me they've seen it as clear as daylight, I can't ignore them, can I?"

"Seen what?" demanded the Squire.

"His ghost."

"Strewth!" said Mitchell.

Woodburn added quickly, "They say it's an unquiet spirit. Fred won't stay in his grave."

"Absurd!" I said, wishing I carried more conviction. You see, I'm constantly being told by mama about psychic phenomena, voices and apparitions, and some of it rubs off, try as you might to take a rational view.

The Squire said, "There was something about this in the paper. He rides around Newmarket on a spectral horse."

"In that case," I said resourcefully, "he won't appear in Beverley. Ghosts only ever haunt one place."

"That's a fact," said Mitchell, though what claims he had as an expert on the supernatural, I cannot think.

I said, "You can tell us the truth, Woodburn. Did you take a bribe?"

The Squire got up from his stool and placed an encouraging hand on the young jockey's shoulder. He said, "You don't even have to speak to answer the question. Just shake your head."

"Or give a nod if the answer is yes," I said with a glare at the Squire.

The rodent features twitched. Woodburn was a very agitated young man.

I said, "You threw away the race, didn't you?"

He dipped his head in confirmation.

"And Archer paid you to do it?"

Another nod.

This was too much for the Squire to stomach. He grasped Woodburn by the nightshirt and picked him off the stool. "What the devil are you saying, you little toad—that the greatest jockey who ever lived was a cheat? Look me in the eye and say it."

"It's true," whispered Woodburn. "As I live and die, it's true, Mr. Baird."

The Squire suddenly went very pale.

Charlie Mitchell, understanding only that the little toad had given offense, stood up and prepared to crush him, but the Squire gestured to him to remain seated.

A flame of triumph leapt up in me. I had proved my case.

Instead of the back room of a humble terraced house in Beverley, this might have been the Central Criminal Court at the Old Bailey. I was ready to take my place among the great forensic lawyers.

It was but a small leap from there to the judge's bench. I told Woodburn gravely, "You have said enough to bring a premature end to your career as a jockey, but it need not be repeated outside these walls if you confess the details fully and frankly. Do you understand?"

"Yes, sir." He fingered the collar of his nightshirt. His hands were trembling.

"How much were you paid?"

"Two hundred, sir."

"To stop Carlton?"

"Yes, sir."

"And when precisely did Archer hand you the bribe?"

"He didn't, sir."

"What?"

"Fred didn't pay me. Captain Buckfast did."

"*Buckfast?*" I heard my own voice pipe ridiculously high.

"He was acting for Fred," said Woodburn, aware that he had some rapid explaining to do. "Fred couldn't do anything without someone watching. People never took their eyes off Fred, so the captain conducted his business for him. He approached me on the first day of the Houghton meeting. He handed over half the money on the day before the Cambridgeshire and the rest on the morning after."

"So you had no dealings directly with Archer?" said the Squire.

"That was the way Fred preferred it, sir."

I believe the Squire winkled out some more from Woodburn about the money and how it was left in a cigar box in a four-wheeler engaged to wait for him at the end of the day's racing, but my concentration was broken. I was thunderstruck at the suggestion that Charlie Buckfast, my assistant, an officer and a gentleman, had not only colluded in the bribery but also actively promoted it, and mentioned nothing of it to me. It was unthinkable. And deplorable. A vicious slander on a dead man.

I wondered whether Woodburn and the Squire had cooked up the story between them. I was tempted to believe this was so, yet I was compelled to admit that Woodburn's account contradicted the

Squire's. According to the Squire, Archer was practically a saint, incapable of anything so underhanded as bribery. Woodburn's statement that Archer was corrupt had shocked the Squire profoundly. Take my word for it; I can tell when a man flies into a temper. His outburst had unquestionably been genuine.

What was I to make of it? I could only assume that Woodburn was unhinged. The possibility had crossed my mind when he had started talking about Archer's ghost, though it has to be said that wiser and more eminent heads than his have entertained such notions. Yet the story about Charlie Buckfast was preposterous. Mad.

I didn't believe a word of it.

Shortly after, we drove back to Brantingham Thorpe. For most of the ride we were silent. Only as we turned into the drive did the Squire ask, "Are you satisfied?"

"Not in the least," I told him candidly.

"Will you still pursue it?"

"To the end, Mr. Baird. To the very end."

He grinned brazenly. "In that case, I'll see you there . . . if you survive."

CHAPTER 19

There were no early risers in Brantingham Thorpe on the Sunday morning. Lady Jessica and her set were not so frisky on an icy December morning when the fires of every sort had ceased to flicker. Breakfast was not even contemplated. The mere thought of renewing social contact over porridge and smoked haddock must have been like a prospect of hell to those nightshirted rovers of the previous night. So I was enabled to slip away at mid-morning, unnoticed by anyone except Sykes, who decently arranged to have me driven to York, where the stationmaster, good man, called up a special train.

I resumed my investigation on the following Tuesday afternoon, 14 December. I traveled down to Newmarket and put up at my private suite in the Jockey Club. I was convinced that my detective quest would be brought to a triumphant conclusion in the town we Turfites know as Headquarters, and so it was, as you shall see.

After a hearty dinner, I passed an instructive evening with Captain James Machell, the fount of all wisdom concerning the Heath and its personalities. Machell is a mournful-looking cove, with a caustic turn of phrase, and he's made many enemies over the years, but I've always found him stimulating company, and as a judge of a horse he's second to none. He'll always be linked in racing memories with Hermit's Derby, in 1867. A week before the race Hermit broke a blood vessel at Newmarket. Henry Chaplin, the owner, wanted to pull out, but Machell patched up the colt and

insisted that it should run and personally backed it to win £3,000.
It got up sensationally at 1,000-15. What's more, when Hermit was
put to stud, he sired many outstanding horses, among them two
Derby winners and one whose name will be familiar: St. Mirin.

This evening the captain was in spanking form, recounting the
latest incident in his unending feud with his neighbor in Newmarket, Carrie Montrose, whom he styled as "that superannuated
scarlet woman." Carrie, it emerged, was back from London with a
young man of twenty-two, whom she had "roused at dawn from his
exhausted slumbers for a ride across the Limekilns." After a night
with Carrie the young man was in no condition for a gallop. His
hack had bolted and thrown its rider and interfered with Machell's
string and there was such a barney between Carrie and the captain
that nobody noticed that the young man had broken his leg.

Our conversation moved inexorably to Archer, and Machell told
me that before their misunderstanding Fred had actually consulted
him upon the advisability of marriage to Carrie Montrose. He had
wanted to know whether it would make him a duke. Poor deluded
Archer! I was convulsed with laughter at this.

From there it was an easy transition to the tall stories that
were circulating of Archer's apparition being seen in Newmarket.
Greatly to my amazement, Machell announced that he had seen
it himself. I wouldn't have bet a brass farthing on that wily old
cynic seeing a ghost, yet he was serious. "I can't get over the poor
fellow's death," he told me. "We had a falling out, I regret to say,
shortly before he shot himself. He told me to back something in
the Seller at Newmarket and it was beaten a head by Wood. Then
I heard from a lady friend in the stand that Archer had told her
to put her money on Wood. I'd had a dreadful week and I was
foolish enough to believe her. When I met Fred in the paddock,
I cut him. Turned my back on the fellow who rode more winners
for me than any other. On the word of a garrulous woman. How
I wish I could turn back the clock! It was the last time I saw him
. . . alive."

I said with due seriousness, "But you believe you've seen him
in spirit form?"

"Last Friday night, sir. I was lying awake—and I'll swear on the
Good Book that I was wide awake—when I saw Archer standing
beside my bed. He was in his jockey's rig, though I can't tell you

whose colors they were. I watched him for a few minutes, and I don't know whether I spoke or not. After a time, he put out his hand and patted me gently on the shoulder, and the action, strange to say, so soothed me that I went to sleep and have slept all right ever since."

I asked how much he'd drunk the previous evening, but he wouldn't be budged. He was certain that Archer's spirit was abroad in Newmarket, attending to unfinished business. Late one evening, a policeman had observed a strange luminous glow in Falmouth House, which had been empty and locked since the inquest. When he had investigated, nobody was inside. Moreover, several of the locals claimed to have seen the ghost on the Heath after midnight, racing over the Cambridgeshire course. Poor Fred was assumed to be still trying to win the race he had never managed to win when he was alive, though, as I pointed out, with no visible opposition it was a walkover, and the great jockey wouldn't have cared for that.

I retired late, and the skeptical reader will be satisfied to hear that I received no visitor during the night, mortal or immortal.

Next morning I started on what was to prove the crucial stage of my investigation. I first visited Heath House, the training establishment where Archer had been apprenticed to the redoubtable Mat Dawson at the age of eleven. The present manager was Mat's nephew, George, whom I had come to see because he was an executor of Archer's will. My purpose: to discover whether there was evidence in the accounts to support Woodburn's story of a bribe of £200.

I was received with due courtesy (a pleasant change after my experiences in Beverley) and shown into the drawing room, which was a veritable museum of the Turf, with Archer prominently represented in two oil paintings and an equine statuette by Edgar Boehm, the sculptor and blackmailer to the Queen. The first punch of the festive season had been prepared for me, and I formed the impression that young Dawson was expecting social conversation. If so, I disappointed him. I pressed my inquiries without preamble.

"I wish I could help, sir," he responded to my question, "and you are welcome to examine the accounts, such as they are."

"That doesn't sound too promising."

"Truth to tell, it's extremely difficult to pin down particular items of spending. Fred made most of his transactions in cash. He was betting heavily toward the end of his life, and he withdrew the money in hefty amounts of up to a thousand at the beginning of each month."

"That doesn't sound like the Tin Man," I commented.

"He earned a fortune and spent it, sir, whatever his reputation for penny-pinching. The ledgers confirm it. Would you care to examine them now?"

Accountancy is as foreign as Timbuctoo to me, so I told him precisely what I was searching for. He ran a finger down one of the columns. Just as I feared, it was impossible to trace the £200 allegedly paid to Woodburn. "Were these accounts kept by Captain Buckfast?" I asked.

"Yes, sir."

"Are they correct?"

"They balance, if that's what you mean, sir."

"But you were saying that up to a thousand a month in cash was withdrawn."

"The entries are here, sir, if you care to look."

"So it's possible that the two hundred pounds we are looking for was actually paid to Mr. Woodburn and didn't appear in the books."

He thought it proper to come to Charlie's defense. "I'm sure Captain Buckfast did all in his power to convince Fred of the need to be more businesslike, but he was hamstrung. For Fred, racing was the only thing that counted after his wife, Helen, died."

"Not quite the only thing," I observed.

"What do you mean, sir?"

"I mean, a thousand a month. Where did it all go—on women?"

The directness of my question shocked him. The family's reputation had to be defended. "Emphatically not, sir. I'm afraid he must have been gambling more heavily than any of us realized."

"And losing?"

"I can't think where else it went." Dawson closed the book.

This wasn't the time to air my theories. I said, "There's another matter I wish to raise. When you were going through Archer's papers, did you come across any documents or drafts of documents suggesting a possible financial arrangement with another party?"

"What do you have in mind, sir?"

"A marriage settlement, perhaps?"

I didn't have the gratification of another shocked response. He asked quite calmly, "Does this relate to the rumor that Fred was planning to marry a certain Dowager Duchess?"

"It could—if there's any evidence."

"I haven't seen it, sir."

Not much point in pressing him further on that subject. "Possibly you came across something else: some indication of a partnership that was mooted with Mr. George Alexander Baird."

"The Squire?" He looked a sight more shocked at a connection with the Squire than with Carrie Montrose. "The gentleman has a sulfurous reputation, I hear."

"Not without foundation," I informed him.

"I can't recall seeing anything about this in the personal papers."

"Possibly not," I said, and added firmly, "I should like to look through them myself."

"I'm sure we can arrange it. They're in a writing desk in Fred's old home, Falmouth House."

"I know the place."

"Yes, sir. I'm afraid it's locked and shuttered at present. We were worried about souvenir hunters."

"Do you have the key?"

"His valet has it: a man by the name of Sarjent."

I remembered Sarjent, the tall young man who'd given evidence at the inquest and afterward made a good job of brushing my hat and overcoat.

"Where can I find him?"

"He should be over there this afternoon, sir. He attends to the horses."

He offered to drive me back to the Jockey Club, but I elected to walk the short distance. It was a crisp December morning, and I don't often have the opportunity to exercise on public roads, so I made the most of my opportunity, missing only my dog Peter for company.

After a reviving lunch I set off on foot again, this time in the direction of Falmouth House. In a matter of minutes, along the Ely Road I spotted the gabled front to my left about three quarters of a mile out of the town. Recalling my previous visit to the house and all that had happened since, I found it difficult to credit that only five weeks had passed.

I walked up the gravel drive toward the unhappy house with its drawn curtains, wondering if it would ever be occupied again. I wouldn't care to live in it myself.

I was making my way around the side and through the kitchen garden toward the stable when a shout of "Oi!" caused me to stop.

He was only a gardener who had emerged from around the wall, and I was prepared to overlook his want of manners, but for some unfathomable reason the sight of him rang alarm bells in my head. He wasn't particularly grotesque. His features meant nothing to me. I could only suppose that his physique and bearing—the disproportionate breadth of his shoulders on a squat body—reminded me of someone obnoxious from my past. I've met so many obnoxious people that this wasn't much help, except that few of them, if any, were gardeners.

He called out, "What do you want?" His voice was so uncouth that I was certain I'd have recognized it if I'd heard it before, but it made no connection in my memory.

I asked for Sarjent, and he pointed me to the building I had been approaching before he stopped me.

It was a four-stalled stable containing a couple of hunters, a carriage horse and Archer's gray hack. A voice hailed me from the saddle room and I found Sarjent the valet there, reclining in a chair balanced on its back legs, smoking a cigar, his long legs draped over the bench on which the harness was meant to be polished.

At my entrance, he practically fell off the chair. Unlike the gardener, he knew me at once, so I capitalized on his state of fright by remarking, "Is this how you serve your ex-master now?"

He dropped the cigar and crushed it with his heel, in the same movement coming to attention like a guardsman. He had the height for the guards, too.

Sniffing the fumes, I inquired, "How can a man of your class afford to smoke Havanas? Did you filch it from the house?"

This stung him into a response. He protested forcibly, "I wouldn't touch Mr. Archer's things. I bought them myself from the tobacconist in the High Street. You can ask him if you want."

I'd been quite favorably impressed by him on our previous meeting. I said cuttingly, "If you wish to address me, kindly have the good manners to do it properly. I've spoken to Mr. Dawson, the executor, and now I'd like to see inside the house."

"Certainly, Your Majesty."

"*Sir* will suffice."

As we crossed the kitchen garden, I looked for the oaf who had first bellowed at me, but he hadn't remained in view. I asked Sarjent, "The gardener I saw, how long was he in Mr. Archer's employ?"

"Parker, sir? Five or six years at least."

"What will happen to him now?"

"He's buying a public house in Cambridge, sir."

"I hope he doesn't shout at the customers."

The experience of entering Archer's darkened house after the stories I'd heard unnerved me somewhat. It smelled musty. A grandfather clock stood silent in the hall. Sarjent showed me into the drawing room where the inquest had been held. He pulled aside the curtains and opened the writing desk for me.

"Would you prefer to be left alone, sir?"

In a haunted house? Perish the thought!

"No," I said as casually as I was able, "you may remain. Have you found a new position yet?"

"I'm proposing to take a year off, sir, to visit my brother in New Zealand."

"You have saved some money, then?"

"Yes, sir."

"Mr. Archer was generous to his staff?"

"I always found him so, sir."

I applied myself to the task of searching through the papers, which were in a fearful mess. I remarked on it to Sarjent, and he said, "They were tidy until yesterday, sir."

"What happened yesterday?"

"Mr. Baird went through them."

I gave him an appalled stare. "The Squire? What was *he* doing here?"

"Looking for something that belonged to him, as I understand it, sir."

"The devil he was!" said I. "Did he find it?"

"I've no idea, sir."

I was manifestly wasting my time if the Squire had got here first. I thrust the papers back into the box and closed it. "Can any Tom, Dick and Harry come in here and search through Archer's private papers?"

It was a rhetorical question, and he had the sense not to answer, though I thought I detected the beginning of a smile at the corners of his mouth.

Determined to put this visit to some advantage, I asked, "How well did you know Captain Buckfast?"

"He was often at the house, sir. He looked after Mr. Archer's correspondence and that."

"So he had occasion to speak to you?"

"He paid us our wages."

"I believe you were asked by the police to identify his body."

"Someone from the house had to do it, sir. The Captain had no family that we ever heard of. So Parker and I performed the melancholy duty."

"Parker the gardener?" I made an attempt to lighten the conversation, which looks callous written down but wasn't intended to be. "A bit of a change from pruning and weeding. Have you heard anything from the police since then?"

"Some detectives were here yesterday, sir."

"Have they interviewed Mr. Abington Baird?"

"This morning, I heard, sir. He was taken into town to answer questions from a titled gentleman who came down special from Scotland Yard."

I don't mind admitting that I took a certain malicious pleasure at the notion of Sir Charles Warren catching up with the Squire.

There was one more important matter to deal with. I remarked, "Doubtless you've heard of the stories that Archer's ghost has been seen."

Sarjent said, "I don't believe them, sir," but I'd observed a muscle at the side of his jaw quivering at the question. That's the sort of thing a detective of my caliber doesn't miss.

"You've noticed nothing here?" I pressed. "There was a report of lights being seen at night."

"I'm never here at night, sir."

"Is anybody?"

"The place is empty and locked up."

"Good thing too," I commented. "It's eerie enough by daylight. I declare it's colder inside than out. Like a tomb. I suppose you wouldn't know where Archer kept his whiskey bottle?"

Sarjent was off like a ticket-of-leaver.

The whiskey was simply a pretext on my part. The few moments I had alone in the room enabled me to cross to the window and unfasten the latch so that it would be possible to open it from outside. When Sarjent returned, I had resumed my position in front of the fireplace.

Warmer and wiser, I returned to the Jockey Club.

But whither next?

First, a hot bath.

Reader, I invite you to join me.

CHAPTER 20

A h, the blissful moment of immersion when the goose pimples go under. I'm a firm believer in the bathtub's restorative powers. Indeed I'd go further. A leisurely soaking clarifies the mind. It may even result in an inspiration. One of the few things worth remembering from an education in the classics is the story of Archimedes. I've forgotten precisely what it was he discovered in his bath, but the truth of the experience reaches down the ages. You relax in the tub, letting the water creep exquisitely over your belly. Suddenly inspiration strikes.

Would you care to try it? I won't insist that you read this chapter in the bath (though it won't come amiss if you are careful to keep the book dry). I won't insist that you read it at all unless you are interested in unmasking the murderess, or murderer, or murderers (to give nothing away except precedence to the fair sex).

What follows is the process of reasoning that led me to cry "Eureka!" when I seized on the truth of the mystery. Kindly understand that I offer this from serious motives and I trust that you will accept it in the same spirit. I have no intention of treating three dreadful deaths as a parlor game. It pleases me to hope that the science of criminology will ultimately profit from my experiences as a detective.

Let us lie back, literally or figuratively, according to circumstance, and consider the essential facts of the case as I did that crucial afternoon in my bathroom in the Jockey Club.

Three people have died violently (I told myself). Fred Archer, by
his own hand; Charlie Buckfast, beaten unconscious and drowned
by two masked men; and Myrtle Bliss, shot through the head by
an unknown intruder.

The deaths of Buckfast and Myrtle occurred after they agreed
to help me investigate Archer's suicide. Therefore it appears that
the key to the mystery is Archer's death. Find the reason for that,
and I may well discover why the others were murdered.

Are we comfortable with that? Shall I run in a little more hot
water?

The verdict of the inquest that Archer's mind was unhinged
by typhoid must be extremely dubious. It rests on flimsy medical
evidence. I'm no doctor, but I speak from personal experience of
the disease, and I have the support of the *British Medical Journal*
that "the fact that acute delirium with delusions, usually of a suicidal character, sometimes comes on during the early stage, will
be new to many." Personally I doubt whether the poor fellow was
suffering anything worse than a feverish chill induced by wearing
insufficient clothes on the racecourse. There was no announcement that typhoid was suspected until he died, and on that day his
temperature was normal, he was able to hold rational conversations
and in the words of several witnesses, including his own doctor,
he was better. It seems likely that the doctors settled on typhoid
for the sake of Archer's family and his reputation. They wished
to exclude the possibility that he killed himself coldly and sanely.

Let us take the more likely supposition that Archer's mind was
sound, and his suicide deliberate. What could have provoked such
a desperate act?

The most obvious cause of suicide is despair. Archer's life had
twice been blighted by death in the last three years: first, the baby
son who lived only a few hours in January 1884; and then, in
November of the same year, his wife, Helen Rose, after giving birth
to their daughter. The death of a child in infancy is distressing but
by no means unusual, as Alix and I can testify. The loss of a wife in
childbirth is not uncommon, either, though harder to bear, I am
sure. Everyone agrees that Archer was deeply affected. To occupy
and distract him after the tragedy, he visited America with Charlie
Buckfast for company. When he returned, his appetite for racing
was undiminished. As a jockey, he was better than ever, winning

four of the five classics in 1885. This year he added his fifth Derby and his sixth St. Leger. Two years passed since his wife's death, so the worst was behind him. He had a two-year-old daughter to live for, and the prospect of many more years as champion jockey.

No, I can't believe that he shot himself out of grief.

On the contrary, he was considering getting married again. Carrie Montrose admitted to me that she had "decided to marry him." He must have given it serious thought because he asked Captain Machell if marriage to a duchess would make him a duke. Fred was twenty-nine years of age; Carrie Montrose, sixty-eight. She is, however, a surpassingly energetic sixty-eight and extremely rich, the owner of the largest stud of thoroughbreds in the kingdom.

Better turn off the hot water now, because we've got to the Cambridgeshire, and that's sure to raise the temperature no end.

Archer rode Carrie's horse, St. Mirin, in the big race and let the world know that he expected to win. According to young Woodburn, a bribe was paid to stop the favorite and leave St. Mirin to take the palm. The plan was foiled when St. Mirin was beaten on the post by an outsider.

My inquiries revealed that the *de facto* owner of the winning horse was the Squire, and that's enough to make anyone smell a rat. The probability that he is implicated in these crimes is inescapable.

Let's consider the three fatalities. Two weeks after the Cambrigeshire, Archer shot himself after uttering those mysterious last words, "Are they coming?" This apparently meaningless question was cited at the inquest as evidence of delirium. I disagree. The patient was better. He was talking rationally to his friends during the morning. According to his sister, his manner was quite normal up to the moment of the fatal incident.

Those dying words cannot be ignored. They may well hold the key to the mystery.

While we're still with Archer I'd like to dispose of another canard. I've heard it suggested that his suicide was due in some obscure way to the constant efforts he was obliged to make to reduce his weight. Certainly he was below weight for a man his size, but so are countless other jockeys. As professional sportsmen they accept the obligations of the job. Lack of food may have made him irritable, but it is most unlikely to have unhinged his mind.

Where else shall I look for an explanation? Was it financial? He was spending heavily in the last months of his life, making large withdrawals of cash, allegedly for betting. He left a smaller estate than was generally anticipated, except by Charlie Buckfast, who managed Archer's business affairs and correctly estimated that the figure would be as low as £60,000. When all's said and done, sixty thou is more than most men earn in a lifetime. Where's the sense in shooting yourself if you've still got a fortune to your name?

The second fatality we must consider was the murder of Charlie Buckfast, which came perilously close to being a double murder. You'll recall that I sent Charlie to Newmarket to keep watch on the Squire. When he got back, he told me that he'd overheard the Squire speak of pressing Archer into a partnership. Acting on this information, he'd broken into Bedford Lodge to look for evidence. The two men he surprised had followed him to London. Two men answering to the same description made their murderous attack on Charlie and myself outside Carrie Montrose's house. Charlie was beaten unconscious and thrown into the Thames and his body was later recovered and identified. I was lucky to escape with my life. As a result, my suspicions of the Squire amounted almost to certainty of his guilt.

And the Squire is linked with the third death, that of Myrtle Bliss.

Myrtle was the Squire's latest plaything. On the night of the Cambridgeshire, he went to London and celebrated his win with her. Buckfast and I subsequently visited the music hall where she was performing. I was still pursuing my investigations when the Squire interrupted us in Myrtle's room in Mile End Road. Later, she wrote offering to assist me. After Charlie's untimely death, I saw her a second time and accepted her offer for help. She went to Newmarket as the Squire's guest, and as my observer. I arranged to meet her in London the following week. To my horror, I discovered her dead in her dressing room.

Tragically bereft of my two assistants, I have since pursued my inquiries in isolation. Naturally, I concentrated on the Squire, because all the evidence suggests that the murders were carried out on his orders. Extract a confession from him, I decided, and he'll readily identify the thugs who carried out his bloody work.

Unfortunately, he outflanked me at Brantingham Thorpe. What is more, he produced Woodburn, and the whole case was turned on its head. I was at first reluctant to believe Woodburn's story that he had accepted a bribe to stop the favorite. If, as he admitted, he was open to bribery, what was to stop the Squire from bribing him to tell me a pack of lies?

Yet Woodburn's admission pleased nobody. The Squire had previously insisted to me that Archer was honest. He didn't expect to hear from Woodburn that a bribe of £200 had been paid to stop the favorite. And I didn't expect to hear that Charlie Buckfast had handed over the money.

Is it conceivable that Woodburn was telling the truth? His confession was like a wink from a bishop's wife: so unlikely that I'd be a fool to ignore it. What are the implications?

For one thing, it means that the Cambridgeshire result must have shocked Archer more than any of us realized, for he had acted dishonestly to guarantee a win for St. Mirin, only to be beaten by a 25-1 outsider. Why take such a risk at the peak of his fame? Was it because his gambling had taken such a grip that he put it before his reputation? Or was it because he heard wedding bells? Was it to please St. Mirin's owner, Carrie Montrose?

Another thing Woodburn's story means, if true, is that Charlie Buckfast held his information back when he and I talked of the Cambridgeshire, and this I find difficult to swallow. True, I had no cause to ask him about an illegal transaction, for I didn't remotely entertain such a notion. But in all our discussions, he never hinted at the possibility.

If Woodburn was lying about the bribery, I can't fathom why. He had nothing to gain by admitting it. He could have denied it, spoken the words that the Squire had wanted to hear and kept his own reputation clean.

Bertie, I think as I straighten my legs and push myself upright, there's something fundamentally wrong with all this. A false assumption somewhere.

And then I shout, "Eureka!"

Do I hear you shout the same, dear reader? Will you commit yourself? Have you reached your conclusion yet?

In that case, let us reach for a towel and climb out, for I almost hear poor Archer's dying words.

"Are they coming?"

CHAPTER 21

Before taking my bath, I had instructed my valet to put out a choice of evening wear that may surprise you: that is to say, the Norfolk jacket, knickerbockers and leggings I generally wear for shooting. It didn't surprise Massie, my valet. He is a dour Highlander who has looked after my wardrobe for so long that he is incapable of being surprised by anything. After high tea in my rooms, I left the Jockey Club soon after dark, having donned an overcoat and deerstalker cap. I believe in dressing to suit the occasion, and this occasion was a ghost hunt.

I had resolved to lay the ghost of Frederick James Archer.

According to the tales being bandied about in the Jockey Club, Archer's restless spirit was quite liable to materialize at one's bedside, but inconveniently couldn't be commanded to make an appearance, so if you wanted a sighting, you were advised to go out on the heath by night and wait for the drumming of spectral hooves. I had a better plan. I was going to call on the late Mr. Archer at his home in Falmouth House, where I had last seen him lying in his coffin, and where the local policeman had reported seeing that "luminous glow."

In my overcoat pocket was the small silver revolver I had acquired from Dougall, my gunsmith, a few years ago at a time when the anarchists were doing their damnedest to bag all the royalty in Europe. No, I don't need telling that a bullet would pass clean through a legitimate ghost; I still felt the need of a loaded revolver, and you may draw your own conclusions from that.

The crisp evening air was a splendid antidote to morbid thoughts. "Ghoulies and ghosties and long-leggedy beasties and things that go bump in the night" hold more terrors indoors, in the shadows cast across a sitting room by a log fire, than out in the lamplight of Newmarket High Street—or so I told myself. In front of the Rutland Arms at the eastern end the waits were giving a brassy rendering of "The First Noel." If anything was creeping up on me, it was the festive season. The shops were full of Christmas cards, and I hadn't addressed a single one as yet. Did you know that the custom of sending the wretched things was started by my dear papa of blessed memory? He still has the most insidious ways of troubling my conscience.

I put the lights of Newmarket behind me and marched intrepidly up the Ely road in the direction of Falmouth House. I'd chosen to foot it because I didn't want carriage wheels announcing my arrival. Ten minutes along that deserted road my confident mood was dented a little by a sign pointing the way to Phantom House. What on earth possesses people to choose such a grisly name for their place of abode? Almost immediately I disturbed a pheasant roosting in the hedgerow, and I don't know which of us gave the louder screech. Worse, I dropped my hip flask and spilled good whiskey on the road.

The house that Archer had built came into view across open ground on my left, the opposite side of the road from the Bedford Lodge estate. Moonlight gleamed on the white barge boards under the gables with an intensity that didn't help my state of mind. However, I drained the dregs of my flask and passed through the gate, whereupon my boots on the gravel sounded like the changing of the guard, so I stepped off the drive at once and took the silent route across the lawn tennis court toward the south side of the house.

If there was anything of a supernatural character inside, it wasn't declaring its presence yet. The curtains were drawn at all the windows, and no radiance showed from within, whether of spectral origin or by courtesy of the gas company.

Emboldened, I approached the drawing room window that I had earlier unfastened, took a grip on the lower frame and eased it up a fraction to satisfy myself that it would still move. It responded readily, so I pushed it up fully, put a leg over the sill and climbed in.

Without wishing to brag, I can state confidently that I have as much experience of creeping around country houses at night as any housebreaker you could name. I picked my way through that, room without disturbing a single ornament. At the door I turned the handle and retained my grip on it until I'd confirmed that the hall was unoccupied.

Where do you start looking for a ghost? Upstairs or down? In the attic or the cellar? I chose the latter.

I can usually be relied upon to remember where the champagne is kept. You never know when these God-given talents will be needed. The cellar door was located in the scullery. In the kitchen I was pleased to discover a candle on the dresser. A smoker is never without his matches, so I put a flame to the wick, opened the cellar door and started down the stone steps with the light flickering fitfully in the draft.

A few steps down, the flame died. I felt for another match and prepared to strike it. Then I paused.

Precisely why, I cannot explain, but I became convinced that I was not alone in the cellar. I can't say that I heard anything, or apprehended it with any of my faculties, unless one believes in a sixth sense.

Better remain in the dark, I thought. Why reveal myself to whoever or whatever is down there? I returned the matches to my pocket, set down the candle and withdrew my revolver. At the same time I pressed my back against the wall and listened.

Nothing.

I waited perhaps half a minute before feeling my way down two more steps, staring into a prospect as black as the Earl of Hell's riding boots.

Then something moved in the depth of the cellar. A slight, but perceptible, sound.

I said at once, "Who's there?"

No answer. Possibly I'd heard a rat; possibly not. With the stealth of one who has tracked the leopard in his time, I crept down the remaining steps to the floor. I probed the darkness with my free hand, feeling for the nearest wine rack. Having located it, I edged along the length of the rack with my fingertips touching the bottles. I wanted to get right away from the place where I'd spoken those two words.

From what I could recall of my previous visit to the cellar with Charlie Buckfast, the racks were in seven parallel rows extending at least sixty feet from end to end. Moreover, there were barrels and other containers stacked along the sides.

I reached the last bottle of the row. My hand probed the darkness and made no contact, but my foot struck against something that scraped the stone floor inconveniently loudly.

I ducked low and held my breath.

The thing I had kicked had sounded remarkably like a piece of crockery, a plate or a saucer, an unlikely object to find on the floor of Archer's wine cellar, which had impressed me as tidy to the point of fussiness when I had last seen it. Even more unlikely was the loaf of bread that my free hand came to rest on: unmistakably a loaf, fresh, crusty and recently cut. The sliced end was soft and springy to the touch.

I had no opportunity to dwell on the significance of this discovery because something was happening at the far end of the cellar. From my position I could make out a faint radiance that threw the joists overhead into relief. It flickered and faded and then intensified.

Oh, Gemini! It was moving toward me between the racks!

If there was a moment when my nerve was put to the test, this was it. I crouched and waited, gripping my gun. I didn't have a clear view. I caught glimpses in the intervals between the bottles. The radiance became brighter, flitting along the row as if it had no substance.

The thing was almost upon me when I fired a shot.

It was meant for a warning shot, and it startled me if nothing else, for I succeeded in shattering several bottles of Archer's champagne, creating a regular fountain of froth and glass.

The light sheered away, revealing to me that its source was nothing more supernatural than a common bull's-eye lantern.

Whoever was holding the lantern took to his heels with a clatter of shoe leather that was most unsuggestive of the spirit world. I set off in pursuit, for he was clearly making for the door. I shouted to him to stop, but he raced up the steps, pausing only to hurl the lantern in my direction before he went through the door and slammed it. Then I heard the key being turned.

I groped my way up the steps and hurled myself at the door, succeeding in confirming how solidly the house had been constructed. My entire physique was numbed by the impact. There was a moment when the air was blue before I thought of using the revolver. I stood back and fired twice at the lock and then gave it an almighty kick that burst through the mortise.

Now where was my quarry? The moonlit interior of the kitchen was as bright as day to my eyes after the cellar. Ahead, the door to the hall swung back on its hinge, informing me that someone had just gone through. I gave chase, caught a glimpse of a running figure, fired a shot over his head and by a happy accident brought down a stag's stuffed head that was mounted over the front door. The fellow instinctively stopped in his tracks as it dropped toward him. Another yard and he certainly would have been brained.

The shock petrified him. He could barely raise his hands when I ordered him to turn around and face me. He was suddenly very pathetic. He was only a pint-sized fellow.

When he saw who I was, he cried out, "God Almighty!"

He was the Squire.

I can't begin to describe how enraged I became at the sight of him. My temper is notorious, but my feelings exceeded anything in my experience. I don't know how I prevented myself from emptying the chambers of my revolver into him.

He was terrified that I would do it. He blathered cravenly for an interval while I contrived to find words adequate to this moment. I had better explain the reason for my outrage, or you may have leapt to the wrong conclusion. The Squire wasn't the murderer. I'd stake Marlborough House to a tenement that he wasn't the murderer. He was a spoiler, a saboteur, a congenital nuisance who had given me a fright, wasted precious time and in all probability allowed the real killer to escape.

Finally I demanded, "What the devil are you doing here?"

"Trying to find out the truth about Archer . . . Your Royal Highness."

"How did you get in?"

"Through the front door. I made an impression of the key when I borrowed it yesterday." He started bleating out some sort of justification: "I'm being persecuted by the police, you know. Sir Charles Warren wants to pin everything on me. The murders, Archer's suicide. What sort of monster do they think I am?

I said, "That's a matter of supreme indifference to me, Baird."

He said, "For pity's sake, sir, I came in here to trap the murderer."

"That much I'm willing to believe," I commented. "There was someone in the cellar, and not many hours ago."

"You found the bread?"

I said with contempt for such a crude assumption, "I had already deduced it." I let him brood on that while I contrived a way of salvaging something from this debacle. If nothing else, I'm used to being in tight corners. And getting out of them. "Against all the evidence, I'm going to have to trust you, Baird," I resumed. "I know where to find the murderer."

"You do?" he whispered.

". . . but I require your help."

"I give it, sir. Unreservedly. Which way do we go?"

"I shall go there alone."

"Is that safe?"

"Far from it, but there are other things to attend to, and I shall have to rely on you."

"Rest assured, sir."

What lip! Imagine anyone resting assured upon the Squire's reliability. However, I had no other choice.

He asked, "Where is it? Where will you go?"

"To Sefton Lodge," I answered. "The residence of the Dowager Duchess of Montrose."

CHAPTER 22

So . . . Carrie Montrose.

My decision to visit the lady and confront her with the truth may strike certain clever readers of mine as obvious and overdue; if you are among them, I doff my deerstalker to you and caution you not to be too complacent. The story isn't over yet.

The plodding majority (God bless you) will want to know what the deuce I was up to. If so, kindly read on.

Sefton Lodge is on the Bury Road, a gray mansion in spacious grounds on the edge of the Heath, across the road from Bedford Lodge, the Squire's headquarters. Next door is a church built by the Duchess as a mausoleum to William Stirling-Crawfurd, her second husband. She buried Craw in Cannes in 1883, and two years later had him disinterred and shipped all the way back to Newmarket to be her neighbor, which was commended in the sporting press as evidence of almost unexampled devotion (the other example being the Blue Room at Windsor, where my late papa's clothes are still laid out each evening with hot water and a fresh towel, twenty-five years after he passed on). The church, by the way, is known as St. Agnes, that being Carrie's middle name.

To save precious time after sending the Squire on his way, I left the road at the first opportunity and hiked across the Severals. The moon was on the wane, yet full enough to throw a pale luminosity over the frosted gallops. It was treacherous going, and I was glad to reach the Bury Road. When Sefton Lodge loomed into view on the right, there were lights at all the windows.

My knock was answered by the same housemaid who had cried "Jerusalem!" when I came dripping from the Thames at Cheyne Walk. I wondered if her knowledge of the Scriptures extended to anything else, but the reception I got this time was disappointing, to say the least. She gave me a cursory glance, turned and called over her shoulder, "It's all right, ma'am—it isn't him."

I can take spontaneous outbursts of awe from servants, but I'm damned if I'll let them ignore me, so I stepped closer to the light, removed my hat and told her cuttingly, "It will oblige me if you now inform your mistress that it *is* him."

She said, "Holy jumping mother of Moses!" and fled.

Unwilling to freeze on the doorstep, I stepped across the threshold into a marble-tiled, oak-paneled hall with a crystal chandelier above me and a staircase ahead. Almost at once Carrie Montrose appeared at the head of the stairs in a black costume glittering with jet. I'd expected to surprise her, but I hadn't pictured it as a scene from a melodrama. She was uncommonly agitated, muttering and making extravagant gestures with her arms. She started swaying so dangerously that I expected her to fall. Instinctively, I moved to the foot of the stairs and stretched out my arms to her.

She clutched the banister rail and called down to me, "Bertie, any night but this!"

I told her with quiet authority, "Duchess, I am waiting to be received."

She shook her head. "It isn't convenient."

I was stung into a sharp rebuke: "Don't be idiotic. Nobody speaks to me like that. I command you to step downstairs at once, or I shall come up to you."

She rolled her eyes most oddly and said, "That's music to my ears, darling—but it cannot be tonight!"

I said with ice, "You misunderstand me. I have come here to question you."

"The answer must be no."

I put my foot on the first stair and she caught her breath in alarm and said, "Don't!"

"Will you come down, then?"

"Impossible."

"Duchess," I said with an effort to be reasonable against all the odds, "you have no choice."

After some hesitation she asked, "Will you give me a moment?"

"If it is brief."

"Kindly wait in the drawing room, then."

I stepped into a room of gracious proportions decorated in pink, with oval panels depicting hunting scenes. Spy cartoons of jockeys were ranged over the fireplace, Archer predictably at the center. To one side was the *Vanity Fair* cartoon by Lib of Newmarket in 1885, with all the elite of the Turf grouped around a figure, supposedly me, though a poor likeness in my opinion. Carrie was depicted to the right of me in her post boy hat and sealskin coat, and above us all was Archer, mounted, I think, on Ormonde.

While I was still identifying the figures, Carrie's voice, close behind me, boomed as if through a speaking trumpet, "I shall stand here in the open doorway."

I turned and asked, "Who else are you expecting?"

"Who else?" Without answering the question she put her hand to her hair and made a great performance of rearranging the russet curls that hung over her ears. The spectacle of Carrie Montrose flustered was novel in my experience. She was like a wasp at a window. She said, "What are you suggesting?"

"Come now, you heard what the maid said when she opened the door to me."

"Ah." She clasped her hands to her throat. "Bertie, I'm in a terrible state."

"That is obvious, Duchess." I gave her a penetrating look. "Is this, by any chance, connected with Archer?"

She nodded about six times. "He's been seen, you know—seen by reliable witnesses. Lord Rossmore. And Machell. Machell is a pigheaded person with no manners at all, but he's nobody's fool."

I said with contempt, "You don't believe in ghosts, do you?"

In response, she started reciting in a voice of doom some doggerel that I remembered having seen in the *Newmarket Journal:*

> "Across the heath, along the course,
> 'Tis said that now on phantom horse,
> The greatest jockey of our days,
> Rides nightly in the moonlight's rays."

I commented, leaving no doubt that I was unimpressed, "I always took you for a down-to-earth sort."

She said dramatically, "If Fred is manifesting himself in Newmarket, he'll come to me. Sooner or later he'll come. When you knocked, I thought it was he."

"He won't need to knock," I pointed out. "He can float through the wall."

She said, "Don't mock the dead, Bertie."

I told her reassuringly, "There's no need to be afraid of ghosts."

"I'm not afraid!" she piped on a note of high indignation. "I want to catch the blighter and ask him why he jilted me."

She was serious too. "Since you're so anxious to see him," I said with calculation, "why not go out on the heath? He may be riding there now."

Carrie shook her head. "I can't leave the house." She pointed her finger at the ceiling, at the same time twisting her features into a look of tortured significance.

Recalling Machell's story of the young man with a broken leg, I remarked in a carrying voice, "I was sorry to hear about the accident to your guest."

She said offhandedly, "Gilbert? He's in no pain. They gave him morphine and he'll sleep for hours."

The remark confirmed what I fully expected to hear: that the cause of her agitated manner had an altogether different origin. I said, "When we last met, I asked you about the Cambridgeshire; in particular, the rumor that Archer paid a bribe to Woodburn. You denied it emphatically."

She said in a distracted voice, "Did I?"

I continued, "Last weekend, I spoke to Woodburn. To my surprise, he confessed that the rumor is true. He said he was paid two hundred pounds by Captain Buckfast."

Carrie passed no comment.

I wasn't standing for evasions. I said, "Duchess, I'm bound to ask whether you are able to confirm this shameful transaction."

Her response to this topped everything, for she nodded emphatically and at the same time said, "Of course I can't confirm it. I knew nothing about a bribe."

"So you deny it?"

She answered, "Emphatically," and at the same time shook her head!

This was strongly reminiscent of that old parlor game called the Rule of Contrary, when the players are given instructions and expected to perform the very opposite action. However, Carrie and I were playing a more dangerous game, and the forfeit could even be death. I said in as steady a voice as I could sustain, "People have been murdered, Duchess. Are you, or are you not, prepared to help me?"

She nodded her head three times and said, "I'm unable to throw any light on the matter. Haven't I made that clear?"

I said, "If you won't speak to me, I'm afraid I shall have to ask the police to question you."

This, as I had expected, alarmed her even more, for she vigorously shook her head and flapped her hands to discourage me.

The reason for the dumb show was by now abundantly clear to me. I lifted my eyebrows inquiringly and pointed at the ceiling, and Carrie responded by enthusiastic nods of the head.

I glanced at the ormolu clock on the mantel. I was sensitive to her message that she wanted me to remain, whatever she'd said to the contrary. Of course I had no intention of leaving yet. I just hoped to God I could rely on the Squire to play his part in the plan.

I said, "Won't you come away from the door and be seated? I don't insist that you stand in my presence. Ladies look better on chairs."

Carrie gave me a piercing look and answered, "That will not be possible." Without pausing for breath she launched into a diatribe about the position of women in society and her lifelong fight to assert her independence. Apparently she wore plaid trousers for hunting in the 1840s, years before Mrs. Bloomer's fashion was taken up. What this had to do with the matter I had come to investigate was far from clear, but I was content to let her continue as long as possible.

What happened next will strain your credulity, I am certain. As I live and die, it is true. At some stage, I stopped listening to Carrie. The idea of ladies in trousers doesn't appeal to me in the least, and my ears had picked up another sound. I wasn't sure whether it was autosuggestion, and I strained to listen more acutely, because it seemed to me that I'd heard the drumming of hooves on turf, and it came from the direction of the heath.

Carrie heard it, too, for she interrupted the oration and asked, "What was that?"

"Something in the fire," I told her to avert the jitters.

She said, "It sounded like a rider to me."

"You're imagining it. Please go on. Did you say tartan trousers? How very diverting!"

Although she resumed, she might have saved her breath, for I didn't listen to another word of it. My heart had doubled its beat and I had to hold down my knees to stop them from shaking. Archer was out there galloping his phantom steed. He had gone by once, and now he was returning.

Carrie stopped. We could both hear the beating hooves now, and they were coming closer, closer. The rhythm slowed from a gallop, to a canter, to a trot.

We stared at each other.

A scream rang through the house. Carrie's maid came clattering from the servants' quarters.

"God save us, ma'am, it's him—the ghost! I know it's him!"

"Be quiet, girl!" Carrie rebuked her. "His Royal Highness will deal with it."

His Royal Highness was already behind the sofa. I had no quarrel with Archer; in fact, we'd got on tolerably well, but now that he was dead, I wasn't insisting on a reunion.

The maid whimpered, "He's in the garden."

To my considerable surprise, Carrie took this as encouragement. She gave the order, "Turn off the gas and draw back the curtains."

I was closest to the chandelier and I didn't mind plunging us into darkness if we were less visible from outside, but I wasn't so rash as to pull back the curtains. Carrie marched across the room and did that herself with one powerful sweep of the arm.

She said in a flat, trancelike voice, "There he is. He's wearing my colors and he's on St. Mirin."

Thinking she was mad, I ventured close enough to the window to check the truth of her statement, whereupon I learned what it means when the flesh creeps. Mine crept like an army of tortoises on the march.

Not thirty yards away on the frost-covered lawn, pale in the moonlight, was a mounted jockey I recognized as Archer. The style, the seat, was his alone, long legs almost straight in the stirrups, so that the feet were visible below the body of his mount; the rounded shoulders and the way of wearing the cap so that the peak jutted upward from his forehead.

Horse and rider were motionless and staring at the house.

"Lord be merciful unto me, a sinner," whispered the maid.

Carrie announced, "I'm going to him."

"No, ma'am!" the maid appealed to her. "Ma'am, it isn't safe!"

But Carrie was off like a lamplighter. For a heavyweight, she moved at exceptional speed across the room and into the hall. I heard the front door being opened before I started to follow. I wouldn't have put a foot outside the door alone, but when Carrie moved off to square her account with the ghost, I discovered that curiosity is the best antidote for a blue funk.

She hadn't even stopped to snatch up a coat. She charged across the hoarfrost in her evening gown, shouting, "Fred Archer, I want a word with you!"

Let's give credit to the horse; spectral it may have been, but the sight of the Dowager Duchess of Montrose bearing down on it must have been terrifying. It stood its ground until she was within a dozen yards, and then it reared slightly, whinnied and trotted away toward an evergreen plantation at the edge of the lawn, its rider allowing the retreat, yet turning his head to see if he was being pursued, which he was.

"Fred, I want to know why!" shouted Carrie.

As far as I was concerned, she was speaking for both of us. I padded after them, all fear dispersed—that is, until they turned behind the evergreens and I heard a scream from Carrie that rooted me in my tracks.

It was a full-bellowed shriek that stopped halfway through, choked off as if she had fainted.

Then I heard a voice say, "Someone pick the lady up, for heaven's sake."

There were people behind the holly bush.

I assumed they were people and not ghosts. I was less certain when a hat bobbed above the level of the foliage: a cocked hat of the sort worn by the late Duke of Wellington. For a petrifying instant I thought the Iron Duke had materialized to add his support to the haunting, doubtless to register a complaint about his damned statue. Then I saw the glint of a monocle, and I remembered Sir Charles Warren.

"You're perfectly safe now, Your Royal Highness," the commissioner told me as I stepped around the holly.

I stared at the spectacle behind the evergreen plantation. Three policemen in shirts and braces were on their knees attempting to revive Carrie Montrose, who was wrapped in their jackets. Another dozen or more with truncheons drawn were watching the house. And the "ghost" of Archer had dismounted and was tying the horse to a tree. He it was who had caused the Duchess to swoon, for he was not Fred Archer, but her archenemy, the Squire.

"You!" I said.

The Squire gave an insufferable smirk. "Did I take you in as well, sir? Not a bad likeness was it? I learned my riding from Fred and my build is similar, so I can give a fair imitation. The horse is a ringer for St. Mirin too."

I snorted my contempt and asked what on earth had justified such a pantomime. It certainly wasn't in my instructions.

He explained, "I alerted the police and brought them here as you ordered, sir. We surrounded the house and waited for a signal from you, but none came."

I said frigidly, "I didn't say I'd give one."

The Squire went on as if he were speaking for Sir Charles Warren and all the police, "As time went on, we became increasingly concerned for your safety. We couldn't send in the police while you were at risk, so we decided to draw you and the Duchess out of the house by some means. Nothing less than Archer's ghost would bring out the Duchess, so I devised this pantomime, as you describe it, and Sir Charles fell in with it. Saved both your lives, probably."

"The devil you did," said I. "We'll probably die of pneumonia."

At this juncture, Warren hissed in my ear, "Do you mind bending down, sir?"

"What?" I was starting to doubt my sanity, or theirs.

"We're about to storm the house," Warren explained.

"To arrest the murderer," said the Squire with damnable smugness, as if some of the credit belonged to him.

Willy-nilly, I found myself cooperating with Warren's request, sinking out of sight like a broadsided galleon.

"How many are in the house now to your knowledge, sir?" Warren inquired.

"To my knowledge? Three. The maid and a young man whose name is Gilbert. He has a broken leg and is sedated."

"And the third?"

"The murderer. I didn't see him. He was upstairs, I gathered from the Duchess."

There was a moan from Carrie. She was regaining consciousness. She said, "I'm innocent. He forced his way in and threatened to murder Gilbert. He was holding a gun at Gilbert's head."

"He still is, Your Grace," said Warren, causing the Duchess to relapse into unconsciousness.

Warren took out a whistle and blew it, and everyone except Carrie stood up and charged across the lawn toward the house. Policemen sprang up from behind walls and hedges all over the garden. A couple of shots were fired. I couldn't tell where they came from. I was keeping my head down.

I found myself in a crowd of policemen waiting by a window, which was presently pushed open by the Squire. "It's all right," he assured us. "He's still upstairs."

Fifteen or more of us clambered over the sill into the drawing room. Warren was already there by the door, directing his men. "Those with guns, step forward," he ordered, and several did.

Someone said to me, "You've got a shooter." He was right. I'd withdrawn it from my pocket as we raced toward the house.

"He's the Prince of Wales, mate," said someone else.

"He can pull a trigger," said the first.

His simple logic galvanized me. This was my moment, and I'd almost allowed it to go by default. The police would not have been here unless I had summoned them. My investigation was about to be brought to a triumphant conclusion, and by Jove I would take charge of it myself.

I ordered Warren to stand aside. He gaped, swallowed and obeyed.

I wish some painter of heroic subjects had been there to record the scene. Standing squarely at the head of the posse, I pointed my gun up the stairs. In a strong, clear voice I addressed my adversary, the killer I had cornered at last. "This is the Prince of Wales. I have twenty armed men down here. Put down your weapon and come downstairs with your arms raised."

We all watched the top of the stairs.

"Be sensible, man," Warren called up. He couldn't bear to keep his mouth shut and leave it to me.

A movement was audible upstairs, a chair being scraped back and something thudding on the floor. Footsteps crossed the landing.

"Keep the arms high," I ordered.

A figure appeared in view. One arm was held high. The other was limp at his side. If you thought all the ghosts in Newmarket had been laid to rest, you were mistaken.

We were looking at Charlie Buckfast.

CHAPTER 23

An awesome silence prevailed as Buckfast descended the stairs without a word and was handcuffed.

I heard the Squire whisper, "He should be dead." A moment later he added with more voice, "Dammit, his body was pulled out of the Thames. It was dressed in his clothes. It was identified."

"By his accomplices," I pointed out, making it plain that I thought any fool would have deduced as much. "Messrs. Sarjent and Parker, the valet and gardener at Falmouth House. I suggest you send someone to arrest them, Sir Charles."

"Sarjent and Parker—at once, sir!" responded the commissioner. He rounded on the luckless senior policeman in Newmarket and said, "Inspector, haven't you attended to this already?"

"Very suspicious characters," commented the Squire, transparently trying to recoup some respect. "Didn't care for them at all."

Of course he impressed no one.

"I suggest you take your prisoner away and ask him some pertinent questions," I advised Sir Charles. Everyone except me seemed incapable of thought or action; bemused, I suppose, by the sensational turn of events. Even Buckfast was staring at me as if I had turned into the genie of the lamp.

Sir Charles said, "Emphatically, Your Royal Highness." Then he cleared his throat, turned extremely pink and asked me in a subdued voice, "Would you care to accompany us to the station, sir?"

I gave him the Saxe-Coburg stare. "That wouldn't be seemly, Commissioner."

"I merely suggested it for selfish reasons: for the benefit of your indispensable advice, sir," he said, groveling.

The wretched fellow hadn't the faintest idea what to say to Buckfast.

I said, "Captain Buckfast, are you ready to do the honorable thing?"

"And confess?" said Buckfast. He drew back his shoulders in what amounted—unintentionally, I have no doubt—to a mockery of the regiment he had once served with distinction. "Yes, sir. I'll make a clean breast of it."

"To the commissioner?"

"Certainly."

I turned to Sir Charles Warren. "That being the case, Commissioner, I shall return to the Jockey Club for supper. If I feel so inclined, I may call at the police station at a later hour."

About 1 A.M., restored to my equable self by good Scotch broth, ptarmigan pie, broad beans and bacon, plum pudding and champagne, I was admitted to the interview room, a narrow, functional chamber with barred windows, whitewashed walls and a stone floor. I sat opposite the murderer Buckfast, with only a desk between us and one puny constable on duty.

The murderer Buckfast. It has a strange ring, hasn't it? The credit for his arrest and detention was mine alone, but I had mixed feelings about meeting him. Believe me, I could think of more agreeable ways of passing the small hours of the night. I knew most of what he was likely to tell me, anyway. However, there were a few minor points to be cleared up, and as you know by now, I'm a stickler for detail.

First I took a cool look at the fellow. Not much over a month ago, I'd appointed him as my assistant. He looked little different from the upright ex-officer, discreet, dependable, who had made such a suitable impression then. The only noticeable difference was the absence of that splendid cavalry officer's mustache, and I couldn't blame him for that.

I refrained from greeting him. The vicious murder of Myrtle was strong in my thoughts.

"I haven't read your statement. I gather that you made a full confession."

He declined to look me in the eye, but he still observed the correct mode of address. "Yes, sir."

"I'm more interested in your motives than what you did. What possessed you?"

A sigh, possibly from remorse, possibly from sheer exhaustion. "I got into deep water, sir."

I was about to remark that he wasn't the only one when it became obvious that he was speaking metaphorically.

"I took advantage of my friendship with Archer. He invited me to manage his business affairs because he was so busy riding and traveling, and it rapidly became obvious to me that he was illiterate and incapable of keeping track of what I was doing. I appropriated his money and put it to my own use."

I said with distaste, "Embezzlement."

"Of monumental proportions, sir. I milked his funds systematically."

"That was deplorable."

"When did you suspect me, sir?"

"Well, it was obvious something decidedly fishy must have been happening when the will was published," I told him. "He should have been worth more than sixty thou."

"He was, to me," Buckfast remarked as coolly as if he were discussing a dabble in the stock market. I was seeing a fresh side of his character.

"Unfortunately for you," I remarked, "someone else developed an interest in him. A matrimonial interest."

"The Duchess of Montrose."

"The indefatigable Duchess."

He grimaced. "And no oil painting, either. You'd think it was a grotesque mismatch. I did, at any rate, but I underestimated the Duchess. Fred was a lonely man after the death of his wife. He lost interest in everything except racing, and of course, he kept meeting Carrie Montrose on the Limekilns and at the racecourse. He raced her horses, and she paid him more generously than any other owner. She flattered him by taking his advice. She was about the only woman he saw except his sister-in-law. One day he told me that Carrie had offered to marry him. He asked me what I thought. I took it as a jest before I realized that he actually wanted my opinion."

"Which placed you in a dilemma."

"Right, sir. If he married the Duchess, questions were going to be asked about his finances. She'd soon be going through the books asking for explanations. My first impulse was to do everything in my power to dissuade Fred. Yet when I weighed it up, it was as sure as fate that sooner or later the Duchess would claim the victory. Her force of personality far outweighed Archer's. So I decided on a different approach. I would throw in my lot with the Duchess."

"Press her claim as Archer's bride," I said, making apparent my disgust.

He nodded. "I would act, in effect, as a marriage broker."

"For financial gain."

"More for self-protection, sir. A chance to put something back in the kitty. I told Carrie that it was Archer's greatest ambition to win the Cambridgeshire. If she could provide him with a winning mount, I reckoned he would agree to marry her. I remember her eyes lit up like a sixteen-year-old with a Valentine. She told me that her colt, St. Mirin, stood a capital chance of winning if Archer was up. Actually I knew that Carlton had the beating of it, but I had a plan, a way of getting out of the fearful mess I was in, and pleasing Archer and the Duchess. I would place a huge bet on St. Mirin—"

"And pay Woodburn a bribe to stop Carlton," I said.

"You found out the truth about that?" said Buckfast with a frown.

"In pursuit of my inquiries," I murmured casually. Perhaps I flatter myself, but I think he was impressed.

He continued, "If Woodburn held off, I was certain that St. Mirin would win, and I would recoup enough to patch up the accounts before I handed them over to the Duchess."

"You meant to quit?"

"Oh, yes, sir. I couldn't abide Carrie Montrose. However, I didn't show it. I talked to her like a younger brother and encouraged her to draw up a draft settlement of marriage. I promised to make sure that Archer rode St. Mirin and sealed the union with his first win in the Cambridgeshire."

"You didn't tell the Duchess about bribing Woodburn?"

"Lord, no, sir. She believed her colt could win fairly and squarely."

"What did you tell Archer?"

"Nothing—except that I had a tip that Carlton was coughing and might be forced to pull out. It worked famously up to a point."

I permitted myself a faint smile. "The point when The Sailor Prince got his nose in front."

"Yes, sir. A disaster for us all."

"Except the Squire."

"Blast him."

Coming from a man who had admitted to murder, the expletive sounded peculiarly tame.

Buckfast resumed, "I was in desperate trouble after the race. Everything fell about my ears. I'd lost another thousand of Archer's money. The Duchess went berserk and sold St. Mirin. She blamed everyone but Archer. She was still resolved to marry him and expected me to work the miracle. Fred was cut up at losing the race. He'd starved himself to make the weight, and he caught a chill soon after. Days passed before I could talk to him on the matter. After that weekend of fever, he rallied."

"Ah, so we come to the day he shot himself?"

"Yes, sir. That's on my conscience, too, though I never intended it, believe me."

"You spoke to him alone that morning?"

"Yes."

"He was able to hold a conversation?"

"Perfectly able. He was fully in control."

"What did you tell him?"

"Everything. I admitted that I'd paid the bribe and told Woodburn it was on Archer's orders. I confessed that I'd embezzled the accounts for over two years and that his funds were dreadfully depleted. I let him know that the Duchess expected to marry him. That, I suggested, would be his salvation."

"What a salvation! How did he take it?"

"He was shocked, naturally."

"Ready to horsewhip you, I should think."

Buckfast cleared his throat in a way that signaled another confession. "Actually I didn't give him much of an opportunity. I told him he had no choice but to marry the Duchess."

"Why?"

"Because if he refused, I would inform the stewards that I'd paid a bribe to Woodburn on his orders. It wouldn't be true, but Woodburn believed it and I was damned sure I could persuade the Duchess to throw in her weight if she knew the stakes. Archer was no fool. He understood the effect of that. He'd be warned off the Turf. His career, his reason for living, would be finished. Even if he refuted the charges, some of the mud would stick. His reputation for absolute integrity would be at an end."

"Charlie," I said. "You killed him."

"He had a choice," Buckfast responded impassively. "He could have married the Duchess and agreed to part with my services and no questions asked. In fact, he did agree. I said I would go to the Duchess and tell her the good news. In a short while, we'd return with a marriage settlement for him to sign."

"He consented to this? You're certain?"

"Absolutely. I went straight off to inform the Duchess."

"Which accounts for his enigmatic last words, 'Are they coming?'" I said. "You and Carrie Montrose. 'Are they coming?' He meant you two."

Buckfast continued with his story, uninterested in my observation. "They said at the inquest that Fred was out of his mind when he shot himself. Quite wrong. It was deliberate. I miscalculated. He wasn't willing to marry the Duchess."

Said without a trace of remorse or compassion! Listening to Buckfast, I understood what sets a murderer apart from other men. It's the logic that recognizes no human feelings.

I said, "You must have been alarmed when you learned that I wished to attend the inquest."

He thought for a moment. "I wasn't worried until you confided to me that you disbelieved the verdict."

A telling remark. I pricked up when he made it. "Ah. With justification, eh?"

"Yes, sir."

"Especially when I told you I proposed to investigate. Not only that, but I wanted you as my assistant! Inconvenient, to say the least."

He had the infernal cheek to comment, "The inconvenience was minor, sir. On the whole, I regarded it as an advantage. I was enabled to lay a false trail. Fortunately for me, you suspected the Squire almost from the beginning, and I encouraged it. I didn't want you going to Woodburn or Carrie Montrose. So I was delighted to be asked to spy on the Squire."

I didn't allow him to rile me. I said evenly, "And did you? Did you carry out my orders?"

"Of course not. I went to Newmarket, but I didn't go near the Squire or Bedford Lodge. I spent the time planning my disappearance."

"Are you telling me that the things you reported the Squire as saying about a partnership with Archer were inventions of yours?"

"Largely, sir. The Squire did once make such a suggestion, but Fred wouldn't hear of it. That was two years ago."

"Good Lord. And the incident at Bedford Lodge—when you broke in and found the two men together?"

"Pure imagination. It fitted in with my plan."

"The plan to make it appear to the world that you were murdered?"

"Yes."

He paused, I suppose, to let me take in the significance of what he had told me. I must have looked slightly dazed. I felt like a fistfighter caught by a low punch.

Figuratively speaking, I stepped out to the scratch again and said, "You'd better tell me what really happened that night on the Embankment."

"First," he said, "I'd like to tell you why it was necessary. You told me before I went to Newmarket that you planned to visit the Duchess. 'Cherchez la femme,' you said."

"I remember."

"That was the worst thing you could have told me. If you and Carrie got together, she was certain to tell you how she nearly married Archer, and soon enough you'd hear about my part in promoting it."

"As it happens, I didn't. I suppose the lady was too proud to give you any credit."

"I wasn't to know that," he said wistfully. "I had to assume the worst, and the worst was that you'd carry on probing until you got to the truth about the embezzlement. It carries a sentence of fourteen years' penal servitude. I couldn't think of any way to stop you."

"I'm very persistent, true."

"So I decided to do a flit. The obvious thing. When I started to plan it, I saw that my best chance was to give the impression that I was dead. Dead, I thought? Better still to be murdered."

"Why? I don't follow the reasoning."

"I pictured it from your point of view, sir. A murder would pull you up with a jerk. Murder isn't the sort of thing the Heir Apparent ought to get involved in. It's a matter for the police. I was confident that you'd drop the inquiry like a hot potato."

"You deceived yourself, then."

"Obviously."

"So you laid your plans in Newmarket?"

"Yes. I needed two men to pose as the Squire's henchmen."

"Sarjent and Parker. They're under arrest. They were picked up this evening in Exning."

Buckfast showed no concern whatsoever. "I knew them well from my two years at Falmouth House. It was my job to hand out the wages, and I knew how much the money meant to those two. They would do anything for more of the ready. Archer's death had put them out of work. As soon as the estate was wound up, they would be finished. I offered them fifty sovereigns apiece to carry out a mock attack."

"They were the brutes who assaulted us on the Embankment."

I had deduced this much earlier, you will appreciate, dear reader. Perhaps you recall my remarking upon the unpleasant feeling I'd had on seeing the gardener's stocky, apelike appearance. Sarjent, too, with his height, matched the physique of the masked man on the Embankment. I gestured to Buckfast to continue.

"I also offered them another fifty to identify the body."

"But whose body?"

"Some unfortunate who was fished from the Thames the same week. Three or four are taken from the river every day, usually by watermen who are paid a shilling by the police to deliver them to Wapping. I went down to Blackfriars and made inquiries in one of the waterside pubs and offered a pound for a clean-shaven male corpse. Next day I had the choice of four. I picked the one nearest to my age and build, took him upriver a mile or so in a small boat, stripped him and dressed him in my clothes and then returned him to the water. A drowned man doesn't much resemble the living version after several days' immersion. But just to be certain, when he was found, and inquiries were made in Newmarket, Sarjent and Parker came forward to identify the body."

"Why wasn't one of your relatives asked to do it?"

"I have no close relatives. The Archer family was too distressed about Fred to perform such a morbid duty, so Sarjent's offer was gratefully taken up."

"What about your arm—your war wound?"

"It wasn't mentioned. Thames Division knew nothing about me. They regarded the clothes and my wallet and other possessions as proof positive. The identification was a mere formality."

Personally, I'd found the description of this gruesome procedure quite nauseating, but Buckfast had related it as calmly as if it were a stroll up the Strand.

I asked, "What happened after you were thrown into the river? You *were* thrown in, weren't you?"

"Yes, sir. It was quite shallow there."

"Shallow?"

"Low tide. Shallow enough for me to wade to the landing platform."

"Good Lord. I thought it was deeper than that."

He gave an unsympathetic shrug. "I watched you thrashing about."

"Where were you?"

"In the water at the far end of the landing platform. I waited until you were out and hammering on the Duchess's door and then I clambered out and rejoined my confederates." He paused. "That should have been the end of Charlie Buckfast."

I waited, allowing him to tell me the rest in his own way.

He said in a more somber voice, "Sir, I regret killing Myrtle. I've already confessed, and I deserve to hang for it. Sir Charles Warren was somewhat taken aback when I brought the matter up. He must have heard that a girl had been shot in a music hall, but I'm sure he had no suspicion that her death was linked with what happened here. I expect you want to know how I could bring myself to commit such a ghastly crime." Buckfast sighed, and it sounded like a genuine expression of self-disgust. "I believed at the time that Myrtle was certain to ruin my plan. Do you remember showing me the letter she wrote you?"

I had an unpleasant intimation that he was trying to implicate me, so I didn't respond.

He said as if to mollify me, "I'm not trying to shift the blame, sir. It was Myrtle's misfortune that you happened to show me her letter. You told me you intended to accept her offer. You still wanted proof of the Squire's dealings with Archer. When I heard that, I was devastated. Not only would she discover that my story of a partnership was a fabrication, but she'd learn that I hadn't been anywhere near the Squire all that week, and I certainly didn't break into Bedford Lodge." He looked away, as if unable to bear my reproach. "That weekend passed slowly for me. My plan had worked like clockwork, and yet Myrtle was capable of ruining it. If you learned that I'd deceived you, I was afraid that you'd go on until you stumbled on the truth."

"Stumbled?" I said, outraged, but he wasn't listening.

He said, "I kept thinking of fourteen years for embezzlement, plus God knows how many more they would give me for conspiracy to attack the Prince of Wales. On Monday evening I took the underground railway to Aldgate and walked through the East End to the music hall where Myrtle was appearing. I found her dressing room. I silenced her with my service revolver."

I shivered. The room felt several degrees colder.

Presently I asked him, "Why did you return to Newmarket?"

"To make my escape. Sarjent knows one of the Yarmouth fishing skippers who was prepared to take me aboard on his next trip and put in at one of the Dutch ports. I decided to lay up meanwhile in the cellar at Falmouth House. Sarjent had the key, you see. The house was empty and locked, and I was undisturbed until yesterday, when the Squire insisted on coming in and nosing about. He came down to the cellar and I had to make a rapid exit. He's very astute, isn't he? I gather that he put two and two together and knew that I was still alive. This happened in broad daylight. Where could I go?"

I ignored his remarks about the Squire, which were obviously said out of malice toward me. Buckfast's manner was insufferable, even allowing that he was a vicious murderer. Answering his question in a tone that left him in no doubt of my contempt, I said, "You went to Sefton Lodge."

"Yes," he said. "I had nowhere to hide, and the Duchess owed me a favor. I'd gone to no end of trouble to try to get Archer hitched to her." The ghost of a smile appeared at the edges of his mouth. "She had a proper fright when she saw me. Hysterics. When you came to the house, I was upstairs holding my gun to the head of her latest paramour. I didn't know that the Squire was outside with the police."

The Squire again. I said curtly, "The Squire acted on my instructions."

He gave me an insolent look that I shall long remember and said, "You needn't worry, sir. If you're thinking about the trial, your reputation is safe with me."

I was amazed at his effrontery. What did he imagine—that an English judge would permit my name to be bandied about in a murder trial?

I said, "I don't require any favors from you, Buckfast. They won't be necessary."

"True, sir."

How true, I failed to appreciate at the time, or after, until I heard the news a few days later that he was dead. He had managed to use his shirt to hang himself in his cell at Cambridge Jail. To the last, he was unpredictable.

And now, my loyal companion through these pages, it is time to conclude my humble narrative and place it under lock and key. What did you think of my investigation? I daresay I was guilty of blunders here and there, and you may be tempted to conclude that there are better detectives than I. Far be it from me to try to convince you otherwise. I shan't fish for compliments. I simply thank you, patient reader, for persisting to the end, as I did, in the pursuit of truth and justice. Thanks entirely to my efforts, a murderer and his confederates were apprehended. Stout work, Bertie! There: I said it for you.

A Note from the Editor

The reader will have drawn his own conclusion about the authenticity of this narrative. It must be extremely doubtful whether "Bertie," either as Prince of Wales or King Edward VII, ever found the time or inclination to write a book. He is known to have left instructions that after his death his personal papers and correspondence should be burned, and Sir Francis Knollys, loyal to the last, carried out the task. Whether a document in a "secure metal box" was ever entrusted to the Public Record Office by the King or Knollys has not been established. The manuscript published here for the first time must therefore be treated with circumspection.

Many of the personalities who peopled these pages are, however, known to have existed, and the reader may be interested to know what became of them subsequently.

Caroline Agnes Graham, Duchess of Montrose, married for the third time in 1888, when she was seventy. Her husband, Marcus Henry Milner, was twenty-four. Her horses were run in Milner's name until 1893, when there appears to have been a rift. She died the following year, at age seventy-six.

The Honorable Christopher Sykes went steadily through his fortune entertaining the Prince. One day his sister-in-law Jessica went to Marlborough House and informed HRH that the Great Xtopher was on the point of bankruptcy. She persuaded the Prince to clear the most pressing debts. When Sykes died in 1898, Bertie attended the funeral at Brantingham Thorpe. Poor Sykes was a source of mirth even at his funeral when, after many attempts and much stifled amusement behind handkerchiefs, it was admitted that his coffin was too long to fit the grave.

George Alexander Baird, the Squire, led life to the full for another seven years before dying in New Orleans at the age of thirty-one, of a combination of malaria, pneumonia and dissipation. He had many successes as a rider and as an owner. In 1887, he infuriated the Turf establishment by declining to lead in his horse, Merry Hampton, after it won the Derby. In 1888, he took Charlie Mitchell to France to fight John L. Sullivan for the heavyweight crown for the second time. After thirty-nine rounds, it was declared a draw.

Sir Charles Warren, Commissioner of the Metropolitan Police, doggedly held office for another two years, despite mounting concern at his incompetence. In 1887, he massed four thousand police and six hundred guardsmen with loaded muskets and bayonets to deal with a demonstration by the unemployed in Trafalgar Square on what became known as Bloody Sunday. He finally resigned in 1888, after mismanaging the Jack the Ripper investigation.

Sir Joseph Edgar Boehm, the sculptor, continued to enjoy the patronage of Queen Victoria and her family. He was created a Baronet in 1889. He died in disputed circumstances the following year. According to the gossip of the celebrated courtesan Catherine Walters (known as Skittles), noted in the diary of Wilfrid Scawen Blunt, Boehm died of a hemorrhage while in the arms of the Princess Louise. The public was informed that death had occurred while he was moving a heavy statue. He was honored with interment in Westminster Abbey.

Frederick James Archer's unhappy spirit is still said to haunt Newmarket. Occasionally when a horse inexplicably swerves or stumbles on the racecourse, Archer's ghost is held responsible by some.

Cocky, a white cockatoo, was kept by Queen Alexandra for many years and outlived everyone mentioned in these pages. After the Queen's death in 1925, Cocky is believed to have been presented to the London Zoo, where it presided over the parrot house until the mid-1930s, with a notice on its perch stating that it was dangerous. Occasionally when Cocky's keeper fed it a large grape, it would mutter, "God bless the Prince of Wales."

Bertie and the Seven Bodies

CHAPTER 1

Splendid! You have opened my book. You are curious about the mystery of the seven bodies and my part in it. If I am mistaken, forgive me. I bid you good day. Kindly close the book and turn to some memoirs of a less sensational character. I recommend *Leaves from the Journal of Our Life in the Highlands*, by my dear mother, Her Majesty, Queen Victoria.

If I am correct in my deduction, bravo! Let us plunge together into the plot. It began innocently enough one spring morning in the year 1890.

"So! You have resolved to go back to nature, Alix," I announced with the air of one who has uncovered an intimate secret.

My pretty wife, the Princess of Wales, shot me a startled look. She was seated at the window in her sitting room at Sandringham. "What did you say, Bertie?"

"You are going back to nature. I perceive that you have finally decided to shed your steel appendage."

She frowned. "Is this a riddle?"

"I mean your bustle, of course."

"Bertie!"

"You can't deny it. This afternoon you wrote to your dressmaker informing her that you propose to wear the new narrow skirts in future."

She was openmouthed with amazement.

Not without satisfaction, I said, "If you want to know how I made this discovery, I deduced it."

"Deduced it?"

"I observed what I saw before me and applied the scientific principles of . . . deduction." I paused, to let the word linger in the air for a moment. Then I directed my gaze across the room. "Upon your writing desk is a candle. The wick is blackened, but the candle is not much used. On a bright afternoon such as this, why should anyone light a candle except to melt sealing wax? I deduce that you wrote a letter. How simple when it is explained!"

Alix said, "There is more to explain than that."

"Quite so. On the floor to your left is an open copy of yesterday's *Illustrated London News* from which you have removed a page. The torn edge is clearly visible and so are the words '*Opposite: the new straight skirt as designed by Monsieur Worth.*' So the chain of reasoning is complete. You saw the picture of the latest fashion from Paris and resolved forthwith to tear it from the magazine and send it to your dressmaker."

She rocked with laughter. "Oh, Bertie!"

"Do my methods amuse you?"

"You couldn't be more mistaken. I haven't the slightest desire to wear straight skirts. They make me look like a beanpole. And I haven't written a single letter all day. I was sewing. At some stage I dropped my thimble. I couldn't see it anywhere on the floor so I lit the candle to look under the writing desk. Some candle grease unfortunately dripped onto the carpet, so I ripped a sheet from the magazine to clean it up before it hardened."

"Alexandra, are you poking fun at me?"

"If you don't believe me, look in the wastepaper basket." I looked, saw that she was right and emitted a bellow of annoyance.

Alix contemplated her fingernails. "Bertie dear, do you think it is wise to persist in this notion that you can be a detective?

The question nettled me, I admit. I responded sharply, "Dammit, one small oversight and I'm branded as a failure. If I'd looked in the wretched wastepaper basket my chain of reasoning would have been different, altogether different. I'm forever being told to find intelligent pursuits and when I do I can't rely on my own wife for encouragement." I turned on my heel and marched out.

ALIX KNOWS THAT MY TEMPER is short and so is its duration. By the next post I received an invitation that altogether restored my humor. A grand *battue* at Desborough in October. Desborough— what a prospect! After Sandringham and Holkham, there's no better shooting in the kingdom. Nine hundred acres in Buckinghamshire. Moreover Desborough Hall is one of the great houses of England, with Tudor banqueting hall, ballroom, gun room, chapel and ninety-odd bedrooms.

"I can't resist it," I told Alix over dinner. "I shall accept."

"Who does the invitation come from?" she enquired.

"Lady Amelia Drummond."

She shifted her head to see around the floral arrangement. "An invitation to shoot from a lady?"

"The widow of Freddie Drummond. Haven't you met her?" I heaved a long sigh to signal sympathy for our prospective hostess. "Perhaps you don't recall? She's easily forgotten, poor soul, rather plain in looks, but making superhuman efforts to keep Desborough on the social map. One feels obliged to show support."

"When did Lord Drummond pass away?"

"Last winter, in tragic circumstances. He was gored by a bull."

"How horrid!"

"Yes, he was a frightful mess, they said. He lingered for six weeks, covered in bandages. Then one morning he sat up, uttered something rather vulgar and breathed his last."

"I didn't catch that. What did he mutter?" Sometimes dear Alix trades on her deafness.

"I think it was 'Oh, bother.'"

"I don't call *that* vulgar. I've heard far worse from Cocky." Cocky is Alix's pet cockatoo. She gave me a searching look and then took a spoonful of Scotch broth. In a few moments she casually enquired, "About what age would Lady Drummond be, Bertie?"

I hedged. "You could look her up in Debrett. I'm not much of a judge."

"Younger than me?"

"Possibly."

"Under thirty-five?"

"Alix, I haven't the faintest idea. Is it important?"

"Conceivably."

LATER THAT AFTERNOON SHE CORNERED me at my writing desk. From somewhere in the clutter of her rooms she had unearthed a copy of *The Tatler* with a studio portrait of Lady Amelia, a ravishing dark-haired beauty in a ball gown cut perilously low. "Bertie, I don't know how you could describe her as plain."

I replied somewhat obliquely, "Where do you keep these old magazines? It smells so musty it must be ten years old at least."

"I looked her up in Debrett, as you suggested. She is still only twenty-seven."

I shut the magazine and handed it back to her. "I suppose you're going to try and stop my sport—just because the invitation comes from a young widow of tolerably good looks."

My dear wife gave me an indulgent smile. "Not at all. When have I ever stood in your way? Of course you shall have your shoot. And I shall come too and offer some sisterly sympathy to Lady Drummond."

"*You* intend to come?"

She smiled faintly this time. "One feels obliged to show support."

And so the visit was set in motion. Francis Knollys, my private secretary, wrote to advise our hostess of my requirements: a suite comprising bedrooms for each of us, dressing rooms and sitting room. Also accommodation for our retinue of equerries, ladies-in-waiting, footmen, valets, loaders, coachmen, grooms and a member of the Household Police, whose duty it is to guard us from anarchists. Then the guest list had to be approved, a crucial matter as it ultimately turned out. Of sixteen names submitted, I struck out three immediately. If one is planning an agreeable week in the country, one doesn't want to rub shoulders with people who have given offense in the past. Nor, if one wishes to shoot, is one obliged to stand comparison with *all* the best guns in the country.

We were left with thirteen names.

"Would you like me to join the party, sir?" Knollys knows my superstitious nature and volunteered at once.

"No," I informed him. "We have more than enough men in this party. We must cross out someone else. Who have we got? Eight gentlemen and five ladies. The balance is fraught with disaster. Who is this reverend fellow, Humphrey Paget? He doesn't sound like a shooting man."

"The family chaplain, sir."

"Ah."

"He buried the late Lord Drummond."

"The best day's work he ever did, from what I remember of Freddie. Better not object to a man of the cloth, I suppose. Who else have we got?"

"Marcus Pelham, Lady Drummond's brother. I presume he's there to perform the duties of host."

"That's as may be, but is he safe?"

"Safe, sir?"

"I wouldn't care to stand with a man who isn't safe."

"I understand he's an expert marksman, sir." Knollys glanced at the list again. "Then there's His Grace the Duke of Bournemouth, who lives on the neighboring estate."

"Dear old Jerry. Good man. Hopeless shot."

"Not safe, sir?"

"Not in the least."

"Shall I strike him out?"

"Better not. The list is pretty undistinguished without him. I'll make sure he's well down the line from me."

"Claude Bullivant. He's a commoner."

"Ah, but he's a card. I like his sense of humor. This is getting damnably difficult."

"'There's Colonel C.D. Roberts, V.C."

"A V.C., do you say? That's our man. Blackball him. We can do without a hero turning the ladies' heads, eh, Francis?"

So the number was painlessly reduced to twelve. I had already run through the ladies' names. Two I hadn't previously met, which lent a certain relish to the week in prospect.

THE SUMMER RAN ITS ALL-TOO-FAMILIAR course: Ascot, Epsom, Goodwood, Cowes. I anticipated the shoot in Buckinghamshire as a change from my customary October *battue* at Sandringham or Balmoral. And a change is what I got. A never-to-be-forgotten week.

CHAPTER 2

Those of my readers who haven't seen Desborough for themselves may care to be informed that it is approached by a mile-long avenue of beeches. It is an extremely large, moated, brick built Elizabethan mansion much extended by its eighteenth-century owners, who added a monstrous Palladian portico at the front and two extra wings. They also coated the Tudor brickwork in stucco, something I find as incomprehensible as putting a pretty face behind a *yashmak*.

We were graciously received. As custom decrees, our host and hostess, Lady Drummond and her brother Marcus, stood at the entrance flanked by their principal servants. Then in a charming, youthful manner Lady Amelia came running down the stone steps to greet us, bunching her skirt for ease of movement and affording glimpses of slender, white-stockinged ankles.

Beside me, Alix murmured, "No longer in mourning, it appears."

The young widow curtsied and gave us her well-rehearsed greeting. She had a most engaging voice, with what I can only describe as a gurgle when she spoke certain sounds. "Welcome to Desborough, Your Royal Highnesses. I hope your journey was agreeable."

"It is becoming so by the minute," I said.

"Your suite is ready, sir, and your servants are installed."

"Capital, my dear. What are the rules of the house?"

She looked uncertain how to respond, so I jocularly explained, "For example, my mother, the Queen, has a horror of smoking, and prohibits it absolutely indoors. At Windsor one evening, the German Ambassador, Count Hatzfeldt-Wildenburg, who cannot live without a cigarette, poor fellow, was discovered in his bedroom lying on the hearth rug in his pajamas, blowing smoke up the chimney. I hope I may light up an occasional cigar in your house without performing gymnastics.

I had brought the dimples briefly to her cheeks and now she found that winsome voice again. "No, sir, there are no rules."

"No rules at all?" I arched an eyebrow. "Isn't that rather reckless?"

She colored charmingly.

Then Alix remarked, "Rules are unnecessary when people know how to behave. Shall we allow Lady Drummond to show us to our rooms?"

Our hostess had spared nothing in making us welcome. Each suite was newly decorated, Alix's in cornflower blue, mine in green and white stripes. Log fires were blazing merrily and producing pretty effects on the crystal decanters.

"When is dinner?" I asked Lady Amelia.

"At half past eight, sir. I would like to present my other guests at eight, if it pleases you."

"I am sure it will please us enormously."

When we were alone, Alix asked what time we were wanted.

"Seven," I said firmly. It's a constant battle with Alix. At Sandringham I have all the clocks permanently put forward half an hour.

She gave me a suspicious look. "That seems rather early."

"It's the country life. Everyone eats early and retires before midnight."

The result was that we got downstairs at twenty past eight.

I spotted a few familiar faces in the anteroom: Sir George Holdfast, of Holdfast Assurance, and Lady Moira, his wife (good people, supporters of many charitable causes, but *so* staid); Claude Bullivant, once the most eligible bachelor in London; and dear old Jerry Gribble, the Duke of Bournemouth, hand on the shoulder of a suit of armor, chatting noisily to a pretty young woman in black velvet. Trust Jerry to lose no time, I thought.

Our hostess made a deep curtsey that Alix later described as theatrical. It didn't offend me in the least. I seem to remember that Lady Amelia's dinner gown was apple green, or it might have been pink. I retain a very clear picture of the corsage, which I am certain was of cream satin, cut distractingly low and decorated with pearl beads. She had her hair bunched high and adorned with a posy of white blossoms. I do like to see a lady's neck and shoulders unadorned except for a few pearls.

Alix said pointedly that we ought to meet the Chaplain.

The Reverend Humphrey Paget demonstrably wasn't one of those clerics who practice fasting as religious observance. He was "Broad" Church, if ever a man was. And we had more in common than that, for he claimed to be a sportsman, in spite of his girth.

"An angler, if I am not mistaken," said I at once. "Did you land many trout today, Padre?"

His face was a study.

"Forgive me," I said. "I have recently interested myself in the science of deduction."

"Deduction, sir?"

"Yes. That distinct and even discoloration around the base of your heels suggests that you recently stood for some time in soft mud. Moreover, your toe caps, although splendidly polished, have several dull patches that could only have been made by splashes of water, say when a catch is landed. These indications, taken together with the knowledge that the River Ouse nearby is well stocked with trout, and the season ends on Saturday next, compel me irresistibly to the conclusion that you are a trout fisherman."

He glanced down at the telltale shoes. Then cleared his throat. "Your acuteness of observation is truly remarkable. Your Royal Highness."

"Anyone could do as well if he applied the method," I modestly remarked, passing on to another guest, a tall, pasty-faced young fellow with eyes like rock oysters. I should explain that the ordeal of meeting me has curious effects on some people. He was introduced as Mr. Wilfred Osgot-Edge, a poet.

"What's a poet doing at a shooting party—writing elegies on pheasants?" I jested.

He was tongue-tied, so Lady Amelia sprang to his assistance. "Wilfred also has the reputation of being the best shot in Buckinghamshire, sir."

"Good for you," I said generously. "A shooting poet."

"It is n-not so uncommon," he stuttered, then seemed unable to expand on the statement.

"Who else is there?" I asked. "I wouldn't care to hand dear old Tennyson a shotgun and stand nearby."

My wife, ever sympathetic towards the nervously inclined, said, "Lord Byron was a sportsman."

"And much else besides." I tried to animate Osgot-Edge with a nudge from my elbow. "Have you noticed how the ladies go pink at the mention of Byron? I really ought to read him."

The poet wound himself up. "I m-must say I like By-By-"

"Bicycling? You *are* an all-rounder."

The poet had no more to contribute. Casting about for deliverance, I caught the eye of Jerry Gribble, the Duke of Bournemouth, still in close proximity to his companion in velvet. "Jerry, you old bore," I shouted across the room. "The lady and I have been winking at each other for the past ten minutes and I still don't know her name."

She was brought to meet me, and I saw at once that this was no shrinking violet. The walk, the shining eyes, the knowing smile, the curtsey—all sang out "actress." Now I'm not one of those who regard treading the boards as the next thing to streetwalking. I pride myself on my encouragement of the dramatic arts.

"May I present Miss Queenie Chimes, sir?"

"Miss *what?*"

The lady giggled. "Queenie, sir. Queenie Chimes."

I said, "Queenie? Queenie? What sort of name is that? I didn't see it on the guest list."

Jerry coughed nervously. "My mistake, sir. I should have said Victoria."

I frowned.

Miss Chimes explained. "Girls who are called Victoria are nicknamed Queenie, sir, after her Majesty."

"Thank you," I told her formally. "The connection is clear to me."

She said, "Do you think it common?"

I stared at her. I am not used to people addressing me so directly. I said, "As a matter of fact, I have a daughter of my own called Victoria"—I paused—"but we don't call her Queenie." And then I smiled.

Everyone smiled.

I resumed, "You're quite right, my dear. Victoria is a common name. I also have a sister Vicky and a niece Vicky. Very common. Very confusing. I shall be happy to call you Queenie. Altogether more distinguished."

Quick to sense my approval of the lady, Jerry Gribble took care to say, "Queenie and I are well acquainted. I would go so far as to describe myself as one of her patrons. She's with Irving at the Lyceum, you know. The great man personally thought of her stage name, didn't he, my dear? She was born Victoria Bell."

The lady gave me an endearing smile. "Bell . . . Chimes."

I chuckled. "I like it! Clever man, Irving. He obviously sees a fine future for you in his company."

"Oh, I don't know if I shall be good enough, Your Royal Highness," Queenie spoke up. She had an alluring, husky voice, as if she spent her mornings drilling the Irish Guards.

"I'm all for modesty," said I. "Are you currently in a production, Miss Chimes?"

"I am preparing a part, sir." Her eyelashes fluttered,

I glanced behind me to make sure Alix was still busy with the poet and said, "Would you care to read it to me?"

At which Jerry said, "It's a nonspeaking role, sir. Have you met Miss Dundas yet?"

"Miss Dundas?"

"The Amazon explorer, Isabella Dundas, a most remarkable person."

At that point the announcement was made that dinner was served. Hastily the remaining guests, including Miss Dundas, the Amazon explorer, were presented to me without time to discuss their remarkable attributes. We formed the procession, Alix, the lady of highest rank, on the right arm of young Pelham, leading us in, the rest following, and Lady Amelia and I last.

The banqueting hall is one of the notable features of Desborough, having somehow escaped three centuries of so-called improvements to the rest of the house. The only embellishments to the original oak and plaster are the escutcheons displayed high on the walls, the heraldic bearings of the Drummonds and their ancestors. Amelia (we agreed to be informal) pointed out her own. As a Pelham, she had a most exotic coat of arms with griffins and birds that I didn't recognize. Alix tried to convince me later that they were harpies.

The hall was such a barn of a place that Amelia had thoughtfully located the dinner table at the far end, where a grand fire was blazing and screens were strategically placed to keep out drafts. A small string orchestra played zestfully as we stepped between the ranks of liveried servants to take our places at the oval table.

The Chaplain said the grace and we were seated. Amelia was to my left, Alix to my right and Queenie the actress directly opposite me, too far off, I estimated, for our feet to make contact unless we sank down in our chairs with our chins resting on the table.

Queenie was flanked by Jerry Gribble and Claude Bullivant, and it was Bullivant, a delightful, black-haired rogue with a moustache as curly as a candelabra, who opened the conversation. "If I were a padre, I think I should object to saying grace on a Monday."

"Why is that?" someone asked.

"Monday, surely, is a padre's day off He's busy all weekend, marrying people on Saturday and taking services on the Sabbath. He's entitled to a rest."

The Reverend Paget gave a half smile and said nothing, so Jerry Gribble took up the running. "The Church is a calling, not a profession. A churchman can never have a day off like the rest of us."

"Oh, he *needs* a day to himself," piped up Lady Holdfast from one end of the table. She was desperately dull, poor old thing.

"I'm sure our friend the Chaplain isn't deprived of recreation," said I, mindful of the trout fishing.

"Perhaps he would care to enlighten us as to how he amuses himself when he is not at his devotions," suggested Bullivant, and all eyes turned on the Reverend Paget.

"I, em, fit in a few private pastimes when time permits," he said. He seemed not to want to own up to the angling.

"Yes, but do you ever get a day off?" persisted Bullivant, wicked fellow, unwilling to let the Chaplain off the hook, so to speak. "How did you pass your time today, for example?"

"Today?" The Chaplain wiped his mouth with the edge of his table napkin. "I was, em, outdoors this morning."

"Fishing for trout?" said Alexandra.

He went extremely pink and twisted the napkin as if he were wringing out washing.

"Out with it, Padre," said Bullivant. "A man of God has a perfect right to fish. St. Peter was a fisherman. Is that what you do?"

"I may have given that impression. Inadvertently." The Chaplain now had his fist wound up in the napkin. "To be truthful, I was officiating at a funeral."

"A *funeral?*" said I.

"And this afternoon?" Alix asked the Chaplain after a pause.

"A baptism."

Mud on his heels and drops of water on his toe caps. I was forced to conclude that I hadn't altogether mastered the science of deduction. To avoid one of Alix's looks, I turned to our hostess and congratulated her on the soup.

This markedly relaxed the atmosphere. The diners turned as one to their neighbors and struck up conversations. I learned from our dear little hostess that she expected a record bag from the week's shooting. The woods were said to be better stocked than the head gamekeeper could remember for years, and it appeared that most of Buckinghamshire would be beating for us.

"Curiously enough, I have never shot here in October," I told Amelia. "I once had a day's cock shooting after Christmas. That must have been when your father-in-law was alive. So you see, most of these guns around the table have the advantage of me. Your brother Marcus, Jerry Gribble, Claude Bullivant, they're all regulars. I don't know about the poet."

"Wilfred? He was at last year's shoot," she said. "He's quick and accurate. But you're wrong about my brother. Marcus was never welcomed here while Freddie was alive."

"They fell out?"

She hesitated. "There was some jealousy between them."

"Over you?"

"Marcus and I were very close as children, sir. Don't misunderstand me, but I think he felt that Freddie broke up the family when he married me."

I glanced at the others along the table. Couldn't see much family resemblance when I studied Marcus Pelham. He had straight, straw-colored hair and one of those pink faces that turn bright red in the sun, or under scrutiny from the Prince of Wales. "And now that you're alone in the world, he's supporting you on occasions such as this. Good man," I said, privately thinking he ought to be tarred and feathered.

I refused to let it spoil my appetite. After the *consommé* came Dover sole poached in Chablis, followed by the dish that never fails to please me: ptarmigan pie. Presently something was said across the table about sleeping in strange houses. It's curious, isn't it, how even when half a dozen conversations are in progress around the table one intriguing remark secures everybody's attention? We all stopped talking except Jerry Gribble.

"Personally," he said, "I never have any trouble. I'm used to sleeping in strange beds."

"Ladies, take note," murmured Bullivant.

"That isn't what I meant. I've slept under canvas, on a train, aboard a steamship, under the stars—"

"In a haunted house?" put in Queenie the actress.

"Not to my knowledge—until tonight," said Jerry.

"Good God—this house doesn't have a ghost, does it?" said Sir George Holdfast in some alarm. His wife gave a horrified squeak.

"Oh, it must have," said Jerry, straight-faced. "In three hundred years it must have acquired one."

"A resident spook!" said Bullivant with relish.

Around me the unease was palpable. It was all very well joking about ghosties over dinner, but before long we'd be shown to our bedrooms by candlelight along dark corridors.

Osgot-Edge the poet spoke up. "I don't believe in gho- gho-"

"Going to bed in haunted houses?" said Bullivant. "Nor I, old man. I shall sleep in an armchair by the fire. You're welcome to join me."

Beside me, Lady Amelia drew herself up to speak. "I know you only say it to amuse, gentlemen, but there's something I would like to say in all seriousness. There is no ghost of Desborough Hall. If there was, I should have heard of it—and I wouldn't have remained here, least of all invited my dearest friends to stay."

"Well said, my dear," I told her and clapped my hands. Everyone did likewise—even Bullivant, looking sheepish—and the congenial atmosphere was quite restored.

Over the roast lamb I surveyed the party and amused myself pairing them off. Queenie of the Lyceum had, regrettably, to be linked with Jerry Gribble; it was perfectly obvious that she had been invited at his request. The Holdfasts looked likely to live up to their name, and they were such a dreary pair that none of us would object. Claude Bullivant was resolutely hacking a path to Miss Dundas, the Amazon explorer, though it was far from clear how she would receive him. The set of her mouth was daunting and her eyes glittered ominously. It crossed my mind that she might be stalking bigger game than Bullivant; once or twice she had looked my way and smiled.

As for the rest, I absolved the Chaplain and Osgot-Edge the nervous poet from any amorous intent, and I could see that Marcus Pelham had eyes only for his sister.

What of the winsome Amelia herself, then? Up to now, she'd been scrupulously charming to everyone, as a hostess should. If you want to know whether I bedded her before the end of the week you had better read on. But one thing you must have gathered: noctambulations would be infernally difficult under Alix's nose and with a jealous brother roaming the house.

I was inquiring from Miss Chimes about Irving's latest production when there was an alarming cry from Lady Holdfast: "A bomb!"

Fortunately, Inspector Sweeney, my bodyguard, wasn't in the room looking for anarchists, or the cook's *pièce de résistance* might have been grabbed and flung out of the nearest window. It was a *bombe glacée Dame Blanche*, a veritable monument of ice cream and fruit carried high on a silver charger by the cook himself in his tall hat to the strains of "See the Conquering Hero Comes."

I am at pains to describe faithfully what happened. The mood around the table, as I recall it, was high-spirited. We shouted "Bravo!" and the cook warmed his knife over a flame before making the first cut. Then the portions were served. Jerry Gribble joked that this was obviously the ghost of Desborough Hall, the *Dame Blanche* herself. Alix asked for a portion with a cherry. Osgot-Edge knocked over his wine in the excitement.

Then Queenie Chimes pitched forward and collapsed—without a murmur—face down in the *bombe*.

CHAPTER 3

Such was the shock around the table that several of us cried out, "Good Lord!" in chorus.

Jerry was the first to come to the aid of Miss Chimes. He placed his hand under her forehead and raised her head.

I had the front view from across the table. The lady's face was thickly coated with white ice cream. Chunks were dropping grotesquely onto the black velvet of her dress. I may say that I've seen the fair sex in disarray of one sort and another on a number of occasions. A lady marked with mud or worse is a not uncommon sight in the hunting field. But one doesn't expect such mishaps at the dinner table. The effect upon me—and I am sure upon us all—was profoundly disturbing.

Jerry's levelheadedness in the emergency was admirable, if unexpected. He was putting his napkin to good use. As he wiped away the ice cream he disturbed one of Miss Chimes's eyelids, and I was alarmed to see almost nothing but white, the eye having rolled upwards. Most of us were on our feet, wanting to assist in some way. "Dead to the world," Jerry said. "Does anyone have smelling salts?"

Lady Holdfast produced a bottle of *sal volatile* from her handbag and Jerry removed the stopper and waved it under Queenie Chimes's nose. Without result.

There was no shortage of suggestions.

"Her nostrils must be blocked."

"We can't stand on ceremony—loosen her stays."

"See if her pulse is beating."

"She ought to lie flat."

"Better s-send for a d-d-"

"There's a sofa through there."

Claude Bullivant scooped the insensible young lady up in his arms and carried her into the anteroom where the sofa was. Amelia unbuttoned the dress at the back, and Miss Dundas the explorer showed how resourceful her Amazon experience had made her. She had fetched the chef's knife from the banqueting hall and she now proceeded to cut the laces of Miss Chimes's stays.

However, there was still no apparent response from the patient. It seemed to me that her skin was too rosy for this to be a simple case of swooning, but the almost pure white of the ice cream still remaining on her hair and clothes may have overemphasized her color.

Then Jerry announced, "Her pulse is beating quite fast."

Everyone voiced their relief.

"Fast—is that a good sign?" I put in as a caution, and no one seemed to know the answer.

"Better send for a d-d-"

"He's right," said Bullivant, "she doesn't seem to be coming round. Suppose it's her heart!"

"God no!" said Jerry, "she's far too young for that."

"You can't be certain," Bullivant pointed out. "I knew a fellow who rowed at stroke for Oxford and collapsed on Paddington Station six months later. Twenty-two years old. His heart gave out."

Holdfast said, "But she hasn't rowed the boat race. All she did was sit down to dinner."

"I was simply making the point that youth is no proof against a dicky heart."

Jerry looked up in alarm. "Do you really think so?"

Amelia said, "I'm going to send for the doctor."

"No." Jerry got up from his kneeling position beside the sofa. "There's a quicker way. I'll take her there myself. We can make her comfortable in the carriage."

Servants were sent to alert the grooms and the coachman and fetch blankets and pillows.

Amelia turned to her brother. "Marcus, you'd better go with His Grace."

"He's got the coachman to help him," Marcus pointed out, rudely, I thought.

"Absolutely right," insisted Jerry, a gentleman through and through. "Don't break up the party. I'll manage perfectly well."

In commendably short time, Jerry's landau was brought to the front of the building. A footman carried Miss Chimes down the steps and lifted her inside and Jerry climbed in. We all watched in tight-lipped concern until the coach lamp had disappeared from sight.

"Wretched luck!" said Holdfast.

"Dr. Perkins will know exactly what to do," Amelia endeavored to reassure us. "He's terribly nice."

"Whatever it is, I hope it isn't contagious like the cholera," said Lady Holdfast.

Her husband said, "Moira, you've never seen a case of cholera in your life."

Distinctly subdued, we trooped back to the banqueting hall, where the servants had cleaned up the mess and rearranged the table, removing the places occupied by Miss Chimes and Jerry, and also our plates. Our portions of the *bombe*, of course, had long since melted. However, the chef, stout fellow, sent up a delicious-looking chocolate balthazar in its place.

"I'm in such a state of nerves," Lady Holdfast ungratefully declared, "that I couldn't possibly face food."

"Well, I can," I informed her. There are times when a firm declaration from me has a good effect on people, and this was one. We all cleared our plates, including Moira Holdfast, and some of us had second helpings.

It was during that polite interval between the finish of dessert and the withdrawal of the ladies that the house steward stepped forward and spoke confidentially to Amelia. I assumed at the time that it had something to do with the serving of coffee.

Thinking of my cigar, I eased back in my chair to afford Amelia a sight of Alix. The nod was given and the four ladies rose, drew on their gloves and removed to the drawing room.

Once we men had closed ranks and lit up, I remarked, "Pity this happened. I thought the young lady looked perfectly bonny when we were introduced. Has anyone met her before?"

The response was negative all round.

"I gather she's an actress, sir," said Holdfast.

"Presumably invited at Jerry Gribble's suggestion," added Bullivant.

"I doubt it," said Marcus Pelham. "My sister is perfectly capable of drawing up a guest list that pleases all concerned. She takes a particular pride in keeping *au fait* with the latest liaisons."

There were some raised eyebrows at that last comment. Bullivant fingered the tip of his moustache. "*There's* food for thought, gentlemen." His brown eyes glittered. "I wonder . . ."

"You wonder what?" said Holdfast.

"I wonder which of us has prior claim on our lady of the Amazon."

"Who is that?"

"You know who I mean—the intrepid explorer, Miss Dundas. Which of us is to be the lucky man? What's the matter—are we all too shy to speak up? Well, in the absence of any other offer she's welcome to beat a path to my . . ." Bullivant's words trailed away as some awful possibility occurred to him. He coughed, glanced towards me and said, "Joking, of course, sir."

I let him squirm for a moment. Then I said, "If it makes any difference whatsoever, Claude, Miss Dundas is completely unknown to me. I never met her before this evening."

He gave a high-pitched giggle of relief.

Young Pelham told us, "The lady is a guest in her own right."

I turned back to Bullivant. "There's a thought to conjure with, Claude: Are *you* a guest in your own right?"

Even the Chaplain joined in the laughter.

Considerately, we got up to join the ladies after one cigar and a glass of port. Left to their own devices after some upsetting occurrence, the fair sex can easily work themselves up into a lather.

Oddly enough, they appeared unruffled. I won't say that anyone made light of what had happened to Miss Chimes, but between us we kept the conversation flowing agreeably. Indeed, I'm sure it would have flowed all evening if only Lady Holdfast had not come up with her paralyzingly stupid suggestion.

"Why don't we have a recitation?"

"Do you mean *poetry*?" I asked, trying to make clear my distaste for such things.

"Certainly, Your Royal Highness. After all, we are fortunate in having a published poet among us. I'm sure we're all dying to hear Mr. Osgot-Edge's work," she plowed on. "I must admit, to my shame, that I, for one, haven't read a line that he's written, and I want to remedy the deficiency at the first opportunity."

Osgot-Edge was even more alarmed than I at this development. He turned crimson and started making incoherent noises.

"It seems he didn't bring his poems with him," I said thankfully.

"That's all right, sir. I have a copy," said Amelia, making her first gaffe of the week. She was disastrously eager to please. "I'll fetch it."

"Before you do . . ." I tossed in another difficulty. "Who will read them?"

Osgot-Edge, poor fellow, said, "I f-fear I c- c-"

I was just beginning to think I'd scuppered the suggestion when Amelia spoke up again.

"Humphrey, *you* can read beautifully."

"Who the deuce is Humphrey?" was on the tip of my tongue. In time, I observed the Chaplain beaming like a lighthouse. The Church and two determined ladies are more than a match for me. I capitulated.

"This one is called 'To an Obstinate Boy,'" the Reverend Humphrey Paget announced when the book had been fetched and we were settled.

> *"He fidgets when the grace is said,*
> *Wicked child.*
> *He should be fed his daily bread,*
> *In the wild,*
> *Where hungrily the king of beasts,*
> *Day by day,*
> *Is heard to roar before he feasts,*
> *'Let us pray.'"*

"Oh, my word," said Lady Holdfast.

"Ha, not bad," said Bullivant. "It's a pun. 'Let us prey.' How about that, Padre?"

"One applauds the intention of the poem without altogether approving of its phrasing," said the Chaplain guardedly.

I glanced across at Osgot-Edge to see how he took the criticism. He was sitting with his head back, staring at the ceiling.

Lady Holdfast said, "If you want the truth, I didn't really like it."

"What are you objecting to?" Bullivant asked her.

"It was too outspoken for me."

"Outspoken? I don't call that outspoken."

"Possibly not, but I think I shall retire before the next one is read out." Which was inexcusable, considering that she was chiefly responsible for inflicting the poetry on us.

"You can't go to bed, Moira," said her husband, quite properly alert to the discourtesy involved.

"Well, I shall retire to another room."

"The poems can't all be as strong meat as that, my dear. I'm sure the Chaplain can find one more suitable to read out."

"Why don't we ask Mr. Osgot-Edge to suggest one?" said Miss Dundas.

"That should see us through till bedtime," murmured Bullivant.

Whereupon I decided to speak up. "Better still, why don't we ask Mr. Osgot-Edge to make a selection of five or six poems that the Chaplain, if he is willing, can prepare, rehearse and read to us another evening?"

"Oh, splendid!" cried Sir George. "I second your suggestion, sir."

I gave a nod and pointed out that the suggestion originated with Miss Dundas. She rewarded me with a tilt of the eyebrow. Peculiar woman, I thought. Not unattractive, however.

The Chaplain and the poet seemed amenable, so we were spared more poetry, at least for the present evening. Instead I regaled the company with my experiences hunting tigers in India and, though I say it myself, it was a damn sight more entertaining.

We called a halt this side of midnight, needing to be up and about quite early next day for the shoot. After the good nights had been said and Amelia had escorted us to our suite I passed a short time gossiping with Alix before retiring to my bedchamber. In view of what follows I had better explain that we have slept in separate rooms for years.

Having confirmed what I would wear next day, I dismissed my valet, washed, prayed for my mother the Queen and good shooting in the morning and got into bed. A comfortable bed it was, too, a spacious four-poster evidently reupholstered for my visit. I do like a well-sprung mattress. My feet found the spot where the warming pan had been, and I believe I was asleep in ten minutes.

Tuesday

CHAPTER 4

The next thing I knew a voice close to my ear, a lady's voice, was whispering, "Are you awake?"

Woolly minded from sleep, I struggled to make sense of it. I had difficulty remembering where I was, let alone whether I'd started the night with a companion. It was too dark to see much. Some hours to go until dawn. Was she a dream? I kept very still and listened.

She repeated, "Are you awake, sir?"

I said, "If we're on sufficiently intimate terms for you to visit me in bed, you'd better call me Bertie. Who are you?"

"Amelia Drummond . . . Bertie."

"Amelia." My brain stopped being bleary at once. I knew precisely what was happening. And on the first night! So bold! I wasn't sure whether to be flattered or alarmed. She was taking an appalling risk with Alix's bedroom just across the corridor.

She said, "I do apologize for disturbing you. I knocked twice, and I thought you must have heard."

She'd *knocked*, on my door!

She asked, "May I light a candle, sir?"

"Bertie—and keep your voice down."

She whispered, "Bertie."

She said it rather fetchingly with that gurgling note in her voice. I responded in a tone equally warm, "Well, Amelia, do we really require a light?"

"I think we do." Amelia cleared her throat. "I regret to say that I am the bearer of bad news." She struck a match and I saw that she was standing beside the bed fully dressed. Bad news indeed.

"What is it?"

"Jerry Gribble has just returned. I sat up to wait for him." Her chin trembled. "Miss Chimes is dead."

"Dead?" I sat up straight.

"She failed to recover consciousness."

"Oh, my hat! That's dreadful. What was it—her heart?"

"I don't know. Jerry thought you should be told at once. He's outside."

"Call him in. You did the proper thing, my dear. Absolutely the proper thing. Forgive me for appearing so confused. Would you hand me my dressing gown?"

Jerry entered the room looking grim. He stood at the foot of my bed with hunched shoulders, taking long, heavy breaths.

I told him to sit on the bed. "My dear fellow, this is too appalling . . . ghastly. When exactly did it happen?"

"Before I reached the doctor's," he told me. "She died in my arms, poor child. Some popping sounds came from her mouth. Like turning off the gas. I knew she was going. I don't think she was in pain. I hope to God she wasn't."

"What a tragedy," I said. "Did the doctor give an opinion?"

"He said it was too early to be sure, but he suspected from my description that she had been in a state of coma, of uncertain origin."

"Coma?"

"She could have suffered a hemorrhage of the brain. I had to take her to the hospital. They'll carry out a postmortem later in the week." He covered his face. "I can't believe this has happened."

The poor fellow was ready to weep, so I did my best to keep him from breaking down by saying gently, "How long had you known her, Jerry?"

"Six months, I think, sir." He was having difficulty in speaking. "We met down in Kent at a cricket match."

"Ah, cricket." A less harrowing topic. "Was that Canterbury, by any chance?"

"No, Gravesend."

We couldn't get away from death. "Gravesend? I know the ground. I know Canterbury better."

"This was definitely Gravesend. The Thespians were playing a team got up by my former brother-in-law, Lord Peterkin. I didn't see much of the game once I got talking to Queenie. She came around the ground selling tickets for the Actors' Retirement Home—the tombola, I mean—and that was how we met. It's such a treat talking to a pretty young girl when you live alone in the world."

"It's a treat in any case, Jerry."

"I'm glad you understand, sir. And she didn't have designs on becoming a duchess. I made it abundantly clear that after two marriages gone to pot I wouldn't consider a third. She understood that."

Amelia spoke. "Jerry, her people will have to be told. Do you know who they are?"

Jerry made a dismissive gesture. "It's all right. She had no living relatives. She told me that herself. I'll arrange everything. I'll give her a decent funeral. Lord, to be talking about a funeral when a few hours ago she was sitting at dinner with us!"

I reached out and put a hand on his shoulder. "Jerry, I think you should have a stiff brandy and get to bed. There's nothing else you can do tonight."

He glanced towards Amelia. She cleared her throat, took a step closer to the bed and said, "With respect, sir, the reason we took the liberty of waking you was to find out your wishes."

"My wishes?"

"This tragic event casts a shadow over the party."

"Without a doubt," I agreed.

There was a moment's silence.

Amelia resumed, "We thought it proper to enquire whether you wished to call off the shoot."

"I see. Out of respect, do you mean?" It hadn't occurred to me. I pondered the matter. My first thought was to soldier on. That's the way of the Prince of Wales, even in adversity. Besides, my charming hostess had gone to no end of trouble and expense to arrange the *battue*. Eighteen months and more of preparation go into any shoot worthy of the name.

Then I remembered how easily things can be misconstrued. I once got into no end of trouble with my dear mother the Queen for omitting to postpone the Marlborough House Ball when Arthur

Stanley, the Dean of Westminster, died. Mama was very attached
to the good Dean. What really put the lid on it was when I had
the funeral brought forward to avoid a clash with the first day's
racing at Goodwood.

Yes, this had to be thought about. On the other hand, the death
of an unknown actress couldn't be compared with the passing of
Dean Stanley. "What do you think, Jerry?" I asked.

After a moments reflection he said, "I think Queenie would have
wished for a quiet funeral, sir. If it gets out that she died at a house
party at which you were present, all of Fleet Street will be there."

"By George, you're right! We don't want to give the press a field
day. If I return home tomorrow, they'll want to know the reason
why. Those blighters can make a scandal out of anything." I turned
to Amelia. "My dear Lady Drummond, with your permission we'll
proceed with the arrangements as planned."

"Certainly, sir, if that is your wish."

"I shall explain everything to your other guests in the morning.
And Jerry . . ."

"Sir?"

"I shan't expect you to join the guns."

"Thank you, sir. I'll go into town and see the undertaker."

"Good man." I gave him a sympathetic smile. "These things
happen. It was the hand of fate."

He got up and left the room. I put my hand to my mouth and
yawned, ready for sleep again, and then realized that the candle
was still alight on the chest of drawers. Amelia was about to follow
Jerry through the door.

"Would you mind?" I asked. "The candle."

Somewhat to my surprise she shook her head and then put her
finger to her lips like a conspirator. She meant to return after
showing Jerry to his room.

Frisky young filly, I mused. After the distressing scene just
enacted I can't imagine how she can be so—what is the word I'm
groping for?—single minded.

And you, dear reader, could be forgiven, nay, applauded, if
you expected me to close the chapter here for reasons of good
taste. However, I must continue, and insist that you read on. What
transpired is not what either of us expected.

She returned, yes, after a short interval. I, meantime, had settled down in the bed, making extra room on the side nearest the door. She had left the door ajar and she crept in, closing it silently behind her, and then paused.

I said whimsically, "This is a little unfair, my dear. I'm in my nightshirt and there you are already dressed for breakfast."

She said nervously, "Your Royal Highness—"

"Come now—it's Bertie between you and me."

"B-Bertie."

"Now you sound like the blessed poet."

"There's something else. It may not be important." Her tone of voice was anything but frolicsome.

I sat up in bed. "What is it? What else happened tonight?"

"After Miss Chimes collapsed, the servants cleared her place at the table."

"I noticed, yes."

"I don't know what to think. I didn't want to mention it in front of Jerry. He was so upset. My butler found something. A small piece of paper cut from a newspaper, *The Times*, I believe. It had been tucked into the frame containing Miss Chimes's name."

"Her place setting?"

"Yes."

"A piece of newspaper? What did it say? Anything significant?"

"It just said '*Monday.*'"

CHAPTER 5

"She was poisoned," said Alix flatly.

We were in her dressing room the next morning and I had just given her the news of the sad business, breaking it to her with particular care. I could well foresee my dear impetuous wife insisting upon our leaving the house forthwith, regardless of my high-minded decision to continue with the shoot. However, she remained calm. I'm afraid it was I who became excitable.

"Poisoned?"

"It was something in the food," said Alix. "That is obvious."

"Oh, Alix, I can't believe that!"

She was intractable. "Where did she collapse? At the dinner table. She was perfectly well until then."

"My dear, that's absurd. People don't murder each other at dinner parties."

"Bertie, you never listen properly to what I say. I didn't say it was murder. I said she was poisoned."

"Isn't that the same?"

"Food poisoning."

"That's equally absurd."

"Not in this house," said Alix in a voice suddenly as prim as a Mother Superior. "I should like to know when Lady Drummond last inspected her kitchen." She paused and eyed me unadmiringly through the mirror on the dressing table. "I have the impression that she would rather visit bedrooms."

"Now that's unfair, Alix. It was quite proper that she knocked on my door last night. I had to be told the bad news, for heaven's sake. And as for your food poisoning, why should it have killed Queenie Chimes and left the rest of us as fit as fleas?"

This time she gave me a look that would have toasted a crumpet. "I shall count the guests at breakfast. And I shall avoid cooked food of any sort. I advise you to do the same."

"I shan't be so ill-mannered."

"You mean you can't make do with a bowl of prunes."

"I mean, my dear, that I have the fullest confidence in the catering arrangements."

When we got downstairs I was told that Jerry had been up before six, had eaten an early breakfast and gone out. He had very decently asked Colwell, the house steward, to pass on his regret at not joining us, either for breakfast or the shoot. It was clear to me that this was a typically considerate act on Jerry's part; he had felt that his presence at breakfast would have put a blight on the party.

The Reverend Humphrey Paget hovered, Bible in hand, at the door of the breakfast room, wanting to know if I would be gracious enough to give the first reading. I rather shocked the fellow by saying that one or two simple prayers from him ought to be sufficient on this and other mornings. He wasn't to know it, but at home I always take breakfast privately, in my rooms, where my morning readings are taken invariably from the *Sporting Life*.

We followed the Chaplain in. It looked a full muster to me, including the house steward, the groom of chambers, butlers and housekeeper, but I was conscious of Alix taking a mental register. I must admit to a tremor of unease when I noticed that Bullivant wasn't present; however, he burst in shortly after, blaming a lost collar stud. I turned to Alix and asked in a whisper if she would now risk a kipper.

After prayers, I thought it fitting to say a few words, firstly of regret at the tragic news of Miss Chimes, then to suggest how best to conduct ourselves in the light of what had happened. I said I had thought hard and long whether to cancel the shoot. The decision had had to be taken early, for the beaters had been called for eight o'clock to start driving in the birds from the fields and hedgerows. The planning for this week of sport had begun more than a year ago, and the arrangements couldn't be altered at the drop of a hat. What with loaders, beaters, stops, pickers-up, drivers and catering staff, we would be using some two hundred personnel. It was the climax of the year for our hostess, dear Lady Drummond, and her gamekeepers. So I ventured to suggest that if any one of us had been called suddenly, like poor Miss Chimes, to our Maker, we would have wished the week's sport to continue regardless, and this was agreed to a man. I added that Jerry would be making arrangements for her to be given a decent, dignified burial in private, which would be impossible if I returned suddenly to Sandringham and the press got to hear of the tragedy. I'm sure that the point was well taken.

The servants withdrew and breakfast was served. Notwithstanding Alix's fears about the cooking, I ate as heartily as I always do before a shoot. It seemed crystal clear to me that the unfortunate Miss Chimes had been afflicted by some seizure of the brain or heart quite unrelated to anything she had eaten.

An hour later, about half past nine, I mounted the dog cart with the other guns, Bullivant, Holdfast, Pelham and Osgot-Edge, and we were driven at a canter to the first stand.

The lofty beech trees of Buckinghamshire are a handsome sight at any season. On this October morning, shafts of strong sunlight imprinted fiery red and gold upon the autumn foliage, and if that sounds poetical, I wonder what Osgot-Edge made of it. He was seated back-to-back with me, spared the agonies of small talk.

Instead I palavered cheerfully with Holdfast, who sat beside me in his deerstalker and tweeds, stout, apple-cheeked and bright eyed with anticipation of good shooting. Away from his insufferable wife he was not bad company at all, and I respected him for his charity towards dumb animals. I'll say this for Sir George: his name is on more horse troughs than any other man of my acquaintance. There's scarcely a cab horse in the kingdom without reason to be grateful to him. Of course, he married an old nag as well.

I remarked, "I suppose you've been shooting here for years like most of the others, George?"

"That's true, sir, except for last year, when I was down with shingles. The coverts are as good as any I could name."

"Sandringham included?"

"Sandringham slipped my mind, sir."

I laughed. "Did you hear the latest story about Harty-Tarty? He made a record bag at Chatsworth."

(Harty-Tarty, readers, is the affectionate name by which my friend the Marquess of Hartington is known. A charming fellow, he is indisputably the worst shot in England.)

"A record bag? Lord Hartington?" Sir George sounded incredulous.

"Yes, he took aim at a wounded cock pheasant which was limping in front of a gate. He bagged it."

"My word!"

"Yes, and with the same shot he hit the retriever which was chasing it."

"Killed it?"

"Oh, yes. And what's more, he hit the retriever's handler in the leg."

"No, that's too much!" said Sir George, doubled up with mirth.

"It wasn't. He shot the Chatsworth chef, who'd just arrived with the lunch."

Ahead was a clearing where two shooting brakes had already transported our loaders and the pickers-up and their animals. The dog cart came to a halt and I stepped down first. As we walked the short distance to the stand, I made a point of giving specific instructions to young Marcus Pelham, "You're our host, so you're the captain of guns today. Treat me exactly as you do the others."

He wetted his lips and ran his fingers nervously through his pale hair. He hadn't expected this. "In that case, sir," he said after a moment's hesitation, "let's make the draw." He beckoned to his head keeper, a short, silver-haired fellow I remembered from my previous shoot at Desborough.

The keeper invited me to pick a disk from his leather pouch. I drew number three. Holdfast was two, Bullivant and Osgot-Edge were four and five, which left one for Pelham.

I marched to my peg, sank the point of my shooting stick into the turf and signaled to my loaders.

"AND WAS THE SHOOTING TO your satisfaction, Your Royal Highness?" Amelia asked me anxiously when the ladies joined us for luncheon after three stands. A marquee had been erected beside the tributary of the Ouse that runs through the Desborough estate. We were enjoying our preprandial champagne whilst the morning's bag was being laid out for counting. It was a scene fit for a Christmas card: well over five hundred pheasants, twenty or more wild ducks, five or six woodcocks and sundry partridges, hares and rabbits.

"Your head gamekeeper is a miracle worker, my dear," I answered. "If I were you, I'd double his wage and recommend him for a knighthood."

"And the beaters?"

"Performed splendidly. The birds were beautifully presented, as fast and high as one could wish."

"That *is* a relief. Some of the men have never beaten before."

"It's always so. If they are well supervised, you get no trouble."

A suitable distance from us, the smocked army of about a hundred and fifty estate workers and farm laborers recruited for the week had grouped around several grand log fires, cooking sausages and onions, or some humble fodder with a smell just as appetizing. I can tell you that I was in grave danger of being lured away from the inevitable quails in aspic and game pie that awaited me in the luncheon tent.

I shall cleave to the memory of that scene by the river, refusing to have it taken from me by what happened after. Thirsty dogs lapping in the shallows; the smoke of the fires curling upwards; loaders at work cleaning the guns; and best of all, the ladies in their elegant walking costumes, looking like birds of paradise, so brilliant were the plumes and feathers in their bonnets. Our hostess, I recall, wore a stunning blue jacket and a jay's feathers in her hatband. "After yourself, sir, who was the most successful?" she asked me with an impish look.

"My dear Amelia, it's not meant to be a competition," I told her, though of course she knew, "but I can tell you in confidence that the poet hardly missed a thing."

"He surprises everyone year after year," she said. "People underestimate Wilfred."

"Is that so?"

"Oh, assuredly so." Something in the way she answered made me prick up my ears.

"It sounds to me as if you know of other talents in his repertoire."

She flushed and laughed. "Sir, I thought we were discussing his sporting prowess."

I changed the subject. "Has Jerry Gribble returned?"

"He hadn't by the time we left the house, sir. There's a lot to attend to, I think."

"Of course."

Presently luncheon was announced and we went into the marquee and took our places at the trestle table. This time I was seated opposite Miss Dundas, who surprised me by straight away asking the name of my gunsmith.

Talking guns with a lady was a novel experience. I suppose I should have realized that she was likely to own a weapon of some sort for use in the jungle. It turned out that she knew my gunsmith, Mr. Purdey of Oxford Street, tolerably well.

"My dear Miss Dundas, we ought to have invited you to shoot with us," I said affably.

Without batting an eyelid she said, "I don't kill for sport, sir. If I am obliged to shoot, so be it. There's no pleasure in the slaughter."

"Do I sense, Miss Dundas, that you don't altogether approve of shooting game?"

Her cool smile told me I hadn't flustered her. "Oh, I'm willing to shoot in self-defense, but I've never yet been threatened by a pheasant."

"You'd eat one, I dare say," I riposted.

"Yes, but I wouldn't stuff my larder with several thousand. There isn't room."

I laughed and so did she. It was the first time I'd noticed how small, even and immaculately white were her teeth. Her complexion, tanned by the tropical sun, certainly showed them to advantage. With the dark brown eyes, she had something of the Celt in her background, if not the Latin. I've always found women of that coloring difficult to resist for long. A whimsical thought occurred to me. Whilst Alix stood guard against the alluring Amelia, perhaps I might manage a discreet adventure with Miss Dundas.

The tiresome Lady Holdfast, seated on my right, broke into my reverie by lightly tapping my knee with her finger.

You're an optimist, I thought, and then I glanced along the table and observed that nobody had yet picked up a spoon.

"Heavens above!" I cried, snatching up mine and scooping up

a chunk of the fruit. "You needn't have waited for me. Damn it all, this is a picnic."

Somebody gave a nervous cough. They still hadn't gone for their spoons.

"Dear Father in Heaven . . ." came the Chaplain's voice from along the table, and I knew that I had made a *faux pas*.

"Didn't notice he was with us," I confided to Amelia after the amen was said.

"Humphrey? He likes to join in the meals," she told me. "He goes about his parochial duties at other times. He looks after the village church as well as our own, you know."

"He must be worn to a frazzle."

She smiled at the notion. "It doesn't show."

THE LADIES STAYED TO WATCH the first drive of the afternoon, in the part known as Roebuck Wood. Folding chairs were put out for them where the pickers-up waited at a safe distance behind the gun stands. I'm never sure whether the fair sex take much pleasure in watching a shoot. Some, I am told, pass the time with their hands over their ears, but I've always had my sights on the birds overhead.

We were rotating positions at each stand so that each gun had a fair day's sport, and I found myself between Holdfast and Bullivant. Young Pelham blew the horn to start the drive and we heard the tapping begin deep in the wood.

How stirring is the rattle of sticks on trees and the screech and churr of startled wildlife—music more thrilling than any I can recall in a concert hall. I waited, flanked by my loaders, picturing the activity in the coverts as the fugitive birds scampered ahead of the beaters. A pheasant has a natural reluctance to take to its wings, and it requires a well-managed beat to put it up precisely over the guns without flushing too many others at once.

This *battue* was faultless. They presented the birds in a long, soaring sequence almost vertically above us. I worked with three guns, receiving from the loader on my right, firing and passing it empty to the other man, never shifting my eyes from the sky. Barrel after barrel the fusillade went on as we picked our targets, swung and fired, dropping the pheasants with steady precision until the cry, "All out, gentlemen," The beaters were at the hedge and the horn was blown a second time to signal the end of the drive.

Ears ringing, I thanked my loaders, took out a cigar and strolled across to the ladies while the dogs were doing their work. The smell of cordite was all about us.

"I never saw such marvelous shooting, sir!" cried Amelia, and I saw Alix give her a sidelong glance.

"What was that, my dear?" I said out of mischief, cupping my ear and drawing closer to Amelia.

"Your shooting is incomparable!"

"Oh, I wouldn't say that. One or two in Europe are at least my equal. We'll see what the bag amounts to."

Alix had turned her back.

The other guns joined us and I noticed Bullivant walk straight up to Isabella Dundas and present her with a long russet tail feather he'd picked up. She fitted it under her hatband and twirled about like a dancer to display it, incidentally affording us all a sight of her ankles. Then she gave him an amused look that I didn't know how to interpret. Claude, I decided, would have to be watched.

Amelia was still at my elbow singing the praises of my marksmanship. The other guns, notably Osgot-Edge, had not been so well positioned to impress the ladies. Even so, I suspected that she was overdoing the tribute, and so, evidently, did her brother Marcus, for as he was passing he prodded her thigh with the blunt end of his shooting stick and said, "Sis, you're making a nuisance of yourself." Addressing me, he said, "Would you care for a nip, sir?"

He held out his brandy flask.

"Not now," I said. "I shoot better with my head clear. Which way is the next stand?"

He pointed. "Beyond the ridge. It should be the best of the day, sir. The birds have already been driven out of their roosting ground into a smaller covert, so when they're flushed out, they fly towards home."

I nodded my approval. A pheasant will always fly better towards home than away from it. "How long will it take us? Shouldn't we start, or the light will go?"

A wagonette had been brought up in case we cared to ride, but I suggested legging it through the wood, and no one demurred. We said our farewell to the ladies, who were being conveyed back to the house to change into tea gowns. I generally find that I have a splitting headache by teatime after a shoot and don't much care what anyone is wearing, but that doesn't stop the ladies, bless them, from parading.

The dead birds were tidily lined up for counting, almost two hundred pheasants, one of the gamekeepers said, bringing our day's bag past seven hundred.

"Somebody missed a few this time," I jested. "I picked off sixty for certain. Seventy, I'd say."

Bullivant asked Marcus, "Do you think we'll take a thousand today?"

"Easily."

I said, "I trust we can improve on that as the week goes on, gentlemen."

Holdfast remarked, "With Jerry Gribble in the party we should."

"I wouldn't count on it," said Bullivant, grinning. "Have you ever seen Jerry shoot?"

"That's enough about Jerry," I told him curtly. Jerry *is* hopeless with a gun, but I won't have my friends ridiculed behind their backs at any time, let alone when they are making funeral arrangements.

With Marcus Pelham leading, we started along a bridle path towards the ridge. Osgot-Edge fell in behind young Pelham, and Bullivant joined him, evidently willing to try for some kind of intelligible conversation. I forgave him a little for his crass remark about Jerry.

I brought up the rear with Holdfast and discussed insurance. I know as little about insurance as I do about poetry, so it was pleasing to discover that according to actuarial tables I can look forward confidently to attaining my sixty-ninth birthday, whereas young Pelham, who is half my age, will be lucky to get to sixty-one. Don't ask me how it works.

The top of the ridge afforded a fine view of beech woods and bracken. We were almost at the limit of the Desborough land. It was bordered by a road, just visible in stretches between the autumn foliage. Everything across the road and as far as the eye could see belonged to Amelia's neighbor, Jerry Gribble. Closer to us, Marcus Pelham pointed out the tower of the family chapel and beyond it the gamekeeper's lodge and some of the tied cottages.

A short distance below us on the slope was the small covert

where the pheasants had been driven in readiness to be put up for the last stand of the day. The army of beaters, conspicuous in their long white smocks, was making its well-disciplined way in silence up the incline and around the covert to begin the drive.

I complimented Pelham on their performance and enquired whether they would get a decent supper at the day's end. Rabbit stew awaited them. My juices stirred and sang a short cantata at the thought.

To cover the sound I said, "I fear we mustn't linger, gentlemen. Let's go down to our positions."

We set off again, skirting the covert.

The last stand of the day was cleverly sited in a hollow with good cover, far enough from the covert for the birds to fan out and reach a challenging height. Our loaders and the dog handlers, who were being conveyed there by horsepower, had not yet put in an appearance, which irked me slightly at the time, but was to prove fortuitous.

Discussing the wind and its possible effect on the flight path of the birds, we continued for some time down the slope before anyone thought to mention an object lying on the open ground selected for the stand. Brownish in color, it might have been a blanket thoughtfully provided in case any of us needed extra warmth at the end of the day: that was my first assumption. Farther down the hill I formed the view that it was a recumbent man, perhaps an assistant gamekeeper sent ahead to meet us. If so, he was in for a surprise when we woke him from his slumbers.

"Is he one of your men?" Holdfast asked Pelham.

"If he is, he won't remain one," said our host through gritted teeth. "Excuse me, while I deal with it." He quickened his step.

Tactfully the rest of us slackened our pace.

Pelham approached the motionless figure, leaned over, grasped the shoulder roughly and attempted to rouse the man. Without success.

Pelham looked up at us. "I think he's dead."

"What?"

"Look."

We gathered around. He was indisputably dead. He had a revolver beside him and there was a hole in his head.

CHAPTER 6

Things spoken in moments of extreme shock tend to look rather puerile written down, so I don't propose to repeat what was said over the corpse. Rest assured that my companions and I were made aghast by our discovery. It was Jerry Gribble.

Young Pelham was the first to make a pertinent suggestion. "I'd better call off the drive, sir."

"The drive? Good God, yes."

"Shall I tell the keepers what has happened?"

"No, no. Can't do that." I gave the matter some rapid thought. "Say that His Royal Highness was called away on an urgent matter of State, so shooting is abandoned for the day."

He set off at a run.

I picked up the fatal weapon and turned it over carefully in my hands. It was a revolver made by my own gunsmith, Mr. Purdey of Oxford Street. There were five more bullets in the chambers. Poor old Jerry, I reflected ruefully: didn't trust his aim even at that range.

Then Claude Bullivant reminded me that our loaders and the dogs would arrive at any minute.

"Head them off, then," I told him. "Which way are they coming? By the road? Get down there and stop them." I waved the gun in that direction, giving Bullivant a moment of unease. "And one more thing, Claude."

"Yes, sir?"

"You'd better return to the house with the loaders. Inform the ladies that we expect to be late for tea." The commands sprang unbidden to my lips. I say it myself, I'm a first-class man in a crisis. I would have made a very able general on the battlefield. I suppose it's in the blood.

Bullivant lingered. "Is that all, sir?"

"Give them our apologies, of course."

"But they'll want to know why."

"We don't want them to panic. Oh, for pity's sake, Claude, you can keep a crowd of females in suspense, can't you?"

I was left with Wilfred Osgot-Edge and Sir George Holdfast for company. I pocketed the revolver and we sat on our shooting sticks and stared at each other.

Holdfast rubbed at his face as if the gnats were troubling him and said through his fingers, "I'm sure you're right to send the loaders away, sir, but it does leave us with a difficulty. What are we going to do with the body? The wagonette would have come in useful."

"Good point." I wished he'd mentioned it before. "How far are we from the house?"

Osgot-Edge almost fell off his stick trying to tell us it was a mile away.

Holdfast said, without, I am sure, grasping the significance of the remark, "Jerry's own house is closer."

I seized on it at once. "That's exactly where I intend to take him. Let the poor fellow be laid out on his own bed." I didn't say so, but I instantly foresaw several advantages to the plan. For one thing it would spare the ladies—and our hostess in particular—some distress. A dead body on the premises is no help at all to a house party. And without wishing to mislead the authorities, we would save them hours of work by letting it appear that Jerry had died on his own side of the fence. You see, when a man puts a gun to his head there has to be an inquest, and it's fearfully boring for all concerned if an entire shooting party has to be questioned by the police.

Far better if he had died at home, Why, it might even have allowed the jury to bring in a verdict of accidental death. For all sorts of reasons, sentimental, moral and legal, you don't want suicide if you can possibly avoid it.

The chance of any other verdict but *felo-de-se* would depend on the medical evidence. I braced myself to look down at the fatal wound. I make no claims to pathological knowledge, but I've seen plenty of injured animals put out of their misery, and I do know what a bullet wound looks like. The hole in Jerry's forehead was circular and singularly neat, suggesting that he had held the revolver at least six inches from his head. If he had pressed the barrel against his forehead, the hole would have been more in the form of a cross or star, due to the gases emitted from the weapon. This was not the case. How fortunate, I thought; anyone examining the body might be led to believe Jerry had fired accidentally. He was always a duffer with guns.

Reader, I can imagine what you are thinking. To be utterly frank with you, I didn't at this juncture entertain any explanation other than suicide. The possibility of murder didn't remotely occur to me. If you had been with me that dread Tuesday and known what I did about Jerry's desolate state of mind, you would have shared my opinion, I'm certain.

Faint voices traveled to us from the depths of the wood, too indistinct to make sense. Marcus must have reached the line and told them their work was over for the day. An unexpected flurry of black and white at the edge of my vision turned out to be a magpie taking to the air. Automatically I swung my hands to the right to receive my gun, regardless that my loader wasn't beside me, and I noticed that Osgot-Edge had done the same. He smiled slightly, then liberally dampened the back of my hand in saying, "S-sorrow."

"You don't need to apologize."

"No, sir. I said s-sorrow."

"I don't think I follow you."

"One m-magpie means sorrow."

I gave him a glazed look. "Really? Is that a superstition? It sounds appropriate, I must say."

"F-from Scotland." With that, he launched into a full rendering of the verse, and I shall spare you the consonantal falterings:

> "One's sorrow; two's mirth,
> Three's a wedding, four's a birth,
> Five's a christening, six a dearth,
> Seven's heaven, eight is hell,
> And nine's the devil his ane sel'."

I thanked him and said I would rather count plum stones. I didn't mean to sound ungracious after his laborious recitation, so I asked, "Are you a native of Scotland, Mr. Osgot-Edge?"

He looked shocked. "D-definitely not. I c-come from a very old English family. Osgot is mentioned in the D-Domesday Book."

There was another disturbance in the thicket and more birds took to the sky.

Holdfast asked, "What do two wood pigeons signify?"

"Pigeon pie if you can bag them," I said.

We understood the reason for their sudden flight when a few moments later Marcus Pelham came briskly from the covert. He informed us that he had spoken to the gamekeepers. The beaters were trekking back. He'd also seen Bullivant turn back the wagonettes and climb aboard one.

"Excellent." I took out a cigar. "Better give them time to get clear." No one showed much inclination to speak, so I did my best to lift the assembled spirits a little. "This melancholy situation reminds me of a letter I once received at Balmoral in response to an invitation. I have a sneaking impression that Jerry might have appreciated it. 'Sir, may it please Your Royal Highness, the laird is honored to inform you that he does not mean to shoot himself tomorrow; but his gamekeepers will be ordered to accompany you and the usual dogs.' Isn't it priceless?"

"Extremely droll, sir," said Holdfast.

Pelham asked, "Is there a plan, sir?"

I told him what I had in mind and he saw the sense of it at once. "In the circumstances, it's the obvious thing to do."

I didn't care for the "obvious," but I was grateful for his support. Unfortunately there's always some wiseacre who thinks he has a better idea: in this case, Holdfast.

"I've been giving it some thought, sir. Do we really need to move the corpse so far?"

"What do you mean?"

"Why not leave him here, just out of sight in the covert? The gamekeepers will find him soon enough."

"You think that's a better plan, do you?"

"Well, sir, it has the merit of being simple. If he doesn't have a gun beside him it will look as if he died accidentally, the victim of a stray bullet."

I rolled my eyes. "And what sort of nincompoop is supposed to have been shooting at pheasants with revolver bullets?"

He reddened. "Ah. I hadn't thought of that."

Pelham said, "Your plan is best, sir."

I turned to Osgot-Edge. He only needed to tip his head in support. I wasn't asking for anything more. His recital of the verse about the magpie must have gone to his head, because he said, "In v-view of last year we d-don't want another shooting accident."

"Too true," said Pelham.

"What happened last year?" asked Holdfast.

Pelham registered surprise. "Weren't you in the party?"

"I had to miss last year. Wasn't well."

"So did I," said Pelham, and grinned. "Wasn't invited. A beater was shot, a lad of fifteen, one of our own estate workers. Pure bad luck that somebody's swing was out."

"Fatally shot?" I asked.

"Yes. Fortunately he had no parents. Not much was made of the incident." He glanced down at Jerry's body. "This is another kettle of fish." After a glare from me, he added, "So to speak. I mean, the death of the Duke of Bournemouth. Really, I'm surprised Jerry shot himself here when he could have done it at home."

Holdfast said, "I don't suppose he was thinking straight."

Osgot-Edge managed to say, "He m-must have wanted us to find him."

It was a shrewd observation. "Quite possibly," I said. "Typical of Jerry. Considerate to the last. He wouldn't have wanted to scare some wretched chambermaid out of her wits, so he made sure his corpse would be discovered by us. Left it to the last stand so as not to spoil our shooting more than necessary."

Holdfast said with a sigh, "Poor old Jerry. He must have been besotted with Miss Chimes to resort to this."

"C-captivated," said Osgot-Edge more poetically.

Then Pelham, smart aleck, shamed us all with his common sense by asking, "Did he leave a note? Have you searched his pockets yet?"

Not wishing to admit that I hadn't thought of it, I said loftily, "We've been too busy discussing what to do with him. Very well, let's see if there's anything." I stooped to examine the body, which was dressed, like the rest of us, in a Norfolk suit. In one of the top pockets my fingers located a tiny slip of paper. I took it out.

Immediately something uncomfortable stirred in the pit of my stomach.

Holdfast asked, "What have you got there, sir? Is something written on it?"

"Just a scrap of newspaper," I remarked, trying to sound unimpressed.

"Anything significant, sir?"

"I doubt it. There's only one word here and that's '*Tuesday.*'"

"Strange. Why would he have that in his pocket?"

"I haven't the faintest idea."

"If you ask me," said Holdfast, "it's unimportant. Probably some system devised by his valet for putting out the clothes in the desired sequence."

It was an ingenious suggestion, and I was so grateful for it that I felt like shaking George Holdfast's hand. I knew he was mistaken, of course, but I couldn't myself think of anything remotely plausible. The great thing was that it seemed to satisfy my companions. They were unaware of the piece of paper that had been found when Queenie Chimes collapsed at the dinner table. Only Amelia, her butler and I knew about that. Even Jerry hadn't been told, which made this fresh discovery puzzling, not to say disturbing.

Taking a grip on myself, I resumed my examination of the pockets.

Nothing else of interest was on Jerry's person. I think I found a handkerchief, some coins and his watch.

A church clock chimed. The afternoon was fast drawing to a close, and there was a job to be done before dark. After some trial and error the four of us contrived a way of lifting Jerry's body by employing our shooting sticks crosswise as a sort of improvised stretcher, for none of us particularly wished to take a grip on the stiffened limbs. It proved an efficient method. There was the occasional stumble, but we reached the road in quite a short time, passed our burden across a stone wall and so entered the Bournemouth estate unseen by anyone. Dense ferns delayed our progress somewhat, and it was a relief to reach a bridle path that led us more swiftly to the landscaped lawns in front of the house.

Twilight was in session by this time and to anyone who chanced to look out a window we would have presented a weird, not to say gruesome, picture as we moved silently across the turf. Presently we came to a steep, stone-lined bank forming what landscape gardeners call a ha-ha, a shelf in the lawn contrived to be invisible from the house. Without needing to discuss it, we lowered the body to the ground and stretched our aching shoulders.

Holdfast said, "Shall we leave him here, sir?"

"Good Lord, no," I said. "Can't do that. We must get him indoors."

"Break in?"

"Really, George," I said in a pained voice. "One of us must go to the front entrance and ask to see the house steward. You, I think, Marcus."

Young Pelham's eyes whitened in the gloom, whether out of stark surprise or pleasure at being asked I couldn't say.

I told him, "Be sure that you speak to the house steward alone. You will break the news of his master's death and you will say that some of his friends have brought him home and are waiting outside. If the man has his wits about him, he'll invite us to bring the body at once to the gun room."

"The *gun* room, sir?"

"Yes, the gun room," I repeated as if speaking to a child. "Any steward worthy of the name would rather his master died accidentally whilst cleaning his gun than by his own hand. He won't need telling."

"Very well, sir."

From our position behind the ha-ha we watched Pelham cross the turf and heard his feet reach the gravel drive. In a moment a light appeared at the front entrance and we dipped out of sight.

There was a long, suspenseful wait.

Finally footsteps crunched on the gravel again, and after an interval Pelham leaned over the ha-ha and informed us that the house steward was ready to receive the body. Between us we used the shooting sticks to hoist Jerry's mortal remains to the higher level. My three companions stood over him.

"What are you waiting for?" I whispered from below them.

Holdfast cleared his throat. "Aren't you coming with us, sir?"

I said, "It wouldn't be appropriate." Nobody spoke, so I added, "I think I've done my share. And it goes without saying, gentlemen, that my own part in this melancholy episode must not be divulged to a living soul. I shall remain here behind the ha-ha until you emerge again from the house."

Another silence greeted this. They made no move to lift the corpse.

I said, "Is there a difficulty?"

Holdfast looked at the others to see if either of them preferred to speak first. "Well, sir, with three of us . . . we'll have to think of another way to carry him."

"Oh, for pity's sake," I snapped. "Pick him up with your hands."

Nothing was said for a moment. Then Holdfast squatted and placed his hands gingerly under the shins. "He's rigid. Like a piece of timber."

Osgot-Edge said, "Rigor m-m-"

"Much easier to get a grip," I said. You can't be fastidious in emergencies. "What's the matter, Pelham?" He hadn't made a move.

"The gun."

"Which gun?"

"The fatal weapon. It's not much help to us in your pocket, sir."

He was right, but I didn't care for the way he chose to mention it. I passed the weapon to Holdfast and said, "Now get on with it."

They bent to the task and took the strain.

Left alone, I perched on my shooting stick and watched the sky turn from purple to black. A breeze was blowing up from the north. I shivered and wondered bleakly whether tea was yet finished at Desborough Hall. My hip flask was empty. My boots pinched. I wasn't relishing an hour's tramp in the dark.

The next thing I heard, some twenty minutes later, was the sound of carriage wheels. I raised my head above the ha-ha in time to see a small carriage driven at a canter from the rear of the house. Three men and the driver were aboard. I was incensed. I was pretty damned sure they were Holdfast, Pelham and Osgot-Edge, and they must have been given transport back to Desborough.

Surely they didn't propose to abandon me?

I snatched up my shooting stick and set off with bent back along the length of the ha-ha in the direction they were taking. The posture was humiliating. It brought to mind the vulgar riddle that I once accidentally overheard from a drunken undergraduate at Cambridge: what is the difference between the Prince of Wales and an orangutan? A nice shock I gave the fellow when I stepped out from behind a potted fern and demanded to be told the answer, which I have to admit was rather clever, though nobody laughed at the time: the Prince is the Heir Apparent and the ape has a hairy parent. Anyway, the mental picture taunted me now as I loped along with my knuckles grazing the turf. And that was not the worst of it. The carriage showed no sign of halting. In despair I threw caution to the winds, stopped, stood at my full height, shouted and waved my shooting stick, to absolutely no effect. They galloped out of sight along the drive.

No doubt you will be as relieved as I was to find that they finally stopped for me at the end of the drive, just outside the main gates. Plodding towards them like a cab horse destined for the knacker's yard, I heard Pelham's voice say, "That's him!" and then, unbelievably, "Come on, matey, stir your stumps. We haven't got all night."

Insolent pup, I thought. I was about to explode when it was made apparent to me that his words were meant for the ears of the driver. He was playacting to protect my identity. George Holdfast, no actor at all, said woodenly, "Give him a hand up, then. It wasn't Charlie's fault we lost our way."

I climbed up and took a seat beside the poet. While I was recovering my breath, Pelham told me in subdued tones how Jerry Gribble's house steward had received the news. The man was worthy of his calling, thank heavens. He had recognized the wisdom of placing the body in the gun room where one of the gamekeepers would find it. They had deposited Jerry on the floor with the revolver beside him and—a nice touch—a bristle brush in his hand for cleaning the barrel.

We barely had time to agree on how much the ladies needed to be told before the carriage drew up at the front of Desborough Hall and Amelia came running down the steps.

"What happened? Has there been an accident?"

I said as I climbed down, "Didn't Claude Bullivant tell you, my dear?"

She spread her hands in a way that conveyed her frustration. "He was very unforthcoming. He simply informed us that you wouldn't be here for tea and then he asked to have a bath. He hasn't appeared for hours."

"That's my fault," I admitted. "I asked him to say the minimum. My dear, we have all had a dreadful shock."

"Someone *is* hurt."

"Jerry Gribble is dead."

She clapped her hand to her mouth.

I put a supporting arm around her and told her gently, "He shot himself, poor fellow. We abandoned our shoot when we learned the dreadful news. We've been to his house and paid our respects. I'm sorry, my dear."

That was the version of events that we had decided would cause the least distress. It was broadly true, if selective with the facts. We had planned it from the highest motives.

The ladies immediately smelled a rat. As if with one mind, they devoted the rest of the evening to wheedling the entire story from us. They were clever. They cornered us separately and got the truth by question and observation. Whilst I was dressing for dinner Alix spotted some blistering on my hands from the stretcher work I'd done with the shooting stick. I didn't admit it right out, of course, but at dinner she took particular note of the other men's hands and they all had blisters except Bullivant and the Reverend Humphrey Paget, who had come in as usual, and was shocked at the news. I think because of the Chaplain's presence, no one accused us of deceit, but significant looks were exchanged. By the time the ladies left the table we men were ready to tell all.

The Reverend Paget left directly after dinner. Perhaps he sensed the crackle of electricity in the air. I can tell you, the brandy did several rounds before we felt sufficiently fortified to rejoin the ladies.

CHAPTER 7

Have you ever noticed that yawning is contagious? About an hour after dinner I put my hand to my mouth and said, "Pardon me." Soon everyone was at it, and when I suggested we send for the candles at ten o'clock there was no dissent.

You may think that the shocks and strains of the day had taken their toll. Not in my case. I am blessed with a very resilient constitution. True, my arms and legs still ached a little from the unaccustomed exercise, but I wasn't ready to turn in. I simply wanted everyone out of the way to permit me a private conversation with Amelia Drummond. So after I had wished good night to Alix I changed into my night things, put on a dressing gown and carpet slippers and quietly returned downstairs.

As I expected, she was still in the main drawing room, going through the next day's arrangements with Colwell, her house steward. The moment I appeared, she broke off and stepped towards me, plainly alarmed by the possibility that the hot water had not been left in my room, or some receptacle had not been emptied.

"Your Royal Highness . . . ?"

Behind her, Colwell bowed and started backing discreetly to the door.

I called to him, "Don't go." To Amelia I said, "With your permission, my dear."

She fingered her necklace and tried to appear composed. "Of course, sir."

I beckoned to Colwell. Amazing how distinguished some domestic servants manage to look behind whiskers. Dressed in a frock coat he could easily have passed for Lord Salisbury, the Prime Minister. If anything, his expression was more noble than Salisbury's. I said, "Yesterday evening when you were clearing the table you found a scrap of newspaper at the place where Miss Chimes had been seated. Is that correct?"

"Quite correct, Your Royal Highness."

"You showed it to Lady Drummond?"

"Yes, sir."

"And to anyone else?"

"No, sir."

"Have you mentioned it to anyone since?"

"No, sir."

"Not even the servants?"

"I never discuss anything with the servants except their duties, sir."

I accepted his word with a nod. "Then I think it would be wise if you continued to keep it to yourself or, better still, forgot about it entirely."

"I shall, sir."

I dismissed him and turned to Amelia. "And now, my dear, if you will forgive me, I would like to put the same question to you."

She looked at me earnestly with her deep brown eyes. "Sir, I have discussed the matter with no one except yourself."

"Not with Jerry Gribble?"

She frowned. "No."

"That is peculiar." I told her what I had found in Jerry's pocket.

Her reception of this information was just as I expected. She blinked, screwed up her face in puzzlement and said, "What on earth can it mean? Was he trying to tell us something?"

"If he was, we knew it already," I commented. "We may not be the best brains in the land, but we didn't need telling that today is Tuesday."

"Perhaps the piece of paper had some other purpose. Did he mean to show that his death was linked with Queenie's?"

"How could he, if none of us had told him about the first scrap of paper?"

"I hadn't thought of that." She reddened.

I said, "You're quite sure you didn't mention it to anyone else? Not even your brother?"

"I swear it, sir."

She looked so hurt at the very suggestion that I grasped her hand and squeezed it. "My dear, I believe you."

Her eyes glistened. "And I am sure Colwell is telling the truth. It is a mystery." A tear started sliding down her cheek.

I felt for a handkerchief and found that I didn't have one in the pocket of my dressing gown, so I stopped the tear with my fingertip. "Chin up. Stiff upper lip."

She managed a wan smile. "Sir, I'm sorry."

Sounding more and more like a page from *The Girl's Own Paper* I said, "What's done is done, and we've got to make the best we can of it. It's up to us all to behave as if we don't even know about Jerry's death. We'll have a full day's sport tomorrow just as we planned."

"Oh, yes, sir." Her face lit up again.

I winked. "I wouldn't object to 'Bertie' when we're alone."

I was given a smoldering look. "That's an intimacy I hardly dare to aspire to, sir."

Reader, how did it happen? One moment we were discussing the death of a dear friend and the next I was flirting. Hadn't I resolved to sidestep Amelia's charms? I am burdened with an amorous nature that undermines all my good intentions. I know better than to fight it.

"Don't be so coy," I chided her. "You used the name more than once in my bedroom last night,"

"True."

"In private, I'm a man like anyone else, as you will appreciate . . . if you are so inclined." I hoped this declaration didn't sound too rehearsed. It had served me well on similar campaigns.

"Oh." She liked it. She was becoming breathless and her efforts to reinflate herself were visibly improving her charms.

Remembering Alix, I said, "But I don't think my suite is best placed for an intimate conversation."

"Nor mine," she said quickly.

I hesitated. "That is a difficulty."

"Not insurmountable . . . Bertie." The way she spoke that word "insurmountable" syllable by syllable made it sound more suggestive than anything in the dictionary or out of it. The "Bertie" came as quite an anticlimax.

I said with a twinkle, "I believe Desborough has ninety-seven other bedrooms."

"But wickedly cold."

"You mean that the fires have not been lit? My dear, neither of us will notice. If we can agree on a room and both succeed in finding it in, say, an hour from now, a warm outcome is assured, I promise you."

She blushed deeply. "Sir, you flatter me, but I am forced to tell you that tonight is inappropriate."

"Inappropriate?"

"Impossible."

"Ah."

So be it, I thought philosophically. You don't argue with a lady over dates. Perhaps I was feeling more *hors de combat* than I had been prepared to admit a few minutes ago.

With, I hope, good grace, I wished her a pleasant night's sleep and returned to my room. In the corridor I fancied I heard a door open briefly and close again behind me, but I paid no heed to it. Anyone who has stayed in a strange house or hotel knows how at any hour of the night if you need to venture along the corridor somebody else will inevitably choose the same moment to walk past. Doors are repeatedly being opened a fraction and timidly closed again.

I turned off the gas, knelt briefly in prayer, dropped my dressing gown, got into bed and gave a genuine yawn. Sleep must have followed quickly.

Do you know, for the second night running, my sleep was interrupted in the small hours? I was in the middle of a stirring dream of a shoot at Sandringham. I was in splendid form, hitting everything the beaters put up. One glorious cock pheasant, a veritable screamer, flew much higher than the rest. I was supremely certain that I would bring it down. I swung the barrel and squeezed the trigger and instead of the discharge I heard a curious squeak and felt a sudden draft on my face. Then there was a muffled thud. I woke at once. The squeak had come from my door handle. The thud wasn't a pheasant dropping from the sky, but my solid oak door being closed.

I refused to be alarmed. For one thing, the dream had left me in a state of elation. For another, I was confident that I was being visited by Amelia. It had been girlish panic that had prompted her to postpone our assignation. After going to bed she had no doubt lain awake in a lather of frustration. Finally, unable to subdue nature any longer, she had come to me, I smiled in anticipation and lay quite still.

Nothing else happened.

Presently I sat up and peered into the gloom. Sadly for my self-esteem, I had to conclude that nobody was in the room except myself. Yet well-made doors with good fittings don't open themselves for no reason.

She has lost her nerve again, I thought.

I leapt out of bed and without even bothering with my dressing gown, crossed the floor and tried the door. The handle gave a squeak identical to the one I'd heard before. I peered out. No one was in sight, but I fancied I heard a floorboard creak nearby, around a corner. This, I decided, warranted investigation.

Pausing briefly to listen outside dear Alix's door in case the noise had disturbed her (it hadn't), I padded off in pursuit. I knew that Amelia's room was not far along that adjacent corridor, and I wanted if possible to catch her before she reached it.

I swung around the corner straight into the arms, not of Amelia, but of her wretched brother Marcus. Like me, he was in his nightshirt and nothing else.

Imagine my confusion.

"What the devil . . . ?"

He had his finger to his lips. "Shh."

I said, "Someone just opened my bedroom door."

He said in a whisper, "Kindly keep your voice down, sir. It was I."

I said, "Young man, you had better explain yourself at once."

As if only just aware of the gravity of the situation, he swallowed, drew himself up and said, "Sir, I'm profoundly sorry. I didn't mean to disturb you. I wasn't expecting to find you in bed."

"Where the deuce did you expect me to be at this hour?" He didn't reply directly. He fiddled with the cuffs of his nightshirt and mumbled something about his sister.

"What are you saying?" I demanded.

"I heard you go downstairs after the rest of us had retired. I knew Amelia was down there, and I assumed . . ."

"You assumed what?"

Before he answered, a door across the corridor opened and Claude Bullivant looked out. "Who's there?"

I said, "Nobody. Go back to sleep."

He closed the door again.

Marcus took the opportunity to change tack. "You're a man of the world, sir. I regret to say that my sister has become—how shall I put this?—rather too liberal with her favors since her husband passed away. I'm afraid the shock unhinged her in this respect. As her only living relative, I don't want her to bring discredit on herself and the family."

I said, "What are you talking about, man? I'm the future King. Where's the discredit in that?"

Pelham hesitated. "You misunderstand me, sir. I don't mean to offend you. I'm perfectly content—indeed, honored—for my sister to, em . . ."

"Concede me the ultimate favor?"

"Absolutely. What distresses me is when she concedes it to any Tom, Dick or Harry who cares to pass the time of day."

Reader, I could scarcely restrain myself from striking him. "That's a deplorable thing for a man to say about his sister, Pelham, and I happen to know that it isn't true. As a matter of fact, the lady was unwilling to welcome anyone to her bed tonight."

He clicked his tongue defiantly and looked away.

His attitude didn't impress me in the least, so I gave him the dressing-down he deserved. I told him to look me in the eye when I was addressing him. Then I told him curtly, "This prying of yours is more offensive than anything Amelia is alleged to be doing. It is underhanded, unreasonable and unhealthy. If you have a modicum of decency you'll find yourself a mistress of your own as soon as possible and let your sister conduct her private life in the way she pleases. Now get to bed and let us all get some sleep."

He fairly slunk away.

I felt better for having spoken my mind. Little did Amelia realize as she lay asleep that she had a champion defending her. Or was she asleep? I had not gone more than a step towards my room when I heard a short, low-pitched laugh behind me. It was female in origin and it sounded so close that I spun around expecting to see the lady standing there.

The corridor was empty.

The laugh came again, clear as anything, wanton, almost a gurgle of pleasure. That's Amelia, I thought. That is definitely her voice and she is playing a game with me.

One of the first rules of noctambulation is to know who occupies the rooms around one. With the help of my valet, I had acquired a plan of the ladies' rooms on the first night, now usefully committed to memory. Our hostess had her private suite up a couple of steps on the left, so I crept towards her door and listened. Teasingly, she was silent again. I gripped the handle and turned it gently. This handle was well oiled. I eased open the door and stepped inside to find myself in Amelia's dressing room. The fire still glowed sufficiently in the grate for me to recognize the gown she had worn that evening, now hanging outside the wardrobe. A heap of white undergarments lay across an armchair and the lower half of a lady appeared to be standing guard beside them, but was in reality her bustle and petticoat.

Having got thus far, I didn't propose to leave without trying the inner door that led to the bedroom. It was ajar. Temptress, I thought. You ran in here just as I came in.

I wasn't altogether surprised to find the bed unoccupied. My guess was that she would be hiding behind the door without a stitch of clothing on. Certain of the fair sex love to exhibit themselves in as stark and dramatic a fashion as possible. The first time I saw the French beauty, Cora Pearl, was at the Café Anglais in Paris when she was served to me on a silver platter wearing nothing but a rope of pearls and a sprig of parsley.

I said in a gravelly voice, "Come on—surprise me, then."

Amelia was not behind the door. She was not under the bed or in the wardrobe or behind the curtains. She was not on the balcony.

I said, "You can come out, my dear. I'm stumped." Silence.

By degrees it dawned on me that I had made a mistake. She wasn't in her rooms. Then where the deuce was she? From where had that seductive laugh come?

I returned to the corridor and stood as near as I could estimate to the spot where I'd heard her voice. There were no obvious places to hide. Not a potted palm or a Ming vase to shelter behind.

Mystified, I waited for another sound from her. When it eventually came, it wasn't nearly so audible. It was more of a sigh than a laugh. Helpfully, it was repeated a number of times, faint, but distinct, and the voice was definitely Amelia's.

The sighing settled into a rhythm. I traced it to the other side of a door just across the corridor from where I was standing. The sound slowly increased in tempo and volume.

Marcus, I thought, you could be right about your sister.

I gave a sigh of my own, gritted my teeth and returned to my room.

There, I counted on my fingers. Not Holdfast; his room was at the far end of the corridor. Not Bullivant; he'd looked out of his, which was on the other side. Not the Chaplain, thank goodness; he wasn't staying in the house. And not Marcus Pelham; he'd gone in the other direction. I was just arriving at the inevitable conclusion when my thought processes were rudely interrupted.

Was it my imagination, or did I hear a distant shout of, "M-m-m-marvelous!"?

Wednesday

CHAPTER 8

Pardon me if I'm mistaken, reader, but did you anticipate a body at the beginning of this chapter? If so, then *you* were mistaken. We all appeared for breakfast on Wednesday morning, if not bouncing with health and strength, at least capable of buttering toast. Osgot-Edge, I'll grant you, made buttering his slice look as laborious as painting a ceiling. Amelia, on the other hand, was more bobbish than ever. She announced, "I'm planning parlor games this evening, so I don't want anyone sneaking off to the billiard room after dinner."

Lady Holdfast, another who managed to be gratingly boisterous, clapped her hands and cried, "Parlor games—how jolly! Shall we have charades? I'm very good at thinking up words."

"Postman's Knock is more fun," said Bullivant.

"How typical of a man to suggest that."

"Hide and Seek," said Alix, who loves nothing better than a romp.

"Definitely Hide and Seek," said Amelia, giving me one of her looks.

I pretended not to have noticed. The previous night's Hide and Seek hadn't pleased me much.

I wasn't allowed to stay silent. "What's your favorite game, sir?" Amelia demanded.

"Ptarmigan," I said, "cooked in a rich gravy and covered with pie crust."

That put a temporary end to the conversation on parlor games.

We started the day's shoot at the place where we had found Jerry's body the previous afternoon. Nothing resembling a wraith rose up from the fatal spot; just regular puffs of gunsmoke as the birds were flushed out. It was a good bag and my mood improved. I made a point of walking across to the game cart and admiring the Suffolk Punch who hauled it. He was sporting his brasses in my honor. "Is he as strong as he looks?" I asked the driver. "I sincerely hope so. You'll have a full load by lunchtime." And he did, six hundred and seventy-two birds. I know, because I won the sweep to estimate the bag. The day was turning out better than I could have hoped for.

THE CHAPLAIN GAVE US A fright at luncheon by arriving with a companion who turned out to be the district coroner, a cheerful, florid-looking fellow called Elston. They had just come from viewing the gun room where Jerry Gribble's corpse had been discovered by his own head gamekeeper. To our enormous relief, it emerged that Elston was an old friend of Jerry's and was satisfied—or willing to be convinced, at any rate—that the death had been accidental. Then Osgot-Edge incautiously asked him, "C-can you tell us about Miss Ch-Ch-"

"Mischance. He means misadventure," I dexterously cut in. "Is that the verdict in such cases, Mr. Elston?"

"Misadventure? Quite possibly, yes, sir."

"There you are then, Wilfred. Have some more game pie." That muzzled Osgot-Edge for the rest of the meal. How imbecilic, to be on the point of mentioning Miss Chimes's death almost in the same breath as Jerry's when we had gone to such pains to separate the two fatalities.

I must say, it made me nervous, as well as annoyed. People are so unpredictable. I might have expected someone like Moira Holdfast to make such a gaffe, but I took Osgot-Edge for a man of intelligence. I could only ascribe his lapse to lack of sleep, and he didn't get my sympathy for that.

All was forgiven by teatime, for that afternoon we increased our bag to over a thousand. Marcus Pelham had arranged for a photographer to record the event, and when we five guns lined up beside the results of our marksmanship you would never have guessed that a cross word had passed between us.

With hearts swelling and heads ringing, we repaired to the house and received the ladies' congratulations over tea. Certain of them, not least my own dear wife, appeared more excited about the parlor games in prospect than our performance in the field, but we forgave them, for they gave us a splendid welcome and the drawing room hummed with good humor. I wouldn't want it to be thought that we had forgotten the tragedies of the previous days; we were all in black ties out of respect—the ladies in subdued colors—and most of the blinds were down, but when all's said and done, you can't toll the knell twenty-four hours a day.

I picked a chair beside Miss Dundas, who greeted me with an amused curl of the lip as if I were some elderly masher about to inflict myself on her company. I didn't expect her to spring up and curtsy, but I'm not used to being treated so casually, and I could have found it irksome. Instead it was curiously stimulating.

She didn't appear to be eating anything, so I recommended the cucumber sandwiches, lowering my voice to add that I really preferred tea seated at a table, rather than having to wait for a parlor maid to pass the plate around the entire room before one saw it again.

She said the way the tea was served was a matter of indifference to her.

"Aren't you eating at all, then?" I asked. "You're not tempted by the egg and cress or the salmon?"

"No, sir."

"You're not unwell, I hope?"

"On the contrary. I feel extremely well. It's just that I prefer not to eat at this time."

"Don't be like Alix," I warned her, speaking close to her ear. "She hasn't touched any cooked food since Monday."

"I am sorry to hear that. Is she ill?"

"Merely careful in view of what happened. She's surviving on bread rolls and sugar lumps. I don't know how long she'll keep it up. Those small macaroons are delicious. Won't you be tempted?"

"Really, sir, I don't require one."

"Yes, but I do. Be an angel and take one for me when the girl comes by."

A crack appeared in her stony facade; she smiled faintly to reveal a tantalizing glimpse of those snow-white teeth. She collected the macaroon and held it elegantly between finger and thumb whilst I consumed the two I had taken. She will be so much more of a conquest than Amelia, I thought as I chewed.

She asked, "Shall I pass it to you now? Then I can take another when they come round again."

"Capital. I had no idea you were so resourceful. The great disadvantage of a shooting party is that it deprives us of the ladies' company for much of the day. How did you spend the morning?"

"Pleasantly enough, sir. Lady Drummond took us on a tour of the house."

"Did she, indeed? Now I suppose you know all the best places to hide—the priest's hole, the secret panels."

She frowned, evidently at a loss to understand me. I said, "The parlor games tonight. Hide and Seek. I shall never find you."

"Oh. Are we certain to play Hide and Seek?"

"Alix will insist on it. Won't you tell me where you propose to hide?"

With the slightest tilt of the eyebrows she commented, "Surely that would spoil the game, sir?"

"Not for me, Isabella."

At the mention of her name a tinge of color sprang to her cheeks. It was the right moment to move on. One needs to judge these encounters with finesse. After all, there was an entire evening to come. I said, "I really must go over and congratulate our hostess on the macaroons. Isabella, you will remember what I said, won't you? I shall be looking to you for hints."

AFTER TEA AND BEFORE SUNSET I took a solitary walk along the drive. Not for exercise or recreation; it was a little obligation that I always put upon myself when visiting a house. In the course of a day I see most of my personal servants, but it's quite possible to go through the week without once encountering the man from the Household Police entrusted with my safety. Inspector Sweeney was on duty at the Lodge, watching the comings and goings, a dreary task.

He came to the door in his braces, with the smell of fried bacon wafting from behind him. His eyes bulged. "Holy kicker!"

I relished the moment. Sweeney is a limpet. There's no other word to describe the way he attaches himself to me whenever I step into a public street. Consequently he is better informed about the intricacies of my private life than anyone else in the kingdom. It was rare—and rather gratifying—to see beneath *his* shell.

"Your Royal Highness—I thought you were safe in the house."

"At ease, Mr. Sweeney. I am perfectly safe," I told him indulgently. "We can afford to relax in the country. I say, have you been cooking?"

"My supper, sir."

"It smells rather appetizing. I think I'll step inside."

I sat warming my hands at the range and watched him finish crisping the bacon, followed by kidneys, tomatoes and potatoes. The Lodge had been put entirely at his disposal during my visit. He was under instructions to remain there except in an emergency. I didn't want him stumbling through the coverts and startling the game.

"Will that be sufficient, sir?"

"Yes. I shall be eating dinner in an hour. Are you quite certain there's enough for both of us? I'll have a rabbit sent up to you if you wish. This is a very toothsome offering, Sweeney. Scrumptious."

The sharing of food has a curious way of encouraging confidences. I found myself talking about poor Miss Chimes and what happened at dinner on Monday evening.

John Sweeney was wise to everything, of course. I believe he knew all about Jerry's death as well, but he was tactful enough not to allude to it.

"Does anyone know what killed the young lady, sir?"

"Not yet. We shall have to wait for the postmortem examination."

"When is that to be, sir?"

"As soon as possible. The coroner will want a report."

"He was here today, sir, with the Chaplain. I challenged them at the gate."

"Good man. Yes, they joined us for lunch, half expecting another corpse, I dare say."

Sweeney grinned and said, "Dying is their living, isn't that a fact, sir?" Which I thought rather witty, and very Irish.

HALF PAST NINE THE SAME evening found me sitting cross-legged on a cushion making a spluttering attempt to smoke a hookah—to the undisguised mirth of the rest of the company, seated around me. On my head was a crimson fez with a tassel.

"Turk," shouted Bullivant.

"Sultan?" called Alix.

"Wait a minute," I protested. "We haven't started yet." The Chaplain struck some chords on the piano that were meant to suggest Asia Minor, and Amelia Drummond made an astounding entrance. She was dressed (if that is the word) in the authentic costume of a Turkish belly dancer with *yashmak,* spangled bodice and purple harem trousers. Her feet and ankles were quite bare. She was rattling a tambourine. Our choice of word in the charade had been suggested by Amelia herself, and now I understood why. She must have ordered the outfit specially from a theatrical costumier. She surprised even me and, I think, shocked some of the company as she stood a yard or so in front of me beating the tambourine and shaking her hips in a most vigorous and distracting manner.

"Oh, I say!" cried Lady Moira Holdfast.

"Corking!" said her husband.

Bullivant called out, "Take a look at Bertie. The smoke is coming out of his ears!"

The game was fast getting out of control, so I stood up and said, "Thank you, Rector. That was the first syllable. We shall proceed at once to the second."

As I ushered Amelia to the door, Bullivant called out, "Encore, if you please!"

What he got instead was Wilfred Osgot-Edge in a solo rendition of the second syllable. Dressed in the suit he had worn for dinner, the poet gave a performance more notable for its understatement than anything else as he paced the room staring at the floor, then got down on hands and knees apparently to examine the carpet. Finally he stood up and stamped his foot.

"Is that all?" asked Marcus.

"Pheasant," said Miss Dundas.

"I beg your pardon,"

"The answer is pheasant. The first syllable was 'fez' and the second 'ant.'"

Alix clapped. "Oh, Isabella, how clever of you!"

"But you didn't wait for the whole word," I protested. "We didn't act the whole word in one."

"We got it without that," Alix pointed out. "Is it correct?"

"Well, yes," I said grudgingly. I could see she was bent on mischief.

She said, "We don't want to see the whole word acted now. I think you should pay a forfeit instead. What does everyone else say?"

Forfeits, of course, are immensely popular when someone else has to pay them. I regret to say that parlor games bring out a decidedly cruel tendency in the national character. The British would rather see punishments inflicted than prizes handed out. There were shouts of support from every side, and the Chaplain gleefully rubbed his hands.

George Holdfast had been appointed forfeit master at the start of the evening. We had agreed to pay our dues as we incurred them, rather than all at the end. "Very well," George said with due severity. "The three of you are to put four chairs in a row, take off your shoes and jump over them."

There was a moment's stunned silence.

"George," protested Lady Moira. "You can't ask His Royal Highness to do that."

"Moira, I'll thank you not to interfere," said her husband through gritted teeth.

"And you can't possibly ask a lady to perform acrobatics."

Goaded into a callous remark that I'm sure he regretted later, Holdfast said, "Why not? She's dressed for it."

I turned to Amelia. "Well, my dear, it seems that no appeal is possible. Do you think you could do it?"

She shook her head. "I think I'd rather be given another forfeit."

"Like kissing me?" suggested Bullivant.

"She'd rather jump in the moat," said Marcus sourly. "Are you going to try, sir?"

"What—kissing your sister?" I said like a shot. "That wouldn't be a forfeit at all."

Marcus scowled and turned pink.

"Put out the chairs," I said, "and let's see if it's possible."

"You have to try," insisted my loving wife.

Just to look at the four chairs side by side brought me out in gooseflesh. "You'd have to be a kangaroo," I said.

Then Osgot-Edge spoke up. "I b-b-believe I can do it."

I could have poleaxed him. This was no time to break ranks. "It seems that we do, after all, have a kangaroo in our midst. Show us how, if you insist," I said airily.

"C-could we hear the f-forfeit again?"

"With pleasure," said Holdfast. "You are to put four chairs in a row, take off your shoes and jump over them."

"I th-thought I heard right." With that, Osgot-Edge removed his shoes, put them side by side and jumped over them. *Over the shoes.*

"Oh, bravo, Wilfred!" cried Holdfast. "He saw through it. A trick forfeit!"

Everyone clapped, including the two of us who hadn't had the wit to guess the catch. Sheepishly, Amelia and I performed the ritual of jumping over the shoes and so paid our dues. I felt extremely peeved that Osgot-Edge—of all people—had bested me.

Lady Moira proposed another round of charades, but she was voted down. After the belly dance, anything at all was going to be an anticlimax.

Alix suggested tentatively that we move on to Hide and Seek.

Marcus Pelham brusquely overruled her. "Spinning the Trencher. Then we can have more forfeits while Amelia changes into something more suitable."

If looks could kill, three of us would have murdered young Pelham on the spot. Alix was piqued at being ignored; I was angry on her behalf; and Amelia, I'm certain, had intended wearing her Turkish costume for the rest of the evening. But in the interest of social harmony we all submitted without a murmur. A silver tray was provided and we arranged ourselves in a large circle, taking turns to spin the "trencher" on its edge and call out the name of another player until each of the party had failed to catch it at least once and so incurred a forfeit. By turns we submitted to whatever indignity was demanded until Amelia reappeared wearing her dinner gown,

"Time for a different game, I think," said Holdfast, and loud support came from every side.

"Hide and Seek?" said Alix.

"I don't know about the rest of you, but I'm parched," said Pelham, pointedly ignoring her again. "Let's have something to drink and then see if anyone can think of a decent game to play." He pulled the bell rope.

His rudeness to Alix had become insupportable. I said in a

voice that brooked no interference, "By all means send for the drinks. They will refresh us for the Hide and Seek that we shall play immediately after."

A silver punch bowl on a trolley was wheeled in. In my time I can fairly claim to have sampled as many punches as a fistfighter, and I've learned to treat them warily. When you take a straight brandy at least you know what you are drinking. If someone hands you a cup of warm liquid with strips of orange and lemon floating on the surface, there's little to distinguish it from the sort of pick-me-up you give an ailing child in the nursery—that is, until it picks you up and throws you through the ceiling.

This particular concoction was heavily based on French brandy, with, I think, additions of white wine and Jamaica rum. I'm willing to concede that there was a hint of calf's foot jelly in the flavor, and a few leaves of mint lay beguilingly among the orange peel, but it didn't beguile me. My eyes watered before I put the cup to my lips.

To my surprise two of the ladies drained their cups and put them out for more. Less to my surprise, they became increasingly noisy, not to say tipsy. Which two? Why, the Ladies Amelia Drummond and Moira Holdfast. Alix had put hers aside after a mere sip, and Miss Dundas had asked for water.

There are almost as many ways of playing Hide and Seek as there are of making punch, so we had to agree to a set of rules. Alix didn't mind which version we played. I think it was Amelia who gave a bosky smile and suggested Sardines.

George Holdfast looked around in puzzlement. "Sardines?"

"Don't you know?" said Bullivant, amazed at such ignorance. "Oh, Sardines is quite the most jolly form of Hide and Seek. It has to be played in the dark."

"Galopshus!" muttered Lady Holdfast.

"One of us has to hide and we all count to ninety-nine and then begin the search. The first to find the hider will quietly join him—or her—in the hiding place. Both must remain as silent as possible. The next to find them squeezes in beside them, and so it goes on until all but one are wedged into the hiding place. Hence the name of the game."

"And the last pays a forfeit," cried Amelia. "Let's turn out the lights and begin."

Sensibly, Bullivant suggested that we first set some limits, or the game would range over the entire house and none of us would ever find each other. It was agreed to restrict the hiding places to the main rooms downstairs. The kitchens and servants' quarters were to be out of bounds.

"Splendid. Who shall go first?" said Holdfast.

"I propose Alix," said Miss Dundas to compensate a little for Pelham's rudeness.

"That's very kind," said Alix, "but I would rather be a seeker the first time."

Lady Holdfast said in a slurred voice, "One of the gentlemen. It ought to be one of the gentlemen. There are more of you."

"How about you, Bertie?" said Bullivant.

Before I opened my mouth, Alix scotched that suggestion. "He's too easy to find. Follow the stale cigar smoke and there he is. We want somebody who'll test us to the full."

"Then it must be Wilfred," Amelia declared. "He's a wonderfully quiet mover."

"Don't we know it," murmured Marcus Pelham close to my ear, before turning to Osgot-Edge and asking, "Are you game?"

The poet checked that his bow tie was still straight. "If you w-wish."

"Very well." Marcus turned to one of the maidservants who had come in to collect the punch bowl and asked her to have the lights turned off. "Better get on your way, Wilfred. We won't start counting until we're all in darkness."

"F-find me if you can, then." And Osgot-Edge hurried away like the White Rabbit.

"That's the morning room that way," young Pelham helpfully informed us. "It leads to the conservatory and the billiard room."

Holdfast said, "Ah, but he might double back in the dark and go through one of the other doors."

"He could, too," said Amelia, sounding quite proud of her poet. "He's like a panther."

About three minutes passed after the trolley had been trundled out. Then one of the maids returned and informed us that all the lights had been extinguished except for the drawing room in which we stood. Pelham dismissed her and turned it off himself.

We started counting in unison. When we got to ninety-nine, Pelham shouted, "Coming!"—and we applied ourselves to the hunt.

I'm sure you'll have gathered, reader, that half the entertainment in the game of Sardines is blundering into other seekers and the other half is squeezing up to the hiders {preferably ladies) after one has found the hiding place. Truth to tell, we weren't in total darkness as we searched, but it was dark enough to excuse a certain amount of horseplay. Before I had moved a step I found myself entangled with Lady Holdfast. Believe me, this was through no desire on my part. The woman rushed at me like a chimpanzee to its trainer and refused to let go. She was aptly named.

I was trapped in the curve of the grand piano, shocked and winded by the force of the attack. To add to my discomfiture, the shrieks and giggles all around were evidence enough that others were having hijinks whilst I was locked in this unwelcome embrace. I wouldn't have credited such strength in a lady of Moira Holdfast's maturity. But she wasn't content to hug me. She had her hands inside my dinner jacket. "I'm going to tickle you," she told me, and added, "but you'd better not tickle me."

Next, I felt my shirtfront tugged out of my trousers and cold fingers on my bare flesh. I flinched at the touch. I quivered. I'm extremely ticklish. I started making hooting sounds.

She said, "I've got you at my mercy now."

Then a voice beside us said, "Is that you, Moira?"

The voice was Sir George Holdfast's.

Lady Moira hesitated.

I didn't. I pushed her hands away and dodged clear. Stuffing my shirt back where it belonged, I bolted across the room and collided with someone at the door to the breakfast room. Someone pretty substantial.

"Who's that?" I asked.

"Your Royal Highness? Oh, my word, I beg your pardon. After you," said he, and I recognized the Chaplain's voice.

"Where have you looked. Rector?" I asked him.

"Behind the curtains in the morning room and in the window seat. He isn't there, sir."

"That's obvious," I said, "or you wouldn't be here. I shall search the billiard room." I groped my way towards a chair and crossed the morning room by passing from one piece of furniture to another. Was it my imagination or did I hear voices ahead?

There was a swishing sound that might have been a curtain being drawn across, or possibly somebody appealing for silence as they heard me approach.

I reached the conservatory—a cold place filled with musty smelling potted plants that had a gray, dead look in the moonlight through the glass roof. I doubted whether anyone would choose such an inhospitable room to hide in, so I moved on, through the door to the billiard room. This was a windowless room, pitch-black.

With my hands probing the space in front of me, I found the table and started feeling my way along its length. Some billiard rooms are equipped with cupboards large enough for several people to hide in, and I proposed to investigate the far end.

There was no need to. I was moving crabwise alongside the billiard table when I felt a touch on my leg.

I said, "God Almighty!"

There were some stifled laughs.

I had found the hiding place. They were under the table. An obvious place to hide, you might be thinking, but allow me to point out that it was extremely clever. If they hadn't given themselves away by laughing, I would have gone straight past. I couldn't see anything when I bent to look.

A voice said, "Who is it?"

"Your husband, my dear," I answered to Alix. "Who else is here?"

"Sh! Someone's coming."

I ducked under the table and in so doing found myself intimately close to a lady. I knew she was a lady because my hand came inadvertently to rest on—forgive me—her thigh and I could feel warm flesh through a fabric that was certainly not the cloth of evening trousers. She placed a cool hand over mine and removed it. Her touch was too light for Alix and not warm enough to be Amelia, and Moira Holdfast in her present inebriated state wouldn't have removed my hand at all.

So she could only be Isabella Dundas.

In the spirit of the game, I edged closer. I got a delicious whiff of some Parisian scent and a sudden jab in the ribs from her bustle, which I was unlucky enough to press against. I gasped.

"Found you!" cried the Chaplain, who had followed me into

the billiard room, and was standing beside the table. Just to make sure, he swung his leg and caught my other set of ribs with the point of his shoe.

I protested painfully.

The Chaplain said, "So sorry, whoever you are. I say, is there room under there for a little one?" He scrambled in, bowled me over and practically suffocated me.

Now there was pandemonium. Others had heard my shout and dashed into the room, desperate not to be last. Bodies hurled themselves into the hiding place, unaware that like some victim of a medieval torture I was bent backwards over the steel bars of Isabella's bustle.

I yelled for mercy.

"Somebody's hurt!" one of the company said superfluously.

"Take care!" said another voice. "It sounds like Bertie."

They made a united effort to find some space for me and I succeeded in rolling off the metal hump.

"Better?" somebody enquired. People do say asinine things at such times.

I didn't reply.

I think it was Marcus Pelham who presently observed, "Well, if there's anyone still trying to find us after that, I'll eat my hat."

"Who's here, then?" asked the Chaplain. "Let's see. Be so good as to answer your names. Lady Drummond?"

One by one, we answered to the roll call like children in school.

"That's everyone," said the Chaplain.

"No," said Isabella. "You called nine names. There are ten of us."

"Nine of us and Mr. Osgot-Edge, who was the hider. There was no need to call his name, because he must have been the first here. Isn't that so, Wilfred?"

There was no response.

"Wilfred?"

"Stop playing games, Wilfred," said George Holdfast.

"Dammit, *we are* playing games," said Pelham testily.

"But we play fair. Speak up, Wilfred. Are you under here?"

"He *must* be, or what are the rest of us doing?"

Nobody supplied an answer. There was a thoughtful interval of about half a minute.

Then one of the ladies made a sound like a steam engine, and it soon became obvious to all that she was trying to stifle a giggle. She gave up the attempt and laughed out loud.

"Is that you, Amelia?" said Pelham.

Amelia erupted into laughter. "He isn't here!" she managed to say between shrieks of mirth. "Claude and I were under here first. We wanted a place for a cuddle. Then Alix came along and we had to pretend we were playing the game." She broke into another peal of laughter. "Wilfred is still hiding somewhere, wondering if anyone will ever find him!"

We had all been well and truly gulled, and now we all joined in the laughter, except, I suppose, for young Pelham, who must have disapproved strongly of his sister's spooning with Bullivant. Even I shook with laughter and hurt my bruised ribs in the process.

"Come now, let's all stand up and see if we can do better this time," the Chaplain exhorted us as if we were at choir practice.

Bullivant said, "I like it here."

"Saucebox!" said Amelia dotingly. My assessment of her as a flirt was amply justified.

"The Rector is right," said Holdfast. "Come on, everyone. One of us will have to pay a forfeit, remember."

There was a distinct reluctance to move. Crushed together as we were, united in the silly error we had made, the party had in some mysterious way attained a feeling of kinship. How odd, that civilized people should become comfortable with each other sitting in the dark under a table—more at ease than they were at dinner, or in the drawing room. If one of us had started to sing, I'm sure we would all have joined in.

However, the game was still on. We turned out to resume the hunt.

"I'm going to look in the library," said Moira Holdfast.

I rather think that she had said it for my ears, so I resolved to go in the opposite direction. I retraced my way through the conservatory to the breakfast room. Someone was ahead of me—George Holdfast, as it turned out, because I heard his voice presently.

He had stepped across to the food lift and opened the door. I heard him haul on the rope and bring up the dumbwaiter. He sounded pleased with what he discovered there. "By George, here you are!"

If this meant he had found Osgot-Edge I was surprised, not

to say shirty. This wasn't playing fair. There wasn't space enough inside the dumbwaiter for more than two or three to hide. And it would be far from safe.

Yet as I crossed the room to join them I sensed that something was wrong.

Holdfast spoke in an urgent whisper, "Wake up, Wilfred." Then, "Oh, Jupiter!"

I was at his side. "What is it?"

He gasped, "Horrible!" Then he grasped my arm. "For pity's sake, keep the ladies away."

CHAPTER 9

I struck a match and held it close to the lift, a damp match, it turned out—or perhaps I moistened it with my hot hand—because the flame refused to ignite the wood. It flared for a second and died, but in that brief effulgence it showed me what George Holdfast had discovered. The dumbwaiter contained the hunched, motionless body of Wilfred Osgot-Edge. The handle of a knife jutted from his chest. A thin streak of blood had trickled down his shirt.

Reader, you may think me obtuse, but I hesitated to believe the evidence of my eyes. I suspected a prank. To understand this, you ought to be aware that it pleases me immensely to play practical jokes on my friends, the more elaborate the better. Anyone as expert as I in leg pulling needs no telling that a private house party is a heaven-sent opportunity. One needs to be more than ever on one's guard against other jokers. So a stabbed man in a dumbwaiter may not be all that he seems. In a bored voice, I said, "Send him down, George."

"What, sir?"

"The lift. See if you can lower it."

He obeyed. The mechanism rumbled and squeaked.

I said, "Not all the way down. We don't want it to reach the kitchen. Stop it halfway." I struck another match. "Nicely done. Now we shan't have to turn the ladies away."

His eyes gleamed like coach lamps. "Didn't you see the knife, sir? Someone stabbed him."

"I wouldn't leap to conclusions if I were you, George."

"That was real blood, sir. Look at my fingers. Still wet." It took the evidence of his bloodstained fingers to convince me that what I had just seen was no tomfoolery. Real blood has a smell that any hunting man can recognize. Suddenly the true honor of what we had just seen struck at me like a serpent. My hand twitched and the match went out.

Somewhere behind us, a board creaked.

Holdfast caught his breath.

I muttered to him, "Say nothing."

"Who's that?" asked Amelia's voice. "Who's cheating? Who's been lighting matches?" She fairly charged across the floor, caught at my sleeve and giggled. "Got you! It's Bertie, isn't it? Let's feel if you've got whiskers."

"There's no need." I struck the next match.

She said, "Two of you! This is all against the rules, you know, two gentlemen collaborating. We ladies are entitled to some help."

I said grimly, "My dear Lady Drummond, I think we should arrange for you to have a cup of strong black coffee."

"Fiddlesticks!" She laughed. "Bertie, I'm not drunk, just a little merry, and where's the harm in that? Besides, we're in the middle of a game. We haven't found Wilfred yet." She gave me a stare. "Have we?"

The black coffee wasn't required. She sobered up appreciably when I told her what had happened. She said, "What in the name of God are we going to do?"

My brain was temporarily addled. I made a performance of lighting another match in hopes of Holdfast suggesting something, but he was no help at all.

From another room came the coarse, now-incongruous laughter of people still trying to play Sardines. Amelia answered her own question. "First, we must stop this ridiculous game and get the lights on. Oh, Bertie, they'll be so alarmed."

Holdfast said, "We ought to fetch the police."

"My thought exactly," said I, crossing to the sideboard to a candlestick I had spotted. I managed to light it before the match went out. "By Jove, yes, we'd better send for Sweeney. He'll help to calm things down."

"Who is Sweeney?"

"My man from the Royal Household Police."

"I hope he can catch the murderer," said Holdfast.

At this, Amelia gave a horrified cry, turned away from us and vomited. Happily the jug from which the porridge was served at breakfast was at hand. That it was murder seemed to have eluded our poor, benighted hostess until this moment. One had to be sympathetic. You don't expect such things to happen under your own roof—least of all when you're entertaining the Heir Apparent.

Amelia soon learned that my presence in the house was more of an asset than an embarrassment. In the next hour I took command, summoning one of the butlers to restore the gaslight; dispatching a footman to fetch Sweeney from the lodge; calling the guests into the large drawing room and announcing what had happened. There was no point in sparing the ladies' feelings.

There were gasps of astonishment all round, and Lady Holdfast swooned, or appeared to (she may have succumbed to alcoholic stupor). Calmly and reassuringly I informed them that the matter was already under investigation.

"Might one be so bold as to enquire who is in charge, sir?" asked the Chaplain.

Without pause for thought I answered, "I am." Then, seeing several jaws drop in surprise, I quietly added, "assisted by Inspector Sweeney, whom you will all meet presently. We shall question everyone in the house and bring this investigation to a speedy conclusion." Taking care not to look in Alix's direction, I then stated my own credentials. "I am not without experience in detective investigations."

"Sir, I hope you'll question the servants first," said Bullivant. "You're not going to find a murderer among present company."

Lady Holdfast, restored to consciousness, piped up, "I think the policeman should be instructed to protect us, or we shall all be murdered in our beds."

"I shall see that a patrol is put on the corridors," I promised. "And as to your suggestion, Claude, yes, we shall shortly summon the servants and question them rigorously."

"Have you any conception how many there are?" said Pelham with his usual want of charm.

"That is immaterial," said I.

"Thirty-seven are permanently in service here," he insisted on telling me. "Twenty more have been hired for the week. To that figure must be added a further thirty or so who are visitors—the retinues you brought with you. I make that eighty-seven at the very least."

"Then have them assemble in the Hall in fifteen minutes," I retorted crisply.

He glared, reddened and marched out.

I glanced at the clock on the mantelpiece. Half past ten. "Unless you have anything germane to impart to me, ladies and gentlemen, I shall now confer with Inspector Sweeney."

That worthy officer, when I received him in the anteroom, was anxiety personified. With his toes turned inwards and a tortured look on his features he gave the impression that he needed urgently to shake hands with an old friend, as the saying goes.

"Not a living soul came in or out of the main gate tonight, Your Royal Highness. It was shut and bolted."

I assured him that nobody held him personally to blame. "I sent for you, Sweeney, because I shall require your help in investigating this brutal crime."

"Me, sir?" he said, performing a terrified jig.

"You're an inspector of police."

"I'm no detective, sir. Bodyguarding is my specialty. I think we should call in the criminal investigation boys."

"Allow me to be the judge of that," I told him brusquely. "What has happened is desperately unfortunate, for Lady Drummond, for her honored guests and not least for me. We can't have it broadcast to all and sundry that I was within an ace of being murdered tonight—because that is what the press will make of it if the word gets out."

"Jesus, Joseph and Mary!" muttered Sweeney, transparently thinking not of me, but his career as a Royal bodyguard.

To reinforce the point I sketched a small, but vivid, word picture. "Imagine Her Majesty the Queen opening *The Times* tomorrow morning. No, Inspector, this is not a case for the common police. You and I are going to solve it together and bring the murderer to account."

"Begging your pardon, if we do, sir, it's bound to come out. There would have to be a trial."

"Not necessarily."

"I don't follow you, sir."

"Better if you don't," I said cryptically.

IT WAS NECESSARY FOR ME to stand halfway up the main staircase to address all the assembled servants, and I had to concede that young Pelham had made a valid point. Normally one has no conception how many domestics are involved in a house party because they are never seen *en masse*. The scale of the investigation came home to me forcefully when I looked down on those serried ranks, the liveried staff to the fore, and behind them so many white caps that I thought of Cowes and felt a touch of *mal de mer*.

I didn't need to inform them of what had happened, of course. The electric telegraph is nothing to the buzz of servants' tongues. I ordered them on pain of instant dismissal without character to say not one word more—except to me or Sweeney—of what had happened. They were not to speak of it to a living soul, now or ever after. I said that we should require from each of them a precise and complete account of their movements between nine and ten that evening. Those untutored in writing were instructed to obtain assistance. The statements would be collected by the house steward and handed to Sweeney by midnight.

After dismissing them I beckoned to Colwell and told him to send four men to the breakfast room to remove the body after I had examined it.

He cleared his throat in the way senior servants do when some impediment to duty is exercising them.

"Well?" I asked.

"May I be so bold as to enquire the destination of the deceased, Your Royal Highness?"

"His destination?" I knew very well what he meant, but I couldn't resist saying, "That's a question for a higher authority than I, Mr. Colwell. Try St. Peter. Or were you merely asking where the men should take the body?"

"That was my meaning, sir."

"I suggest somewhere removed from the house, some outbuilding that will serve as a temporary mortuary. What's that place beyond the kitchen garden?"

"The game larder, sir."

"Ah."

"There is a harness room attached to the coach house that is not in use, sir."

"Well, then. You've answered your own question."

"Yes, sir."

He still seemed reluctant to move, so I said, "Is there something else?"

Colwell cleared his throat again. "If I may venture to make a suggestion, sir . . ."

"What?"

"You asked me to send four men to the breakfast room."

"Yes."

"That would involve conveying the gentleman's remains through the state rooms to the main entrance and down the steps. If, instead, sir, we lowered the dumbwaiter to the scullery, the men could carry their melancholy burden through the tradesmen's entrance without further inconvenience to the guests."

It was a fine point of decorum, weighing respect for the dead against the sensibilities of the living. As a means of conveyance for a corpse, and a gentleman's corpse at that, the dumbwaiter was hideously inappropriate. However, since Osgot-Edge was already in there, he might as well be removed at the most convenient level.

I gave my consent. "We'll do it as tastefully as the circumstances allow. I shall proceed to the breakfast room with Inspector Sweeney and examine the body there, at the top of the shaft."

"Very good, sir."

"You will assemble your men in the scullery and when the signal is given, er . . . what is the signal?"

"There is a speaking tube, sir."

"I shall give the instruction down the tube and you will lower the dumbwaiter."

With that settled, I snapped my fingers at Sweeney, who was edging towards the cloak room, and we returned at once to the breakfast room. There, I instructed him to close all the doors and raise the dumbwaiter.

My confidence drained as Sweeney hauled on the rope. Suppose, after all, this *had* been a practical joke, and Osgot-Edge was poised to leap out, alive and smiling. Or suppose the merry jester had contrived to escape, leaving the dumbwaiter empty. I would look pretty silly after my solemn speeches to all and sundry. I'm sure it

was this uncertainty that stopped me from feeling a proper sense
of grief or regret at his passing. I couldn't shake off the suspicion
that I was being duped.

So you will understand why I breathed a sigh of relief—no, let's
be truthful, I practically cheered—when the corpse came into view
with the knife still protruding from the chest. It was propped up
in a sitting position in the cramped space, but it looked decidedly
more dead than it had by match light.

"God help us," said Sweeney in a whisper.

I ordered him to withdraw the knife from the body.

"Is that wise, sir?" he asked. "Shouldn't we be leaving it for the
police to see?"

"Sweeney, you are the police."

"That is a fact, sir."

"Do you have a handkerchief?"

He was silent for a moment. "What would I be wanting with a
handkerchief, sir?"

"You wipe the blade with it. We don't want to ruin our clothes.
Take the one from his top pocket, then. Keep it ready in your left
hand and withdraw the knife with your right."

He braced himself and grasped the hilt. The blade came out
easily. He wiped it clean and handed it to me.

So far as I could judge, it was a bone-handled kitchen knife,
used, presumably, for cutting meat or vegetables. I ought to say
much used, for the blade had been worn to a virtual spike. It was
extremely sharp. No great strength would have been required to
have plunged such a weapon into a man's chest, so I could not
exclude the possibility that a woman had committed the crime.

"We must ask the cook whether this is one of her knives," I
told Sweeney.

"I'll attend to that at once, sir."

"No you won't. Not yet. Go through the pockets." Starting with
the jacket, he made a painstaking search of Osgot-Edge's clothes,
handing each item to me. Truth to tell, the harvest didn't amount
to much: another handkerchief, a pencil and some loose change.

"Are you sure there's nothing else in the top pocket? No slip
of paper?"

He pulled out the lining to show me.

I decided to tell him about the pieces of paper found with

Queenie Chimes and Jerry Gribble. "I was half expecting to find another scrap with 'Wednesday' written on it," I admitted. "It's a good thing we didn't."

"It is and it isn't," he said with Irish logic. "If it was there it would raise the unpleasant possibility that Miss Chimes and the Duke were murdered; but as it isn't, we don't have much to go on."

"Come now, we've hardly begun our inquiries," I said with my usual optimism. "Can you use a whistle?"

His blue eyes regarded me with mystification.

I reached for the speaking tube and handed it to him, I've never been obliged to whistle for anything.

Comprehension flooded over his features. He pulled the whistle from the tube and blew on it.

I took it from him. "Colwell, are you there?"

The answer came up, "Your Royal Highness?"

"We have finished up here."

"Very good, sir."

The ropes tightened, the pulleys squeaked and Osgot-Edge went down like the setting sun.

"Is the scoundrel apprehended?" was the question that was flung at me when I returned to the drawing room. It came from the Chaplain.

The tense faces of the guests regarded me in a way that I didn't find at all agreeable. It was as if they blamed me for what had happened. Obviously they had worked themselves up into a frightful lather. Even Alix looked faintly skeptical of my authority.

I informed them that inquiries were vigorously underway. Written statements had been demanded from all the servants, and by the morning we expected to have a list of possible suspects. Meanwhile it would be sensible if each guest appointed a trusted servant from his own retinue to stand guard outside his bedroom door for the night.

"I've arranged that anyway," said Holdfast. "I think we should issue them with weapons from the gun room."

"Oh, do you?" said Amelia. "And what do you suppose will happen if one of us is compelled to visit the bathroom in the night?"

"Forget the guns," said Bullivant. "Better issue us with jerries instead."

It was a measure of the crisis that nobody smiled.

The guns were rejected by common consent. Presently the footmen arrived with the candles to escort us to our rooms. Holdfast took out his watch. "Good Lord, it's almost Thursday already."

While the party was starting to disperse, Alix chose her moment to draw me aside. "Bertie, I insist that you send for the police. This isn't the time to play your detective games."

I reminded her that Sweeney was a policeman.

She said, "Sweeney wouldn't recognize a clue if it turned a double somersault and bit him on the nose. He's a bodyguard, not an investigator."

I said, "I hope you haven't spoken in these terms to anybody else."

"Of course not! They'd panic if they knew. You're trifling with their lives, Bertie—with all our lives. There could be another murder in the night."

"My dear, I'll make you a solemn promise. If anyone else is killed tonight I shall send for the detective police at once."

"That will be too late for the unfortunate victim." It was no use arguing with her. I said, "I think I shall sleep in your bed tonight."

Just as I hoped, she was derailed by the remark. We've had separate rooms for years. "Where do you propose that I should sleep?"

"Next to me."

"Bertie, how *could* you—when a murderer is at large?"

"I think you misunderstand me, my dear," I said piously. "My thoughts are exclusively devoted to the personal safety of the lady I love and cherish more than any other."

Her lip trembled as it does when I remember our wedding anniversary. No more was said about sending for the police.

There was a diplomatic cough from somewhere behind me. I turned and saw Colwell the steward and took a few steps towards him, well out of Alix's earshot.

"Did you convey the body safely to the coach house?"

"Yes, sir. I have locked the harness room."

"And have the servants produced their statements?"

"Almost all have been handed in, sir."

"Excellent. Give them to Sweeney as soon as possible. Tell me, do some of the servants live out?"

"There are some from the village, yes, sir."

"Are they discreet?"

"I believe I can vouch for them, sir. We had an unfortunate incident last year and it was kept from the village. We pride ourselves on a very loyal household."

"That may be so," I said, "but tonight's affair is rather more sensational than some boy shot by accident. Mr. Osgot-Edge was murdered, no question of it."

"I still have confidence in my staff, sir."

"Good, but it may be prudent to issue a further warning to anyone leaving the house."

"No one is going off duty tonight, sir."

I gave an approving nod. Colwell was a credit to his office. He lingered, glancing about him to see if he could be overheard.

A warning pulse started beating in my temple. I said, "Is there some other matter that you wish to bring to my attention?"

"There is, sir. We made a rather disturbing discovery when we removed the body from the dumbwaiter. A piece of paper, tucked under his leg. I took the precaution of pocketing it before anyone else had an opportunity to read it. In view of the scrap of paper I found on Monday evening when Miss Chimes collapsed, I thought this may be relevant to the investigation."

"What did it say?"

"I have it here, sir." He handed me a piece of newspaper. And of course you are correct, reader. It had been cut from the *Times* and the word printed on it was "Wednesday." But that was not all. Something else had been added by hand, in black ink, so that the message in its entirety read: *Wednesday's Corpse.*

I was forced to conclude that I was dealing not with one murder, but three. *Wednesday's Corpse* implied that the deaths labeled *Monday* and *Tuesday* had been planned and executed by the same evil assassin.

Thursday

CHAPTER 10

I believe it was about 1:30 A.M. when Alix said, "Bertie, if you don't mind, I would like to get some sleep tonight."

I told her not to be such a killjoy.

"But I can scarcely breathe! I really must object."

"My dear, you never used to. In fact I was given to understand that you found it quite agreeable."

"Yes, but not in bed. How much longer are you going to be?"

"I suppose I've finished," I said, reaching for an ashtray to extinguish the objectionable cigar butt. "I thought it would help me concentrate, but I can't say I've reached any rational conclusion."

She grasped the bedclothes tightly and made a performance of turning over. "Murder isn't rational. Kindly turn out the lamp, would you?"

I obliged. But I remained sitting up in the dark, unable to rest until I had made more sense of the evenings appalling discovery. Queenie Chimes had not, after all, collapsed from natural causes; she had been poisoned. Jerry Gribble hadn't committed suicide; he had been shot. Osgot-Edge had been stabbed, and the murderer had claimed all three like a sportsman bagging game.

I shuddered.

Murder isn't rational, Alix had pointed out, yet calculation must have played a part in these killings, for the pieces of newspaper had clearly been cut from the *Times* beforehand and left like calling cards. The killer was boasting: *Look at my tally—a murder a day. Be sure and credit the deaths on Monday and Tuesday to me as well as Wednesday, won't you?*

I couldn't imagine why anyone should want to murder three innocent people—a trio so different as a pretty actress, a middle-aged Duke and a poet. Admittedly Queenie and Jerry were lovers, so they may have been killed as a brace, if you'll pardon my persisting with the sporting idiom. But I could think of no other connections.

Well, you'll have gathered the direction my thoughts were taking. It seemed to me that the victims had been picked off like prey, impersonally, for no other reason than that they happened to be guests in Desborough Hall at this time. Such callous slaughter is not unknown. I can't expect my twentieth-century reader to have heard of the East End murders committed in 1888 by a seeker of publicity known to the press as Jack the Ripper. At the time they made a considerable sensation. He wrote letters challenging the police to catch him, but up to now he is still at liberty. I tell you candidly, sitting in that darkened room, I could foresee a campaign just as brutal and alarming as the Ripper's—in fact more alarming, because it was aimed not at streetwalkers, but people of refinement.

If this murderer is a publicity seeker, I told myself, then my conduct in the case is amply justified. Silence catches the mouse. He wanted the world to know about these daily killings and the telltale scraps of newspaper left beside the bodies. I frustrated his plan. Not even my fellow guests are fully aware of what he has done. So I have trapped him into adding something to his calling card.

Wednesday's *Corpse.*

The addition had been written in a crude, spidery copperplate hand, probably disguised. John Sweeney had by now collected his statements from the servants, but I doubted if we would learn much by comparing their handwriting with that of the murderer. Half of them were sure to be illiterate and must have asked others to assist them.

Alix interrupted my thoughts by saying, "Bertie, are you proposing to sit up all night?"

I said, "I'm thinking."

"Can't you think lying down? There's a draft down my back . . . What are you thinking about?"

"A piece of paper."

"Notepaper?"

"It's of no importance."

She clicked her tongue in annoyance. "It must be important, to keep you awake like this. Does it have some bearing on what happened to poor Wilfred?"

"I can't say."

"Bertie, you're hiding something from me."

I groaned inwardly. My dear wife is remarkably tolerant of my activities. She seldom protests or interferes, but she will not abide flannel.

She would have prized the truth from me, syllable by syllable, so I surrendered the whole bloodcurdling story of the week's events without more ado, and I must say she took it with commendable *sangfroid*.

"*Wednesday's Corpse?*" she repeated. "How melodramatic—as if every day brings a fresh fatality."

"It does," I said.

"I do dislike that word 'corpse.' It sounds so final."

I said, "It's curtains for some poor blighter, however you put it."

"Yes, but 'body' is less horrid, don't you think? *Wednesday's Body.* This murderer has no feeling for the English language."

"That's rich," I said, "coming from a Dane."

"Who are you to criticize, a Saxe-Coburg who rolls his *R*s?"

Alix and I have had this exchange many times before. It descends rapidly into mild vulgarity, but we find it amusing. I think we both welcomed it as a temporary relief from the grim events of the day. Finally the banter ran out and we went silent.

After an interval I asked her, "Were you trying to make a serious point?"

"About the word he used? I don't know. It sounds out of place. And yet . . ."

"And yet what?"

"I'm not sure."

She yawned.

I eased myself under the bedclothes, stretched and turned on my side. I was almost asleep when Alix piped up from her side of the bed.

"It scans."

"Mm?"

"'Corpse.' It's only one syllable, so it scans. Like the word 'child' in the rhyme. *That's* why he used it."

"Which rhyme?"

"Oh, Bertie, don't be so dense! You know it. Everyone knows it:

"Monday's child is fair of face.
Tuesday's child is full of grace.
Wednesday's child is full of woe.
Thursday's child has far to go.
Friday's child is loving and giving.
Saturday's child works hard for a living.
But the child that is born on the Sabbath Day
Is bonny and blithe and good and gay."

In the darkness I scratched my beard thoughtfully. Of course I knew the verse. I'd had it recited to me often enough in the nursery. I was a Tuesday child, full of grace. I'd rarely listened to what was said about the children born on other days of the week.

Sounding very like my old governess, Alix said, "Now substitute the word 'corpse' for 'child.'"

I saw the point. However, I wasn't much impressed by it yet, though I did my best not to trample on Alix's feelings. "Yes, it fits up to a point. Monday's corpse was Queenie Chimes, fair of face, certainly. Tuesday's was Jerry, and if His Grace the Duke of Bournemouth doesn't fit the rhyme, I don't know who does. Full of grace by birthright, bless him. But there the coincidences end, I'm sorry to say. I wouldn't describe Osgot-Edge as full of woe. He was a cheerful fellow, a bit of a lady's man on the quiet. No, my dear, it doesn't match up, I'm afraid."

She said, "Perhaps his poetry was full of woe."

"Woeful, I'll grant you," I quipped. "No, to be fair what he wrote was meant to be amusing. Do you recall the poem that was read out to us on Sunday evening? That line about the lion saying 'Let us prey' probably went over your head, my dear, being Danish. It was a pun. Did your English tutor teach you about puns?"

Alix said, "Something you feed to an elephant?"—and I suspect that she smiled in the dark.

We lapsed into a drowsy silence. I may even have dozed a little.

Suddenly Alix startled me by saying aloud, "I've got it! Wilfred Osgot-Edge."

I said, "You're talking in your sleep."

She said, "His initials. It's his initials—W.O.E."

"Woe?" I propped myself up. "*Full of woe!* Alix, you're right! You must be!"

"Don't sound so surprised, then."

There was another pause, filled, this time, with a spate of mental activity.

Finally I said, "What day is it?"

"Bertie, you know. It's already tomorrow. Thursday."

"Refresh my memory. What was the line about Thursday?"

"'*Thursday's child*'—or *corpse*—'has far to go.'"

"Far to go . . . Oh, my hat!—Miss Dundas, the explorer!"

I GIVE ALIX HER DUE. She objected strenuously to my calling on Miss Dundas in the middle of the night. I would have expected no less. Clearly I was putting my personal safety—not to mention the future of the realm—at risk. I could have been struck down by the killer as soon as I stepped outside the bedroom door.

However, I was adamant. Perhaps I'm too gallant for my own safety, but I rather relished myself in the role of protector to Miss Dundas. And as I explained to Alix, no one else except the murderer knew the danger the lady was in. I had a responsibility to warn her. A moral responsibility.

For that, I was treated to a few uncomplimentary remarks about my morals that need not be repeated here. Alix also complained that I wasn't showing sufficient concern for her safety, and refused to spend the rest of the night alone, so I had to ring for her woman-of-the-bedchamber, Charlotte Knollys. Poor Charlotte, plucked from a warm bed upstairs, burst in seconds later in a flannel nightgown expecting heaven knows what emergency. Upon seeing me she gave a cry of dismay and put her hand to her curlers. In the confusion I stepped past her through the open door.

Immediately four or five faces stared at me. I'd quite forgotten the servants on guard outside the bedroom doors. Decently clad as I was in dressing gown and slippers, I nevertheless felt slightly foolish carrying the poker I'd picked up for protection; however, I think they were more ill at ease than I. Tucking the poker under my arm like a swagger stick, I marched past them without a word along the corridor to Isabella Dundas's room.

It was disturbing to discover that hers was the only door without a guard. I tapped lightly and got no response, so I tried a second time, with a firmer knock.

Nothing.

I glanced over my shoulder and immediately the five pale faces watching me rotated like lighthouse lamps and looked the other way. I gripped the door handle, fully expecting to find the door locked.

It opened. I stepped inside, into a more profound darkness. "Miss Dundas?"

No reply. This was not encouraging.

I took a step inwards, hands probing the space in front of me, while behind me the door shut with a thump loud enough to waken the dead.

I said, "Isabella?" and still elicited no response. Becoming increasingly perturbed, I felt in my pocket for matches and then cursed my negligence; I'd left them in Alix's bedroom.

I suppose it was pride that stopped me from returning immediately to fetch them. I didn't relish the looks I would get in the corridor. Instead I chose to proceed as well as I could without a light. After all, it was just another bedroom to negotiate in the dark, I told myself, to keep up the proverbial pecker. This wouldn't be the first, or, one trusted, the last.

Such blind faith!

One step forward was all I took. Without warning I felt my ankles gripped by a cord of some description. It tightened so suddenly that I keeled off balance and crashed to the floor. Immediately I was smothered by some all-enveloping fabric and trussed up, notwithstanding my strongly voiced objections.

And would you believe nobody came to my aid? That's the penalty of being of the blood Royal: people are only too happy to dance attendance on you for as long as you conduct yourself according to protocol, but the moment anything untoward occurs they are too timid to come forward. I had to wait, practically suffocating, until my captor chose to loosen the bonds. Fortunately, it wasn't long. I was aware of a sawing motion at my neck that I sensibly and correctly took to be the cord being severed. Then the blanket—for that was what covered my head and torso—was drawn back from my face like a cowl and I found myself staring first at a knife blade gleaming in candlelight, and beyond it at Miss Dundas.

She said without a trace of remorse, "So it *is* you."

"Would you have liked a fanfare?" I said with sarcasm. "If you were here all the time, why the deuce didn't you speak up?"

She said, "Sir, I had to be certain. After all, it could have been someone impersonating you. I'm sorry if you had a shock, but an undefended lady is entitled to take reasonable steps to protect herself when a murderer is afoot."

"Reasonable!"

She said, "You're more fortunate than you realize. You could have found yourself dangling by your heels from that beam above you. If you'd been a baboon I wouldn't have hesitated. Don't look like that, sir. I was about to explain that this is a simple hunter's trap. I used to rig one up when I camped in the jungle. Ideally I'd have used rope and a good, strong net, but sashcord and a blanket had to suffice tonight. Allow me to finish untying you and then you can tell me why you're here."

With as much dignity as I could salvage, I remarked, "I merely looked in to save your life. I have reason to believe that you are next on the murderers list."

She gave that amused curl of the lip that I had noted before. In the circumstances I excused it as a nervous reaction. "Surely there isn't a list?"

"I'm afraid that is the inescapable conclusion," I told her. I explained about the cuttings from *The Times* and the rhyme linking each of the victims to a day of the week.

"So you interpret 'far to go' as fitting me?" she said with that smile still lingering about her mouth.

"No one else in the party has traveled so far, or is ever likely to," I answered.

After a moment's reflection she said, "Perhaps the words are meant to apply in another sense. Have you considered that?"

"You had better explain."

"Well, without wishing to alarm you, sir, it might be thought by some that the throne of England is the very height of society. In that sense you, the Heir Apparent.

I said, "No, no. That's too far-fetched for words." She finished loosening the cord around my ankles. "Well, sir, now that you have warned me—and I thank you for that—I shall rig up my trap again."

"Extremely wise."

"Then I think we can safely go to bed."

After this astonishing remark I stared saucer-eyed at Miss Dundas. In my time I've met more than my share of ladies who fit the appellation of "fast," but never one who came to the point without a hint of passion, not a sigh, nor a blush. It was as matter-of-fact as putting on a shoe, and, to be candid, just about as stimulating. After all, I was here on a mission of life and death. True, there was a certain piquancy to visiting a lady in her bedroom, but I wasn't expecting a tumble. Even a courtesan would have pulled up the drawbridge under present circumstances. To hold her at bay, I said, "That's very agreeable, my dear, but rather sudden. Wouldn't you care for some liquid refreshment? I see you have a decanter and some glasses here."

She cleared her throat. "It seems that I expressed myself badly. I propose, sir, that you return to your bed and I to mine."

"Ah." A misunderstanding. The wind returned to my sails. "No, I shall remain here."

"I beg your pardon."

"I said I shall stay here. Your life is in grave danger, Isabella."

She gave a sigh and ran her hand through her hair, which hung loose over her nightgown. "Sir—"

"Bertie."

"Bertie, then. I appreciate your concern, but it won't be necessary."

I said, "I'll be the judge of that, my dear."

"I can protect myself."

"Of that I am certain," I said. "However, I have taken it as my solemn duty to protect everyone in this house by apprehending the murderer. Having rather cleverly deduced that this room is earmarked for the next crime, I intend to remain here until I've made an arrest."

"Couldn't you wait outside the door?"

"And advertise my presence? No, no. I must surprise the villain."

Overwhelmed by the force of my reasoning, Miss Dundas applied herself to re-erecting her man trap, with some assistance from me.

When the job was done, she said, "I think I will investigate that decanter. Will you join me? By a fortunate oversight two glasses seem to have been provided."

A fortunate oversight! You might be familiar, with jungles, I thought, but you don't know much about the secret ways of country house parties, Isabella.

She climbed into bed with her Madeira and I sat high-mindedly in the armchair.

"Who will it be?" she asked presently. "Whom do you suspect?"

"If I knew for certain," I answered guardedly, "I would already have made the arrest."

"I can't think who would wish to murder me," she said after taking a sip of Madeira.

"I dare say each of the victims would have ventured the same comment."

"Oh." She drew up her knees and clasped them over the bed-clothes. "Are these murders without cause, then?"

I didn't answer. I didn't know.

"Really," she went on, "one ought to consider what the victims had in common, apart from being here this week. An actress, a duke and a poet. What about Queenie, the first to be killed. What do we know about her? She was with Irving's company at the Lyceum, wasn't she?"

"I gather so, in a small capacity, a nonspeaking role. I found her charming and inoffensive."

"I didn't speak to her," said Miss Dundas. "She was shepherded closely by Jerry Gribble."

"'Shepherded,'" I said. "That's a delicate way of putting it. Jerry would have liked that. Yes, there's no doubt she was included in the party as company for Jerry. They met at a cricket match six months ago, he told me. She was selling tombola tickets. Poor fellow, he had a fatal weakness for the ladies."

She tilted an eyebrow.

"Well he was twice divorced," I said. "He made it clear to Queenie that he wouldn't be getting spliced a third time."

She asked, "What happened to the ex-wives? Perhaps there was resentment if they fell on hard times later."

"And saw him shepherding pretty young actresses, do you mean? Good thinking. But I have to tell you that Angela, the first Duchess, died in childbirth after she married a French count; and Polly, the second, lives very comfortably in New Orleans, happily married to a ship owner."

"I wonder whether anyone else bore some grudge against Jerry?" she persisted.

"That's hard to imagine. He was a dear fellow, a gentleman in every sense, the salt of the earth."

"Twice divorced?"

"But utterly without blame. The judge found the wives at fault in each case."

She rolled her eyes upwards; precisely why, I couldn't say. "Well, Bertie, if you're right, Miss Chimes and Jerry Gribble were two delightful people who gave no offense to anyone. What of Wilfred Osgot-Edge? He was a more complex person than the others, was he not?"

I pondered this for a moment. "Because he was a poet, d'you mean? That may be so, but I found him straightforward enough. When he succeeded in putting more than two words together, he generally had something practical to say."

"Yes, I rather admired the efforts he made to be sociable. I think what I mean is that poetry and shooting are difficult to reconcile—the one creative and the other destructive."

"Forms of self-expression," I explained. "Perfectly understandable for a fellow who is tongue-tied to write down his thoughts in verse. And what a tonic for his confidence to shoot better than the blighters who show him up in conversation. He was devilish fast on the trigger."

Miss Dundas signaled a spicy remark by clearing her throat. "I formed the impression that he wasn't exactly slow in other matters."

"Matters of the heart?" said I, mindful of what I had heard in the corridor the night before.

She smiled faintly. I'm sure she knew Osgot-Edge had winkled his way into Amelia's bed. Nothing in a country house at night escapes the notice of the fair sex.

Never one to beat about the bush, I said, "Our charming hostess might be able to enlighten us further on that subject. Come to think of it, the frolics yesterday night might have given someone else a motive for murder."

"Jealousy?"

"Exactly."

We had no need to say it. We both thought of Amelia's brother, Marcus.

"Be that as it may," I said. "There's still no connection I can see with the other deaths."

She evidently agreed, for she said, "Looking at it another way, have you made a list of possible suspects?"

Impressed, I commented, "My word, Isabella, you are well informed. Do you read the police reports?"

"No," she said. "Detective stories. Cheap and trivial, but they pass the time on long sea voyages. It seems to me that this is a case in which opportunity may be more indicative than motive."

"My thought exactly," said I. "Would you care to elaborate?"

"If you kindly pour me another Madeira." She held up a finger. "I mean nothing else, Bertie. I can drink this stuff and stay sober till kingdom come."

I said as I collected the decanter, "I'm the Prince of Wales, my dear. It's my destiny to wait for kingdom come."

When she'd taken a sip, she said, "Opportunity, then. Queenie Chimes, it appears, was poisoned. Something, presumably, was added to one of the dishes she had at dinner. Who was in a position to poison her food?"

"Someone in the kitchen. The waiters. The dinner guests."

"Can you recall who was sitting on either side of her? I think one was Jerry Gribble."

"Who was the other? I know—Claude Bullivant! By George, he was, and doing his best to frighten us all by saying there was a ghost in the house. Frighten us, or distract us, I ask myself."

She moved on without showing much respect for my observation. I had already noticed that she was rather partial to Bullivant. "Then there was the shooting of Jerry Gribble. Was opportunity a factor there?"

"Less so," I said. "He'd been dead some time when we found him." I tossed in my bit of medical jargon as if I was constantly using the term. "*Rigor mortis* had set in. My estimate is that he died shortly after breakfast, before we started the shoot. Almost anyone could have fired the fatal shot—servants, beaters, people from the village, or any of the party."

"Probably not one of the kitchen staff, however," said Miss

Dundas astutely. "After breakfast they must have been fully occupied preparing the picnic lunch."

"Which brings us back to the guests," I mused. "And the third
murder. Whoever stabbed Osgot-Edge succeeded in doing it under
cover of darkness as we were playing Sardines. There shouldn't
have been any servants about. It points emphatically to someone
involved in the game." I clicked my fingers. "Who was it who suggested Osgot-Edge should hide first?"

"Not I," said Miss Dundas. "I suggested your wife, Her Royal
Highness, if you remember, and she declined."

"Yes, and then Bullivant suggested me, and Alix made some
comment about a trail of cigar smoke. Do you know, I think it
was Amelia who put Wilfred's name forward?"

"It was."

The full import of this took a moment or so to digest. I fingered the top button of my nightshirt. "And it was Amelia who
drew up the guest list and invited us here in the first place."

CHAPTER 11

M y suspicions of Amelia may strike the reader as deplorable.
She had gone to no end of trouble and expense to provide
a good week's sport, welcomed us warmly to her house and put
the best rooms at our disposal, and now I was willing to regard
her as a modern Lady Macbeth. I can only say in mitigation that if
the wretched King of Scotland (his name escapes me) who came
to stay with the Macbeths had been as circumspect as I, then he
would have survived and Shakespeare could have put his talent to
better use. Too many of the Bard's plays are about the untimely
ends of kings and princes for my liking. Personally, I find more
to admire in Gilbert and Sullivan, but that's to digress.

Back to Amelia. If our hostess *had* been planning the demise
of several ladies and gentlemen of her acquaintance, she was
well placed to do it. She had issued the invitations, subject to
my approval, of course, planned the menus, allocated the rooms
and she, better than anyone, knew the house, its corridors and
staircases, entrances and exits. The poisoning of Miss Chimes, the
shooting of Jerry Gribble and the stabbing of Osgot-Edge were all
within her capability, given that she was better placed than anyone
else to choose the appropriate moment and make good her escape
from the scene of the crime.

Was I being uncharitable? You will have an opportunity to judge.

Meanwhile, I prepared to stay awake seated in the armchair,
waiting for the murderer to spring the trap. In my right hand was

the length of sashcord I would pull at the critical moment. Across my knees lay the poker I had brought from Alix's room.

Miss Dundas said, "Would you mind if I blow out the candle?"

I gave my consent and promised to remain alert, adding the wish that she would sleep soundly. To be frank, I hadn't the slightest expectation that she would. It amazed me soon afterwards to hear her breathing lengthen and take on the regular tempo of slumber. What self-possession, I thought—to be capable of sleep when a murderer might enter the room at any moment! Quite extraordinary. I could only put it down to habituation, the many times she must have bedded down in her tent in the Amazon jungle while untold dangers lurked outside. Or because she felt safe with me as her protector.

Quite soon the armchair began to be uncomfortable. Pins and needles spread up my left leg even though I shifted my position several times. Moreover I was wrestling mentally with the knowledge that only half the bed was occupied and the probability that Miss Dundas was only pretending to be asleep in an effort to suppress her natural excitement at my physical proximity. I found myself wondering whether I could work the man trap from a recumbent posture.

Of course it was out of the question and I didn't seriously entertain it. I took my responsibility seriously, which was just as well, because presently I heard a sound, muffled, but not to be dismissed. Outside, close to the bedroom, something had moved. I tightened my grip on the poker and watched the door.

Miss Dundas stirred. "What was that?"

"I don't know," I whispered.

"Let them step right in before you pull the cord," she cautioned.

I held my breath.

Another sound came, a thud, too heavy to be a creaking floorboard. I felt the hair rise on the back of my neck. You see, the sound didn't come from outside the door. It came from the French window. Someone was on the balcony. Slowly and with stealth, the handle was being turned.

There was I, seated with my back to it, waiting to trap someone at the door. Reader, I did the only sensible thing—dropped the sashcord and ducked behind the bed.

I heard the curtains flap. I was conscious of a draft from the window and with it a distinct whiff of scent. Everything I had deduced was coming true except the means of entry. The only uncertainty left was the weapon Amelia proposed to use. I decided against raising my head to find out.

You may imagine the shock it was to hear a masculine voice say in a curiously unthreatening tone, "Isabella, are you awake?" To say that I was taken by surprise is an understatement. I was dumbfounded.

He repeated her name and I was too stupefied to recognize his voice until he said, "Bit of a liberty, eh? Didn't like to think of you alone in here, not after some of the looks you gave me. You're a damned fine looker, if you want to know."

I boiled inwardly. The voice was Bullivant's.

"Be a peach," he went on in this disgraceful vein, "Say you're gasping for me. Don't hold it in. I brought you these. Picked by moonlight."

He'd filched the last roses from the garden, the blighter, which explained the perfume I'd noticed.

Miss Dundas said, "Kindly keep your distance, Mr. Bullivant. I am holding a knife."

"I'll be jiggered!" said Bullivant on a high note of indignation. "You're not afraid, are you? Good God, I wouldn't take a lady by force. That's not the ticket, not the ticket at all. I wouldn't say a kiss and a cuddle is the summit of my ambition, but if that's as far as you care to go on this occasion, Isabella, I'm your man."

You may imagine my outrage at this unseemly declaration. It took a moment to satisfy myself that Bullivant wasn't bent on murder, but when I fathomed that his boorish behavior was meant to win the lady's favors I was almost as appalled as if he *had* meant to kill her. In the nature of things one doesn't normally hear how other fellows broach the question, but if this was typical of the English gentleman then all of us might as well go back to painting ourselves with woad and clubbing any passing lady we admire. Whatever became of old-fashioned chivalry, sweet nothings and honeyed words? One bunch of roses stolen from someone else's garden didn't impress me much—nor Miss Dundas it seemed, who said acidly, "You're *not* my man, Mr. Bullivant, and you won't be anybody else's if you so much as touch me."

To which he said, "Fiddlesticks. What have you got to lose, my beauty? Surely not your Sunday School certificate?"

This was more than I could stomach. I stood up, no, sprang up, and said, "That's unforgivable, Bullivant."

He uttered my name as if a fire had broken out.

Fairly flinging my words across the bed, I continued, "If I hadn't been speechless with disgust I'd have stopped you earlier. How dare you molest this lady?"

"Sir, I didn't know you were here," he protested lamely.

"That's immaterial," I told him.

"I didn't molest her," he said, more confident now.

I said, "You did worse. You insulted the lady. You molested her verbally, cast an aspersion on her reputation. I heard it."

"You weren't meant to."

"You'd better apologize at once."

"Sir, I do, most humbly."

"*To the lady*, Bullivant, to the lady."

Miss Dundas surprised us both by striking a match to light the candle at her bedside. She said, "No apology is necessary, or desired. There has obviously been a misunderstanding for which I must bear some responsibility, at least. Mr. Bullivant and I have had several conversations in the last few days and it is not impossible that he gained the impression that I was amused by his blandishments. Not that I had in mind a visitation by night, I hasten to add."

Her statement silenced us both, so she went on, "Three unexplained deaths in the house are not conducive to romantic trysts, I would have thought. And with all those servants standing guard in the corridors—"

"That's why I climbed over the balcony," said Bullivant. He turned to me, the blighted hopes still lingering on his features. "But if I'd known you were here, sir, I wouldn't have ventured from my room. Frightful gaffe."

I pointed out firmly, "I was engaged in investigating the crimes."

"Ah." Bullivant sounded as if a doctor were examining his tonsils. As an expression of belief it failed to carry conviction.

"What is more," I informed him, "my detective duties require me to remain here for the rest of the night."

Bullivant seemed to understand this, even if he didn't altogether appreciate it. He said, "You'd like me to return to my room, sir?"

I nodded. "By the same route you entered, and you can take the roses with you. They're covered in greenfly."

CHAPTER 12

You may wonder how I felt towards Isabella Dundas after that unseemly incident with Bullivant. After all, she had admitted to the possibility that her light behavior had encouraged the man. I had been led to assume that she was indifferent to my own good looks and winning ways. Well, not to mince words, I was peeved. I'd gone to her room from the highest motives, ready to deal with a murderer. I hadn't bargained on a lover. All this, of course, was trivial compared to the matter under investigation, but one has one's pride. I resumed my armchair vigil in a chastened mood. It improved towards morning, about 5:30 A.M., when the lady offered to change places with me. She'd slept sufficiently, she told me, and now I deserved a turn in the bed. I didn't decline the offer.

Nobody else disturbed us until the maid came with tea and bread and butter. Miss Dundas had stepped deftly around the trap to take the tray in at the door. She offered me the cup (there was only one), but since I prefer cold milk to tea in the morning, I took what was in the jug and used the glass tumbler beside the bed.

All things considered, I felt agreeably refreshed. In one sense the chance to snatch some sleep had been a blessing, but it was all time that I could ill afford from my investigations. The murderer remained at large and the threat to Miss Dundas was not removed. If my judgment counted for anything, she would be in mortal danger for the rest of Thursday. I told her firmly that I wouldn't be leaving her side until Inspector Sweeney reported for duty.

Madam said with a click of the tongue, "That's going to be inconvenient." But as she had already dressed by this time, it was clear that the inconvenience would be mainly on my side. She said, "Would it simplify matters if I packed my things and left?"

"Went home, do you mean? No, no," I told her. "That's no guarantee of safety. Come along to my rooms while I get into some clothes."

She rightly pointed out that we ought to dismantle the trap in case the chambermaid became enmeshed in it. "What an anticlimax," she remarked as we untied the cords. "You were the only catch all night."

Everyone had gone to breakfast by the time we emerged from her room, so we were spared any embarrassment. I'm not unused to being caught out, as they say, but I would resent winks and nudges after a night of what the lady aptly, if unkindly, characterized as anticlimax.

Whilst I dressed with the door ajar, she leafed through a magazine in the adjacent sitting room, turning the pages with a quickness that conveyed her ill humor. She called out to me, "Really it's no different from the so-called savages of the Amazon."

"What?" I said, caught hauling up my trousers. I looked to see if some mirror was embarrassingly positioned.

"These pictures of fox hunting in—what is it called?—*Fur and Feather.*"

I said, "You're not comparing what goes on in the jungle with the hunt?"

"Why ever not?" she answered. "The meet is a tribal ritual, after all—the Master of Foxhounds and the stirrup cup and the horn and the 'Tallyho' and the 'View Halloo.'"

"That's sport."

"Dressed up to the nines to chase a verminous animal across country, catch it, kill it, cut off its tail and blood the novices? The only difference I can see is that the Amazon hunters catch their prey to eat. You stuff it and call it sport."

"You're talking like a blasted socialist," I told her testily.

She started to laugh and then stopped abruptly with a sharp intake of breath.

"What is it?" I said. It was a horrid moment. Dreadful possibilities flitted through my brain.

Then I heard a too-familiar voice ask stiffly, "Is the Prince of Wales through there?"

Alix didn't wait for a reply. She stepped into my dressing room and said, sounding depressingly like my mama, "Bertie, I have been waiting for you to accompany me to breakfast. It's five past nine already. Everyone must be waiting downstairs."

"My word," I said, recovering my wits. "Is it so late? I overslept, my dear."

"You were supposed to have been preventing another murder."

"Oh, I did," I answered. "Miss Dundas has come through the night safely, as you see. I guarded her room while she slept. Took a nap towards morning, when I was satisfied that the immediate danger was past. How are you this morning, Alix? Did you manage to get some sleep yourself?"

Ignoring that, she asked, "How do you propose to pass the day—taking care of Miss Dundas?"

I told her with dignity that I would be delegating that responsibility to Sweeney at the earliest opportunity. "I must start my inquiries in earnest. I shall interview everyone."

"You'll have to hurry, then," she said. "The Holdfasts are about to leave, if they haven't gone already. Their carriage is at the front door and their trunk has been loaded. I saw it from my window."

"I can't allow that," I said. "Damn them, they can't! Stay with Miss Dundas, would you?" and with that, I fairly stormed downstairs.

Sir George Holdfast was in the entrance hall, already in his overcoat saying goodbye to Amelia. When I demanded what the deuce was going on he gave a feeble shrug and blamed his wife. "Moira is extremely agitated, Bertie. She hardly slept at all last night. She is resolved to leave."

I said adamantly, "You must tell her that I cannot allow it. As I made clear last night, I have instituted an inquiry into these regrettable deaths. You will each be required to make a statement about your movements and what you remember of the circumstances leading up to the murders."

He said in a shocked voice, "You don't regard Moira and me as suspicious persons?"

"George," I answered slowly, spacing out my words, "it would look suspicious if you defied my instructions and left the house."

I had him collared and he knew it. "I'll speak to Moira," was all he said.

Having weathered that crisis successfully, I went in to breakfast, where everyone waited ravenously for morning prayers. I gave them a profuse apology. One short prayer from the Chaplain and we all dipped in the trough, so to speak. After the first pangs were satisfied, I thought I had better take precautions in case anyone else had ideas about leaving. I ordered them to assemble in the morning room at half past ten, a measure of my resolve considering that it restricted breakfast to a meager hour.

Subdued and ill at ease, they filed in.

"It isn't more bad news?" Amelia asked me in confidence. She was still my principal suspect, but I have to admit that her concern sounded genuine enough.

I shook my head and gestured to her to sit down. "Are we all assembled?" I asked. "We seem to be short of several people."

Marcus Pelham grinned unpleasantly. "Haven't you heard?"

Amelia gave him a glare and said, "There should be eight of us, sir. The Chaplain asked me to give you his apologies. He has to take his Scripture class at the village school."

"Eight it is," said Holdfast after a glance around the room. At bottom he was a sound fellow and a good support.

"Splendid." I launched into my announcement, putting it to them in a positive manner that brooked no interference. The investigation, I informed them, was already well advanced. Statements had been collected from the servants, and Inspector Sweeney (who was at my side, looking pale) had spent much of the night comparing them. We were now about to begin the second stage of our inquiry, namely the questioning of the present company. It was imperative that they remain in the house for the rest of the day.

The moment I stopped talking, Pelham inquired, "What have you learned so far, Your Royal Highness? Have you found any clues?"

"Clues? What are they?" cried Lady Holdfast, lifting her feet off the floor and staring about her as if they were cockroaches.

"Ignore him," said Amelia. "He reads the police reports in the newspaper and he wants to impress you all."

"Actually, a clew," Pelham insisted on telling us and spelling the word, "is a ball of thread. Anyone who knows the classics must remember the clew that Ariadne gave Theseus to unwind behind him as he went through the labyrinth at Crete. So in its modern rendering, Lady Holdfast, a clue—c-l-u-e—is anything that guides or directs one in an intricate case. Proper detectives always look for clues."

"Oh. Have you discovered any?" asked Lady Holdfast, trying to sound calm again. "Do tell us, Your Royal Highness!"

I was cautious. For one thing I didn't want to alarm people by telling them about the pieces of paper found with each of the bodies and the significance I attached to them; for another, I meant to deprive the murderer of the attention she (or he) was seeking. In that way, we might lure her (or him) into the open. So I said, "We are far advanced with our investigation and we only require your help to bring it to a swift conclusion."

"You can speak frankly to us," said Pelham.

"That is exactly what I have done."

"And we support you to a man," said George Holdfast. "Who do you want to question first, Bertie?"

"Our hostess," said I.

Amelia turned pink.

"And, in due course, each of you," I added.

"Don't leave out the Chaplain, will you?" said Pelham. "He could be a vital witness. He was here last night, remember, and he was at the table on Monday when Miss Chimes collapsed. He's as warm a suspect as anyone else."

"Fie on you!" said Lady Holdfast. "A man of the Church?"

"The Chaplain will be invited to assist us," said I. Then Alix quietly added, "And Claude Bullivant?"

"Claude?" I said. "Isn't he here? I thought we were all present."

"Oh, my word!" cried Lady Holdfast. "What's happened to Mr. Bullivant?"

"We counted eight," said Amelia, "But we must have included Inspector Sweeney."

Her brother said, "Then where the devil is Bullivant? Did anyone tell him about the meeting?"

George Holdfast asked, "Has anyone seen him since last night?"

Miss Dundas cleared her throat to speak. I cut in gallantly, "Yes,

I saw him in the small hours. I expect he overslept, like me. Better send a servant up to his room."

So we adjourned. The man sent to rouse Bullivant returned shortly to report that he wasn't in his bedroom. I was unperturbed. Bullivant wasn't earmarked as the next victim of our killer; in no conceivable way had he "far to go." But it did cross my mind that he might have come to grief climbing over balconies by night. So I ordered a search of the immediate grounds. Another mishap, from whatever cause, would not be good for morale.

Amelia lingered in the morning room, waiting to be questioned. Catching her eye, I said, "It's a fine morning. Why don't you put on a coat and we'll take a walk outside?"

I turned to Sweeney and instructed him to stay with Miss Dundas.

"Shall I question her, sir?"

"Better not. Just guard her like a crock of gold, Sweeney."

"Depend upon it, sir." And he couldn't resist adding, "Protection duty is my proper function."

So I stepped outside the house with its pretty owner and escorted her slowly along the gravel path that led past the croquet lawn to a rock garden. "This is a fine pickle, Amelia," I said without preamble. "What's behind it?"

She looked up at me uncertainly, her hazel-green eyes glistening moistly. I must say she appeared a picture of fragility in her black coat with beaver trim and matching hat. "I wish I could understand."

I said sternly, "You had better try. The plain fact is that you invited a number of guests to your house and three of them are dead. They were not killed at random. They were chosen victims. If I understand it right, you prepared the guest list."

She took a quick, frightened breath, yet still had the temerity to say, "It was sent to Marlborough House for your approval, sir."

"I know that," I said curtly. "The names were your choice, were they not?"

She hesitated. "Well, yes."

"No one else influenced your choice? Your brother, possibly?"

"Marcus? No, I didn't consult him. The list was my own absolutely."

"Hm." This was becoming more damning by the moment. Time for a smoke, I thought—one reason why I'd suggested an interview outside. I put a match to a Tsar that I had ready in my pocket. "You had better tell me why you chose this particular set of people."

We walked on for some distance before she replied, "They had to be guests who would meet your approval, sir."

A pretty low punch. I refused to let it wind me. "That wasn't the only criterion, surely?"

She said, "As it was a shooting party, I nominated the guns first. Your name was top of the list. Then I selected several gentlemen I considered worthy to stand with you, old friends who shot here when Freddie was alive. Sir George, Wilfred, Claude and Jerry. All distinguished people. Marcus had to be included to act as host. Oh, and the Chaplain attends all the social events at Desborough. Really it was quite obvious who should come. I did include another neighbor on the original list."

"The V.C.?"

"Colonel Roberts, yes. He's new in the county. I met him at the Hunt Ball. Knowing that he was a sportsman and a gallant soldier, I thought he might be suitable, but you struck him out."

"So I did. Thirteen on the list. That was tempting the fates. I did your Colonel a good turn, as things turned out. He might have been dead by now."

She shivered. "Don't! It's too horrible to contemplate."

We had come to a bench overlooking the croquet lawn, so I suggested we sit down. "Now you can tell me how you selected the ladies. That is, apart from Alix and Lady Holdfast."

"Who does that leave? Queenie Chimes and Isabella Dundas. Well, sir, I first met Queenie at the Church garden party. It was well known locally that she came to stay at Jerry Gribble's house for occasional weekends, and the poor man really wasn't himself without her. As for Isabella, I wanted to include a lady of character, someone with sand in her boots, so to speak. She gave a very impressive lecture at the Beaconsfield Geographical Society last January and I was introduced to her afterwards. We corresponded and she accepted my invitation. Without disrespect to the other ladies, I felt that her presence would add intellectual weight to the female side of the party."

"But you didn't know her before last January?"

"I'd read about her in the magazines, that was all."

"You bear her no ill will?"

"Quite the contrary! Why do you ask?"

"No matter. And you say that your acquaintance with Queenie Chimes was slight?"

"I met her on three or four social occasions in this neighborhood."

"You didn't disapprove of her morals?"

"Sir, if I had, I would not have invited her to Desborough. I'm not a prude." She looked away, across the croquet lawn. "I believe I know what you're thinking. But if I'd wanted to do away with Queenie for some unfathomable reason, I'd be a fool to do it in my own house in full view of all those guests. And I wouldn't have dreamed of shooting poor Jerry. He was a darling, one of our oldest and best-loved friends."

"Since you've mentioned Jerry," I said, "was there any breath of scandal locally about his liaison with Queenie?"

"I couldn't say. I don't listen to gossip."

"I was thinking of people who knew the wives he divorced and may have felt angry that he should now take up with an actress."

"Plenty have behaved worse than that," she replied. "It wasn't as if he was still married." Then she shot her hand to her mouth. "Oh, dear! I mean nothing personal, sir, really, I don't."

I shook my head. "You won't embarrass me, Amelia. But I shall expect you to answer a personal question with the same candor. Was there ever any suggestion that Jerry might marry you after Freddie died?"

Her cheeks turned scarlet. "Jerry? He was twice my age."

"He was twice Queenie's age."

"I was speaking for myself."

"Ah, but from Jerry's point of view, you were his neighbor, a pretty widow he'd known for years. It would be strange indeed if he hadn't given some thought to your future. May I have an answer to my question? Did he ask you to marry him?"

There was a pause, followed by a sigh. "It's painful to speak of. He didn't propose. He said after two marriages he had a horror of front pews. He wanted me to live with him, to live in sin. Of course I refused. I made light of it, and we remained friends. He was charming about it. I don't know to this day how serious he was. Please, I wouldn't want this mentioned to anyone else. I was never Jerry's lover."

Her statement impressed me. Jerry's maxim about the front pew sounded so typical of the things he trotted out. But if I believed Amelia, my theory ran aground. If she hadn't been jealous of Queenie Chimes and angry with Jerry, what motive had she for killing them?

Stumped for the moment, I moved obliquely to the matter of the other victim. "If you were to take a lover, he would have to be a younger man?"

She stood up. "I'd like to walk on, if you don't mind. It's cold sitting still."

"Such as your poet," I said, flicking the ash from my cigar.

She didn't deny it, which was a point in her favor. Instead she asked, "Sir, perhaps you will tell me what is behind that observation?"

"Certainly. I happen to know that Osgot-Edge visited your room the night before he died." I saw the muscles flex at the side of her face. "Suppose, for the sake of argument, you *had* killed the other two, and Osgot-Edge found out and was profoundly shocked that the lady he loved could be capable of murder—"

"You are wrong!"

"—then you had a motive for killing him as well."

"I did not!" Her eyes managed to glisten with tears and burn like beacons at the same time. "Yes, he was my lover. That is the *only* thing you said that is true. Wilfred was a kind, courageous, gentle-hearted man. Whoever killed him is a demon." With that, she broke into a fit of weeping and ran away from me.

This was dreadful. I had overstepped the mark. I couldn't allow the interview to end tike this. I tossed away the cigar and ran after her. "Amelia!"

Unhappily, my running is usually done astride a hack. The lady was too fast for me. She ran up the steps of the house and through the door before I reached the staircase. She was still sobbing pitiably.

I pounded up the steps after her, sounding like a bulldog with bronchitis, through the hall and into the morning room. Six pairs of eyes stared at me.

"Next?" said Marcus Pelham.

CHAPTER 13

"Has Bullivant appeared yet?" I asked.

Inspector Sweeney gave me a persecuted look, then told me not only that the search for Bullivant had been unproductive, but that people were becoming agitated.

"Probably he went for a long walk," I said. "I dare say he'll appear for luncheon."

"Might I have a private word with you, sir?" Sweeney asked. Before we had withdrawn to the far end of the room he said, "I wouldn't describe myself as a detective, sir—"

"I know that," I said through gritted teeth, "but you don't have to broadcast it to all and sundry. Keep your voice down."

"This Lady Holdfast, sir. She's acting like a guilty person, saying over and over that she wants to leave the house as soon as possible. She's giving her husband the devil of a time, sir."

"Pure nerves," I told him.

"I'd be nervous myself if I'd murdered three people, sir. She has a wild look in her eye. I wouldn't care to meet her with a dagger in a dark room."

"That may be so, Sweeney, but I need something more to go on than a wild look."

"I thought I'd mention it."

"And you have."

"You could question her next, sir."

"And give her the excuse to leave? No, she'll have to wait.

Return to your bodyguarding. That's what you do best. Leave the conduct of the case to me."

I fingered my watch chain and thought what on earth shall I do next? Interview another suspect. Young Pelham will do. But when I crossed the room, he had gone.

"If you're looking for Marcus, he went up to see what he could do for Amelia," Alix informed me without looking up from her needlework. "She was plainly distressed when she came in."

The notion of Marcus Pelham comforting his sister was so unlikely that it warranted investigating. Instead of sending for him, I went upstairs myself, just as I approached Amelia's room, the door opened and Pelham emerged. He closed it, hastily, I thought. "How is your sister?" I inquired.

"Resting. She wants to be quiet for a while. She seems wrought up. I promised her she wouldn't be disturbed before luncheon."

"How thankful she must be."

He frowned at me. "Thankful?"

"To have a dear brother to comfort and protect her," said I with a straight face. "You had better escort me downstairs, hadn't you, seeing that I was the instrument of her distress? I want to put some questions to you anyway. Let's see how you stand up to the inquisition."

He grinned sourly.

I took him through a different part of the garden, past borders where forlorn chrysanthemums lingered into the autumn on stems with shriveled leaves. "Where does this lead?" I asked.

"I couldn't say."

Ungracious pup. "Have the good manners to address me properly, would you? Surely you know the garden well?"

He shook his head.

I warned him, "You're testing my patience, laddie."

"It's true," he said defiantly, and then added tamely as I conveyed my displeasure with a look, "Sir. I'm as much of a stranger here as yourself. This is the first year I've been invited to shoot at Desborough. I wasn't welcome when Freddie was alive and I'm only here now because my sister needs a man to act as host."

"What was Freddie's objection to you?"

"He found out that Amelia was paying off my debts from time

to time. Bloody Freddie would cheerfully have seen me in the poorhouse."

"How did the debts arise? Do you gamble?"

"Not to excess." Sensing, correctly, that I would erupt if I heard one more boorish word from him, he added "sir" as an afterthought and volunteered some information. "This may seem difficult to credit, but my sister and I had a strict upbringing. Our father was an archdeacon. In the last century there was money to burn in our family, huge estates, rents, all a gentleman could want. Then one morning, out of the blue, Grandfather Pelham—Sir Hugh, as he was—heard the call of God. He renounced his life as one of the gentry and studied to become a parson. He found the scriptures difficult to master, so he was never admitted to holy orders, but he made sure that my father and my three uncles all wore the cloth. The Pelham estates were given to the Church because the Bible tells us not to lay up treasures upon earth."

"That's a text I've pondered more than once," said I. "I'm not much of a theologian, I admit, but I would have thought that handing over one's inheritance to the Church of England would put the Church itself in danger of laying up treasures. No, I take it as an injunction to spend generously while one has the means, don't you?"

Young Pelham wasn't much of a theologian either. He sidestepped the question. "Well, enough was provided for my school fees and Oxford and then I was supposed to take holy orders myself, but I rebelled. I wasn't suited for preaching, damn it."

"That is evident."

"I'm with my eighteenth-century ancestors in spirit."

"In spirit, but not in funds."

He nodded.

I said, "How thoughtful of your sister to have married a rich man like Freddie Drummond!" Provocative, I grant you, but the sarcasm rolled off this young man. We walked on in silence for a stretch and entered a walled vegetable garden. I may have appeared quiet, but as we strolled among the ranks of savoys I was busy revising my opinion of Marcus Pelham. Until then I had put him down as a man unhealthily infatuated with his own sister and jealous of any fellow who showed the slightest interest in her. Apparently I had been mistaken. The interest wasn't incestuous. It was pecuniary.

He was afraid of someone marrying her and putting a stop to the payments.

I said, "Don't you have any private income at all?"

"A few stocks and shares, sir. Not enough to survive on."

"You're being uncommonly frank."

"I've seen the way certain people are looking at me. I don't mind being unpopular, but I dislike being under suspicion. I want you to know why I'm here, and it isn't to murder the guests."

"You know on which side your bread is buttered."

"Exactly."

"And at the same time you can observe what progress, if any, her lovers are making."

He gave me a surprised look. "Now *you're* being uncommonly frank, sir."

"Isn't that a fair comment?"

"Well, yes."

I said, "Let's speak plainly, shall we? We both know that your sister has a liking for masculine company."

He muttered resentfully, "You could put it more plainly than that."

"That's plain enough. We're gentlemen, when all's said and done. My point is this. Any lover of Amelia's who is not a married man must be considered a potential threat to your income, isn't that so?"

He picked a Brussels sprout off its stalk and tossed it at the wall. "Not necessarily."

Unmoved, I went on, "Freddie conveniently died. But there were others lining up to replace him. Jerry Gribble was a widower and Osgot-Edge a bachelor. You may well have decided to protect your future by killing them both."

He made a show of being amused. "Jerry and the poet—to stop them marrying my sister? That's rich!"

I waited for the bluster to subside.

It took a moment or two for the gravity of the charge to penetrate. Then he said more earnestly, "Before you put a noose around my neck, sir, there's an obvious flaw in this. What about the other victim? Why should I have killed Queenie Chimes? She was Jerry's mistress. If what you say is true, I would have wanted Queenie to stay alive and keep Jerry out of Amelia's skirts."

I mulled it over for a few paces. "That has a certain logic, I grant you. However, a really cunning murderer knows that logic will defeat him, so he commits an illogical crime. One more death is neither here nor there to a man who is resolved to murder twice. He kills Miss Chimes to obscure the pattern of his crimes." This ingenious theory sprang practically unbidden from my lips. I found it so persuasive that I said, "You'd better give an account of yourself. Where were you sitting at the table that first evening when Queenie collapsed?"

Perhaps it was the chill of the air, but I fancy that the color rose to his cheeks now that he sensed how serious I was. His tongue flicked nervously across his lips. "The Chaplain was on my right and the Princess of Wales on my left. If you want to know who sat on either side of Queenie it was Jerry and Claude Bullivant," he added.

"That is of small consequence," I pointed out. "Anyone could have tampered with the food before it was served."

"Only if they visited the kitchen. I did not."

"Then the poison could have been placed in the drink she had in the anteroom."

"You had better speak to Colwell about that. He served the aperitifs."

"I have every intention of doing so," I said, slightly ruffled, wishing I'd thought of this before.

A certain smugness spread across his features. "When all's said and done, Colwell is just a glorified butler. Have you considered the possibility that the house steward did it? Perhaps he has a grudge against the upper classes."

I ignored the observation and pressed on. "Let us consider Jerry's murder. It was perfectly possible for you to have fired the fatal shot on Tuesday in the hour between breakfast and the start of the shoot."

"It was perfectly possible for any of us to have fired it, not excluding the ladies. And as for the stabbing last night," he said, anticipating my question, "the same holds true. We were all there in the dark. It wasn't my suggestion to play Sardines, by the way, Your Royal Highness. I dislike the game. The only game I suggested all evening was Spinning the Trencher, and if that incriminates me, what hope is there for any of us?"

This, I thought, was too bumptious by far, so I commented, "You may not want a noose around your neck, Pelham, but you sound increasingly like the counsel for your defense. Have you been rehearsing?"

His lower lip protruded sulkily. After an interval I asked, "Do you happen to remember who did suggest Sardines?"

"My sister." To this unbrotherly admission he saw fit to add, "Anyone might have made the suggestion, given that we'd promised to play some form of Hide and Seek."

"Quite." I didn't need reminding that the Hide and Seek had been Alix's suggestion.

He said, "I don't think Amelia is capable of killing anyone. She wouldn't hurt a fly."

We had reached the limit of the vegetable garden, so we returned by a second path, a decision we might have reconsidered had we known that it led past the pigsties. I said wryly, "You were speaking of flies?"

Pelham pulled a face and said, "It's offensive. She'll have to get rid of them."

I remarked, "I happen to have quite a healthy respect for pigs. We rear them on the Sandringham estate. Highly intelligent creatures. You can train them, you know. And they make few demands. They'll eat anything you give them. Anything. You could put a dead sheep in there and not a bone would remain."

"I'm obliged to you for the information, sir, but I definitely don't kill sheep," said Pelham.

I gave him a sharp look and his eyes glittered in amusement. It *was* amusing in a morbid way, and I was forced to smile as well. If he supposed my suspicions were any the less, he was mistaken. As soon as we reached the fresher air of the flower borders, I brought up the vital question of the guest list. "When did you first see it?"

"Towards the end of May, I should think."

"Five months ago. Were you consulted about the choice of guests?"

"No, sir. My sister showed me the final list after you had approved it."

"But you were given the names as early as last May?"

"Amelia had persuaded me to act as host. The least she could do was tell me who had been invited."

"Had you met any of them before?"

He thought for a moment. "All of them except yourself and Her Royal Highness."

"Every one—including the three who are dead?"

He nodded.

"Queenie Chimes?" I said in surprise. "Where did you meet her?"

"The first time? On the landing outside my rooms in Chelsea. She dropped her umbrella down the stairs and I opened my door and picked it up. She sent me a ticket for the Lyceum and we had supper after the play."

"When was this?"

"Last winter. January, I think. The play was *Julius Caesar* and she was in the crowd scenes."

"'Friends, Romans, countrymen . . . '?"

Ignoring my apt quotation, he went on, "As it happens, she was impossible to spot in the costumes they wore, but of course in Romano's afterwards I praised her performance to the skies. She was easily pleased. I saw her in something else on another occasion—*Much Ado About Nothing*. She played a gentlewoman then. I wasn't so flush that week, so we had a one-and-sixpenny supper in Kettner's and walked home. In case you care to know, sir, there was never anything improper between us."

"A pretty girl like that? Surely you didn't take no for an answer?" Leaving that aside, I turned to the interesting implication of what he had just told me. "It emerges, then, that you knew Queenie before Jerry did. They met at a cricket match a mere six months ago—something about tombola tickets."

"Queenie told me, yes."

"So you knew she was Jerry's mistress?"

"I gathered as much, and my sister confirmed it when she showed me the guest list."

"Weren't you infuriated? I'm sure I would have been."

He shook his head. "As I tried to explain just now, my association with Queenie amounted to nothing more than a few visits to the Lyceum, followed by supper. One doesn't turn down the chance of seeing Irving. Queenie was gracious enough to invite me, so I treated her to supper. That's all. I wasn't jealous of Jerry Gribble and I wasn't angry with Queenie."

"You don't need to raise your voice," I told him. "The point is taken."

He said, "From the way you spoke, sir, I thought you were still accusing me of murder."

"Everyone is under suspicion except me, laddie," I told him. "And I want to know more about the guest list. Quite obviously, the whole case hinges on it. You got the names from your sister in May, you said? Did you discuss them with Queenie Chimes?"

"Naturally, when I knew she was included. She was curious to know who else was coming and I told her. It didn't mean much to her. I don't think she'd met any of us except Amelia, Jerry and me."

This young man and his sweeping statements! I was forced to put him right. "On the contrary, I suggest that a list like that would mean a great deal to any young lady capable of reading the newspapers. She must have heard of Miss Dundas, the explorer, and probably Osgot-Edge. George Holdfast's name appears on just about every list you see of subscribers to charitable causes. And I haven't even mentioned the Princess of Wales and myself."

That silenced him, which hadn't been my intention. We were fast approaching the house again and I still had a crucial question to put to him about the guest list. To gain a few minutes, I asked, "What's that small building at the end of the rose arbor?"

He took it for a trick question. "I wouldn't know, sir. As I told you I'm almost a stranger here."

"Of course. Shall we find out?" As we stepped out, I said, "Does the name of Colonel Roberts mean anything to you?"

"The V.C.?"

"Evidently, it does. Do you know the man?"

He was bright pink again. "No, sir. I heard from my sister that you struck him out of the original guest list, that was all."

"You wanted to know why, no doubt?"

"I was curious, yes."

"Thinking perhaps that Roberts was a social pariah for some unsavory episode in his past? You were wrong, then. It was simply a matter of reducing a list of thirteen names to twelve. I happen to be superstitious."

"I see."

Looking at the wood and stone structure ahead, I said, "I believe it's a well."

"So it is."

"Did you mention Colonel Roberts to Queenie Chimes?"

"No, sir."

"He's a local man, isn't he? Is it likely that he would have heard that his name was put forward and rejected?"

"I don't know, sir. You had better ask my sister." Pelham may have added something else. If he did, I have no record of it. My attention had switched to something quite different, and much more arresting. On the low brick wall surrounding the well was a scrap of newspaper weighted down with a stone. I moved the stone aside and picked up the piece of paper.

Do I need to tell you the word that was ringed there?

CHAPTER 14

"Thursday?" Puzzlement was written large on Marcus Pelham's features and horror much larger on mine. He shook his head. "What can this possibly mean?"

I rattled out an order. "Get some men here with ropes and grappling hooks. Hurry!" Even as I spoke I was striding with all speed towards the house. In the morning room, five anxious faces, alerted by the urgency of my approach, stared at me: Alix, the Holdfasts, Sweeney and—I was heartily relieved to see—Isabella Dundas.

Explanations had to come later. I told them simply that I believed someone had fallen down the well.

Predictably, Moira Holdfast whimpered and sank facedown into her husband's lap. The others stood up and fairly showered me with questions: how did I know and where was the well and was it an accident and was the person alive and shouldn't we call for help?

I appealed for silence and asked, "Has anyone seen Amelia since she went upstairs?"

The clamor ceased.

She spoke from behind me, and gave me quite a start. "I'm here." She had followed me in. She said, "It isn't Marcus, is it?"

I shook my head. Pandemonium returned.

Shortly after, however, utter silence reigned as we stood around that stupid well like characters in a nursery rhyme, except that it was a human being down there and a grappling hook was being lowered. Marcus had rallied the head gamekeeper and three of his men. From the way coil after coil of rope dropped out of sight it was evident that the well was exceedingly deep. The chance of anyone surviving a fall was negligible.

At length, the gamekeeper gave the order to stop unfurling. The end of the rope was passed across the windlass and two of the men commenced to haul it up. "It's no good," said one. "There's no weight on the end." So they lowered it again. They had no better success. This procedure must have been repeated a dozen times. Then they brought the hook to the surface and discovered nothing more on it than mud.

An hour passed. Alix complained of the cold and returned to the house with Amelia. Most of the others followed soon after, but I remained, and so did Pelham. In desperation more hooks were lowered. The clash of steel carried up to us faintly, depressingly faintly. Three hooks proved to be no more productive than one. In fact the ropes became entangled and hindered the operation.

In the next hour a hamper of lunch was sent out to us and the men ate and worked the ropes by turns. Nobody had the temerity to suggest that I might have been in error, but the comments each time an empty hook was brought to the surface became increasingly despairing. It wasn't a matter of offensive language or outright defiance. The skepticism a man can put into the simple word "no" is quite sufficient to express his feelings. I was left in no doubt that if I had relaxed my vigil and left them to their work I could expect no result whatsoever.

I don't exaggerate when I say that almost four hours elapsed before I was proved to be correct. An evening mist was closing in on us when one of the men announced, "It feels like something."

We all moved closer and peered into the void.

"Careful, now," I cautioned. "Don't snatch at the rope. Bring it up gradually, hand over hand." To be just, they did their best. For a few seconds they appeared to be raising a considerable weight. Then the rope slackened abruptly.

"Bloody hell!" said Pelham, and I think he spoke for everyone.

At my insistence they hauled the grapnel to the surface, and a good thing, too, for one of the flukes had a torn scrap of fabric attached to it, a strip of silk, maroon in color, patterned with small white stars. It was some three inches long, tapering to a point. Clearly it had been ripped from a garment, for there was a buttonhole at the wider end that I observed had been torn at the edge, presumably when the weight of the body was taken up. I eased the piece of material over the point of the fluke and examined it. Then I passed it to Pelham, who remarked that from the size of the buttonhole it appeared to have come from a waistcoat.

"Yes, but do you recognize it?" said I.

He did not. He muttered something about clothes having no interest for him.

I said, "I shall show it to Alix. She is acutely observant of people's dress. She will certainly know if she's seen it before."

And Alix did, when I returned to the house and showed it to her. Without hesitation she told me, "It's from Claude Bullivant's waistcoat. I know the pattern. He wore it on Tuesday evening. Bertie, how dreadful!"

I answered cryptically, "Yes . . . and no." I had better mention here that I hadn't passed those hours beside the well in a state of passivity. From the moment I had seen who was left alive in the morning room I had concluded that the body down there could be no one else but Bullivant's. After that I had set my mental powers the more demanding task of accounting for his death. The explanation had not come quickly, but when it did, it had all the simplicity of the truth. And, as I indicated to my dear wife, my conclusion was not wholly pessimistic.

I decided to communicate my findings to the company; they had not had much to cheer about. When they were assembled in the drawing room, comfortable in their chairs, teacups in hand, I took up a position beside the fire. "My friends, I propose to tell you a story. Bear with me, please. It has a particular relevance to things I wish to tell you later. Some years ago I heard of a sportsman, a shooting man, who was unwise enough to speculate heavily on some venture in the Stock Market that failed. He was ruined, irredeemably. So he put on his Norfolk suit and collected his shotgun and whistled to his favorite retriever and spent the day on his estate contentedly bagging game until the sun set. Then he returned to the house and took his bag book off the shelf and entered his tally. I believe it amounted to some fifty wildfowl and a dozen rabbits. Finally he added his own name to the list. Then he blotted the ink, replaced the book on the shelf and shot himself."

I smiled, so George Holdfast took the cue and chuckled, encouraging some of the others to titter self-consciously. No doubt the story would have gone down better after a good dinner when the ladies had left the table.

"What is more, there was an inquest and they brought in an open verdict." I capped it with all the aplomb of a music hall comedian. "Nobody had thought to look in the bag book."

After an uneasy silence Alix asked, "And what is the point of the story, Bertie? Does it have a moral?"

"I was about to come to that," I said. "First, I must offer a small apology to most of you. In the course of my investigation of the shocking events of this week I thought fit to keep certain information to myself. The murderer left some clues."

Moira Holdfast dipped down and gathered her skirt against her ankles. Swarms of clues still infested her fevered imagination.

I continued, "I deemed it prudent to say nothing about these clues at the time. On the evening when Miss Chimes collapsed at the table, a scrap of newspaper with the word '*Monday*' on it was found at her place setting. The next day, when Jerry Gribble was found dead, a similar piece of paper was in his pocket."

George Holdfast perked up. "I remember. It said '*Tuesday.*'"

I nodded. "And after Mr. Osgot-Edge was stabbed, we found yet another piece of newspaper bearing the day of the week, except that this time a word had been appended, so that it read '*Wednesday's Corpse.*'"

Horrified gasps compelled me to pause.

"It was obvious to me by this time," I continued in the same calm, authoritative tone, "that this was a murderer who was not satisfied with mere killing. He wished to advertise his crimes. He was issuing a challenge. The pieces of paper left beside the bodies were, in effect, a conundrum, and it was the work of a few minutes to resolve the puzzle." Out of the corner of my eye I noticed Alix set down her teacup and fold her arms. I hoped she wasn't about to interrupt. "The key to the puzzle is the rhyme familiar to us all. 'Monday's child is fair of face' and so forth, the word 'corpse' being substituted for 'child.' So simple." Alix shifted again and I moved on swiftly to explain the relevance of each line of the verse to the respective victim.

They stared at me like owls in a thunderstorm.

"So when I was walking in the grounds this morning with Marcus and spotted yet another scrap of newspaper, this time on the walled surround of the well, I knew exactly what had happened."

"I don't quite follow," Pelham interrupted me. "I thought the rhyme to which you referred went 'Thursday's child has far to go'?"

"So it does."

"But we believe that Claude Bullivant is at the bottom of the well. I cannot conceive of any sense in which that line of verse can be applied to him."

Not without satisfaction, I said, "Then it would seem that our murderer is too clever for you, Marcus. Let us remember how ingenious—or devious—he has been up to now. 'Fair of face' we can take as a literal description of the first victim, poor Miss Chimes. The second line, 'full of grace,' was a play on words, a reference to Jerry's Dukedom. And 'full of woe' was, we deduced, a reference to Wilfred's initials. Each interpretation of the verse has been different, so why shouldn't Thursday's bring yet another variation?"

"Well, it's all Greek to me. 'Far to go'?" said Pelham, and the murmurs around the room suggested that it was all Greek to the rest of them.

"If any one of us fitted the description, it would have to be Isabella," added Holdfast.

"A reasonable assumption," I acknowledged. "I made it myself at one stage, and of course I took sensible precautions to safeguard Miss Dundas. However, the murderer had someone else in mind—Claude Bullivant. And the phrase 'far to go' is a reference not to his way of life, but to the way he met his death."

After some hesitation, Alix said, "By falling down the well?"

"Now you see it. The man had far to go, indeed. That well is extremely deep. I doubt whether we shall ever recover his body, which is, perhaps, what he intended." I remained alone in a sea of blank faces, so I said helpfully, "Cast your minds back to the story I told you a few minutes ago about the man who entered his own death in the bag book. That, I suggest, is what Bullivant did."

"Killed himself?" said Holdfast, his voice rising in astonishment.

"After putting out the piece of newspaper," said I.

"With all respect, Bertie, I find that uncommonly difficult to

believe," said Holdfast. "He wasn't a melancholic sort at all. Far
from it. I can't see Claude doing away with himself."

"What you can't see, George, is the totality of the mystery. I
don't blame you. It would tax many a trained investigator. Before
Claude Bullivant did away with himself, as you put it, he had done
away with three others. I put it to you that he is the murderer."

"Claude?"

The faces around the room were satisfyingly aghast.

I said, "Just like the man in the story, he went on a solitary hunt
and then added himself to the tally."

"You're telling us he killed Miss Chimes and Jerry and Osgot-
Edge? Why?"

"Why does anyone resort to murder? Either he was mad, or
bad. I cannot be more precise than that. His motive is somewhat
clouded, I grant you, but one is confident of a clear view before
much longer. At this moment I wanted mainly to reassure you that
your lives—indeed, all our lives—are no longer at risk."

"Thank God for that!" cried Moira Holdfast.

"Let's also thank His Royal Highness," said her husband with
his customary tact.

There were murmurs of support, rather muted, I have to say.

Miss Dundas, who had sat through my explanation in conspicuous silence studying the tea leaves in her cup, now joined the
conversation—using a tone I didn't care for at all. "Apart from
the fact that he is dead," she remarked, "is there anything whatsoever about Mr. Bullivant that would suggest he killed people?"

This, I thought, was pretty unsporting considering what she and
I knew about Bullivant's erratic behavior in the night. I wasn't so
ungallant as to let the company know that he'd climbed over the
lady's balcony expecting a tumble, but to my mind it was a strong
indication of guilt. Of all the party, only the murderer could have
known that it was safe to philander.

Rather to my surprise, Marcus Pelham sprang to my defense.
"I'll tell you one thing. Bullivant was sitting next to Queenie
Chimes on the night she died. He was better placed than any of
us to tamper with her food."

"So he was!" said Amelia.

"Don't sound so surprised," her brother rounded on her. "You
drew up the seating plan."

Miss Dundas remained unconvinced. "But why would he have wished to kill Miss Chimes?"

George Holdfast gently chided her, "My dear, you're asking for the motive. Bertie just told us that he doesn't know yet. The main thing is that it's all over. We can sleep safely in our beds tonight."

A comforting statement, you might think, but it almost caused a domestic tiff. Moira Holdfast said, "If you think I'm willing to spend another night in this house after what has happened, George, you're woefully mistaken. Our things are packed and we're leaving within the hour."

Amelia was up from her chair before the words were out. "What are you implying, Lady Holdfast? I've heard more than enough of your slurs on my hospitality. Nobody was murdered in bed. Nobody. You make it sound as if my house is verminous."

"Your manners are," retorted Moira Holdfast. "Not to mention your morals."

"Moira!" George rebuked her.

Amelia caught her breath at the enormity of the insult. She would certainly have struck Lady Holdfast had I not intervened. Just as she raised her wrist I grabbed it. I appealed to them both, "Ladies, please! Decorum, decorum!" To salvage a little dignity for them I added, "We have all been subjected to intolerable strains, but the danger is over now. Let us be thankful that we are alive." I was about to add, ". . . to tell the story," but stopped myself in time. I didn't want anyone telling the story. I'm only telling it now in the knowledge that it will be under lock and key until long after all of us are dead.

Lady Holdfast redeemed herself slightly by saying that she regretted her last remark, but she still intended to leave as soon as possible. Amelia was led to a chair where she remained sullen and ashen faced.

Then Alix enquired of me brightly in her singsong accent, "Is the house party over, then? You found your murderer, Bertie. That is all we have to decide, is it not?" She can be embarrassingly direct with her remarks.

I strolled back to the fireplace, thinking actively. "Well, the case has been brought to a conclusion, it is true. It's out of the question, of course, to resume the shooting tomorrow . . ." I hesitated.

Miss Dundas—another lady whose questions struck into you

like bolts from a crossbow—said, "May I ask what you propose to do about Mr. Osgot-Edge?"

"Osgot-Edge?"

"Unless I am misinformed, his body is still in an outhouse somewhere. What is to become of it if we all go home?"

"Fair comment," I said, buying time to think.

"Sir, we ought to inform the police," said a voice at my ear that had not spoken for some time.

"Sweeney, how many times do I have to remind you that you *are* the police?" I smiled at Miss Dundas. "You're absolutely right, my dear. Of course the poor man must have a decent burial. I shall speak to the Chaplain. We'll have a private funeral before the weekend."

"Shouldn't there be an inquest?" asked Alix.

I gave her a look that she recognizes—not one that I am often forced to resort to—and she was silent. Turning to Amelia, I said, "You knew Wilfred better than any of us. Did he have any family?"

"There's a brother in the Indian Civil Service."

"Based abroad, then?"

"In Bombay, I was informed."

"That's all right. You can write him a letter. He wouldn't get back in time for a funeral in any case. Be so good as to send word to the Chaplain that I would like to speak to him urgently, would you?" To Alix, I said, "That, I think, is the answer to your question, my dear. Some of us may wish to stay on for the funeral. I see no reason why Lady Moira should remain, if it would upset her, or any of the ladies, come to that."

So it was agreed that the Holdfast carriage should be summoned. George very decently insisted on staying. His insufferable wife, he said (he didn't really say it; I did), was capable of traveling to their London residence in the company of her maids. As for himself, there might be some way in which he could be useful to me and Amelia. I thanked him for his support.

Then Alix announced that she, too, proposed to leave. I suppose I ought to have expected it; there wasn't much prospect of parlor games in the next day or two. I tried to persuade her to delay her departure until the morning, but she was insistent that she would rather spend the night in her own bed at Marlborough House however late she got there, so I ordered the carriage. In the privacy of her suite I told her I hoped she understood why it was necessary for me to remain.

Making a fine distinction she said, "I understand why you feel it is necessary to stay. I didn't expect you to return with me."

I squeezed her hand to show my appreciation. "What will you say when they ask why you came home?"

She lifted her shoulders. "If anyone really wants to know, I shall say the party didn't turn out as I expected."

"That's true."

"I think we should all respect the truth, Bertie."

"I couldn't agree more, my dear."

"Will you keep yourself to yourself when I am gone?"

I frowned and tried to look puzzled.

She said, "Leave them alone, Bertie. One is too clever and the other is anybody's. Get some sleep, you old ram. You are looking tired."

"Tired, but not unsatisfied," said I, letting the remark make its impact before I added, "You haven't congratulated me yet."

She stiffened—and when Alexandra stiffens she could stand in a sentry box. "Congratulate you—what for?"

"My detective work, of course. Another case brought to a brilliant conclusion."

She sighed. "Oh, Bertie, I despair of you. You don't really believe Claude Bullivant was a murderer? He was killed like the others. Isabella Dundas was right. There's no motive. All the evidence you have is circumstantial."

This from my own wife set me back on my heels. "Of course there's a motive," I told her scornfully. "I shall find it. See if I don't." I was so astounded by what she had said that I felt like quitting the room immediately. I believe I would have done so if I hadn't thought of a devastating riposte. "If there's any truth in what you say," I told her, "the murderer is still at large. How can you even think of going back to London knowing that your husband is in risk of his life?"

She tilted her head defiantly and said, "You're welcome to come with me,"

"My dear Alix, it's utterly out of the question. I shall be here until Osgot-Edge has had a Christian burial and all the other matters are tidied up."

"Tidied up—or hushed up?" she said insensitively. "It's the same old story wherever we go, isn't it, Bertie? Avoid a scandal at all costs."

"This time I'm blameless. I can't be faulted."

"That's a matter of opinion. I warned you not to play at being a detective. You brought this botheration on yourself, beloved, and now you want to sweep it under the carpet. Stay here if you must. I don't think you'll be murdered. All the murders up to now have fitted that rhyme, and if there are to be any more, I don't suppose the murderer will deviate from it. What's tomorrow?"

"Friday."

"Friday's corpse is loving and giving. The loving might apply to you, but not the giving. You're not ungenerous, but I wouldn't say you're noted for it. That must be someone else. Then there's Saturday. Saturday's corpse works hard for a living. Even less likely. And the corpse that is killed on the Sabbath Day is bonny and blithe and good and gay. Bonny and blithe I grant you. Gay, yes. Much more gay than good." She made a wafer-thin space between her thumb and forefinger. "The good is a small measure."

"Well," I said cuttingly, "if I want home truths, I always know where to get them."

"Yes," said Alix. "But I don't want you to think I'm indifferent to the perils of this place, Bertie. Just to be sure, I've had a quiet word with Sweeney. After I've left he's going to move into my suite and keep a special watch on you."

CHAPTER 15

I was pocketing my handkerchief after waving goodbye to Alix when a pony and trap trundled up the drive with the Reverend Humphrey Paget aboard, so I remained at the foot of the staircase to thank him for answering my summons so swiftly. Having eased his weight ponderously from the carriage to the gravel, the Chaplain performed an odd maneuver. He dipped his head, as if uncertain whether protocol required him to bow to me, and then proceeded to rub each shoe in turn against the back of his opposite trouser leg. No doubt about it—the fellow was buffing up his toecaps to discourage me from another demonstration of the science of deduction.

We mounted the stairs together and entered the hall, where Amelia received him in what was by her standards a lackluster manner, a fleeting smile and a limp hand.

As soon as we were alone in the drawing room the Chaplain commented, "Poor Lady Drummond! The burden of these tragedies is more than she should be asked to bear. It's too cruel!"

"Did you hear about Bullivant?" I ventured.

"The dreadful news was in the note she sent. Such a cheerful fellow, I always thought, may the Lord rest his soul. Is he still . . . ?" He pointed downwards.

I nodded. "The men will try again tomorrow, no doubt. In many ways it might be a mercy if he is never brought up. Probably you didn't hear that we suspect him of having killed the other three."

His eyebrows reared up like flying buttresses. "My word, no! That is unbelievable."

"On the contrary, Padre. It is obvious."

Now his fat features absorbed the shock and became more guarded and the eyes narrowed. "Did you deduce it, sir?"

I was beginning to find the Chaplain tiresome. I said as if to a child, "It's the only possible explanation. But to return to the topic of Amelia and her distress, I should like for her sake to keep the events of this unhappy week from being bandied abroad."

"How very considerate."

"I shall do everything within my power, Padre, and I look to you for support."

"You shall have it, sir." And in case I doubted his credentials he declared sanctimoniously, "As a pastor it behooves me to give comfort and succor to all who require it in this transitory life."

"Capital. So I dare say you wouldn't mind burying one whose life turned out to be more transitory than any of us expected?"

"Oh?"

"I should be obliged if you would lay the poet to rest as soon as possible."

"Mr. Osgot-Edge?"

I nodded, tempted to say that I didn't know of any other dead poets wanting a quick funeral. "Would you care for a cigar?"

He took one and his hand shook. "Has Mr. Elston the coroner been informed, sir?"

"About Wilfred? No, we haven't troubled the coroner. He's busy enough, I am sure, with Queenie Chimes and Jerry Gribble."

He clasped his free hand to his mouth and drew the fingers downwards as if trying to locate his chin in the fleshy surrounds. "Forgive me, wouldn't it be somewhat presumptuous to consign a stabbed man to his grave without an inquest, sir? Not that I wish to be obstructive."

"I'm glad to hear it, Padre." I struck a match. As he drew close to light up the cigar I added, "On occasions one is justified in bending the rules. You and I know that Osgot-Edge was murdered in this house and we know who did it. But the whole of the kingdom doesn't have to be told. Fearfully distressing for Lady Drummond, not to mention the rest of us."

"Does he have a family?"

"Osgot-Edge? A brother in India. I'm willing to serve as chief mourner myself. A private ceremony in the village church tomorrow. What say you?"

There was a pause. Then: "Might I help myself to some brandy, sir?"

"I'll join you. Didn't I hear from somebody that you organized a private funeral last year for a young gamekeeper who was shot?"

"Accidentally shot, sir. On that occasion there was no question of deliberate murder. The boy happened to stray ahead of the beaters. One of the guns heard something in the thicket and took a shot at what he supposed was a wounded bird."

"Who fired the shot?"

"I didn't witness the incident, sir." He had his back to me, pouring from the decanter. Interesting, isn't it, how much you can tell about a man's state of mind by looking at his back?

"But you know who fired it?"

"The members of the shooting party resolved to treat the incident as a closed book after the boy was buried." He handed me a glass. "The poor lad was an orphan so we laid him to rest in the village churchyard the next day."

"I must insist that you answer my question, Padre. Who was it who shot the boy?"

He sighed. "Sir, in all humility I beg of you to respect the confidentiality of this information. It was Mr. Bullivant."

"Bullivant?" I got up and walked to the window. "I should have guessed. Things are beginning to fall into place. Who else was of the party—Jerry Gribble?"

"Jerry, yes."

"Freddie Drummond, of course?"

"Er—yes."

"Osgot-Edge?"

"Yes." You'd have thought every "yes" was a slate from the roof of his church.

"Any other guns?"

"No, sir," he said with relief.

But I hadn't finished. "And the ladies, apart from Amelia? Miss Chimes, perhaps?"

"No, sir. There were no other ladies present."

"How dreary. I do think a complement of ladies makes for a more agreeable atmosphere, don't you?"

He didn't answer. Perhaps it wasn't a fair question, though I've known parsons who would have answered strongly in the affirmative.

Returning to matters more pressing, I said, "Well, Padre, how soon can we have the funeral?"

DINNER WAS DESTINED TO BE a subdued occasion that evening, so I had no qualms about telling them between courses that we would bury Osgot-Edge on Saturday at noon in the village churchyard. The ladies—that is to say, Amelia and Miss Dundas—immediately fell to debating what they would wear. Marcus Pelham quizzed me on the formalities—the need to obtain a death certificate from a doctor and the difficulties attendant on employing an undertaker. Fortunately I was able to pass on the reassurance that the Reverend Humphrey Paget (who had murmured something about a choir practice and taken to his heels after the interview with me) was hand in glove with Dr. Perkins and Mr. Hibbert, the gentlemen who fulfilled those offices in the district. Osgot-Edge's death would go down as heart failure and he would be buried in a nightshirt buttoned to the chin. The Chaplain, the doctor and the undertaker were not unused to cooperating to cause the least embarrassment to the families of the departed. In country districts such as this, death had an inconvenient habit of occurring during bouts of inebriation or infidelity that would have caused no end of humiliation to the bereaved had our resourceful trio not combined to circumvent it.

George Holdfast then remarked, "And Bullivant? Will he be buried at the same time?"

I said, "Between ourselves, George, I think it unlikely that we will succeed in raising him. As I mentioned to the Chaplain, the sensible procedure may be to say the burial service at the top of the well."

"And block it up after?"

"Exactly."

Amelia broke off her description of a crepe bonnet to say, "Nobody has used it for years."

Holdfast said, "What's your source of water, then? Are you on the mains, my dear?"

"I've never enquired."

"Might be prudent to find out."

To finish the evening on a less depressing note, I suggested a few rubbers of bridge. How often have I been grateful for my pack of playing cards when more boisterous entertainment is unsuitable to the occasion. One has to say it: the Royal Family is so numerous that Court mourning is practically the norm. And when one is obliged to show respect each time some European Grand Duke gives up the ghost, it's no wonder that I can deal the cards as smoothly as a Mississippi sharp.

Seeing that we were five in number, Pelham said with more tact than I thought he possessed that he would go and look for Sweeney for a game of billiards, leaving Holdfast and yours truly to get up a four with the two ladies. I partnered Isabella Dundas, who seemed to understand my calls like the sounds of the jungle, and we lost only one rubber all evening. There was no acrimony from the other side, either. In fact, Amelia's good humor was quite restored, for Holdfast repeatedly praised her play and claimed that all the mistakes were his own. I'm sure it was a tonic for us all to pass two hours without once referring to the dreadful events of recent days.

We had a final drink and some warm sausage rolls soon after midnight and sent for the candles. Cheery good nights were exchanged, though I have to say that we sounded awfully like provincial actors speaking lines.

Upstairs, it was comforting to see a light under the door to the rooms Alix had so recently occupied. I dismissed the footman and went in to have a few words with Sweeney, whom I discovered to be mother-naked, a curious, hairy specimen of manhood among the pink bed hangings and cornflower-blue walls. He grabbed his nightshirt and apologized.

"Not at all," I told him. "I never knock on bedroom doors, so it isn't the first time, although I will say I've made prettier discoveries. I hope you gave young Pelham a pasting."

"The billiards, sir? Not at all. I should have played him for matchsticks. He's a regular demon with the cue. Did you learn anything over the card table?"

"Quite the reverse. Miss Dundas and I gave a lesson in bridge to Sir George Holdfast and Lady Drummond, if that's what you mean."

"I'm glad to hear it, sir. Actually I was enquiring about the case."

"The investigation? That's over, Sweeney. Didn't you hear? Bullivant killed the others and then did away with himself. What is more, I have now deduced the motive. Would you be interested to hear it?"

"I'm all ears, sir."

"I wouldn't have said so when I opened the door just now." I got a sheepish grin for the quip. It was slow in coming, but no matter. I used the time to settle into an armchair and light a cigar. "Be seated, man. You don't have to stand on ceremony now. You can get into bed for all I care. Now, the key to this case is a very unfortunate incident that happened a year ago. It was mentioned to me first by Osgot-Edge after Jerry was shot. Pelham gave me the gist of the story and later the house steward referred to it obliquely, but I had to prize the crucial facts from the Chaplain this evening. A boy was accidentally shot and killed at last year's shooting party. By Claude Bullivant. Did you know that?"

"I did not, sir."

"The lad was without parents, so the Chaplain was persuaded to conduct a funeral with all speed and in the utmost privacy, and the members of the shooting party pledged themselves to regard the incident as a close secret. And of course the servants were instructed on pain of dismissal not to mention it to anyone. Bullivant must have spent some sleepless nights, but as time passed and nothing more was said, it seemed that the accident really had been successfully swept under the carpet. So successfully, in fact, that Lady Drummond had no qualms about holding another shooting party at Desborough this autumn and inviting me as her principal guest and Bullivant as one of the guns. So we all arrived expecting a fine week of sport, and on the first evening one of the party was poisoned—Miss Queenie Chimes, the Duke of Bournemouth's doxy. And who was seated on her left at dinner? Claude Bullivant."

Sweeney's face was a study,

"Why was the lady murdered?" I mused. "Have you any suggestion, Inspector?"

"None, sir."

I shamed him with a shake of the head. "You must tell me what you think of mine, then. There was rather more to Miss Queenie Chimes than met the eye. She was a scheming young woman, an adventuress, as Her Majesty the Queen would put it, and I'll tell you how I know. I have it from Marcus Pelham that before Miss Chimes met Jerry she contrived a meeting with Marcus and invited him to the Lyceum. Did I tell you she was an actress in Irving's company? Well, he was presented with tickets on several other occasions and she met him for supper after the performance each time. However, I have Pelham's word that it wasn't a romantic fling, and I believe him. Queenie was pumping him for information, Sweeney. He put it down to natural curiosity. I'm convinced he was mistaken. Somehow or other that young woman had learned about the shooting accident. Someone had talked. So this minor actress, trying to exist on the paltry money Irving pays his underlings—and Irving is notoriously close—this hard up, scheming little supernumerary saw a way of putting the information to profitable use."

"Blackmail, sir?"

"Pray allow me to continue. She befriended Marcus, thinking that he would be her *entrée* to this year's shooting party, but inconveniently for her plans, Marcus isn't a lady's man, so she had to look elsewhere. She settled on Jerry, who had chalked up two marriages and two divorces and still hadn't learned to resist the flutter of eyelashes. In no time she was at his side wherever he appeared. And when the invitations to the shooting party were sent out, Queenie was on the list."

I paused. "What I am about to say now is conjecture, Sweeney, but I think you will agree that it provides a credible explanation of the ghastly events that happened later. I believe this artful young woman must also have made some sort of approach to Claude Bullivant and thoroughly alarmed him. Months ago, before she met Jerry, I think she tried her damnedest to win her way into Bullivant's affections, and when that didn't work because he guessed what she was up to, she threatened to expose him as the man who shot an innocent youth and failed to report it to the proper authorities."

Mystification had been creeping over Sweeney's features. "What I don't understand, if I may interrupt, sir, is why Miss

Chimes went to all these lengths just to get an invitation to a shooting party."

Policemen can be deplorably dense on occasions. "It wasn't just a shooting party. She heard that I—the Prince of Wales—was being invited."

"Oh."

His mouth still stood open like a crocodiles, but I kept my temper and explained, "She saw it as a way of insinuating herself into my company. She'd calculated that a Royal patron could work wonders for her prospects as an actress. Without mentioning anyone in particular, she wouldn't have been the first to benefit from my interest in the stage, I'm bound to admit. Does that explain it to your satisfaction?"

"Thank you, sir."

"Let us examine the consequence. When Bullivant learned to his horror that Miss Chimes was being invited to Desborough, he was in ferment. He was convinced that she would blurt out the story of what happened last year, to the extreme embarrassment of himself and all the others who had helped to conceal the incident from public knowledge. He could foresee the effect upon me, Sweeney. I was certain to be outraged at finding myself embroiled in a scandal through no fault of my own. I would be compelled to leave at once. And Bullivant would become a social pariah."

"What did you say, sir?"

I sighed. "A pariah, Inspector. An outcast. Society is not merely founded on family, school and so forth. It requires consent. I could rattle off a dozen names of people of impeccable pedigree who have forfeited that consent by misconduct of various kinds that has become public knowledge. They are pariahs. When invitation lists are drawn up, their names are not included. If they ask to join our clubs we blackball them. If they appear in public, at the races or the theater, we cut them. That is the prospect Bullivant faced—through one interfering actress. Understandably, he was beside himself with anger and humiliation. So he decided to silence the woman. He obtained some poison and brought it with him to Desborough. He slipped it into her food or her drink at the first opportunity, at dinner on Monday evening, when he happened to be sitting next to her. She collapsed, as you know,

and died on the way to the doctor's, in Jerry Gribble's arms. And
the next morning, Jerry himself was shot through the head. Can
you account for it now?"

"Mr. Bullivant killed them both?" said Sweeney, in manifest
disbelief

"Yes, and I'll tell you why. I think Jerry didn't tell me the truth
when he got back that night. He said that Miss Chimes died without
recovering consciousness. I believe she did speak. Before she died,
she managed to tell him that Bullivant must have poisoned her,
and why. What a terrible accusation! No wonder Jerry was in such
a distracted state. And no wonder he concealed the truth from me.
He decided to confront Bullivant with it at the first opportunity,
which was in the morning, after breakfast. They must have walked
or driven away from the house to discuss it. And when Bullivant
realized that Jerry knew he had committed murder, he took a gun
from his pocket and shot him. Two deaths."

"Two deaths," Sweeney echoed. "And two to go."

"Let us consider the next, then. Osgot-Edge must have been
killed for the same reason. He was one of the party last year.
He was part of the conspiracy. Osgot-Edge was a shrewd fellow,
Sweeney. After two mysterious deaths, he must have been deeply
suspicious. Unfortunately, he made the same mistake as Jerry,
attempting to take the matter up with Bullivant. It sealed his fate.
Bullivant plunged a knife into him the same evening. And with
Osgot-Edge's death, each of the guns from last year had perished,
except Bullivant himself."

Sweeney gave a long, low whistle. "That is a fact, sir. There's
no denying it."

I said, "You can go through the survivors: Pelham wasn't invited
last year because Freddie couldn't stand the sight of him; George
Holdfast went down with shingles; and I was at Sandringham."

"Speaking of the late Lord Drummond, sir, do you think his
death could have been murder?"

"No, no. He was gored by a bull last winter. Pure accident. Any
other questions?"

"Well, sir, there's Mr. Bullivant's death."

"Yes?"

"How do you account for that, sir?" He was being fearfully
obtuse, and I let him know it with my tone of voice. "Obviously

suicide. He knew that I was on the trail and getting closer by the minute. There was no escape, so he jumped."

There was an interval of silence.

Sweeney said finally, "It's a peach of a theory, sir. Beautiful."

"It's more than a theory, Sweeney. It's the explanation."

"The explanation, yes." He lowered his eyes as if something embarrassed him and fingered the hem of his nightshirt.

I said, "Out with it, Inspector. Have you thought of a snag?"

"Not at all, sir. Not a snag. More of a loose end. It's the little pieces of paper. I'm trying to think why he left them beside the bodies."

"Well, I suppose as some sort of distraction, to deflect us from the truth."

"But they fitted the rhyme, sir—which you cleverly identified. Monday's corpse is fair of face. If the theory—pardon me, the explanation—is right, Mr. Bullivant poisoned Miss Chimes to keep his secret safe. He wasn't expecting to kill the others. That happened later, when they tumbled to what had happened."

"That is correct."

There was another pause. "Well, sir, I may be out of order here, but it seems to me that the person who left those bits of newspaper must have known on Monday that he was going to kill his second victim on Tuesday and his third on Wednesday." He hesitated. "And another on Thursday."

I stared at him, stunned. He was absolutely right.

He added, "And so on."

Friday

CHAPTER 16

"*And so on.*" The force of those words, spoken so softly in Sweeney's Irish lilt, as if on a note of apology, was devastating. My beautiful explanation was in ruins. The murders hadn't been contrived to silence people who found things out; they must have been premeditated, intricately and cold-bloodedly planned. Alix's words came back to taunt me: "*Oh, Bertie, you don't really believe Claude Bullivant was a murderer? He was killed like the others.*"

I suppose if I were asked which of my personal qualities has contributed most to such successes as I have chalked up as a detective I would have to say in all modesty my quicksilver reactions. When I am blown off course—and it happens to the best of investigators—I refuse to be run aground. I instantly reach for the tiller, so to speak, and chart a more promising course.

"Sweeney," I said, "you and I must act at once, or I fear the murderer may strike again."

"You're right, sir."

"Of course I'm right. It's past midnight and this is Friday. Another day, and another victim—unless we prevent it. Friday, Friday—what does that suggest?"

"Would you be thinking of the little verse, sir?"

"I would, Sweeney, I would. 'Friday's child'—Friday's corpse—'is loving and giving.' Which of the party could be so described? That is the burning question."

"No doubt about it, sir."

"You have the answer?"

"No, sir. It's the burning question, that's for sure."

I sighed. Plainly it was too much to expect that my bog trotting assistant would have a constructive idea in his head. He'd picked a hole in my hypothesis, but ask him for a thought of his own and he was stumped. He fingered his left ear lobe as if it might assist his mental process.

"Well now, there aren't many of us left to choose from," I pointed out with the patience of an old nanny. "Lady Drummond and her brother Marcus, Miss Dundas, Sir George Holdfast and myself. I don't include you."

"Thank you, sir."

"Although the murderer might," I added, seeing the look of complacency that was spreading across his features. "Your turn may come tomorrow. Saturday's corpse works hard for a living. That would exclude everyone else but you." I paused to let it take root. "However, let's not anticipate. The obvious candidate for tonight is Sir George. I can't think of anyone in the country more loving and giving. I wouldn't mind a guinea for every charity he supports. You must have seen his name on the horse troughs."

At that moment Sweeney wouldn't have known a horse trough from an elephant. He was thinking about Saturday's corpse.

"We have a duty to warn him," I went on, raising my voice. "Sir George Holdfast, Sweeney. His life is threatened."

He had stopped fidgeting with his ear. He was tugging at his lower lip now.

I said, "Do you hear?"

He said, "Do you suppose it could be referring to one of the servants, sir?"

"What?"

"Works hard for a living."

"Sweeney, I despair of you. I don't believe you heard a word I was saying. Do you possess a dressing gown?"

"No, sir."

"Never mind. Pick up the candle and follow me."

Few places are so drafty as the corridor of a country house by night. The candle was blown out straight away and we had to pause to reignite it. Holdfast's bedroom was around a turn and at the end. I stepped out boldly. Anyone hearing my tread could have been in no doubt that my purpose was urgent. Sweeney padded barefoot behind me, doing his best to keep up and guard the flickering flame.

I halted at Holdfasts door and instructed Sweeney to knock. There was no reply from within, so we entered.

"Nobody here," Sweeney intoned in a voice of doom.

"I can see that," I said tersely, flinging open the wardrobe. The suit George had worn that evening was hanging there among the others. "No obvious sign of foul play," I commented in the reassuring manner of Scotland Yard, though my heart was pounding a knell. I looked into the cupboards, under the bed and out on the balcony. "He could be anywhere in the house or grounds."

"Do you think we're too late, sir?" Sweeney asked.

I said phlegmatically, "I think we are justified in ascertaining which of the guests are where they should be, in their bedrooms."

Sweeney's eyes gleamed in the waxlight. "Sure and if anyone is missing, we'll know why. We'll be arresting the murderer tonight and putting a stop to his crimes, sir." His voice positively throbbed with expectation.

Without another word I strode out to the corridor and stopped at the first door on the right, which I knew to be Pelham's, and thrust it open. Bed springs creaked and Marcus's voice demanded, "What the deuce . . . ?"

Sweeney held the candle high.

"Merely making sure," I announced. "You may go back to sleep." We withdrew and closed the door.

We ignored the room opposite, the one formerly occupied by Osgot-Edge. Sweeney, a veritable bloodhound now, trotted ahead of me and grasped the handle of the next.

"One moment," I cautioned him just in time as I saw which door it was. "I think it would not be wise to make a sudden entrance here." In my mind's eye I saw Sweeney hanging by his heels from the beam while Miss Dundas prepared to eviscerate him with her hunting knife. "Better knock and wait."

Presently the lady's voice sang out clearly from within, "If that is who I think it is, I'm honored by your gallantry, sir, but I'd rather fend for myself. I wouldn't care to repeat what happened last night."

"As you wish, my dear." With a look at Sweeney that defied him to put any construction on it, I gestured to him to move on. Isabella Dundas was in her room and that was all we needed to know. There remained one room to check—Amelia's—and the attentive reader will recall that I had originally plumped for her as my principal suspect before succumbing to the theory that Bullivant was responsible.

Sweeney stationed himself on the step outside our hostess's door and gave me a doglike look.

"Leave this to me," I told him, reaching for the handle, but it turned before my hand made contact.

The door opened six inches and a face stared out, the broad, ruddy-cheeked face of Sir George Holdfast. He looked at me as bold as a cabman and spoke my name.

And I spoke his. For the moment I had nothing to add. Sudden death was so much the vogue in this house that I'd mentally killed him off. It was like seeing a ghost.

He asked, "Is everything all right, sir?"

I said, "That is a question I should address to you. You weren't in your bedroom." And even as I spoke, the mystification cleared. He was barefoot and wearing a nightshirt. What an old goat! No sooner had he waved goodbye to his wife than he was partnering Amelia at cards, trumpeting every hand she played and buying his ticket for a mattress jig.

"Were you looking for me, sir?"

"Out of concern for your personal safety, George," I told him. "I had reason to believe that your life is threatened, and when I walked into an empty bedroom I feared the worst. Obviously I need not have worried. Lady Drummond is within, I take it?"

He lowered his voice. "Yes, sir, but things are not as they appear."

I said, "Save your breath, George. You and I are men of the world and Sweeney wasn't born yesterday."

His face twitched as if a wasp had stung him. "Sir, the reason I'm here is that Amelia invited me to come."

I said acidly, "Bully for you!"

"No, please allow me to make this clear. She isn't entirely convinced that Bullivant committed the murders, and she reasoned that I—with my reputation for supporting good causes—fitted the epithet loving and giving."

"Which you obviously do. I'm sorry we interrupted."

"Sir, you interrupted nothing!" The old hypocrite's motives were as spotless as the bottom of a birdcage, but he would insist on justifying his tumble with our winsome hostess. "What I am trying to say is that Amelia blames herself for these tragedies. She feels that if she hadn't invited us to Desborough to shoot, none of this would have happened. In spite of your reassurances to the contrary, she is fearful of yet another dreadful event tonight, and for her peace of mind I was persuaded to pass the night in here upon a made-up bed on the ottoman, where I shall come to no harm."

I gave him a penetrating look and said in a voice that only he and I could hear, "That remains to be seen."

His eyes widened and I saw the first spark of doubt there. He whispered, "Surely you don't suspect . . ." He pointed over his shoulder.

"George, I wouldn't be in your shoes for all the tea in China." It was an unsuitable thing to say because he wasn't wearing shoes, but it made its point.

"Oh, Jerusalem!"

Just then Amelia called out, "Georgie, darling, I'm getting cold like this. There's a wicked draft."

He clapped a hand to his face. The fruits of passion had suddenly turned sour. In desperation, he asked me, "What can I do?"

"Not much to please a lady, if I'm any judge." Cruel, I admit, but it was rather galling to hear Amelia call him to her bed. More helpfully, I added, "Make an excuse."

To my utter surprise and confusion, he did. He turned and informed Amelia, "It's His Royal Highness, my dear. I believe he has something of a confidential nature to impart to you. He has recommended me to return to my room, so I'll wish you good night." With that, he stepped into the corridor, dipped his head in some kind of salutation and moved off at speed towards his bedroom.

"Shall I make sure he comes to no harm, sir?" volunteered Sweeney, quick to seize on a chance of bodyguarding as a change from looking into bedrooms.

I nodded. Holdfast had to be protected. Sweeney handed me the candle and set off in pursuit.

Events were moving with bewildering speed, like a lantern show that is running out of time. Next, I heard a movement from inside the room and Amelia looked around the door, her black hair hanging free like a gypsy girl's. "Bertie, you're dressed."

I said, "I haven't been to bed."

"Do come in. Corridors are so public." She grabbed my free hand and drew me firmly inside and closed the door. She was wearing a silk kimono like the young ladies in Mr. Whistler's pictures. It was quiveringly clear that she was unconfined by other items of clothing, but as you will have perceived from my reference to fine art I meant to keep my thoughts on a higher plane.

"What a lark!" she gushed. "What on earth did you say to George to get rid of him? Never mind. I've had some fizz, so you'll have to forgive me if I'm too forward. Or would you like me to send for some more?" Her eyes gleamed.

It's no secret that I excite the fair sex to an exceptional degree. I'm used to them becoming quite giddy in my presence. Whether this interesting effect arises from my Royal blood, or the cut of my clothes, or my blue eyes, or the charm of my personality is not for me to say; whatever its origin, I cheerfully accept it as a fact of life.

I suppose I had better give you the reverse of the coin: I'm readily aroused by a pretty woman, sometimes too readily for my own good. This time, I meant to keep myself in check, for this pretty woman might also be a murderess. "Thank you," I said in answer to her offer of champagne, "but I'd rather have a cup of cocoa, if you would be so kind. And more of those sausage rolls." While she rang for a maidservant, I placed the candlestick on the mantelpiece, picked up a poker and attended vigorously to the fire, which had burned low.

She said, "I'm going to blow out the candle. I love the firelight, don't you?" She came so close as I crouched on the hearthrug that she nudged my shoulder with what I shall politely call her hips. She said, "What a splendid flame! I shall warm my knees." She parted her kimono to reveal as pretty a set of pins as you would ever see. "Bertie, this is such a surprise! I didn't think it possible that you would visit me like this."

"Why not?"

"After our talk in the garden today—or is it yesterday now?—I thought you had decided I was to blame for all the horrid things that have happened."

I said in all sincerity, "Yes, I spoke too harshly. I came after you to apologize. I came up here to explain, but your brother said you wouldn't wish to be disturbed." On an inspiration I added, "This is the first opportunity I have had to make amends."

"How gallant." She put a hand on my shoulder and slid it over my collar, letting a fingertip stroke the curls at the back of my neck, a pleasant sensation were it not that my knees wouldn't support me any longer in the crouching attitude.

I stood up and she took it as a cue to move towards me, almost nose to nose, saying, "Do you feel safe with me now—or would you care to search me?"

Such temptation! You'll be encouraged to learn that I resisted. Well, to be strictly accurate, her maid knocked and she went to the door to give the order. I took the opportunity to seat myself in an armchair and take out my cigar case. "You don't mind if I smoke?" I asked her when the door was closed again.

She gave her permission, of course, and made some remark about the cold, so I told her to find a shawl, or something, to which she said coquettishly that she knew better ways of getting warm and ran across the room to the fire and pulled the kimono fully open, stretching it out like a flag. I had the draped view from the rear, I must hasten to emphasize, but I was still subjected to the shape of her body behind the silk silhouetted by the flames, and very provoking it was, I can tell you.

To subdue nature, I made a performance of lighting the cigar. I was reluctant to speak in case she turned about and gave me the front view. But she wrapped herself up again and said, "Bertie, in case you are wondering why, the reason I invited George to my room was because I'd abandoned hope."

I couldn't resist a chuckle at that.

She said solemnly, "I had better rephrase that. I didn't dare hope or aspire to a visit from you. Oh dear, I confess that I have been thinking of it constantly, ever since Monday night when I came to your room with the news that Miss Chimes was dead and you appeared for a moment to misinterpret my reason for being there. But it seemed so unthinkable, so open to censure until . . ."

"Until this evening when Alix left," said I, matter-of-factly, to help her out.

"Well, yes—and you appeared anyway to suspect me of murder."

"I suspect everyone," I told her genially.

"But mainly me?"

Ducking that, I said, "I can't think why a lady would invite a number of old friends to her house and kill them one by one."

"She wouldn't and she didn't," said Amelia. She hesitated, and then added in a small, tight voice, "But she's guilty, and ready to confess."

Every muscle in my body tensed. "What?"

"Yes. A confession, Bertie. Do you want to hear it?" I glanced rapidly about the room, suspecting a trick, looking for the hidden weapon that she meant to kill me with the moment she had told me the truth.

She approached and leaned right over me, with her hands on the arms of the chair, her face within inches of mine, the faint fumes of champagne on her breath. "I plead guilty to desires of the flesh, Bertie."

"Oh."

"There! I've said it." And having said it, she flopped into my lap like a Channel swimmer who has reached the shore.

I was quite unable to prevent it without risk to each of us from my cigar. She pressed her face against mine as I shifted my legs to accommodate the rest of her anatomy.

I would like it to be known that even under this extreme provocation I endeavored to keep my detective duty paramount. I said, "Is that all?"

She didn't answer. She was unbuttoning my waistcoat.

I persisted, "Is there nothing else that you meant to confess?"

She answered, "There is nothing else. Please don't cause me to weep again. This has been such a wretched, ill-fated week, but tonight I want to forget all the horrors we have had to endure. You have been a tower of strength, Bertie, so resolute and so manly."

"Decent of you to say so," I remarked, caught slightly off guard.

Her hand moved inside my shirt. "Please take me to bed," she murmured.

I was fast succumbing. There are limits to every man's resistance and my limits are shorter than most. In ordinary circumstances I wouldn't have held out for half so long. It's not in my nature to disappoint a lady. However, I had one more card up my sleeve. "What about the cocoa and sausage rolls?"

She giggled. "I told the maid to leave them outside the door." That giggle was irresistible.

And now in the interests of decorum we move forward in time by an interval I am unable to document. I lost track of time, and when I might have consulted my watch it was still in my waistcoat pocket somewhere on the floor across the room.

Amelia said, "Do you mind cold cocoa, or shall I send for some more?"

I said, "I'll take it cold. I'm devilish thirsty."

"No wonder!" She went to the door and picked up the tray and carried it to the commode on her side of the bed. "Sugar?"

I propped myself up on one elbow, mainly, I confess, to look at her in the pink, and a sublime spectacle she was. "Sugar—yes."

I was feeling agreeably fatigued, as one does, and relaxed, so it says much for my vigilance that I spotted what she was doing. *She had a bottle in her hand and she was pouring a pale liquid into one of the cups.* You may imagine what I immediately suspected.

My first impulse was to shout, "Poison!" and snatch it from her, but some instinct made me decide on a less dramatic course of action. I sat back submissively against the pillows and allowed her to hand me whichever cup she selected. I then asked her if she would fetch my cigar case from my jacket.

She said with a smile, "I do believe you enjoy seeing me prance about the room in a state of nature."

"Emphatically."

The moment her back was turned, I leaned across and switched her cup of cocoa for mine. Cruel, do you think? If it *was* poison, it had been meant for me. If it wasn't, no harm would come to her.

She climbed into bed. We each had a sausage roll and drank our cocoa. I found mine slightly bitter to the taste and added some sugar.

Presently I found myself slipping down in the bed. My eyes were heavy-lidded.

Amelia said, "Aren't you going to smoke a cigar after all?"

"No, I feel drowsy now, uncommonly drowsy."

"That's good," she said. "We should both get a good sleep. I took a large dose of chloral with mine. It's a habit, I'm afraid. I had trouble sleeping after Freddie died, but this stuff really knocks me out. Sweet dreams, Bertie."

CHAPTER 17

Normally I am one of the charmed few who can wake refreshed at the crack of dawn unable to fathom why the rest of humanity prefers to linger in bed. So it was puzzling, not to say infuriating, for me that Friday morning to find that lifting a leg off the mattress was a feat to be equated with tossing a caber. I made a number of attempts and, shameful to relate, dozed in the intervals.

By degrees I dimly registered that the cause of my lethargy must have been the chloral hydrate I had swallowed the night before. The taking of sleeping drafts is, I gather, a widespread practice among the fair sex, but I have never had any truck with it. So when at the umpteenth attempt I succeeded in getting a foot to the floor, my mood was thunderous. Nor was it helped by the discovery that Amelia's side of the bed was empty; she, it appeared, having had no difficulty in getting up.

Mother naked, I stumbled across the room and looked into her dressing room, which felt like the North Pole, and revived childhood memories of winter mornings in Buckingham Palace. The balcony windows were wide open.

I braved the cold and put my head outside in the hope that fresh air might sharpen my wits. The balcony afforded a frost-blanched view of a small walled garden with bits of stone statuary and gravel walks lined with box hedges. A pond at the center had gray ice floating on the surface.

One deep breath was enough. My legs wobbled. The scene

changed to a snowstorm, as if someone had given a shake to one of those ornamental glass orbs containing water and a miniature village. The snow, of course, was in my head. I staggered forward and grabbed the iron railing, telling myself that a cigar would have been a better remedy than fresh air.

Presently my vision clarified. I could see the gravel below the balcony. And—reader, forgive me for the shock this will cause you, for it was a paralyzing shock to me—I saw another corpse.

She lay in a posture of terrible finality, with her head turned at an angle that could only mean that her neck was broken. One arm was trapped beneath her body and the other was fully extended, the palm resting upwards. She was still in her nightdress, leaving one of her legs exposed almost to the knee.

My first impulse was to rush downstairs and cover her decently. Pausing only to pull on a few clothes of my own, I dragged a blanket from the bed and hared down the nearest staircase, through the first door I reached, which happened to be a baize one, and out through the servants' hall past a group of goggle-eyed maids. My mental faculties were responding to the emergency, thank heaven, and my legs were functioning too.

Outside, I scarcely had time to spread the blanket over Amelia's body before Colwell the house steward joined me, summoned, I suppose, by the maids. With admirable *sangfroid,* he asked whether he could assist me in some capacity.

"You can tell me where everyone is," said I. "Mr. Marcus Pelham, for one."

"Mr. Pelham is in the breakfast room waiting for morning prayers, sir, together with Sir George Holdfast. They are being observed by Inspector Sweeney from the serving hatch."

"Ah." The last I had seen of Sweeney was when he had volunteered to make sure Holdfast came to no harm. He was still on duty, no doubt blithely believing that he had thwarted the murderer.

"Miss Dundas has ordered breakfast in her room this morning," Colwell continued.

"But someone has seen her?"

"One of the maids."

"Good." I paused to consider which course of action was appropriate to this latest outrage, which had shocked me more profoundly than any of the others, as you will appreciate, for reasons of a character too intimate to dwell upon. That it was murder I had no doubt. Murder had been done within a few feet of the place where I had lain drugged and asleep.

Colwell cleared his throat. "Might I enquire what is under the blanket, sir?"

I stooped and uncovered the face.

"I feared so," he said in a flat voice.

I replaced the blanket. "That's a curious remark. Surely you didn't know that Lady Drummond was killed?"

He raised his eyes to the balcony above us. "I didn't know it, sir, but in all the circumstances, it was a reasonable deduction."

I refrained from asking him how he deduced it. I said, "I think it would not be prudent to speculate any further. Leave the detective work to me, Colwell."

"I shall, sir."

"And be so good as to ask Inspector Sweeney to join me here at once."

LATER THAT MORNING AT MY request our tragically dwindling party assembled in the drawing room—a mere half dozen of us, and that included the Chaplain, who had remained after breakfast to discuss the arrangements for Saturday's funeral. They may have been few in number, yet they spread themselves around the whole of the room, not, I have to say, to appear more numerous, but to keep at a safe distance from each other.

"You all know by now that our dear hostess is dead," I said.

"Rest her soul," added Sweeney, earning an "Amen" from the Chaplain.

"I discovered Lady Drummond in her private garden under the balcony of her dressing room. Having examined the scene, I concluded that the fatal act had been committed within the hour. The signs were very instructive. For one thing, her clothes were almost unmarked by the frost."

"And for another?" said Pelham with his usual impertinence.

"May I remind you, Mr. Pelham, that we are in mixed company? Graphic descriptions of violent death are manifestly unsuitable for the drawing room. Take my word for it that your sister was killed between six and seven o'clock this morning."

"Killed?" spoke up Miss Dundas. "Are you quite certain it wasn't an accident, sir?"

"Utterly."

"She could have fallen from the balcony, could she not?"

"That was a possibility until we examined the, em, body," said I.

"So far as I am concerned, you may speak frankly, sir, since I am the only lady present."

I gave a shrug. "As you wish. Inspector, would you explain?"

Sweeney said, "She hit the ground head first and her neck was broken. We found pieces of gravel embedded in the scalp on the left side of the skull. But we also found injuries on the other side of the head that could not have been caused by the fall. It seems that she was first attacked in the dressing room."

I took up the account. "I went to the dressing room and found the weapon—a poker. It was lying on the floor. Her attacker evidently struck her twice and then opened the balcony windows and pitched her over the railing to make certain she was dead."

With a glance in the direction of Miss Dundas, George Holdfast put in, "Or perhaps to give the impression that she caused her own death."

I shook my head. "This murderer doesn't wish us to be in any doubt, George. We found the usual calling card, the scrap of newspaper with 'Friday' printed on it. It was wrapped around the poker."

They heard this in horrified silence.

Holdfast said in what sounded suspiciously like a complaint, "Bertie, I don't understand the logic of this. Last night you came to warn me that I was the likely victim. Friday is the one who is loving and giving. It fitted me. And now we find that Amelia was killed."

Marcus Pelham had observed an understandable silence since learning of his sister's murder. Now he said, "If it's love you're talking about, no one was more loving than Amelia."

"How true!" the Chaplain said sanctimoniously and got a glare from Pelham.

"Loving and giving," said Pelham. "She gave herself to all and sundry."

The Chaplain gasped.

"Shame on you, sir!" The rebuke came from Holdfast, and I think he spoke for us all.

Pelham glared at him. "That's the giddy limit, coming from you. Where were you last night when His Royal Highness knocked on your bedroom door? Let's have the truth."

Not liking the drift of this at all, I said, "I'll ask the questions, gentlemen."

"But it's obvious," the loathsome fellow insisted on continuing. "Find out who was sleeping with Amelia and we've got our man. Who else could have attacked her in her own dressing room?"

"Pelham," I addressed him coldly. It was definitely time to pull rank. "I am trying to make allowances for the grief you must be suffering, but there are limits. I warn you not to overstep them." To the company in general I said, "We estimate that the murder took place between six and seven this morning. I must insist that each of you tell me where you were at that hour."

Pelham refused to be subdued. "When you say each of us, you mean Holdfast and me. We're the only suspects left. Well, I can tell you that I was in bed till gone seven—and I mean my own bed. The maid had to wake me up to give me my morning tea."

There was a stirring of petticoats across the room. "Pardon me," said Isabella Dundas, "but I will not be dismissed by Mr. Pelham as if I don't exist. I am as capable of wielding a poker as anyone else." This extraordinary claim secured everyone's attention, but the rest of her statement came as an anticlimax. "As it happened, I did not leave my bedroom all night, and I had breakfast served in my room at half past eight."

So all eyes turned to Holdfast, but it was Sweeney who spoke up. "I can vouch for Sir George, sir. I kept watch on his room all night. He didn't leave it until after the murder was discovered."

"Thank you, Inspector," said Holdfast,

Pelham said, "Well, I'm not satisfied. I'm entitled to an explanation. This is my sister who was brutally murdered by one of you. We all know Sir George wasn't in his room at the beginning of the night. I heard the Prince and the Inspector go in there after they woke me up. I heard the doors being opened as they searched the place." He turned to Miss Dundas. "Didn't you overhear it?"

"Actually, yes. I did."

"Where was he, then?" Pelham triumphantly demanded. "Why won't you tell us where you were, Holdfast?"

"Pelham, these insinuations are not only misconceived. They

are deplorable," I reproached him. "Since the matter has been raised, I had better state that Inspector Sweeney and I traced Sir George to Lady Drummond's suite shortly after midnight. I cautioned him as to the danger I believed he was in, whereupon he left immediately."

To which Holdfast added, stressing every word, "And I returned directly to my own bedroom."

To my immense relief—and everyone's, I fancy—this squashed Pelham. He had been ready to convince us that Holdfast was the murderer, and now I had driven a coach and horses through his theory. George wasn't a murderer. He wasn't much of a philanderer, come to that.

For my part, I saw no purpose in regaling the company with an account of the way I spent the night. I wasn't under suspicion of murder. I was conducting the investigation. (And if you, the reader, harbor the slightest suspicion that I might somehow have committed the crimes, I would have you know that such thinking is not only preposterous, but tantamount to treason, even if you *are* expecting an ingenious solution.) Instead, I said, "It seems we shall get no further like this, so I shall be pursuing other lines of inquiry. I trust that nobody has thoughts of leaving, because I must insist that you remain at Desborough until further notice. We know enough about the methods of this murderer to be assured that no one else will be attacked today."

"What of tomorrow?" said Miss Dundas.

"I expect to have the case solved by then. But in any case tomorrow is Saturday, and according to that wretched verse, Saturday's victim works hard for a living, a description which can in no way apply to people of our class, with one obvious exception."

Sweeney crossed himself.

The Chaplain then asked if we still wished to proceed with Osgot-Edge's funeral on Saturday and I told him I saw no reason to alter the arrangement. Pelham not unreasonably announced that he wished to talk to the Chaplain about a funeral for Amelia, and I dismissed the meeting.

Sweeney was at my side in a twinkling. "Sir, I don't think we should wait. It's obvious who did it. Let me run the beggar in. He'll blow, I guarantee."

I said, "The only thing that's obvious to me, John Sweeney, is that you want an arrest before tomorrow. Who do you mean, by the way?"

He screwed up his face at my obtuseness. "Pelham."

"On what grounds?"

"It comes down to three people, sir, and didn't we just eliminate Sir George? He couldn't have killed Lady Drummond because I was watching his room when the murder occurred, and he didn't so much as put his nose outside the door. That leaves Miss Dundas and Pelham. Why would Miss Dundas kill all those people, even if she's capable of it? She didn't know most of them from Adam before she was invited here."

"Very well, tell me Pelham's motive."

"The inheritance, sir. He's her nearest relative. She had no children and I don't suppose she made a will. He stands to inherit Desborough and all the Drummond estates."

"That has a certain cogency to it," I agreed, and then set him back on his heels with the comment, "but you have to explain why he murdered four others before he killed his sister."

I could almost hear the sound of dredging from his head as his brain labored. "Well, sir," he finally said, "he's a misanthrope."

"A *what?*" I was acquainted with the term, but I needed a moment to ponder its relevance to Pelham.

"A misanthrope. A despiser of mankind. I haven't heard a generous word from the man all week. He's as bitter as aloes."

"I'll grant you that."

"His sister married money and cold-shouldered him, that's about the size of it. He wasn't welcomed here until Lord Drummond died and Lady Amelia was stumped for a man to lead the shoot, with you being here and everything. She turned to Marcus for help and he agreed to come, but he was still eaten up with bitterness. And it wasn't just his sister who made him envious—it was the people the Drummonds had invited here in previous years. He hated them all and he wanted them to suffer, so after agreeing to come, he devised a plan. He would kill his sister and inherit the lot, but to disguise his motive he would make it one of a series of murders, one each day. He would knock off the people he despised most, the ones who had been preferred to him. And then he refined it some more by thinking of the verse, and the idea of the pieces of paper."

"To play cat and mouse with us, do you mean?"

"That's it in a nutshell, sir. He wanted to see you suffer."

"It sounds rather Irish to me, Sweeney," I told him. "How did he know that the people he wanted to murder would fit the verse?"

"They didn't, sir—not all of them. The very first one—fair of face—for example. Obviously that had to be a lady, but he didn't want to give himself away by killing his sister first, so he had to think of someone else. He picked Queenie Chimes. He'd met her in London, if you remember, so he knew she was pretty, and that was her death warrant—a pretty face."

"And the others?"

"Well, there were two that happened to fit the verse, the lines about Tuesday and Wednesday. He must have chosen it because they were so appropriate. Full of grace for a duke, and full of woe for a man whose initials happened to spell out the word."

"That's obvious."

"Indeed, sir. But Thursday, being far to go, tested his ingenuity somewhat, so he pushed Mr. Bullivant down the well. He could have done that to any of us, but he picked Mr. Bullivant because, like the Duke of Bournemouth and Mr. Osgot-Edge, that gentleman had been invited to previous shooting parties when he, Marcus, was *persona non grata*, if I have the expression right, sir. All three of those gentlemen fell foul of his envy."

"Continue."

"So we come to the fifth death, that of his sister, the one that would make his fortune. He claims to have been in his bed all night, but we only have his word for it."

I said, "Presumably the maid will confirm that she brought him tea at seven or thereabouts."

"But there's no certainty that he was in his own room at six or half past. I think he murdered her and got back before the maid served the tea. And that isn't all, sir. Have you noticed how little grief he has shown since his sister's horrible death?"

"That was typical of the man," said I. "He lacks breeding. He has none of the finer feelings one expects of a gentleman. However, I don't think we can lay a murder at his door just because he doesn't know how to behave."

"As you wish, sir. But there's another thing I found indicative, and that was the liberty he took with his own poor dead sister's reputation when he said she was loving and giving—and left us in no doubt that he meant it in a most disagreeable sense."

"That *was* unnecessary," I agreed.

Sweeney became fearfully agitated at this. "Begging your pardon, sir, that isn't correct. The reverse is true. Pelham wanted to demonstrate that Lady Amelia's death was just one more in the series, so it *was* necessary, indeed it was vital, that he fitted her character to the verse. Then you and I wouldn't recognize this as the crucial murder, the one that provides the motive and gives him away. Have I made myself clear, sir?"

"My dear fellow," I said, "I'm mightily impressed. I didn't know you were capable of such a penetrating analysis of the case. It's a fine illustration of that saying of Dr. Johnsons, to the effect that when a man knows he is to be hanged in a fortnight, it concentrates his mind wonderfully."

"*Hanged*, sir?"

"Hanged in a fortnight or murdered tomorrow—the upshot is the same. As I said, you made a very persuasive case. However, it's mostly conjecture, isn't it? Inspired, I'm sure, but short of real evidence."

"That's why I want to run him through the mangle, sir. Squeeze out the facts."

"I'd rather you didn't."

His entire face drooped at the angle of his moustache, but I didn't relent. Proper detective work isn't a matter of putting people through mangles. Marcus Pelham might be the only suspect left, but we wanted cast-iron evidence, not a confession squeezed out under duress.

"Look at it this way," I said in a kindly tone. "If you and I are right about Pelham plotting all this to murder Amelia, then he has just accomplished his object, so there shouldn't be any more murders. Anyone such as yourself, who can be said to work hard for a living, need have no fears about Saturday. Isn't that so?"

"True."

"If, on the other hand, he feels that you are dangerously close to unraveling the truth, I wouldn't give twopence for your chances."

His eyes bulged for a moment and then glazed over with gratitude. "I didn't think of it like that, sir."

CHAPTER 18

Now, a small confession from me.

Sweeney's theory had impressed me mightily—more than I cared to show. I would have been proud to have thought of it myself, which was awfully galling, considering that he was supposed to be a duffer fit for nothing more intelligent than bodyguarding duties. He had convinced me utterly that Pelham was our man, and if only I'd worked it out for myself I would have said by all means put the murderous blackguard through the mangle.

Instead, I sounded the cautious note that you heard at the end of the last chapter, because—here's the confession—I wanted to salvage some credit for myself. The grand unmasking of the culprit would have to be delayed. I had my growing reputation as a detective to consider. Now that we could pin the murders on Pelham, I reckoned I could put together some impressive evidence to show that my investigations had led triumphantly to the right conclusion.

Poor old Sweeney: you should have seen his stricken look when I said, "Well, have you finished? Don't you have something else to report?"

"I beg your pardon, sir?"

"The proof—the clincher. Out with it, man."

"I've told you all I know, sir."

"Come, come," I protested amiably. "You've saved it up for last, haven't you? You were keeping watch in the corridor all night. You must have seen Pelham come out of his bedroom and enter

Amelia's room. And you must have seen him returning after the deed was done."

"No, sir."

"You didn't? But you were there."

"I was there, sir, and I wasn't," he said as only an Irishman could. "It's true that I kept watch on Sir George's room, but I wasn't in the corridor. That would have been too conspicuous. I spent the night in the linen cupboard opposite. I had the door ajar to keep an eye on Sir George's door, but I couldn't see along the corridor."

"That's a confounded nuisance. I thought you must have seen Pelham enter Amelia's room."

"I'm sorry."

"Are you telling me that your splendid theory is entirely supposition? We need a witness—at least one witness."

"There were no witnesses, sir," he said flatly.

"Sweeney, you are mistaken. Depend upon it, someone saw the murderer this morning."

He hesitated. "Was it you, sir?"

What neck! But it was no use denying where I had passed the night. I gave him my most frigid stare and said, "I was asleep at the time."

For that, I was subjected to a stare almost as frigid. In Sweeney's opinion, if anyone had some questions to answer, it was me. All this must have added to his festering resentment, but I really preferred not to go into the story of how I had swallowed the chloral.

He said, "All the others were asleep as well, sir, or so they claimed."

"So they claimed."

We seemed to have reached an impasse, so I started thinking aloud, which is worth trying when all else seems to have failed. "Not everyone could have been in bed when the murder was committed. There must have been people up and about between the hours of six and seven: the servants, Sweeney, the servants!"

"True," he said without animation.

"How easy it is to overlook them!" I said, since the brilliance of my reasoning seemed to have passed him by.

He didn't so much as nod his head. His night in the linen cupboard had left him thoroughly out of humor.

I continued, "Why didn't we think of it before? The housemaids who brought the morning tea—let's have them up and hear what they have to say. I'll see them at once."

He lingered. "May I make a suggestion?"

"Well?"

"Leave the maids to me, sir. They'll be too scared of you to say a blessed word."

"My dear Sweeney, I can state without fear of contradiction that I have more experience of coaxing tongue-tied females to speak than any man in the kingdom. The secret is to put them at their ease. Sympathy and understanding do the trick—and my sympathy and understanding are unequaled. Now jump to it, blast you!"

I took his point, to a degree. Housemaids aren't used to being spoken to by anyone above the station of housekeeper. In certain houses they are expected to turn and face the wall if they happen to meet one of the family in the corridors. To be summoned upstairs to answer questions was daunting enough. To appear before me was another thing again. However, it couldn't be ducked. If there was a scrap of decent evidence to be unearthed, I wanted it.

The maid who was ushered in presently was no more than fifteen years of age by my estimate, a dumpy, black-haired child who curtseyed awkwardly and kept her head bowed. Her name, Sweeney announced, was Sarah.

"Step closer, Sarah. I won't eat you. How long have you worked here?"

She took a short step towards my chair, watching the carpet as if it were a cliff edge.

Sweeney said smugly, "She's nervous, sir."

"That is evident. Did you understand my question, Sarah?"

Sarah moved her head slightly and said nothing.

"Let's try something more simple. How old are you?"

"Fifteen."

"Sir," Sweeney prompted her at once, and her mouth clamped shut, not from insolence, but sheer panic.

I turned to Sweeney and asked whether he had succeeded in finding any other servants.

"I did, sir. There's another maid outside the door. Shall I ask her to step in?"

"No. Be so good as to join her, would you?"

There was a stunned pause. "As you wish, sir." He turned and made his way to the door, reddening noticeably around the back of the neck.

"So you are fifteen, my dear?" Without Sweeney's petrifying presence, Sarah the maid would soon respond to my charm.

She gripped the lace edge of her apron and managed to agree that she was, indeed, the age she had said.

"And at what hour did you rise this morning?"

"Half past five, sir."

"That's early. I expect it was quiet. Was anyone else up and about?"

"The kitchen maids, sir. They get up at five, to clean and light the range."

At least a dozen words! "And what are you exactly—a chambermaid?"

"An under housemaid, sir."

"What is your first task each morning?"

"Cleaning grates."

"How many?"

"Twelve, sir."

"And when the grates are cleaned?"

"I make the morning tea."

"What time is that?"

"Quarter past six."

"So early?"

"Tea for the housekeeper, sir."

"Of course. Did you take tea to anyone else this morning?"

"Yes, sir. St. George."

"St. George, you say?" I didn't correct the girl. I rather enjoyed the notion of Holdfast as one of the company of saints. Lady Moira, I privately decided, was his dragon. "What time was that?"

"Seven o'clock."

"And did you take tea to anyone else?"

"Only Mr. Pelham, sir, just after."

"Mr. Pelham. Is that your daily duty, taking tea to Sir George Holdfast and Mr. Pelham?"

"And bread and butter, thinly sliced, sir."

"At the same time each day this week—about seven o'clock?"

"Yes, sir."

"Splendid. This isn't so agonizing, is it? Now, Sarah, I want you to think carefully about this morning. When you entered Mr. Pelham's room with the tray, did you knock first?"

"Oh, yes."

"And he called you to come in, I expect. Did he answer at once?"

"I think so."

"So you went in. Was he sitting up in bed?"

"No, sir. Lying down."

"Then what did you do with the tray?"

"I waited for him to sit up. Then I handed it to him."

"Was anything said?"

"I wished the gentleman good morning. He didn't speak, sir."

"Did you happen to notice anything irregular in the room?"

Creases of mystification appeared around the bridge of her nose.

"Things out of place," I explained. "Anything suggesting he might have got up in the night."

Just when the answers had been coming freely, she turned scarlet and stared at the floor again.

Reading her thoughts, I said, "I don't wish to know if he used his chamber pot. I want to know whether he had left the room, possibly only a short time before you entered. Is it light by seven these mornings?"

"Yes, sir. Sunrise is half past six."

"Did you notice whether the curtains were still drawn?"

"They was, sir."

"Was there, perhaps, the smell of a candle?"

"I can't remember."

"Did you happen to notice his dressing gown?"

"It was hanging on the back of the door, sir."

"Bedroom slippers?"

She shook her head.

It was evident that this avenue of inquiry was leading nowhere, so I tried another. "When you brought the tea to these gentlemen, you passed Lady Drummond's door, is that correct?"

"Yes, sir."

"Did you, by any chance, see anyone go in or out of that door?"

"No, sir."

"Did you meet anyone in the corridor?"

"Only servants, sir."

"No gentlemen or ladies?"

"No, sir."

"Did you hear anything from inside Lady Drummond's room—a shout or a scream or even the sound of people talking?

"It's more than my job is worth, sir."

"What do you mean?"

"Listening at doors."

"Oh, indeed. I'm sure you wouldn't do such a thing. But you might have overheard something as you were passing."

She shook her head. But she made clear her wish to help by adding, "You could ask Singleton."

"Who is he?"

"It isn't a man, sir. She's waiting outside."

"Doesn't she have a Christian name?"

"I don't know, sir. She's the lady's maid."

The social distinctions below stairs are every bit as rigid as our own. "Then would you ask Singleton to step in here? You are dismissed. It goes without saying that none of what we have discussed should be repeated to a living soul. I mean that, Sarah. Do you know what will happen if you gossip?"

"The Lord will find out, sir, and I will surely burn in hell."

There was nothing I could profitably add. The interview had been pretty unproductive, but I suppose you can't expect a fifteen-year-old to supply the entire case for the prosecution.

I looked more hopefully at Singleton as she entered, a figure of more poise, at least twice the age of Sarah, with pleasingly mature proportions, and reddish-gold curls kept tidy by a white ribbon. She had a neatly proportioned face. A little powder over the shiny parts and she could well have passed for a lady.

Sweeney sidled up to me and asked stiltedly whether I wished him to remain.

"Provided that you don't interfere," I told him in confidence. "Simply observe. Leave this entirely to me and you will see how diplomatic one has to be in coaxing them to tell what they know." Then I bestowed a broad, disarming smile on Singleton. "Thank you for waiting. I believe you are the lady's maid."

She answered, "Yes," and immediately covered her face with her apron and burst into convulsive sobs.

"Oh, my hat!" I said. "What on earth is the matter?"

She didn't respond. I doubt if she heard me, the wailing was so terrific.

Now, if there's one thing I cannot cope with, it's a female who pipes her eyes. Having fathered three daughter's I ought to be equal to the challenge by now, but I am still at a loss each time it happens. I sprang up to offer Singleton my handkerchief and she ignored it and howled even more loudly. I walked around her once and put my hand on her elbow and murmured what I thought were consoling words. As those didn't work, I told her sharply to pull herself together, whereupon she turned and fled.

Then I became aware of Sweeney's malignant eye on me. "Don't just stand there, damn you!" I thundered. "Go after her. Calm her down and bring her back in a better state of mind."

Fully fifteen minutes passed before he returned with the wretched woman. The tears had stopped, thank heaven, but her face was fearfully puffed up.

"What do you think?" I asked Sweeney.

"I think she can take it now, sir."

"All I did was mention her job,"

"That was the trouble, sir. She's lost it."

"Really?"

"Well, she's the lady's maid and the Lady is no more."

"Ah." There was undeniable logic in what he said. I made a second start with Singleton. "I didn't ask you here to talk about your personal prospects, but I'm sure that every effort will be made to find you another position, if that is what distresses you."

For a moment I thought we were in for a repeat performance. The eyes glistened again. She said, "I'm dreadfully sorry, Your Royal Highness. I wasn't crying for myself. I was crying for my mistress, God rest her soul. It's horrible . . . so cruel. Lady Drummond treated me so kindly always. Three years, I've been her lady's maid."

"And you can render her a final service by helping me to discover exactly what happened," I said.

"I would if I could. I know nothing, sir."

"I'll be the judge of that. I have some simple questions. What time did you rise this morning?"

"Half past six, sir."

"And what are your duties in the morning?"

"I take tea on a tray to my Lady's room at half past seven, sir, and a jug of hot water for washing twenty minutes after. This week I have done the same for Miss Dundas."

"Do you mean that you go into their bedrooms?"

"No, sir. Not into my Lady's room. I was instructed to knock and leave the tray and the jug on the floor outside the door."

"That was the arrangement this morning?"

She modestly lowered her eyelids. "All the week, sir."

Poor Amelia—her secret hopes laid bare. "So you had no reason to enter the room this morning? Did you hear anything when you knocked?"

"There was no answer, sir."

"Did that strike you as peculiar?"

"No, sir. I supposed that it was not convenient for my Lady to respond at that minute."

Discreetly expressed. "Now tell me, did you happen to see any other person in the corridor?"

"Nobody except servants, sir."

Virtually identical to the answer I had got from Sarah the housemaid.

Singleton added, "The corridors are fairly swarming with servants at that time, delivering the tea and the jugs of water and clean shoes."

"People you know?"

"Not all of them, sir. We've had so many extra below stairs this week that we had to take our meals in sittings. Some of them have left, but there are still plenty who are strangers to me, such as Sir George's retinue and your own."

"I understand. So it would seem that nobody had any reason to enter Lady Drummond's rooms between six and seven this morning."

"No servant, anyway." She frowned thoughtfully and put her hand to her mouth.

"Is there something you wish to add?" I asked.

"I don't know if it's my place to mention it, but the chambermaid found a cigar butt under the bed when she swept my Lady's room this morning."

"No," I said rapidly, "it wouldn't be significant. Could have been there for days, you see."

She reddened. "The rooms are swept and dusted every morning, sir."

"So after you left the tray outside the room," I firmly resumed, "what did you do?"

"I returned to the kitchen and brought up the tray for Miss Dundas."

"Ah. And what was your arrangement with that good lady?"

"Miss Dundas comes to the door when I knock, sir."

"I know." Hastily I explained, "That is to say, I would expect it. She is an explorer, trained to react to the slightest sound. Did she have anything to say to you?"

"She ordered breakfast in her room, sir, for half past eight. I was to pass on the message that she wouldn't be down for breakfast."

Everything these servants had told me appeared to confirm the statements already made by the guests. I tried yet another tack. "As the lady's maid, you must have known Lady Drummond more intimately than any other person in this house."

That almost made her purr. "I dare say that is true, sir."

"You looked after her clothes and attended to her hair. You must have had many conversations."

"Oh, yes."

"I want to ask you about the things she may have said to you in the last few days. Did she admit to any fears?"

"Fears?" Singleton pondered the question. "I don't know about fears. She was extremely agitated about the dreadful things that happened, but I don't think she knew fear. She was the bravest lady I ever had the good fortune to serve, sir. She bore Lord Drummond's dreadful accident last year with wonderful fortitude."

"So I gathered, but I'm talking about this week. Did she pass on any suspicion she may have had about the person responsible for the tragic events?"

"No, sir."

"Did she speak of her brother at all?"

"Mr. Marcus?" She gave me a sudden guarded look. "I would rather not speak about him, if you will forgive me, sir."

"Why is that?"

Her mouth quivered. "If I am to seek a position in another household, I shall require a character, and I shall have to approach Mr. Marcus to see if he will supply me with one. There is no one else who can do it now. I wouldn't like to repeat anything to his discredit."

"*Is* there anything to his discredit?"

She lowered her face.

I said, "If there is, you must tell me. What did you hear from Lady Drummond?"

And much to my disappointment, she spoke as if she meant it, "My mistress was utterly loyal to her brother."

"Utterly—or blindly?"

"That is not for me to say, sir."

"But you have your private suspicions, I gather."

"They are not of any consequence."

"I shall ask you something else, then. You said just now—I'm quoting your own words—that the house is fairly swarming with servants early in the morning. Do you think it was possible for the murderer to have entered and left Lady Drummond's rooms without being seen by one of the servants?"

"It is most unlikely, sir."

"Did anyone in the servants' hall mention seeing anything suspicious this morning?"

"Not that I am aware of."

"Thank you, Singleton. I have no further questions at this juncture. I should think you will get the character reference you want, and if I were you, I would ask for it without delay."

"You see?" I said to Sweeney when we were alone again. "Perfectly amenable and extremely helpful."

Those black eyebrows of his reared up.

"What's the matter now?" I said.

"*Helpful* sir?"

"Vitally so. We learned that Pelham wasn't seen going into the room or out of it. One of the servants would certainly have noticed him. What do you deduce from that?"

"He could have got in there sometime in the night, sir, before the servants were about."

"And when did he come out, do you suppose?"

"After he'd killed her."

"Which we estimate as sometime between six and seven, when the corridors were thick with servants. No, Sweeney, that won't wash."

He said without much conviction, "Then he must have remained hiding in the room until later."

I shook my head. "The housemaid found him tucked up harmlessly in his own bed when she brought the tea just after seven o'clock."

Sweeney was obviously stumped.

I put a hand on his shoulder. "Come upstairs and I shall demonstrate how it was done."

CHAPTER 19

Iled Sweeney briskly upstairs to Amelia's dressing room, which felt like the North Pole when we stepped inside, because the balcony windows still stood open. Sweeney hastened to close them.

"What on earth do you think you are doing?" I demanded with a frost of my own. "We're not here for the sake of our comfort, you know. We are about to reconstruct the crime. Pray leave them as you found them and step into the bedroom."

"I beg your pardon, sir."

"Right. I shall be the murderer, you the victim."

He did as instructed, while I remained in the dressing room.

"Close the door and lie on the bed as if you are asleep. Have you done that?"

A muffled, "Yes, sir."

"Good. Now listen for a disturbance. When you are convinced that you have heard something, enough to waken you from your slumbers, get up from the bed, cross the room and step in here to see what is the matter. Not yet. I am going outside." So saying, I moved to my position, not in the corridor, as he would suppose, but *on the balcony*, pulling the windows gently together.

I waited a few moments and then rapped on the glass. Through it, I presently saw the connecting door open and Sweeney emerge. Just as I had anticipated, he crossed to the dressing room door without a glance in my direction, and looked out into the corridor.

I tapped again and he spun on his heel, saw where I was, and gaped like a cuckoo.

"Look alive, man!" I shouted, for I was in danger of perishing from exposure out there. "Come over here and let me in."

He shook his great befuddled head as he admitted me.

"So," I said, "having gained entry, I take two strides to the fireplace like so, snatch up the poker like so, and strike you across the skull, which we shall have to leave to the imagination. You fall to the floor. Well, do it, man!"

He sank to his knees.

"I drop the poker, stoop and carry your unconscious, dead or dying body to the balcony. On your feet, Sweeney—I'm not going to risk a hernia for this." I took a firm grip on his arm. "Through the open window you go, out to the balcony and over the edge." As we advanced to the iron railing, Sweeney grabbed it like a drowning man and held on. I said, "You don't have to panic. This is only a demonstration. Do you see how it was done?"

"No, sir."

Reader, who could have blamed me if I had tipped him over? "What, then, is the difficulty?"

"How did the murderer get here, sir?"

"Get where?"

"Onto the balcony."

I said cuttingly, "Take a look to your right."

He did as instructed. "Well, I'll be jiggered!" He was looking, as you may have surmised, at the balcony of the room next door, a mere arm's length from where we stood. This wing of the building was so designed that pairs of balconies jutted from the facade at regular intervals. There was a long stretch of wall before the next pair, so Amelia's balcony was accessible from its neighbor to the right, but no other. Even Sweeney in his jittery state saw the significance. "Anyone could climb from there to here."

"And back," I said, "after committing murder."

"So that was why no one saw him in the corridor. He climbed over the balcony." He gave a whistle, which was rather *infra dig*, but gratifying in its way. "Smart of you to think of it, if I may say so, sir."

"You may."

"Such a thing would not have occurred to me in a million years."

"That I am willing to believe." I basked in his admiration for a short while, without troubling to mention how I had got the idea. You will recall that two nights before I had seen Claude Bullivant enter Isabella Dundas's room by way of the balcony.

"The next question is," Sweeney remarked with ponderous calculation, "whose balcony is that?"

"You ought to know. We looked into the room last night."

"Mr. Pelham's?"

"Correct."

He made a fist with his right hand and punched it into the palm of his left. "We've got him now, sir, thanks be to God!"

"Not yet," I cautioned. "We have merely established a possibility. We need proof that he entered the room this way. Clues, Sweeney, clues."

"Like a footprint on the balcony, sir?"

"A bloodstain is more likely. There was blood on the poker."

"But he dropped the poker, sir."

"There could have been blood on his hands, or his clothes. I propose that you climb over and see what you can find."

"Would you be asking me to climb onto Mr. Pelham's balcony, sir?"

"Precisely."

"Suppose he's in his room."

"He's downstairs. We saw him a minute or two ago."

"Sure and that's the truth," said Sweeney limply. He hoisted one leg awkwardly over the rail and reached for the other balcony. He had difficulty getting a foothold, and I didn't assist him. The point of the exercise was to demonstrate how easily a man could manage it alone.

He completed the maneuver eventually. A younger man such as Pelham could practically have vaulted the rails.

"No signs of blood here, sir."

"Examine the windows. Are they marked at all?"

"They are spotless, sir. Shall I come back?"

"Certainly not. See whether the windows open." When that suggestion came to nothing I said, "Very well. Remain where you are. I shall go into the room and open them from the inside."

I don't altogether approve of entering other people's bedrooms without invitation or permission, but this was a murder investigation. Who could say what damning discoveries I might make: a bloodstained garment possibly, or a copy of *The Times* with the name of the day cut out.

Not a soul was in the corridor when I stepped out of Amelia's room. I moved the few yards to Pelham's door, grasped the handle—and felt the horrid sensation of its turning independently. The door swung inwards and Marcus Pelham stood there, all teeth and charm.

"Do come in, Your Royal Highness."

I said on a high note of disbelief, "You were downstairs."

"And now I am here. As the only surviving member of the family, I thought it proper to make myself available. Won't you come in, sir?"

Naturally I was wary, but he appeared not to have any murderous weapon to hand. "How did you know I was at your door?"

"I watched Inspector Sweeney climb onto my balcony. I cannot imagine why he should essay such an acrobatic feat except in the performance of his duty as a bodyguard. I therefore concluded that I was about to be graced by a Royal visit." He rounded off this sarcastic piece of insolence with a faint smile. He knew very well that I hadn't expected to find him in the room.

I said, "You wasted no time in coming upstairs."

"I followed you up," he admitted without turning a hair. "The obligations of host fall entirely to me now that my poor sister is no longer with us. I am at your service, sir, ready and willing to render assistance."

"Very well," I responded, treating his humbug as if I believed every word, "you can begin by opening your balcony window and inviting Inspector Sweeney to step inside. He's of more use as a bodyguard in here than out there."

"So I would have thought," said Pelham. "He's the one whose life is threatened."

"Why do you say that?" I asked at once.

"He'll catch pneumonia out there."

He approached the window and reached for the bolt. The wretched Sweeney saw his approach, dodged sideways and pressed himself against the railing in the corner, trying without success to escape from view, a mortifying spectacle. "I seem to have startled him," Pelham remarked.

I declined to comment. I was observing the attempt to open the window, which was in itself an action of overriding importance to the investigation. Sweeney's personal comfort was of no account compared with this. Pelham was having some difficulty, or so he wanted me to think.

"It's the devil to shift," he said.

I let him struggle a moment, and then told him to stand aside. I discovered that he had not been bluffing. The window *was* stuck fast. I had to put my shoulder to the frame to move it, and then I only succeeded at the fourth or fifth attempt. There was a rasp as it finally yielded and flakes of paint came away from the wood.

"No wonder," said Pelham. "It must have been given a coat of paint last summer and closed before it was dry, with the result that the surfaces stuck fast. Shoddy work. Step inside, Inspector, we're not discussing you."

Sweeney entered without a word. He didn't need to pass any comment. His look was eloquent enough. He had seen the efforts to open the windows. He could see the paint flakes on the floor. He knew, as I did, that those windows hadn't been opened in months. Our theory—no, let's be brutally honest—*my* theory had just been exposed as impossible.

CHAPTER 20

So the hounds had bayed in vain. I was obliged to spend the rest of the day in the kennel, so to speak, gnawing at the bones of my theory and finding precious little meat. Reluctantly I was forced to conclude that my suspicions about Marcus Pelham had got the better of me. Try as I might, I was unable to fathom how he could have got into Amelia's room and out of it unseen when the corridor was swarming with servants. In fact, I couldn't fathom how anyone had managed it.

In bed that night (with a gundog and his handler on guard outside my bedroom door) I resolved to toss out all the suspicions and prejudices I had accumulated and adopt a more objective method. Emulating Scotland Yard, I would marshal the facts of the case and make a "wanted" portrait of the murderer.

Five deaths had to be accounted for. Five deaths in five days, and apart from the obvious fact that the victims were all members of our house party, the only thing they had in common was the piece of paper left beside or upon each of the bodies. Beyond doubt the murderer had left those clues for a purpose. The deaths were linked to a few lines of rhyming folklore. What could one deduce from that?

First, those lines of verse fitted the victims so aptly that the guest list must have been known to the murderer some time in advance. To put it in legal jargon, the crimes were premeditated.

Second, the daily killing was clearly presented as a challenge, or a taunt. We, the people under threat, were invited to guess who was to be next and we had been outwitted so far.

Third, this murderer was willing to take risks. The leaving of clues was a dangerous indulgence.

And fourth, it had taken exceptional foresight to calculate that the house party would not be abandoned and the police called in after one, two or three murders. The killer had banked on my personal refusal to embroil the office of Heir Apparent in a sensational case of murder. That stuck in my gullet.

Have a care, Bertie, I cautioned myself—the good detective strives to be impartial at all times.

With a firm eye on the facts, I characterized the murderer as a plotter of ingenuity and foresight, one for whom mere killing was insufficient satisfaction, who treated it as a macabre game, to baffle and taunt the victims. Unhappily, the description fell short of a physical picture. Age, height, build, hair, eyes, dress, marks or peculiarities. I wasn't even certain of the culprit's sex.

And this night was bringing us to Saturday. My thoughts became unscientific again and drifted back to my fellow guests, the remaining members of the house party, no doubt lying awake, like me, asking themselves the dread question, "Could I conceivably be described as one who works hard for a living?" George Holdfast, Marcus Pelham and Isabella Dundas. I did not seriously consider as possible victims Sweeney and all the servants; the killing had been confined to legitimate guests, and so I expected it to continue—unless and until I put a stop to it.

Holdfast, Pelham, Miss Dundas and myself. Survivors, thus far. You may wonder why any of us lingered any longer in that house of murder, and it is difficult to explain, but I will try. Two of the party had already chosen discretion as the better part of valor, of course, and who could blame them? But since Alix and Lady Moira had left, a sort of understanding had grown up. We who remained were all, in our different ways, dogged, self-reliant individuals with our own private reasons for refusing to leave. A sense of moral obligation played a part in my own case, and, I am sure, in others; there was an unspoken pact between us that no one else would quit until this monster was caught. Call us brave, if you must. The same dauntless spirit built the greatest Empire in history.

Besides, if anyone had packed his bags at this juncture we would all have smelled a rat.

Saturday

CHAPTER 21

Have you ever gone to bed with a problem to resolve and found that when you woke up you had the answer? That was what happened to me that Saturday morning. But before you shout "Unfair" and protest that no self-respecting detective relies on dreams to resolve his cases, let me make myself clear. This wasn't a dream. I was roused by Wellard, one of my footmen, who brought me my usual glass of cold milk, and the sight of him prompted me to say, "What time is it?"

"Seven o'clock, sir."

"Seven, eh. Is it busy out there?"

"Busy, sir?"

"In the corridor. Servants going this way and that."

"Well, yes. Quite busy, sir."

"I dare say you're getting to know the other servants."

"Not to any noticeable degree, sir. Each retinue tends to keep to itself."

"So if you pass someone in the corridor, the chances are that you won't know who they are?"

"I'm afraid that is so, sir."

I sat bolt upright, alert to the importance of what my questions were revealing. "Now tell me this, Wellard. Would you recognize any of the guests if you passed them in the corridor?"

"The guests? Certainly, sir."

This wasn't the answer I wanted to hear. "How? How would you recognize them?"

"From their clothes, sir. They are not in uniform as the servants are."

"Never mind what they wear. Do you know any of the guests by sight—by face alone?"

"No, sir. My duties confine me to your suite and the servants' quarters."

"As I thought." I beamed at him with approval. "That is all I wanted to know, Wellard."

Thus, without fuss or fanfare, I finally grasped the key to the mystery. It was clear to me how the murderer had been able to pass through the house unremarked and unchallenged—*by posing as a servant*. This week Desborough was stuffed with visiting servants, and in most cases one flunky didn't know another from Adam—or from Pelham, or Holdfast, or Miss Dundas.

BREAKFAST FOUND THE FOUR OF us still alive and in pretty good spirits considering that the day held nothing more in prospect than a funeral. It was a fine day, too; the sort of sunny October morning when one ought to be off to Newmarket for the races, but the blinds were down and two mutes with crepe-covered wands were on duty at the front door. In the absence of the Chaplain, who had excused himself from leading the morning prayers, I said a brief grace and dismissed the servants. Then I enquired of Pelham what arrangements had been made.

He surprised me with an effusion of information, cheerily communicated. "The funeral service is at noon, sir, in the family chapel in the Hermit Wood, for reasons of privacy. It is not much used, but the Chaplain thought it more appropriate than the village church. The carriages are called for half past eleven. The hearse will lead the cortege, followed by your carriage, and then ours—Miss Dundas and Sir George riding with me. After a short service the burial will be in a plot to the rear of the chapel."

"It all sounds most appropriate, as you say. Apart from my presence, is anything required of me?"

"I think Wilfred will be sufficiently honored by your attendance at his funeral, sir."

I nodded. "Yes, it will be something of a departure for me—and much more of a departure for him, come to mention it." I thought this rather droll, and waited for the faces around the table to respond, which they eventually did. "True, I'm not often seen at the funeral of a commoner. I have to draw the line somewhere, or I could spend the whole of my time in graveyards. However, I'm pleased to pay my last respects to this fellow. Even more reason why we don't want any of today's doings reported in the press. You're quite sure we're the only mourners?"

"Yes, sir, except for the undertaker and his assistants."

"Don't forget the sky pilot," Holdfast jovially put in. Turning to Miss Dundas, he added, "The Chaplain, my dear—a term sailors use for the clergy."

She said evenly, "Thank you. I am not without experience of sea voyages."

The rebuke was lightly delivered, and Sir George gave a wry nod and smile. His avuncular presence had been a support to us all through this harrowing week. The amiable gleam had never left his eye. If anything, it had gotten brighter since Lady Moira's departure. In fact, looking about the table, I found it well nigh impossible to cast any of my companions as the scheming, stony-hearted assassin I had divined as responsible for the murders. Isabella Dundas looked perfectly demure in a simple black dress overlaid with jet beads that I suppose she would otherwise have worn for dinner one evening. She had her reddish-brown hair gathered to a chignon and fastened at the side with black combs. Women of her stamp are equal to every contingency. If we had all been transported to the moon she would still have found something correct to wear. As for Marcus Pelham, my opinion was mellowing. The tragic death of his sister seemed to have made a man of him. The adolescent scowl was less evident. He even showed commendable concern for someone other than himself by asking, "How is Inspector Sweeney this morning? No ill effects from yesterday, I trust?"

"Apparently not," I answered.

"Only I haven't seen him."

"I dare say he's about his business," said I.

Miss Dundas looked up and asked, "Did the Inspector have a bad experience yesterday?"

"A little time outside without an overcoat, that was all."

"He did look somewhat *distrait* towards the end of the day," she remarked. "I do hope nothing is amiss, sir."

None of us said any more about Sweeney until later.

OF NECESSITY, THE FUNERAL OF Wilfred Osgot-Edge was without much ostentation, even if it is imprinted on my memory forever. There were few of the trappings of these occasions. True, Hibbert the undertaker supplied us with hatbands and cloaks, but that was the extent of it. I had refused to have my pair of grays dyed black, so they weren't fitted with sable plumes, which would have looked silly. The hearse, of course, was drawn by plumed horses; Hibbert himself walked in front, which was heroic considering the state of the going, and the mutes and pallbearers also made the short journey on foot. We proceeded at the best gait they could manage along a sticky cart track through the wood, stopping at the lych-gate, where the Reverend Humphrey Paget stood waiting. As so often happens, the horses drawing the hearse marked our arrival with a mournful neighing—probably in protest at the tolling of the church bell.

While the pallbearers stepped forward to shoulder the coffin, I stood back with the others. The family chapel was a gloomy-looking stone structure with a small bell tower heavily encrusted with lichen. Although I doubt if it was more than a hundred years old, its location had exposed it critically to the depredations of nature. I didn't relish stepping inside. Pelham nudged my arm and offered me a hip flask. My first reaction was to take a nip, and then I thought better of it. After all, I told myself, there was a one in three chance that the funeral was Pelham's doing. A moment later, when I saw him put the flask to his lips, I wished I had been more trusting.

Hibbert nodded to the Chaplain and we followed the coffin through the lych-gate. The path was thick with moss and ivy, and one of the pallbearers stumbled slightly. But the dead and the living all got inside without serious mishap and the service commenced. The Padre had my backing when he steamed into his words like an express train, for the pews had no padding and the smell of mustiness was quite overpowering. None of us meant any disrespect to Osgot-Edge; I'm sure he wouldn't have wished any of us except his murderer to feel uncomfortable on his account.

In a strange way Osgot-Edge contrived to make his spiritual presence felt. When the Chaplain first said, "Let us pray," I was reminded of that poem about the obstinate boy and the lion that we'd heard recited on the first fateful evening. Curiously enough, on that occasion it had been the Chaplain who had read it to us. "*Let us prey.*" When he spoke the words for the second or third time, my thoughts, shameful to relate, took a sacrilegious turn. I was prompted to ask myself whether I might have overlooked a possible suspect.

My skin prickled at the thought. *A man of the cloth?* Surely not. I tried to remember whether the Reverend Humphrey Paget had been present in the house each time a murder had been committed. Certainly he had been at dinner with us the first night, when Queenie Chimes was poisoned. Moreover, he had joined us for lunch in the marquee on the day Jerry Gribble was shot.

"Amen," said the congregation.

On the night Osgot-Edge had been stabbed to death, the Chaplain had played with gusto in the parlor games.

"Psalm Ninety," announced the Reverend Humphrey Paget, "'Lord, thou hast been our refuge.'"

On the morning Bullivant was pushed down the well, who had led us in morning prayers? I particularly remembered, because everyone had been waiting when I arrived.

Could the Reverend Humphrey Paget possibly have entered the building secretly in the small hours of Friday morning disguised as a servant and murdered Amelia? Her own family chaplain?

As the words "Let us pray," were spoken yet again, I knelt and silently asked forgiveness for my unholy suspicions, and at such an ill-chosen time. I am sorry if this offends my more devout readers, but I fancy that a still, small, sporting voice said, "Hold your fire, Bertie, but keep your shooter loaded."

The service in the chapel came to an end and we shuffled silently from the pews and followed the coffin outside. The ground we traversed was fearfully overgrown with damp, rotting bracken. I did my best to beat a path with my stick while Miss Dundas, accustomed to the jungle, took a grip on her skirts and stepped in behind me.

I should explain that this wasn't in any sense a regular churchyard. There were no graves that one could see. I imagine that there was a family vault beneath the chapel where the Drummonds were interred, and where Amelia would be laid to rest in a day or two. Osgot-Edge, not being family, was accommodated outside, close to the drystone wall that enclosed the consecrated ground. We duly positioned ourselves around the grave and saw the coffin lowered. Four suspects and me. And I'm glad to say that the interment was completed with due reverence. We paid our respects and moved away. I told Pelham that I would now appreciate a nip from his flask.

He made the unnecessary remark, "So poor Wilfred is laid to rest."

"That was my understanding of what happened."

"A nicely conducted service, I thought, sir. It went well."

"Without a stutter," said I.

He missed the irony. "We can be grateful to the Chaplain."

"Yes, I intend to have a word with him." I handed back the flask. "Why don't you and the others drive back to the Hall for lunch? I'll join you later."

"Just as you wish, sir." He hesitated as his features creased into a look of genuine concern. "Is it safe?"

"What exactly do you mean by that?"

"I mean out here in the open, without your bodyguard. No one has seen hide nor hair of Inspector Sweeney."

I assured Pelham that I would take care of myself and he went back to Holdfast and Miss Dundas. I raised my hat to the lady and made clear my intention to be independent by picking my way through the bracken towards the far side of the chapel. They were soon out of sight. Presently I heard their carriage move off. Soon after, the hearse left as well. I had noticed the Reverend Humphrey Paget reenter the chapel by a back door, presumably the vestry, so I was alone, apart from an estate worker who had started the work of filling in the grave. The man was soon lost to view as I made my way around the building.

I was in no hurry to question the Chaplain. If possible, I wanted to remove a lingering doubt from my mind, only I hadn't reckoned with the bracken, which was knee-high, even after the recent frost had brought it down some feet from its full summer glory. Hacking with my stick and looking to right and left, I progressed methodically towards the lych-gate until I spotted what I was seeking, surprisingly close to the path that the cortege had used as we entered the chapel.

I had discovered a gravestone, a plain, rectangular slab of granite jutting up from the ground and almost obscured by the bracken. A few swings of my stick enabled me to read the inscription, which was recent in origin:

ROBERT BELL
Died October 20, 1889, aged 17
Gone, but not forgotten

Not forgotten, but almost lost to view, I reflected wryly. This was, of course, the resting place of the youth accidentally shot a year ago by Claude Bullivant. Decent of the Drummonds to have had a stone put up for him. *Gone, but not forgotten.* Only a couple of days ago I had been inspired to concoct an entire theory out of the fate of this boy and Bullivant's consequent difficulties. A misfounded theory, as events had proved beyond doubt, but I had wanted to see the grave for myself. I still had a strange intimation that it had a bearing on our present difficulties.

And now, with a thrill of discovery, I understood why. I understood almost everything about the Desborough Hall murders.

CHAPTER 22

I didn't have long to savor the moment. I flung myself to the ground at the sound of gunfire.

I lay still and waited, flat to the ground. I knew the identity of the murderer now, knew it for certain. This was no empty boast, as you will discover, reader. If you flatter yourself that you could have matched my success as a sleuth, then you had better name your suspect at once, without sneaking a look at the last pages of the book.

For the benefit of those who prefer to remain mystified until the last possible moment, I shall continue to unfold the events as they happened. Obviously this was not the time to step forward and unmask the murderer.

Two shots had been discharged. If thirty years' experience of shooting counted for anything, I knew they had been fired from a double-barreled shotgun, in which case the firer was probably reloading at this minute—or already taking aim. One can never be certain about the effects of echo in the vicinity of a building, but it seemed to me that the shots had come from somewhere close to the chapel. Nor could I be entirely sure that I was the intended target. Now that I considered the matter, I hadn't noticed shot being sprayed in my vicinity.

I wasn't comforted. I remained motionless, praying that my black clothes were not conspicuous. The sensation of helplessness made me shake with rage. If I *was* the target, the contest was so uneven. Even a wretched game bird has a sporting chance. What chance had a burly middle-aged man out there in the open equipped with nothing more effective in defense than a walking stick?

The boundary wall was twenty yards or more behind me. If I could run that far without being shot, I would still have the devil's own job to get out of the firing line. Scrambling over walls isn't the sort of exercise I am accustomed to taking. And the lych-gate was at least forty yards away. So I settled for discretion and a face full of damp foliage.

The extra shots I expected were not discharged. There followed a long, tense time when nothing happened except for a colony of rooks returning to occupy the chapel roof and tower which they had noisily abandoned. I wished I had their confidence.

Finally I risked raising my head sufficiently to peer around the gravestone. A patch of taller and more verdant bracken was to my left. I considered whether it was worth scrambling on my stomach for ten yards to get some better cover. I stared in the direction of the chapel and saw no sign of life. Yes, I would risk it.

First I removed the mourning cloak, made a bundle of it with the silk hat and walking stick and pushed them under some fronds. Then I started a passable imitation of an Indian scout, leaving the shelter of the gravestone to drag myself forward on elbows, hips and knees. No shot came. I crossed the divide and collapsed breathlessly into the denser foliage. Sanctuary.

I lay on my stomach for a few minutes recovering my breath. I reckoned that I could stay there in reasonable safety for an indefinite interval. Until dark, in fact. There was no point in taking unnecessary risks. It wasn't just a matter of saving my hide; the future of the realm had to be safeguarded.

I was tempted to light up a cigar, but smoke signals would be taking the scouting to excess, so I rolled onto my side.

To my absolute horror, I saw the mistake I had made. I stared back at the way I had come. My route through the bracken was flattened into a track so obvious that I might as well have unrolled a red carpet and stood a guard of honor on either side. Any fool could tell where I was. All the subterfuge had been useless. I would have done better to have stood up and walked. In fact, I would have to move somewhere on foot, and fast.

Someone was approaching. I could hear steps on the gravel by the chapel door.

A dash for the lych-gate was out of the question now. It would make more sense to look for a sheltered place behind the chapel or, better still, inside. Gingerly I raised my eyes above the level of the foliage. Ahead was another oasis of tall bracken. I got up and bolted towards it. Out of the corner of my eye I had a blurred impression of the figure by the chapel door. I ducked down. In one more gallop I could get out of range on the far side of the building. I took a deep breath and was off like a rabbit.

I tripped, staggered, put a hand to the ground and kept my footing by the sheer force of my onward rush. I didn't mean to stop until I reached the chapel wall. Suddenly a pheasant rose up screeching and brushed my face with its tail feathers. It didn't stop my charge. Nothing but a cartridge would do that.

So when I glimpsed something red and white below me, I leapt over it and ran on. It wasn't as startling as the pheasant because it didn't move. Not startling in that sense, but in another. It was a glimpse of death.

The white object was the Reverend Humphrey Paget's surplice. Do I need to say what the red was? The Chaplain had been shot through the head. It wasn't a sight that a susceptible reader would wish me to describe, or that I should care to. Anyone who knows the power of a twelve-bore will have an idea of its effect at close range.

I lurched on until I flattened my hands on the chapel wall. I felt ready to vomit, but I dared not stop. Somehow I had to stay in control, get inside the vestry and lock the door behind me. I groped my way to the door, grasped the handle, turned it and let myself in. As it slammed shut, I leaned against it and breathed a great, shuddering sigh. That sigh stopped prematurely.

I was looking into the twin barrels of a shotgun.

The shock was profound. I failed to understand how it was possible. I was not capable of understanding. My brain had not fully absorbed the horror of the Chaplain's death, and now I faced my own destruction. I am not at all proud of the spectacle I presented. I wanted to plead for my life. I merely gibbered.

I was at the mercy of the murderer, and she had now revealed herself. She was Miss Queenie Chimes.

The lady should have been dead, but she was not. She was standing with the shotgun leveled, her finger against the trigger. She was not an apparition. She had not, after all, been killed. You must take my word for it that I wasn't in the least surprised. I had deduced that she was the murderer the moment I had seen that gravestone.

She *did* succeed in taking my breath away when she said, "You can sit down, Your Royal Highness. I shall not shoot unless you make it necessary. But I shall continue to aim the gun at you. There is a chair to your left."

I wanted to protest about poor Paget, but the words would not leave my lips. I sank onto the chair. Queenie Chimes remained standing in the center of the vestry, which was furnished with a row of empty clothes hooks and a cupboard. She was dressed in a riding habit and silk hat. Appropriately she favored the color of mourning. I could recall the black velvet dress she had worn when I had seen her last. The signs of strain showed more strikingly in her face than they had that Monday evening, but she was well in control of herself.

She lowered the gun to the level of my chest. "You *do* remember who I am?"

I nodded.

She said, "Are you unable or unwilling to speak?"

I succeeded in saying, "Miss Chimes, or do you prefer Miss Bell?"

"I don't mind very much how you address me. So you found the grave? I saw you searching for it."

"The grave, yes. Am I correct in deducing that Robert Bell was your brother?"

"My dear brother Bob." A glaze of moisture came over her eyes. "My family. All the family I had in this world until he was murdered."

I said as gently as I could, "If you are speaking of what happened a year ago, that was an accident, surely."

The mouth twitched and she said with bitterness, "Yes, call it an accident. Dismiss it. Just an orphan boy who happened to stray into the line of fire. An unfortunate incident, not worth canceling the shoot for. They didn't. My brother wasn't killed outright, you know. He was hit by scores of pellets, and in terrible pain, but it was inconvenient to call a doctor or take him to a hospital while the shoot was in progress, so they had him carried to the nearest cottage and left in the care of an old woman of eighty who tried to comfort him with hot milk. The shooting party went back to slaughtering pheasants. Three hours after the shoot was over a footman was sent to the cottage with a flask of brandy. That was all the interest that any of them took. Sometime after midnight my poor brother died of his wounds. Do you know what they were doing in the Hall that evening? Singing around the piano."

"Such insensitivity!" I said, trying to show sympathy without sounding insincere. "I'm profoundly sorry. One can only assume that nobody realized how serious the injuries were."

She let out a harsh, indignant breath, "If he had been one of theirs—a brother or a son—do you suppose they would have abandoned him like that? Bob's death need not have happened. They were responsible. And they knew it. They buried him in secret without an inquest. The servants were instructed never to mention it, or they would be dismissed. He wasn't even buried in a proper coffin. One of the estate woodmen was given the task of making a box from unseasoned timber." She pressed her lips together. "I can't bear to think of it."

I said in a futile attempt to assuage the bitterness, "They provided a decent stone for him."

"Pardon me, they did not. I paid for the stone when I learned how my brother had died and been left in an unmarked grave. I had it delivered here without any indication of who had sent it. Each of them assumed that one of the others had ordered it in a fit of conscience. So it was erected as a headstone, and touched nobody's conscience at all. You saw how the grave was overgrown."

Still trying not to antagonize her, I remarked, "Then the words on the stone were your choice. *Gone, but not forgotten.*"

She gave a laugh bereft of any amusement. "What restraint I showed! My first thought was to have the truth engraved there. *'Cruelly struck down and allowed to die.'* But my plan was already made, you see. I couldn't put it at risk."

"Your plan?"

"The Drummonds and their friends made the mistake of believing that Bob was alone in the world. They thought he could be buried and forgotten."

"So the words on the stone are not without point," I commented.

"They didn't know of my existence. Bob wasn't one to talk about his past—it was too painful." She sighed, "You see, as children we were separated after both our parents were called to God. On top of the grief, we had to endure loneliness. Sometimes cruelty. Yet we kept in touch. Don't ask me how—it was God's work. We were only young children, but we refused to be cut off from each other. The tie of blood was too strong. As the elder child, I felt responsible, even after we had both grown up. So I knew that Bob had gone to work on the Desborough estate, and when my birthday came and I heard nothing from him, I was worried. I came here to see him and no one would tell me what had happened to him. Their lips were sealed, but I could see in their faces that a tragedy had happened. Finally by sheer persistence I found the old woman in whose cottage he died. She was brave enough to tell me the dreadful truth. It was almost a relief to know for certain. Yes, I traveled back to London feeling gratified. Can you understand that?"

I nodded.

She said, "Later it turned to grief, of course, and self-pity. Then anger. Outrage. Blind fury at those monsters who had conspired to cover up their crime. It was a crime, you know, failure to report a death."

"I'm sure that is so."

"The greater crime was letting him die. The law might not hold them responsible for that, but I did. I blamed them. The outrage didn't diminish. If anything it grew as I learned what it truly means to be alone in the world. I lived with my anger for a time. I tried to subdue it, I really did, and eventually I succeeded. I achieved a sort of calm by planning vengeance. I vowed to kill everyone who had conspired in Robert's death, every member of that house party including the chaplain who buried him." She paused, I suppose to see the effect of this statement.

The effect upon me was that I remained outwardly impassive whilst privately thanking my stars that all my shooting last year had been done at Sandringham and Balmoral.

She continued in the same toneless voice, "I was saved the trouble of disposing of Lord Frederick Drummond. He was gored by a bull."

"That much I know," said I.

"Five others remained. I set myself the task of finding out everything I could about them. As a first step, I contrived to meet Marcus Pelham and gain his confidence. He had not been one of the party, but he was worth cultivating because he took particular interest in his sister's social attachments."

"Indeed he did."

"I learned from Marcus what I hoped to hear—that another shooting party was to be held at Desborough."

I gave a nod. "And did he tell you that I was to be the principal guest?"

"That was a mishap I had not foreseen," she said without realizing how tactless a remark it was. "Alarming at first, I confess, but the more I thought about it, the more I saw the opportunity it presented."

"In what way?"

"Well, an unexplained death in the house would put Lady Drummond and her brother into an appalling quandary. They would want to avoid the matter becoming public knowledge."

"For reasons which you need not go into," said I.

She gave me an unsympathetic glance. "I contrived a mysterious death with shocking possibilities of scandal—an actress who collapses at the dinner table in front of the Prince of Wales. Everyone's instinct would be to conceal it from the police and the press, to behave as if nothing had happened."

"Which everyone did," said I. "And now I discover that there was no dying actress, unless you have a twin sister."

"I don't. There was no dying actress. There was an actress pretending to die."

"Extraordinary behavior!"

"It was necessary. It enabled me to test the water, so to speak, and discover how everyone would react. And it removed me from all suspicion."

"This is all very cunning and ingenious," said I, "but I fail to see how it was done."

"With a convincing performance," she said with just a hint of self-congratulation.

"I'll grant you that—but we had Jerry Gribble's word later that you died in his arms. Collapsing is one thing, dying is quite another. There must be limits to what an actress can achieve. Jerry was no fool. I can't believe that he was taken in by this performance of yours. And what of the hospital? They know a corpse when they see one."

She said with an air of contempt, "We didn't go near the hospital. You're perfectly right about Jerry. He wasn't taken in. So far as he was concerned, we were playing a very artful practical joke on the rest of you."

"A joke?"

"You must understand that I had planned this for months. I first met Jerry at a cricket match."

"I know."

"Yes, but it wasn't a chance meeting. I contrived it. I set out to win his affections, which was all too easy."

"If I may say so, you're extremely single-minded."

She let out a short, audible breath. "He didn't inflame me with passion, I assure you. I yielded to him simply to get myself invited to Desborough Hall. Before we arrived I persuaded Jerry to conspire with me in the practical joke I mentioned. He knew how much you enjoyed a good hoax. The idea was that I would pretend to collapse at dinner on that first evening. Jerry would take me off supposedly to the doctor. Later he would return and say that I had died in his arms."

"Strange sort of joke," I commented.

"Yes, but the next night I would start my haunting. I would come back as a ghost. Don't you remember the talk of ghosts that first evening? We would have no end of fun scaring the living daylights out of all of you—or so Jerry believed. Of course I had no intention of dressing up as a ghost, but I gather that Jerry succeeded in convincing you that I was dead. I arranged to meet him the next morning at one of the stands where you were due to shoot later on. He told me proudly that everyone was taken in. I resisted the temptation to say that the joke was on him. I simply shot him and put the gun in his hand."

"And left a piece of newspaper in his pocket."

"Yes."

"Why?"

"Why did I shoot him? I've explained. He was one of that group who allowed my brother to die."

"I meant why the piece of paper?"

"Ah. The verse. It was something I thought of at an early stage to embroider the plan. I once heard somebody address Jerry as "Your Grace" and that inspired the idea. It happened that Wilfred Osgot-Edge had initials that fitted the line for Wednesday, so I arranged to kill him on Wednesday. It wasn't difficult to fit in the others."

"You were taking a risk by leaving clues."

"Not much of a risk. If anything, it was a diversion from my real motive. Anyone could cut out words from *The Times*. That gave nothing away. I did it to mystify you all, and you in particular, Your Royal Highness."

"Me?"

"It's well known that you relish a challenge, whether it's racing your yacht or shooting with the best guns in Europe."

"Granted."

"You've never been known to walk away. I was confident that you would see out the week in hopes of outwitting me. And if you were willing to remain at the house, so would my victims."

I said, "I hope you're not implicating me in this plot."

She ignored me and asked, "What time is it?"

I felt for my watch and incidentally became aware of the disgraceful state my clothes were in. "Just after two o'clock."

"I can't remain much longer. I've told you what drove me to do these things."

"What do you propose to do now?"

"I shall dispose of you first—"

"What?"

"Lock you up whilst I make my escape. There's a room at the top of the tower that I have used from time to time this week. No doubt someone will find you there before the day is out.

"You don't intend to injure me?"

She said as if such a treasonous thought had never crossed her mind, "Why should I wish to do you any harm? My brother's death isn't on your conscience, is it?"

"Emphatically not," I said, then sensed that I ought to add something. "And I deplore the way he was treated. My dear lady, I can assure you, if I had been one of the party—"

She raised the shotgun a fraction. "Let us go upstairs, then."

"Is that all you're proposing to tell me?"

"On your feet, please. I'll tell you about the others as we go. I want you to open the door behind me and walk down the aisle to the main door. Just to the left of it you'll see the steps."

I obeyed, hoping fervently that there wasn't anyone left in the chapel. When there's a gun at your back you don't want unexpected things to happen. The place appeared to be deserted, thank the Lord. I started down the aisle with Queenie Chimes in close attendance. "Am I right in supposing that you masqueraded as a servant?" I asked.

"Yes. I'm well accustomed to acting the role of housemaid. I could come and go as I pleased. Very few of the servants knew each other. I meant to kill Mr. Osgot-Edge in his bedroom, but an opportunity came earlier, when you all played Sardines."

"How did you know that Osgot-Edge was to be the hider?"

"I was one of the maids who served the punch."

"And nobody recognized you?"

"Of course not. Nobody gives a servant a second look. I was in apron and cap and that was disguise enough. When the game started and the lights were out, I pursued Mr. Osgot-Edge and stabbed him with a kitchen knife." The dreadful statement defiled our surroundings, although she had spoken it in a voice as commonplace as if she were reading the liturgy.

I asked about Bullivant's murder.

She said, "That was simple. I wrote him a note supposedly from Miss Dundas suggesting a dawn assignation at the well. He was so dumbfounded when he saw me that he quite failed to notice the poker I had concealed behind my back."

"You attacked a man of his strength with a poker?"

"He had no opportunity to use his strength. I said, 'Look behind you!' He turned his head and I swung the poker. He fell without a sound. Then I heaved him into the well."

"Thursday's corpse has far to go."

I stopped. We had reached the spiral stairs that led up the tower. "And Amelia—Lady Drummond? You posed as a servant to enter her dressing room and attack her?"

"Yes, that was more dangerous than I anticipated. Move on, Your Royal Highness. Up the stairs, and not too quickly. I had been led to believe by the servants that Lady Drummond took chloral and would be lethargic, to say the least. I intended to use the poker again. It had proved so effective against Mr. Bullivant. However, she was out of bed when I entered the room and she put up no end of a fight. I don't believe she was drugged. Finally I struck her with the poker and tipped her over the balcony."

"Why did you kill her? Surely she wasn't one of the guns?"

"Neither was the Chaplain, but I killed him. They condoned it, you see. They conspired with the others to cover up what they had done. And surely a woman with a spark of compassion would have gone to visit the wounded boy."

"Yet you characterized her as loving and giving."

"She was, where men were concerned. Didn't you know?"

Her remark was so far beneath contempt that I declined to answer it. Instead I said, "So Saturday's corpse was the Chaplain. How inconvenient that he didn't fit the epithet by being a wage-earning man."

She had an answer to that. "As a clergyman he had a benefice, or a living, as it is commonly known. I don't know how hard he worked, but he did it for a living."

We had reached the top of the stairs. Ahead was a door. I hesitated. "And is the killing complete? What of the corpse who was killed on the Sabbath day?"

She said, "After all, you are not quite so perceptive as I supposed. Didn't you take note of the date on the gravestone? My brother was shot on Saturday and died on Sunday. He was the one who died on the Sabbath Day. *Bonny and blithe and good and gay.* Every word was true of Robert. Yes, it's all over now."

But it was not.

CHAPTER 23

I stood facing the door. "Do you wish me to open it?"

"If you please." Her tone as she fairly barked out the words belied the suggestion that I had any choice in the matter.

As I reached for the handle I told her, "You must make allowances—I'm not accustomed to opening doors." This was true, but I *am* conversant with the principle of turning a door handle. I made the remark—in a carrying voice—to announce our presence, and my predicament. It was not impossible that someone was listening nearby. "It's jammed, I think," I added.

"It can't be."

"You didn't lock it, perhaps?"

"No."

"You are welcome to try it yourself," I offered. "The handle turns, but the door is stuck fast. Do you wish to try?"

"Put your shoulder to it."

"Not with a shotgun against my back. If you stand clear, I'll do the best I can."

"Very well." The pressure in the small of my back eased. She said, "I won't hesitate to shoot if necessary."

I told myself that if a certain party *had* overheard us, at least he could be trusted not to put my life at risk. Heroics weren't in order here. I stepped up to the door and made a show of resting my shoulder against it while glancing back at Miss Chimes. She had the twelve-bore trained on me. She had backed against the curve of the wall two steps from the top and she was totally in shadow except for a pale menacing glint from her eyes.

You will have gathered that the door was not jammed at all. I offered up a short, silent prayer and pushed it open.

The speed of what happened next is impossible to convey. In one sense it was instantaneous and in another terrifyingly slow. The door swung inwards. The room was unoccupied. I stepped inside and to the right in an endeavor to put the wall between me and the shotgun. Then my blood ran cold as shots were fired. How many I could not say, for the echoes in that small space hammered at my eardrums. I flung myself to the floor and covered my face. Bits of shot, stone and plaster spattered about the room.

If anything, the silence that followed was harder to endure than the shooting. I lay hunched and trembling, a trapped beast awaiting the *coup de grâce*.

I heard no footsteps approach, yet they did. My shoulder was gripped. I opened an eye and saw two feet a short distance from my face. Large feet, wearing black socks. The voice of Inspector Sweeney asked, "Are you hurt, sir?"

I opened the other eye.

"It's impossible to say. I am numb, completely numb." I pushed myself up to a kneeling position. "Is she . . . ?"

"Two shots through the heart, sir." He proudly held out his hand. A revolver lay across it.

"You weren't in the room?"

"No, sir, I was on the stairs below her. I took off my boots and followed you up, staying just out of sight around the curve of the stairs. As you stepped into the room, I crept into a firing position and pulled the trigger twice."

"I suppose I had better congratulate you."

"Bodyguarding is my job, sir."

"You have made the point several times this week, Sweeney. There's no need to harp on it."

"I beg your pardon, sir."

I got to my feet and brushed myself down. "Was it unavoidable to shoot the lady?"

"She was pointing a shotgun at you, sir, and after what she did to the Father . . ."

"Whose father was that?"

"The priest."

"Oh, the Chaplain. Ghastly. Did you actually see him shot?"

"Yes, sir. I was too far off to do anything about it. I was guarding you, as my duty requires."

"I didn't notice you."

"I try not to be too obvious about it, sir."

I frowned. "If you were guarding me, Sweeney, how was it that you allowed me to be taken prisoner?"

He ran his tongue guiltily along his upper lip. "I lost sight of you after the Father was shot, sir."

"I was facedown in the bracken." I paused as a possibility occurred to me. "A short while afterwards I spotted a figure by the lych-gate. Was that you?"

"Yes, sir—making a search for you."

"You put the fear of death into me. So it was you I ran away from, blast it, straight into the vestry where Queenie Chimes was lying in wait. A fine bodyguard you are!"

Presently we made our way downstairs, and not without difficulty, for we had to step over Miss Chimes's body. She still had the shotgun cradled in her arms. She had squeezed the trigger at the moment she was hit, and the pellets of shot were everywhere, making Sweeney wince as he stepped on them with his stockinged feet. He collected his boots and we returned on foot to the house.

I left Desborough Hall within the hour and I have not returned since. There was time only to inform young Pelham what had happened and to make my farewells to Isabella Dundas and Sir George Holdfast. Sir George decently agreed to remain behind and impress upon the police the need for discretion. As I informed you more than once in these pages, he was a stalwart. He was also a personal friend of the Chief Constable of Buckinghamshire.

CHAPTER 24

When the inquests into the deaths of the Reverend Humphrey Paget and Victoria Bell, also known as Queenie Chimes, were held, a letter that Miss Chimes had penned to Mr. Henry Irving was read out. It had been found in a pocket of her riding jacket, and it made clear her intention to resign from the Lyceum company. It went on to state that she intended to justify her actions to the press before surrendering herself to the law, and that she was sorry for any unwanted publicity that might come the way of Irving and her friends at the Lyceum. From that, I gather that if she had not been shot she would have made her way to some newspaper office to give them what would have been a sensational story, unthinkably damaging in its consequences. As it transpired, the inquest found that Queenie murdered the Chaplain and was herself shot by some person unknown. On instructions from the Chief Constable of Buckinghamshire, no more inquiries were made into the matter.

UPON MY RETURN TO SANDRINGHAM, I found Alix in a strange mood. I had rather relished giving her an account of my investigation, but she disappointed me by professing some sympathy for the murderess. Admittedly, Queenie Chimes had a genuine grievance against her victims, but her revenge was out of all proportion to the original offense. I said as much to Alix and cautioned her not to permit her heart to rule her head.

She said, "Well, I can only hope that the whole sorry episode has been instructive for you, Bertie."

"Instructive—certainly," said I.

"Will you now admit that you ought not to have interfered?"

"*Interfered.* Alix, my dear, if you remember, I was sent an invitation."

"Which you accepted with alacrity."

"It was a perfectly proper invitation to a shoot. I wasn't to know that it would result in wholesale carnage—not of the human sort, anyway. What am I to do—cut myself off from society in case of a repetition? If you have your way, I shall end up like Mama, a fusty old recluse."

"I think the Queen is not so cut off from the world as you suppose."

"She's blinkered."

"Not necessarily, Bertie."

I heard a warning note. "What has happened?"

"A message arrived from Windsor this morning. The Queen commands you to visit her urgently." She sat back in her chair and paused before mildly asking, with maddening irony, "What do you deduce from that, my dear?"

A Note to the Reader

In the first volume of the so-called *Detective Memoirs of King Edward VII*, entitled *Bertie and the Tin Man,* the reader was cautioned that it was extremely doubtful whether "Bertie," either as Prince of Wales or King, ever found the time or inclination to write a book. It is even less likely that he wrote a second volume.

Unless one believes in automatic writing, everything in these pages should be taken as fiction.

Bertie and the
Crime of Passion

CHAPTER 1

Sandringham, May 1899

Paris.
  Paris.
  Paris.

No good at all. Do you notice how the pen twitches each time I form the word? I suppose not, if you are reading these memoirs of mine in print, but you can take it from me that in my own fair hand the effect is just as if a spider had walked through the ink.

It is hardly surprising.

I'll try once more.

Paris in 1891 was the setting for one of the most audacious adventures in my secret career as an amateur detective.

That, I think, is legible.

Eighteen ninety-one, the year I saved the *Sûreté* from obloquy. I must guard against embroidering the account, for these things sometimes grow in the telling, and I was so occupied in the drama that I kept no journal. Fortunately, certain other documents have survived, including several letters to my dear wife, Alexandra, the Princess of Wales (who was visiting her family in Copenhagen at the time), and I shall refer to these to curb excesses of the imagination.

The start of the adventure is sharp in my memory. Picture me at breakfast in my suite at the Hotel Bristol in the rue du Faubourg Saint-Honoré, where I arrived the previous evening with my faithful Irish terrier, Jack, and thirty-odd servants. Only the delights of Paris could tempt me year after year, each March, across the freezing Channel. It is the most enchanting of all cities. A surprising claim, you may think, from a future British sovereign, but I must be truthful. London is not in the business of enchantment, for it is the capital of the world, a masculine metropolis, soberly dressed, commanding respect, not adoration. I suppose of all our native cities, Edinburgh holds the most appeal, but for all its Caledonian charm, Edinburgh will never let you forget that it is built on granite. I definitely prefer Paris. I remember vividly toward the end of my first visit there, at thirteen, pleading with the Empress Eugénie (I adored her) to allow my sister and me to remain. She said she fancied that my mama and papa could not do without us, to which I retorted, "Not do without us? Don't fancy that, for there are six more of us at home, and they don't want *us*."

My secretary, Francis Knollys, ever the brake on my spirit of adventure, but a good fellow for all that, put his grizzled head around the door. His timing is uncanny, for I had just finished the last croissant in the basket.

"What is it, Francis?" I inquired as I shook the crumbs off the napkin.

"Your engagements for the day, sir."

"Not many, I trust?" One of the problems with Paris is that it's a honeypot for royal visitors, and if I don't watch out, I find myself doing nothing but visiting and receiving cousins and nephews.

"The Duc de Rheims will call at ten."

"That, I can endure, so long as he doesn't insist on standing beside me." (I should explain that the duc is a beanpole at least six feet six inches tall.)

"Madame Bernhardt is coming at eleven."

"Sarah! Now *she's* in proportion, charmingly in proportion."

"And luncheon with the Comte d'Agincourt has, unfortunately, been canceled at his request."

"Canceled, Francis?" This news surprised me. I didn't have any objection to time in hand, so to speak, with the bewitching Bernhardt, but Jules d'Agincourt was an old friend who wouldn't lightly have broken a luncheon engagement. "Did he offer a reason?"

"He apologizes profusely, sir."

"Of course he does, but what is behind this?"

"He characterizes it as a family crisis."

"Is that all? My family is permanently in a state of crisis."

"That was all he said, sir."

The matter continued to exercise me until the lady known across Europe as the Divine Sarah arrived to pay her compliments, wrapped in a cloak of gray velvet. My friendship with this peerless scrap of flesh and bone goes back more years than I care to name, to a first night at the Odéon, when she played the Queen of Spain in Hugo's *Ruy Blas,* with an exquisite coronet of pearls and lace fastened high on her red hair. She mesmerized me. I think it was, above all, the voice, that incomparable sound that ranged from the purity of a blackbird's song to the power of the great bell of Notre Dame. You may think I exaggerate; that, I promise you, was the effect on me that night. I fell in love with Bernhardt. All Paris fell in love with her. Such is my devotion that one evening I actually joined her on the stage to play the part of the corpse of her murdered lover in Sardou's *Fédora*—a splendid lark that only the French could appreciate, Sarah weeping over me as I lay in my shroud longing for a cigar and trying not to cough.

"Sarah, my dear!"

"Bertie." We embraced. The French are terribly demonstrative, so don't let your imagination run riot over a bear hug from Sarah. For some unfathomable reason, she had never entirely capitulated to my charms. Being French, she didn't mind everyone believing she had—which made my situation all the more frustrating. But I still adored her and looked to the future with confidence.

"So kind, so kind." I spoke in French, of course. I have spoken the language since my youth.

"What is it you are saying?" she asked.

"You are so kind."

"Ah—but why?"

"Why, your coming to see me here. You know I'm not too comfortable visiting your house."

She waved her hand dismissively. "In Paris, it's no scandal. It's nothing."

"I know that, Sarah. There's another reason. The last time, if you remember, a monkey sat beside me on the sofa."

She threw back her head and laughed at the memory.

I inquired charitably, "Do you still have the little creature?"

"Darwin? Yes. He's very friendly."

"I would rather be friends with you. And is the lion cub still in residence?"

She shook her head. "Stupid people complained about the smell when he got large. He wasn't smelly. It was hardly noticeable. I donated him to the Jardin des Plantes. But I still keep a cheetah and the parrots."

The sure way to charm Sarah is to talk about her menagerie, all of which, believe it or not, is housed in domestic rooms at her house in the boulevard Pereire. I don't mind talking about our dumb friends (my wife, Alix, is dotty about them and keeps a cockatoo in her rooms), but I draw the line at sharing a sofa with a monkey.

With nice timing, Jack trotted in and sniffed La Bernhardt's boots. For this understandable curiosity, my terrier was snatched up and hauled to her bosom. He endured it philosophically.

"What is the gossip?" I asked, steering the conversation into more familiar waters.

"About you—or me?" asked Sarah.

"About everyone else, of course. Is there anything I should be told about the Agincourts?"

She gave me a penetrating stare with those Cleopatra eyes. "When did you arrive?"

"Last night."

"Haven't you heard about the man who was shot at the Moulin Rouge last week?"

"A man shot?" I spoke so sharply that Jack gave a yelp and leapt from Bernhardt's arms. "Not Jules d'Agincourt?"

"No, not Jules."

"Thank God for that. You'd better tell me, Sarah. Jules was due to call on me today and has canceled. There was some message about a family crisis."

"A family crisis!" This innocuous phrase caused a hoot of laughter. The refinements of polite conversation are quite foreign to Bernhardt.

"Come, come," I said. "If someone was shot and it concerns the Agincourts in some way, I demand to be told."

She said, "Do you remember Rosine?"

"The child?"

"A child no longer, Bertie."

"Little Rosine was the victim? That's dreadful! She used to sit on my knee and play with my watch chain."

"Stop leaping to conclusions, Bertie. I'm trying to tell you that Rosine blossomed into the most beautiful woman in Paris."

Coming from Bernhardt, this was uncommonly altruistic, and I told her so.

She angled her head in a pose that emphasized her flawless neck and said, "I'm a grandmother now."

I said—and meant it, "That, I refuse to believe, Sarah."

Having fished for her compliment and landed it, she returned to the sinister matter under discussion: "Rosine became engaged. It was her fiancé who was killed."

"At the Moulin Rouge?"

She nodded. "The papers are full of it. I'm surprised you haven't heard."

"I haven't looked at a paper since I got here. An accident?"

"Accident, my aunt! In a dance hall? It was cold-blooded murder, Bertie."

"My word. That would certainly explain why Jules felt unable to call on me." I stood up, my sleuthing sense alerted. "Have they arrested the assassin?"

"The Sûreté?" She rolled her eyes upward.

"Then I must find out whether I can be of assistance."

Sarah now introduced a note of caution. "It may not be exactly as I described it. You know what the newspapers are like."

"You don't have to tell me, of all people, about the newspapers, my dear."

"Everyone likes to dramatize a little."

"Speaking of drama," I said, my thoughts galloping ahead, "what are you playing at the moment?"

"Nothing."

"Resting—is that the expression?"

"Hardly. A week from today, I embark with the Bernhardt Troupe on a world tour, commencing in New York."

"Excellent!" I told her. "In that case, my turtledove, you may join me in unraveling this mystery." Momentous decisions are sometimes taken lightly. Bernhardt had never seen me in fearless pursuit of a murderer. Who could tell what effect Bertie the

Detective might have on her? This could be the opportunity I had waited twenty years to grasp.

But she pursed her lips ominously.

"No, Bertie."

"No, Sarah?"

"I am insulted."

I stared at her. "But why?"

"I will not be likened to a turtle, even by a prince."

"A turtledove, my dear. That is something else—a pretty bird renowned for the purity of its note and the constancy of its affection."

"*Tourterelle.*"

"What did I say?"

"*Tortue*"

A foolish error, particularly as I've consumed gallons of turtle soup in my time. "But you will accompany me?"

"Impossible. I have to pack for the world tour, Bertie."

"How many trunks?"

"Seventy-five."

I blinked in disbelief "For the entire troupe?"

She opened her hands in a gesture of helplessness. "For my simple needs."

"You mean the costumes you wear in the plays?"

"No, no, the costumes travel separately, in fifty-six enormous crates. The trunks contain my personal clothes."

I resisted the impulse to comment; after all, it was her own fortune that funded this more-than-adequate wardrobe. "But you have a maid, surely. She'll do the packing. Trust her."

Without committing herself, Sarah asked, "Bertie, how exactly do you propose to investigate this mystery, as you term it?"

"I shall visit the Agincourts and offer my services. I am not without experience as a detective."

"A surprise visit?"

"Exactly."

"Royalty on the doorstep—is that fair, Bertie?"

"I shan't expect a fanfare, if that is what you mean. They're old friends, Sarah. I've known Jules for twenty years. Damn it all, he's not far short of royalty himself."

She clicked her tongue at my last remark and said, "We had a revolution, Bertie."

I refrained from pointing out that since 1789 France had crowned two emperors and three kings. "Well, am I to call a cab?"

"A cab?"

"I'm sure you don't approve of carriages in your republic."

She put her tongue out. She can be extremely vulgar on occasion.

I informed Knollys simply that I was going for a drive with Madame Bernhardt. Knollys doesn't regard my detective escapades with unqualified approval. Come to that, he didn't look overjoyed at the prospect of my sharing a carriage with Sarah. The poor fellow has more than enough worries, so I try not to add to them.

Montroger, the main residence of the Agincourt family, is a short drive out of the city, on the road to Versailles. We used a closed landau and Sarah prattled on so much about her forthcoming world tour that I was beginning to regret recruiting her as my assistant. I was mightily relieved when the main gates of the park came in view, because she had only reached Chicago and there remained at least eighteen months of the itinerary to discuss.

Montroger is probably smaller than Sandringham, but I wouldn't stake my inheritance on it. These Louis Quinze mansions, all shutters and balconies, can be deceptive. I must say, it looked strikingly like a house in a fairy story, with a glittering patina of frost on the gray slate roof.

Sarah insisted on remaining in the carriage while I went to the door. She was uneasy about our arriving unannounced, and I suppose she was right. The advent of the two of us, the Prince of Wales *and* the first lady of the French theater, might have been daunting. I took the view that, if nothing else, our arrival would succeed in distracting the family from their trouble.

When I announced myself, the girl who answered the bell behaved much as I expected, with a touch more Gallic hysteria than one experiences in England. I'm well used to it. I make more informal calls on my friends in France than is generally realized, and the domestics always act as if the Day of Judgment is at hand. It's to be expected, and I blame nobody, as I always make clear.

That first panic over, the girl admitted me to a reception room where there was a decent fire and a copy of *Le Monde*. I found nothing about the murder. I went to the window and waved the newspaper sociably to my companion, sitting chilled to the bone in the landau.

"Bertie, *mon ami!*"

I turned to greet my dear old friend Jules, immaculate as always in a morning suit and pale purple cravat. He crossed the room and embraced me in the French fashion, regardless that his cheeks got rasped in the process.

"You must forgive me for descending on you. I received your message that you have a family crisis," I explained, "but I couldn't allow that to prevent me from seeing my old friend."

His eyes moistened. They are a very emotional nation. He held on to my right hand with both of his. "Such grief!" Of course, I'm translating here. What he actually said was, *"Quelle douleur!"* and the way the French have of speaking the phrase makes it immeasurably more heartrending than the English equivalent.

How can I depict Jules in words? Unprepossessing in physical terms, slight in stature, with a long, lined face and a nose that preferred to hide behind a cigarette, and usually did, he nonetheless exuded charm. "But it is so uplifting to see you, Bertie. Let us drink champagne."

I mentioned to Jules that Bernhardt was freezing to death outside.

He gave a little gasp of amazement at the news, said that he was doubly honored, and insisted on going in person to the carriage to invite her inside. It says much for his character that he could still be so hospitable.

The shivering Sarah was escorted in and given cognac in preference to the bubbly. Because she was so cold, she remained wrapped in the cloak and her fur bonnet, striking a Napoleonic pose in front of the fire. Jules knew her well; how well, one prefers not to inquire, but then, Sarah is such an institution that most of Paris behaves as if it knows her intimately.

In the circumstances, small talk about the family was going to be difficult, so once we had the glasses in our hands and had drunk one another's health, I trotted out the old maxim that a trouble shared is a trouble halved and asked Jules if he cared to speak about the matter.

He gave a slight sigh. "It is a tragedy, Bertie. I never dreamed that such a calamity could devastate my family. Rosine, my only daughter—do you remember Rosine?"

"The last time I saw her was at Biarritz. She must have been about thirteen."

"She's twenty now, a young woman. Exquisitely beautiful. I'm not expressing a father's biased opinion, Bertie; I'm quoting *Le Figaro*. But *beautiful* isn't the word that would spring to mind if you saw my little Rosine now. She is racked with grief. I even begin to fear for her sanity, she has taken this so badly. And her mother, Juliette, of course, is in a state of profound shock. You must forgive us if neither of them comes to be presented."

"Jules, I wouldn't dream of disturbing them," I assured him, recalling Juliette as a domineering woman who wanted the family and everyone else to dance to her tune. Her state of profound shock was a happy escape for us.

Sarah added with more tact than I thought she possessed, "It is more than enough that you are willing to receive us."

In a low, expressionless tone that was so unlike his usual conversation, Jules gave us the salient facts. "Rosine became engaged two weeks ago to a young man called Maurice Letissier. The Letissiers are well regarded, a family who have occupied the same château in the Loire for three centuries. I know the parents well, and—without being snobbish—they are the sort of people one hopes one's daughter will live among."

"They race horses," I remarked, to indicate that I'd heard of them.

"Yes, indeed. They have stables at Longchamp, just down the road. I don't think Maurice was actively involved in the racing. His sport was shooting."

"What did he shoot—grouse?"

"Waterfowl mainly, I believe."

"So what happened? Was it a loose gun?"

"No, no. I'm coming to that. All this is frightfully confidential, Bertie. There's been far too much in the newspapers already."

I assured him warmly, "You may depend on me. I've held the press at bay for most of my adult life. And I'll vouch for Sarah's discretion."

Jules nodded. "I can vouch for that myself."

Bernhardt turned her eyes up to the ceiling as if she were in direct communication with the Almighty. I'd seen her do it before, when playing Jeanne d'Arc.

Satisfied that we could be trusted, Jules informed us, "The engagement was announced a week ago last Saturday and the civil marriage was to be on the twenty-third of June, followed by a church wedding the next day."

"So soon?"

Bernhardt said, "Bertie, in France we don't go in for long engagements."

"The details of the marriage contract were settled in a most civilized way between the families," Jules went on to inform us. "I found Letissier senior a charming fellow to deal with. On Wednesday, the young couple dined with the Letissiers at the château, and on Friday we took them out to Magny's."

"Magny's. I frequently dine there myself," I told him. "Was it an agreeable meal?"

"The food, you mean? Absolutely. One couldn't fault it."

"And the conversation?"

"Oh, Juliette, as usual, had more to say than the rest of us put together. If possible, the engagement had made her more animated than ever. It was an ambition fulfilled. Not that the rest of us were silent, but you know how she can be. We talked until almost eleven and then went on to a dance hall."

"Saucy!"

"Oh, it was Rosine's idea. She'd planned all week that we would end the evening that way. According to our daughter, everyone is going to the Moulin Rouge near Montmartre these days. Respectable people."

"I've been there," put in Bernhardt, begging the question.

Jules went on: "Rosine insisted that it was terribly chic and there was supposed to be a marvelous cabaret. I've heard of such places before and I was none too enthusiastic, but Maurice said it was a stunning idea, so I felt obliged to fall in with the suggestion. You can't really stand in the way of a young couple when you're celebrating their engagement. Off we went."

"The four of you?"

"Five. We had Tristan with us—didn't I say?"

"Tristan?"

"My son. Rosine's young brother. He's eighteen now, in his

first year at the Sorbonne. Naturally, the dance hall had his vote, too. We arrived about half past eleven, when the place was filling up with people coming from the restaurants. I was reassured to find that we weren't by any means the only party wearing silk hats, although it wasn't exactly the Alcazar. Some of the women we passed in the hall were blatantly *cocottes*."

"And good luck to them," said I smoothly, at the same time giving him a broad wink, for I happened to know that Bernhardt's mother had been one of the sisterhood.

"Oh, certainly," he succeeded in saying. "We were shown to a table at the edge of the dance floor and served with drinks. A band was playing for general dancing, so by turns we joined in, and I must admit that it was amusing to tour the floor with some of those exotic characters who patronize the place. Then at midnight, the floor was cleared and the cabaret announced. When I say 'cleared,' I'm referring to a space at the center not much larger than this room. In fact, it was the signal for people to crowd onto the floor in significant numbers and it rapidly became obvious that we would see nothing unless we abandoned our table and joined them, so we did. I remember feeling anxious about pickpockets." Jules sighed. "Pickpockets! If I'd known what was about to happen, I'd gladly have settled for having my pocket picked. We found ourselves in the thick of the crowd, with a partial view over the shoulders of people ahead. There were others behind us; everyone very excited, for this was one of the nights when La Goulue performed."

"That creature!" said Bernhardt.

Perhaps I should explain here that the lady who rejoiced in the soubriquet of La Goulue, "The Glutton," was at this time (1891) at the height of her fame, a performer of outrageous dances verging on indecency, yet unquestionably one of the chief attractions in Paris. Bernhardt's contempt may have been mixed with some envy.

"First we had the cancan, of which I saw very little from our position, although the music, so-called, was deafening, and then La Goulue was announced and made her entrance.

She need not have bothered so far as I was concerned, because all I could see of her was the strange topknot of carroty hair that is her trademark, but her partner, a tall, thin man of grotesque features known as Valentin, was more visible in his top hat, leading her in a surprisingly subdued dance. All around us, people were calling out and straining for a better view. It was not unlike being close to the winning post at the races. I'm telling you all this because of what happened shortly after. The *chahut* was announced and the tempo of the music quickened."

"*Chahut?*" I said dubiously, for the word means "uproar" or something similar in the French argot.

Bernhardt rapidly informed me that it was a dance, an old-fashioned dance recently revived and made notorious by La Goulue and others and involving two athletic feats, *le grand écart* and *le port d'armes,* high kicks that required the dancers to perform the splits in the upright position while balanced on one leg.

"*Chahut,* it became in the literal sense," Jules resumed, "for just as the dance was reaching its climax, the dancers leaping like beings possessed, the music at crescendo, the crowd shrieking encouragement, there were two deafening explosions close at hand. I felt a terrific jolt the first time and another immediately after as people reacted, uncertain whether it was part of the performance. There were some screams and I caught the smell of cordite, though I still didn't fully understand what had happened. Maurice, you see, was still on his feet, though mortally wounded by two shots in the back."

"Dreadful!"

"Yes, it was. The pressure of the crowd kept him upright. There was some screaming from hysterical people, but I think no one appreciated that murder had been committed on the floor of the Moulin Rouge until the dancers stopped uncertainly and the crowd drew back. I gripped Maurice under the armpit and someone else was on his other side. Between us, we were holding him up. We let him down gently to the floorboards. He made no sound. I believe he was already dead. Of course a doctor came forward and after a few minutes we moved him to a dressing room. I could, see myself that it was a matter for a detective, not a doctor."

"What an appalling crime," I said. "Is no one apprehended? There must have been a hundred witnesses."

Jules gave a Gallic shrug. "The Sûreté are investigating. They say paradoxically that too many witnesses are an impediment. It is difficult to find an assassin in a crowd."

"But who would want to shoot the young man? Did he have enemies?"

"None that my family has heard about."

"Could it have been a case of mistaken identity?" (You can see how actively my brain was working, reviewing each possibility.)

"They simply don't know, Bertie. Goron himself is at work on the case."

"Who's that?"

"Goron—*chef de la Sûreté.*"

"Is he any good?"

He stared at me as if I had insulted the tricolor.

Bernhardt told me, "Marie-François Goron is a legend in Paris. He arrested Allmayer, the King of Rogues, and Pranzini, the triple murderer."

"But he has failed so far to find the killer of young Letissier," I remarked in a way that deflated them both. "Jules, I myself am not inexperienced as a criminal investigator. A mere amateur, yes. The resources of the Sûreté are not at my disposal. No gendarmerie, no whistles, no capes. However, I have Madame Sarah Bernhardt to assist me, and—without denigrating Monsieur Goron—I venture to suggest that she and I are as capable of solving this mystery as anyone else in Paris."

Bernhardt turned to me as if I'd tugged her bustle. Fortunately, poor old Jules didn't notice. He was far too occupied trying to think what to say to me.

I saved him the trouble. "Of course you are about to remark that I shouldn't undertake so dangerous an assignment. It has been said before, Jules, and more than once. I appreciate the sentiment each time I hear it, I give my thanks, and then I ignore it completely. Good Lord, we're the oldest of friends. I can't turn my back on you in this hour of crisis."

His face creased with emotion. "Bertie, don't think me ungrateful—"

"Never," said I, placing a hand masterfully around his shoulder. "The decision is made. Tonight Sarah and I shall visit the Moulin Rouge to see where the poor young man was murdered."

CHAPTER 2

Feeling hungry, we stopped at the first wayside hostelry on the road back to Paris. The choice was a happy one, as it turned out, even though, amazingly, the patron failed to recognize either of his visitors. We had the dining room to ourselves, simply furnished, with a good log fire and an enormous dog asleep on the hearth rug—that is, until Bernhardt decided to embrace the "poor dumb creature." Nothing can be taken for granted where she is concerned. Having told me she was famished, she ordered onion soup and nothing else, while I lunched on chicken liver pâté (much of which Bernhardt fed to the dog), followed by roast quails in a mysterious and quite delicious sauce. On inquiry, I was advised that this small establishment employed its own *saucier,* who had no other duties. I expressed surprise, giving Sarah the opportunity to quote Voltaire's unkind remark that England is the country of one sauce. Unkind and untrue, as I pointed out, for what are applesauce, mint sauce, and bread sauce? She had no answer.

The shooting at the Moulin Rouge was hardly a suitable topic for luncheon, so I reminisced about the Jules d'Agincourt I'd known on happier occasions, at the races and down at Biarritz. "He is unfailingly kind. On one occasion, we took the children for a picnic in the country and the Agincourts came with us. This must have been about 1874, when Eddy, my eldest, the Duke of Clarence, was nine or ten. I say it myself—because I'm damned if I'll allow anyone else to say it—Eddy can be extremely tiresome when he's not watched. His sister Louise had brought with her a favorite doll, which at some point in the afternoon went missing. There was such a chorus of lamentation, with Victoria and Maud joining in, that for some peace and quiet we grown-ups were compelled to make a search of the area. I was convinced that Eddy was responsible and threatened to send him home directly if he didn't at once tell us where he'd hidden the wretched doll. The queen is always telling me that our children should have been whipped from infancy as we were, and I suppose they *are* inclined to rampage when excited, but Alix and I have never cared for corporal punishment. Well, to cut the story short, Jules informed the party in all seriousness that he'd spoken to a bluebird, which had told him that Elizabeth, the doll, had met some pixies and been taken to fairyland. If there were no more tears, he solemnly informed us, Elizabeth would be returned to Louise before midnight with a gift from the fairies."

"What a charming notion!" said Bernhardt. "Had he found the doll?"

"Yes, but in no condition to return to a sensitive little girl. Someone had taken a knife to it. Most of the stuffing had spilled out.

"Eddy?"

"I fear so. I was so angry that I was ready to forget my principles and warm his backside there and then until Jules persuaded me to ignore the incident, pointing out that every boy has done something destructive at some stage in his youth. That night, the doll, invisibly repaired, with, I believe, an entirely new torso, was returned to the nursery. When Louise found it the next morning, there was a crystal-bead necklace around its throat and a larger one beside it, for the child to wear. Typical of Jules's kindness."

"He's such a lovable man," murmured Sarah.

"He's not alone in that," I was quick to remind her, "but he has a remarkable understanding of children. I'm sure that Rosine and the boy must have had a blissful upbringing. This horrible murder—you *have* finished your soup, have you?—has obviously affected poor Jules the more because of his closeness to Rosine."

"Do you think he is too close to see?" said she.

"I don't understand you."

"Sometimes a father who dotes on his daughter refuses to believe that she is human, a woman, with a woman's desires."

Bernhardt is so used to projecting her voice that she must have been audible in the kitchen. I cautioned her to speak more softly. "Are you suggesting that there may be a second young man in Rosine's life?"

She gave a nod.

"A *crime passionnel*, eh?"

"Look at the circumstances," she said. "The girl has just become engaged and pouff! The man is shot down in front of her. It shrieks of jealousy to me."

"So we look for the rejected lover?" To be truthful, I was more than a little skeptical of the theory. Bernhardt's passionate imaginings *would* run to melodrama of this sort.

"You don't sound impressed, Bertie," she commented. "Do you have a better proposal?"

"For the moment, yes," said I. "I shall try the crêpes suzette."

That evening I wrote a short letter:

> *Hotel Bristol*
> *Paris*
>
> *My dearest Alix,*
> *Paris without you is indescribably dull. Weather barely tolerable—a wind from the North Pole, I am informed. Compelled to wear flannel underclothes, which always make me appear corpulent. But that's enough of me. This morning, I called on Jules d'Agincourt, our old friend of years past. The poor fellow was in low water, his prospective son-in-law having been dreadfully murdered in a Montmartre dance hall. Do you remember little Rosine, his daughter? Unbelievably she is grown up and the victim was her fiancé. The top man of the Sûreté is investigating and no doubt will make an arrest shortly. Scant consolation for the Agincourt family.*
>
> *I shall endure a few more days of walking the dog here before taking the train to Cannes.*
>
> *Kiss Toria and Maud for me. And my parents-in-law if I am in better odor this visit.*
>
> *Ever your loving Bertie*

The same evening, I escorted Sarah Bernhardt to the Moulin Rouge. Sometimes in the pursuit of the truth, one is obliged to venture into places one wouldn't normally patronize and make a show of enjoying oneself.

Montmartre is a revelation by night. No city in the world has as many restaurants and dance halls as Paris, and this is where most of them are concentrated. There's nothing special in that, you may say, but you should see their names written in flames in the gas festoons outside every one. You should see the magic lantern projections making spectacular sights out of dull stone walls. Above all, you should see the Moulin Rouge.

This temple for worshipers of the cancan was built by Charles Zidler in the year of the Paris Exposition, the same year that they erected that monstrosity, the Eiffel Tower. The mock windmill outlined with red electric lightbulbs has been described as an excrescence on the boulevard de Clichy, but personally I find it less offensive to good taste than Monsieur Eiffel's so-called miracle of engineering on the Left Bank. We approached the Moulin by landau from the rue Blanche, and long before reaching the top of the rise we could see the night sky glowing crimson. The sense of anticipation was irresistible to a woman of Bernhardt's sensibilities. She squeezed my hand and said, "*Là là,* Bertie!" Swathed in sealskin trimmed with sable (nothing was said about the dumb creatures who had supplied their hides), she brandished an ostrich-feather fan that she seriously suggested she could use to conceal her identity. Of course we were recognized the moment we stepped from the carriage.

One enters through a lobby hung with posters and peopled with vendors of flowers, bonbons, and less innocent wares. I paused at a flower basket to buy a knot of spring flowers for my companion's bosom and we were importuned by a dozen other sellers. A few choice words from Bernhardt ensured a passage through the glass doors to the foyer, where the reek of cheap scent and face powder assailed us. The demimondaines were there in force.

"Your Royal Highness, Madame Bernhardt, we are deeply honored." Some functionary of the establishment had spotted that we were of two minds whether to continue with this adventure and had darted forward. "Would you care to visit the gardens first, or would you prefer to take a table in the ballroom? At this very moment, Zélaska, the queen of the belly dance, is performing inside the plaster elephant from the Exposition. There are merry-go-rounds, shooting galleries, and donkey rides—whichever you desire."

We told him that we desired a table in the ballroom.

"And I should like to speak to the manager, if that is possible," I added. "Would you kindly ask him to come to our table?"

"Your Royal Highness—"

"'Sir' will suffice."

"Sir, I am the manager, Georges Martineau." Georges Martineau had the sort of physique that makes me feel slim. When he bowed, his face practically disappeared into his several chins.

"I am pleased to hear it. First, Monsieur Martineau, we should like to visit the cloakrooms."

He cleared his throat. "If I may be so bold as to offer advice, sir, you may prefer to retain your coats. It can be drafty in the ballroom."

I said frigidly, "Thank you for your advice, monsieur. Now, would you show us to the cloakrooms?"

(Answering a call of nature, I confide in passing, is no simple matter for members of my profession. The rest of the population appears to believe that the Lord provided royalty with a superior system of plumbing, but, alas, He did not.)

Comfortable again, we were shown to a fairy-lit table on a balcony overlooking the dance floor. The blare of what sounded like circus music was deafening at first; the orchestra—I use the term ironically—seemed to be engaged in mortal combat to see which instruments would prevail, the drums, cymbals, or trombones. Mind you, no one was interested. The players might have been silent, for all the attention they were getting. Every face was turned in our direction. And what did they see? Yours truly still in hat and opera cloak; Bernhardt rashly slipping off her sealskin to reveal one of Monsieur Worths creations, white cashmere ornamented with silver braid, with an antique silver girdle. Sarah is not a beauty, not by conventional standards, but I have to say that she always contrives to look stunning.

While Martineau called for champagne, I surveyed the scene of the recent crime. The ballroom was as big as Victoria Station and quite dazzling to the eye, thanks to abundant chandeliers, globe lights, and mirrors. Drinks were being served at small tables around the edge, and behind the massive pillars supporting the gallery on

either side of the long hall, people were promenading. At least, one
hopes that is what was going on. The lighting penetrated there only
dimly and some of the promenaders in my view presented a rather
Babylonian character. In the center, dancing couples wearing hats
and coats cruised sedately around the wooden floor, observed by
others chattering—and if they weren't chattering, I'm sure their
teeth were, for there was a wicked draft coming from the gardens.
I took out a cigar and our host stepped forward to light it.

"Now, Monsieur Martineau," I said, "shall we see the cabaret
presently? I can't sit here shivering for long."

"Very soon, sir."

"And is the lady known as 'The Greedy One' performing
tonight?"

"La Goulue—yes indeed."

"How did she come by such a name?"

"I think the explanation may be vulgar, sir. She is known for
her amorous tendencies."

She was not alone in that; I avoided Bernhardt's gaze. "And is
the man called Valentin also here tonight?"

"Le Désossé—yes."

"The what?"

Bernhardt said in English, "'The Boneless One.'"

"He is there now, just below us," said Martineau, pointing to
an exceptionally thin man—a veritable beanpole—partnering a
woman wearing a faded yellow coat and a black feather boa. I'm
no judge of dancing, but I could see with half an eye that they
were moving more elegantly than any other couple on the floor.
It was a bizarre spectacle because Valentin—this man guiding his
partner with such sinuous grace—had one of the ugliest faces it
has been my misfortune to see, his nose like the sharp end of a
pickax, poised over a huge spadelike pointed jaw. He wore a battered stovepipe hat with a decided downward tilt, as if to hide as
much as possible of the disaster. By the same token, his suit was
cut to draw attention to those supple limbs, the trousers tailored
like tights.

"Will he appear in the cabaret, as well?"

"Oh yes. He dances every dance, each night, sir. He can treat
a waltz in a hundred different ways. The women queue up to
partner him."

"No wonder," murmured Bernhardt. "The man is fascinating."

To restore some balance to the conversation, I observed, "I dare say dancing with such an ugly fellow tends to lend attraction to the lady."

"Oh, Bertie—he's a joy to behold!"

I turned to a more interesting topic. "Monsieur Martineau, I learned that there was a fatality here on the dance floor quite recently."

A quiver went through Martineau's more-than-ample flesh. "That is correct, sir, but I assure you we have taken steps—"

"I've every confidence, or we wouldn't have come," said I. "Where were you when the incident occurred?"

"On the step beside the orchestra. I announce the cabaret from there."

I glanced across to the wooden bandstand where the dozen or so instrumentalists were housed. "And where did the shooting take place?"

"Across the floor from there."

"How much did you see?"

"Very little, sir. Like everyone else, I heard the shots."

"This was during La Goulue's performance?"

"Yes, in the *chahut*. I suppose the assassin chose the time when everyone's attention was on the dancing. They crowd on to the floor for a better view and there's a tremendous crush. You'll see presently. There were two shots, followed by some screaming. The orchestra stopped playing and presently a man dropped to the floor."

"Someone must have seen the man with the gun."

"Apparently not. No one has come forward. The shots were at close range, sir. I imagine that the murderer had the gun secreted inside an overcoat."

"Come now," I persisted, "the people around must have been aware of what happened. You can't tell me that if some idiot standing next to you fires a gun, you don't look to see who he is."

"Your Royal Highness, I couldn't agree more—in theory. With the utmost respect, you haven't experienced the crowding when La Goulue performs. People jostle for position, trying to get a view between the hats. You may turn your head, but you are unlikely to get a sight of what is happening below shoulder level. The shots were deafening even from my position across the room. It was impossible to tell with any accuracy from where they had been fired."

His explanation was beginning to sound plausible. "How many people were present that evening?"

"At least five hundred. Friday is a popular night."

I turned to Bernhardt. "A curious paradox. If you wish to commit murder and get away with it, choose the most crowded place you can find." Then I asked Martineau, "How soon did the police arrive?"

"Within a very short time, sir. I sent for them immediately. We moved the unfortunate young man to the dressing room and they came soon after."

"You stopped the entertainment?"

"Naturally."

"And I suppose some people left the dance hall?"

"Practically everyone. It would have been impossible for me to detain them. I was trying to comfort the Agincourt family. Such a tragedy!"

"But the show goes on," commented Bernhardt acidly. "You opened your doors again?"

"Not until this week, madame. Monsieur Zidler, the owner, discussed it with Detective Chief Goron. The police were in favor. They wanted to interview some of our regular clients. The only way was to reopen. I've had detectives here every night asking questions. It isn't very good for business."

"Have they learned anything useful?"

"Not to my knowledge, sir. Monsieur Goron describes the case as an infliction."

"I'm sympathetic if he has to spend his evenings getting chilled to the bone," said I. "No wonder some people are stamping their feet." In fact, in the last few minutes the drumming of leather on wood had become distracting.

"They are impatient for the cabaret, sir," answered Martineau sheepishly.

We detained him no longer.

A drumroll signaled his arrival beside the bandstand, and I saw precisely what he had meant. There was excited shouting. People were already gathering on the floor, coming in from the gardens and down from the galleries, more than I'd realized were in the building—and this was supposed to be a thin attendance. You could see their breath mingling with the cigarette smoke on the cold air. Bernhardt was all for our joining them, but I didn't relish being squeezed by Parisians reeking of garlic and tobacco.

Martineau shouted, *"Mesdames et messieurs, le cabaret!"* A cheer drowned the rest, except for ". . . La Goulue!"

A gangway had to be forced in the circle before several dancers could run in, gripping their skirts. Behind them, alone, making the entrance of the star performer, strutted the woman known as La Goulue, in a red and white polka-dot blouse and black skirt, a black ribbon around her throat. She appeared preoccupied, eyes down, indifferent to the reception she was getting. I should have realized that it was done for effect, because suddenly she flung back her head, stared straight up at me, gave an evil grin, and shouted, "'Ello, Wales!"

A great cheer from the audience greeted this overfamiliarity and I raised my hat in response—to their greeting, not hers. Hers was infernal cheek and I was not amused. If I hadn't been there for a very good reason, I'd have left at once. I'm told that the lady is known to present her rear view on occasions, flicking up her skirts to display the scarlet heart embroidered on the seat of her drawers. I'm no prude, but I have to be thankful that she spared me that spectacle.

I shall be generous. What followed went some way to expunging the incident. Rarely have I watched a performance as exotic, acrobatic, exceedingly naughty, and hugely entertaining, but I shall not dwell on it here except to say that La Goulue transformed vulgarity into art. Other dancers joined her in the so-called quadrille— unrecognizable as the sedate dance of that name performed in English ballrooms—but one's eyes were only on this virago with the Psyche topknot and the kiss curls who flung herself into each movement with lunatic abandon, high kicking, shrieking, whirling, and leaping.

The climax was the *chahut* with Valentin. Now, I've watched the cancan performed in other places, and, believe me, it is tame compared to the *chahut.* If the cancan is mainly skirt and petticoats, the *chahut* is—let us not duck the truth—all legs and drawers. As if goaded by the antics of her partner, La Goulue flung her black-stockinged, diamond-gartered legs ever higher and grabbed her foot with her hand, regardless of the expanse of white thigh she was revealing in the midst of that froth of lace. Now she released the foot and let it go higher, higher, as if to kick the chandelier above her: *le grand écart.* Scandalized shrieks from ladies in the audience only encouraged her more. Spinning on one foot, then the other, wriggling and bending, vulgar and athletic, witty and alluring, she went through her repertoire of movements. Some of the contortions appeared impossible as she repeatedly performed the splits while standing on one leg. And always Valentin le Désossé was there to complement the movements, his gargoyle of a face expressionless, even when, in a final dervish-like gyration, La Goulue spun with one foot high above her head and finished by kicking the hat from her partner's head. Valentin, being the artiste he was, retained his dignity by catching the hat and replacing it in one movement.

Did I say I wouldn't dwell on the performance? Obviously, it made more of an impression than I realized. I must add that the cabaret went on for some time after and nothing came up to La Goulue's *chahut.*

It was past midnight when we left. Bernhardt had overindulged in champagne and was beginning to become embarrassing in ways that I'd rather not go into, except to state that I have always insisted on decorum in public places, whether in Paris or anywhere else.

My investigation—if it could be so termed at this early stage— had not advanced so far as I would have liked, and I took the opportunity to put some more questions to Martineau while he escorted us toward the exit. "I take it that Letissier was dead before you got him to the dressing room?"

"You're speaking of the incident the other evening, sir?"

"Does it sound as if I'm discussing the racing form?" I said with sarcasm.

He reddened appreciably. "You must forgive me, sir. I was instructed not to discuss the tragedy."

"Who by?"

"The owner of the Moulin Rouge, Monsieur Zidler. It is not good for our reputation."

"Your *what?*" said I, wondering if I had heard correctly.

"To come back to your question, Monsieur Letissier was killed on the dance floor, sir."

"There were no last words?"

"I believe not."

Thus the frustrating difference between reality and fiction, I reflected. There are always dying words in a detective story, the half-finished sentence that only the investigator can interpret. "And—you must tell me if I have it wrong, monsieur—you removed the body to the dressing room and called the police?"

"Yes, sir."

"Who was present?"

"The family Agincourt, sir. The comte, the comtesse, and their daughter and son. Also a doctor and his wife who were in the audience and certain of the performers who used the dressing room."

"That La Goulue creature?"

He shook his head. "This was the gentlemen's dressing room, sir."

"I can't imagine that would trouble her. Was Monsieur Zidler present?"

"No, sir."

"And was anything said that threw any light on the mystery?"

"Not while I was there, sir."

Bernhardt gave an exaggerated yawn and leaned her head against my arm. My tolerance was severely strained. I asked Martineau to see if our carriage was waiting. Once he was out of earshot, I reminded Sarah why we were there. She said she was ready for bed and I said she'd made that transparently clear. She drew herself away from my person and promised to behave.

"You'll have gathered that I'm taking a personal interest in the case," I told Martineau when he returned. "Was any suspicious person seen here on the night of the murder?"

"That's impossible for me to answer, sir."

"Presumably you know the sort of clientele you get. They come to enjoy themselves. You'd notice anyone of a furtive demeanor?"

"That may be true, but my duties don't permit me to study everyone who enters and leaves the place."

"Is there anyone who does?"

We had reached the foyer. The answer to my question was all around us in the shape of members of the scarlet sisterhood.

Bernhardt cackled like a parrot and said in English, "I 'ope you're feeling strong, Bertie."

I disregarded her.

Martineau coughed nervously and said, "There is one of our habitues who may be willing to assist you, sir. He knows most of the working girls. They confide in him."

"A pimp, do you mean?" I said, shocked.

"No, sir, the artist, Toulouse-Lautrec. He is responsible for several of the posters that you see around us."

I had vaguely registered that there were some particularly grotesque drawings displayed on the walls. They were all over Paris, on posters in the boulevards. Valentin and La Goulue were pictured in a crude representation of the dance. To my eye, all the drawings looked unfinished, as if the artist had wisely decided to abandon them. "If that's the best he can do, I'd hesitate to call him an artist."

"He's here most evenings, sketching," Martineau said. "I haven't seen him tonight, however. His studio is not far from here, at twenty-one rue Caulaincourt."

"Was he here on the night of the shooting? "

"Yes, he was one of the last to leave."

"And you say that this Lautrec converses with the wretched creatures around us?"

"He paints them. Sometimes he visits the houses where they, er, conduct their business and paints them. They all know Toulouse-Lautrec."

"He sounds utterly depraved."

Bernhardt whispered in my ear, "Bertie he is a nobleman. He is the Count of Toulouse-Lautrec Monfa."

CHAPTER 3

Hotel Bristol
Paris

Dearest Alix,

And how is Fredensborg this year? It cannot be more tiresome than Paris, where the racing has been canceled because the turf is frozen. That is not the whole story. The theaters are half empty because the plays are all written by philosophers. The latest craze, would you believe, is an importation from London or New York that seems destined to supplant the traditional French café; it is the "bar," complete in many cases with a British barman. I don't come to Paris to sit up at a counter and stare at a row of bottles. You can judge how desperate I am for recreation when I inform you that I have decided to dedicate this morning to art! As you well know, I can't tell a Leonardo from a Landseer, but I propose to visit the studio of a painter who is all the rage, I gather. I saw some of his work yesterday, scenes of Parisian life (interiors) done with a certain flair, though I can't imagine that his style would pass the selection committee of the Royal Academy. Not to prolong your curiosity I shall now reveal that he is a count, from one of the oldest families of the provincial aristocracy, the Toulouse-Lautrecs and the visit will be mainly social. Mind, I shall probably inform my new friend the count that my wife paints admirable watercolors. It's a pity you can't be here to give him

*some advice, because his colors seem to me to lack the restraint
that is so characteristic of your little masterpieces.*

*No news of the police inquiry into the murder of that young
man I mentioned in yesterday's letter. I decided to drive out to
Montroger and visit the Agincourt family to express our sympathy and see if there was anything one could do—unlikely, but
at such times the support of old friends can be a solace. Jules,
poor fellow, is visibly depleted by the blow that this has dealt to
his entire family. The others were too grief-stricken to meet me.
I gather that they were all present in the dance hall when the
wicked deed was perpetrated.*

*I am constantly looking out for a letter from Fredensborg, but
I suppose tomorrow is the earliest I can hope for. My love as
always to you, Toria, and Maud.*

Your becalmed Bertie

Bernhardt really is the limit. She gave me no clue as to what I
might expect on my visit to Toulouse-Lautrec; I think she wickedly
relished seeing me in a state of confusion.

By day—by a sharp, clear day in March at any rate—Montmartre
is another place from the one I portrayed in the previous chapter. The *bon viveurs* had abandoned the quarter before dawn and
the residents in respectable employment had left in droves for
Paris soon after, so apart from the occasional nursemaid, we saw
nobody. Rue Caulaincourt, where the count had his studio, was
a few minutes only from the Moulin Rouge (which, like most of
the pleasures of this world, is a disappointment in daylight). We
stepped from the carriage into a street of respectable bourgeois
dwellings that must have been built about twenty years before.
Number 21, a three-storied apartment building with tall, shuttered
windows, was at the corner of another street, the rue Tourlaque,
giving it the novelty of a second address. The third-floor window,
on the angle of the corner, had obviously been enlarged.

"That will be his studio."

"What time is it, Bertie?" Bernhardt asked me.

"A few minutes after noon. Even an artist should be on his
feet by now."

We made ourselves known to the concierge, who was clearly
a dyed-in-the-wool republican, for without batting an eyelid she

asked whether *Monsieur* Toulouse-Lautrec was expecting us. Left to myself, I would have informed the lady at once how persons of rank are addressed. However, Bernhardt subscribes to the view that a Parisian concierge ranks as royalty in her domain, and perhaps she is right. After an ingratiating speech from Sarah, we were permitted to pass. The count, as we had surmised, lived on the third floor, the one with the studio window.

"You'd better tell me if you've met him," I said to Sarah while we were climbing the stairs, since she seemed to be on familiar terms with most of the French aristocracy, and I needed to know whether a formal introduction would be necessary.

"No—but I have seen a photograph."

"That's not the same thing at all."

"It 'elps," she said in English, with an impish glint in her eyes that I didn't understand. Each time I think back, I become more reproachful of her conduct that day. I am not without experience in the machinations of the fair sex, but, believe me, Bernhardt is irredeemable.

I knocked.

There was no sound of movement inside so I knocked again, trusting that the concierge would not have sent us upstairs if the count had been away from home.

After a considerable delay, I heard someone coming.

"He was in bed," murmured Bernhardt.

The door opened a fraction. The shutters must have been across, because it was difficult to see inside. A whiff of cognac crept into my nostrils and that was all. I put my face closer and still saw nobody. Then the light from outside caught the shimmer of a pair of spectacles at about the level of the door handle. I assumed that a poor-sighted child had answered our knock. Bernhardt hadn't mentioned that the count had a family. I bent lower and started to say in an avuncular tone, "Good morning, would you kindly ask your . . ." when my words trailed off, because the crack in the door had widened sufficiently for me to see that the child had the head of a grown man sporting a mustache and beard. My sense of shock was the greater because, not to mince words, he was an ugly fellow, swarthy, with an overlarge nose and thick, moist lips. He was dressed in a flannel nightshirt that reached to the floor.

I am not sure how much of my astonishment showed. I know Bernhardt—the wicked hussy—would tell me if I inquired, but I have never given her that satisfaction.

I managed to say, "Sir, I must apologize. We have clearly called at an inconvenient time."

He adjusted his pince-nez and after an uncomfortable interval said, "Yes." There was another pause for reflection before he thought fit to add, "If you are who I think you are, I would have wished to receive you in better circumstances . . . Your Royal Highness? And . . . Madame Bernhardt?"

In the circumstances, it was as gracious a welcome as we could have expected. I nodded and took a step back. "No doubt you would prefer us to call again."

He opened the door fully. "On the contrary, sir. I can make myself more presentable, but I doubt whether I can make my studio more presentable, and since you have seen me already . . ."

One could only admire the little man's composure. When I say "little," I should qualify the word. I once met a truly little man, General Tom Thumb, who was just over three feet in height. Toulouse-Lautrec was almost five feet, but it is a trick of perception that anything a few inches below the norm appears freakish. To compound his difficulties, he walked woodenly and used a stick.

We were admitted to the studio while its owner hobbled back to his bedroom to change out of the nightshirt. Presently, we overheard subdued voices, and one was unmistakably female.

"Can you believe it?" I whispered to Bernhardt.

"He's popular with the ladies," she whispered back.

"A little fellow like that? He must have hidden charms."

She smiled. "They call him 'The Coffeepot.'"

I turned away. I can't in honesty say that I admired his paintings any more than the posters. There was a vast canvas lying against one wall that depicted a group of drinkers at—I think—the Moulin Rouge. It had been painted in reddish browns, ochers, and pale greens, with some black areas for the men's hats and overcoats. The people were drawn with some facility, but to my untutored eye, the brushwork was slapdash, the perspective faulty, and the whole scene at such an impossible angle that the drinks looked about to tip off the table.

"Do you recognize anyone, Your Royal Highness?" Toulouse-Lautrec had reappeared, decently attired in a morning coat and check trousers. Before giving me a chance to comment, he touched his stick against a figure in the background. "That, of course, is me, with my cousin, Tapié de Céleyran, the tall man."

"And the woman adjusting her hair must be La Goulue," I was pleased to be able to add.

"Ah, you know La Goulue, then?"

"We saw her perform last night."

"A phenomenal dancer. Let me show you some other examples of my work."

This, I realized too late, was fraught with embarrassment. He assumed that we wanted to buy one of his pictures. Why else would well-to-do strangers call? With the best will in the world, I didn't want a Toulouse-Lautrec adorning the walls of Sandringham.

He was tugging out canvases from a great stack behind an easel, and the strain on his small physique was all too apparent. "I am looking for one I did of an Englishman, an artist I know who studied at the Slade School."

Impulsively, I uttered a complete untruth. "It is your posters I admire the most, monsieur le comte."

He turned and the pince-nez flashed. "Oh, I don't use the title."

"But you are a count, are you not?"

"It doesn't make any difference to my painting, sir. People here in Montmartre call me Toulouse, or Lautrec, or Toulouse-Lautrec, or simply Henri. I was named after the Comte de Chambord, the pretender to the throne of France, but I am not interested in the royalist cause. I am a disappointment to my father."

"You don't see many of your own class?"

He laughed. "Not in Paris. Sometimes in Albi, by force of circumstance."

"So you wouldn't know the Comte d'Agincourt?"

"We have not been introduced, if that is what you mean. I know the gentleman in the sense that I would recognize him. I sketched him at the Moulin Rouge last week."

Bernhardt clapped her hands in delight. "Marvelous! Was that the night the man was murdered?"

"Yes, madame."

"You were sketching the dancers?"

"The dancers, the onlookers, the orchestra, anything that caught my interest. I am often there."

Bernhardt's eyebrows soared like pheasants at a shoot. "Then it is possible that you sketched the man who fired the fatal shots."

"If I did, madame, there is no way of telling who he was. I saw no one pointing the gun at the victim."

"May we look at your sketches?" She was ahead of me, I have to admit. I was thinking of ways of getting out without having to buy a picture.

Toulouse-Lautrec said, "I thought you were interested in the posters."

I said quickly, "The sketchbook interests us more."

Bernhardt said, "May we see?"

"I am sorry, madame, but you may not."

"You refuse to show them to us? We are extremely interested."

"That is evident."

"And if I offered to buy them . . ." suggested Bernhardt after a pause.

"I would be unable to accept."

"But why? What is there to be secretive about?"

"That is not the point."

"But it is. What if His Royal Highness demands to see them?"

He was silent, but the expression on those fleshy lips didn't give me any confidence that a royal command would do the trick.

Bernhardt is used to getting her own way and was becoming shrill in her protests. "Don't you see? A murderer is at large and the pigheaded attitude you are taking may lead to a second killing."

He said, "I never heard anything so ridiculous."

The dispute was fast becoming detrimental to our investigation, Bernhardt was pursuing it so vehemently. The painter and she were liable to end up screaming at each other if I didn't intervene, so I said, "If you will allow me, Sarah, I think we should explain to monsieur le comte why we are here."

She gave a sigh of impatience and capitulated by sitting on a chaise longue and folding her arms.

With the absolute candor of one gentleman addressing another, I explained that I was investigating the murder of Letissier for two good reasons: the first, that I was a longstanding friend of the

Agincourt family; and the second, that I was doubtful whether the Sûreté were capable of solving the crime.

"You can do better than the Sûreté?" asked Toulouse-Lautrec, sounding more skeptical than impressed.

I said, "I have had some modest successes as an amateur detective. Monsieur Goron of the Sûreté has admitted that this is a baffling case. I am not baffled. With the support of Madame Bernhardt, I am actively pursuing the murderer."

Bernhardt blinked and fortunately said nothing.

"A dangerous pastime, surely?" He picked up a sketchbook and I thought for a moment that my candid statement had won his cooperation, but then he opened the book at a blank page and reached for a piece of charcoal. "Kindly hold the pose, Madame Bernhardt." With no more preamble than that, he pulled a stool across the floor, climbed onto it and commenced a drawing of Sarah as she sat in her attitude of pique. "Have you considered the danger? The assassin has killed once, and that is enough to earn him a kiss from madame la guillotine. Why should he not kill a second time and a third? One kiss is all he will get. No, please keep your head quite still, madame. This will not take long."

I said deviously, "Perhaps if you cooperate, Sarah, my dear, monsieur le comte may be persuaded to show us the rest of his sketchbook."

Bernhardt said in a long-suffering voice, "He'll want me stretched out naked for that."

The artist smiled. "I am open to negotiation."

"I am not," said Bernhardt.

He worked fast. A passable likeness was already taking shape on the paper, although whether it would please the sitter was another question, for it picked out signs of middle age that Bernhardt probably never noticed when she looked in a mirror. I privately resolved not to submit to a sketch.

But I was not immune to his satire. "You must be familiar with Sue, Your Royal Highness," he remarked while continuing with the drawing.

"Sue?" I frowned, uncertain where this new avenue was leading and not caring for it. I'm not in the habit of discussing ladies of my acquaintance with comparative strangers.

He preserved me from making an ass of myself by saying, "Eugéne Sue, the author of *Mysteries of Paris*."

"A writer? I don't get much time for reading."

He said, "Forgive me, then. I thought perhaps he was your inspiration. Sue's chief protagonist is a prince, Prince Rodolphe, who visits the dens of iniquity and studies the habits and careers of thieves and murderers, exposing injustice and crime."

I said firmly, "Sir, I do not frequent dens of iniquity."

To which Toulouse-Lautrec replied cryptically, "I do. My best work is done in dens of iniquity." He held the sketch at arm's length and studied it. "You may move if you wish, madame. I have finished." He jumped off the stool.

"May I see?" Bernhardt reached for the sketchbook.

"Certainly. You may keep it." He tore out the sheet with her portrait and handed it to her. He was not parting so lightly with the rest of the book.

Poor Sarah—my sympathy went out to her as she frowned at the all-too-penetrating likeness. She said, "Is that how I look?"

The little man had the grace to say, "No. That is how I drew you, madame."

To forestall a second demonstration of his skill, I said, "We shall not detain you much longer, monsieur. There is much to do. It would oblige us greatly if you would give us your recollection of the fatal incident at the Moulin Rouge."

"Is that your reason for calling?"

"Yes."

With a shrug, he said, "My recollection will be no better than anyone else's. The cabaret was announced and a crowd formed on the dance floor as usual. Among them were the Agincourt party, new faces to me and quite helpfully positioned opposite me—I sit at a table on the dance floor—so I sketched them rapidly without knowing who they were, the distinguished older man and the youth so similar in feature that he must have been the son, and the mother built like a ship's figurehead and the rather pale, beautiful daughter."

"And the victim?"

"The man who was killed—yes. Like the father, he was in a silk hat and looked ill at ease so close to the dancers, who are rather risqué in their movements. These were thumbnail sketches, an artist's notes, of no practical value to anyone except me. Presently the *chahut* began with La Goulue and Valentin le Désossé as usual attracting all the attention. The next thing I recall were the two reports. People screamed. The dancing stopped and, as the audience drew back, the young man dropped to the floor. His hat fell off and I remember being surprised to discover that he was bald. Understandably, the people with him were very distressed by the attack. The victim was there some time before they removed him to the dressing room."

"Did you go over to see?" asked Bernhardt.

"No, madame, I am not very mobile. I continued to sketch the scene from where I was sitting."

Bernhardt's bluster hadn't succeeded in prizing the sketch book from Toulouse-Lautrec, so I decided to appeal to his sense of duty as a citizen. I literally stood over him and said with authority, "I really must insist that you show us your sketches of that evening. However rudimentary they may be, they are evidence, and one shouldn't withhold evidence, you know."

Rubbing his hands vigorously to remove the charcoal dust, he said, "Sir, I would not dream of withholding anything from you or Madame Bernhardt. If I had the sketchbook here, you would be more than welcome to examine it. Unfortunately, I do not. It is in the hands of the Sûreté. Monsieur Goron was here last week and took it away. I can only refer you to him."

I was so taken aback, I could only repeat the statement. "Goron has the sketchbook?"

"He is a very astute policeman."

Bernhardt spoke a word that I cannot possibly translate here; the effect is strong in the French, but several times stronger in our own tongue.

Without disguising my disappointment, I said to the artist, "You could have told us this ten minutes ago."

"I am sorry. I was of two minds. Monsieur Goron particularly instructed me not to gossip to anyone about his visit."

"I'd hardly categorize a statement to the English heir apparent as gossip," I remarked. "However, it seems you acted from the very best motives, monsieur le comte."

"I assure you there is nothing to be learned from the sketchbook," he said to mollify us—and I thought I detected a nuance in the way he spoke, the promise of something he was tempted to mention.

Whereupon, Bernhardt atoned for previous lapses by shrewdly asking, "Were you able to assist the police in any other respect?"

Toulouse-Lautrec vibrated his lips and looked away from us. I was sure there was some other matter he was tempted to bring to our attention if only we could coax it from him.

I said tentatively, "Something overheard?"

He shook his head.

Bernhardt said, "Something you wish you had mentioned to the police but didn't?"

This drew no immediate response except that he shuffled across to the bedroom door and drew it shut. Turning, he said in a modulated tone clearly not for the ears of the person on the other side of the door, "There was the matter of the gun."

"The gun?" I said, my hopes revived. "You saw the gun?"

"Whether it was *the* gun, the murder weapon, I can't say with certainty," said he. "I saw a gun. It was after most people had gone. Because of my stature and my slowness in walking, I like to let the crowd leave before me. I was left alone in the ballroom, although there were still a number of police and other people in the dressing room where the dead man had been taken. I was at my table finishing a drink. The lights had been turned down, so I suppose I was inconspicuous, even more inconspicuous than usual. I heard the sound of someone coming from the dressing rooms. A man, a tall, thin man, crossed the floor of the ballroom, which is the most direct way to the foyer, and I noticed that he put a hand in an outer pocket of his overcoat and took out a pistol, silver in color."

"*Mon Dieu*," whispered Bernhardt.

"He glanced briefly at it and then transferred it to an inner pocket and walked swiftly toward the exit."

I sent up a rapid prayer and asked, "Did you get a clear view of him?"

"No."

"Damnation."

"But he had a profile easily recognized. He was the dancer, Valentin le Désossé."

I felt my skin prickle. "La Goulue's partner?"

He nodded. "I didn't inform the police. You see, I know Valentin quite well. We have not been on the friendliest of terms of late, but he is still someone I would not wish to incriminate. I'm certain he could not have shot Letissier. He was dancing the *chahut* at the moment the fatal shots were fired. Letissier must have been facing him. Everyone was facing him, watching him. How could Valentin have drawn a gun and shot a man in the back?"

"It seems an impossibility," I conceded.

Our informant nervously fingered his necktie. "Now that I have told you, sir, I must entreat you to exercise discretion with this information. I would have spoken to Valentin myself if we had not fallen out over a poster he objected to. It requires more courage than I possess to visit him in the knowledge that he carries a gun."

"Is he dangerous?"

"How can one tell? Do you think you could speak to him without alarming him?"

"I shall have to, if I value my life," said I.

"And keep me out of it?"

"I make no promises, monsieur le comte, but we shall do our best. Where is he to be found?"

"His real name is Renaudin. He has a wine shop in the rue Coquilliere, near Les Halles."

CHAPTER 4

Les Halles has a vile reputation. It is known as the belly of Paris for the obvious reason that it is a food market in the center of the city, but to anyone who has visited the area, a more disagreeable symbolism is suggested. The market halls are surrounded by narrow, malodorous streets and alleys of intestinal complexity. Most of them date from the Middle Ages. It is a pity Baron Haussmann didn't flatten the whole of this squalid slum when he modernized so much of Paris during the Second Empire. The driver of our landau could hardly believe that people of our class intended to venture there, and I had doubts myself when we came to it. Passing down the rue Montmartre, you have no conception of what lies ahead. At some point, we left the busy commercial street and trundled through a cobbled lane lined with houses black with years of grime, almost every window boarded over. Regardless of the bitter cold, groups of men in clothes I would be ashamed to dress a scarecrow in, many of them barefoot and all of them stained the color of coal heavers by exposure to dust and mud, huddled in doorways, plotting the devil knows what. These, surely, were descendants of the agitators who had fomented the Revolution. The least decrepit and—to my eye—the most threatening wore the black jerseys of apaches, cut low at the neck and armpits, their arms covered only by a crust of grime. Some of these unfortunates no doubt resided in the slums of this street, but many were homeless, for there are no workhouses in France.

"We must be mad," I remarked to Bernhardt, "coming to this place to look for a man with a gun."

She said, "Bertie, I would cheerfully follow Valentin anywhere. He fascinates me." Which didn't address my concerns at all.

The rue Coquillière, when we reached it, proved to be slightly less odious than the lane we emerged from, yet not a street I would care to linger in. At the end closer to the actual market halls, a crowd of costermongers had surrounded a fellow in a countryman's blouse. He was doing nothing more provocative than carrying a huge empty basket on his arm. We were unable to hear what was being said, yet we could see plainly enough that they were prodding and goading him, and when the hapless wretch dropped his basket to defend himself, they kicked it into the middle of the street and pushed him into it, a spectacle that had them holding their sides with laughter.

With unfortunate timing, our cabman asked, "Where shall I put you down, sir?"

"As close to Renaudin's wine shop as possible. Do you know it?"

He did, and fortunately it was some distance from the thugs we'd just passed, a small establishment sensibly barricaded with iron bars in front of the window and casks of wine behind the glass. Bernhardt insisted on joining me, so after I'd helped her out and shooed away some ill-disposed dogs, I asked the driver to wait for us. He said he couldn't guarantee it; if he saw someone preparing to rob him, he'd be off and it would be up to us to find our own way home. I was indignant and told him so, threatening to have his license confiscated, but in his position I would have said the same.

The interior of the shop was built like a barricade. None of the stock was in reach. A sturdy counter supported two large casks, allowing just a small space between in which an unsmiling fat woman was framed. The bottled wine, the little one could see of it, was on racks behind her. No customers were ahead of us, so I asked if Monsieur Renaudin was available.

"What do you want?" the woman rudely demanded.

I remained civil. "Just a few words with the owner, madame."

"I'm his wife. What's wrong with me?"

I was tempted to tell her, but Bernhardt got in first. "This is His Royal Highness the Prince of Wales and I am Sarah Bernhardt.

Now will you kindly ask Monsieur Renaudin to step out from wherever he is?"

This impressed Madame Renaudin enough to make her turn her head and shout, "Visitors!"

It sounded as if we'd found Valentin at home. His wife remained staring at us as if we were from Timbuktu, and I suppose we might have been, for all the people of refinement she had seen from behind her counter. She was better scrubbed than the brutes in the street, yet she had the same Neanderthal cast of face, and one could well understand why Valentin spent most of his nights at the Moulin Rouge.

The scrutiny was becoming unnerving, so I occupied myself by looking around the shop—not that there was anything of interest, just more casks, some crates of empty bottles, a broken chair, and cigarette butts liberally scattered across the wooden floor. I glanced up at the crossbeams and saw last summer's flypapers still suspended there with their victims adhering to them. Then I happened to look beyond the flypapers to one of the darkest corners, copiously draped with cobwebs, and something moved— something too large for a spider.

My first thought was that I must have seen a bat, but I was wrong.

"What is it, Bertie?" Bernhardt asked me.

I was about to say that I was damned if I knew, when there was another slight movement from the same corner. Two eyes were watching me. Whatever it was up there had blinked. Bernhardt had seen it, too. She's an extraordinary woman. I don't think she has any fears at all. She crossed the floor to get a closer look and immediately there was a sound, the scraping of wood against wood.

I moved closer for a better view. A sliding hatch had just been drawn shut: a spy hole. Someone had been watching us from upstairs.

I said to Bernhardt, "We'll have to go up. I'm sure he's there."

Rapid footsteps from upstairs punctuated my statement. I looked for a way around the counter and found it barred by casks. Our progress might have stopped altogether if Bernhardt hadn't said, 'Look, Bertie, one of them is on hinges. It must be a door." And she was right. A cask had been sawn down the middle and fit- ted with hinges and a hasp and staple. I unfastened it and went through, only to meet a sturdier barrier in the person of Madame

Renaudin. Now that I saw the entire lady and not merely the portion framed behind the counter, I had a petrifying memory. In my youth, there were women known as dippers employed at Brighton and other seaside resorts to supervise the bathing machines and plunge the wretched bathers into the waves. These grinning harpies would stand for hours fully clothed up to their hips in water. Consequently, the only women who could endure the cold were very fat. The sight of Madame Renaudin reminded me all too vividly of the mountainous creature employed by my parents to force me screaming into the sea at Osborne at the age of six.

"Don't stand there, Bertie!" Bernhardt urged me and gave the woman—who would have made six of her—a volley of abuse worthy of the roughest fishmonger in Les Halles. Our way was cleared.

I mounted the first stair and prudently called out, "We are friends and admirers, monsieur."

If the man upstairs heard, he wasn't persuaded to remain. A strong draft from an open window hit our faces as we reached the landing and I caught sight of a trousered leg being lifted over the window ledge at the end of the passage. I dashed to the window and looked out.

Valentin—for it was he, beyond all doubt, in his battered top hat and brown suit—had shinned down a drainpipe into the yard at the rear of the shop and was in the act of climbing over a wall.

I shouted his name, and he ignored me. He jumped into the yard of the neighboring house and—so far as I could tell without falling from the window—ran inside the building.

"Aren't you going after him?" demanded Bernhardt, at my side. She seemed to think I was capable of matching Valentin's agility.

I looked at the drainpipe and knew it wouldn't support me. "Better to meet him the other way." Suiting action to the words before Bernhardt disputed them, I ran downstairs, dodged around the still-shocked Madame Renaudin, through the shop and into the street in time to see Valentin's thin form bolting like a startled gazelle toward Les Halles, with two dogs in pursuit. He must have come straight through the house next door to make his escape. He was a very frightened man.

Our carriage was still outside and there was a chance that with horsepower we might get closer to the fugitive. As soon as we had climbed aboard, I urged the driver to use the whip.

Like most cabbies in my experience, this one was a pessimist. "You want me to catch him? It's not possible, monsieur." "Of course it's possible," I said tetchily. "A horse is faster than a man, and you have two."

He didn't argue the point any more, but he had to turn the carriage, and then I was forced to admit that his opinion had been sounder than mine. We had lost sight of Valentin. Refusing to be defeated, I ordered the driver to take us with all speed as far as the first of the market halls, the weird umbrella-like structures of cast iron and glass where it was obvious Valentin must have gone to avoid pursuit. We would take our chances among the market fraternity. Having heard Sarah's repertoire of abuse, I almost pitied the fishmongers.

By this time, the business of the vegetable market was over and only a handful of tradesmen remained, sweeping and tidying up. They didn't include Valentin, so we penetrated farther. There are ten halls altogether, two ranks of five, with narrow streets behind. *Halls* is a misnomer, really, because they are open on all sides but roofed over with glass, supported by iron girders. We hurried through what must have been the meat and fish markets by the odors that lingered, eventually to reach the last hall, a more salubrious area where flower stalls were still in place and people were buying and selling blooms that I suppose had come from the warm south. Oblivious of any who may have recognized us, we darted this way and that, looking up the gangways. Some of the stalls were tiered so high that even a man of Valentin's stature could easily dodge behind them and be missed.

This was an obvious place for a man to be hiding, and I told Bernhardt as much. Imagine my satisfaction, then, when we caught sight of Valentin again. He appeared briefly between two stalls only about twenty paces from us, the nose and chin unmistakable.

Bernhardt shrilled, *"Là! Là!* Bertie!"

Valentin didn't turn in our direction, but he must have overheard Bernhardt's cry, because he immediately started running toward the far end of the market.

Now, I'm fit for most things in this life, but running isn't my sport and never was. Never mind running—a quick walk leaves me gasping for breath. I'm perfectly sure that even Sarah Bernhardt could outpace me if she was suitably attired; skirts tend to hamper the fair sex in feats of athletics. So it was pointless for either of us to go haring after Valentin. Resourcefully, I did the best thing I could think of—climbed onto a flower stand to observe the direction he was taking.

A vase or two of daffodils were tipped over in the process, for it was actually a handcart about three feet high fairly packed with flowers, and it required quite some agility to step up there. Bernhardt did her best to pacify the lady owner while I ignored the rumpus and watched Valentin weaving between the stalls at a speed I could never have matched. I kept him in view until the moment he left the hall by the southeast side.

"Right—let's get after him," I said, climbing down and knocking over more pots in the process. This time the stall holder didn't shout at me. I think Bernhardt had convinced her that she would get a royal warrant—*HRH Albert Edward, Prince of Wales, kicked over some vases on this stall in March 1891*—and instead she insisted on attaching one of her broken daffodils to my lapel, just as if it was St. David's Day.

We made the best possible speed across the hall and found ourselves in a street heaped with rubbish from the markets, where children were scavenging for anything edible.

"We need some sous, Bertie," Bernhardt told me, and without waiting for a response, she turned to the children and asked which way the tall, thin man in the top hat had gone.

The urchins looked expectantly in my direction. I have never found room in my pocket for anything so humble as a sou, so I had to part with several francs before we got the information we wanted. The thin man, they told us, had gone in the direction of the rue des Innocents.

Paris street names bear no resemblance to their character. The prettily named rue de la Lingerie down which we passed was unspeakably shabby and the rue des Innocents, with which it connected, seemed consecrated to venery, for there were streetwalkers parading even at this hour of the afternoon. This actually proved helpful, because two of them knew Valentin from the Moulin Rouge and had just seen him enter a place known as the *caveau*.

The waiter behind the bar in this establishment, a man of saturnine looks, said nothing when we inquired, merely pointed downstairs—down a set of narrow stone stairs between plastered

walls covered in penciled drawings and inscriptions that I hoped
Bernhardt passed without noticing, because the ones I saw were
unfit for even the most emancipated lady to inspect.

This was the *caveau* proper, a vault divided into three by arches
that lent the place a quaintly ecclesiastical air; indeed, I learned
later that this had formerly been a charnel house. It was now fitted with gas jets, by the light of which we could see six or seven
derelicts at a wooden bench engaged in a game of dominoes. A
blind man was playing a mournful tune on an upright piano. In
one dim corner, a couple were locked in a passionate embrace.
In another, trying to hide behind a newspaper, was Valentin le
Désossé.

Up to this point, I have to state that the lady at my side had
shown as much pluck as I, perhaps more. This was my opportunity
for a show of derring-do. Without a thought for personal safety, I
said, "Monsieur Renaudin, a word, if you please."

To my horror, he lowered the newspaper and revealed a silver
gun in his right hand, pointing at my chest.

I turned rigid. I think one is supposed to speak calmly to a man
holding a gun. I was dumbstruck.

There was a loud bang. I gasped and swayed back, certain that I
was shot, but the sound I had heard was a domino being slammed
on the table behind me. Rough men turn this innocent parlor
game into a show of aggression. It surprised Valentin, too. His
hand jerked up and he fired a shot into the ceiling. The report
was deafening.

Pandemonium followed. I threw myself to the floor to avoid
being hit and so did Bernhardt. The domino players tipped the
table over and sheltered behind it. The blind pianist grabbed his
white stick and blundered into the wall, his free hand groping for
a door that wasn't there. The young lovers fell off their chair and
disappeared under a flurry of petticoats.

As for Valentin, he was so shocked that he dropped the gun.

At this juncture, I acted with commendable presence of mind
by grabbing the stick from the blind man and using it to hook the
gun out of Valentin's reach. Bernhardt snatched up the weapon,
stood upright, and pointed it at him. Without a word, he raised
his hands. I got up from the floor myself and murmured to Sarah,
"Bravo!"

Behind us, everyone except the blind man was escaping up the stairs. If Valentin couldn't hold a gun without shooting into the ceiling, what would a woman do?

She would cope perfectly well, I was confident—for about two seconds.

Inconveniently, quite a cloud of dust had been raised by the commotion and poor Sarah suddenly erupted into a fit of sneezing. I grabbed the gun, which, through no fault of her own, she was waving about like a conductor's baton.

Pointing it steadily at Valentin, who had turned deathly pale, I told him, "You can put down your hands, but keep your distance."

He obeyed, his grotesque features rigid with terror.

I told him, "You have some explaining to do, monsieur."

It was some time before he succeeded in saying anything, and then it was only to ask, "May I sit down?"

We all sat down except the blind man, who was still pawing the wall. Bernhardt got up to reunite him with his stick and steer him to the stairs. Someone at the top shouted, "Are you all right down there?"

"Everything is under control," I called back, "and we should appreciate a few minutes' privacy."

Valentin said in a rush, "Monsieur, I appeal to you, while you continue to point that thing in my direction, I cannot speak a word. Not a word, not a word." A nice example of self-contradiction. He was talking nineteen to the dozen. The idol of the Moulin Rouge, the disdainful dancer who set female pulses racing, was reduced to a gibbering wreck.

Satisfied that he was no threat, I lowered the gun and examined it. A fine example of the gunsmith's art, I concluded. A silver revolver, elaborately chased on the side plate and along the barrel—a gentleman's gun, beyond question. I have one like it in the gun room at Balmoral, a useful weapon for putting a wounded animal out of its misery. I rested it on the table, out of Valentin's reach, but sufficient to signal that I was not proposing to shoot him. By now, his fit of hysteria had calmed somewhat. I would have introduced myself and Bernhardt, but it might have sent him into another paroxysm, so I contented myself with saying, "You had better tell us how you acquired the weapon."

He had gone silent now, his features rigid, producing a strong resemblance to those monstrous statues one sees in illustrations of Easter Island.

I prompted him: "This was at the Moulin Rouge, was it not?"

He managed to nod his head.

"On the night the man was shot there?"

"Yes."

"You've found your voice, then?"

He said, "Are you from the Sûreté? You sound like an Englishman."

"We are independent investigators. Please go on."

"Will you respect what I say as confidential?"

"Depend upon it."

"Then yes, I saw the man shot at the Moulin Rouge. That is to say, I heard the shot." His hand went to his throat. The scene was obviously vivid in his memory. "It happened right in front of me when I was dancing with La Goulue. A tremendous report, followed immediately by another. Everything stopped and a young man dropped to the floor."

"Did you see who was behind him?"

"No. I was looking down at the victim. I was very shocked." His brown eyes studied me intensely, making some kind of appeal. "Paris is a terribly dangerous city. I live in constant fear of being murdered. That's why I kept the gun."

"You're running ahead of your story, monsieur."

"I'm sorry. After the shooting, the poor fellow was carried to the gentlemen's dressing room. I believe there was a doctor in attendance, and the Agincourt family. The police arrived and went in. Most of the audience had left the building by that time and so had La Goulue and the other girls. I would have gone with them except that my overcoat was still in the dressing room and I didn't like to interrupt. I waited some time. The ballroom was empty."

"Not entirely empty," said Bernhardt. "You overlooked Toulouse-Lautrec."

"Don't we all?" I quipped, but my wit was lost on Valentin. "Pray continue."

"When I went in, the corpse was lying on a table, covered with a blanket. The family were talking agitatedly. I think the young girl was crying and the father was trying to comfort her."

"Who else was there?"

"The two policemen. The doctor had left. There was a middle-aged lady talking to the police."

"The comtesse," I said.

"And a youth."

"Tristan, the son. No one else?"

"No one else."

"Did you speak to any of them?"

"It seemed inappropriate. I raised my hat, picked my overcoat off the hook, and left. Only when I was outside did I put my hand in the pocket and find the gun there."

"You're telling us it was in the pocket of your coat?"

"I don't know how it got there, monsieur and madame. I swear I don't know."

"Why didn't you show it to the police immediately?"

"I was afraid."

"It was your public duty, surely?"

His mouth tightened. "You don't know our police. They would think I was the prime suspect. Anyone from Les Halles is labeled as a criminal."

"But you were dancing when the shots were fired," Bernhardt pointed out. "Hundreds of witnesses must have seen you."

"If the police find a man in possession of a gun at the scene of a murder, they are not interested in witnesses, madame. They expect a confession, and they usually get it."

All this was said with an intensity that I found persuasive. However, the story begged two important questions: Why did the murderer deposit the gun in Valentin's overcoat, and when?

Unless plausible answers could be found, Valentin's part in the affair could not be dismissed as innocent.

"If you are so fearful of the police, monsieur," said I, "why did you not dispose of the gun? They might have called on you at any time and found it in your possession."

Deep creases appeared under Valentin's eyes and for a moment I thought he would burst into tears. "You don't believe a word I've said."

"On the contrary," I told him with a trace of impatience, "I am doing my damnedest to find the rational explanation for your behavior."

"But I have told you. Les Halles is a jungle. Savages roam the streets in gangs. Through no fault of my own, I have a conspicuous appearance. To some of these brutes, my face is an incitement to violence. Returning late at night from dance halls, I have been set upon and assaulted three times. I go in constant fear of my life. Is it so surprising that when a gun is put into my pocket I should think twice about keeping it for protection?"

My thoughts returned to the bullying we had witnessed in the rue Coquillière in broad daylight and it wasn't difficult to put myself into Valentin's shoes walking home sometime in the small hours, fearful of what might be lurking in every doorway. I wouldn't care to attempt it without arming myself. Yes, the opportunity to carry a gun might outweigh the dangers of being found in possession of a murder weapon.

I picked up the revolver again and examined it closely to confirm something I had noted before without fully absorbing its importance. The implications, I now realized, were devastating.

"What is it?" Bernhardt asked.

I didn't respond. Instead, I asked Valentin, "Have the police questioned you about the murder?"

He rolled his eyes upward. "They keep coming back to the Moulin Rouge. I was questioned last Monday by the *chef de la Sûreté* himself. He simply asked me what I saw when the shots were fired. Nothing was said about what happened to the gun. I didn't lie to him, monsieur. It wasn't mentioned."

"Then with luck, you won't hear from him again," said I, a statement so morally irresponsible that I drew a gasp from Bernhardt, who had the grace to stay silent after that. "I suggest, monsieur, that you take some lessons in pugilism, because I can't allow you to keep the revolver."

"May I go?" he asked, relief flooding across the furrowed face.

"Let us all go," I said. "The air in this cellar can't be improving our health."

In the rue des Innocents, the lamplighter was busy. We watched Valentin's spindly figure scuffle into the dusk and then we made our way in the opposite direction as far as the rue Saint-Denis, where with some relief I succeeded in hailing a cab.

"Bertie, what are you going to do with the gun?" Bernhardt asked anxiously when we were aboard.

"It's safe with me," I assured her.

"It ought to be taken to the police. I think we should have escorted Valentin to the police, whatever he said. You can't allow sympathy for the man to outweigh civic duty. The revolver is vital evidence."

Her pious tone needled me somewhat. "I'm aware of that, Sarah, and I, of all people, don't need lectures on civic duty. I think you may form another opinion if you examine the weapon." I took it from my pocket and handed it to her.

She turned it over in her hands. "Is there some doubt that this is the gun used in the murder?"

"No doubt, so far as I'm aware," I said. "But if you will look closely at the chasing on the side plate above the trigger, you may understand why we are not at this minute speaking to the *chef de la Sûreté.*"

She held it close to her eyes and waited for the carriage to pass a streetlamp. "Well, I see some kind of emblem engraved in the silver. Is that what you mean? A shield with something written under it in Latin. I don't read Latin, Bertie."

"Look above the shield, at the crest."

"The letter A surrounded by these curly bits, do you mean?"

"That is precisely what I mean, Sarah. You are looking at the coat of arms of the Agincourt family. Unless I am very mistaken, the weapon that killed Maurice Letissier was from their private armory."

CHAPTER 5

That evening, I dined with Sarah Bernhardt at Magny's, where the cuisine has never failed to please. You will recall that the Agincourt family dined at this highly regarded restaurant on the night of the murder, so our visit was mainly investigative in character. Smile at the "mainly" if you wish, but who would deny that Sarah and I had earned a decent dinner after risking life and limb in Les Halles? Besides, there was much to discuss and my brain works best over a toothsome meal.

My companion was ravishingly dressed in another of Monsieur Worth's creations, sky blue damask lavishly trimmed with embroidered lace and pearls. As usual, she wore white gloves to her armpits, for she is terribly conscious how thin her arms are. At her breast was a magnificent brooch with the letters *LN* worked in diamonds. Without too blatantly staring at this area of the lady's anatomy, I spent an interesting time trying to decipher the significance.

"Who is he?" I asked eventually. "A lover?"

Smiling, she gave an evasive answer. "This brooch? I've had it more than twenty years."

"Yes, but whose initials are they?"

The emperor's.

I blinked. "You and Louis Napoleon . . ."

"My reward for a command performance, Bertie." Now her eyes mocked me wickedly, inviting me to decide whether the gift had been earned on the boards or in bed. I knew she'd had scores of lovers, but until that moment I had confidently assumed none of them outranked me.

Slightly piqued, I said, "Personally, I think messages in jewelry should be more discreet. My engagement present to Alix was a ring with six stones—a beryl, an emerald, a ruby, a topaz, a jacinth, and a second emerald."

I let her puzzle over this for a while before explaining that the initial letters of the gems spelled my name. "But of course," I was quick to add, "I could not duplicate the gift for another lady, however intimate a companion she might become."

"That would be unforgivable," she agreed, then added coquettishly, "but you would think of some other keepsake for such a lady, if one existed. You have a fertile imagination, Bertie."

"A fertile imagination, but poor credit with Monsieur Cartier, I'm afraid," said I, not entirely untruthfully. "These days, a monogrammed handkerchief is the very best keepsake I can run to."

She laughed, not believing a word of it. After all, we were dining at one of the finest restaurants in Paris. Who would believe that the Prince of Wales was so underfunded by his own nation that he was obliged to borrow from his foreign friends? Who would believe that he was prey to moneylenders touting for trade who virtually laid siege to the Hotel Bristol?

Over some delicious Ostend oysters garnished with anchovies and radishes, I returned to the vexing question of the murder of Letissier. "We can't duck it, Sarah. That revolver belonged to the Agincourt family."

"Can we be certain?"

"There is no question, my dear. In my youth, I was given an excellent grounding in heraldry and it is quite a passion of mine. I can recognize a coat of arms, be it English or French."

She said she didn't doubt me, but she felt it right to point out that it was Valentin le Désossé, and not one of the Agincourts, who had been caught with the gun in his possession.

I said, "That is immaterial, in my opinion. Valentin's coat happened to be hanging in the dressing room and the murderer slipped the revolver into the pocket."

"For what reason?"

"In case the police decided to conduct a search."

She set down her knife and fork and sat back in her chair to meditate on the matter. She had scarcely touched her oysters, but then her appetite is birdlike.

"If you're not going to finish those . . ." said I.

"Please do." She pushed her plate toward me. "Bertie, let us be clear about this. You are suggesting, are you not, that one of the Agincourt family must have fired the fatal shot?"

"That is the obvious conclusion," I concurred.

"Meaning Jules or his wife, Juliette."

"Or the daughter, Rosine."

"Or the son . . . what was his name?"

"Tristan, a mere lad of eighteen."

"Young males on the threshold of manhood can be very anti-social, Bertie."

"Insufferable. I've had two of my own," I reminded her while I helped myself to oysters from her plate.

"Then you don't need telling how disorderly the male of the species can be at that age."

I gave her a sharp look to satisfy myself that the remark was innocent. No one is more stern a critic of my two sons than I, but I won't hear them maligned by anyone else. I took a sip of Chablis. "I must have met Tristan when he was a small child, but I've no idea how he turned out."

"Nor I," said Sarah.

"It's a queer fellow who shoots his sister's fiancé in the back."

She said, "It's just as queer when the girl's parents do the deed."

"Or the girl herself."

A twitch of the mouth, the tiniest movement, told me that Bernhardt, too, had her suspicions about Rosine. "She faced a lifetime tied to this man."

"She'd agreed to marry him."

"Do we know that, Bertie?"

I gazed at her in mystification.

She explained, "The father's choice of a son-in-law doesn't always coincide with his daughter's."

"Sarah, do you know something? Is there a lover?"

"Intuition, pure intuition."

I told her candidly, "We should be dealing in facts, not fancies."

"All right. Do you know for a fact that Rosine loved Maurice Letissier?"

"Come, come, Sarah," I chided her. "People of rank don't marry for love. They do it to produce sons." As I spoke, I was all too aware how difficult this would be to convey to Bernhardt, the love child of a courtesan. Poor Sarah had loved many men and married only one, a Greek, on a whim of passion, and he had been utterly unsuitable, addicted to morphine, which had killed him at forty-two. How could a woman of her romantic nature and experience understand the fine discrimination that goes into the uniting of two young people of family? "In society, you marry the girl your parents invite to sit next to you at dinner. Love is what happens with someone else, preferably after you have produced an heir."

She said, "You can't legislate for love, Bertie. It can happen at any time."

"I know that only too well, my dear."

"Didn't you have lovers before you married?"

"I was not without experience," I said guardedly, "but I am a male. Young ladies of Rosine's class are entirely ignorant of such matters, and rightly so."

"In England, possibly," said Bernhardt with disdain. "You are in France now."

The task was hopeless. She didn't understand a word I was saying, and anyway, we were interrupted by the first violin from the quintet. He was at liberty among the tables, playing at people with a view to francs, so I finished the oysters to a rendering of some mournful chanson. I paid him and pushed the plate aside. "The only certainty is that we are faced with a domestic murder. Another visit to Montroger is essential."

The fish course I had chosen was salmon trout with whitebait. Before I could intervene, she sent hers back and asked for a smaller portion.

I told her, "I could have helped you with that."

She said, "Bertie, shouldn't we take that gun to the police?"

"Keep your voice down," said I.

"It may be important to their investigation."

I told her confidentially, "This may be a case the Sûreté should not be encouraged to pursue. Jules d'Agincourt is an old friend."

She frowned. "Are you seriously suggesting that we should obstruct the police in their inquiries?"

"I wouldn't *obstruct* them," I said in a shocked tone. "I'm merely proposing to pursue an independent investigation, subject, of course, to Jules's permission, and if you and I succeed in unmasking the murderer, the outcome must be more satisfactory from every point of view."

"But the murderer is almost certainly one of the family."

"Exactly. And the family is one of the oldest in France. They can deal with it in their own way. They won't want their name besmirched in the courts."

"Bertie, I don't think the police will approve of this at all."

"I'm not seeking their approval, my dear."

For this, she treated me to a lecture on the French system of justice that I won't bore you with, the gist of which was that an examining magistrate wouldn't take any more kindly to interference than the police. I listened with restraint, finished my fish course, called for the next wine, a Saint-Estèphe, and repeated that we would definitely make a second visit to Montroger in the morning.

She said, "You haven't listened to a word I said."

"Every word, my dear," said I. "Call me old-fashioned if you wish, but I put loyalty to an old chum above kowtowing to magistrates and policemen."

"Loyalty to an old chum! It's not a matter of sentiment. It's dangerous," she said.

"Why?"

"Well, if one of them is a murderer . . ."

"Oh, that won't arise," I reassured her. "No, no, the great advantage we have over the police is that we can go into the house as friends of the family. I've done this before, Sarah. I'm an expert at lulling the guilty into a sense of security. Now, I think the waiter is approaching with your pheasant and truffles. Let us enjoy the meal. Do you know, I'm beginning to get an appetite?"

And, my word, Magny's excelled themselves. The bird was roasted to perfection, those truffles looking like ebony apples. There's much to be said for the skills of a French chef, as I conceded to my companion, deftly moving the conversation into a different area of controversy. "But of all the cooks I have known, I award the palm to Rosa Ovenden, an Englishwoman of Cockney descent. Delightful creature. She is cook to Lady Randolph Churchill."

"And before that, she was kitchen maid to the Duc d'Aumale at Chantilly," Bernhardt said in a way calculated to undermine my claim. "Then she joined the staff of the Comte de Paris. She learned everything she knows from French chefs."

Warily I said, "You know the lovely Rosa, then?"

"I have sampled her cooking."

"Weren't you enslaved?"

"I wouldn't put it in quite those terms. She is an adequate cook of simple meals."

I would not be downed. Bernhardt is no more generous to her own sex than she is to foreigners, so I relished telling the story I had been leading up to. "The first time I met Rosa, I had no idea of her occupation. I was attending a shooting party at Chieveley Park and happened to slip into the dining room sometime before dinner in search of something to keep me going. I was not the first. At the sideboard was a stunning creature dressed in a white gown and sipping champagne. We chatted agreeably and I found her so charming that I couldn't resist planting a kiss on her cheek before leaving. But later when we all sat down to dinner, this vision in white wasn't at the table. Somewhat disappointed, I made inquiries of my hostess and it was revealed to one and all that I must have kissed the cook. After a moment's embarrassment, I laughed and then everyone else laughed, too, though a little uneasily. Then my hostess charmingly declared that I must have guaranteed them an excellent dinner."

Bernhardt forced herself to smile. The French sense of humor leaves much to be desired.

However, Monsieur Magny judged it a suitable moment to approach the table and ask if we were enjoying our meal. I assured him that the fare was delicious and Bernhardt added waspishly, "Incomparable."

I told Magny that we would appreciate a few words with his headwaiter and his sommelier over coffee.

Before that, I enjoyed a savory dish of quails garnished with peeled grapes, accompanied by Chambertin 1884, followed by some splendid rum babas and chocolate patisseries. Bernhardt had long since placed her napkin on the table, but she joined me in coffee and a small *chasse café* in the form of a cognac.

Having verified that the headwaiter remembered meeting the

Agincourt party on the evening of the murder, I asked him whether he had been able to observe their demeanor toward one another.

He said, "Your Royal Highness, I noticed nothing untoward."

I said, "You don't have to be discreet just because you're talking to me, my good man. Be candid. Were any harsh words spoken between them?"

The fellow was a typical stuffed shirt. You could tell straight away that he was going to say nothing of substance whatsoever. "I was not in a position to hear very much of what was said, even if I had been disposed to listen, sir."

"Of course, but you must have sensed the atmosphere at the table. Were they convivial?"

"Cordial would be closer to it, sir."

"Cordial? They were celebrating a betrothal. 'Cordial' sounds like a funeral. No high spirits? Toasts to the happy couple?"

"None that I noticed, sir."

"Do you recollect who was in the party?"

He described the four Agincourts and Letissier.

"At least we're talking about the same people," said I in some frustration. "No one joined them, I suppose?"

"I believe not, sir."

"Did you sense any unease at the table?"

"Unease, sir?"

He was a washout. A headwaiter should be as vigilant as a bride's father. This one's daughter could have married the sweep and he wouldn't have noticed.

"Be so good as to ask the sommelier to step over, will you?"

I suppose it is in the nature of their work, but sommeliers in general are more forthcoming than headwaiters. This one was not much taller than Toulouse-Lautrec, Oriental in feature and indeterminate in age, but with a disarming grin that displayed some wide gaps in his teeth. Yes, he had attended the Agincourts' table and brought them champagne. To his eye, they were going through the motions of an engagement party without the expressions of joy normal on such occasions. "Madame la comtesse had much to say, very much, and it seemed to discourage the others."

"What was she talking about?"

"Whenever I approached the table, the subject of her discourse was the impossibility of finding reliable servants."

"They were discussing the servant problem at an engagement party?" said Bernhardt in disbelief.

"The comtesse was expounding her views, madame. It was not a discussion. She held forth from the hors d'oeuvres to the savories and no one seemed willing to change the subject."

"Perhaps she was giving advice to the young couple," said Bernhardt.

"No doubt you are right, madame."

"There must have been some breaks in this monologue," said I.

"Once started, the comtesse is like—" He stopped himself.

"A steam engine? We know the lady," said I. "However, one of the party was murdered later in the evening, as I'm sure you know. Are you able to tell us anything at all about the others at the table? The daughter, for instance?"

He put a hand to the silver corkscrew that he wore on a chain suspended from his neck and stroked it thoughtfully. "May I be frank, sir? She is a stunningly beautiful young girl, but that evening she was not so radiant as others I have seen on similar occasions. Her eyes should have flashed like the chandeliers. They were almost opaque."

"How extraordinary! And her manner?"

"Demure and dignified."

Sarah exchanged a glance with me that said I had better take seriously her theory about a lover.

"Tell us about the others," I urged the man. "About Letissier. How was his behavior?"

"My impression was that he was not displeased. Slightly ill at ease, perhaps, but no more than one would expect when his new fiancée was looking so wan. Yes, I would say that he was acting normally under the circumstances. And the comte, too, was doing his best to raise the spirits of the party by ordering some excellent wines. He knows the great years and he is generous enough to order them."

"But he wasn't interrupting his wife?"

"You mentioned that you know the comtesse, sir?"

"Point taken. That leaves the son, young Tristan. How was he holding up under *Mamans* dissertation?"

"When he wasn't actually eating, his eyes were on his sister, sir."

"Interesting. He was sensitive to her mood, I take it?"

"That is difficult for me to say, sir."

I nodded. The sommelier had more than compensated for the headwaiter's blandness and I thanked him warmly and put something into his hand.

I gestured to Magny and called him to the table. "We have had an excellent evening, patron, so I shall let you into a secret about one of your confrères. It was some years ago in another restaurant and the Swiss waiter was making pancakes for me beside the table on one of those contraptions."

"Flambé?"

"Exactly. Unfortunately, the poor fellow betrayed some nerves and it was quite obvious that he was burning the first one. It was thin as lace. I told him not to be dismayed but to baste it immediately with curaçao and brandy, which he did. The result was delicious. That evening, we had discovered a new delicacy. He asked me if I would permit him to name it after his sweetheart. I suppose I could have insisted that he name it after me, but I am magnanimous about such matters. Instead of crêpes bertie, we gave the world crêpes suzette."

"*Magnifique,* Your Royal Highness!"

"Is this true?" said Bernhardt.

"You can ask the waiter concerned. He has an establishment not far from here. His name is Cesar Ritz."

Magny held up his hands, bereft of speech.

"All of which leads me to add," I continued, "that a few crêpes suzette and a little more champagne would not come amiss at the conclusion of this excellent meal. What do you say, Sarah?"

CHAPTER 6

Knollys, my private secretary, was fussing as usual when I called at the Bristol next morning to walk my dog.

"We had no idea where to look for you, sir."

"Splendid," I said.

"But your bed wasn't slept in."

"Francis, this is Paris, not Balmoral," I told him good-naturedly. "The city wakes up at night. You should get out and see for yourself. Meet a charming mademoiselle and take her to a show and dinner afterward. It'll do you no end of good and you'll very soon understand why my bed wasn't slept in."

He said, "I'm fifty-three years old, sir."

I said, "Well, I hope if I'm spared to live so long I won't consider it an impediment to pleasure. Oh, I appreciate your concern, Francis, really I do, but it isn't necessary."

As it happens, I was a little tetchy from having spent another innocent night with Bernhardt. After Magny's, the lady had insisted on visiting an extraordinary entertainment in the boulevard de Rochechouart, with a notice outside that proclaimed: *Le Mirliton, for Audiences that Enjoy Being Insulted.* A vulgar man called Bruant, dressed in velvet and a wide-brimmed hat, had fulfilled the promise with a series of unrepeatable songs and repartee that Sarah found enchanting but that I didn't particularly care for. I put up with it manfully until dawn was breaking, seeing that she was so enraptured, and then took her for an early breakfast, but afterward

I fell asleep in the cab on the way back to her apartment. It was the driver who wakened me in front of the Bristol, acting, he said, on Madame Bernhardt's instruction, she having left the cab and paid our fare.

"What do you have for me this morning?" I asked Knollys. "Any post?"

There was a letter from Fredensborg—at last.

Fredensborg Castle

Beloved Bertie,

I am writing this at once in response to your letter, which has just arrived. What dreadful tidings for the Agincourts! Such a kind, devoted family. I remember Rosine as a pretty child in ringlets and I can scarcely believe that she is old enough to have become engaged—but then our own darling boys grew up too fast. Life moves on so rapidly and so much that one has to face is cruel. God knows, we have had our share of heartbreak, but nothing so violent as this tragedy that the Agincourts must endure. When you send our condolences to Jules and Juliette (and Rosine, of course), be sure to mention that they are in my prayers.

And now, my dearest, I venture to say something that you may find difficult to accept. I have never sought actively to curtail your freedom, nor would I, but these are difficult times—you said to me yourself that we are walking on eggs until that disagreeable business about the game of baccarat at Tranby Croft is resolved in the courts—and I have a strange presentiment that out of your generous nature you run the risk of becoming involved in the unhappy event that has befallen the Agincourts. You declare confidently that the Sûreté will make an arrest shortly, but what if they do not?

Bertie dearest, we both know that from time to time you have interested yourself in an active way in cases of murder, and yes, I admit, the guilty parties were eventually apprehended. This time, if the opportunity arose, you would be in no position to usurp the role of the detective police, and even if you were, the risks of being misunderstood are too appalling to contemplate. Paris may seem like a second home, but you are still in a foreign country. Their methods are not ours. With Tranby Croft hanging over us,

we cannot afford more misunderstanding and the scandal that
always comes in its wake. So I implore you most earnestly not to
involve yourself in the Agincourts' tragedy, however much your
chivalrous feelings may prompt you.

Now to other matters. If Paris is so cold—and I can believe
it, for we have twelve degrees of frost in Copenhagen today—why
don't you travel immediately to the Riviera? I am sure Francis
Knollys would make the arrangements speedily. He never seems
entirely relaxed in Paris. And I do not like to think of you in a
state of boredom.

For me, here in the castle, life is tolerable, though I do wish
they would serve something besides currant jelly for dessert. It is
a great consolation to have Toria and Maud with me and we
play loo every evening, but I think constantly of Louise, praying
that she will not deliver prematurely. I am determined to be home
in good time.

Write again soon, my dearest. Remember I shall look first at
the postmark to see where you are.

Ever your devoted Alix

Poor Alix! She is utterly loyal to her aged parents, but in truth,
every hour she spends in Fredensborg is like a prison sentence.
Part of the problem, I think (though she never admits it), is the
difficulty of communication, for the old couple are both very deaf
and so is Alix. A family conversation sounds like the Trooping of
the Color.

The rest of the letter was predictable, and of course matters had
moved on so rapidly since it was written that Alix couldn't possibly
expect me to follow her advice in every particular. What a good
thing her thoughts were so taken up with Louise's pregnancy and
the forthcoming arrival of our first grandchild.

I stuffed the letter into my pocket, called for my terrier, Jack,
and went for a stroll in the Champs-Elysees. The sun was out at last.

For the rest of the morning, I was forced to take a nap.

JULES D'AGINCOURT WAS SURPRISED TO see Bernhardt and me on
his doorstep a second time, but he took it in good part. Having
invited us inside and poured us cognacs, he said, "I need not ask
why you are here. The police are getting nowhere."

"Have they been back?" I asked.

"The *chef de la Sûreté* himself had long interviews yesterday with Juliette and Rosine. But he should be making his inquiries in Montmartre, not here."

I gently disabused him of this opinion. "Jules, the police may not be so far astray as you believe. They do not know it yet, but this was found hidden at the Moulin Rouge on the evening of the murder." I handed him the revolver with the Agincourt coat of arms.

He let it rest on his hands and stared at it in silence for a long time.

Finally he said in a voice tremulous with emotion, "Found at the Moulin Rouge?"

"And recovered later by Sarah and me."

I watched him keenly. After all, no investigator worthy of the name can permit friendship to get in the way of the truth. Those patrician features and the pale blue eyes and the lines around them that formed into an expression of absolute geniality when he smiled (and you always expected him to) had to be treated as suspicious. I had always taken his intelligence to be a force for good and never known any cause to doubt that assumption, but I understand enough about human nature to know that in extremis a clever mind may be artful in deceit.

His lips formed a word and then closed as if his voice was unable to function. He made another try. "You said the police are not informed yet?"

"That is so."

"It means . . ." He was unable to go on.

I said, "We believe the truth is to be found in this house, Jules."

He lowered his head. I can't begin to tell you how distressing it was to see my old friend in such a state of shock, but I had to be firm with him.

I lifted the revolver from his open palms. "We have a choice. We can hand this to the police. Or we can conduct our own investigation here, in the family and among friends."

He managed to say, "The latter."

I told him that in that case we would require his cooperation in persuading the rest of his family to submit to questioning.

The voice tried to be steady. "I shall see to it."

"Not yet," I said. "Before we go any further, Sarah and I would like to know where this gun was kept."

"It's from the gun room. All the firearms are kept there."

"May we see?"

The way to the gun room was through the dining room and the smoking room and across a cobbled courtyard. He led us there and pushed open the door.

I said, "You don't keep it locked, I notice."

"There is a key," he pointed out.

"Yes, but it's not much use if you don't remove it when the door is shut."

"Bertie, I've never had reason to lock it—or never thought I had," Jules said, sounding sheepish. He pushed open the door.

Reader, I have seen the gun rooms of every great house in England and Scotland and, believe me, this would have ranked among the finest. Oak paneled and as high as a coach house (which I dare say had been its original purpose), it was furnished with twenty or more rosewood gun cabinets, each holding a dozen shotguns. The walls just below the open beams were hung with the mounted heads of animals bagged by Agincourts over half a century, including wild boar and some big game. At a lower level were a series of exquisite oil paintings of hunting scenes. They were interspersed with photographs of shooting parties. The floor was carpeted and dominated by two magnificent tiger skin rugs. The morning newspapers lay undisturbed on a table. The pleasant smell of cigars lingered. A black retriever was asleep on the hearth, at least until Bernhardt gave a cry of delight and woke the poor beast.

I am not by temperament a sybarite, but I could easily picture myself resorting to this companionable room on a foggy morning when shooting was impossible, fanning my hands in front of the huge log fire before settling into one of the leather lounging chairs with a glass of sherry and a volume of Surtees (or his French equivalent) from the bookshelves behind the door. In fact, the atmosphere was more to my liking than the smoking room. In no way could one think of the room simply as an armory.

"I spend many a cozy hour in here," Jules said, reading my thoughts. "I've never cared to keep it locked."

"So anyone may come in?"

"Yes."

"Including the ladies?" Bernhardt inquired, looking up from where the dog was lying in a most undignified position having its chest massaged.

"Certainly, when they wish."

"And do they?"

"Not as a rule, but occasionally they'll come for a newspaper or a book."

"Or a gun, if they had a use for it," said I, quick to catch the drift of Bernhardt's questions.

Jules missed the point entirely. "The ladies in this house don't go in for field sports."

"Where do you keep the pistols? I don't see any on display."

"They're in the top drawer of the gun cabinet at the end, or should be," Jules informed us. "We possess four revolvers, all engraved with our coat of arms." He went to the cabinet he had pointed out and opened the drawer. It was not kept locked, I noticed. Clearly, no one had seen any reason to enforce security.

"How many are left?" I asked with a strong hint of irony. To tell the truth, I was not a little shocked by the easy access to the weaponry. Given that Jules liked using the room to lounge in, you would think that he'd still see the wisdom of keeping the cabinets locked.

"Three."

I looked inside. The silver guns lay in no particular arrangement on the black velvet lining among a scattering of loose cartridges. "Would you by any chance have checked this drawer in the past few days?"

He shook his head. "I had no reason to."

"So you had no idea that one of these revolvers was missing?"

"No idea at all." He looked apologetic, but what use was that?

"Tell me, Jules, in the week of the murder—that is, the days before the murder took place—do you recall any visitors, anyone who might conceivably have come in here?"

He fingered his cravat as he made an effort to remember. "No, we've had no visitors recently, other than Maurice, rest his soul. Lord, I shouldn't say this, but I wish there *were* someone else."

"Is there any one of the servants you might suspect of taking the gun?"

"The servants." He sighed and frowned. "Most of my staff have been with me for years. I can't believe they would steal from me."

"It's not so unusual," said Bernhardt, trying to be helpful. "I once caught my maid wearing my underclothes. I found out only when my pet monkey got under her skirt and made her jump onto a chair. A lady's maid wearing a Breton-laced petticoat from Beer's! My God, she was out of my house in thirty seconds."

"Sans petticoat?" said I.

"Sans everything except the mark of my boot on her derriere."

Jules listened blankly. Not even an image like that would lift his spirits.

At my suggestion, we prodded the fire into more activity, threw on a couple of logs, and sat in front of it in the huge leather armchairs. Sarah had already draped herself on one of the tiger skins, where she could fondle the by now utterly shameless gundog. I wanted Jules to relax sufficiently to tell us how young Letissier had met Rosine and how each member of the family had reacted to the prospect of this outsider becoming one of them. He began with much sighing and hesitation, as if the exercise was too painful to undertake, but with no end of coaxing from Bernhardt and me, he gradually became more fluent.

"How were they introduced?" He echoed my question. "I think it must have been at a dinner party."

"A dinner party?"

"It could have been somewhere else," he hedged. "A salon. No, it was supper in Cubat's."

"I know Cubat's," I said, for he was speaking of one of the better restaurants in Paris. Cubat was the former chef to the Tsar, and the Romanov family know how to eat well. "So they met over supper?"

"It was during the Grande Semaine the year before last. 1889, the year of the Exposition."

"The Grande Semaine. No wonder your memory was hazy," said I.

The Grande Semaine, reader, is the climax of the Paris season, a week of racing in August followed every night by balls, parties, and suppers that last until dawn, a social program so exhausting that it can only be undertaken in the knowledge that immediately the week is over, everyone departs for the summer resorts.

Jules explained, "The whole thing was got up at Longchamp

by some Yankee millionaire in a straw hat who was looking in at all the boxes, announcing, 'Cubat's at midnight. See you there.' It became quite a joke along the racecourse. As soon as one of us spotted a friend, we all chanted in chorus, 'Cubat's at midnight. See you there.' And so we had to be there."

"All the family?"

"Yes, Tristan had finished at the lycée."

"Cubat's must have been crowded that night," Bernhardt prompted him after a longish pause.

"Crowded, oh, yes. But it was a gloriously warm evening and the tables were laid in long rows in the garden. A candlelit supper. No prearranged seating. Americans like informality, don't they? And that was how we found ourselves at a table with Maurice Letissier. He was seated at the end, as if he was presiding, and in a way he did, because the waiter couldn't get to everyone along the table, it was such a crush. Maurice called us all to attention at the appropriate moment and announced the soup of the day and so on. He did it all with great charm and wit."

"You were impressed by him?"

"One couldn't fail to have been."

"Was he handsome?" Sarah asked.

"Not by conventional standards, but he was very animated, very articulate, and I'm sure the ladies found him attractive. He sported a particularly fine mustache. He was seated beside Juliette and for once my dear wife didn't monopolize the conversation. She was intrigued by the young man."

"And where was Rosine seated?"

"Along the table, on my left, close enough to observe Maurice without exchanging too many words."

"Was it love at first sight?" Bernhardt asked.

"I think he fell for Rosine straight away, yes. His eyes hardly left her."

"And Rosine?"

Jules hesitated. "She was only eighteen at the time."

"An impressionable age."

"That's a fact!"

My remark had hit the bull.

"Well, you may as well know that Rosine was already in love with someone else," he added. "Someone utterly unsuitable."

At this, Bernhardt sank her hand so powerfully into the retriever's furry chest that the creature gave a yelp and scampered under the table for refuge. "So there *is* a lover."

Jules covered his mouth as if he'd said too much.

"Unsuitable in which way?" I pressed him. When he declined to answer, I said, "I realize how delicate this matter must be, Jules, but clearly it has some bearing upon our investigation. I must insist that you tell us."

He shifted in the chair. "Sarah, you will understand what I am saying, but bear with me while I explain our French customs to Bertie. We are old-fashioned enough to believe that marriage is a contract between families. A bride must accept that she takes not only her groom for better, for worse, for richer, for poorer, but his entire kith and kin. It is more than a personal matter; it is a joint-stock affair. There is a matrimonial settlement. A French mother doesn't cry on the wedding day because she has lost a daughter; she rejoices at gaining a son."

The speech seemed like flannel to me. "This is not so different from marriage among English people of rank, as I was trying to explain to Sarah only yesterday," I commented, leaving him in no doubt that I was irritated at being lectured on French customs.

"Ah, but it must be handled with delicacy in France," he said with want of tact. "We have to abide by the Code civil. If a daughter of twenty-one or older should choose to defy her parents and promise herself to some young man of her own choice, and if the parents will not give their consent, she may make what is called a *sommation respectueuse,* a kind of extrajudicial protest. After three such *sommations,* if her parents continue to resist the match, the Code allows her to marry the man whatever his character and habits."

"Good Lord!"

"Be he a vagrant, a philanderer, an anarchist, anything," Jules added. "It is diabolical."

"But it is the law," said Bernhardt firmly, and for a moment I feared that she was about to give us a lecture on the rights of women. To my great relief, she spared us that.

"So do you see the difficulty parents labor under?" Jules went on. "We are not insensitive to our children's wishes. Matchmaking is a delicate process that continues for some time until a desirable partner is found. Parents—and I suppose I should say mothers, for they are usually the more instrumental in the process—will make discreet inquiries about the circumstances of prospective families. If suitable, they will approach the other parents and suggest opportunities of acquaintance, such as garden parties, or croquet, or dinner parties."

A little wearily, I said, "Jules, old friend, this is all very familiar. Remember, I have three daughters and two sons, and only one is married."

"Yes, but your daughters aren't threatening you with a *sommation respectueuse*," he blurted out.

We were coming to the crux of it.

"Has Rosine resorted to that?"

"She can't. She is not twenty-one yet, but she will be next October."

"And who is the young man she so admires?"

"He is not young at all, Bertie. He is older than I am."

"Come, come," I said in disbelief.

"He is a worthless painter called Morgan and he is fifty-one.

"Well, I'll be jiggered!"

Bernhardt for once was lost for words.

Jules informed us, "She met him in church, of all places."

"That's some consolation, surely?" I commented. "The fellow can't be entirely bad."

Jules quickly put me right on that point. "He is a pagan. He followed her in there to talk to her when she was arranging the flowers. The ladies of the district take turns to decorate the village church. You'd think your daughter was safe to perform a pious duty like that unchaperoned. I gather Morgan happened to be in the churchyard in front of his easel when he saw my little Rosine coming up the path with her basket of flowers. He went in and started a conversation with her, just like that. No one introduced them. In a house of God, Bertie!"

"It does seem sacrilegious," I agreed. "When did this disgraceful episode take place?"

"Sometime early in the summer of '89."

"Before she met Letissier?"

"Yes. She is totally infatuated with Morgan. I can't understand it."

Bernhardt said to console him, "The ways of the heart cannot be analyzed, Jules."

"Yes," he said, "but this is an old man. He's over fifty."

"That's not so old," said I, with my own half century looming in November. "The difference in ages is cause for comment, I grant you."

"Well, he looks a damn sight older than he is," Jules said. "It's the long beard streaked with gray that does it, I suppose, and the scruffy clothes."

"You've met him, then?"

Our host spread his hands in a gesture of helplessness. "Last summer, Rosine invited him to paint a landscape of the park. We've had him wandering about the estate ever since. The gardeners kept asking if he was a tramp. I had to tell them he was there by invitation. I don't know what the girl sees in him."

Bernhardt made the obvious point that some young girls were attracted to older men. "It's their experience, their urbanity—"

"Not forgetting their money," said I.

"Not in this case," Jules put in. "Morgan is practically without a sou. His paintings don't sell. He says he doesn't care about material needs. Mind you, he makes short work of lunch when it's brought to him on a tray."

"You made him welcome, then?"

"We tolerated the fellow, Bertie. I didn't want him sitting at my table, so I had the meals sent out to him."

"But you met him yourself?"

"I went to look at his painting out of curiosity. I didn't have the slightest suspicion that Rosine was in love with him. I thought we were helping a poor painter as a charitable gesture. She had mentioned that she'd met him at the church, which was true, and I assumed they had been properly introduced. She'd said after painting the church he was looking for other local scenes to render in oils and I gullibly agreed to give him the freedom of our estate. We French have a high regard for the arts, as you know."

"Is he a talented artist?" Sarah asked, like me looking for crumbs of comfort.

"Did I call him an artist?" said Jules, by now quite pink in the face just talking about the man. "If I did, it was a mistake. He's one of these Impressionists—all dabs of paint in garish colors straight from the tube. He does the whole thing in two hours. You have to stand ten meters away before you can pick out anything at all in the picture, and then it's very crude in outline. He'll never sell anything, as I keep telling Rosine."

"Was he civil when you met him?" I asked.

"Depends what you mean by civil. He didn't have much to say. Didn't even have the decency to put his brush down. And he didn't once look me in the eye. I didn't object at the time. I put it down to eccentricity. After all, I didn't know I was speaking to a prospective son-in-law."

"Is that what he has become?" said I.

"Heavens, no, Bertie. I'm speaking from the point of view of my deluded child."

"You said they met two years ago. When did you meet him yourself?"

"Last summer, when he started painting here. The fellow hasn't gone away yet. Sometimes he sleeps in empty buildings on the estate. And he appears to think that he has carte blanche to roam across my land with his easel at any time. He was painting a snow scene within a hundred meters of the house when I last saw him."

"Haven't you warned him off?"

Jules sighed and shook his head. "I've always tried to be civilized in my dealings with local people, and they respect me for it. I gave permission for Morgan to paint on my land without specifying that it was only for a limited time. He's done no damage. He closes gates after him. If I ban him from the estate, I've got to justify my action."

"But if he was pursuing Rosine—"

"He wasn't, not in any obvious way. He was clever, you see. If there was any pursuing, it was Rosine who did it. She goes riding around the estate every day—has done for years, and I can't stop her. I'm sure she knows where Morgan sets up his easel. I'm not suggesting that there was any misbehavior. She's a virtuous girl and I trust her. But if I put a ban on Morgan, it won't be his reputation that suffers in the village; it will be Rosine's."

"So he does have carte blanche."

"Well, now that you point it out, I suppose he does," Jules admitted. "But only to paint, not to fraternize with my daughter."

"Rosine was promised to another."

"Exactly."

"You and Juliette thought him suitable, I take it?"

"Maurice? Well, I wouldn't have promoted the engagement otherwise," said Jules, still tetchy about the whole unfortunate business. "He was from an excellent family, decently educated, completed his military service with some distinction. And he had a very confident, charming manner. Juliette and I discussed him and decided after making some inquiries, as responsible parents do, that we should meet the Letissiers. It was easy, because they are racing folk, as you know, and I'm a member of the Jockey Club, so I got a mutual friend to introduce me to Letissier senior. It was arranged that our families should meet at a costume ball given by the von Winslows."

Bernhardt boldly asked, "Did you consult Rosine?"

"Of course. She said at first that she wasn't ready yet to meet young men, but she was twenty, for heaven's sake, as I had to remind her. In the end, she said she was willing to accompany us to the von Winslows'. Maurice paid particular attention that evening to Rosine, who later agreed that she could find nothing to object to in his character. Juliette, as mothers do, pressed his case as a prospective husband. Perhaps she pressed too hard."

"Why do you say that?"

"Because Rosine resisted. Juliette, being the kind of woman she is, pressed all the harder. By degrees, we began to learn the reason—our child's infatuation with the painter. One day, she told us that nothing on earth would induce her to marry anyone else, in spite of the fact that Morgan was in no position to support her. We were appalled. We had some tearful scenes, I can tell you, and it went on for months. Eventually, Rosine saw sense, or Juliette's iron will prevailed, and the engagement was agreed. Believe me, Bertie, I wouldn't have let Juliette make such an issue of it if I hadn't believed myself that Maurice would be a good husband."

"So the engagement went ahead."

"Yes, it was announced—what is it?—just over two weeks ago and the wedding was arranged for June, as I mentioned."

"And I commented that it seemed a short engagement," said I.

"We don't require long betrothals in France, as you do across the water. No young man in this country will seek a wife before he is in a position to marry her." Jules was proud of his nation, and I don't blame him for that. I didn't take him up on the point, but I don't necessarily agree that short engagements are something to wave the flag over. Couples who rush to the altar may have something on their consciences.

Bernhardt asked another penetrating question. "Did Rosine stop seeing the painter?"

Jules looked shocked. "I assume so."

"Did you and Juliette insist on it?"

"I don't think we gave her an ultimatum. She agreed to marry Letissier and that was enough."

"She still goes riding each day?"

"Yes."

"And Morgan is still about?"

"I haven't heard that he has left. But I really can't see that this is a matter you should pursue." He was becoming twitchy, tugging at his hair and crossing his legs. As if unable to contain himself, he sprang up from the chair and put another log on the fire and then stood staring at it.

I said quickly, "Depend upon it, Jules—Sarah and I will employ the utmost tact in questioning young Rosine. Is she now in a calmer state of mind than the other day?"

"I believe so."

"She'll see us, then?"

He took this as his chance of escape, offering to go and look for her at once. The dog, too, made a dash for freedom.

The minute Jules was out of the room, Sarah said, "He's hiding something from us, Bertie. He's a dear man, but he hasn't told us everything."

I thought it proper to exert my authority as the senior detective in this team. "Let's not make unfounded assumptions, Sarah. You have to understand that his family are now under suspicion of murder, of the murder of a young man they were supposed to be embracing as one of their own. That must be a terrible blow to any father—and the Agincourts are one of the most respected families in France. No wonder he is guarded in his replies."

She said, "One thing is very clear. He feels extremely guilty about forcing this engagement on his daughter. And another thing, Bertie—there is a lover. One of my assumptions, at least, proved to be true." She followed this with a triumphant long look that reminded me of my mother when Mr. Gladstone lost the election.

I said, "Personally, my dear Sarah, I look at these matters with an air of detachment. That is the mark of a good detective."

She said, "Yes, but what have you detected?"

Quick as a nun's kiss, I answered, "A new suspect."

"Morgan?"

"Yes . . . a *crime passionnel.*"

She said, "That was my suggestion,"

I said, "But we didn't know about Morgan then. He had the motive and the opportunity. He was permitted to roam freely around the estate. It wouldn't have been difficult to pick his moment to come in here and steal the gun. He'd only have to find his way into the courtyard and open the door. As one of those Impressionist people, he must know Montmartre and the Moulin Rouge. And as Rosine's confidant, he must have known that the family were going there that evening with Letissier."

Bernhardt said after a stunned pause, "Bertie, you're doing so brilliantly on your own, do you really require an assistant?"

CHAPTER 7

I was in the act of kissing Sarah Bernhardt when we were interrupted.

Let me explain the kiss. My clever deduction about Morgan,
the painter, had the curious effect of demoralizing poor Sarah.
You see, she hadn't thought of it first. She was practically inconsolable. As she expressed it in a faltering voice, she felt that her
contributions to the investigation were so puny that she would
be better employed packing her trunks for the Bernhardt World
Tour. Do you know, I'd almost forgotten by then that she was the
world's greatest actress.

She sank into one corner of a large leather sofa and managed
to look pitiably small and the very picture of dejection. Quick to
reassure her, I sat beside her and said that her questions to Jules
had been uncommonly helpful. She was my support.

She said, "I'm just a crutch, am I?" And a gleaming tear escaped
from the corner of her eye and rolled down her cheek.

Now it has often been written that Bernhardt is so skilled an
actress that she can weep at will, but I prefer to believe that this
tear was involuntary.

What could I do but draw the poor waif to me and embrace her?

Next thing, we were up from that sofa like rocketing pheasants
when a voice said, "Who are you?"

The speaker was a youth in a brown suit. He was a more paunchy
version of Jules and I took him, correctly, to be the son, Tristan.

Dark and disapproving, he stood just inside the door with a shotgun in the open position over his shoulder. When I say that he resembled Jules, I should qualify the description. The boy lacked his father's slightly languid manner. But the eyes of that disturbing light blue color so unusual in a dark-haired man were unmistakably those of Jules's son.

Allowing that we had arrived at Montroger unannounced, it was not unreasonable that Tristan inquired who we were, and I introduced Bernhardt and myself. The lad pricked up his eyebrows, blushed, and gave a courtly bow.

Bernhardt said, "You must be Tristan."

"Yes, madame."

"We are waiting to meet your sister," I informed him without any reference to the scene he had chanced upon. Never go into explanations when you're caught spooning. "Your father went to fetch her."

Tristan said, "How typical of Father."

"What do you mean by that?"

"I don't mean to be disloyal, sir, but he won't find her. She's out riding. She goes riding every afternoon at this time. Father is terribly absentminded." He rested the shotgun on a table.

"What were you shooting? " I asked with an effort to be at my most amiable.

"Rabbits, sir. Do you mind if I attend to my gun?"

"Please do. Any success?"

"Five, actually." He went to a drawer and took out a cleaning kit.

"So you're a good shot?"

"Better than average, sir." He attached the swab to the cleaning rod in a practiced way and pushed it into the bore.

"Have you ever used a revolver?"

He looked up. Those blue eyes were as still as the frost on a window. "It's an unreliable weapon, sir."

"You have fired one, then?"

"Only for amusement." The young man was beginning to impress me. He was mature in manner, polite without obsequiousness. I've noticed that most French children are quicker to mature and more socially adept than our own. This, I am sure, is because they join their parents in the dining room at an age when ours are confined to nursery meals.

"I'm sure you know that your sister's fiancé was shot with a revolver," I said, watching for his reaction.

He nodded. "So I was informed, sir."

"But you were there."

"I heard the shot, sir. I didn't see the type of gun that was fired. If I had, I would have told the police."

He would make an impressive witness in a court of law, I thought, if it should ever come to that. "The detectives questioned you, then?"

"They questioned us all, sir. Not one of us saw the gun. How could we? It was fired from behind."

"Whom were you standing next to?"

"My father, I suppose."

"You must know, Tristan."

"With respect, it isn't so simple, sir. There was jostling. Everybody wanted a good view of the dancers. I had a tall woman with a wide hat in front of me, so I moved to the right to see better. When the shot was fired, I wasn't literally next to Father, but I was close by. I turned to see what had happened and Father was beside Maurice. My sister, Rosine, was on Maurice's other side."

"And your mother?"

"She stood next to Rosine, I think, sir." He put down the gun and it was obvious that there was something else he wanted to say. "If I may be so bold, why are you asking these questions about my family?"

I said evenly, "Because your parents are valued friends of mine and I want to find out the truth about this tragedy. Did you like Maurice Letissier?"

He frowned. "He wasn't family." As if to soften the response, he added, "My sister didn't really want to marry him."

"Is that your observation, or did she tell you?"

"We all knew it, sir."

"You felt some sympathy for her, I dare say?"

He gave me another ice blue stare. "That's no reason to kill a man, is it, sir?"

This had developed into a duel and I wasn't sure who was winning. I said, "Your parents clearly approved of Letissier."

He parried with, "Sir, I think my parents would prefer to speak for themselves."

Bernhardt cautioned him, "Have a care how you speak to His Royal Highness."

He immediately apologized, but I didn't press the question. To be frank, I had some sympathy for the boy's point of view. I still feel pain remembering my elder sister Vicky, at seventeen, being married to Prince Frederick of Prussia, even though the marriage tuned out to be a happy one and Fritz one of the finest and noblest of men. The tie between brother and sister is stronger than most people realize. I was fifteen and I wept for Vicky, I don't mind admitting. For the whole of her adult life, she has written to me regularly and I have always scribbled something back at once, notwithstanding my dislike of writing letters.

Tristan had picked up the gun again and was working methodically on the bore with a bristle brush. He wasn't skimping.

I said, "You shoot regularly, do you?"

"As often as I can, sir."

"Every day?"

"That would be impossible, sir."

"You attend the Sorbonne?"

"Yes, sir." He smiled faintly. "We get a few hours for private study."

"You don't have lodgings nearby, as some students do?"

"No, sir, I live here."

"And bag a few rabbits when you can fit in the time, eh?"

I winked and he grinned more readily.

"And have you ever seen anyone except your own family in here?"

"The servants attend to the fire and sweep up, sir, but it's very unusual for anyone else to come in. That's why I was surprised to discover you and Madame Bernhardt."

"I'm sure." Passing smoothly on, I said, "Tell me about the servants. How many live in?"

The question was never answered because before the words were out, we all heard a shot fired, followed immediately by the screeching of rooks alarmed by the sound.

Tristan dropped the shotgun he was cleaning. "What on earth . . ."

A rash of gooseflesh afflicted me. I'm accustomed to gunfire, but not sudden, unexpected gunfire. I said, "Should anyone be out there shooting this afternoon?"

"Absolutely not."

"The gamekeeper?"

"He's laid up with sciatica."

"Does anyone in the family use a gun?"

"Father. But he's in the house, isn't he? The shot came from outside."

I said, "I think we should investigate."

We all stepped outside, across the yard, around the stables to an open area with a view of the estate. Nobody was in sight, and the colony of rooks was settling in the trees again. The vista before us reminded me rather of Sandringham, the flat meadowland made interesting by clumps of trees and small woods. We could probably have seen a great distance if the mist had not been so reluctant to lift.

I said, "It's anyone's guess where it came from. Do you get poachers?"

"If we do, they don't come in broad daylight, sir."

"Then who do you suppose it was?"

He didn't answer.

Some scuffling and panting at our feet signaled the arrival of Bernhardt's friend, the black retriever. It nuzzled her skirt companionably. From behind us, Jules appeared, striding from the house. He called sharply, "Ezra!" and the dog came obediently to heel.

"What are you doing here, Tristan?" he asked. "I thought that shot just now was yours."

"No, Father. I was in the gun room."

"Then who the devil is shooting on our land?" Jules said. "I'm sorry about the language, Sarah, but this is very irregular. Would you mind fetching my field glasses, Tristan?"

While his son went on this errand, Jules explained that he hadn't yet been able to find Rosine.

I said, "We were told she is out riding."

"Of course she is," said Jules. "Should have thought of that." As another thought struck him, he put his hand to his mouth. "If Rosine is out riding and some idiot is loosing off a gun, she could be at risk. I don't care for this at all, Bertie."

None of us cared for it particularly, but there wasn't a lot we could do to remedy the situation. The glasses, when they were brought, didn't assist us.

Then came two more shots.

They echoed across the entire countryside, but there was no mistaking the direction they had come from.

"Just beyond the wood," said Jules, pointing to a copse a good half mile away practically enshrouded in mist. "Infernal cheek! I'm going to saddle a horse and ride over there. Would you excuse me, Bertie?"

"Excuse you? If you have a nag strong enough, I'll join you," I offered.

Whereupon, Bernhardt gamely said, "I'll come, too."

"We ought to be armed," said Tristan, making it clear that he meant to be one of the posse.

Within a few minutes, all four of us set off across the turf at a canter, Bernhardt riding sidesaddle as if she'd done it all her life. My days of riding to hounds were over and I was grateful to find myself on a mount more used to trotting than galloping, a strong, broad, underbred mare. Out of courtesy, Jules and his son went ahead to take whatever risks might be involved in engaging the enemy first, and fine horsemen they were, both of them, each with a shotgun slung across his back. They were soon out of sight.

By the time Bernhardt and I reached the copse, I was glad of slower progress as our beasts picked their way through dead bracken. Bernhardt remarked that I looked red in the face and asked if I was winded. This was her way of asking me to pause awhile, for I'm sure it can be no comfortable experience trotting sidesaddle across a field, so out of consideration, I halted.

"We'll go to the rescue when they need us," I told her with a confident air. "Actually, I would hazard a guess that young Tristan can see off most of the perils lurking in these parts. He knows how to handle a gun."

"He knows more than that," said Bernhardt. "I thought him remarkably self-assured for eighteen."

"Without the deplorable manners so typical of adolescence," I concurred. "At his age, I was the despair of my parents. I overate and was bone idle. They had diet sheets prepared for me and they stopped me wearing carpet slippers."

"Carpet slippers—how decadent, Bertie!" said Bernhardt, smiling. "When I was seventeen, I made my debut with the Comédie-Française."

"That was precocious."

"It was disastrous."

She didn't expand on the statement, and I didn't press her. "The question is," said I, "how seriously should we consider Tristan as a suspect?"

"I rather like the boy," Bernhardt remarked.

"That's beside the point."

She said, "I thought Morgan was our suspect. He sounds contemptible."

"We can't eliminate all the others just because they're nicer people," I told her as gently as possible, because I didn't want her piping her eye again. "Personally, I'd be more than satisfied to find that Morgan is the murderer, but until he confesses to the crime, we must keep an open mind about the Agincourt family."

"Very well."

"I was about to say that when investigating a murder, you have to take stock of each suspect's opportunity and motive. Tristan had the opportunity to fire the fatal shot. He uses the gun room regularly, so he knew where to find a revolver. He was at the Moulin Rouge on the night in question."

"But what would have been his motive?"

"Sympathy for Rosine, being dragooned into marriage with a man she didn't love. Boys can be very protective of their sisters. Tristan is on the verge of manhood, at the mercy of his glands."

She frowned, uncertain of my drift.

I explained, "Lads of that awkward age often feel compelled to prove themselves in some way."

"By murdering somebody?"

"That would be an extreme case," I admitted. "However, one should never underestimate the glands." I took out a cigar and put it to my lips, deciding that I'd probably said enough on the matter.

"Are you speaking of aggressive tendencies?"

"Er, yes, that sums it up nicely." I struck a match.

Then Bernhardt said in the most innocent of tones, "I thought you meant that he was in love with his sister."

The match went out.

"Then the motive would be simple jealousy," she explained.

I was deeply shocked. "A brother and sister? I don't care for that."

"Neither do I," said she, "but it can't be discounted. Never underestimate the glands."

We might have continued this unedifying discussion for some time had it not been for a sudden sound behind us, a definite rustling in the bracken. My steed whinnied in fright and reared, and I only stayed up with the greatest difficulty.

"What is it?" Bernhardt asked.

It was black and breathless. It was Ezra, the retriever.

We resumed our progress through the copse until the view opened up. We must have been climbing without being aware of it, for a considerable tract of parkland lay below us. At the foot of the declivity was a stream where some rather scrawny sheep had come to drink. There was a derelict cottage with some of the eaves exposed. In front of it, we could see Jules and Tristan. They had dismounted and were about to enter the ruin, their guns held at the ready.

"What are they doing?" Bernhardt asked.

"They appear to believe someone is holed up in there," said I. "There aren't many other places he could be. Let's watch for a moment."

It was fascinating as a spectacle, better than watching the Volunteers on maneuver in Windsor Park. Jules appeared to be guarding the front, while Tristan, bent low, prowled around the walls to the rear. We couldn't hear what was said, if anything. I imagined they would invite the occupant (if one there was) to step out, for it was a safer procedure than walking into a possible ambush.

"Bertie."

Peeved at having the sport interrupted, I said, "Yes?"

Bernhardt said, "Look at Ezra."

"What?"

"Look at the dog. He's behaving strangely."

I turned and saw exactly what she meant. Ezra was obviously stalking something in the bracken behind us, his belly low to the ground as he emitted a peculiar growling sound. "A rabbit hole, I dare say," said I.

"I think not," said my companion. "There's something there, something quite big."

Just as I turned, Ezra gave a full-throated bark and leapt into the patch of brown and sodden bracken.

There was a scream, but not from Bernhardt and certainly not from me.

"Someone's there!" cried Bernhardt.

A man leapt up, wild-eyed, stocky, with the waxed mustache that many Frenchmen have. His tawny-colored hair was cropped and he looked very like a rat. Ezra had him by the sleeve of his brown overcoat, but the man swung the dog away with remarkable strength and bolted toward the thickest part of the wood. Ezra gamely stood upright again, gave a vigorous shake and set off in pursuit—with me in pursuit as well, still in the saddle.

The rat-man didn't get far. Ezra somehow contrived to get between his legs and he tripped heavily, hit the ground hard and groaned. My mare almost trampled him.

I didn't dismount. The fellow was craven, as I'm sure I would have been with a black retriever on my chest, with its teeth sunk into my collar, growling ferociously.

"Ezra, that will do!" I commanded, but the dog ignored me. "Ezra, you can stop now. Ezra!"

It was Bernhardt who succeeded in calling off the dog. When she said, "Heel, Ezra," the beast immediately desisted and ran to her, wagging its tail. The fuss she had made of it in the gun room had paid a dividend.

Unarmed as I was, I had no fear of the man.

"On your feet and sharp about it!"

He rose unsteadily from the bracken, now a pathetic little figure in a brown overcoat, his shirt collar ripped from its moorings, his face smeared extensively with mud and one end of his mustache dangling where the wax had snapped. He had angry brown eyes under bushy eyebrows. The epitome of a trespasser caught in the act.

"Hands away from your pockets," I ordered him, remembering the shots that had started us on this manhunt. He might well be carrying a pistol. "Now, remove the overcoat and let it drop to the ground."

With a scowl, he obeyed. The coat fell in a heap on the bracken. Rather to my surprise, he was wearing a passably decent gray pinstripe under it.

"And the jacket, if you please."

He protested, "Monsieur, it's cold and I suffer from asthma. Can't you hear my breathing?"

I said, "Do it!"

The jacket joined the overcoat.

"Step away from the coat. Any tricks from you, my man, and you'll answer to the police—that is, after the dog has finished with you. Waistcoat."

He looked up at me with malevolent eyes before removing the waistcoat.

To be quite certain he was unarmed, I could have insisted that he remove his trousers, as well. Out of respect for Bernhardt, I spared the fellow that indignity. He looked pretty unthreatening in his suspenders and shirtsleeves.

"Now, you had better identify yourself."

He shivered, gave me a murderous glare, drew in a breath, and wheezed. "I am Marie-François Goron, *chef de la Sûreté*."

CHAPTER 8

My Dearest Alix,

Yes, I am penning this from wicked old Paris, but do not despair, for I shall be leaving directly for the Riviera. Nothing can detain me here any longer.

I remember complaining the last time I wrote that Paris was becoming tiresome, or dull, or both. I am happy to report a distinct improvement. In fact, today has been a bracing experience. I thought I had better drive out to Montroger, the Agincourt residence, to convey the kind thoughts and condolences you expressed in your latest. (Before you throw up your hands in alarm and declare that I ignored your appeals, I went merely out of a sense of obligation to you and our old friends the Agincourts. Detective investigation was furthest from my thoughts.)

Jules was deeply comforted by your concern. I didn't see Juliette, but I met their son, Tristan, now grown up to be a fine young man of good intelligence and cultivated interests, too. He is a keen sportsman and we had an intelligent exchange about shooting. But I mustn't digress. I gave your message to Jules, and he particularly asked me to let you know how much your support means to him. With the best will in the world, I couldn't prevent our old friend from asking me for an opinion about the murder.

He insisted once again on giving me all the grisly details and it was soon transparently obvious to me that this was a crime of passion and that the culprit was young Rosine's lover, a man of mature years, a painter by the name of Morgan. He is one of the Impressionist school and seems to lurk around Montroger ostensibly to paint scenes, but in reality to effect assignations with Rosine, who is quite besotted with him, notwithstanding her betrothal to Letissier. Impressionism in Morgan's case is the pursuit of an impressionable young girl.

We were discussing these matters when the sound of gunfire came suddenly from outside. No one had permission to shoot on the estate, so Jules and his son saddled horses and rode off to investigate. I observed them from a safe distance while exercising their dog. As you know, there are few activities I enjoy better. I assure you, Alix, my dearest, I was well out of range of any gun. But you may imagine my astonishment when Ezra, the retriever, discovered a man skulking in the undergrowth. Ezra and I between us treated the ruffian with the severity he deserved for giving us such a fright.

Now this is the bombshell. The wretched man turned out to be Monsieur Goron, the most senior policeman in Paris. A fine pickle! Fortunately, Goron's powers of detection were sharp enough to tell him who I was, or I might have found myself in a French clink. He and I were soon on better terms, but he kept his distance from Ezra.

Goron, it emerged, had been keeping watch on the same derelict building that Jules and Tristan were about to search. Several of his officers, also in plainclothes, were hidden at vantage points nearby. After carrying out the most intensive investigation lasting almost two weeks, the Sûreté had reached the conclusion that I had come to in five minutes: namely, that Morgan the painter was Letissier's murderer. Morgan was known to be in the ruined house, supposedly for some kind of assignation with young Rosine, who goes riding at this time each afternoon. I was relieved to learn that she had not yet been seen. Morgan was certainly armed, for he had bagged a rabbit before entering the house; these were the shots we had heard.

This was alarming, because Jules and Tristan had posted themselves at either end of the building and might any minute go in! We were not close enough to warn them of the danger. But it all ended benignly, with Morgan stepping outside, unarmed, and being apprehended at the point of Tristan's shotgun. The police closed in and made the arrest. The painter is now being questioned at the Sûreté.

You may imagine the sense of relief at Montroger that the Agincourt name has emerged from this affair unsullied. No opprobrium can be attached to young Rosine, for the lawyers will make it clear that she had no foreknowledge of the murder. Morgan plotted his dastardly crime independently, motivated, no doubt, as much by pecuniary gain as passion. Few will have any regrets when he goes to the guillotine. He is no great loss to the world of art if his painting is anything like the other Impressionist works I have seen. If I had my way . . . No, better not say it to one who takes so much pleasure in fine art.

Now, to far more important matters. I have it on excellent authority from Fife that Louise is in the pink of health and the doctors are entirely satisfied with her progress. There are no indications of premature labor, so you may continue to enjoy the games of loo and—dare I say?—the currant jelly for a few weeks yet.

Give my love, as ever, to your pretty antagonists at the loo table. I think of them constantly, as I do of my own darling wife.

Showers of kisses, Bertie

"Francis."

"Sir?"

"I shall be going to the Théâtre des Variétés tonight with Madame Bernhardt. I see from the paper that they have revived one of my favourite operettas, *La Belle Hélène,* and I must on no account miss it. Have the hotel reserve my two boxes on the pit tier and send two decent armchairs. The furniture in French theaters is impossible to sit upon for more than ten minutes."

"I shall attend to it, sir."

"Tomorrow we leave for Cannes."

"Very good, sir." An expression of the most ineffable relief spread over Francis Knollys's face. He regards himself as my unofficial moral guardian (by appointment to HRH the Princess of Wales), and while Cannes is not without its temptations, it possesses fewer than Paris. The worst that has happened there (in the view of Francis) was the year I attended the Battle of Flowers dressed as Old Nick, in a scarlet costume and with horns attached to my head. Everyone but Francis thought it a marvelous lark.

Memories. While sitting beside Bernhardt in the gilded splendor of the Théâtre des Variétés that evening listening to Offenbach's matchless music, my thoughts drifted back more than twenty years to another Belle Hélène, dear little Hortense Schneider, who for one glorious season instructed me personally in *La Gâieté Parisienne*—until word got back to Windsor and I was given a jobation by Mama for neglecting Alix.

"Bertie!"

I sat forward with a start. The crystal gasolier had been turned up for the interval.

Bernhardt—dressed fetchingly in lemon-colored taffeta that rustled when she moved—turned to me with eyes narrowed and declared, "A tear has just rolled down your cheek."

I said, "The story is very moving, don't you agree?"

She said, "You were remembering an old flame."

I shook my head.

"We Frenchwomen aren't so dense as you think, you know," she said. "Your conquests here are well known."

"Name one, then."

"One!" She laughed. "The Princesse de Sagan."

"Jeanne is an old friend," I said.

"An old friend with an absent husband," said she, as if that settled the matter, and then she started counting on her fingers. "The Duchesse de Mouchy, the Duchesse de Luynes, Giulia Beneni, known as La Barucci, the Comtesse de Pourtalès, the Baronne de Pilar, the Baronne de Rothschild, Émilienne d'Alençon, Madame Kauchine, Liane de Pougy, Cora Pearl—"

"She's Irish," I pointed out.

"French by inclination. Where was I?"

"You've used up all your fingers," said I.

"Then I can start again. The widow Signoret, the Comtesse de Boutourline, Miss Chamberlayne, Hortense Schneider, Yvette Guilbert, Jeanne Granier—"

"This is the silliest nonsense," I broke in, for it was obvious that she intended to continue for some time. "And you haven't mentioned the only one I'd be willing to admit to."

"Who's that?" she demanded fiercely.

"Sarah Bernhardt."

She thought a moment, frowned, and blushed. "But you and I have never—"

I placed my hand over hers. "You didn't listen properly. I said I'd be willing. It was an offer, not a boast."

She clicked her tongue and said, "You've had too much champagne."

With more than a hint of invitation, I told her, "We are partners, successful partners, my dear. We solved the murder together. Tonight is for celebration."

She said, "The police solved it without our help."

"But we were absolutely right in our deductions. Morgan was the murderer and it was a crime of passion, just as you said at the beginning. More champagne, partner?"

Charming as the music was, when the show resumed, my concentration had gone. I spent the whole of the second act making mental lists, counting furtively on my fingers. Sarah had been wrong over several names, but I hadn't challenged them. It would only have strengthened her suspicions about those that I didn't challenge. There's no winning a game like that. Besides, there were others she might have mentioned, and hadn't.

At the end of the performance, she turned to me and said without prompting, "That was naughty of me. I got carried away. In my case, it *was* an excess of champagne."

I said, "In mine, an excess of lady friends, apparently."

She laughed and leaned toward me for a kiss, which she received. Then she said, "Let's eat at Maxim's."

I had to be careful here. I pondered the matter with a judicial expression before saying, "Do you like caviar?"

"I adore it," said Bernhardt with a little quiver of anticipation.

"The caviar at my hotel is quite the best I've tasted," said I.

"Oh, I couldn't possibly eat at the Bristol," she said at once. "I'm sure the food is divine, but we'd be seen."

I said, "That, surely, would be a cause for congratulation. Most ladies of my acquaintance—" I stopped myself just in time. "If you wish to be discreet about it, my dear, I have a key to a back door. We shall eat in my rooms and no one will hear of it."

Of two minds, she said, "I do think Maxim's would be simpler."

Not for what I was planning. I said as if the world was coming to an end, "This is my last night in Paris. Tomorrow we leave for Cannes."

This did the trick. She said, "Then let us both be quite clear, Bertie. I would be coming only to try the caviar."

I said, "I don't think it will disappoint you, my dear."

And we took a carriage almost to the Bristol. I say "almost" because I instructed the driver to put us down at the Place Beauvau and we walked the short distance to the hotel. I shepherded Bernhardt to the back door and not a soul spotted us. There were two flights of back stairs to negotiate, but it was exceedingly quiet and poorly lit. At the first landing, my companion stopped unexpectedly, faced me, tipped my hat upward, put her arms around my neck, and kissed me passionately.

Then she said out of the blue, "Did I tell you that to reach the stage door at the Théâtre des Variétés you go up the Passage des Princes?"

Bemused, I said, "Really?"

She said, "In the profession, that is what we call Hortense Schneider—the Passage des Princes."

It was a wicked slander on a dear old friend, but I couldn't stop myself from smiling.

Humor is the best aphrodisiac. On the next landing, I returned the kiss with interest and told my own Schneider story. "One royal admirer of Hortense was Ismail, the former khedive of Egypt. Once when he was at the spa at Vichy, he got bored with the cure and told his equerry to write to Hortense. But through a mistake, the letter was delivered to an American salesman called Harold Schneider. This gentleman could not believe his good fortune when he read, 'By order of the khedive, a suite is reserved for you at the Grand Hotel at Vichy and your presence will be to Ismail as an oasis in the desert.'"

Bernhardt clapped her hands in delight. "And what happened?"

"Believing a large order was in prospect, Harold Schneider took the first train to Vichy and, my word, he was impressed by the welcome he got at the Grand. He was taken up to the suite, which was full of flowers. There were chocolates and champagne. Feeling tired from the journey, he got straight into a relaxing bath. Shortly afterward, the door opened slowly and Ismail peered around it to look at his oasis."

"Wonderful!" said Bernhardt with relish.

"Whether the coconuts stayed on the palm tree is not recorded."

At this, she burst into such a belly laugh that I had to warn her to keep her voice down. After the trouble we'd gone to, I didn't want one of my staff discovering us. However, we negotiated the corridor leading to my suite—Bernhardt so paralytic with my story that I was holding her upright (no hardship)—and I let us in.

"What an elegant room!" She let the cloak slip off her shoulders and attempted a pirouette, compelling me to catch her again.

We held each other in a close embrace.

I murmured, "Let's postpone the caviar."

Sarah gave me a lopsided smile. "Coconuts instead?"

It was at this more-than-promising moment in my romantic career that I happened to glance over Sarah's shoulder and was subjected to a surprise no less than if I had been knocked down by a London omnibus while strolling up the Champs-Elysées. Against the wall opposite, inconspicuous between a satinwood secretary and a tall fern in a brass pot, was an upright chair. Upon the chair, motionless, sat a young woman in black. Neither of us had noticed her upon entering, we had been so occupied with each other.

What could I do next? I said gently to Sarah, "Don't be alarmed, but we are not alone."

She said muzzily in my embrace, "Mm?"

My paramount concern was not to create a panic. In a voice as even as a billiard table, I told her, "Sarah, there is a third person in the room." Then I relaxed the embrace, allowing Sarah to turn around and see for herself.

Before I could get any further in unraveling this mystery, Sarah reached her own conclusion, and it was not to her liking. "*Mon Dieu!* I have never been so humiliated. What sort of perverted creature do you take me for?"

"Sarah, for pity's sake," I protested, "I don't even know this young lady."

"Then it's even more vile than I thought. Don't ever speak to me again, you . . . you Bluebeard!" She snatched up her cloak and dashed from the room.

Naturally, I went after her, but she refused to stop. I called down the stairs, "Sarah, will you listen? I don't know who she is or how she got in there." I ran down the first flight of stairs after her, but she was far too quick for me. All that I saw was the end of her cloak trailing around the corner.

Whatever may be said about me—and plenty is—I am not a bad sportsman. In a fair contest, I can take defeat as well as the next man. This was palpably unfair. I trudged upstairs simmering with resentment and frustration. Worse was to follow, for the commotion had brought most of my retinue out of their rooms to find out what was happening. Just about every door in the corridor stood open and they goggled at me as if I was the Wild Man of Borneo: my valet, footmen, brusher, equerries, lord-in-waiting, groom-in-waiting, pages, even my dog, Jack, was there barking.

Knollys, in a purple dressing gown, stood at the head of the stairs and said in his unctuous voice, "Can I be of assistance, sir?"

I said loudly enough to be heard by everyone, "You can tell the gallery that the poppy show is over for tonight." When all the doors were closed, I said to Knollys, "Now perhaps you will account for the young woman who is sitting in my room."

"Is she still there?" he said. "Oh, my word, I forgot all about her."

"You invited her in, I take it?" I demanded acidly.

He fiddled with the tassels of his dressing gown as if milking a cow. "Sir, I had no idea she would still be here at this hour. She arrived much earlier this evening. I thought you had gone for a short walk before dressing for the theater. I meant to explain when you came back."

I said, "You must have taken leave of your senses to allow a person we don't know from Adam to install herself in my suite. It has resulted in extreme embarrassment for me. Aside from that, she could be out to assassinate me. An anarchist."

Knollys cleared his throat in a way that suggested I was mistaken. "I beg your pardon, sir, but the young lady in there is not unknown to us."

I said with certainty, "She's a stranger to me."

"She is Mademoiselle Rosine d'Agincourt, sir."

"Rosine?"

"I thought you knew her, sir."

"Years ago. What does she want?"

"She won't say, except that she insists on seeing you, sir, about a matter of surpassing importance."

"Something to do with the murder?"

"I would imagine so."

"And she is still here at this hour? It's past midnight. She must be desperate."

My evening was already a lost cause. Bernhardt was convinced I was debauched. My staff had seen me in undignified pursuit. I hadn't eaten yet. And now there was this young girl waiting to drown me in tears because her lover was going to the guillotine.

I should never have stayed in Paris. Alix was right. She is always right.

CHAPTER 9

She was still seated, half hidden by the fern. And she still looked petrified.

"Why don't you come out from there?" I suggested with admirable restraint, considering the embarrassment I had suffered. "I won't eat you."

After some hesitation, she rose and curtsied, keeping her eyes modestly averted from mine. I had been led to expect beauty in this young lady and the description could not be faulted. She possessed a type of French face that I have seen nowhere else in Europe and it is difficult to convey in words, but I shall try. Superficially, the hair is dark, the face oval, eyes deep set and olive or brown, nose straight or with the slightest curve, jaw well defined. You'll have noticed that I left the mouth till last. This is deliberate. Of the features in this singularly French face, the mouth is the most characteristic. The lips are precisely defined, yet fuller and more prominent than you might think perfection requires. The flesh above and below the mouth contrives to curve outward at the edge of the lips, giving the merest indication of a pout, as if confident of a kiss. The effect is charming. The lady may be a paragon of virtue, yet incapable of changing the promise in her expression. I have even been amused to spot these kissable mouths among certain sisters of the church.

"Well, Rosine, I have been told who you are," I informed her, doing my level best to be dignified again. "Frankly, I didn't recognize you just now, as you must have gathered."

She said in a low voice, "Yes, Your Royal Highness."

"I was not expecting you to be here."

"No."

"You have been waiting some hours, I was told. May I send for some coffee or tea, or would you care for a drink?"

"No thank you, sir."

"Then you had better sit on the sofa and tell me why you are here. Would you like to remove your cape?"

Under the cape, she was dressed in a mourning gown buttoned to the neck and with no ornamentation whatsoever. She positioned herself opposite my armchair, demurely at one end of the sofa, her gloved hands nervously fingering the strap of her handbag. Her tragic demeanor and appearance could not fail to arouse sympathy.

"My dear, after waiting so long you had better not waste your opportunity," I prompted her compassionately. "You have my undivided attention."

"They have taken poor Glyn and he is innocent!" she blurted out.

"The painter?"

"Yes, sir. He is falsely arrested and I don't know what to do!"

"This *is* the man called Morgan you are speaking of?" said I, knowing full well that it must be; I was being pedantic merely to let her know that I would not be sunk by a tide of emotion.

"Yes, sir. Glyn Morgan." She gave me a penetrating look. "He is a countryman of yours."

I was wary and probably sounded so. "The name sounds Welsh to me." Between ourselves, reader, it is good advice to be wary of the Welsh. A nation with so many chapels must have sinners in abundance to give the preachers employment.

"Forgive me, sir," said Rosine. "But you are the Prince of Wales."

This, I thought, despite that "forgive me," shows want of tact. I may be obtuse at times, but it isn't necessary to remind me who I am. Worse still, she takes me for a Welshman. "And you believe he is falsely arrested?"

"I know it. Glyn didn't murder Maurice. He is the most gentle of men. An artist. Artists don't kill people."

"You'll have to think of something more significant than that to save him," said I. "I was with Monsieur Goron of the Sûreté this morning and he is in no doubt. Morgan had a powerful motive and an opportunity second to none. They expect to get a confession very soon."

She was saucer eyed. "Sir, that is monstrous! They are treating him as if he is guilty. The truth is that Glyn was as shocked as any of us when the shot was fired."

"Oh, really!" said I at once, for not much escapes me when I'm hot on the scent. "So he was definitely present at the Moulin Rouge that night?"

She put her hand to her mouth like a child who has spoken out of turn. "Didn't you know that?"

"I had my suspicions."

"You won't mention it to the police?"

I said, "I'm sure they will have heard it from Morgan himself by now. If he is innocent, what possessed him to go there?"

"He knew that my parents intended to take us there after we had dined. He said . . ." She lowered her eyes modestly. "He said he wouldn't be denied an opportunity to see me."

"Even in the company of your fiancé?"

"Glyn's love for me is unshakable, sir."

Incredible as it may sound to the reader, this made sense to me. You would think the sight of his heart's desire on the arm of his rival would have rubbed salt in the wound, but the Welsh are second to none in the art of suffering.

"Did he speak to you or any of the party?"

"No, sir. He merely observed us."

"And you, in turn, observed him?"

She blushed. "Well, yes. He took care to stand at some distance from us, or my father would have recognized him."

"I can imagine," I said with conviction. I could picture all too vividly the infatuated painter pacing the outer reaches of the ballroom. "And did he continue to keep his distance for the whole of the evening?"

A shrewd question, which caused her to hesitate. "Until Maurice was shot, Glyn did not venture anywhere near us."

"But after the shots?"

"Naturally, he was anxious to know whether I had been hurt. In the confusion, he appeared at my side and asked if I was all right. My parents didn't notice. They were too occupied with what had happened to Maurice, but my brother saw Glyn in conversation with me." She pressed both hands to her cheeks. "Tristan may have told the police. Oh, how a noble action can be misconstrued!"

I said to calm her, "It is best to know the worst of it. Tell me, where was Mr. Morgan standing at the moment the shots were fired?"

"Sir, I do not know. I lost sight of him when the dancers appeared."

Morgan sounded as guilty as Cain to me. "And after he spoke to you, did you see him again that night?"

"No, sir. He left with everyone else."

"Have you seen him since?"

She colored a little. "Yes, sir."

"Does he profess to be innocent?"

She said with a catch in her voice, "Sir, he is innocent. I know it."

I said reasonably, "That wasn't what I asked, my dear. The question is whether Morgan himself has told you he is innocent."

She answered with fervor, "But there's no need! Glyn is incapable of committing such a wicked crime. The possibility has never been mentioned between us."

I said, "The police won't flinch from asking him."

"That is what terrifies me."

Trying not to distress her more, I commented, "If he is innocent, as you say, he need have no fears, nor should you."

"You do not know Marie-François Goron, sir."

"Do you?"

She shivered. "He has an evil reputation. He will get the answer he wants, regardless of whether it is true. Glyn is doomed."

"Then why have you come to me?"

"Because you are the Prince of Wales and all of Paris respects you. The police would be compelled to listen to you."

This I could not deny and I rather liked the way she expressed it. Flattery would not have impressed me in the least, but she was speaking the truth. No one was better placed than I to intervene. I was seriously tempted to play the gallant prince coming to the aid of the maiden in distress. Young Rosine sensed it and shed a tear. Because I cannot abide women who weep, I gave her grounds for hope. "If I am to be of any use at all in this matter, I must know exactly what has happened between you and the painter."

She uttered a shrill cry as if unable to believe her ears and then answered in a rush of words that ended in another fit, of weeping, "Sir, I don't know whether I understand you correctly, but nothing has happened. Nothing! Nothing!"

I got up and poured two cognacs, the smaller for her.

She said, "Sir, if that is intended for me—"

I said sternly, "You will drink it. You are becoming hysterical."

"I am not allowed."

"You are commanded. Every drop, before we speak any more of this."

It was only a small measure. She obeyed, screwing up her face as the spirit warmed her throat, then taking the rest like medicine. Not the way to treat fine cognac, but it had the desired effect. She said, "It makes my head feel strange, as if I am floating."

"It will pass. Now, I was told by your papa that you first met Morgan in the village church."

"That is correct." She gave me the story almost exactly as I had heard it from Jules.

"You make him sound like a young man, but I am told he is over fifty," I said.

"I don't think about his age when I'm with him. Glyn is so much more charming than boys of twenty. He is wise and he sees beauty in everything. He may lack material possessions, but he is infinitely rich in talent and vision."

"You mean his painting?"

"Sir, I mean his mind. What is painting but marks on a canvas? His mind directs the brush."

"Forgive me, I haven't seen his work," said I, striving to keep the conversation from becoming too ethereal. "He is one of the group who call themselves Impressionists, is he not?"

"Glyn would not be fettered to any movement. He is happy to spend many a long hour discussing theories of art with people like Monet and Renoir, but he is a free spirit."

He sounded to me like a windbag. "And you have been meeting him regularly? You had better be frank with me."

At this, the color might have risen to her cheeks, but she was already flushed with the cognac. "I can't deny it, sir. Glyn has lately been painting landscapes in the park around Montroger—with my papa's permission, I must add. I go riding each afternoon, and that is when we have tended to see each other."

I was amused by the innocent-sounding "tended to see each other," as if she cantered past him with no more than a wave of the whip. "Where do you meet—in that ruined house?" When she hesitated, I said, "For heaven's sake, child, I'm not going to stand in judgment."

"We meet there sometimes, yes," she answered, adding quickly, "but in no way could our meetings be construed as shameful, or furtive. We have conversations, marvelous, inspiring discussions about art and poetry and the meaning of life. Everything Glyn says is so . . . so liberating."

Perhaps fatigue was setting in, or perhaps I am becoming jaded as I approach middle age, but all this talk of poetry and philosophy struck me as depressingly juvenile. Don't misunderstand. I can respond to a young girl's beauty as well as ever I did, but some of the drivel they talk is depressing. Give me a lady of maturity every time, only let her be passably handsome, as well. "And did you discuss the murder?"

"Only to agree that killing can never be justified."

"He said that?"

"No, sir, I did. But Glyn did not demur."

I fetched the decanter and poured more cognac into both glasses. She gave me the look of a trapped deer as she put hers to her lips and took a gulp. I selected a cigar from my case and trimmed it thoughtfully. "There is something I ought to point out to you, Rosine. If, as you maintain, your friend Morgan is innocent of this murder, some other person must be guilty. Now we know that the revolver used by the murderer came from the gun room at Montroger. The inescapable conclusion must be that one of your own family shot Maurice Letissier. Have you considered this possibility?"

"I cannot bear to think about it."

"Four people," I pressed her, "including yourself."

She said passionately, "I didn't kill Maurice."

"I'm relieved to hear it. That leaves your parents and Tristan." She put down the brandy glass and covered her eyes.

After a pause, I said, "If you know of anything suspicious . . ."

She was silent.

I took some time over lighting the cigar. "Let us talk about the victim. You and Letissier were first introduced during the Grande Semaine two years ago, I gather from your papa."

"Yes, sir." She proceeded to give me her version of the candlelit supper at Cubat's, which didn't differ markedly from her father's, except that she told it in a tone of icy disenchantment.

"You said that your mama was seated beside Letissier and got on well with him."

"She declared him to be the most eligible young man she had met since my father," Rosine admitted.

"But you did not? I sympathize, my dear. If anything is calculated to turn one against a prospective suitor, it is the enthusiasm of one's parents."

"I didn't dislike Maurice," she told me. "He was a good conversationalist. Anyone who can keep my mother from talking for minutes at a time must be a social asset. He was handsome, too, with a big mustache that he got rid of recently. He should have kept it, because his hair was rapidly getting thinner on top—he was practically bald, in fact." She hesitated, conscious that she might have given offense. "I know it happens to some gentlemen, most gentlemen, but not when they are young."

"It was probably inherited," said I.

She said generously, "I think all gentlemen look better with mustaches. And beards, ideally."

"How right you are!"

"But even if he'd been the most handsome man in the world, I couldn't have brought myself to love him," she declared. "By then, I had already met Glyn, and beside Glyn, Maurice was shallow. Papa arranged a dinner party with the Letissiers—a real ordeal—when I was supposed to succumb to Maurice's endearing personality. I did not. He was amusing, attentive to me, and paid me compliments, but he couldn't compare with Glyn."

"Did you say this to your parents?"

"Of course—from at least the time it was made clear to me that they wanted him as a son-in-law. When I told Mama about Glyn and she learned that he was a poor painter more than twice my age who despised the sort of life we led, there were terrible, painful arguments. Mainly, the onslaught came from Mama, because she has always had the most to say in our family, but Papa made it clear that he supported her. It went on for many months. Cruel things were said on both sides. They even suggested I must have allowed Glyn to seduce me, which was a vile slander and showed how little they understood Glyn or trusted me. And I threatened them with a *sommation respectueuse.* Do you know what that is?"

"Yes," I said, "your papa explained. You can enlist the Civil Code to marry against your parents' wishes. After three declarations, you are at liberty to wed the man of your choice."

She nodded. "But I didn't tell them that Glyn and I would never marry."

"Oh." This pronouncement took me so completely by surprise that I bit on my cigar and ruined it.

"Glyn doesn't believe in marriage," she explained. "He says it was invented because most people are too weak willed to trust each other. He believes we should be free to make whatever arrangement we like with the partner of our choice. It can be just as binding as a formal marriage if we choose, but it should be no concern of the church or the state."

"He *is* a freethinker. So he had no intention of marrying you?"

"Absolutely none. That is why, in the end, I agreed to marry Maurice."

I frowned, unable to follow her reasoning. "But you say you loved Morgan."

"I still do," she said with conviction. "I have never wavered."

And who could doubt her, even if the brandy glass was wavering perilously? I was hearing things I would never have heard without the aid of the cognac.

"So why marry a man you do not love?"

"Because after a married lady has provided her husband with a son, she may take a lover," she confided, her eyes shining at the prospect. "Have I shocked you, sir?"

"No," I said after a moment's thought. "You have just persuaded me to speak to the *chef de la Sûreté.* If Morgan had no intention of marrying you, then the obvious motive for murdering Letissier is removed. This was not clear to me until a moment ago. It is imperative that this information is communicated to Monsieur Goron. I shall visit him in the morning."

She sprang up from the sofa and reached for my hand. "Sir, you are a hero! *Un preux chevalier!* Let us drink to your success!"

"I think not," said I, reaching for her glass. "I shall arrange a carriage to take you home and a maid to escort you, and I think it would not be wise to have another drop of brandy before you meet your parents and explain why you were out so late."

After she had gone, I ordered the supper I had denied myself for so many hours. Feeling famished, I chose for my main course *côtelettes de bécassines* à *la Souvaroff,* a snipe dish guaranteed to quell the pangs, for the bird is well stuffed with forcemeat and foie gras and the whole is grilled in a sow's caul and served as cutlets with truffles and Madeira sauce. On reflection, I was mistaken to choose a fish dish quite so substantial as sea bass, coming after pea soup, because by the time everything was served, the night was well advanced, and my stomach didn't take kindly to the horizontal position that the rest of my constitution demanded. In consequence, I sat up in bed for some hours regretting the French version of plum duff that completed the meal.

Between interruptions I need not go into, I reflected on what I had learned from Rosine. Far from confirmed by the arrest of Morgan, the identity of the murderer was once again a mystery. Of course I could not ignore the possibility that Rosine had lied to me to enlist my support. She had the intelligence to deceive, I was sure, and she would do anything to secure Morgan's release. Yet her statement that he rejected marriage as an institution fitted the impression I had gained of the man. If he had not killed Letissier to thwart the match with Rosine, what could have been the motive? It was certainly time I met him and formed my own judgment.

CHAPTER 10

Carrying an armful of daffodils, I called early next morning at Bernhardt's lair, 56 boulevard Pereire, resolved that the misunderstanding of the previous evening would be put right. Our friendship was too precious to sacrifice for want of a few words of explanation. Besides, I wanted Sarah in support when I tangled with Monsieur Goron of the Sûreté.

Her factotum, Pitou, received me. Pitou is a failed violinist who at some time in the past insinuated himself into the Bernhardt establishment and will never leave. I had forgotten he existed until he opened the door and stared at me with his spaniel eyes.

"Pitou, my dear fellow!"

"Your Royal—"

"Is she up and about?" I asked.

"Madame Bernhardt?"

"Who else? I must see her at once."

"Sir, begging your pardon, that is impossible."

"Why—is she in the bath?"

"She gave me instructions."

"She is laboring under a whopping misapprehension. Are the animals at liberty in the house?"

"Not the larger animals, sir."

"Stand aside, then. I'd like to come in."

Poor Pitou. He was in a fearful dilemma. Clearly, Bernhardt had banned me from the house, but it was not in the man's character to stand in anyone's way, let alone mine. He is one of nature's doormats.

I strode into the entrance hall. The house is furnished like a rajah's palace, with exotic rugs and cushions everywhere, and hardly a square inch of wallpaper to be seen for oil paintings of Bernhardt in various dramatic roles.

Her voice came from upstairs. "Who is it, Pitou?"

I gestured to Pitou to remain silent. In a servile tone, I called up, "A gentleman delivering flowers. Flowers from Wales, madame."

Bernhardt said, "That's not Pitou. My God, if it's that philandering old goat from England, I'll castrate him with my bare hands." She rushed to the top of the stairs, where she could see me. "It is, you monster!" She grabbed a vase and hurled it at me. It smashed a yard from my feet.

Somewhere in the house, a parrot cackled at the prospect of a fight.

Forty-five minutes later, forty-five minutes I shall not dwell upon except to state that I needed at least thirty of them to secure a hearing, a carriage left the boulevard Pereire to convey Bernhardt and me to the Île de la Cité, that island in the Seine that houses not only Notre Dame but the Palais de Justice and the Préfecture de Police.

"I don't know why I agreed to this," Bernhardt complained to me halfway down the avenue Marceau. "This place has an evil reputation."

"You agreed because an innocent man is incarcerated there," I said tersely, not wanting more of her tantrums. "And because, like me, you want to know the truth about the murder at the Moulin Rouge."

"What use will I be? You are perfectly capable of talking to Goron."

"Yes, but who will talk to the prisoner? From what I know of Morgan, he is a rampant anarchist. The very notion of royalty is anathema to him. He'll regard me as the enemy. But we know he is susceptible to feminine charm. You'll coax the truth from him."

She clicked her tongue and stared out of the window.

"And more importantly," I added, "I can't bear to be apart from you."

Millions of women would have given their eye teeth to hear

words like that from me. Not Sarah Bernhardt. She made a vulgar sound with her lips.

I must admit that when we crossed the Pont Neuf, I shuddered, for, like Bernhardt, I knew the vile history of the Ile, the unspeakable sufferings that people of refinement had endured there. I have heard that the island is a warren of underground tunnels, more than twenty miles of them linking countless cells and dungeons with the Préfecture; the sinister Conciergerie, where, during the Terror, thousands of the aristocracy spent their last days; and the Palais de Justice, where those bloodthirsty hags, the *tricoteuses*, would look up from their knitting and cry, "To the guillotine!"

I wouldn't say it to a Frenchman, but in these supposedly more enlightened times, the concentration of police, prison and law courts on one small island is itself sinister, to my mind, laying them open to the suspicion of summary justice.

We were put down outside the Préfecture at 36 quai des Orfèvres, our driver having assured us that the Sûreté also had its headquarters there. We made ourselves known to the guard and were permitted to enter.

It was an intimidating place with a high ceiling, where voices echoed, and the stone floor reeked of disinfectant. After a short hiatus while the usual panic ensued at an unexpected royal visit, we were escorted upstairs to where the *chef de la Sûreté* presided, in a barn of a room overlooking the river. Marie-François Goron was behind a large ebony desk. He had the grace to stand and receive us properly and I noted an improvement in the state of his mustache since our last encounter in the bracken at Montroger. The ends were beautifully waxed. But he still looked an unlikely policeman, stunted in height and wheezing with the effort of getting up. This time, he was wearing pince-nez; a shipping clerk, conceivably, or a teacher of Latin. Never the top detective in France.

Not wanting to declare my hand too soon, I inquired how the investigation of Morgan was progressing.

"Satisfactorily," he said, equally guarded. "Forgive me, I was not expecting such distinguished guests." He snapped his fingers and some minion working at the opposite end of the room brought chairs for us. "May I presume that you have fresh information touching on the case?"

"Presume whatever you wish, my dear fellow. We would like

to speak to Mr. Morgan," said I, refusing to be drawn into some kind of interrogation.

Goron regarded me speculatively over the pince-nez. "With what purpose, Your Majesty?"

I could not be certain whether the way he addressed me was calculated sarcasm or a foreigner's gaffe, so I ignored it. "He is, I believe, a British subject."

"That is true, sir."

"It is the practice in civilized countries to enable foreigners in custody to be visited by their consuls."

"Certainly."

"The British consul is the representative of the queen. If you wish to go to the trouble of verifying with the consul that I have my mother's authority to make this visit . . ."

"Good Lord, that won't be necessary, sir," said Goron, faced by the specter of a diplomatic incident. "He is being held downstairs, but I can have him brought up. He has already been questioned intensively."

"With what result?"

Goron gave that peculiarly French shrug that involves every muscle in the upper half of the body and conveys absolutely nothing.

"Then has he admitted anything at all?"

"It is too soon, I think, sir." The implication was clear. Goron expected to extract a confession regardless of how long it took. "I will have him sent up."

"No," I said astutely. "We would prefer to see him in the place where he is being held."

The pince-nez flashed. "Whatever you wish, Your Royal Highness, but it is not very agreeable down there." He gave a patronizing smile. "Madame Bernhardt may care to remain here."

Which showed how little he knew of Sarah. She wasn't the frail female. She gave him a murderous look and said, "Monsieur, I didn't come here to twiddle my thumbs in an empty office."

Goron shrugged again, took a key from his desk drawer, got up, and unlocked a door to our left. He led us along a paneled corridor and down an iron spiral staircase to a level that felt markedly colder, a dimly lit brick-lined passage that appeared to stretch to infinity. A uniformed warder stepped in behind us without a word, the keys at his belt clinking. "Be careful of your clothes, madame," Goron cautioned Bernhardt. "There is mold on the walls."

A row of cell doors presently came in view and we stopped outside one. The turnkey took down a lantern from a ledge opposite and lighted it. Then he made a selection from his key ring. Goron turned to us and said, "I would advise you to remain outside for a moment."

Presently, an evil-smelling bucket was conveyed from the cell. Even without it, the place was not the most fragrant I have ventured into.

The lantern's flickering light showed us a standing figure wrapped in a blanket. The face was broad, the eyes focused above our heads, the mouth down turned in defiance. With the blanket and his fine growth of beard, Morgan looked not unlike some Old Testament prophet.

"You have just been told who we are, I take it?" I said in English, to put him at his ease. "Would you care for a cigarette?"

He gave a nod.

In fact, we all lit up, including Bernhardt, for cigarette smoke was much to be preferred to the odors latent in the cell. Morgan's hand shook when I held the flame to his cigarette, due more, I am certain, to the cold than his state of nerves. He had the deep-sunken dark eyes of the Celt and they glittered with offended pride. He betrayed no sign of being unmanned either by his predicament or my presence.

I explained that Bernhardt and I were taking a personal interest in the case, adding that we had spoken yesterday to Rosine d'Agincourt.

"Rosine?" His eyes narrowed. "Have these bastards arrested her as well?"

"No, no. She came to see me. She asked me to take up your case with the Sûreté."

"She's plucky."

At this point, Goron interrupted to ask if we would conduct the conversation in French, and I answered that I had no objection, provided that we could be frank. He gave me a stare that I took to be his consent.

"You heard that," I addressed Morgan in French. "How are they treating you?"

"Abysmally," he replied, and went on to say in fluent French, "I have not been given a bite to eat since I was brought here yesterday. They keep me in this stinking cell in darkness and bring me out every two hours for interrogation. I have had no sleep. I am chilled to the bone. They don't believe a word I say. What do they expect—that out of hunger and despair I'll confess to something I didn't do?"

I turned to Goron. "Did you know about this?" Before the *chef de la Sûreté* could respond, Morgan cried out, "Of course he knows, the bugger. He is my interrogator."

Goron flicked ash from his cigarette and remarked, "Prisoners who persistently insult their questioners can hardly expect us to provide privileges."

This incensed me. "Basic meals are not privileges, Monsieur Goron. The man has not been convicted of any crime. He is cold and hungry. I insist that he is fed at once. And he requires another blanket. Kindly arrange this with the warder."

Goron was apparently unmoved—until Bernhardt turned her cannon on him. "What are you waiting for? Can't you understand, you cretin? You make me ashamed to be French. Have some breakfast brought in for Monsieur Morgan, and a good one, or we shall go straight from here to the Minister of the Interior. This place may stink to hell, but we can make a bigger stink, believe me."

It was a mite excessive and I had my doubts what result it would bring, but the mention of the minister was decisive.

Goron capitulated, while muttering, "This is flagrant interference." He gave a nod to the turnkey and the man left the cell.

In a complete change of tone, Bernhardt said almost seductively to Morgan, "Monsieur, are you innocent?"

"Innocent of what, madame?"

Slightly nonplussed, she said, "Of the crime of murder."

"Of course I am not a murderer."

"It may not be so obvious to others as it is to yourself. Speak up. This is your chance."

He said, "I'm a simple painter. All my life I have only wanted to paint. I should be out there now."

I said, "Tell us about your friendship with Rosine d'Agincourt."

He drew his blanket more closely around him. "I refuse to implicate her in this."

Bernhardt addressed him with the air of the grande dame she sometimes became when it suited her. "You had better listen to me, Monsieur Morgan. The only reason we are here is because that young lady went to extraordinary trouble to persuade us to come. She loves you. She believes in your innocence. You won't get her into trouble by speaking the truth. You owe it to her to speak out."

Just how prickly a character Morgan was became apparent when he responded to this uplifting statement by saying, "Look, I've been battered by questions most of the night. They threaten me with the guillotine one minute and promise me my freedom the next. Why should I believe anything you buggers say? How do I know you're not hand in glove with the Sûreté?"

I was about to admonish the fellow for using unparliamentary language in front of a lady, but just in time I realized that he was doing it to provoke me. Given half a chance, he would have lectured me on the iniquities of the monarchy. I said in a tone that admitted no nonsense, "Mr. Morgan, if you don't need our help, we'll cancel the breakfast and leave you as you were. There are other places I would rather be this morning, I can assure you."

Almost certainly it was the threat to his breakfast that did the trick. Morgan inhaled on his cigarette, blew out a cloud of smoke, and said as if we were his oldest chums, "All I ever gave Rosine was a few kisses. Poor little scrap, she was put through the mangle by those pigheaded parents of hers, trying to shackle her to Letissier. She came to me for the sympathy they should have given her. They're her own flesh and blood, for Christ's sake. Rosine is just a pathetic young girl with romantic ideas about people like me who ignore the chance of a comfortable life for the sake of art. I could have taken her to my bed anytime I wanted, and she would have let me, but I didn't, not once. When I want a woman, I know where to get one. Is that what you wanted to know?"

His blunt speaking didn't derail me. I responded firmly, "The way you conduct your private life is of no consequence, Mr. Morgan. The point is, would Rosine have married you?"

He gave a bleak smile. "She had childish ideas of eloping with me. Can you imagine? I'm over fifty, for God's sake. I told her I don't believe in marriage. I'm a painter, first and last. I'm in no position to keep a wife. I can't even keep myself."

"I thought you Impressionists made a decent living," I remarked.

"I'm not any kind of '-ist,'" he said sharply. "Anyway, you have to be an Academy painter to make a decent living, and I'm not one of those fossils, thank God. But don't go thinking that there's money in Impressionism. Most of that bunch are from the bourgeoisie. They had money in the bank already, or they wouldn't have survived—Manet, Degas, Bazille, Sisley. Old Pissarro dresses like a pauper, but he's bloody rich. Renoir and Monet were not so flush, but they feathered their nests as Salon painters first, both of them. Made themselves secure and then turned their coats. I'm the bloody fool who tries to do it on a shoestring. I've known one or two others who tried and starved, or went mad. As I told young Rosine time and again, it wouldn't be fair to take a wife."

"You didn't actively discourage her?"

"I didn't send her away, if that's what you mean. I pitied her."

"How did you feel when she finally agreed to the betrothal?"

He glanced upward as if the answer were written on the cell roof. "Not surprised, to be frank. She had no choice, really. Her parents were always going to get their way in the end. We talked about it. She had this idea that if she presented Letissier with a son, she would be free to take a lover. She made me laugh. Not bad to be thinking so far ahead when you're still a virgin. She was serious, though."

"You would have us believe that she did all the chasing, yet you went to the Moulin Rouge on the night of her engagement dinner."

"Ah, we've come to it now," said Morgan bitterly. "This is what they kept asking me all night."

"You don't deny you were there?"

"Certainly I was there, but I didn't put two bullets into Letissier."

"Why did you go at all?"

"It was a chance to get a squint at this young buck she was being mated with."

This wasn't the version I had been given by Rosine, and I didn't care for the vulgar way he expressed it, but it struck a note of truth. We had been given opinions of Morgan by Jules d'Agincourt and his daughter and neither altogether matched what was presently being revealed to us. "Did you speak to him?"

He stared back as if unable to believe I'd asked such a

preposterous question. "I may be a fool, but I'm not that daft. I wasn't there to make a scene. I kept my distance."

"Kept your distance all night?"

"Until after the shooting, anyway."

"How much did you see of it?"

"Practically nothing. I was across the room with a full glass of beer. I didn't want it spilt in the rush, did I? I heard the shots and thought some maniac was loose. I bolted into the garden with some others. Lost most of my beer in the process."

"Did you return to the ballroom?"

"Pretty soon, yes. Someone said a young toff in a silk hat and dinner jacket was the victim. I thought of Letissier and went to see. A lot of people had run out, like me, but there was a cluster around Letissier. He was in the middle of the floor. The comte was kneeling beside him and the comtesse was talking to people, asking what they saw. I think a doctor was there. I saw Rosine with her brother, a little back from the group. She was holding her arms across her chest. Thinking she might have been hurt, I went over to ask. She hadn't been hit. She was in a state of shock."

Bernhardt unexpectedly asked, "What was she wearing?" Morgan stopped, his flow of thought interrupted. "A blue dress, I think, Prussian blue, if that means anything to you, and a velvet cape over it, dark gray or black, with gold fastenings. People keep their coats on at the Moulin Rouge this time of year."

What this had to do with the fatal incident we were discussing was far from clear, and I was nettled by the interruption. Some of the fair sex think of little else but fashion. Until this moment, I had had a higher opinion of Sarah Bernhardt.

"You were saying that she was in a state of shock," I reminded Morgan.

"Yes. Oh, and she had one of those small black bonnets that are high tone now, with an ostrich-feather trimming."

I turned to Bernhardt and said cuttingly, "Do you have the picture now, or would you like to know about the shoes?"

She glared at me and I am sure she was about to say something sulfurous when the door opened and the breakfast was brought in on a tin tray. The turnkey placed it on the stone shelf that also functioned as the bed. And he handed Morgan an extra blanket that he'd slung over his shoulder.

I told Morgan he had better make a start on the food. He needed no second bidding and started wolfing bread rolls as if he hadn't eaten for weeks. I suppose he'd had little else to look forward to. To my eye, it wasn't much of a breakfast, but then if he'd been sitting at the best table in the Ritz, he would have been served nothing more appetizing than coffee and rolls. The French have no conception of what the first meal of the day should consist of. They don't even give it the status of a proper word in their language, calling it the "little luncheon." (They don't go in for afternoon tea, either, indulging instead in what is called a "five o'clock" at a public tearoom, where you nibble at pastries that could be consumed in a mouthful. Not a poached egg in sight.)

Goron was becoming restless. He asked if we had finished the interview and I told him frigidly that I would advise him when we were ready to depart.

He said morosely, "The prisoner has all morning to eat."

Unmoved, I said, "I would prefer to see for myself that he is allowed to finish what is in front of him."

One thing was certain: I had not made a friend for life of the *chef de la Sûreté.*

Only when every crumb was consumed did I prompt Morgan to resume his narrative.

"I told you practically all of it," he said. "I can't tell you who fired the shots, but it wasn't me. Rosine urged me to leave at once. I think she was alarmed that her father or someone would think I was the killer. Well, it could have looked suspicious, me being there. I took her advice and left on the double."

"You left the building immediately?"

"Isn't that what I just said?"

The man's uncivil tone wasn't helping his cause, but the conditions he'd been kept in were enough to test anyone's temper. I strove to remain tolerant. "You didn't go into the dressing room?"

He shook his head. "Why would I do that? I don't even know where the dressing room is. Are they going to release me now?"

Goron gave a sarcastic laugh. "You think you have talked your way out of here, do you? You think all these lies have fooled me? You are as guilty as hell, and you will confess; you will confess."

I said witheringly, "If he is kept in these appalling conditions and deprived of the most basic necessities, I am sure he will confess,

Monsieur Goron. There can't be a person alive who would not. I demand to be told your reasons for detaining Mr. Morgan."

"Sir, I'll do better than that," said Goron with the confident air of a man who knows more than he has revealed. "Kindly step upstairs and I'll show you the evidence."

"Evidence?" said Morgan. "You've got no bloody evidence. You've got nothing on me."

I said, "We should like to see it at once."

"And so would I," said Morgan with disbelief.

Goron said tersely, "Not you."

Bernhardt made a heartwarming speech, pure Joan of Arc, promising Morgan that he would not be forgotten, and then we left the wretched fellow to endure more hours in the darkness and the cold.

The barnlike office upstairs now seemed homely and agreeable. "You will appreciate why I was reluctant to invite you to the cell," Goron said as we drank coffee together. "The conditions are harsh, but there is a method to the treatment. I am an educated man, not a torturer. I have studied law enforcement intensively and achieved considerable success in interrogation. These days one does not resort to the thumbscrew and the rack to get the truth from a man unwilling at first to supply it. Morgan is a typical case. Intensive questioning is the first step. We keep the suspect literally in the dark and question him at regular intervals. Food and water are sparingly given and sleep is discouraged. But he will not be quartered in the dark cell for many more hours. We shall move him to a pleasantly lit one. He will be offered an adequate meal and wine in return for a statement. I am confident he will supply it—or we shall begin the whole process again." He extended his hands elegantly, as if he had just informed us how simple it is to lace one's shoes.

I couldn't stomach much more of this. I said, "This statement you expect to extract is the one that will incriminate him."

"Certainly."

"But what if he is innocent of the crime?"

"That is not my opinion," said Goron.

"Now look here. I came to this place pretty sure in my own mind that he was guilty. Having heard what he has to say, I am far from convinced."

"Nor I," chimed in Bernhardt.

"We thought this was a simple *crime passionnel*," I continued. "It seemed obvious that he was a jilted lover driven to murder by young Rosine's decision to wed Letissier. But having listened to the man—"

Goron interrupted. "Not a *crime passionnel*. Oh no. Morgan is too old for that. Young Rosine d'Agincourt—who knows he is guilty, by the way, but won't admit it—would like to believe it is a *crime passionnel* but she is deluded. The passion is all on her side. On his side, there is calculation." He took off the pince-nez and polished it. "Consider. Morgan is an unsuccessful painter. He lives a hand-to-mouth life, occupying empty houses when he can. He meets the young girl, Rosine, rich beyond his imagination. Sees an opportunity, not of romance, but of money and patronage. She is flattered by his foreign charm, by the romantic idea of the artist as her lover, and he sets out to insinuate himself into the Agincourt ménage. He gets permission to paint on their estate and takes up residence in a derelict cottage, where he bestows secret kisses on the girl."

I said, "All this may be true. He may be on the make, but a murderer? I have grave doubts."

"I'm coming to the murder," said Goron. "Does anything I have said conflict with what you have heard?"

"It's one possible interpretation," I conceded. "Please go on."

"Then Letissier appears on the scene. After being put through the mangle by her parents, as Morgan colorfully expresses it, Rosine is persuaded to become engaged. For Morgan, this is a disaster. He is about to lose the milch cow he has reared so diligently. If Rosine goes, he will surely be turned off the estate. He will lose his place of abode. He will no longer be able to tap Rosine for gifts of food and money, as I'm sure he did. So he decides to do away with Letissier. He acquires a revolver—from where, I do not know yet, but I have strong suspicions, and I will confirm them. In the Moulin, he picks his moment to perfection and shoots when everyone's eyes are on La Goulue. In case Rosine should suspect him, he appears at her side briefly to inquire whether she was hit. Then he leaves. A cold-blooded murder, carried out with cunning. He will confess. If not by tonight, then sometime tomorrow."

I didn't care for Goron's methods in the least, but I was

compelled to admit that he had laid his case before us persua-sively. I was swaying back to the conclusion that Morgan was guilty.

Bernhardt was less impressed than I and wasn't afraid to say so. She told Goron, "You promised to show us some evidence. All you have given us are theories."

"No," said Goron with a thin smile. "I have given you coffee. I thought you would enjoy that first. If you would like to see the evidence, be so good as to step into the next room with me."

We got up and followed him into a smaller room. And one couldn't deny that it was stuffed with evidence. Two trestle tables practically groaned under the weight of items connected with the case. A uniformed policeman was at work there, inscribing labels. With a wave of his hand, Goron dismissed the man from our presence.

Most of the objects already had labels attached to them. I noted a dinner jacket laid facedown to display two holes with scorched edges below the left shoulder. Beside it was an overcoat similarly holed. In case we missed the significance, there were postmortem sketches of the victims back and chest. The spent bullets had been recovered and were laid on a sheet of white paper. There was a floor plan of the ballroom at the Moulin Rouge. And there was a large sketchbook.

I picked up the latter and started turning the pages. Bernhardt, eager not to miss a thing, came to my side. Toulouse-Lautrec's excesses with the pencil were unmistakable. If that was art, give me a photograph every time. Without question, this was the sketchbook he had been using on the night of the murder.

"You will find what you're looking for if you start at the back," said Goron with a supercilious air.

I continued to examine the pages in the proper sequence, refusing to hurry. In my own good time, I came to a series of sketches recognizably made at the Moulin Rouge. They included people seated at tables and standing for the cabaret. As the little artist had insisted when we interviewed him, most of the drawings were rudimentary, barely recognizable as likenesses. I picked out one standing group that might have been the Agincourts. Then I turned the page and saw the final sketch, a more carefully exe-cuted study of a group of eight or nine figures clustered around a prostrate form that could only have been the corpse of Maurice

Letissier. Mercifully, it was drawn from a foreshortened viewpoint, the hairless top of the head the most notable feature. Somewhere to one side lay a silk hat. Beside the victim, two figures were kneeling, one—presumably the doctor—supporting the head; the other, leaning over him in an attitude of concern, undoubtedly Jules. It was a simple matter to pick out the pigeon-chested Juliette, standing beside a man of vast girth I recognized as Martineau, the manager of the Moulin Rouge. Juliette had her mouth open, holding forth as usual. Slightly to the rear but just recognizable was Tristan, in the floppy black tam-o'-shanter that you see everywhere in the Latin Quarter, standing with his sister Rosine and the bearded figure of Morgan.

Goron stepped closer and jabbed a finger at the likeness of Morgan. "Proof positive that the suspect was there that night. I confirmed it with Lautrec. He knows Morgan as a fellow artist, of course."

Making no comment, I closed the sketchbook and returned it to where I had found it.

The other table was heaped with paraphernalia that I assumed had been brought here from the cottage at Montroger where Morgan had been arrested. There were cups, plates, and cutlery; some clothes; a stack of canvases; an easel; a box of paints and brushes; and a double-barreled shotgun and some cartridges.

"Your Majesty, have you heard of Cesare Lombroso?"

I looked across to Goron, who was now holding a large leather-bound book open at a page with a bookmark inside.

"An Italian?"

"The professor of criminal anthropology at Turin University, a man of genius who has made exhaustive studies of the criminal class. This is his book, *L'Uomo Delinquente.* Do you know Italian, sir?"

"*Criminal Man?*" I hazarded.

"Precisely. Professor Lombroso examined the physical characteristics of over seven thousand convicts and reached the interesting conclusion that criminals may be recognized by their physical appearance. This is the fruit of his research, a standard work of reference for investigators. The indispensable guide to the malefactors it is my job to find. Look at this page of murderers, for example. Note the receding foreheads, the heavy jaws, and the characteristic ears."

I took the book from him. The illustrations showed an unlovely set of profiles, but no more intimidating, I would have thought, than a picture I could recall of the bishops of England and Wales. Beside me, Bernhardt thought otherwise. She said in a tone of high alarm, "Oh, Bertie! Look!"

"I think you have anticipated me, Madame Bernhardt," Goron said smugly.

"This one in the bottom row," said Bernhardt in a shocked whisper.

"I am glad you agree," murmured Goron.

I studied the portrait to which Sarah was pointing. Undeniably, there was a distinct resemblance to Morgan. "I suppose if the beard was slightly fuller . . ." said I.

"The beard is of no significance, sir," said Goron. "Criminal anthropology is based on the physical features that cannot be altered. The criminal type can be recognized as the modern embodiment of primitive humanity. The typical criminal exhibits the ferocious instincts of uncivilized man. The shape of the head, the structure of the features and their relative sizes—these are the significant indications. The man downstairs conforms in every significant particular to the archetype of a murderer."

"I'm sure you're right," said I. "But this fellow in the row above looks uncannily like my brother Affie, the Duke of Edinburgh, and he's no murderer."

"Pure coincidence," said Goron. "Does your brother have long arms?"

"Not that I have noticed."

"The criminal type always has arms longer than the average. We have measured Morgan's and found them to be two centimeters longer than the norm."

"He's a large fellow."

"He also has acute eyesight, another criminal tendency."

"Really?"

"The evidence is overwhelming."

"I shall suspend judgment," said I, closing the book and returning it to him. The science of criminal anthropology didn't impress me at all. "And speaking of evidence, I cannot see the point in labeling some of these objects. What's this shotgun, for example?"

"It was recovered from Morgan when we arrested him. You will recall that he was shooting rabbits that morning. We found these cartridges in his pocket."

"But the victim was killed with a revolver. What is the significance of the shotgun?"

Goron picked it up and handed it to me. "Examine the metal plate inlaid into the stock. That is the Agincourt coat of arms. The gun was removed from the gun room at Montroger—clear evidence not only that Morgan stole this weapon but that he had access to a variety of weapons, including revolvers."

I may have reddened slightly. Certainly I cleared my throat in an embarrassed way. It happened that in my pocket was the murder weapon. I had fully intended to hand it over, having foreseen that this meeting would be the opportunity to unburden myself of something for which I had no further use. To retain it any longer could lead to embarrassment, even incrimination. By producing it now, I seemed to be sealing Morgan's guilt, but one should not manipulate justice.

"What is this?" asked Goron when I placed it on the desk.

"Well, if you of all people don't know, I fear for Paris," said I, recovering my poise. "It's a six-chambered silver revolver and it was found in the pocket of an overcoat left in the men's dressing room at the Moulin Rouge on the night of the murder. You will note that the arms on the side plate are those of the Agincourts."

He stared at the gun without moving a hand toward it. "How did you acquire this?"

"By vigorously pursuing inquiries."

His eyes locked with mine and I discerned some respect in them, but antagonism also, and the antagonism was driving out the respect.

I said loftily, "I am not at liberty to say more, except that the owner of the overcoat is unquestionably innocent. The murderer placed the gun in the pocket at some time after the shooting but before everyone left the dressing room. The coat's owner found it when he put on the coat to leave the ballroom."

"Is it loaded?"

"I removed the remaining bullets." Taking three from my other pocket, I placed them beside the revolver. "One shot was fired at the time the weapon came into my possession."

Goron's eyes widened. "I shall need to know more than you have seen fit to tell me, Your Majesty."

"Royal Highness," I said with formal coolness. "You must accept my word that what I have told you is true."

Bernhardt spoke up. "Monsieur, I can vouch for every word that His Royal Highness has spoken. I was present when he acquired the gun from the person concerned."

Goron picked up the revolver and examined it. "This is certainly the Agincourt coat of arms."

"It reduces the number of suspects by several hundred," I remarked to pacify him. "It will save you no end of time."

"When did you acquire the revolver?" Goron demanded.

"Quite recently."

"The details are confidential," reiterated Bernhardt.

Goron said, "Like the shotgun, apparently, it was stolen from the Agincourts."

"That, we cannot say for certain. It comes from the gun room at Montroger, without any question. I have seen the cabinet where it was kept. Neither the gun room nor the cabinet is kept locked."

"You have already checked these matters?"

"Yes."

"So you acquired the gun before today?"

"A fair deduction. But I shall give nothing else away."

"It seals Morgan's guilt," stated Goron with certainty. "This is fascinating. He must have meant the gun to be found, or why would he have gone into the dressing room and dropped it into someone's overcoat pocket? He could have walked off with it and thrown it in the Seine. What made him change his mind?"

We were silent.

"I'll tell you," said Goron. "He wanted the Agincourts to come under suspicion"

"But why?" said Bernhardt "They were his providers, if all that you have said is true."

Goron brooded on this for a moment. "It begins to look as if something very provocative happened on the day of the murder. Suppose the comte chose this day to banish Morgan from Montroger. After all, Rosine was now engaged to Letissier. It was most undesirable that she should continue to rendezvous with the painter. The comte must have spoken to the fellow and told him to go. Morgan was so incensed that he used one of their own revolvers to kill the wretched Letissier and then left it to be found. Naturally suspicion would fall on the family."

"In that case, why did he continue after the murder to trespass on the estate?" said Bernhardt—cleverly, I thought. "Wouldn't it have been more sensible to leave the district?"

"No." The *chef de la Sûreté* was adamant. "That would have looked suspicious. He kept his nerve and stayed, confident that the revolver would be found and point inexorably to the guilt of one of the family. If it had been handed to me on the night of the murder, as Morgan intended, he would not be in custody now. I might well have suspected someone else." He smiled. "A few minutes ago, I was ready to accuse you of obstructing the work of the Sûreté, Your Highness. I was mistaken. Quite inadvertently, you have foiled Morgans cunning deception."

CHAPTER 11

After that, I need fortifying," I told Bernhardt. "Shall we find ourselves some lunch?"

This being a fine morning, the first promise of spring, we strolled in the sunshine as far as the Pont Michel and crossed to the Left Bank, to the boulevard Saint-Michel, or Boul'Mich, as it is known to all Parisians. At the top end, it is lined with cafés and restaurants catering to every nationality. We walked past several where we would have looked conspicuous. The Vachette was filled with elegantly dressed Africans from, I would guess, Madagascar and Martinique, who would, I am sure, have welcomed us. A band of cadets of the Ecole Polytechnique in their cocked hats had occupied the Soufflet; and the Café Steinbach was emphatically given over to Germans drinking beer at fifty centimes a glass. We wanted a table on the sunny side of the boulevard, and we finally settled for a discreet place in the third row outside the Café d'Harcourt, where the English tend to congregate, and ordered aperitifs. I suppose the weather had put people in a larky mood, because we could hear much laughter from the other tables. A pretty grisette unselfconsciously lifted her skirt to place a handkerchief in her stocking top, whereupon a young man at another table created much amusement by slyly imitating her, slipping his matchbox into his sock. It was difficult to credit amid this gaiety that people were languishing in dark cells just across the bridge.

I made an effort to dismiss the thought. "Cannes is calling to me," I told Sarah. "Do you think if I left this afternoon I could be there before midnight?"

She turned to me and placed her hand over mine. "Bertie, you can't leave Paris."

Ever the optimist, I took this to mean that she wanted to rekindle the flame so unkindly extinguished the previous evening, but she added immediately, "We must do something about that odious little man."

"Goron?"

"Unless we stop him, he'll force a confession and an innocent man will go to the guillotine."

"Oh, I don't think that's likely," I told her. "No one but Morgan could be the murderer."

She said nothing, making her disagreement clear by staring across the street as if I was no longer at the same table.

Tolerantly—for I knew she was genuinely troubled—I reminded her that her own country's law has its safeguards. "It isn't only up to Goron. The *juge d'instruction* will see that the police are conducting the investigation properly."

She was unconvinced. "Can you imagine a magistrate who would disbelieve the famous Goron?" Turning to face me, she said in a tone that was almost accusing, it was so forceful, "Bertie, you conscripted me as your assistant and now you must listen to me. Morgan is innocent. I understand him, because I, too, am an artist. I value my talent above all things. Morgan cares too much about painting to put it at risk by killing a man. His supposed motive for the crime isn't at all convincing. Look, the man has been living on the edge of poverty all his life. If he's ejected from the cottage at Montroger, so what? It's no different from all the other hovels he's had to leave for want of payment. This has been his way of life; he expects to be asked to move on. Why should he suddenly become so angry about it that he commits murder—and not even the murder of the man who evicts him? Why kill Letissier? Why not Jules?"

I had no answer.

She said, "This is a simple man, not Cesare Borgia."

I nodded. She'd argued with her usual clarity and there was a certain amount of good sense in what she said. Goron's version of events had sounded plausible enough in the Sûreté. Here in the sunshine, I was being swayed again. "The case against Morgan looked cut-and-dried before we met him, when we thought it was a *crime passionnel,*" I conceded. "But we're asked to believe something else. Whatever one may say about Morgan, he isn't a frustrated lover."

"He's too old for that nonsense," Bernhardt said sweepingly. It was meant to support what I had said, so I let it pass.

I said, "I just can't conceive of one of the Agincourts murdering Letissier."

She looked at me with intensity. "You must face it, Bertie—one of them is guilty."

"They're respectable people. I've known them for years."

"The daughter and the son?" said Bernhardt sharply. "You told me you hadn't seen Rosine since she was a child and you couldn't remember Tristan at all."

"My dear Sarah, their parents are people of refinement."

"No one—not even you—can make statements like that with absolute certainty," she told me. "All my life people I took to be respectable have given me shocks."

"I dare say you gave some in return," said I.

I meant the remark lightheartedly, wanting to relax her. Instead of smiling, she put her hand to her mouth and looked away. What was in her mind, I cannot say for certain, but I'd once heard the story from another source that at eighteen she had met a Belgian nobleman, the Prince de Ligne, at a masked ball. At the end of the evening, this young man in the costume of Hamlet had presented her with a rose. Enchanted by his charm and blond good looks, Sarah had given herself to him. Some weeks later, her prince was having a housewarming and unkindly neglected to invite her. Being Sarah, she arrived dramatically on his doorstep and informed him that she was expecting his child. He told her with appalling cruelty that she should realize that if she sat on a pile of thorns she would never know which one had pricked her, and he sent her away. To her eternal credit, she had raised their illegitimate child with no help from de Ligne. Her son Maurice was now himself married.

The waiter asked for the order. Bernhardt, as usual, had no appetite and settled for a brioche and black coffee. I ordered plovers' eggs, followed by salmon, lamb cutlets, and stewed fruit.

"I have always taken the view that a man in my position should eat lunch," I explained to lighten her mood. "My brother-in-law George, the king of Greece, eats frugally at lunchtime, thus causing his guests to swallow their food in gulps for fear of being caught conversing with their mouths full, because George will keep asking them questions. With me, there is no risk of anyone choking to death."

She said without the glimmer of a smile, "Bertie, I keep thinking back to something that poor man Morgan told us. He said that after the shots were fired, he went across to Rosine, supposing that she might have been hurt."

"That's right."

"He said she was standing quite still, a little apart from the group surrounding Letissier. She appeared to be in a state of shock and—the phrase I particularly noted—her arms were across her chest."

"Well?"

"That was when I inquired what she was wearing. Remember?"

"All too vividly," said I. "I wasn't expecting the interrogation to stop for an excursion into fashion."

"Yes, but do you recall what Mr. Morgan told us?"

"My dear, I was too peeved to listen."

"He said she was wearing a velvet cape, dark gray or black."

"Ah," said I, trying to keep up.

"A cape, Bertie." Her eyes widened encouragingly, but I wasn't able to supply the comment she expected. Too impatient to wait, she said, "She had her arms across her chest, but nobody could see them because she was wearing the cape."

"Oh, I don't think that's important," said I. "He probably guessed she had her arms folded from the shape of the cape. The elbows would project a bit, like so."

A small sigh escaped her lips. "I wasn't questioning that. I was speculating that if she was holding a revolver, nobody would be able to tell."

"Rosine—with the revolver? You're not suggesting that *she* fired the shots?"

"Certainly I am," she said, and she would have thumped the table as well if it had not been so rickety. "She's the obvious suspect now. She was infatuated with the artist. Everyone agrees on that, including herself."

Smiling, I said, "It's our old friend the *crime passionnel* after all, is it?"

She frowned. It was no joking matter to Sarah. "Yes, and why not?"

"My dear, if Rosine is the guilty party, why did she come to see me last night? A murderer doesn't assist the investigation."

"She was driven to it. The man she loves—the man she killed for—is being unfairly accused of the crime. When she shot Letissier, she didn't expect her lover to be arrested. She came to you hoping you could use your influence to free him."

"Which I have failed to do."

"Only because Rosine didn't tell you the whole truth. Bertie, if only for the sake of Mr. Morgan, we have to go back to Montroger and get her to confess."

Hotel Bristol
Paris

My dearest Alix,

The quickest of notes to let you know that in spite of my best intentions I am delayed in Paris another day. One more wearisome engagement that Francis Knollys couldn't put off. Rest assured that my next letter will be sent from Cannes.

Ever your loving,
Bertie

Imagine my dismay when we were received not by Rosine, but her garrulous mother. The French have a phrase—*"une femme formidable"*—that is so apt for Juliette d'Agincourt that it must stand. It would lose something in translation. If you have no French at all, let me put it another way. Occasionally before a dinner, I have secretly slipped into the dining room and switched the place card of one of the fair sex. I once did it for Juliette—to locate her as far from me as possible.

This dowager was in what I believe was known as a Directoire costume, an attempt to disguise a bulging middle with stays that creaked each time she moved. The top layer was dark green plush—the material footmen's breeches are made from—and looked most unappealing. I had to remind myself firmly that Juliette was a crucial witness and we needed to speak to her.

Not much chance of that. She was going like a barrel organ. "Your Royal Highness, Madame Bernhardt, you shouldn't do this! Jules has gone to Paris for the day. He won't forgive himself for missing you, and I'm in no state to welcome you properly. You'll have to excuse me. You'd like to speak to Rosine, I was told, but she is indisposed today. It's to be expected after all she's been through. I say 'indisposed' and it sounds like a mild dose of indigestion, but she's suffering terribly, poor child. This tragedy has affected us all in different ways. Such an enormous shock. I detest shocks, don't you? I swear that dear Jules has grown a crop of silver hairs he never had a month ago. We hardly ever see Tristan except at meals, and then he is silent as the grave. Would his age have something to do with it, do you think? He goes out shooting by the hour. As for me, I'm quite unable to do any tapestry for the shaking of my hands."

She paused for a breath and I seized my chance. "Would you be good enough to let Rosine know that we are here? She may rally a little at the news, I fancy."

"What news?" she said, her eyes the size of donkey droppings.

"The news that we are here."

The droppings shrank to rabbit size. "Oh, I thought you were going to say that Morgan had confessed. The sooner he does, the better for us all, including Rosine. How can I persuade her that this parasite she calls her friend is utterly without morals, capable of absolutely anything? He would have seduced her. That was the only thing he had in mind, you know. That was why he was lurking about the estate for months on end like some horrible tomcat. I'm sorry to sound indelicate, Madame Bernhardt, but this is the reality we had to face. The guillotine is too quick for a man like that. He deserves a lingering death, like being eaten alive by crabs."

"So far as we know, Madame la Comtesse, the worst he is guilty of is a few stolen kisses," said Bernhardt with such scathing hostility that my own skin prickled.

"He's under arrest, isn't he?" said Juliette. "You don't get arrested for kissing. He's a murderer. No one else had any reason to shoot poor Maurice. Well, did they? Did they?"

"Juliette, kindly be so good as to let Rosine know that we are here," I repeated before Bernhardt got another word in.

"She won't come down," our hostess stated as if it was carved in stone.

"I am not insisting that she comes down."

"Very well." She rang for a servant and started up again before either of us opened our mouths to speak. "What exactly is your interest in this dreadful business? This is the third time to my certain knowledge that you have visited Montroger in as many days. Jules said something about your wanting to solve the mystery, but the Sûreté have solved it."

"Not to our satisfaction," said Bernhardt.

With nice timing, a manservant answered the summons and prevented Juliette from launching into another tirade. She instructed him to convey our message to Rosine.

Precisely as he closed the door, I said, "To answer your question, Juliette, I like to think of myself as a friend of the Agincourt family, and I would be a poor friend if I failed to apply my deductive talents, such as they are, to unraveling the mystery. Sarah has generously agreed to join me in the quest. Up to the present, we are far from satisfied that the truth of this matter has been revealed. In fact, it would oblige us greatly if you would answer some questions."

She made her most unlikely statement so far. "I'm sure I can add nothing to what you have been told already." And immediately she contradicted herself with another outpouring of words. "If you want to know about poor Maurice, rest his soul, I would have welcomed him as a second son. He would have been perfect for Rosine—amusing, handsome, sophisticated, and with a private fortune. From an old French family, properly educated, completed his military service with distinction, a most able sportsman—what else could one look for in a potential husband? Naturally Jules and I urged Rosine not to miss her opportunity. The silly minx took her time deciding, but girls do sometimes, and she had this loathsome person Morgan doing his best to distract her. She has always had a wild streak and anything vaguely bohemian holds a fascination for her. Gypsy violins, circuses, and sensational novels. When she was just a child she wrote a love letter to a Bretonne onion seller. What I'm saying is that we had to steer her gently in the right direction."

"From what I heard, you had to wrestle with the tiller," said I, "and there were rough seas, too."

"She told you that? She dramatizes everything. What she needs, as I pointed out so often, is a husband who will steady her, not some vagrant painter hoping to live off her money."

"Does she have money?"

"Eighty thousand francs in trust from her late grandfather. She'll inherit on her next birthday. I kept telling her, if Morgan wasn't out to seduce her, he was certainly a fortune hunter."

Bernhardt opened her mouth to speak up for Morgan, but I preempted her, enunciating my words with an emphasis that brooked no interference. "Perhaps you will give us your account of the events leading up to the murder."

"It was supposed to be a celebration," Juliette recalled. "The betrothal was announced on the Saturday after Jules gave his consent. On the Wednesday, the happy couple dined with Maurice's parents at the château and on the Friday we took them to Magny's and the Moulin Rouge. That was at Rosine's insistence—her bohemian streak. I'm sure Maurice would have preferred something more conservative, like a visit to the opera. Our willful daughter had her way, and how calamitous it was!"

"At the beginning, was it an agreeable party?" I asked.

"Perfectly."

"Rosine—"

"Behaved impeccably," said Juliette. "All the tantrums were behind us. She was charming to Maurice and took his arm. I really believed that evening that we could all forget Morgan. It was a blissfully happy family occasion. Tristan was with us, being unusually sociable. Whatever we may say about our son and his moods, he adores his sister. Always has done. And of course it was a great thrill for a boy of his age to be taken to the Moulin Rouge."

"He's a boy no longer," I pointed out.

"To his mother, he is," said she.

"Do you recall any of the conversation over dinner?" said I, knowing that she had dominated it.

"I think we discussed the wedding and what we would all wear. I told them about our own wedding in Nantes Cathedral, waiting behind the beadle in his cocked hat and red sash while he knocked three times with his staff at the great west door and then following him up the aisle to the wedding march from *Lohengrin*. I was dressed in ivory-colored silk with—"

"Was there agreement about the engagement—Rosine's, I mean?"

"Of course. I told you it was harmony from beginning to end."

"No disagreements over anything?"

"None whatsoever. Bertie, I don't know why you keep hinting at misunderstandings. There were none. We all left Magny's together and took a four-wheeler to the Moulin Rouge—a place I shall never set foot in again. I could hardly hear myself speak for the band, and there were scarlet women at the entrance."

"Nonetheless, you went in."

"If it had been up to me, we wouldn't have. What could one say? This was the engagement party. To have objected would have soured the whole occasion. I caught a glance from Jules and I knew he was shocked, but, yes, we refrained from saying anything. Inside, it was pandemonium. So many people of all classes. The dust, the noise, the smell of cheap scent, the drinking. Quite revolting. The whole thing was a terrible mistake, a nightmare."

"You were given a table?"

"Yes, actually on the dance floor at the edge. I made a show of enjoying myself. I'm not in your class as an actress, Madame Bernhardt, but I can put on an act when necessary. I danced a waltz with Jules—in our coats, if you please, because it was so cold in that barn of a place—and I also took the floor with Maurice. Tristan wouldn't dance—he's at a sensitive age, so I didn't press him. At some point, there was a fanfare or a drumroll or something and the cabaret was announced. I remember thinking, thank the Lord for that, because when it's over we can all go home. Everyone got up and formed ranks around a small space in the center of the floor. We wouldn't have seen a thing if we'd remained at our table, so we were obliged to join in."

"Now, this is important," said I. "How precisely were you standing in relation to one another?"

"'Precisely' doesn't come into it," said Juliette. "We were in a seething mob. I've never been so frightened. If I could have escaped, I would have done so at once, but there were people on every side of us. It was vile, finding oneself cheek by jowl with total strangers."

"Where was Rosine?" I persevered.

"Somewhere to the right of me, beside Maurice. I tried to keep hold of her arm, but we got detached in the crush when the dancers appeared."

"And Jules and your son—where were they?"

"On Maurice's other side."

"So you and Rosine were to his left and the two men were to his right?"

"More or less."

"Did you spot Morgan?"

"If I had, I wouldn't have known. I've never met the man. He must have come from behind us. It was all too simple in the melee. That grotesque dancer, the one they call La Goulue, appeared and there was a surge from behind. The next thing, there were two loud bangs and poor Maurice had been shot in the back. After some confusion, the crowd parted enough for it to be obvious that he was collapsing. Jules and another man were holding him up. The dancing stopped and a doctor was found and Maurice was carried to the dressing room, but he was already with his Maker, poor boy."

"Do you remember who was there—in the dressing room?"

"Apart from ourselves, do you mean? The doctor, of course, and a lady I presume was his wife. A disgustingly fat man I took to be the manager. I couldn't tell you his name."

Bernhardt supplied it. "Martineau."

"It means nothing to me. Two policemen arrived and asked us no end of questions. And some of the performers came in to collect their clothes."

"How did your daughter receive the news that her fiancé was dead?"

"Bravely. She went pale, uncommonly pale, but she didn't weep at all. She conducted herself with dignity, as she did at the funeral."

"The funeral? When did it take place?"

"It was on the Monday after he was shot."

"Was there no postmortem examination?"

"That was on the Saturday morning. They verified that he died from bullet wounds—as if we didn't know!"

"And the funeral?"

"A modest ceremony at the church where the Letissiers

worshiped and where the couple would have been married in a few weeks. So tragic!"

"Did Maurice live at the château?"

"No, I believe most of his time was spent in Paris. He had an apartment."

We both hesitated, disturbed by the sound of some creaks as someone descended the stairs and then the rustle of skirts outside the door.

"Do you happen to have the late Monsieur Letissier's address?" I asked Juliette.

"There's no point in going there now. It's probably let to someone else. Good apartments are much sought after."

"Yes, but do you have the address?" My patience was at snapping point.

She went to a writing cabinet, sifted through some papers, and produced a calling card bearing Maurice Letissier's name and an address in the rue Tronchet.

"I am obliged to you, Juliette," I said graciously, "and, unless I am mistaken, your daughter is waiting outside the door to see us. We shall not detain you any longer."

"Oh, I'm quite content to remain," she offered.

"We'll call you back if we require another consultation," I countered.

"Don't you want me here?"

I said, "Juliette, my dear, you and I have known each other long enough to be frank without giving offense."

"You *don't* want me here." She turned scarlet and left the room.

I looked across at Bernhardt. She went to the door and admitted Rosine, still in mourning, in a bombazine dress that made her face appear quite spectral.

"Did you see Glyn?" she asked. "Are they going to release him?"

"We saw him," said I.

"And he will not be released," Bernhardt quickly added, sparing her nothing. "The Sûreté are confident that he will confess."

The rigor of this announcement startled me. I knew that Bernhardt now regarded Rosine as the chief suspect, but the way she said it was almost triumphal. The so-called frail sex can be ruthless with each other when an opportunity beckons.

Understandably, Rosine turned to me, her young face contorted with despair. "Sir, didn't you tell Monsieur Goron that Glyn had no reason to murder Maurice? Didn't you tell him that Glyn doesn't believe in marriage?"

"That was made abundantly clear to Monsieur Goron," I assured her.

Bernhardt said, "Goron has enough evidence to sink a battleship—the proof that Morgan was there: a sketch of him standing beside you after the fatal shots were fired."

"That doesn't prove that Glyn fired them," Rosine protested.

"He found Morgan in possession of a gun from the gun room here and he has proof that the murder weapon belonged to the Agincourt family. And if that isn't enough, he is able to demonstrate from a scientific study of criminal anthropology that Morgan has the classic features of a murderer. He showed us Professor Lombroso's book and the resemblance is extraordinary."

Tears streamed from Rosine's eyes. "I don't understand. He's a peaceful man, not a murderer."

"This evidence was not entirely conclusive, my dear," said I, trying to offer some consolation.

Which Bernhardt capped by saying, "But the confession will seal it. The guillotine awaits him."

Rosine covered her face and sobbed. The reason for Bernhardt's pitiless treatment of the young girl was of course apparent to me. She wanted to provoke a confession. But I don't think she is aware that her training for the stage has given her such a devastating force of utterance.

After a while, Rosine managed to say between sobs, "He would have told me if he'd done it. He's completely honest. I've never known anyone so truthful."

"You value the truth, do you?" said Bernhardt, resuming the inquisition. "Are you truthful yourself?"

"I try to be."

"And do you believe in God?"

"Of course."

"Then would you swear before God that you didn't kill Maurice Letissier?"

CHAPTER 12

All the way back to Paris, I had to listen to a tirade against Rosine d'Agincourt, for, in spite of the repeated denials we had just heard, Sarah Bernhardt remained convinced that we had just been talking to a murderess. The Divine Sarah would blithely have applied the thumbscrews to extract a confession. Call me a cynic if you wish, but I think there was more to this hostility than mere certainty of murder. I couldn't help noting that Bernhardt had lost all sympathy for Rosine since the night we had discovered that winsome young lady in my hotel suite.

"Good Lord, it's almost six already. I'll get you back directly to the boulevard Pereire," I offered, to give myself some respite. "Why don't you join me later for dinner at the Bristol?"

"A night in prison has more to recommend it," said she unkindly, but we were at cross-purposes; she was still proposing ways of persuading Rosine to confess.

I repeated my invitation.

She heard it this time, thanked me, and explained that she was compelled to devote the evening to preparations for her world tour. She said she had never relied so much on her domestic staff as this week.

"May I assist?"

"I'm grateful, Bertie, but packing a trunk requires absolute concentration, don't you find?"

"I don't think I've ever packed a trunk myself," I confessed.

"As I thought," said she, smiling in a superior way. "Perhaps we may meet tomorrow."

"Just as you wish," said I indifferently, and shouted the instruction I had long ago discovered was understood by any cabman in Paris. "*Chez Sarah, s'il vous plaît.* And after that, the rue Tronchet."

Bernhardt swung around to face me accusingly. "You're going there tonight—to Letissier's lodging?"

"I can't put it off. Not while that poor wretch Morgan is freezing to death in a dungeon."

"Then I shall come with you."

I revised the cabman's instruction.

The rue Tronchet runs between the boulevard Haussmann and the Madeleine, a good address, convenient for the Champs-Elysées and the Opéra and free of the crowds who throng the boulevards. Already the lamplighter had been by and it was becoming obvious that the brass fittings on most of the doors had been polished that day. As is customary in Paris, we let ourselves in and entered the hall. There was an aroma of dried lavender. The concierge, a small, beak-nosed, bespectacled lady in the black merino dress so favored by elderly Parisiennes, came swiftly to inspect us. In no way intimidated when we introduced ourselves, she informed us tartly that she disliked the theater and disapproved of tides.

For this impertinence, Bernhardt was very abrupt with her, but she seemed almost to expect it. These widows who scrape a living by guarding apartment houses are a despised species. You see, the concierge takes in the post and receives visitors and watches the comings and goings of the residents. In short, she knows too much for anyone's comfort except her own. She is a potential spy and informer.

Mindful that we needed the woman's cooperation, I pointed out jovially that at least we weren't hawking matches or onions. We were calling merely to inquire about her former tenant Monsieur Letissier.

"He is gone," she said.

"We know," said I. "We wish to speak to you, madame."

She melted at the *madame* (I think she *did* have a sneaking respect for rank) and actually invited us through a door, divided like a stable door, to her personal domain, a tiny room equipped with strategically placed mirrors, a single armchair, a reading lamp, a stack of newspapers, and two linnets in a cage. Bernhardt squeezed in there somehow and I remained in the doorway.

I said untruthfully, "What an agreeable room. You have the advantage over us, madame."

"Why is that?"

"We don't know your name."

"Bergeron."

Madame Bergeron went on to inform us that she had told everything she knew to the *chef de la Sûreté*. My hopes plummeted. Would I go anywhere that had not been swept of every clue by Goron?

"Have you come from the Sûreté?" she asked.

"I won't deny that we visited them today, but we have no connection with the police."

"I'm glad to hear that. You should have seen the mess they left."

"Yes, please."

She stared uncomprehendingly.

"We would like to see the mess," I said as if to a child.

"You're too late. The apartment has a new tenant. The elderly lady from the top floor moved down there yesterday. Three flights of stairs are difficult for her these days, so it suited her better."

"What has happened to Letissier's property?"

"Everything the police didn't take was collected. The removal men came two days ago. His father was here to supervise. A charming old gentleman."

"Could we view the apartment?"

"I told you, it isn't convenient."

To avert a sharp riposte from me, Bernhardt said quickly, "There would be nothing to see except an old lady, Bertie."

Reluctantly, I had to agree. "How long was Letissier living here?"

"Three or four years."

"In that time, you must have formed some impressions about him."

A muscle rippled in Madame Bergeron's wrinkled cheek. "I don't gossip about my tenants."

"It wouldn't be gossip, madame. Maurice Letissier was murdered. It is salient information. It will all be made public at the trial."

She brought her hands together nervously. "There is to be a trial?"

"There must be, if they don't release the man they are holding."

"Have they caught someone?"

"The wrong man, we think. We want to prevent them from bringing him to the courts. It's a waste of everyone's time, particularly yours."

"What does it have to do with me?"

"The trial, madame."

She gasped. "Would I have to go before the court?"

"As a witness, almost certainly. Yes, I would bank on it if I were you," said I, watching her eyes bulge. "Let us hope we can arrive at the truth in time to stop it coming before the court. Was Letissier temperate in his habits?"

She was so shaken by the prospect of a trial that she stopped stonewalling. "I wouldn't say so. He had no job so far as I could tell. He was one of the idle rich we had a revolution to get rid of, coming home at all hours of the night, sometimes not at all. He would be away for days on end. Never warned me in advance. Never told me why."

"Women?" suggested Bernhardt.

"You have it in a word, madame."

But we wanted more than a word. "Did you actually see him with women?" I asked.

"Of course. I don't tell lies. He was quite good-looking when he first came. He had more hair then. He lost it very quickly."

"These women . . ." said I.

"Some came here . . . as visitors."

"For immoral purposes?"

She drew in a sharp breath. "I don't permit that. The ones I admitted were proper ladies, to my eye, not demimondaines, or I would have sent them away. But what went on outside these walls was no concern of mine."

"Indeed," said I, confident of hearing more, even if it was no concern of hers.

"Once I saw him in broad daylight leaving the Montyon."

Bernhardt muttered confidentially to me, "Don't ask, Bertie."

The concierge continued, "If he'd worked for a living, he wouldn't have had the energy for that sort of how-d'you-do."

"You seem to have taken a strong dislike to the young man."

"I keep this house respectable, monsieur."

"That is apparent. You mentioned lady visitors. Would you happen to know any of their names?"

"No."

"Would you describe them?"

She removed the glasses from her face and closed her eyes in thought. "The first one he introduced as his sister. She had red hair and a foreign accent, like a Pole. Then there were two dark-haired ones, decently dressed. I can't remember which came first. Good-looking, both of them, but they didn't visit more than twice."

"When was this?"

"I don't know. The first year."

"So this was all some time ago, then?"

She gave a nod. "He kept getting sore throats and headaches last winter and that stopped his philanderings. Migraine, he told me it was, but I think it was jaundice. His skin took on a yellow look. I had to get the doctor to him several times."

"We're interested in the recent past, madame. Did he receive any lady visitors in the past few weeks—since Christmas, let us say?"

"The only one who . . ." Her voice trailed away. She was unwilling to go on.

"Yes, madame."

She replaced the glasses and examined me afresh. "Why do you want to know?"

I reminded her, "We are looking for the truth about your former tenant, madame. We believe the Sûreté may be in error."

She said, "I told the detectives everything I am telling you."

"And they appear to be ignoring it," said Bernhardt smoothly.

"Do you think so?"

"It is obvious to us."

Sucking in her cheeks in a way that didn't enhance her attractions, she said, "I may not have said quite enough to the Sûreté about this young lady. To tell you the truth, I felt rather sorry for her the last time I saw her. I wouldn't like to think she had anything to do with Monsieur Letissier's horrible death."

Bernhardt placed a supportive hand over Madame Bergeron's arm. "We must not suppress anything, madame. What was she like?"

"Quite young, younger than some of the others. No more than twenty, I would say. Good-looking, if not beautiful. Very slim. Dark hair, brown eyes, pale skin. No rouge. An intelligent face. Demurely dressed. A little taller than you, madame."

"How did she wear her hair?" Bernhardt asked with some excitement. "With curls at the front, like mine, in the Greek style?"

"No, more of her forehead was visible. She had a parting at the center and the hair was combed back and fastened behind."

"And it was definitely dark?"

"Chestnut."

Bernhardt turned to me and gripped my arm. "It must be her. Bertie, it must be!" She asked Madame Bergeron, "Did you discover her name?"

"No, madame."

Bernhardt sighed.

The concierge continued. "She must have come four or five times altogether at the beginning of the year before last, on Sunday afternoons. I think they went walking on the boulevards and came back for tea. I'd almost forgotten about her until a few weeks ago and then she reappeared one afternoon, asking to see him. That was when I felt so sorry for her. She had altered. She was pale and tight-lipped and her eyes had gone red at the edges, as if she had suffered. It was a striking change."

"She came alone?"

"That is what I said."

"Did he invite her in?"

"Yes."

"For how long?"

"Half an hour. No more. Then they went out together, I suppose to find a cab, because he came back soon after."

"Did they appear affectionate?"

"Quite the reverse. He was cool toward her. When they came downstairs, they kept a distance from each other as if they'd just had an argument. She controlled her feelings as well as she could when she passed me, but I would say she was burning with resentment."

"Did they speak in your presence?"

"No."

"You could tell her state of mind from her face alone?"

"Her face, her posture, everything about her. Monsieur, she was incensed."

"And you're quite certain that this was the companion he had promenaded with on the boulevards?"

"There's no question. She recognized me, too. It was only because I knew her by sight that I didn't ask her name."

Bernhardt turned and gave me a triumphant look. However, I was not entirely convinced that the mysterious visitor must have been Rosine. True, there were similarities in the description. The color of Rosine's hair and the way she wore it matched what we had just been told and the age was about right. But we had heard nothing until today about the young couple taking walks along the boulevards. Rosine hadn't mentioned it, nor had any of her family. My understanding had been that she had resisted all her parents' attempts at matchmaking until shortly before the betrothal was announced.

I turned back to the concierge. "You said that the visit this young lady made was a few weeks ago. Can you be more precise?"

She gave that tiny movement of the shoulders that in France means a vague dissent.

"In point of fact, it's two weeks since Letissier was murdered," I remarked. "Was that the day she came?"

"No, it was before then—the weekend before." She hesitated. "I think it might have been the Sunday."

"Think carefully, madame."

"Yes, it was Sunday afternoon. I had been to Mass in the morning and I discovered a hole in one of my black lace gloves. I was repairing it when she stepped into the hall. I remember dropping it when I got up to speak to her."

"And she left after a short visit and you haven't seen her since?"

"That is correct."

We seemed to have extracted all that the concierge had to tell about the unhappy young lady. "Did Monsieur Letissier receive any other visitors prior to his unfortunate death?"

"No, monsieur."

"He went out more than once in that last week of his life, I gather?"

"Yes, a number of times. He was often out."

"Dressed for dinner?"

"On the Wednesday and the Friday. He told me he was dining with his parents on the Wednesday. They were having a small party to celebrate the betrothal."

"Yes, we heard about that. He didn't bring his fiancée here that evening?"

"No."

"Nor at any other time?"

"She has never been to this house," Madame Bergeron said as confidently as if it was a response in church.

Bernhardt was quick to take her up. "How can you be certain that the young lady you mentioned just now was not the fiancée, Rosine d'Agincourt?"

"Because she was someone else."

"But you can't be sure!" Bernhardt rounded on her. "How can you know? From the description you gave us, they sounded identical."

If Bernhardt's supposition was right and Rosine, in some distress, had made an unscheduled visit to Letissier on the Sunday before he met his death and left soon after in a state of burning resentment, we had a fresh insight into the case. It was quite conceivable that by the Friday the anger had formed into a resolve to kill Letissier.

"Mademoiselle d'Agincourt has never set foot inside this house," the concierge insisted.

"If you've never seen her, how can you say·that?" cried Bernhardt.

The old woman gave her a glare and selected a newspaper from the neatly stacked collection she had beside her. It was the *Petit Parisien,* one of those gossipy papers so beloved of the masses. She turned the pages until she found what she wanted. "There is Rosine d'Agincourt." She opened the sheet fully to a graphic report of the murder and handed it to Bernhardt. The likenesses of Rosine and Letissier were reproduced side by side halfway down the column. "I tell you that is not the lady who called here."

The artist had caught Rosine rather skillfully. She was portrayed in a dark dress buttoned to the neck and a small hat with a straight brim. Probably the original sketch had been made at a salon, where the prettiest girls are regularly drawn. The *Petit Parisien* would have copied her likeness from some magazine for the beau monde and altered the clothes to fit the solemn character of the report.

"She was thinner in the face and her mouth was quite different," the concierge went on to say. "Her lips were finer than this. And the eyes were not so large, nor so wide apart. This is definitely someone else."

Bernhardt refused to believe her. "But this is only a newspaper. There are pictures of me in the papers that my own mother wouldn't recognize."

"The picture of Monsieur Letissier is exactly like him," declared Madame Bergeron with finality.

"But men are so much easier to portray. Look at Rosine's hair. It is exactly as you just described it."

"The face is somebody else's, madame." She would not be budged.

I had one more card to play. "You informed us earlier that the police left Monsieur Letissier's rooms in an untidy state."

She became animated at this. "Untidy? I should have said disgusting. A pigsty. They tipped everything all over the floor and took what interested them. They put nothing away afterward."

"Did you tidy it yourself before the removal men came?"

"Of course I did. There was nobody else to do it. The tenant was dead."

"What did you do with the rubbish, madame?"

"I threw nothing away. It wasn't mine to dispose of."

"But what did you do with it?"

"I tidied it."

"Put things away, do you mean?"

"Yes, and stacked them together."

"And when the father came with the removal men, did they take everything with them?"

"Yes." From the way she pressed her lips together, it was obvious that she wanted this to be the last word on the matter.

"Absolutely everything?"

She gave a nod and turned to speak to her birds. "All right, I'll feed you presently."

I said, "I can't believe they took everything. Food, for instance? There must have been stale bread."

"They left nothing of value, monsieur."

"Ah. But they left something?"

"They tossed some rubbish into a tea chest."

"For disposal? Is it destroyed yet?"

"There was nothing of value."

My patience was at an end. "Madame, I know very well that you expect to sell any rags for a few sous. We are not here to deprive you, but we would like to examine the contents of that tea chest. Now, where is it?"

"In the cupboard under the stairs."

"Then we'll pay you a fair sum and take it with us," said I with satisfaction.

She was dubious, and no wonder. You don't expect the Prince of Wales to take away your rubbish. In the end, I had to bribe her with a louis d'or for the privilege. And our driver demanded five francs before he would heave the tea chest on board.

In the carriage, Bernhardt's pent-up anger erupted. "Silly old witch. She'll be laughing her head off now."

"Why?"

"She's a louis better off for a box of stinking rubbish, and what is more, she's sent us on a wild-goose chase."

"If she has, I'm not aware of it," I commented.

"Oh, come on, Bertie! You weren't taken in by all that nonsense about the mysterious woman who visited Letissier?"

"Nonsense?"

"Well, she didn't fool me. It was Rosine, of course."

"Do you really think so?"

"She was protecting Rosine by pretending it was someone else."

"Why would she do that?" I added, not unreasonably, "If she didn't want the truth to come out, why mention the visit at all? No, I'm inclined to believe the old lady. Two years ago, Rosine wouldn't have called once at Letissier's apartment, let alone five times. She wouldn't have been seen dead there."

"They'd been introduced."

"Yes, but she'd already gone dotty over Morgan and she couldn't bear to think of Letissier as a suitor. You're mistaken, Sarah. This mysterious caller must be an entirely different woman. We have a fresh suspect."

"That's it!" said Bernhardt turning her artillery on me. "You can't bear to think that one of the Agincourts is the murderer. You're only too pleased to have someone else to pursue, even if she's a figment of that old woman's imagination."

I answered stiffly, "If that's your opinion, I see no point in discussing this any further. I shall find the young lady without any help from you and you will eat your words."

She laughed mockingly. "Find your Cinderella, then, Prince Charming. Dark, twenty, average height. There can't be more than ten thousand girls like that in Paris. It may take a year or two of trying to fit the slipper, but, knowing you, that will be no hardship."

"Sarah, that's below the belt!"

She said, "A choice of phrase that sums it up exactly."

We parted on frigid terms outside her house. Nothing was said about another meeting.

In case there was any bounce left in me, a strong letter from Alix was waiting for me at the Bristol:

Fredensborg Castle

Beloved Bertie,

My worst fears are confirmed. After all your promises to depart for Cannes, you are still in Paris. How could you mislead me so, knowing that I am half a continent away and helpless to protest? I can think of only two possible circumstances that could detain you. The first, your perennial weakness, I can only trust to the Almighty to control and I pray night and morning that He will help you obey all His Commandments, but especially the one that you find most difficult to keep. The second possibility, this ambition of yours to be a criminal investigator, would be easier for my heart to endure, but it troubles my head, for I can see dreadful danger resulting from it.

Yesterday's French newspapers have reached here and I am better informed now as to the facts of the Moulin Rouge Murder Case (as it is described). My dearest, I am more than ever seized with the certainty that you should have nothing to do with it. There seems no doubt that this was a crime of passion and that Rosine d'Agincourt is at the heart of it. Whoever killed the young man Letissier was driven by a force we seldom see nakedly revealed in England (and never, I think, in Denmark). It may seem trite to say so, but the French are a passionate people, Bertie. Where your typical English murderer is a doctor who poisons for profit or a wretched wife seeking escape from an unhappy marriage, your Frenchman (or woman) may kill from motives we little

understand. Their crime is not calculated; it is not really mur-
der as the English understand it, but slaughter in the heat of
passion, vengeful and violent. Stand in their way and you risk
being another victim. That is why I urge you with all the love I
have to leave the Sûreté to do their own investigating.

The Agincourts are old friends, I know. But you have visited
them to express our concern, and in all conscience that is as much
as friends can be expected to do.

Believe me, I fear for your life.

Ever your loving wife, Alix

I read it twice in my bath. I was mightily pleased to get into a bath
after sifting through the rubbish in the tea chest we had brought
back from Letissiers lodgings. More of what I discovered anon.

Alix fusses too much, but she is nobody's fool, I told myself as
I read the letter a third time. Perhaps she was right. The French
may murder from motives that we—the more placid races of
Europe—get out of our systems on the grouse moor. I would think
afresh about motives.

After dressing for dinner, I found Knollys hovering in my sitting room.

"You found your letter from Her Royal Highness, sir?"

"Thank you, Francis. Yes."

"She is quite well, I hope?"

"Fretting, as usual, that's all."

"About anything in particular, sir?"

"No, it's to be expected after a couple of weeks in that god-
forsaken castle."

"Ah."

"And now I'm going to dine at the Jockey Club."

"Very good, sir." He gave his diplomatic cough. "Shall we be
leaving for Cannes tomorrow?"

"I doubt it, Francis. I have some unfinished business here."

He frowned. I had a strong intuition that he knew the contents
of Alix's letter. He wouldn't have opened it. Of that, I am certain,
for he is a man of honor. But Alix is perfectly capable of writing
to Knollys as well as to me.

CHAPTER 13

You may wish to cast a discerning eye over the inventory I made of the contents of the tea chest from Letissier's lodgings:

Shirts, linen 3
Collars, starched 5
Nightshirts, linen 2
Vests, cotton 4
Drawers, men's 3
Garters, women's 14
Newspapers, various 7
Magazines, various 9
Programs, theater 22
Postcards, vulgar 31
Bread, loaf, moldy 1
Cheese, moldy 1
Wine bottles, empty 6
Toupee, brown 1
Soap, toilet 2
Soap, shaving 1
Brush, shaving 1
Razor 1
Medicaments, various 38
Toothbrush 1
Tooth powder, tin 1

The list gives no idea of the unpleasantness of my task, for the decaying food had imparted an odor to everything in the chest. In the interests of the investigation, I persevered to the end, and it was a huge disappointment. I knew, of course, that the Sûreté or Letissier's father must have taken away everything of obvious interest, such as his address book, pocket notebook, photographs, letters, and visiting cards, but I took the view that a detective worth his salt should be able to find clues in the most unpromising material.

The rubbish that remained told me nothing I didn't already know. The collection of naughty postcards testified to his interest in the fair sex and the garters confirmed that his studies had progressed beyond theory, but I had already learned as much from the concierge. Letissier had sown some wild oats, but which young man of spirit has not? The newspapers, magazines, and theater programs were innocuous. That left the clothes, the food, the toiletries, and the medical items. Oh, and the wig. People may poke fun at such things, but you won't hear an unkind word from me. Premature thinning of the hair can cause no end of anxiety, and I can perfectly understand a young man's wish to hide the effect from public view.

The quantity of pills and potions may strike the reader as excessive; Letissier was obviously a man who tried many remedies and persisted with few. Just as well. He had enough laxatives to relieve a constipated elephant: castor oil, black draft, Epsom salts, rhubarb pills, senna pods, cream of tartar, Seidlitz powders, calomel, Glauber's salts, and, in case your stomach hasn't already stopped you reading this list, jalap. I was led to wonder if this was typical of the average Frenchman's medical chest and, if so, what was so binding in the diet. So it was reassuring to find several large bottles of logwood to arrest the laxative effect if necessary. In addition, there were Dr. Clark's pills for headaches; cough mixtures galore; a variety of ointments and poultice mixtures; several sorts of bandages; and—looking to recovery—tonics such as sarsaparilla and chamomile. Finally, there was a bottle said to contain Van Swieten's liquor, with no information as to its use.

If it seems wasteful to discard good medicine, ask yourself if you would be willing to take the potions and pills that belonged to a dead man. The inspection complete, I packed everything back in the tea chest and summoned one of the hotel staff to dispose of it at once. You may think my decision premature; you would not if you had smelled the contents.

I was never so glad to get into a bath.

IT WAS TOO MUCH TO expect that I would meet Letissier senior at the Jockey Club that evening. To tell the truth, I had entertained a small hope of finding him there, knowing him to be a member. Instead, I dined with old friends and talked agreeably of other matters.

The evening was not devoid of interest, however. I was looking for a well-placed armchair for a smoke when I spotted Jules d'Agincourt dozing in front of the fireplace. This was no great surprise, for it was his usual haunt. Jules was too much the gentleman ever to say so, but I'm sure the club was his main refuge from Juliette's interminable babble.

I sent for cognacs, occupied the chair opposite, and disturbed his slumbers. Once properly conscious, he greeted me warmly and we soon got down to talking of matters that interested us both. I gave him a resume of my investigation so far.

He was clearly impressed. "You've left no stone unturned, Bertie."

"Oh, I wouldn't go so far as to say that," I told him. "I haven't questioned the victim's father."

"I doubt if he'll have anything to add," said Jules. "A father is the last person to ask about his son's private life."

"Do you really think so?"

"Well, what is your experience? Do you have the slightest idea what the Duke of Clarence gets up to when he isn't at home? Or George? Young colts will canter, as the saying goes."

I gently rotated the cognac in my glass before answering, "Who am I to read the riot act? I was a fearful trial to my parents."

"I'm a fine one to talk," said Jules. "I don't know what Tristan gets up to at university. You just have to trust them not to get into trouble."

This seemed a promising avenue to explore. "Tristan strikes me as capable of looking after himself."

"Confident to the point of brashness," said Jules with candor. "I was hoping he would learn more respect for his elders at the Sorbonne."

"He is unfailingly courteous to me," said I.

He appeared not to have listened. "It's a bumptious generation,

Bertie. Lord knows what the world will be like when they have charge of it."

I said, "I warmed to your son when we met. And he clearly has a high regard for his sister."

His face lit up. "I think you're right. They've always been close, those two."

"Did Tristan approve of her choice?"

"Morgan?"

"I meant young Letissier, actually."

"*Our* choice, then. I've never discussed it with Tristan. I think he had some sympathy for Rosine when Juliette and I were singing Maurice's praises too loudly and too long. But I'm damned sure he wouldn't have liked Morgan for a brother-in-law."

"That wouldn't have happened, would it?" said I. "Marriage was furthest from Morgan's thoughts."

"I must take your word for that."

"Do you doubt it?"

"The man had a powerful hold over her. Still does. She was ready to go to him whether he married her or not. She's my only daughter, Bertie. I love her dearly. She may doubt it, but I do. I couldn't bear to see her throw away her life on a penniless artist."

"Is that why you championed Letissier so vigorously? A young man of excellent family capable of supporting her, even if she loved another?"

"Bertie, marrying for love is a luxury for the lower classes."

I gave a murmur of assent.

He added bleakly, "One thinks as a parent that one is acting from the best motives."

"Do you blame yourself?"

"For what happened at the Moulin Rouge? Absolutely."

"You shouldn't, you know."

We were silent for an interval, staring at the flames steadily devouring the logs. Neither of us would say outright that the wrong person was sitting in a dungeon in the Île de la Cité; the alternative was too painful to face.

Finally, Jules said, "If you speak to old Letissier, what do you hope to find out?"

"The identity of the young woman who visited Maurice on the Sunday before he died."

"It's a blind alley, Bertie."

"Why do you say that?"

"He won't know of her existence."

"One thing I have learned about the science of detection is never to make assumptions," I told him, and it sounded an excellent maxim. "I must trace that young woman and question her. And—forgive me, old friend, but you and I know what is troubling you—there is no possibility that she is Rosine. The concierge was adamant that she is someone else."

He sidestepped the mention of his daughter. "A new suspect?"

"Assuredly."

"You seriously believe this woman might be the murderer?"

"Consider the few facts we have," said I. "She visited young Letissier on four or five occasions the year before last. It's reasonable to assume that she believed herself to be his friend, if not his lover."

"You just said you never make assumptions," Jules remarked without his customary tact.

"What I meant is that I never allow them to put me off the scent," I told him smoothly. "This young woman, as I was about to say, probably had ambitions of becoming the next chatelaine. Maurice's engagement to Rosine must have come as an appalling shock. As Shakespeare said, 'Hell hath no fury like a woman scorned.'"

"Did Shakespeare say that?"

"Actually, my dear fellow, I've no idea."

"It begs a question," said he.

"Perhaps it was Byron, then."

"I'm speaking of the mysterious young woman, Bertie. If she is the murderer, how did she acquire the revolver from my gun room?"

Trying to sound as if the question had been steadily in my thoughts, I answered, "That is one of the matters I intend to explore with her."

"Will you speak of this to the *chef de la Sûreté*?"

"Goron? Not yet."

"You want to present him with a fait accompli, is that it?"

"Nothing less will do, Jules. Goron is convinced that Morgan is the culprit."

I might have added that in either case, the good news was that the Agincourt family was absolved of all suspicion, but Jules

wouldn't have drawn much consolation from that. He had seen
his name bandied in the popular newspapers for day after day and
there was the prospect of a criminal trial to come in which the
Agincourts would feature as the principal witnesses. No, there was
not much good news for Jules, whatever the outcome.

I changed the subject to horses.

I LEFT BEFORE MIDNIGHT AND hailed the first cab that came by,
a humble fiacre.

"Do you know the Montyon?"

"You're from England," said the cabman.

"I'm aware of that, thank you."

"But you speak with a German accent."

"The way I speak is no business of yours."

"The Montyon—do you know it?"

"That is the question I just asked you," I told him testily.

He said, "Are you the Prince of Wales, my lord?"

"Yes." It wasn't much of a discovery on his part, seeing that I
was standing on the steps of the Jockey Club, where I am so well
known.

He said, "The Montyon—that's an introducing house. Do you
know what I mean?"

"I should like to be driven there, whatever it is."

"Just as long as you know what to expect, Your Highness."

I got in. Naturally, I had some inkling that the address had
a certain notoriety. The concierge had been scandalized at seeing Letissier emerge from its portal "in broad daylight." Anyone
like me, who had once sat down to dinner at a private party and
been served with a "dish" consisting of the notorious courtesan,
Cora Pearl, upon a silver salver, naked except for a deftly placed
sprig of parsley, was unlikely to be shocked by anything the Hotel
Montyon had to offer.

We clattered across Paris at a canter. I had quite forgotten
to ask which district we were to visit and so it was some relief to
observe top hats and white shirtfronts on the streets we traveled
through. In fact, the Opéra presently came up on the left, so we
must have passed close to Letissier's apartment in the rue Tronchet.
Turning left, we crossed the boulevard Haussmann, so coming to
the rue de Provence.

"Voilà, Your 'Ighness."

The Montyon sign was in elegant lettering illuminated by a gas festoon. I tipped the driver generously, when really I should have saved my money. You can't buy silence from one of his profession. However much I bribed him, he was sure to gossip about his "fare."

I was received cheerfully with the title of monseigneur by a merry-eyed, Titian-haired young *cocotte* who stepped forward and took my hat, coat, and cane as if it went without saying that I had come to stay. She radiated such charm that I am straining to recall what the surroundings looked like. I have a fuzzy recollection of a small foyer handsomely decorated in gilt and white; a chandelier reflected in mirrors on three of the walls; chairs with striped satin covers; a crimson carpet; and a piece of marble statuary that would not have been out of place in a drawing room at Windsor Castle.

"I should like to see the proprietor, if you please," I said.

"But of course, monseigneur," said she. "Do you wish me to mention your name?"

The way this inquiry was worded was the first indication that the place was anything but innocent. "You may say that, um . . . Lord Tennyson has called," said I, thinking slyly that the reputation of the poet laureate could do with pepping up.

She went to a table in the corner and picked up a speaking tube. A few minutes after, I was shown into a paneled room furnished with two sofas and some potted ferns. A petite, well-groomed woman occupied one of the sofas, a sweep's brush beside her—or so it appeared until the brush barked at me. The breed I think is known as an affenpinscher, or monkey dog. This specimen was small, black, and bristly and it yapped throughout our conversation, simply asking to be stuffed up a chimney.

"What an honor, Lord Tennyson," the woman said, rising to shake my hand and steering me toward the vacant sofa. She was, I suppose, about sixty, although these days I find a lady's age increasingly hard to judge. This dowager, anyway, made me feel at least ten years her junior. With her tight gray curls, lace collar, and rigidly corseted posture, she could have passed for a headmistress, which I suppose, in a sense, she was. "And how gracious that you should ask to meet me first. Gentlemen visiting the Montyon are not always so punctilious."

"Really, madame?"

"They forget the courtesies. Their mind is on other things. Please sit down."

"Thank you."

"Will you be quiet?" She lifted the dog onto her lap in an attempt to calm it down. "We have not had the pleasure of welcoming a man of letters before. Of all English poems, "The Charge of the Light Brigade" is my favorite."

This hit me like a ton of bricks. I had not counted on a madam with a knowledge of English poetry. If she also knew how long ago the thing was written, I was exposed as a charlatan.

"I won't bore you by asking you to recite it," she said with a sweet smile, and I sent up a prayer of thanks for that. "I may ask you to sign the visitors' book later."

I stammered, "Th-that will be a pleasure." This woman knows very well that I am not Tennyson, I thought. She recognized me the moment I came in and is out to enjoy herself.

In a voice pitched high to be heard above the noise from the dog, she said, "We are a famous establishment, patronized by numerous gentlemen of influence and distinction. Politicians, members of the French Academy, men of letters. Guy de Maupassant, the celebrated writer, was often here. You must have heard of his story *La Maison Tellier*, as illustrated by Edgar Degas, the well-known artist. *La Maison Tellier* is the Montyon, thinly disguised."

"Really?" said I.

"Yes, we are part of the great fabric of French literature. If you happened to find the facilities here to your satisfaction and felt inspired to write a few lines of verse in the book, I would, of course, be deeply honored. Monsieur Degas presents me with a pastel drawing each time he visits the house. I have a stack of them now. Strictly between you and me, they're not my idea of art, but the paper is wonderful on wet days for keeping paw marks off the carpets. But you're not here for conversation."

"On the contrary, madame," I interjected. "It is conversation that I want, a consultation. All I am seeking is information."

She smiled graciously. "Rest assured, my lord. With such a distinguished clientele, we positively encourage conversation. This is not the sort of house that hurries the choice. Ample opportunity will be given for you to arrive at a decision and if—by some mischance—we cannot make an introduction that delights you, you will be at liberty to leave without obligation."

I said, "Madame, you misunderstand me. I am not here for an introduction."

"What is it you want, my lord?"

"I am seeking a certain young lady—"

"So that's it!" she interrupted. "You know whom you want already. Excellent. Who is it?"

The confusion had to end at once. Painstakingly, I explained that I was an English private detective making inquiries into the recent murder at the Moulin Rouge. I admitted that Lord Tennyson was my assumed name and that for reasons of security I was unable at present to reveal my true identity—which was about as frank and open as I could afford to be.

She chose to treat all this as an elaborate excuse. She would not be shaken from the conviction that I had come to sample the wares, even when I made it clear that I was willing to pay as much for information as for intimacy. She wanted more than money. In fact, I was offered the freedom of the house, whatever that involved. It was the honor, she said, the seal of approval. She knew who I was all right.

Finally, I told her straight that when I wanted a tumble, I didn't have to go to a brothel for it. We were talking the same language at last.

She'd read in the papers about Letissier's murder and she remembered him making use of the Montyon. He'd been a regular at one stage.

"Did he have a regular girl?" I asked.

"Mimi was always his first choice."

"Mimi."

"Yes. She was the favorite. Brunettes appealed to him."

"Is Mimi here? I would like to meet her. To speak to her, that is."

"You're lucky," she said. "She is much in demand. At this minute, she is available." Thrusting the dog to one side, she got up and walked straight toward the wall and pushed a piece of paneling that opened inward. I followed her into a less austere room papered in pink, which, if not exactly homely, was at least reposeful. Here, demimondaines in black stockings, thin peignoirs, and little else lounged on divans. Cheap scent in the air took the harsh edge off the reek of Turkish cigarettes. Nobody looked up. They were not on duty, for this was, in effect, their common room.

Madame clapped her hands for attention. "Where is Mimi?"

"Mimi? Taking a bath," said one, and pointed to a door.

We were back in the part of the hotel that clients were meant to see, a carpeted corridor with gilded lamps and paintings of fruit and poultry. A roar of ecstasy from behind a closed door signaled that one of the team, at least, was gainfully employed. Upstairs we went and along another handsomely furnished corridor. Madame opened a door at the end and I met Mimi.

She was standing naked in a hip bath, with her back to the door, as delightful a spectacle as I'd seen that week, gleaming wet and glowing bright pink from the Plimsoll line down.

"*Mon Dieu*—close the door; it's drafty!" she cried before turning around. Then, hands on hips in a pose of confrontation, with no thought of covering those parts that ladies rarely put on display, she added, "And don't I even get time for a bath now?"

I pulled the door shut and Madame picked a towel off a chair and handed it to Mimi. "This gentleman isn't a client. He's a detective from England."

"A policeman?" Now Mimi pulled the towel protectively around her shoulders. She had her brown hair tied on top of her head with a white scarf to keep it from getting wet. I noted mentally that it was curly, naturally curly. She was too buxom, anyway, to fit the description of the slender young creature the concierge had seen visiting Letissier. But Mimi was not unattractive. Eyes suddenly turned saintly regarded me from above a mouth just too pert to complete the effect. "I've done nothing criminal."

"You're not in trouble, mademoiselle," I told her. "I want to ask about a gentleman you may remember. Why don't you step out of the water and dry yourself? We don't want you catching your death of cold."

This considerate suggestion was well received by Mimi. She toweled her torso perfunctorily and exited from the bath. "Would you hand me my dressing gown, monsieur? It's hanging on the door behind you."

When I turned back with it, she was naked again and so close to me that I could feel the warmth from her. She flaunted herself shamelessly as she slipped the garment on and tied it loosely around her waist, leaving her Junoesque bosom uncovered until last, like the curtain closing at the end of a good play. Had I been alone with her, the temptation to applaud might have been too strong to resist.

We moved into an adjoining dressing room. Madame came, too, not wanting to miss a word. Mimi took the chair in front of the dressing table and turned it to face us. "Which gentleman?"

"Maurice Letissier."

"I thought so."

"You knew him well?"

"I knew him intimately, and you know it or you wouldn't be here, would you? But I wouldn't say I knew him well. In this profession, monsieur, you get to know the animal in them, not the man. If they say anything at all, it's about the business at hand."

The madam put in quickly, "And that's of no interest to you, monsieur."

"Did he ever speak of other women—other ladies—he knew?"

"No."

That one brief word was a crushing blow. "You're quite sure? It's important."

"I have no reason to lie to you, monsieur. I'd have remembered if he had."

"He was a regular client, I understand."

"For a time—only two or three months, and never more than once a week. He was just another job to me, but I'm sorry he was murdered. If you think I'm going to tell you who did it, I haven't the foggiest idea."

"When did you see him last?"

"It must be a couple of years ago. He'd stopped coming here by then. We met by chance at the Exposition."

She was speaking of the great event of 1889, when for six months the Champ-de-Mars with its awful Eiffel Tower had been the sensation of Europe. "You just happened to spot him there?"

"Yes. I wasn't working at the time. He was with a student. I suppose she was giving him what he wanted, because he didn't pay for it here anymore."

My expectations soared like a skyrocket. "A student? What was she like?"

"Dusky, when I saw her."

As we all know, rockets fizzle out and plunge. "Dusky—like a native, do you mean?"

"Not really." She gave a chuckle. "It was cocoa oil, or something. She was supposed to be a seller of bead necklaces in the bazaar in the Indian Pavilion. They employed students to dress up as foreigners all summer."

"Was she dressed as an Indian?"

"That's what I said."

"Then how can you be certain that she was a student?"

"Because Maurice introduced us."

"He introduced you—his *cocotte?*"

She laughed. "He had no choice. I marched up to him and greeted him. He turned bright pink when he saw me, but I wasn't going to tell her where he'd met me. I'm not mean. She was in her second year at the Ecole de Médecine."

"Her name?"

"Claudine."

"Is that all? No surname?"

"Monsieur, he knew me as Mimi, nothing else. He couldn't introduce one of us with the full name and not the other."

"So she was a medical student by the name of Claudine. Is there anything else you can tell me about this young lady?"

"She didn't need stays. She was as thin as a stem." This was promising. "How was her hair dressed?"

"In the Indian style when I saw it—combed straight back from the forehead and plaited."

"Unusual," I remarked. "I thought curls were all the rage these days."

"Hers was straight and long."

This fitted the description the concierge had given me. "And dark?"

"Quite brown."

"Any particular shade?"

"Brown is brown to me."

It was too much to hope that she would say chestnut. "What color were her eyes?"

"Brown, if I remember right. I only saw her for a couple of minutes."

"Mimi, this is of the utmost importance. Are you quite certain she was his friend—more than just a passing acquaintance, I mean?"

"Anyone with half an eye could see they were in love, monsieur."

"And you haven't seen her since?"

"No."

I thanked Mimi sincerely. My visit to the Montyon had been well rewarded, and I said so—whereupon the madam informed me that the night was young and once again offered me the freedom of the house, so to speak, before I collected my hat and coat. Politely, I expressed myself more than satisfied already.

I escaped without signing the visitors' book. Madame had to be content with a wink and an *"Au revoir."*

CHAPTER 14

I ordered an early breakfast—using the English word, which they understand in the Bristol—and was ready to leave by nine. Almost too quick for Francis Knollys, who had expected to find me still in my dressing gown when he came in with the letters.

"Not another blasting from Fredensborg, I hope?"

"No, sir. Some invitations."

"Decline them politely, would you? I haven't a moment to spare, Francis. I'm just off to the Left Bank."

"Before you go, sir, there is something you may wish to cast an eye over." He conveyed disapproval in his tone, as if the casting of the eye would be akin to playing cards on Sunday.

This, of course, intrigued me.

"It is a letter addressed to me as your private secretary, sir. The writer doesn't reveal his or her identity."

"One of those, is it?" said I, less interested. Anonymous letters telling me how to conduct my private life are frequently sent to me at Marlborough House and Sandringham, but in France they are a rarity. "What's the gist, Francis?"

"I think you should read it yourself, sir."

It was inscribed in the sort of immaculate copperplate that betrays no clue as to the writer. The sender gave no address.

The Private Secretary
His Royal Highness the Prince of Wales
Hotel Bristol

Sir,

It has come to my notice that His Royal Highness the Prince of Wales is taking a personal interest in the investigation of the recent death of Monsieur Letissier at the Moulin Rouge. It would oblige me greatly if you would convey to His Royal Highness some information that may expedite the inquiry. I was present at the Moulin Rouge on the evening in question and I can state from personal observation that the man Morgan being investigated by the Sûreté is innocent. At the moment the fatal shots were fired, Monsieur Morgan was outside the hall, in the garden. I swear that this is the truth. Justice will be done if His Royal Highness will use his undoubted influence to secure the release of this unfortunate man.

For reasons of a delicate nature I am unable to divulge my name, but, believe me, sir, this statement is true.

A witness

"This is manna from heaven," said I with some excitement. "Thank you for bringing it to my attention. Damned shame he's so coy. *'Reasons of a delicate nature'* presumably means someone else's wife was with him at the Moulin that night."

"Or someone else's husband, sir. It could have been written by a lady."

"Sharp thinking, Francis."

"Not at all, sir."

"If only you were more sympathetic to my investigative work, we could form a highly effective team."

He gave his diplomatic cough. "I do have other obligations, sir."

"Look, this is too important to delay. You'd better telephone the Sûreté and ask that scoundrel Goron to come here directly. Don't tell him what it's about. Just say we have been handed something pertinent to the case."

"Weren't you leaving for the Left Bank, sir?"

"I was. This is too urgent to put off."

To his credit, Goron responded promptly to the summons and arrived at my suite within half an hour. With his cropped hair and mustache and a brown overcoat reaching almost to the floor, he looked more like the popular idea of an anarchist than the *chef de la Sûreté*. He wouldn't accept my invitation to sit down.

"I assume that Mr. Morgan is still in custody," said I without a hint of reproach.

He answered with caution, "Yes, sir."

"You heard my opinion on the matter yesterday and I didn't invite you here to prove a point, you understand. I'm simply doing what any responsible person would do and handing you a piece of evidence that has come my way."

He took the letter and read it rapidly. Then attempted to hand it back.

"You are welcome to keep it," I offered.

He sniffed. "No, thank you. It's of no interest to the Sûreté." He tossed the letter onto a coffee table.

At this, I'm afraid my cordiality slipped. "What do you mean 'of no interest'? This is independent evidence that Morgan is innocent. I'm sorry if you find it disagreeable, Goron. You've wasted your time on that wretched man Morgan, and you may not care to admit it, but you can't turn your back on the truth."

"It isn't the truth," said he in his uncouth way. "Two letters like this, in the same hand by the look of it, were sent to the Sûreté. They say the same thing."

"This person wrote to you as well?"

"Yes, and it just confirms my opinion that Morgan is the murderer."

"Come now, Goron, you can't duck the truth when it stares you in the face. Someone goes to the trouble of bringing this to your attention, an educated person, judging by the way he expresses himself—"

"Or herself," said Goron.

"I was about to add that. I have an open mind," I told him pointedly. "Someone goes to all this trouble and you disbelieve them?"

"Yes."

"I find that deplorable. I am bound to say that your conduct of this case is irresponsible in the extreme."

He said with a shrug, "I'm sorry you take that view. Good day, sir."

"Don't you dare turn your back on me after all the trouble I've taken to help the Sûreté."

He stopped by the door and half turned toward me. Then he said with a fish-eyed stare, "That letter must have been written by one of Morgan's friends in a futile attempt to provide him with an alibi. If you remember, Morgan told you himself, and he has told me repeatedly—I have it in a signed statement—that he was in the hall with a glass of beer when the murder took place. He claimed that he kept his distance. He only went into the garden *after* the shots were fired, because he thought some maniac was loose in the hall. The letter contradicts him. Either Morgan is lying or the letter writer is lying. Whichever it is, that letter does him no service at all."

I was speechless. Goron was right, damn him. I remembered now.

He said with a supercilious air, "I'm not ungrateful for the information, sir."

I nodded.

"If there's anything else . . ." he said.

"That was all," I told him curtly, privately resolved that the next time we crossed swords I would have the whole case solved beyond an iota of doubt.

CHAPTER 15

The sum of all the words I have exchanged in twenty years with the head doorman at the Hotel Bristol wouldn't amount to a conversation. Unfailingly, he wishes me good morning in English and doffs his cockaded blue top hat and thanks me for the coin I press into his gloved hand, but that is the extent of it. If it wasn't for his magnificent cavalry mustache, one wouldn't remember him from year to year. This morning, he surprised me.

"Begging your pardon, Your Royal Highness."

"Did you speak?"

"Begging your pardon . . ."

"Yes?"

"I hesitate to mention it."

"By all means do."

". . . and it may be nothing at all, but you may care to know that there is a man who follows you, sir."

"*Follows* me?"

"Probably you wouldn't have any cause to notice him. The only reason I spotted him is that my duties oblige me to stand here for long hours looking across the street. Do you see the carriage at the front of the cab rank, sir? He is there now, obscured by the horse. If you bend down a little and look under the horse's belly, you can see his legs."

The doorman and I must have presented a curious spectacle,

stooping to stare under a horse. However, I saw a pair of brown-trousered legs.

"The minute you step into a carriage, sir, that man will climb aboard the cab and follow you. And when you return, he'll not be far behind. He was there when you returned last night."

"Was he, by George?" I said as I resumed the upright stance.

"I thought it my duty to mention it, sir."

"How right you are!" said I, handing him a louis d'or and trying not to imagine what the more sensational newspapers would make of my visit to the Montyon the previous evening, for who else could my pursuer be but a reporter? "What does this damned jackal look like?"

"Average in height, sir. A youngish man, thickset, bearded, probably under thirty. Wears a brown bowler hat and a black overcoat."

"I'm obliged to you, doorman. He'd better watch his own back in future." I climbed into my carriage and told the driver to take me to the Ecole de Médecine. As soon as we were in motion, I looked for the spy from the press through the small window at the back of the fiacre and saw no more than I expected to see; it is quite impossible to distinguish one cab from another unless one is a horse.

We crossed the river at the Pont des Invalides and started along the Left Bank, eventually reaching the rows of booksellers' stalls where people stand in the cold leafing through dusty tomes. In the most exciting city in Europe, they have their noses in secondhand books! I always feel as if I am venturing into alien territory when I visit the Latin Quarter. I'm unsuited to formal learning, it has to be said. Neither Oxford nor Cambridge (I attended both) succeeded in convincing me that the academic life has anything to commend it beyond meeting a few like spirits and shirking lectures with them and I've no reason to think that a year at the Sorbonne would have made a scholar of me. The failings were all mine, of course—and would have been all too obvious if I had ever submitted to an examination. The mere sight of the columned portico of the Ecole de Médecine sent a shiver up my back.

Needs must, however, and presently I was in the registrar's office inquiring into students past and present with the name of Claudine. One, I discovered, had left last year and as many as five were currently enrolled. Two in their first year could be eliminated

from my investigation, for the young lady I sought had been a
student already at the time the Exposition opened in May 1889. I
jotted down the addresses of the others: two second-year Claudines,
named Lacoste and Pascal, and one third-year, named Collomb.

The easy part was accomplished.

Middle-aged gentlemen inquiring after female students are
viewed with extreme suspicion, I learned when I called at Mademoiselle Lacoste's address. Claudine was not at home, the concierge
informed me—and that was all she would say in answer to a variety
of perfectly civil questions. I fared no better at Claudine Pascal's;
in fact, I was threatened with the police.

The treatment I received was dispiriting, not to say humiliating.
I didn't trouble with the third address; there had to be another
way of contacting the young ladies, I decided, but what was it to
be? I had the driver return me to the Ecole de Médecine, where
I inquired where the three Claudines would be in attendance for
lectures. You would think the registrar would know, but you would
be wrong. Students' timetables were subject to modification at
short notice, so they might be attending a doctor on his rounds
at the hospital, or in the laboratory, or the library, or with a tutor.
My best plan, I was told, was to ask another medical student. And
the best place to find a student at this minute would be at Père
Adolphe's, known as Folies-Cluny, where numbers of the species
congregated for lunch.

A noisier, more boisterous hostelry than Père Adolphe's doesn't
exist. The racket could be heard from Boul'Mich—and this was
some way down a side street. One paid twelve sous at the door and
edged in sideways between bodies, at the grave risk of having *le bon
bock* poured down one's shirtfront. An unlimited supply of liquor
was included in the admission price. The place was an extraordinary shape, scarcely wider than an omnibus, yet three times as
long. At the far end was a tiny stage with an upright piano being
played robustly while a chanteuse did her damnedest to be heard
above the din of several hundred students in earnest conversation.

A glass of bock was thrust into my hand by a serving wench
who nudged me laughingly in the stomach. I was on the point of
asking her to introduce me to a medical student when someone
placed a hand on her derriere and she wheeled around and kissed
him. I moved on.

Suddenly, I was eyeball-to-eyeball with a face I knew. Plump around the jowls, clean-shaven, and with ice blue eyes.

"Tristan!"

"God!" he exclaimed.

"Not quite," I remarked, "but not far short."

"I mean, Your Royal—"

I said, "Less of that. I'm incognito here."

"What are you doing in this place, sir?"

"The same as I was doing when I saw you last—investigating. Today I'm looking for medical students."

"You're in the right place, then. We're surrounded by them."

"How does one tell?"

"By the tammy—the tam-o'-shanter. If the border is mauve, he's a medic. Care to meet one?"

Thus it was that I presently found myself bellowing questions in hopes of being heard by Jacques, a personable second-year. Jacques hadn't the foggiest idea that the Bertie he was addressing was of the blood royal. I was just a fish out of water to him. In fact, he took me for a fish looking for tasty bait.

"Claudine? At your age?"

Tristan said, "Careful what you say, Jacques."

"Let him speak freely," said I. "This is too important."

"If you mean Claudine the *poitrine,* she's spoken for," said Jacques. "She goes about with a third-year called Roland."

"Is she dark and slim?"

"You fancy the brunettes, do you, Bertie? No, she's blond and you couldn't by any stretch of the imagination call her slim."

"What is her name?"

"Pascal. The other Claudine in our year is called Lacoste. She's more your type. Dark and slim."

"Does she have straight hair?"

"You *are* hard to please. No, it's curly, very curly."

"Are you being serious?"

"Absolutely. Her mother must have spent some time in Africa."

Tristan said, "Jacques, we are not playing games."

"Neither am I," said he. "Claudine Lacoste has tight black curls. Ask someone else if you like."

I said, "We believe you. I understand there is a third-year student with the name of Claudine."

"She'll be all of twenty," Jacques said, poker-faced. "A little old for your taste. I don't know her name."

"Collomb."

"How is it that you know so much and haven't met her? She's here somewhere. She must be. She always comes in at lunchtimes."

"Is she—"

"Brunette? Yes. Lift me up, will you? I'll have a scout." Tristan and I put down our tankards and hoisted Jacques above the level of the heads. I was doubtful whether he would see anything through the cigarette smoke, but he announced that he had spotted Claudine Collomb near the piano. In a moment, all three of us were prizing our way through the crush. To add to the din, the pianist was giving a rendering of the "Anvil Chorus" and half the room was joining in.

"This is Bertie, from England. He is quite frantic to meet you, Claudine."

"What?"

"Bertie, from England."

I pumped the limp hand of a young lady who—I was overjoyed to discover—fitted the descriptions I had gotten from the concierge and Mimi, even to the dejected expression last noted at the house in the rue Tronchet. The dejection may have owed something to the discovery that it was I, not Jacques, who wanted the chat. With his dimples and wide eyes, Jacques was just a puppy, but puppies are irresistible to the fair sex.

"May we talk outside, mademoiselle? It's impossible here."

"What do you want?"

Jacques put an arm around Claudine's waist and drew her forward. She came like a lamb. All the way out to the street, I was praying that I'd struck gold this time. I could understand Letissier being attracted to her; she had an air of nunlike melancholy redeemed by remarkable beauty.

Outside, she said, "What is this all about?"

I explained that I was looking for a medical student by the name of Claudine who had sold beads in the Indian Pavilion at the Exposition. For the moment, I kept Letissier's name out of it.

She devastated me by saying, "I didn't work at the Exposition, monsieur. I come from Grenoble and I go home every summer. You've mistaken me for someone else."

"Have you ever met Maurice Letissier?"

"Who?"

She wasn't bluffing, I was certain. She was genuinely bewildered by the questions. I apologized and let her return to the mayhem. With a shrug and a smile, Jacques went also, his hand on her shoulder. If nothing else, I thought resignedly, I have just played Cupid.

Tristan hauled me out of my brown study. "Sir, what does all this have to do with the murder of Maurice?"

I led him away in search of a quieter place for lunch. The young man had gone to some trouble to assist me, so I would take him into my confidence. The eating house (restaurant would be a misnomer) catered to students. When I tried ordering oysters, I was told curtly by the patron that he would tell me what we would eat. It was soup, followed by whiting, followed by *poulet* Henri IV. He was not the sort one argued with.

The advantage of this arrangement was that for once in my experience of eating in France, the courses were served promptly. The soup was a vegetable concoction, piping hot and delicious.

After hearing the gist of my conversations with the concierge and the demimondaine, Tristan commented, "Rather intriguing, sir."

"I would call it highly promising," said I. "Do you see how infuriating it is that not one of these girls in the Ecole appears to be the Claudine who knew Letissier?"

"If she exists—as I am sure she must—what interpretation do you place on her behavior?" he asked.

"It's crystal clear. The friendship between Claudine and Letissier was well established a year ago. He saw her regularly and invited her to his rooms a number of times. She was a young student, less experienced than he. Quite possibly he led her to believe she was his one true love. He took advantage of her innocence and thought little of it. Soon he tired of her. He had a wide circle of women friends. Then Claudine heard of his engagement to your sister. On the day after the announcement—the Sunday before the murder—she made her visit to his apartment to express her outrage. Probably he was dismissive in a way that hurt her deeply. She resolved that if she could not have him, neither would Rosine. At the Moulin Rouge the following Friday she shot him."

After a moment's thought, Tristan said, "It is persuasive, sir, except for one matter."

"The gun?"

"Yes."

"I have pondered over that and I have an explanation that may fit the facts. As you know, it was taken from the gun room at Montroger. Letissier was a sportsman, was he not? A wildfowler?"

"That is so."

"Did he ever shoot on the Montroger estate?"

His eyes widened. "On several occasions."

"Then he used the gun room, did he not?"

"He borrowed our guns, yes."

"So it was conceivable that if he wanted a revolver—say, for protection—he may have pocketed one from the drawer in the gun room at Montroger?"

He hesitated. "Took it deliberately, sir?"

"Let us say borrowed it."

"But Maurice was a gentleman."

"Not quite the gentleman your father took him for, as more than one young lady could attest."

"That is becoming clear."

"You will accept that under the lax arrangements in the gun room the gun's absence is unlikely to have been noticed."

"I wouldn't argue with that." His thoughts ran ahead. "You deduce that he had the revolver in his rooms and that Claudine found it and resolved to kill him?"

"At the next opportunity."

"My word!"

The soup plates were cleared and the whiting put before us, *en colère*, their tails in their mouths. I was reminded how much one misses by dining in the most-touted Paris restaurants. One is easily deceived into thinking that no other fish are eaten except salmon, turbot, sole, and trout. The delights of herring, conger eel, skate, and *dorade* have to be sought in the small family-run houses in the side streets, the places patronized by priests and students. Helpings are plentiful in cheap restaurants, too. I have always regarded myself as a gourmand rather than a gourmet; it is impossible to like food if you do not have a decent appetite. It was obvious from the way he attacked his plate that Tristan agreed with me.

"Your theory about the murder becomes more persuasive by the minute, sir."

"Or by the glass?" said I as I topped us both up with Chablis. "There is one flaw, unfortunately."

"What is that?"

"This murderer appears not to exist."

"Oh, I don't think you should abandon hope, sir."

"Hope is not enough, Tristan. I must take active steps to find this elusive young lady."

"I'm sure you are right, sir. She is unlikely to come forward."

"But who is she? I was convinced that the girl we spoke to, Claudine Collomb, was telling the truth. When I mentioned Letissier's name, she had no idea what I was talking about. And if Jacques was to be believed, the others, Pascal and Lacoste, have to be dismissed because they look nothing like the descriptions I was given."

"You are certain she was at the Ecole de Médecine?"

"Mimi was certain, and I'd lay money on Mimi's memory."

We continued in this vein for some time, relishing the excellence of the meal and deploring our inability to solve my problem. The chicken was served and eaten, then cheese, fruit, and coffee.

"What is the time, sir? I should be going to my lecture."

"Half past two."

"I wish I could have been of more help, if only for Rosine's sake."

"Why, precisely?"

He flushed.

I added rather deviously, "I know you have a brother's concern, but she isn't under suspicion, is she?"

He said, "She thinks of Morgan all the time. I hate to see her suffering."

He left me at the table smoking and reflecting that Morgan ought to be on my conscience, too, after the hopes we'd raised in his prison cell. It was not impossible that the poor wretch had been persuaded to sign a confession by this time. I finished the cigar in a pessimistic mood.

I tipped the patron more than he expected and asked if by some chance he knew of a medical student called Claudine. He shook his head. I got up to go. As I rose from the table, so did a young man across the room. He picked a brown bowler hat off a chair.

"Who is the young man over there?"

"I have never seen him before, monsieur," said the patron. "He came in just after you did. He is one of those who sit for two hours over a *consommation*. I wish I could afford to be so idle."

"I'm sure he wasn't idle," said I.

"What is he, then, a poet? "

"Probably not a poet, but a writer of sorts."

On my way out, I gave the fellow a penetrating stare, leaving him in no doubt of my disapproval, if he wasn't the reporter following me, there was no great harm done. If he was, I would know his coarse features, the thick brown eyebrows and the great trough of a mouth, the next time.

I strolled the streets of the Latin Quarter in the thin spring sunshine for a while, stopping occasionally to look behind me. If my pursuer was there, he was being less obvious about it. Eventually, my steps took me for the third time to the Ecole de Médecine.

"Not one of those students by the name of Claudine is the one I seek," I told the clerk in the registrar's office. "I have checked them all."

"When did you say she was in attendance, monsieur?"

"Two years ago. She took a job at the Exposition in May 1889."

"In term time?" He snapped his fingers. "You should have mentioned this before. She must be the one who had to give up her studies, stupid girl."

"Named Claudine?"

"Or was it Cloette?" He tapped his chin. "No, Claudine, I'm sure."

"You said she was stupid. Did she fall behind with her work?"

"No, monsieur. She was pregnant."

"Pregnant?"

It was a shock that left me speechless for some time after that. If this was really Letissier's lover, the case took on a dimension I had never considered until now.

The clerk was running his finger down a list. "Voilà! And it *was* Claudine—Claudine Jaume."

"Jaume. Would you kindly write it down for me?"

"Perhaps I was unkind to call her stupid," said the clerk, reaching for a pen. "They only have to make one mistake, and she was a charming girl, not the sort you'd expect to get into trouble. Others I could name give their favors at the drop of a hat and get away with it."

"Did she have the child?" I asked.

He didn't know. The Ecole had lost touch with her.

I asked if he had Claudine Jaume's address. Upon checking, he was able to tell me that during her time as a student she had lodged in the rue du Chemin-Vert, across the river; but he was uncertain where she had gone after giving up the course.

I must have betrayed signs of exasperation, because he asked me to wait while he made inquiries of one of his colleagues. The consensus was that Claudine Jaume still lived at the same address.

I took a cab there directly.

The district was northeast of the place de la Bastille and might as well have been Timbuktu. I suppose it afforded cheap lodgings within a miles walk of the Ecole de Médecine. Frankly, it was shabby, if not a slum.

After instructing the driver to be sure to wait, I ventured across to a door that stood open. No concierge here; simply some crudely scribbled names on scraps of paper pinned to the newel post at the foot of the stairs. I was profoundly pleased to see that one of them was Jaume. She occupied room eight.

Up the uncarpeted stairs I went, taking care to keep my gloves off the grimy banister rail. Behind one of the doors on the ground floor, a dog was howling. This was not a comforting place in which to find oneself. I stepped up sharply to the second floor and the third. Just as I reached the top stair, a door opened and an old crone in a black shawl with a face like a walnut looked out and said, "Who do you want?"

"Mademoiselle Jaume, if you please. Which is number eight?"

"She's gone."

"Gone out, do you mean?"

"Done a moonlight flit with her bastard child a couple of weeks ago. I'm not sorry. It was a miserable brat, forever crying."

My spirits plunged again. My murderer was on the run. "Are you sure of this? Did you speak to her?"

"People don't speak much here. It's obvious, isn't it? And by the way, if you think I took any of her stuff, you're mistaken. It was that gang downstairs and their friends. Filthy scavengers."

I moved past her to the room at the end. A figure eight was marked in chalk on the wall. The door was ajar, so I stepped inside.

The scavenging had been thorough. Not a stick of furniture

remained. The garret Claudine Jaume had occupied was a mess of broken china and paper, as if a mob had fought over her possessions. Threads of torn fabric hung from the rings on the curtain rod. There were sheets of what I took to be lecture notes, apparently ripped from exercise books for the blank paper remaining. Scattered among them were nutshells, cabbage stalks, and hardened orange peels.

I said to the old woman, "Who are the people downstairs who did this? Which room?"

She said, "The one with the dog. You'd be a fool to go in. It's a vicious tyke, and they're not at home. They have a barrow in Les Halles."

"I suppose you have no information where Mademoiselle Jaume went?"

"She'd be a fool to tell me, wouldn't she?"

I returned downstairs and this time the dog registered my approach by a low growling that made my blood run cold. I knew the likely result if I tried the door.

Instead of going out through the front, I turned the other way along the passage, past a stone sink that probably serviced the entire house and through a door into a small yard. My idea, if possible, was to peer through the window of the room so ably guarded by the dog. The window was shuttered and bolted. However, I made an interesting discovery in the yard. A number of items had been heaped against a wall, among them some medical textbooks in too tattered a state to have been worth selling, a moth-eaten shawl, and a collection of pots and bottles. My contention, made earlier, that nobody has any use for other people's medicines, was borne out here. I found a well-known cough mixture, some liver salts, and a number of jars, among them one of green glass with a black lid and an Ecole de Médecine label. The powder this jar contained was white and gritty. I didn't care to taste it. Unhelpfully, someone had gone to some trouble to scratch away the part of the label that would have named the contents. At least it appeared to confirm that I had found Claudine Jaume's lodgings, so I pocketed the jar.

But the trail was cold.

CHAPTER 16

"**B**ertie, what was the powder in the jar?"

"Arsenic."

Sarah Bernhardt and I were in a café just off the Champs Elysées near the Arc de Triomphe—neutral ground. We both had some pride at stake. She had declined to come to my hotel and I had refused to set foot inside her house. It was that efficacious modern instrument, the telephone, that had restored communication between us, a call from Knollys to milady's servant Pitou. I knew that she would be unable to suppress her curiosity if I dangled the bait of a vital clue in the Letissier case. After some token reluctance, she had consented to meet me for no more than a drink.

This was *l'heure verte,* the absinthe hour, in Paris, when business has ceased and the businessman sets aside his troubles at work and makes an interlude before facing the troubles at home. He buys his evening paper in the kiosk and takes it to the café, orders the French national drink, and enjoys an hour of quiet contemplation.

Without wishing to denigrate the French palate, I dislike the licorice flavor of absinthe and prefer a glass of cognac, and had ordered one. Bernhardt was supplied with a thimbleful of Madeira. Diplomatically, I didn't refer to her wounding remarks the last time we had spoken. The account I gave her of my latest discoveries made the point far more effectively. What a blunder to have doubted the existence of Claudine Jaume!

"Arsenic? Are you certain, Bertie?"

"As night follows day, my dear. I had it analyzed by the best chemist in town, at the pharmacy in the rue Washington. He described it as a compound of arsenic. He was appalled that it was not labeled as a poison."

"Why would Claudine Jaume possess such a dangerous substance?"

I smiled cryptically. "It is not impossible that she used it to put down rats or mice. I'm sure vermin are common in the area where she lived."

"Does one buy rat poison in that form?"

"She didn't buy it. She was a medical student. She took it from the laboratory."

"To put down for rats?"

"Don't ask me. I am not an expert. If rat poison is required at the royal residences, someone else looks after it and says nothing to me."

"You don't really believe she kept the arsenic to kill rats, do you?"

"That isn't the point, Sarah. The fact that she possessed the stuff at all is what matters. Thank heaven I had the good sense to pick it out of the rubbish heap in that yard."

She traced a gloved finger pensively around the rim of her wineglass. "Do you think she was a poisoner?"

"What I *think* is of no importance," said I mischievously, for I meant to make the most of this. "A detective assembles evidence and makes deductions."

She said with her sledgehammer tact, "Oh, Bertie, don't be so blessed pompous. What was she up to?"

"Consider her situation—a poor student living in a tenement slum. Because she is pretty, she was befriended by Letissier, and there's no disputing that he was a rake and a seducer, charming by all accounts, but utterly unscrupulous. Unbeknown to her, he had a string of females in tow and—as if that was not enough—frequented an introducing house. He toyed with young Claudine for a time, brought her home to his elegant rooms in the rue Tronchet, impressed her with his wealth and breeding. Then came the day when she was obliged to tell him he had made her pregnant. Precisely how the fellow reacted, we cannot say for certain; except that he declined to do the gentlemanly thing."

"You mean marry her?"

"Of course. Is this a reasonable thesis up to now?"

"Go on," said she impatiently.

"As we saw for ourselves, Letissier was a copious taker of medicines."

"He had a large supply, but we don't know how many he took," she corrected me.

"Sarah, do you want me to go on?"

"Very well."

"Quite soon, he became rather unwell. Last winter, he complained to his concierge of sore throats and migraines. He filled his medical chest with laxatives and tonics. Moreover"—I raised a finger—"his hair was falling out."

"Is that indicative?"

"Most certainly."

"Of poisoning?"

"According to the chemist I consulted, the classic symptoms of chronic arsenical poisoning include general malaise, headaches, dryness of the throat, diarrhea alternating with constipation, jaundice, and falling hair." I paused and gave her a steady look.

"The concierge mentioned jaundice."

"And loss of hair," said I.

She frowned, taking in the implications. She believed me now. "How would she have administered the arsenic?"

"She could have added it to anything he took regularly—sugar, salt. Or she could have tipped some into a liquid. There was that stuff in a medicine bottle."

"Van Swieten's liquor."

"Yes, it was practically empty. If that was some kind of tonic he took each day . . ."

She leaned forward, an expression of awe written over her features. "Bertie, did you work this out yourself? I'm going to need another drink."

I called the waiter, and when it was ordered, I rested my case for an interval. The café was filling and most eyes were on us; people find it hard to believe that in Paris I behave as others do—although I suppose not many others share a table with Sarah Bernhardt. Then my attention was taken by someone who had just come in. He appeared to be distributing folded pieces of paper, placing one on the corner of each table. I watched this procedure curiously. Some picked up the paper, unfolded it, and read what was written inside, but the majority conspicuously ignored the gift, even if they had nothing else to distract them.

"You mentioned chronic poisoning," said Sarah. "By that, you mean steady doses rather than one lethal amount?"

I nodded. "That way, it is less likely to be detected by the victim. He just assumes he is ill. All she had to do was tip some arsenic into one of the preparations he took."

"But in the end, it wasn't the arsenic that killed him; it was two bullets."

"Granted," I admitted serenely. "All I am asking you to believe is that Claudine Jaume intended to kill Letissier. She possessed the arsenic and he exhibited the symptoms. In the end, she lost patience and shot him."

"Bertie, it wasn't a question of losing patience," Bernhardt said in some excitement. "She was bitterly angry in the end."

"Angry?"

"Yes—at the news of his engagement to Rosine. We know she made one more visit to his apartment on the Sunday before the murder, obviously to appeal to him to acknowledge the child he had sired."

I nodded. Of course I had deduced this already, but I can be generous when others talk sense. However, it was my dogged persistence that had led us to the truth, and I didn't want Bernhardt stealing this scene from me, so I said firmly, "She found a revolver there, a revolver Letissier himself had acquired from the gun room at Montroger. Let us say borrowed. She secreted it in her handbag, took it away with her, and shot him at the next opportunity, at the Moulin Rouge."

"Oh no."

I glared at her. "What is wrong now?"

She stared back defiantly. "Claudine didn't shoot him. That's far too fanciful. You've been amazingly clever up to now, Bertie. Don't spoil it."

"What are you saying—that after all this, you don't believe she did it?" said I, flabbergasted.

"This complicated theory about the gun," said she. "It contains some doubtful assumptions, to put it mildly. First he steals the thing and then she does—really stretching credibility. You don't understand women at all."

"That's rather sweeping."

"I withdraw it, then. I'll rephrase it. You have overlooked the explanation that I, as a woman, find transparently obvious."

I greeted this with the frigid silence it deserved.

"What happened is this," she told me. "Claudine appealed to Letissier to do the gentlemanly thing and marry her and found him unsympathetic. Her remedy was not to shoot him, but to expose him. If he wouldn't disclose to his fiancée that he had fathered a child, she would. She went to Montroger and told Rosine the truth about the man she was to many. As I have maintained from the beginning, it was Rosine who shot Letissier, and for very good reason. You have supplied the motive, Bertie. I salute you." She gave me a sweet smile. "Between us, we have arrived at the truth."

"Whoa there," I said. "I can't agree with that."

"Why not? If Rosine is the murderer, you don't have to explain how the fatal weapon came into her possession. It was already there, in the house where she lives."

"But she didn't do it, Sarah."

The drinks came. To our left, the fellow distributing pieces of paper was still going diligently about his business, not missing a table. A few people unfolded the papers and looked at the contents. The majority did not trouble.

Bernhardt would not be subdued. She had to wring an admission from me. "Bertie, don't be so dense. You must see that Rosine's motive is overwhelming now. Not only was she being forced to marry the man she didn't love; she'd learned that he'd fathered someone else's child."

"I may be naïve where women are concerned," I said with heavy irony, "but if your theory is true, isn't it far more likely that she would appeal to her parents to call off the engagement? She had just been handed a very persuasive reason not to marry Letissier."

"Appeal to her parents, after all that had gone before? " said she with a sharp note of scorn.

"Wouldn't Jules and Juliette support her?"

"No."

"Why not?"

"Because they are not bourgeois, Bertie. In the circles the

Agincourts move in, they take a more tolerant view of a young man's indiscretions. They wouldn't see his conduct as an obstacle to marriage. To make an issue of it would be a social gaffe. It would neither be understood nor supported by the people they fraternize with."

"That must be debatable," said I.

"It isn't. Jules d'Agincourt is an old-fashioned aristocrat. His promise had been given to the Letissier family. He would see it as his duty, a matter of family honor, to insist that the marriage took place. Privately, he might have had strong words with the young man and insisted that he make Claudine some kind of settlement and would never repeat the adventure, but that is the most he would do. The engagement would stand."

I was about to insist that Claudine Jaume had a stronger motive than Rosine, but I was in imminent danger of being overheard, so I took a sip of cognac instead and watched the man with the folded papers approach our table, put one down for us, and move on.

Just as I started to put my hand out, Bernhardt grabbed my wrist. "If you do," she warned me, "he'll demand two sous. Only the tourists fall for it."

"But what is it?"

"A form of begging. He's dumb, or pretending to be. This paper has printed on it the key to the deaf-and-dumb language. If you are curious enough to touch it, he'll notice and take that as consent. Watch him now. He'll visit all the tables again collecting the papers, and his dues."

It was a new form of enterprise to me. Habitues of the cafés are regularly approached by sellers of parakeets, puppies, toffee apples, roses, plaster figurines, walking sticks, and sexual favors. In most cases, one may examine the goods, more or less. In this instance, you paid to have your curiosity satisfied. You were unlikely to keep the paper, for who wants to study sign language? So it was nearly all profit.

Therefore, we ignored the piece of paper.

Rather than debating Claudine Jaume's behavior any longer and provoking another argument, I switched to a less, controversial matter and informed Bernhardt about the anonymous letter that had come that morning and my conversation with Goron. "I really believed it to be the proof of Morgan's innocence," I said. "You may imagine my mortification when Goron pointed out that it didn't square with the statement Morgan himself made to us."

"Who would have sent it?" she asked.

"Some well-meaning friend of Morgan's, according to Goron."

Her eyes narrowed and she drummed her fingers on the table. "Rosine, perhaps."

"Oh, I shouldn't think so."

"Bertie, she went to the length of visiting you at the Bristol to protest his innocence, so she certainly wouldn't stop at writing you a letter."

"But unsigned?"

"Without question, if she felt it would lead to his release. It was a decently written letter, you said, an educated letter?"

"Yes."

"It wouldn't have been written by one of his artist friends, then. Most artists are practically illiterate. I would be fascinated to compare it with Rosine's handwriting. Do you still have it?"

"At the hotel."

"Keep it, Bertie. It could be a vital clue."

"Goron doesn't think so."

"Goron is an idiot."

On that, at least, we were in accord. Pensively, we sipped our drinks. I remarked in the spirit of cooperation that even though our theories on the murder differed, we would both dearly like to speak to Claudine Jaume.

"Perhaps the landlord has a forwarding address," Bernhardt suggested.

"I wish it were so," said I. "Unfortunately, all the evidence is that she did a flit. She left her possessions behind."

"Perhaps she couldn't pay the rent. It would be due soon. All rents must be paid by April eighth, the next quarter day."

"Sarah, she is on the run because she is a murderess." The dumb man was on his round for the second time, and I took a franc from my pocket. Thanks to Bernhardt, I hadn't fallen for the trick, but I admired the poor fellow's enterprise. He deserved a tip.

"That's too much," Bernhardt scolded me.

"This is his lucky day, then. I never carry sous."

The man gave me a nod for my generosity. Instead of picking

up the paper, he placed a finger on it and slid it across the table toward me. Then he moved on.

"My, you're honored!" said Bernhardt. "They don't usually let you keep it."

"May I look at it now?" said I, unfolding it. And then I frowned.

"What is it?" she asked.

"Not sign language, for sure." I turned to look for the dumb man, but he had left the café.

A message was inscribed in pencil:

> *7 rue Alexis*
> *8 p.m.*
> *Claudine Jaume*

I handed it to Bernhardt and said, "Where's the rue Alexis?"

"Across the river."

"Do you think I should go? It may be a trap."

"Of course we must go," she said, slipping smoothly into the plural. "She wants to prove to us that she is innocent."

"But she isn't innocent. How did she know we were here? I don't care for this, Sarah. I don't like the way it was done. I don't care for it at all."

CHAPTER 17

I was deeply suspicious of the message. A strong, almost-supernatural impulse urged me to ignore it. I was hearing another message, the words my own wife had written to me: "I can see dreadful danger . . . Believe me, *I fear for your life.*" My dear, devoted Alix was speaking to me as passionately as if she was sitting at the table.

Whatever my failings (and I admit to plenty), I am no coward. It wasn't a blue funk that made me hesitate, it was loyalty to Alix. And there were also practical reasons for caution. There was the knowledge that if I took up Claudine Jaume's invitation, she would have the advantage over me. Up to now, every action of mine had been my own choice; she couldn't possibly have predicted where I would go next or what I would discover about her. Now the advantage would swing to her. She had named the time and place.

There was, of course, another consideration. I had been handed a matchless opportunity of catching up with her. To reject it was to throw in the towel.

Bernhardt, seeing me of two minds, said, "If you like, I'll go and meet her by myself. She doesn't frighten me in the least."

Ignoring the barb, I said, "Where exactly is the rue Alexis?"

"Near the Champ-de-Mars, where the Exposition was."

"We'll go together. I think there's time for another cognac first."

"Dutch courage?"

I preserved a dignified silence while pinching her under the table.

A little after half past seven, we hired a closed coupé. Paris was about its business as gaily as ever in the lighted streets and boulevards, the strains of violin and harmonium from the restaurants and brasseries competing with the clink of harness and the clatter of hooves along the roadways. Beside me, Bernhardt behaved as if we were blithely out for an evening of food and fun like everyone else. Leaning half out of the window, she gave me a commentary on everything outside, mocking the stuffed-bird trimmings on other women's hats, urging me to sniff the appetizing odors wafting from open doors or to wave to friends she spotted in other carriages.

I was silent, unmoved, a coiled spring.

What was Claudine Jaume's game? I kept wondering. Why risk a confrontation with me when she knew—she surely knew—I suspected her of murder? And I was at a loss to understand how she had discovered precisely where to reach me with the message— and recruited the dumb man to deliver it. The whole thing was mysterious and extremely unnerving.

Somewhere along the avenue Kléber between the Arc de Triomphe and the Trocadéro Palace, Bernhardt said, "Chin up, Bertie. Even if Claudine did it, which I dispute, I don't think she'll kill you."

"You forget something. I am the only person in Paris who believes she is a murderess. My life is definitely at risk."

"Then I shall make it very clear that I don't share your opinion," said she, unable to take anything seriously that night.

Our carriage swung around the terraces of the Trocadéro and crossed the Pont d'Iéna. I was so preoccupied that I failed even to comment on the ugliness of the Eiffel Tower when it loomed up, fully illuminated and soaring to the stars. We veered left and skirted the Champ-de-Mars for a few minutes before venturing up a short unlighted street.

"You said rue Alexis, monsieur?" our cabman called down.

"Number seven. And be sure to wait for us if you want the fare."

They were tall tenement buildings. The darkness may have restricted my observation, but it seemed to me that Mademoiselle Jaume's new address was even less desirable than the last. Most of the houses were boarded up and one end of the street was just a heap of rubble, left over, I guessed, from the Exposition.

"I should have armed myself," said I.

"To meet a woman with a baby?" said Bernhardt.

"A murderess who shot a man in the back."

"Allegedly," said she.

"It's not a risk that one should take."

"But she doesn't have the gun any longer."

"She is also a poisoner."

"Don't drink the coffee, then."

We got out. Boards had been nailed across the windows of number seven, not just on the ground level but to the roof. It looked most unlike a domestic habitation. The front door was solid wood apart from a small recess halfway down that was protected by an iron grille. I knocked boldly. After some delay, a hatch behind the grille slid open and a pair of dark eyes inspected us.

Stooping, I said, "We are here at the invitation of Mademoiselle Jaume." I had no intention of announcing our identities, not to a pair of goggling eyes.

The scrutiny continued.

"Jaume," I repeated. "Mademoiselle Claudine Jaume."

The hatch closed, the door opened a short way, and I had my first shock of the night. Behind it was a dwarf, a proper dwarf about a foot shorter than Toulouse-Lautrec and with a head too large for his body. He was dressed in a cockaded red turban, white shirt, black suede waistcoat, pink satin pantaloons, white stockings, and red Turkish slippers with pointed, curling toes.

"How many cognacs did I get through?" I muttered to Bernhardt. Then I told the little man, "I think we must be mistaken. We wanted a young lady."

He piped, "Claudine Jaume?'

"Well, yes."

Then he beckoned me inside. Naturally, I stepped back to let the lady pass through the door first, but Bernhardt had an extraordinary effect on the dwarf. He raised both hands to bar her entry and jabbered something excitedly in his own language, which was neither Bernhardt's nor mine.

"The lady is with me," said I in a civil tone calculated not to excite him more. "We are together."

He shook his head vigorously and wagged a finger at Bernhardt, who said, "This is utterly absurd."

"For some occult reason, he doesn't wish you to enter," I said superfluously.

"Who the devil is he?" said she.

"By his dimensions, he appears to go with the door," said I. "The peephole is exactly his height."

"He can't be the concierge, can he? Well," she said, articulating her words as if she was on the stage, "it's apparent that *Sarah Bernhardt* is persona non grata here."

But the dwarf didn't exactly jump to attention at the sound of Bernhardt's name. He continued to stand in her way, scowling ferociously.

She said, "You'd better go in without me, Bertie."

"That's out of the question."

She said, "I shall wait in the cab. You go in."

I was reluctant to leave her outside, for my own convenience as well as hers. I'd counted on her support in extracting the truth from Claudine Jaume. I made one more attempt to communicate our intentions to the dwarf, this time introducing myself as the Prince of Wales and my companion as the celebrated Madame Sarah Bernhardt.

I might as well have said she was Medusa. He shook his head so hard that the turban swiveled.

Sarah told me, "You're wasting your breath, Bertie. You'll have to go in alone. If it's a misunderstanding, you can send for me, but don't send him. If he wags his little finger at me once more, I'll pick him up by the seat of his pink satin pants and toss him in the river." She strutted back to the waiting cab.

I called out to her, "I have an uncommonly nasty feeling about this."

She retorted, "Oh, get on with it, Bertie! I shan't wait out here forever."

The dwarf pulled the door fully open. With a troubled sigh, I stepped inside. He shut out Paris with a thud.

At least the hall was carpeted, which was an improvement on Claudine's previous address. A miserly light gave me little chance to inspect the interior. It was as much as I could do to follow the bobbing turban along a passage that eventually led completely through the house, down a couple of steps, and into what looked like a conservatory but turned out to be a glass-sided corridor that evidently connected number seven rue Alexis with another building.

"Where are you taking me?" I demanded without any expectation of being understood.

Of course I was given no answer.

The dwarf opened a door at the end and gestured to me to go ahead. Having begun this bizarre adventure, I was obliged to continue it. Greatly to my surprise, I stepped into a spacious, well-lit octagonal room with a tiled floor and a fountain playing in the center. An ornate wooden screen exquisitely carved in an Ottoman design formed the surround. Four archways were incorporated in the screen. A number of marble benches provided the only furniture. Looking up, I saw that this elegant place was sited under a large cupola painted deep blue and intricately decorated with stars, crescents, and lozenges.

Behind me, the door shut, and to my disquiet, I heard a bolt forced home with vigor by the dwarf on the other side. I was abandoned in this alien place. I stood uncertainly, extremely doubtful now that Claudine Jaume would materialize. I could think of no possible connection between an unmarried mother and this vestibule of what appeared to be a Moorish palace. I had never heard of such a building in Paris. One could only speculate that it was one of the many exotic pavilions put up for the Exposition. I thought they had all been dismantled except Monsieur Eiffel's enormous offense to good taste, but obviously this place, too, had been reprieved.

The Exposition must be the connection, I thought. Claudine was employed here. Mimi, the demimondaine, had told me of meeting Claudine with Letissier in the Indian Pavilion. Obviously, she had come to know this building while she was working at Champ-de-Mars. I felt a little easier in my mind at having worked this out for myself. That wretched dwarf had undermined my confidence.

Then a naked man walked in.

I had better qualify that. He was wearing sandals. He also carried a towel. Regrettably, he carried it without the slightest concession to decency. He was an unprepossessing sight, too, pink as a flamingo, corpulent, hirsute, and without any attribute that I would have thought worthy of putting so flagrantly on display.

I cleared my throat to attract his attention or he would have walked straight past, I am certain. "Do you speak French, monsieur?"

He hesitated, stared at me as if I were the naked man, gave a Gallic shrug, crossed the floor to the archway opposite, and disappeared from my view.

I am not used to such rudeness.

I followed him. Through the archway on the other side of the screen was a tiled passageway with latticed half doors to a series of cubicles that I took to be changing rooms. The man's head and torso were visible in the nearest of these. He turned and stared at me over the half door with the expression of a horse reluctant to be saddled.

I said with such deference as I could muster, "You must excuse me. I am a visitor. Do you happen to have seen Mademoiselle Jaume?"

He said in a squawk of outrage, "Mademoiselle? Where?"

"That is my difficulty. I don't know where. I was brought here."

"Brought? Who brought you?"

"A Turkish dwarf."

"Oh?"

"Before that," I went on, "I received a message, but that needn't concern you." I was beginning to sound as confused as I felt.

"A message?" said he dubiously.

"To come here and meet Claudine Jaume."

"You came to this place to meet a woman? How did she get in?"

"I haven't the faintest idea."

He said, "Well, who are you?"

"The Prince of Wales."

This was the last straw as far as he was concerned. He said firmly, "Just move away from me, will you? I'm sure somebody will come for you."

Crushed, I gave up. I would be better employed making a tour of the cubicles in search of somebody who would help me. And so it turned out. I had not gone more than a few steps when a figure—a clothed figure—approached from the opposite direction. My rising hopes dived again when I saw what clothes they were. He was dressed like the dwarf in baggy trousers and a turban. However, I could now be reasonably certain of one thing that had gradually been dawning on me: I was in a Turkish bath and this was an attendant. Make of it what you will, reader, and you will probably be as mystified as I was.

Ever the optimist, I said in French, "Good evening, can you help me? I am the Prince of Wales and I was directed here in the expectation of meeting a young lady, Mademoiselle Jaume."

The attendant smiled, nodded, pushed open the door of the nearest cubicle, and ushered me inside.

"I don't think you understand," said I.

He pointed to a towel hanging over the door, as if that explained everything.

"But I haven't come for a bath."

He folded his arms in a way that I could easily have taken as menacing. They are muscular fellows, these Turkish bath attendants.

My beleaguered brain struggled to make sense of this pantomime. There had to be some logic to it, some reason why I had been led or lured here. Clearly, I was in the gentlemen's section of the baths. Perhaps Claudine had sought sanctuary in the ladies' half—if such a facility existed. I had once been shown a postcard of a French painting in the Louvre of twenty or more ladies in a state of nature disporting themselves in a Turkish bath (presumably in Paris), drinking tea, playing a mandolin, and passing time in other ways I shan't go into, except to state that it wasn't the sort of place where a man would have been welcomed. It made me curious how the artist (a man) had obtained permission to set up his canvas. I remembered noticing an unusual feature, and that was that the painting had been circular, giving the impression of a view through a window, or peephole. Knowing mankind's insatiable curiosity, it would not surprise me to know that there were secret arrangements between the attendants of both sides of the baths. No, I would not abandon hope of meeting Claudine Jaume.

There remained the matter of my clothes. Clearly, I couldn't walk around a Turkish bath in a silk hat and overcoat. On the other hand, one feels so vulnerable with only a towel for protection. An English gentleman is not comfortable in the buff. In London, I occasionally visit the Jermyn Street Turkish bath, which is conveniently close to my club. There, bathing drawers are de rigueur. The likelihood of obtaining a pair in this place was negligible. The French are shameless in their attitude to the human form.

I came to the reluctant decision to remove all my clothes, reflecting, as I stepped out of my trousers, that the dwarf, after all, had acted properly to exclude Sarah Bernhardt from this baring of the flesh. I'm not coy where Sarah is concerned and I can't believe she would object to parading au naturel, but who could say what sights lurked in the inner sanctum of the baths?

Taking care to tuck the towel securely around my middle, I slipped my feet into the sandals provided. Only then did my attendant unfold his arms and allow me out of the cubicle.

"Now will I have your cooperation?" said I with a withering stare.

He took a step back and pointed to a set of swing doors, making it patently clear that he would not be coming with me. Wisps of steam were escaping through the slot at the center.

I pushed open the doors and entered a white vault. The heat inside was palpable. The modern Turkish bath is supposed to function with hot, dry air, but they are always full of vapor and it was far from easy to see anything. It took some time before my vision adjusted sufficiently to show me another set of doors ahead, streaming with condensation. The idea is that one progresses through a series of rooms of increasing temperature. This was merely an antechamber. Staunchly, I persevered. The second chamber was so hot that I felt the moisture rolling steadily down my torso. It was necessary to remain some minutes there before even thinking of moving on, so I sat for a while on one of the marble benches provided. No one else was present. If I had come here from choice, I would have endured the sensations in the happy knowledge that I was purifying my blood, protecting myself against scrofulous diseases, gout, sciatica, rheumatism, corpulence, baldness, and ennui. Because it was involuntary, I resented every second of it. I was beginning to suspect that I had made myself a laughingstock. Bernhardt would think this risible if I emerged pink faced to announce that I'd been through a Turkish bath and learned absolutely nothing.

Passing swiftly through another sweltering room, I penetrated to the steam room itself. There, I was obliged to halt. It was the nearest thing to hell that I am ever likely to encounter. I held the door open a moment and the steam rushed past me as if I was in a railway tunnel—traveling *outside* the train. I couldn't see much at all. There was no other way through, so I took a deep breath and stepped into this inferno and out by the opposite door as swiftly as possible.

Then, by contrast, blissful cool air. I pushed open the doors to a grander room, in fact an atrium, a place of classical pillars and tall arches, the very center of the hammam. Immediately in front of me was a huge temptation, a pool of water that I could tell at a glance was ice-cold. Had I been totally confident of privacy, I would have discarded the towel, stepped out of the sandals, and plunged in. However, one has one's standards of decorum. Through the vaporous air (it was still tropically warm in here), I had spotted two fellow creatures, and one doesn't parade naked in front of strangers, even though these two were inert. They were lying facedown on the vast marble platform at the center of the room that is used for massage. So far as I could tell in the conditions, they were not female.

A third figure, a boy of Eastern features in a blue loincloth, appeared from behind a column and gestured to me to join the others on the platform. One is frightfully vulnerable facedown; however, I submitted. I don't know if the heat saps one's resistance, but at that minute the prospect of being horizontal was peculiarly appealing.

When the boy eased the towel from underneath me, I didn't even murmur. I lay there like a beached porpoise. He commenced to massage me by pressing lightly with his fingertips on my neck and shoulders, working downward to my feet, which he chafed assiduously to remove hard skin from the soles.

I was lulled into a state approaching sleep when the second, more vigorous stage of the massage began. Unknown to me until this moment, a second masseur had arrived, an adult. I opened my eyes and saw him, huge, solemn and silent, in loincloth and turban and with a black beard, just as he grasped my wrists and jerked them suddenly from under my head to engage in what felt to me like a tug-of-war with the boy, who gripped my ankles. My spine stretched and my limbs ached. Not satisfied with that, the man immediately tried another maneuver, pressing his knee into the small of my back and pulling hard on my shoulders until the joints cracked. I've had Turkish massages before and I know about the joint cracking, but this was more like the Inquisition. Of course, the manipulations are well founded, subscribing to a ritual universal in the Muslim world, differing only in the degree of energy expended by the masseur. This fellow was herculean. Ignoring my groans of protest, he attacked every joint in my body from the toes to the fingertips with sudden twists and savage jerks, the sole purpose of which was to achieve the audible crack of bone and gristle that signals success. He was inexhaustible, and turned me over like an omelet several times. At one stage, he was standing on my chest, kneading my ribs with his bare feet. The next, he grabbed my arm to raise me up while he pressed his foot against the opposite thigh.

I have no idea how long this torture persisted. He signaled the end of it, as they invariably do, with a sharp slap across my buttocks. To me at that stage of the process, any indignity was welcome if it brought respite. I felt as if my entire body had been taken apart and reassembled. I swear that no muscle, ligament, or nerve had escaped his attention.

I flopped on the marble, panting.

As if from another world, a voice said in French, "Your Royal Highness?"

I remained supine.

"Mustafa is unequaled at his trade. You will feel the benefits later, Your Royal Highness."

I wouldn't have troubled to raise my head if the voice had not sounded familiar. I couldn't trust my ears alone. I hauled myself onto an elbow and stared across the marble surface at the naked form of the *chef de la Sûreté*.

CHAPTER 18

My first thought was that the dreadful mauling I had just received had affected my brain. With my blood in its parboiled and turbulent state, was it any wonder that I should experience hallucinations? I blinked twice, fully expecting to remove Marie-François Goron from my field of vision. But when I looked again, he appeared more substantial than before. His cropped hair glistened with sweat and his fat face was crimson. The wax had melted from his mustache and the tufts at each end had sprouted and sagged.

He raised himself to his hands and knees and crawled toward me across the massage dais like a large naked baby—a spectacle too ludicrous to be a figment of my imagination.

The squelch of his potbelly coming to rest beside me on the marble removed any lingering doubt. I won't say I was reassured; I preferred the illusion.

I sat up and said, "This can't be a coincidence."

He grinned sheepishly.

I was incensed. "I came here in the expectation of meeting someone else. Instead, I am the victim of an ambush. I have been forced to strip, then pummeled, mauled, and beaten. Every joint in my body has been tugged out of its socket—and now I know exactly whom to blame."

He raised his shaggy eyebrows in pretense of innocence and two beads of moisture rolled down his cheeks. "May I respectfully suggest that you lie still and relax, Your Royal Highness? Mustafa would like to complete the shampoo."

"Shampoo?"

He nodded.

The effrontery of this charmless clown took my breath away. Nobody on this earth, not even my mother, the Queen, refers to my receding hair, however obliquely. When I managed to find words, I told him, "This is beyond belief! Who do you think you are to make offensive remarks about my appearance?"

"Sir, I think you misunderstand me. *Shampoo* as the Turks understand it is a massage of the entire body, not merely the head. You have just had the manipulation and it can be rather nerve-racking to hear one's joints cracking, but that is the way they do it. The embrocation is the next stage. I think you will find it more agreeable. While Mustafa does his work, we can talk."

"Never mind Mustafa. I demand to know why I was lured here."

"Understandably," said Goron. "It was a necessary stratagem and I apologize for it. I needed as a matter of urgency to speak to you in private, without Madame Bernhardt in attendance."

"Bernhardt? All this because of Bernhardt? It's preposterous. If you wanted a word in private, you should have asked."

"Ah, but she would have taken it as a challenge," said he. "She hates being excluded from anything. This is one place where I can be assured of meeting you alone. At this time of the day, the bath is hardly used. Actually, I come here several times a week. It is the most discreet location for a meeting between gentlemen."

"*Discreet* is hardly the word I would use," I commented. "Parading in the buff is not my idea of discretion. Couldn't we have met in a club?" By declining to answer this, except with a sigh and a shake of the head, he intimated that his reason for bringing me here was too compelling to delay any longer. Making it plain that I was seething over what had happened, I resumed the prone position beside him—only because I was immensely curious to learn why he had tricked me into coming here. "Well, if this is the way the Sûreté conducts itself, I'm glad your methods haven't crossed the Channel. I take it that the message I was handed in the café was from you?"

"That is so. The man distributing the notes was one of my officers."

"How did he find me?"

"Another of my men has been following you for the past two days."

"I was not unaware of him," said I smoothly, quick to remember the fellow in the brown bowler hat. The fact that I had taken him for a newspaper reporter was of no importance. "You should teach him to be less obvious."

Goron sidestepped the criticism. "I became concerned about your activities. There was serious danger that you would undermine my investigation."

"By finding out the truth, do you mean?"

"No, sir. If I thought you were likely to find out the truth, I would have no cause for concern."

"Except the trifling inconvenience that you arrested the wrong man," said I with a shaft of irony that was deflected by Mustafa planting a blob of cold cream between my shoulder blades. "Jerusalem!"

Goron said, "Morgan is guilty."

To which I retorted, "That's the fallacy of French justice. You presume a man is guilty when he's innocent and has no chance of proving it. Is he still rotting in your prison?"

"He is still being questioned, yes."

"Hasn't he confessed yet? He must have a will of iron."

"I can vouch for that," he said with feeling.

Mustafa had smeared the cream liberally across my shoulders and was kneading my flesh with his fingertips, and I have to say that he was producing quite tolerable sensations.

I told Goron, "You are completely wrong about Morgan. The murder was committed by a woman."

His response was to yawn without even covering his mouth. "You mean Claudine Jaume? That is impossible."

"It most certainly is not. She was Letissier's lover before he met the Agincourt family. She bore his child and when he rejected her, she understandably became incensed. She visited him on the Sunday before the murder to beg him not to marry Rosine. All this is indisputable."

"I don't dispute it," said Goron, yawning again.

I would not allow his want of manners to deter me. "It was a classic French crime, the rejected mistress driven to a desperate act, a *crime passionnel*. I would have told you everything in time to arrest her, but I was hot in pursuit. If you had not inveigled me here under false pretenses, I would certainly have caught her. She must be up and away by now."

He said indifferently, "Up and away? Yes."

I hesitated. "Do you know this for a fact?"

"Yes, sir."

"Then in the name of justice, why didn't you detain her?"

He said flatly, "Because she is dead."

"Dead?" I stared at him, aghast. "How do you know?"

"I have seen the body. When you remarked that she is up and away, I could not disagree. It is true in a metaphysical sense. Whether she is up or down, it is difficult to say, but she is certainly away."

Only a French detective could have talked metaphysics at a moment like this. "How did she die?" I asked, still unwilling to believe him.

"Suicide, we believe. Her body was recovered from the Seine, near the Pont des Arts. A child's body was also found. Both have been identified."

"Already?"

"Already."

He gave the information in such a colorless way that I was beginning, after all, to accept it as fact.

"If this is true," I commented, "it's dreadful. She took the child's life as well as her own?"

"No, sir. The evidence suggests that the child was dead before entering the water. The most likely explanation is that Claudine killed herself from grief and had the dead baby in her arms when she jumped from the bridge."

"Grief, you say. Let's not exclude guilt."

"I'm not excluding it, sir. She was a tormented young woman."

As if by mutual consent, a silence descended. We respected the gravity of death, regardless that the deceased had sinned more than most. For an interval, the only sound was the rubbing of Mustafa's hands across my back.

I was dumbfounded by Goron's statement and, if the truth be told, crushingly disappointed. After so much diligent detective work, I had looked forward to unmasking the murderer myself. Was that too much to have hoped?

"I suppose she didn't leave a note, a confession?"

"No note," said Goron.

"It's so unsatisfactory this way."

"Yes."

Mustafa grasped me firmly by the hip and shoulder and turned me to face upward, this time dropping the towel strategically over what an intimate friend of mine once called the crown jewels.

"Anyway, her suicide is tantamount to a confession of murder," said I.

"No, sir," said he flatly.

I gasped at his obtuseness. "You're not still insisting that Morgan did it, not after this?"

"I am more certain than ever," he insisted. "Claudine couldn't have murdered Letissier."

"Why ever not?"

"Because her body was found six hours before he was shot."

I sat bolt upright and pushed Mustafa away. "That's impossible."

Goron also heaved himself up. "I don't tell lies, sir."

"That's rich! What do you call it when you inveigle me here with a note supposedly from a woman who turns out to be dead?"

"I'd call it deception—in the interest of justice."

"Don't talk to me about justice, Monsieur Goron. You've deceived me from the outset," said I. "This is the first I've heard of her death. You didn't mention it when I came to see you at the Sûreté headquarters."

"I was unaware of it then. The bodies lay in the morgue unidentified for a fortnight. The girl's father, Felix Jaume, an hotelier, came up from Nantes yesterday because she hadn't written. She always wrote two letters a week to her family. After he'd described her to me, he was shown the body. He recognized his daughter at once, her face, her clothes, her crucifix, the comb she wore in her hair."

I shook my head. It is painful to reject an explanation one has firmly believed to be the truth. I would have staked my reputation on Claudine. Yet now that I cast my thoughts back to the conversation I'd had with the old woman who was her neighbor in the house in the rue du Chemin-Vert, she had told me that Claudine had done a moonlight flit with the baby two weeks previously. Two weeks—the interval matched Goron's information.

I said, "It would appear that I may be in error."

Goron gave a magnanimous shrug (which looks odd when given by a naked man).

I said, "I suppose I should thank you for mentioning it in private."

"You need not," said he, adding, after a significant pause, "All I would ask, sir, is that you now leave the Sûreté to complete its work."

This I did not particularly care for. I said, "I see no reason to abandon the case, if that is what you mean."

He frowned.

"I'm damned if I'll give up," said I. "The tragic death of this young woman must have a bearing. It can't be coincidence."

"She killed herself because her baby died," said Goron.

"It was also Letissier's baby, remember."

He pressed his hand to his head and gave a sigh like the ebb tide. "Sir, I wouldn't have brought you here—wouldn't have gone to such lengths—unless there were overriding reasons to ask for your cooperation. This unhappy episode can only inflict more grief and distress on those already mourning the death of young Letissier. I am thinking of his parents in particular, decent elderly people who have not the slightest idea that their son fathered an illegitimate child. If you had met them and seen their suffering already, as I have, you would not wish them to be dealt this additional blow. Without wanting to be overdramatic, I fear that a further tragedy might be the result."

I said, "I shan't trouble the Letissiers unless it becomes absolutely necessary. My suspicions point me in another direction."

"And which is that?"

"Back to the Agincourts, I'm afraid. I say that with a heavy heart, Monsieur Goron. I am a family friend."

A look sprang into his eyes that I had not seen before, and it was akin to the look of a child caught raiding the pantry. "The Agincourts? They are just as vulnerable," he said quickly. "Surely you can see that? The daughter, Rosine, was engaged to Letissier. The parents welcomed him as a future son-in-law. In recent days, they have had to endure repeated interrogation by the police and the press, not to mention you. They have seen their name bandied in the cheapest newspapers and they have borne it all with dignity. To heap this fresh infliction on them would be to invite more press sensations, more wagging tongues in the cafés and on the boulevards. We can spare them that, Your Royal Highness."

"Spare the Agincourts—or spare the Sûreté?" said I. "You nailed your colors to the mast when you took in Morgan as your prime suspect, didn't you?"

He said, "That is immaterial."

"On the contrary, it's so material, you could make a convict suit out of it, my friend, and it might not fit Mr. Morgan. If the news of this tragedy gets to the ears of the examining magistrate, he may not be so impressed by a forced confession."

He said with vitriol, "You exceed yourself, sir."

"We shall see. I have not the slightest intention of surrendering the case to you. I may have been mistaken over Mademoiselle Jaume, but no more mistaken than you are over Morgan. I shall persist in pursuing the truth, Goron, whatever the cost to peoples sensibilities. If necessary—who's that?"

My attention was distracted by a movement at the other end of the massage dais. Someone had stood up and was creeping away. I couldn't see him clearly through the vaporous atmosphere and he was swallowed altogether by steam billowing from a door he went through, but I can tell when a man's movements are furtive.

"Just another bather," said Goron.

"That's the steam room," I pointed out. "He's gone the wrong way."

"That's his choice," said he.

But I wasn't satisfied. I remembered taking note of two recumbent figures when I had entered this place. The shock of meeting Goron had dismissed the second from my mind. That mysterious person, whoever he was, had been well placed to eavesdrop on our conversation.

"I'm going after him."

Goron said, "Don't."

That galvanized me.

I swung my legs off the dais and dashed across the atrium, past the cold pool, skidding dangerously on the wet tiles and just staying upright. When I tugged open the door, steam fairly rushed out and hit me like a solid mass. It was a lunatic act to subject oneself to the experience without first becoming inured to heat in the purgatory of the other heat chambers. But if the man I was following was so keen to escape, then I was keener still to follow. Inside, the shock of the heat made me stagger. With eyeballs popping, heart thumping, and my entire body streaming, I groped toward a stone bench supposedly provided for the patrons to disport themselves upon—if their physiques could endure the experience. No one was there, so I shuffled to the other side. There I found a set of steps. The ventilators belching out the heat were high above me, near the ceiling, and it was a test of bulldog courage to mount the steps, increasing the agony. The only reason I submitted to it was that I had glimpsed through the billowing steam a pair of legs about four steps above me. Whoever was up there, he would be blistered all over if he stayed for long.

I braced myself and ascended two steps. The legs above me became sharper to my vision. I could see the calves, dark where the hair was flat to the skin, and the thighs, slender yet solid. As I watched, the muscles tensed.

I should have been more wary. I hadn't expected violence. One of the feet swung at me and caught me in the chest, pitching me backward. I might have been thrust on the tiled floor and seriously injured. However, my instinctive reaction to the attack was to grab the foot. I held on. I *did* fall backward, but slowly, tugging my assailant with me. We ended together in an ignominious heap at the bottom of the steps.

We were soon back on our feet, both of us, because the heat of the tiles was searingly painful against delicate areas of flesh. Before I could get a look at him, the man mounted the steps again—on the principle, I suppose, that the high ground was tactically easier to defend, but this time I was close behind. He was slight in stature; I'd gleaned that much from our encounter. I'm no Eugene Sandow, but I reckoned with my superior weight I could subdue him.

The problem was that the higher one went up the steps, the closer were the ventilators belching out the steam. I got almost to his level and grasped an elbow that he tried jabbing into my midriff. I held on as well as I could with the steam gusting into my face. He was a doughty antagonist, because he twisted one of his legs behind my own and forced me to relax my grip under the threat of losing my balance. Then, before I was steady again, he secured an armlock around my neck.

My face was forced down brutally. Below the ventilators at the top of the steps was a large semicircular cistern half filled with steaming water and lined with sediments of gray clay. My head was being inched toward it and the searing sensation on my skin made me cry out. To come into contact with the enamel edge would result in terrible burns. I was so close and the heat so terrific that I could not tell whether I was already being scalded.

The Marquis of Queensberry's Rules weren't written for people in the process of being casseroled. My only hope of escape was to go below the belt, so to speak. Groping like a blind man at a door, I found his most vulnerable point, squeezed with all my strength, and twisted. He emitted a roar of pain and relaxed the armlock. But you are right: I did not relax the hold I had on him. Holding tight, I braced and drew back from the wicked heat. My efforts toppled us both off the top step. We slithered down the steps together, staying upright only because we held on to each other. At ground level, I let go and pushed him away. I was practically expiring from the heat and the exertion. The only thing in the world I wanted was to get out of the steam room. I staggered to the door, pushed it open, and took a running jump into the cold pool.

Sinking thankfully under the surface, I thought, I shall never order a cooked lobster again.

I came up for air in time to see a pink blur at the edge of the pool, followed by a mighty splash. My antagonist had taken the same escape route. I rubbed water from my eyes and waited for him to surface.

I blinked. "You?"

He groaned, gave me a long look across the rippling water, and said, "For pity's sake, keep away from me, Bertie. I can't take any more."

He was Jules d'Agincourt.

You may imagine my confusion, I said, "I had no idea it was you."

"I won't make a run for it, I give you my word," said Jules. "I'm not even sure if I can walk after what you did to me. Just let me stay in this water."

When Goron, the far-famed *chef de la Sûreté*, came to the side of the pool and offered to help me out, I declined. I said in a dignified way, "You'll be better employed attending to your confederate."

I won't say Goron's shamefaced look was worth the indignity I had suffered. But it was some consolation.

DRESSED AGAIN, THE THREE OF us met over mint tea in the tea-room of the hammam, a blessedly cool, secluded place with a fountain playing.

Goron had taken time to marshal his defense. "Your Royal Highness, allow me to explain why I invited the comte to be present when I met you in the bath," he said in an emollient tone.

"To eavesdrop," said I. "I understand now why you chose this place. It's ideal for eavesdropping."

"That wasn't the spirit in which it was done, sir. The comte was deeply troubled about the distress your, um, investigation was capable of inflicting on innocent people like the Letissiers and his own family."

"*Distress?*"

"In all innocence, of course. But I shared his concern. We at the Sûreté had serious worries that your activities might interfere with the process of the law."

"This is really too absurd," said I.

He continued doggedly, "I agreed to arrange a meeting with you. And you're correct in suggesting that this place seemed the ideal choice, because it enabled the comte to be present but unseen. He would be well placed to come forward, if necessary, and use his influence—"

"You don't have to go on," I cut in. "It's all transparently clear. Frankly, Monsieur Goron, I am more interested to know why my old friend the comte crept away like a thief in the night—or tried to."

"Because you impugned his family, sir," said Goron. "No sooner had I convinced you that Claudine Jaume could not have committed the crime than you pointed your finger at the Agincourts."

"Are you suggesting that he beat a retreat rather than defend his family's good name?"

"He avoided an unpleasant scene."

"I think you are mistaken." I glanced in the direction of Jules, who had stayed conspicuously silent. "That isn't the conduct of a gentleman and Jules is a gentleman through and through, regardless of the dustup we had this evening. Isn't that so, Jules?"

My old friend looked at me bleakly and, to my astonishment, said nothing. Now, I'm as prone to error as anyone else (some would say more prone), but I know the ways of the aristocracy of Europe. Jules would defend his family like a tiger, whatever their failings. "Jules?"

His silence was a revelation. In that moment of scintillating clarity, I understood.

Reader, I rumbled him.

"You killed Letissier."

After a moment's stunned silence, Jules said, "Yes, I admit it."

"What?" said Goron, jerking upright as if his name had been called by Saint Peter.

Jules said in a tone drained of all emotion, "Bertie is right. I shot Maurice Letissier. I have behaved abominably. You must release that poor man Morgan. He is innocent."

"When did you discover this?" Goron demanded of me as if *I* was the guilty man.

I ignored him. Addressing Jules, I said, "You were the sender of that anonymous letter—the one insisting that Morgan was innocent."

"Yes—and the others to the Sûreté. I did everything I could, short of confessing, but this man took no notice."

Goron reddened. "The information you gave us was flawed. Morgan wasn't in the garden when the shots were fired. He was in the hall."

"Jules didn't know that," said I. "All he knew was that Morgan didn't fire the shots. As a man of honor, he couldn't allow an innocent man to be accused, so he invented what he thought was a watertight alibi for him. He didn't know that Morgan's own statement contradicted it."

Goron's hands were clasped in front of him and his knuckles were white. "If this is true, it's astonishing."

"You dismissed those letters as unimportant," said I. "A more alert investigator recognized them as clues." (The attentive reader may recall that this was Bernhardt. I would have given her the credit if she had been present, but the distinction would have been lost on Goron.) "Jules, you had better explain what made you into a murderer."

The word unsettled him. He shuddered and ran his hand through his hair. "The immediate cause, I suppose, was meeting Claudine Jaume."

"By chance?"

"No, she came to me. I knew nothing of her existence until the Wednesday before. She wrote a letter asking to meet me in front of the Madeleine at noon the following day. It was a simple letter in an educated hand and I decided to act on it. I took her to a quiet café and she told me the story that you know, of her *affaire de coeur* with Maurice, about the love child and her attempts to persuade Maurice to acknowledge the child and come to some arrangement for its upkeep. Over the last days, the child had become sick to the point of death. In desperation, Claudine went to Maurice's apartment to make one more appeal for money, to pay for a doctor's attention. He sent her off without a sou and now she was appealing to me. Of course I did what I could to help. Tragically, the help came too late."

"Did you confront Letissier?" Goron asked.

"Maurice? Of course. I did it discreetly, on the Friday. I told him frankly that I thought he should have the decency to help the girl. One might forgive his peccadillo with Claudine, if that was all it had been, but as a gentleman he was honor bound to make provision for the child. His reaction was to tell me that Claudine was lying, that he had never been intimate with her. I didn't believe him. The girl had been convincing—utterly convincing—and Maurice was not. And if he was prepared to lie to me over this matter, I didn't want him marrying my daughter."

"What was his answer?"

"He challenged me to break off the engagement. He said if I muddied his reputation, he would be justified in muddying Rosine's and he went on to allege deplorable things about her."

"With Morgan?"

"Yes—and I am sure they were untrue, but you know how scandal is spread in society. He fully intended to ruin her life if I intervened. What could I do as a father? Throw my daughter to a jackal like that—or risk her being slandered as a slut? I couldn't allow it, Bertie. I had to remove the threat. I decided to kill him."

I nodded. "The rest we know. You don't need to tell us how it was done, except one thing. After shooting him, whatever possessed you to put the gun into Valentin's overcoat pocket?"

He gave a shrug. "Incompetence. I didn't think ahead. After I shot him and he was carried to the dressing room, I realized that the police would be called and that any of us might be searched for a weapon. The coat pocket was the only hiding place I could find. It didn't occur to me that the owner of the coat would collect it while we were still in the room. I was in no state to think clearly."

We became silent. Each of us, I suppose, was imagining the devastation this would wreak in the Agincourt family and in the larger family of Parisian society. I almost wished I had left the Sûreté floundering in its own incompetence. But then an innocent man would have been executed.

CHAPTER 19

There is a postscript to this case.

More than a year later, Sarah Bernhardt arrived in London to fulfill the latest engagements of her world tour, and naturally I attended a performance and visited her dressing room. Capricious as ever, she declined my offer of supper at the Savoy and instead proposed tea the following afternoon. She said tea would be more discreet. I suggested breakfast as a compromise and got a ticking off. She was most anxious not to cause offense to Alix while in London, and I am sure on reflection that she was right. Those two formidable ladies have always respected each other.

A world tour can be tedious in the telling, and I was resigned to hearing how the Bernhardt troupe had been received at every stop from Amsterdam to Zanzibar, but to my relief, Sarah had called at Paris enroute to London, so she had more intriguing news to impart when we met at a quiet corner table toward the back of Elphinstone's, the tea shop in Regent Street.

"That dreadful Rosine d'Agincourt, Bertie!"

"Rosine? What has she done?"

"Married an American millionaire."

"Good Lord! I thought she'd sworn undying love to the painter—what was his name?—Morgan, the fellow I saved from the guillotine."

"I told you she was not to be trusted. It appears that she was wrong about the undying love. It was puppy love."

"Well, I don't suppose Morgan is brokenhearted. All that passion was too much for him to handle. He'll have to find someone more his own age."

"He has," said she. "The gossip is that he's living at Montroger now."

"On the estate?"

"In the house, as Juliette's lover."

I choked on a cucumber sandwich. "Did you say Juliette?"

"She is more his age."

"Yes, but she hated him. She called him a parasite."

"A lady can change her mind, Bertie."

"He's not her type."

"Who can tell? With Jules gone, she needs someone else to talk to. I'm sure he'll earn his keep."

When I'd adjusted to the shock, I nodded. "It still seems insensitive, not to say callous. Poor old Jules. He deserved better from his family after the dignity he showed, and right to the end. I read about his execution in *The Times*. I gather he went bravely."

"Nobly."

"I think about him often," I added. "That a decent man like that should feel driven to murder—quite appalling. It occurred to me that there could have been a much more satisfactory outcome to this wretched business."

She leaned forward eagerly. "What is that?"

"Well, we know that Claudine Jaume did her best to poison Letissier with arsenic."

"Do we?" said she archly.

"My dear Sarah, I thought your memory was better than that. She possessed a jar of the stuff. I took it to the chemist for analysis, remember? And Letissier displayed the classic symptoms of slow poisoning—gastric problems, headaches, loss of hair, and jaundice. Now, this is the point: if only the poisoning had succeeded, Jules need not have shot him. Claudine would have taken her own life, anyway, after the baby died. And Jules would still be alive to this day!"

The corners of her mouth twitched. I thought for a moment she was deeply moved, but she scolded me instead. "Bertie, that's the silliest nonsense. After all these months, I can't believe you

still don't know the truth of it. The arsenic wasn't for poisoning.
It was medicinal."

I shook my head. "Sarah, this is no joking matter."

"I mean it. I'm serious. Claudine was taking it for her condition."

"Taking arsenic?" I was utterly skeptical.

"Yes."

"For her condition? You do mean when she was, um"—I cleared
my throat—"expecting the child?"

"No, Bertie. She had the pox."

"Good Lord!" I looked about me. "Keep your voice down. Do
you mean . . . syphilis?"

She gave a nod. "I am not conversant with the condition, but
the treatment is well-known. You take arsenic or mercury in tiny
amounts."

"Sarah, how can you possibly advance such an unedifying
theory?"

"Bertie, she caught it from Letissier. He was a roue. He went
to whores."

I winced, certain that the entire tea shop was listening. "I
don't dispute that, but it was never suggested that he contracted
a disease."

"He did," she insisted. "And I'll tell you how I know. Do you
remember the medicines you found in his lodgings at the rue
Tronchet? Among them was a bottle of Van Swieten's liquor. I
made inquiries. It is a preparation made from sublimate of mercury dissolved in alcohol and water and it is the standard remedy
for chronic syphilis."

"Oh."

"She favored arsenic—I suppose because she found it easy to
acquire—and he used Van Swieten's."

"Really?"

"And what is more," she said, "all those symptoms you described
for arsenic poisoning are characteristic of the pox in its secondary
stage. The stomach upsets, the sore throats, the headaches—what
else?"

"Loss of hair."

"Alopecia."

"Jaundice."

"Hepatitis."

"And they are . . ."

"Characteristic of the second stage. It lasts up to three years."

I took a sip of tea. I'd lost my appetite for the sandwiches. The cakes would not be eaten, either. "If this is true—and I admit you make a strong case—why didn't Jules speak of it when he confessed? Wasn't he aware of the truth?"

"I'm sure he knew," said she. "What happened is this. When Claudine met him in the last days of her life, she was in despair. She showed him her dying baby, another victim of the disease."

"He didn't mention it to me."

"Bertie, he wouldn't," said Bernhardt with such an outpouring of feeling that I was quite subdued. "Jules was a gentleman to the last. He regarded what that poor girl told him as confidential. But he was appalled that Letissier—having infected Claudine and her child and ruined their lives—should still insist on marrying his daughter. When he saw Letissier and heard his lies, his absolute denials, he felt he had no choice but to shoot him. That was the real motive. But he went to the guillotine without mentioning it once."

I needed no more convincing.

She said, "Do you believe me now?"

I nodded. "I am a father myself, and, I hope, a man of honor. I understand why Jules acted as he did."

I wouldn't have added anything else, but Bernhardt, being Bernhardt, couldn't let an opportunity go by. "So it was, after all, a crime of passion, as I always insisted."

"I don't agree," said I. "Jules wasn't driven by passion."

"No, but the source of it all was one man's promiscuity."

"Well, if you put it like that, yes."

"Thank you."

"But you chose the wrong suspect. You kept telling me quite mistakenly that Rosine was the guilty party." I softened my expression. "However . . . I could be persuaded to forgive you, my dear. We have at least two hours before the play begins."

She missed my drift entirely, she was so indignant. "Who are you to talk about mistakes? You suspected Claudine. You were just as much at fault as I."

"Very well," I said, wanting a truce. "We were both mistaken."

"But I was right in saying it was a crime of passion, wasn't I?"

"Yes, I already said so."

She gave a faraway look. "Love is dangerous. It isn't worth it, Bertie."

"What do you mean dangerous? It's perfectly safe with me, I assure you."

She smiled. "It isn't you, Bertie. It's the hat."

"Which hat?"

"The hat that just came in. Unless I'm mistaken, it belongs to my dear friend the Princess of Wales."

And it did.

A Note to the Reader

Anyone coming freshly to this series of detective stories may be interested to know that in an earlier book, reference was made to the detective memoirs of King Edward VII having been deposited in a sealed metal box in the Public Record Office. A hundred-year embargo was placed on publication. This might explain why biographies of the king published prior to 1987 contain no reference to his career as an amateur sleuth.

However, in an afternote from the editor, readers were advised that it was highly unlikely whether Bertie, either as Prince of Wales or king, ever found the time or inclination to write a book. This publication of this volume should dispose of all doubts.